FIGHT CLUB

"How's this?" one of the other men asked and threw a punch himself. Once again John L. danced aside and the aggressor lost his balance.

"Get him!" the first man shouted.

Two men ran forward to attack John L. but he threw two left jabs that landed with sledgehammer effect, knocking both men off their feet.

John L. danced back. He was breathing heavily, Clint could see, but not because he was tired, rather it was from excitement.

"Who's next?"

The first man said, "Wait," and moved to join his partners. The other men helped the two fallen men to their feet.

"There's nine of us and one of him," the spokesman said. "Let's just all take him at once."

"Gentlemen," John L. said to Clint and Bat, "I just might be in need of your assistance here."

Clint and Bat stepped forward and flanked the pugilist, facing the nine men together.

"Three against nine," the man said to his eight companions. "Still in our favor."

"That's funny," Bat said. "I was thinking how outnumbered you all were, now."

DON'T MISS THESE
ALL-ACTION WESTERN SERIES
FROM THE BERKLEY PUBLISHING GROUP

THE GUNSMITH by J. R. Roberts
Clint Adams was a legend among lawmen, outlaws, and ladies.
They called him . . . the Gunsmith.

LONGARM by Tabor Evans
The popular long-running series about Deputy U.S. Marshal
Long—his life, his loves, his fight for justice.

SLOCUM by Jake Logan
Today's longest-running action Western. John Slocum rides
a deadly trail of hot blood and cold steel.

BUSHWHACKERS by B. J. Lanagan
An action-packed series by the creators of Longarm! The
rousing adventures of the most brutal gang of cutthroats ever
assembled—Quantrill's Raiders.

DIAMONDBACK by Guy Brewer
Dex Yancey is Diamondback, a Southern gentleman turned
con man when his brother cheats him out of the family fortune. Ladies love him. Gamblers hate him. But nobody pulls
one over on Dex . . .

WILDGUN by Jack Hanson
Will Barlow's continuing search for his daughter, kidnapped
by the Blackfeet Indians who slaughtered the rest of his family.

THE GUNSMITH

TALES FROM THE WHITE ELEPHANT SALOON

J. R. ROBERTS

JOVE BOOKS, NEW YORK

This is a work of fiction. Names, characters, places, and incidents are either the product of the author's imagination or are used fictitiously, and any resemblance to actual persons, living or dead, business establishments, events, or locales is entirely coincidental.

TALES FROM THE WHITE ELEPHANT SALOON

A Jove Book / published by arrangement with
the author

PRINTING HISTORY
Jove edition / November 2001

All rights reserved.
Copyright © 2001 by Robert J. Randisi.
This book, or parts thereof, may not be reproduced in any form
without permission.
For information address: The Berkley Publishing Group,
a division of Penguin Putnam Inc.,
375 Hudson Street, New York, New York 10014.

Visit our website at
www.penguinputnam.com

ISBN: 0-515-13182-2

A JOVE BOOK®
Jove Books are published by The Berkley Publishing Group,
a division of Penguin Putnam Inc.,
375 Hudson Street, New York, New York 10014.
JOVE and the "J" design
are trademarks belonging to Penguin Putnam Inc.

PRINTED IN THE UNITED STATES OF AMERICA

10 9 8 7 6 5 4 3 2 1

PART ONE
FORT WORTH

ONE

When Clint Adams rode into Fort Worth, Texas, his only intent was to visit his friend Luke Short, who had opened a hugely successful saloon and gambling hall called the White Elephant Saloon. He didn't know exactly where it was located, but he knew it was on Exchange Street. While he rode along Exchange looking for the saloon, he noticed how much Fort Worth had grown. Once a major cow town, it was now a full-fledged city, and he could see why his friend had been having such success with his new venture.

Short had come to Fort Worth and opened his business with his friend Jake Johnson, after he had sold his interest in the Long Branch Saloon in Dodge City. Clint and Bat Masterson and some other friends had helped Short get out of Dodge in one piece, as a full-fledged war had erupted between the little gambler and the town. Clint hoped his friend was doing better in Fort Worth than he had done in Dodge.

Finally he came upon the White Elephant, and was impressed. It was easily the largest saloon and gambling establishment he'd ever seen outside of Portsmouth Square in San Francisco. Farther along the street he found a livery where he put Eclipse, his Darley Arabian, in the capable hands of a liveryman. Most Texas liveryman were experts with horses, and this one was no different.

"Quite an animal," the man said.

"Thanks."

"Wouldn't be interested in selling him, would ya?" The man was in his fifties, and had all the earmarks of a man who had spent many years handling horses. He had scars on his arms and hands from bites, and was missing a piece of one finger. "I'll give you a fair price."

"Not interested," Clint said.

"Don't blame ya," the man said. "I had a horse like that, I wouldn't sell him, either. Don't worry, I'll take good care of him."

"I appreciate it," Clint said.

"Need directions to a place to stay?"

"No thanks," Clint said, "I'm staying with a friend, but I would like to leave my bedroll here with the saddle and my rifle."

"Sure," the man said. "I'll watch everything. Mind if I ask where you're stayin'?"

"The White Elephant."

"Luke Short's place," the man said, his eyes lighting up. "Best place in town."

"For what?" Clint asked.

"Name it," the man said. "Food, booze, gambling,

women . . . can't beat the White Elephant. You a friend of Short's?"

"That's right," Clint said, and he left without introducing himself and before the man could ask him who he was. He didn't need word circulating that he was in town even before he had a place to lay his head.

He walked back up Exchange Street until he reached the White Elephant. He paused again to take a good look at the impressive front facade before finally going inside. Here, his friend's good but expensive tastes were clearly evident. There were crystal chandeliers, oil paintings on the walls, mahogany gaming tables covered with green cloths. There were drapes made of rich materials, thick carpeting, and waiters serving drinks to the patrons.

The bar was also made of mahogany with some marble inlay, and ran almost the length of the huge room. Clint thought that his friend, a gambler most of his life, finally had the place he wanted and deserved.

While there was gambling going on at the moment, the place was certainly not in full swing. It was early in the day, and the place was quiet except for the occasional sound of a roulette wheel turning or chips landing on chips.

He went up to the bar and one of the two bartenders, both young men with slicked-back hair, wearing vests, came over to him.

"Can I help you, sir?"

"I'd like a beer, please."

"Yessir, comin' up."

The man drew the beer and brought it over to Clint in a long-stemmed beer glass. Clint sampled the brew and found it excellent, good flavor, excellent body, and extremely cold.

"How is it?" the man asked.

"It's wonderful," Clint said. "I almost feel human again."

"Been on the trail?"

"That's right."

"Must be hungry, then."

"Starving."

"We got the best steaks in town."

"And I'm going to have one," Clint said, "with all the trimmings, but first I want to see your boss."

"Mr. Short?"

"That's right."

"Is there something wrong?"

"No," Clint said, "I'm a friend of his. Is he in?"

"I think he's in his apartment upstairs, with Mrs. Short."

Clint had not seen the beautiful Hettie in a long time.

"Could you tell him I'm here?"

"Yes, sir," the man said. "And your name?"

Clint sighed. It was very rarely that he told someone his name and did not have to withstand some sort of surprised reaction. This would be no different.

"It's Adams," he said, "Clint Adams."

The man stared at him with no sign of recognition, and said, "Yes, sir, Mr. Adams, I'll tell him."

TWO

Clint remained at the bar, nursing his beer because he knew if he finished it he'd have another, and he didn't want to have another until he had something to eat.

Instead of sending someone to fetch Luke Short, the young bartender decided to go and get him himself. Clint didn't expect Short to come down the stairs as quickly as he did, outpacing the young bartender easily.

Short was not a tall man—no joke intended—but he had a tremendous energy, which sometimes tended to burn him out. As he approached with his hand outstretched, Clint could already see the signs. His friend had a thriving business in a still growing city, he had his wife, Hettie, and should have been happier than ever. And yet the man approaching him with outstretched hand and a smile on his face looked anything but relaxed.

Only a close friend would be able to read the signs.

7

• • •

"Clint, by God!" Short said, grabbing Clint's hand and pumping it. "I've been expecting you all year."

"Took me a while to get here, all right," Clint said. "Quite a place, Luke. Looks like you finally hit the mother lode."

"You'd think," Short said.

"What's that mean?"

"It means," Short said, "let's have another beer. Andy?"

The young bartender had finally reclaimed his place behind the bar, catching his breath from trying to keep up with his boss.

"Yes, sir?"

"Two more beers. Bring them to my table."

"Yes, sir."

"Luke," Clint said, "I wanted to have something—"

"And bring Mr. Adams a steak dinner."

"Yes, sir."

"Thank you, Luke," Clint said.

"Come on," Short said. "Let's have a seat. I've got to talk to you about something."

The two men walked to a table that was in a corner, so that two of the four chairs had their backs to a wall. Clint and Short took those chairs.

"What's wrong, Luke?"

"What makes you think something's wrong?"

"Because you've got even more energy than usual," Clint said. "You're not looking as dapper as you usually do."

"I look bad?" Short demanded, touching his face.

"Not bad," Clint said, "just not as dapper as usual. It would take someone who really knows you to tell."

"What else?"

"The way you pumped my hand," Clint said. "You've got a real problem you think I can help you with. I mean, you've been glad to see me before, but not that glad."

Andy came over with the beers and said, "Mr. Adams's steak will be out shortly."

"Thanks, Andy," Short said.

When the bartender withdrew Clint said, "I'm all ears, Luke."

"Do you know Jim Courtright?"

"Long-haired Jim Courtright? That one?"

"That's him."

"I've met him," Clint said.

"What do you think of him?"

Clint made a face and said, "I don't think he'd ever be one of my best friends. A little on the too-shady side."

"Exactly."

"What's going on?"

"He showed up in town a while back, tried to use his reputation to procure himself a badge."

"Didn't work?"

"No," Short said. "He's got a lot of friends in Fort Worth, but nobody would give him a badge."

"And so?"

"He got himself a partner and opened a detective agency," Short said. "Calls it the 'T.I.C. Detective Agency.' The 'I' between the 'T' and 'C' is actually an eye."

"Very clever. What do the initials stand for?"

"Nobody knows."

"Who's the partner?"

"Another reprobate known as Charley Bull."

"I don't know him."

"You know my partner, don't you?"

"Jake? Sure, I knew him when he was marshal here. Why?"

"He and Courtright are friends."

"So?"

Now it was Luke Short's turn to make a face. He sat forward in his chair and said, "Clint, I'm afraid I'm going to have to kill Jim Courtright."

THREE

"Or be killed by him."

Clint stared over his mug at his friend's face and saw that he was deadly serious.

"What's going on, Luke?"

"He and his partner have started a lucrative business," Short said. "They're shakin' down saloon owners."

"Oh."

"Yeah, right," Short said. "I'm not about to start paying for protection."

"Has Courtright come to you and your partner yet?"

"Not to Jake," Short said, "just to me."

"What's the difference?"

"I don't know," Short said. "I don't know that he thinks there *is* a difference."

"What did you tell Courtright?"

"Just what I told you," Short said. "I'm not about to start paying him and his partner."

"And what did he say?"

"We made some remarks about each other."

"Like what?"

"I talked about the Frenchman he was recently acquitted of havin' killed in New Mexico, and he said the same thing about me and Charley Storms."

"You killed Storms fair and square."

"I know. And he backshot those Frenchman and managed to get acquitted."

"All right," Clint said, "so some hot words were exchanged. Did you tell Jake?"

"I did," Short replied.

"And what did he say?"

Andy arrived with Clint's steak dinner and both men sat back while he set it down.

"Anything else, boss?"

"More beer."

"Yes, sir."

"Go ahead and eat while we talk, Clint," Short said. "You must be hungry."

"Tell me more," Clint said, while he cut into the inch-thick piece of beef.

"Jake wants to pay him," Short said. "Says we should consider it part of the cost of doin' business."

"Protection doesn't come under that heading," Clint said.

"That's what I told Jake."

"Could he and Courtright be in it together to shake you down?" Clint asked.

"I thought about that," Short said, sitting back and stroking his mustache. "I'm still thinkin' about it . . . but no, I don't think so. We're doing too good here, Clint. The top names come here to gamble against each other, and again me. Bat and Wyatt have been here, Chisum, Rusty Coe, hell, even Horace Tabor comes here."

"The Silver King."

"Right. Rolls into town in his private railroad card and stops in here to play faro or poker against me. We got the best people in the city coming here to eat. High society and business people. Our menu rivals Delmonico's in New York. No, there's too much at stake for Jake to turn against me."

"All right, then," Clint said. "Did he talk to Courtright?"

"Yeah," Short said, "he said Courtright's got it in for me and he ain't gonna let go. He doesn't care that Jake's involved."

"So what happened then?"

"Courtright sent Bull in to intimidate me."

"Uh-oh."

"I didn't kill him," Short said. "I had one of my bouncers give him a bloody nose and throw him out. I'm tryin' not to kill anybody, Clint. I don't want a repeat of what's happened to me in other towns, like Dodge. You fellas had to bail me out of that."

"Wasn't your fault, Luke," Clint said. "You won't bend when it comes to your businesses. I respect that."

"I'm startin' to branch out, Clint," Short said. "Got other businesses goin' in Fort Worth. I don't want to blow it this time. I'm happy here, Hettie's with me—"

"What's Hettie say, Luke?"

Short sighed. "Hettie thinks like Jake, that I should pay."

"So then pay."

"I can't," Short said, trying to contain his anger. "I won't!"

"So what do you want me to do?" Clint asked. "Talk to Courtright? Threaten him?"

"Just stay around awhile," Short said. "Be seen here. Maybe he'll back off."

"I could talk to him—"

"Let's try it this way first, Clint," Short said. "In fact . . . yeah, yeah, this is good." Short sat forward, warming to his subject. "Yeah. . . . I'll give you a piece of the place. If he finds out you're part owner, he'll back off."

"I don't want to own a piece of it, Luke," Clint said. "It belongs to you and Jake."

"Take a small piece," Short said. "You've more than earned it over the years."

Clint thought it over while he continued to decimate his steak.

"What will Jake say?"

"If it gets Courtright to back away Jake will be all for it," Short said. "I'll talk to him, don't worry."

"Good steak," Clint said, to give himself time to think.

"Good as Delmonico's?"

"Better."

Short beamed.

"So why wouldn't you want to own a piece of a place that's got better steaks than Delmonico's?"

Clint put down his knife and fork and said, "Well, I guess you've got a point."

"You'll do it?"

"I'll buy in."

"You don't—okay," Short said, cutting himself off. "You can buy in . . . for a dollar."

"Okay," Clint said, "but once the crisis is over you'll buy me out."

"Fair enough."

"For two dollars!"

Short laughed.

"You've already figured a way to double your money."

Clint handed Short a dollar and the two men shook hands. That was how Clint became a 1 percent of 1 percent owner of the White Elephant Saloon.

FOUR

Later that evening Clint had dinner in the restaurant of the White Elephant Saloon with Luke and Hettie Short and Jake Johnson. He got there first and was shown to Short's table. When his friend entered with Hettie Short, Clint stood and she rushed into his arms.

"It's been such a long time," she said, kissing his cheek.

If anything Hettie was more beautiful in her thirties than she had been as a younger woman.

"It's good to see you, Hettie," he said.

She pressed her cheek to his and whispered urgently in his ear, "I'm so glad you're here!"

They all sat down to await the arrival of Jake Johnson.

"I understand you own a piece of us now," Hettie said.

"A very small piece."

"Well," Short said, "it's no one's business how small a piece."

"What about Jake?" Clint asked.

"I only told him that I sold you some of my percentage," Short explained. "He doesn't know how much."

"And how much do you own?" Clint asked.

"Let's just say," Short answered, "the majority share."

Short was always closemouthed about his businesses— at least, the ownership aspects of them.

"Here he comes now," Hettie said, and she said it with an obvious dislike for her husband's partner.

"Sorry I'm late," Jake Johnson said. "Good to see you, Adams."

"Jake."

Johnson said and added, "Although I'm not sure why you're here, or why we needed another partner."

"Just a minority partner, Jake," Clint said. "I won't try to change anything."

"I should think not," Johnson said. "This place is a gold mine the way it is." He was older than Short by about ten years, a large, florid-faced man.

"That's good to hear," Clint said.

"Shall we order dinner?" Short asked. "My dear?"

They chatted over dinner, but Johnson took every opportunity to question Clint's investment in the White Elephant. Before dessert Hettie announced that she was going up to the apartment.

"No dessert?" Clint asked.

"Not if I want to maintain by girlish figure," she said. She kissed Clint's cheek and said, "Jake." Then kissed her husband and left. That fact that Johnson was the only man she hadn't kissed seemed to leave him miffed.

"I don't know why she doesn't like me," Johnson said.

"I'm at a loss to explain that myself," Short said.

"Maybe," Clint said, "she doesn't like the company you keep."

Johnson narrowed his eyes.

"Meaning what?"

Clint shrugged.

"Maybe she doesn't like your friends."

"Well, she doesn't have to, does she?" Johnson demanded. "It's not me she's married to, is it?"

"No," Clint said, "it isn't."

Suddenly, Johnson seemed to get it.

"Oh, I understand now," he said. He looked at Short. "You told him about Courtright."

"Well, of course I did," Short said. "As an investor he has the right to know everything."

"Ah!" Johnson said, taking his cloth napkin from his lap and tossing it on the table. "I told you I'd take care of Jim, Luke."

"But you haven't, Jake," Shirt asked, "have you?"

"It takes time!" Johnson stood up.

"No dessert?" Clint asked.

"I've lost my appetite," he said, and stormed out.

"Well," Clint said, "that went well."

Jake Johnson left the restaurant, went to his office to retrieve his hat and coat, and then took his gun from the desk drawer. It was small, a gambler's gun, and it fit in his coat pocket. He then walked through the saloon and left by the front door.

"How's the peach pie?" Clint asked Short.

"The best you'll ever have."

"Do you think Johnson will go to Courtright?"

Short smiled and said, "He's probably on his way right now."

FIVE

Jake Johnson found long-haired Jim Courtright at another saloon down the street. It was small and nameless and catered to a clientele that either couldn't afford the White Elephant or weren't welcome. Courtright was sitting alone and the tables immediately around him had been vacated. Everyone had heard the stories about his temper, and how quickly he would bring his twin Colts into action.

Johnson joined him at the table.

"Drink?" Courtright asked.

"No, Jim," Johnson said, "I don't want a drink."

"Then why are you here, Jake?" Courtright asked. "You gonna ask me to lay off again?"

"I thought I might," Johnson said. "Luke won't be pushed, Jim."

"And I won't be ignored."

"Nobody's ignoring you, Jim."

"Why did you even go partners with him, Jake?"

"Because he's got a midas touch, Jim," Johnson said. "Every business he's ever run has been a success."

"And then he gets run out of town."

"He has a problem with people, sometimes," Johnson said. "He's working on it. That's why he hasn't come after you, yet."

"That might work in my favor, Jim," Courtright said. "He might give in rather than fight me."

Johnson sat back in his chair. He didn't like this, being caught between two friends, one of whom was his partner.

"He may not have to fight you, Jim."

"Whataya mean?"

"I mean we got a new partner, me and Luke."

"And who would that be, Jim?"

Johnson hesitated for effect, then said, "Clint Adams."

Courtright sat forward in his chair, his hand tightening around his beer mug.

"The Gunsmith is in town?"

"That's right."

"And he bought in?"

"Right again."

"How big a piece?"

"I don't know," Johnson said. "He bought in from Luke."

Courtright's eyes were glittering, and Johnson didn't like the glassy look.

"Did Short bring Adams in? Did he ask him to come?"

"I don't know that, either."

"He did," Courtright said, "I know he did. He doesn't want to face me himself. He thinks that by bringing the Gunsmith in it'll make me back off."

"It would make me back off," Johnson said.

"Well, not me," Courtright said. "I ain't afraid of Luke Short, and I ain't afraid of Clint Adams, neither."

"Jim . . . you better check with Bull on this."

"Bull goes along with me," Courtright said. "I'm the senior partner in our agency."

Johnson knew this was a crack about his letting Short be the senior partner, but he believed what he said about Short, and Luke was proving it. He was fast becoming the king of gamblers in Fort Worth.

"Well," Johnson said, standing up, "I was just tryin' to warn you, is all."

"Warn Short," Courtright said. "If he sends Adams after me I'll kill him—I'll kill 'em both. You tell him that. In fact, you tell Clint Adams, too. If he comes after me he better be ready to die."

"Okay, Jim," Johnson said, "I'll tell them."

"Then there'll just be you, Jake," Courtright said. "Are you gonna pay?"

Johnson stared at Courtright.

"I thought we was friends, Jim."

"We are, Jake," Courtright said, "but I don't let friendship get in the way of business. You ought to know that."

"I know it now, Jim," Johnson said, "I know it now."

SIX

Clint and Luke Short stayed in the restaurant to have another drink. Clint had beer but Short went for brandy.

"Hettie certainly doesn't look happy with Jake Johnson as your partner."

"She's not."

"Why?"

"She doesn't like the company he keeps."

"Who?"

"The likes of Jim Courtright."

"And you say Courtright actually has friends in Fort Worth?"

"Oh yeah," Short said, "but none of them are allowed in my place."

"So where do they go?"

"Anywhere else."

"Like where Jake went right now?"

"Jake probably went to tell Courtright you were a new partner," Short said. "Maybe he also thinks that'll make Jim back off."

"Well," Clint said, "it would be nice if that was true. What do you think?"

"I'm hoping it will," Short said, "but do I think so? No, I'm afraid I don't."

"So it'll come down to guns."

"Courtright's good," Short said.

"How good?"

"Not as good as you . . . or me."

"But you don't want to kill anybody."

"What is it about me and people?" Short asked. "I'm a nice guy, ain't I?"

"I think so."

"I've got friends," Short went on. "I can't be all that bad if I've got friends."

"But you said Courtright's got friends, too."

"Well . . . everybody can't be all bad."

"Will his friends back his play?"

"His partner will," Short said. "I don't know about his friends—especially when they hear you're in town."

"Luke," Clint said, "does Hettie have anything to do with you not wanting to kill Courtright?"

Short scratched his cheek and said, "You're a smart man, aren't you?"

"Sometimes."

"She's never seen me kill a man," Short said. "I don't want her to. Is there anything wrong with that?"

"No," Clint said, "nothing."

"I'm not asking you to kill him for me, Clint," Short said. "I wouldn't do that. If it comes to that I'll do it myself."

"Maybe," Clint said, "I can keep Hettie from seeing it."

"That," Short said, "would be helpful."

Short left the restaurant first to go upstairs and see Hettie. He told Clint that he would be in the saloon later. Then he would take him to the upstairs gaming room.

"Upstairs room?"

"You'll see," Short said, and left.

Clint sat and finished his beer. The peach pie had been delicious, as Short had promised. In fact, all of the food had been as good as advertised. Now he was curious about this upstairs gaming room.

He finished his beer and left the restaurant in time to run into Johnson coming back in.

"Adams," Johnson called out.

"Jake."

"We need to talk."

"Okay."

"Come into the saloon with me."

He walked off, assuming Clint would follow him. He was tempted not to, but he wanted to hear what the man had to say.

He followed.

Courtright waited in the no-name saloon until Charley Bull came walking in. From the relaxed look on his face and the way he was moving he knew that Bull had spent the afternoon with a whore. Bull got a beer from the bar and then joined Courtright at his table.

"Jim," Bull said, greeting his partner.

"Bull," Courtright said. "You smell like perfume."

"Yeah," Bull said, smiling.

"I've got news."

"About what?"

"The White Elephant."

"Short gave in?"

"No," Courtright said. "No, he didn't He got himself another partner."

"Big deal?" Bull asked. "Who would that be?"

Courtright smiled.

SEVEN

"Have a seat," Johnson said.

"Why don't I get us a couple of beers?"

"Sit," Johnson said. "I'm the boss. I'll have somebody bring two beers over."

Clint didn't bother mentioning that he was also the boss. He sat down.

"What's on your mind, Jake?"

"Wait."

He waved to the bartender, then made a series of signals that the man—not Andy—seemed to understand. The man drew up two beers and carried them over to the table.

"Thanks, Dan."

"Sure, boss."

"Oh, Dan," Johnson said, "this is Clint Adams."

Dan looked shocked and said, "Uh, nice to meet you, Mr. Adams."

"Dan."

"Tell the other boys, Dan," Johnson said. "Mr. Adams is a new partner. He gets anything he wants, understand? Just like me and Luke. Get it?"

"I get it, sir," Dan said. "I'll talk to the others."

"That's all, then."

"Yes, sir."

"Thanks, Dan," Clint said, because Johnson hadn't.

Dan nodded and left.

"Okay, Jake," Clint said, "what's up?"

Johnson swallowed half his beer before speaking.

"I just came from seeing Jim Courtright."

"I'm not surprised."

"I can't talk him out of pushing Luke."

"And?"

"And I can't talk Luke into paying him."

"And why should he?"

"Because it would be a small price for doing business," Johnson said. "And it would be a peaceful way out of this."

"I can't argue the second part," Clint said, "but Luke won't do it . . . ever."

"I know," Johnson said.

"And don't ask me to try to talk him into it."

"That wasn't my intention."

"Then what is your intention?"

"To try not to lose a friend."

"Luke?"

"I'm as good a friend to Luke as I am to Jim," Johnson said, looking worried, and sincere. "I don't want to lose either one, and I sure as hell don't want one to kill the other."

Clint studied the man for a few seconds.

"I believe you, Jake," Clint said. "So what do we do?"

"Did Luke ask you to come here and kill Courtright?"

"No."

"Then why did you choose to come here at this time, when there's trouble?"

Clint hesitated, then said, "I'm going to say I don't know, Jake, but I do know that I'm usually around when Luke's in trouble. I don't know how that happens."

"Coincidence?"

Clint made a face. He hated that word.

"I don't know."

"Courtright thinks you're here to do Luke's fighting for him."

Clint laughed out loud.

"Luke does his own fighting."

"What about Dodge?"

"What about Tombstone?" Clint asked. "Luke outgunned Charlie Storms one to one. In Dodge City he was outnumbered and we went in to help."

Johnson turned his beer mug round and round on the table. Clint sipped from his.

"So what do we do?" Johnson asked. "How do we resolve this?"

"Courtright's not going to back down, is he?"

"If anything," Johnson said, "he's looking forward to facing you. I can't do anything to stop him."

"So I may be making things worse by being here," Clint observed.

"No," Johnson said, running his hand over his face in a drywash. "No, Jim's gonna come for Luke sooner or later. That's gonna happen, whether you're here or not."

"So we're pretty much stuck in the middle."

"I guess."

"I was pretty much ready to think badly of you, Jake," Clint said. "I'm sorry for that. I believe you are a good friend to Luke."

"And you," Jake said. "I only wish I could get Hettie to see that the way you do now."

"Well," Clint said, lifting his beer mug in a silent toast, "one thing at a time, Jake."

Jake Johnson lifted his mug and said, "I agree, Adams. One thing at a time."

Before Clint drank he said, "Call me Clint, Jake."

EIGHT

Before dinner Luke had shown Clint to his room on the second floor. It was opulent, certainly a room befitting a partner. But Clint had not seen the rest of the second floor, and was shocked when Luke Short took him up there.

"This," Short said, "is where most of the big gambling gets done."

The room stretched out the length and width of the building. Where the downstairs had to make room for the bar, and for the restaurant, up here every inch was used for gambling.

"Are those *women*?" Clint asked. "Are there women up here gambling?"

"Keno," Short said. "They love it, and we'd be losing money not letting them come in."

"My God," Clint said, "is that Hettie playing?"

"Yes," Short said. "She's discovered it, and it keeps her busy."

"I've never heard of keno," Clint said.

"It's a simple game involving numbers," Short said. "Not for the likes of us. You'll be more interested in the poker setup. Come on."

Short had taken Clint up a front staircase, and now took him to the back of the room where the poker tables were. One of them was empty.

"Who's that table for?" Clint asked.

"That's for us," Short said.

"You and me?"

"Not you and me against each other," Short said, "you and me and Jake against whoever wants to play us."

"Jake plays?"

"Not much, anymore," Short said. "Usually if someone wants to come in and specifically play against me, that's the table we use."

"You mean," Clint said, "if they come looking to play against the best."

"Don't let Bat hear you say that," Short said. "He thinks he's the best poker player in the country."

"Well," Clint said, "don't tell Bat, but I think it's you."

"I appreciate that," Short said, "but do you know who I think has the potential to be the best?"

"Who?"

Short turned to face his friend and said, "You."

"Me?" Clint laughed. "I'm not in the same class with you and Bat, or even the likes of a Ben Thompson."

"You could be in anyone's class, Clint," Short said. "Bart, Brett, even that fella Hawkes."

"You're flattering me, Luke."

"I'm serious," Short said. "Don't forget, I've watched

you play for a long time. If you concentrated on the cards, and nothing else, I think you could be the best."

"Well," Clint said, "I appreciate it, Luke, but I think my days of concentrating just on the cards are past. If I did that now I'd be dead in ten seconds . . . like Hickok."

"I know it," Short said, "don't think I don't know it."

"This is quite a setup," Clint said. There were crystal chandeliers up here, too, rich mahogany carpeting, and the smell of expensive cigars. "Quite a setup, Luke."

"And part of it is yours."

"Yep," Clint said, "one percent of one percent."

"More, if you like."

"No," Clint said, "let's just keep it the way it is, why don't we? Until we see what happens."

"Fine."

"Anybody up here I know?" Clint asked.

"Not right now."

"What about town gentry?"

"In about another hour we'll have statesmen and businessmen up here playing poker. Right now why don't we get a drink. I've also got a private room off to the side there, for drinks and games."

"Let's go."

Short showed him the way and, with a wave, brought over a waiter wearing a vest.

"Yes, sir?"

"Two beers, Leon."

"Comin' up, sir."

They entered the room which had one large, round, green felt poker table.

"Luke," Clint said, "you've truly built a place for the Knights of the Green Cloth to come and play."

"Sit down."

Clint took a seat at the big poker table, and Short sat opposite him.

"I've got one question."

"What's that?"

"The noise," he said. "If you and Hettie and Jake—"

"And you."

"And I . . . live up here . . ."

"I've got that covered," he said. "Between the gaming room and the apartments I had a sixteen-inch wall built, and filled it in with sawdust. We can't hear a thing."

"Seems like you've thought of everything," Clint said.

"Well," Short said, a faraway look coming into his eyes, "almost everything."

NINE

"Courtright?"

"It's not just Courtright," Short said. "It's just the fact that it's anybody. I attract them, Clint, men who want to start trouble."

"Tell me about it," Clint said, wryly.

"Oh, I know," Short said, "you've always attracted the young gunnies who want to try you. With me they're not after my reputation, they seem to be after my success. Why can't I just be a success without attracting trouble?"

"Maybe because if you were you wouldn't be Luke Short. Come on, Luke, who doesn't attract attention when they're successful?"

The waiter, Leon, returned with their beers, set them down and withdrew.

"You seem to have your waiters well trained."

"So far."

"No women? No saloon girls?"

"Later tonight," Short said. "You'll meet them all."

"What did Hettie have to say about them?"

"Jake did the hiring of the girls," Short said. "I hired the waiters and the dealers."

Short sipped his beer and returned to the subject they had previously been discussing.

"All right, so maybe I'm paranoid, but even this Court-right trouble is a little different. I just can't bring myself to pay protection, Clint."

"I don't blame you, Luke," Clint said, "but maybe there's a way you haven't looked at this."

"Oh? What way?"

"Hettie's way," Clint said. "What does she say you should do?"

"She says I should follow my conscience."

"Do you think that's really the way she feels?"

"Yes," Short said. "She loves it here, Clint. She gets to play keno, she shops for all the newest fashions, we're both in the same place at one time . . . she doesn't want it to change."

"It'll change if Courtright kills you."

Short waved his hand.

"I'm not worried about that."

"Because you're leaving her well off?"

"Because Courtright ain't gonna kill me," Short said. "I can handle that two-gun tinhorn."

"From the back?"

Short stared at Clint.

"You think he'd shoot me in the back?"

"Who knows?"

Short chewed his lip.

"You might be right," Short said. "If he did that, that

would leave Hettie partners with Jake. She wouldn't like that."

"I meant—"

"I know what you meant," Short said. "You meant maybe I should pay Courtright to keep him from shooting me in the back. I'm thinking of how I would be leaving Hettie if he did."

"I don't think Hettie would care who her partner was," Clint said, "once you were dead."

"You."

"What?"

"You can buy me out."

"What? I told you, one percent of one percent is—"

"No, I mean you could buy me out just until we resolve this business with Courtright. If I did end up dead, you'd own my share. If I come out of it alive, you just sign it back over to me."

Clint thought a moment, and then said, "Well, all right, if that's what you want."

"We can draw up the papers, sign them, and just leave them in my desk to be opened in the event of my death."

"Like a will."

"Right."

"Okay," Clint said. "I'll go along with that, but that doesn't solve the problem at hand."

"No, it doesn't,"

"Whose the law here?"

"Marshal named Sullivan," Short said.

"Any good?"

"He's no Jake Johnson, but he can break up a fight at the saloon."

"Any other law?"

"A police department."

Clint made a face.

"I'm not sold on those uniformed departments, with a chief of police."

"I'm not either, but we've got one."

"Who's the chief?"

"Irishman named O'Doul."

"What's his relationship with you?"

"Cordial."

"And what would happen if you killed Courtright on the street, or vice versa?"

"Whichever one of us comes out alive would be arrested," Short said, "and tried. The city of Fort Worth don't hold with gunfights in the street."

"And Courtright's friends?" Clint asked. "Do they extend into the police department, or the city fathers?"

"Not that I know of."

"Maybe the law can talk to him."

"No," Short said, "the law has pretty much been looking the other way as far as protection goes."

"Why?"

"Because they're too busy trying to make gambling and drinking illegal," Short said.

"There's a temperance movement here?"

"Oh, yeah."

"So they'll go at it from that direction," Clint said. "If they abolish drinking and gambling there'd be no reason for a protection racket."

"Exactly."

"So for now Courtright has a free hand."

"Uptown, downtown, across the tracks, the stockyards, it don't matter," Short said. "Courtright has a free hand right now."

"That's a problem," Clint said.

"That," Luke Short said, "is the biggest problem."

TEN

Short told Clint that he always made sure he was downstairs to greet the high rollers when they arrived.

"Want to come with me, now that you're a partner?"

"No," Clint said, "you go ahead. I'll sit here and finish my beer."

"And then what?"

Clint smiled.

"I haven't decided yet. I had a long day. Maybe I'll just turn in."

"This early?"

Clint spread his hands.

"Maybe not."

"All right," Short said. "If I don't see you later, I'll see you in the morning. I always have breakfast around nine."

"Nine sounds good."

Short nodded and left the room. The waiter, Leon, came

in a few minutes later and asked Clint if he needed anything else.

"I'll just finish what I have, Leon. Thanks."

"Yes, sir."

As the waiter withdrew someone else entered the room and Clint stood up.

"Oh, sit down," Hettie Short said. "Finish your beer. Do you mind if I sit with you a minute?"

"Luke just left—"

"I know," she said. "I saw him. May I?"

"Of course."

She sat in the seat recently vacated by her husband.

"Clint," she said, "I need your help."

"I'll do what I can, Hettie."

She hesitated, then blurted, "I want you to keep Luke alive."

He smiled. "I can do that. I've done it before, and he's done it for me, many times."

"I realize that," she said, "but this is different."

"I know it is," Clint said. "You have a life here and you don't want it to be ruined."

"That's a true statement," she said, "as far as it goes."

"And how far does it go?"

"Not far enough," she said. "You see, 'we' have a life here, Luke and I. That hasn't happened very much before. He traveled a lot while I was left behind."

"I know that."

"Well, I'm not left behind this time, Clint," she said. "I like what we have here, and I don't want anyone to ruin it."

"And who's—"

"I'm sure Luke told you about Jim Courtright, the man who wants him to pay protection?"

"Yes," Clint said, "I just wasn't sure that you knew."

"Oh, I know everything," she said. "You see, that's a condition between Luke and I for coming here, that I be in on everything—and I have been."

"I see."

"Luke won't pay, Clint," she said. "He never will."

"I know that."

"I want you—I would like you to make Jim Courtright go away."

"And how would you like me to do that, Hettie?"

She looked away and said, "I don't care."

"Do you want me to kill him?" Clint asked. "Is that what you're asking me to do?"

"I'm asking you to save your friend's life," she said, looking at him again, boldly this time, eyes flashing. "That means by not allowing him to be killed by, and not allowing him to kill, Jim Courtright. And I don't care how you do it."

"Hettie—"

"That's all I have to say," she announced, standing up. "I—I don't wish to talk about it anymore."

"Hettie—" he said, but she rushed out without giving him a chance to get any further.

Well, he'd seen everyone involved now and been asked to do what he could by them—all except one man.

Jim Courtright.

ELEVEN

When Clint left the room he took his empty beer mug with him and handed it directly to Leon.

"Thank you, sir."

"Leon, what did Mr. Short tell you about me?"

"Sir, he said you were now one of my bosses," Leon answered. "Is there anything else you need?"

"Yes," Clint said, "don't snap to attention every time you see me. Relax a bit."

"Yes, sir," Leon said, almost clicking his heels.

"Thanks."

Clint took a turn around the room and noticed that already the intensity on the floor had changed since he first came up with Short. It was almost crackling in the air, like lightning, and it was a heady thing. He suddenly felt more awake and alive than he had all day.

Still, he didn't feel like sitting in on any games if it

45

was going to become known that he was now a partner. Rather he thought he'd simply look the entire operation over, as a new partner would. It was during this inspection that he saw the woman.

Unlike most of the women in the place, who were playing the new game, keno, this one was playing poker.

She had lots of luxurious black hair and skin like creamy milk. Obviously, she did all of her working and playing indoors, away from the sun. As he watched her play it was as if she suddenly became aware of him. She looked up right at him and smiled. He smiled back and continued to watch as she took money away from the four men she was playing poker with.

The game was five-card stud and she played with confidence. He got close enough to see the cards on the table, and to watch the house dealer to see if he was helping her. A woman like that, she could get all the help she needed from a man with no problem. However, this dealer seemed to be working a straight game, no marked cards, and no cards coming off the bottom.

It was a high stakes game, too, and he assumed that some of the men in the game must have been the businessmen or statesmen Short had been talking about.

The lady, however, was a gambler, pure and simple.

Or not so simple.

Although she was aware of him watching her, and even looked up at him once or twice, it did not distract her from her game. She continued to take the men's money in a very efficient fashion, and it frustrated them.

In fact, it frustrated one man so much he had to speak up.

"Damn it," he said, "the cards are just fallin' for her,

ain't they?" He was well dressed, in his mid-forties, and Clint couldn't make up his mind if he was a businessman or a statesman. He certainly wasn't a gambler, not the way he played cards. He had the money to play in a high stakes game, but not the skill.

And when a man lacked skill he almost invariably blamed the cards—or someone else.

He looked at the dealer, who appeared to be about thirty, and asked, "Wouldn't be dealin' her cards, would you, son?"

The dealer remained calm.

"Same as I'm dealing you, Mr. Cabot."

So the man was a regular, recognized by the dealer.

"Oh, not the same as me, son," Cabot said, "not hardly. Seems every time she needs a certain card—bang—it falls right there for her. When I need it . . . well, it's someplace else, ain't it?"

"Henry," one of the other men said warningly.

"Mr. Cabot?" the dealer asked. "Are you saying I'm cheating?"

"Hell, son," Cabot said, around a big cigar, "I'm just makin' observations." He let out a big cloud of blue smoke along with a laugh. "Ain't nobody said nothin' about cheatin' . . . yet."

The dealer put his cards down as all of the players looked at Cabot—except the woman. She looked up at Clint with mild amusement.

"Mr. Cabot?" she said.

"Ma'am?"

"Would you like your money back?"

Cabot laughed again and looked around the table.

"You offerin' to give it back?"

"No, sir," she said, "I'm proposing to let you try to win it back."

"How so?"

"In a private game," she said, "for increased stakes, with the dealer of your choice."

"The little lady wants to play me head-to-head?"

"That's right," she said, "if the other gentlemen don't mind? I understand there's a private room available up here?" She looked at the dealer.

"Yes, ma'am, that's right, but I'd have to clear it with one of my bosses."

The woman looked up at Clint and asked the dealer, "Is that one of your bosses?"

The dealer looked at Clint and said, "Yes, ma'am. That's Mr. Clint Adams."

Two things happened then. Clint realized that the word had gotten to most if not all of the employees that he was now a partner and two, all of the players turned in their seats and looked at him.

TWELVE

Clint agreed to the private game, with him as the observer. The choice of dealer went to Henry Cabot, who was a regular at the club and did, in fact, have his favorite dealers.

"I choose Walter."

Clint looked at the young dealer and asked, "Is Walter working tonight?"

"Yes, sir," the young man said. "He's downstairs."

"And what's your name?"

"I'm Frank."

"Frank, why don't you go downstairs and tell Mr. Short what's happening up here and ask him to send Walter up."

"Yes sir. And me?"

"Close this table until you speak with Mr. Short. He'll tell you what to do next."

"Yes, sir."

"And Frank . . . don't take this personal."

"No, sir."

As Frank went off to do as he was told Clint turned to the table and said, "We haven't been formally introduced. I'm Clint Adams."

"Henry Cabot," the man said, without waiting for the lady to speak.

"Mr. Cabot," Clint said. "And ma'am?"

"Not ma'am," she said, seemingly amused by it all. "My name is Lillian Farmer, Mr. Adams."

"It's a pleasure to meet you, Miss Farmer."

"Lillian," she said, "please."

"All right, then," he said. "Lillian, Mr. Cabot, if you'll come with me I'll take you to the private room."

"Uh, Henry," the other man—who had spoken in a warning tone to Cabot before—said.

"Yes, Douglas?"

"Do you have any objection to us watching?"

Cabot looked around the table at the other three men.

"I have no object if the lady doesn't," Cabot finally said. "I'd be happy to have an audience watch me take her money."

"Ma'am?" Douglas Colter asked Lillian Farmer.

"I have no objection, Mr. Colter. The more the merrier." She looked at Cabot, then at Clint. "I tend to thrive in front of an audience, anyway."

Clint got Cabot and Lillian set up at the table in the private room, with the other men standing around the table waiting for the game to begin. He waited outside for the dealer to arrive, and when he did he was with Luke Short.

"What's going on?" Short asked.

"Two of your customers want to go head to head."

"Cabot is one of them?" Short asked, almost in a whisper.

"Yes."

"He's a fool," Short said, "but a good customer. Loses a lot of money here every night."

"Well," Clint said, "tonight he's been losing it to a lady."

"Lillian Farmer?"

"Yes, how did you know?"

"She's the only woman around here who doesn't play keno," Short said. "Clint, if she beats him badly there's going to be hell to pay."

"What kind of hell?" Clint asked.

"He's a very bad loser," Short said. "In fact, he's the worst kind of loser."

"The kind who makes excuses every time?"

"Right."

"The kind who blames the cards."

"And the dealer."

"He requested this dealer," Clint said, indicating Walter, who was standing off to one side looking unaffected. He was also young, like Frank and most of the other waiters and bartenders.

"Yes, he usually plays at Walter's table."

"Is there a relationship going on between the two?"

"You mean does Walter deal him seconds?"

"That's what I mean."

"No, I'm sure not."

"I watched Frank deal," Clint said, "He's very good."

"Frank deals an honest game."

"I know."

"All my dealers do."

"That's good."

"But that doesn't mean Cabot won't complain."

"Let him," Clint said. "I, for one, want to see this woman take him for a bundle."

"You, for one," Short said, "just want to see the woman."

"Well," Clint said, "there's no reason for you to stay up here, Luke. Walter and I will have everything under control."

"You're gettin' right into this, aren't you?"

"Why not?" Clint asked. "At the very least it'll make for an interesting night."

"More than interesting," Short said. "Okay, Clint, this is all yours." And with that he walked away.

"Walter?"

"Sir?"

"Are you ready?"

"Yes, sir."

"Do you get intimidated while you're dealing?"

"No, sir," Walter said. "Never."

"Not even by a beautiful woman?"

Walter smiled. He was a handsome young man, one who would probably do very well with the keno ladies. He hesitated before answering the question.

"I've dealt to Miss Lillian before, sir."

"And to Cabot?"

"Oh, yes, sir."

"What's your impression of him?"

Again, he hesitated before answering.

"May I speak frankly about one of our patrons, sir?"

"I'd prefer it."

"It is my belief, sir," Walter said, carefully, "that Mr. Cabot is a born loser."

"Walter," Clint said, "that is my impression exactly."

THIRTEEN

Clint and Walter stepped into the room and Walter took his place at the table. The only three people seated were the dealer and the two players. Clint would watch, along with the other three interested parties, from a standing position.

Walter produced a new deck of cards and allowed both players to examine and approve them.

"Deal," Clint said.

"Five-card stud?" Walter asked.

The players agreed.

From the position in which they were seated Lillian would be the first to receive a card. This didn't seem to upset Cabot. Clint couldn't help but wonder at the man's apparent confidence. Judging from the way he played, where did such confidence come from?

As luck would have it, Cabot won the first three hands,

and his best hand was a pair of aces. The cards had been falling for Lillian in the other game but not, apparently, in this one.

Not for a while, anyway.

Cabot had recouped most of his losses by the time the tide started to turn. He was riding high, very happy, talking and laughing while Lillian remained silent throughout. Occasionally, she'd exchange a glance with Clint— glances which he thought were saying quite a bit.

Leon, the waiter, came in and out with drinks for the players and the spectators. None for the dealer. Clint offered Walter a break after an hour, but he declined.

"I'll deal as long as they want to play."

At one point Short stuck his head into the room and beckoned Clint to come out.

"How's it going?"

"Cabot's won back most of what she took in the other game, but I think the momentum is beginning to swing her way, again."

"How long will this go on?"

"Until one of them quits, I assume. Why? Do you have another private game?"

"No," Short said, "no other game tonight, Stay with it, then. I'll circulate for another couple of hours and then check back before I turn in for the night."

"Right."

"By the way," Short said, "you were asking about girls. They're working downstairs right now."

"That's okay," Clint said. "I've got a woman up here I'm finding fascinating."

"Lillian?"

Clint nodded.

"Good luck."

"How do you mean?"

"Well," Short said, "Lillian is pretty much known as a cold fish around here."

"Around here? In the White Elephant?"

"No."

"In Fort Worth?"

Short shook his head, then said, "In Texas."

"Ah."

"Maybe you're the one to thaw her out, though," Short said. "Lord knows I've seen you do it before."

Clint thought about the glances she'd been tossing his way, some of them positively hot, in his opinion.

"Well," Clint said, "I get the feeling she's already partially thawed."

"Then I say again," Short answered, "good luck."

FOURTEEN

Slowly the money began to go back across the table to Lillian's side. Clint knew that in a head-to-head poker game the action often switched sides. The only way for someone to win was for the game to be called while they were ahead. He could see from the way it was going that neither player was going to do that, and it was going to have to fall to him to call "Last hand," at some point.

He wouldn't do it now, though. Lillian seemed to be getting the cards again, and as the game had been mostly Cabot's right from the beginning he wanted to give her the chance to get back.

The spectators, however, were beginning to fall by the wayside. One by one they announced they were leaving, wished good luck to the players, and faded away, until there were only four people in the room: the dealer, the two players, and Clint.

Clint watched the action and was able to gauge when the players were about even. To call the game at that time would have done no one a service. They began to play evenly for a while, each taking a hand in turn, and he watched carefully to see which way the luck was going to swing next.

Then, suddenly, there was a big hand in progress. He could feel it. In fact, Walter looked up at him after the third card was dealt, as if he knew it, too.

Cabot had a pair of aces on the table, and Lillian had a pair of tens. They were matching stares while Cabot pondered his bet.

"Your bet, Mr. Cabot," Walter said.

Cabot gave Walter a slow, long look and said, "I know it's my bet, son."

Walter shrugged and sat back to watch the play.

Cabot turned and looked at Clint.

"All right to up the bet?" he asked.

"If it's all right with the lady."

Both men looked at Lillian, who simply inclined her head in a nod of agreement.

"A thousand," Cabot said.

"Up a thousand," Lillian said, immediately.

"I've got two aces here, lady."

"I can see, Mr. Cabot."

"And you raise me a thousand on tens? Am I supposed to think you have a ten in the hole?"

"You're supposed to think we have two more cards coming, Mr. Cabot," Lillian said.

"Well, it's going to cost you to get those two cards," Cabot said. "I'll call your thousand and raise you five."

"I'll call," Lillian said.

"Ha!" Cabot said, as if causing her to call and not raise was some sort of triumph.

Clint was shaking his head, unbeknownst to Cabot. He could see Lillian reeling the man in. The whole night was apparently coming down to this hand.

Walter sat forward and dealt out the fourth card to each player. Cabot received a ten while Lillian got a useless three. While the ten did not improve Cabot's hand it boosted his confidence because it was a card Lillian could have used.

"Five thousand," he said, with a smile.

"Raise the same," Lillian said. Cabot frowned.

"Are you watching the cards, woman?" he asked.

Her raises were having the desired affect on her opponent. He was growing agitated that she apparently did not respect his aces.

"There's a raise on the table, Mr. Cabot," Walter said.

"I know it!" Cabot snapped at him.

Walter left the deck on the table, folded his arms and sat back.

"Your five," Cabot said, counting out his money, "and ten more."

Cabot slapped his hand down on the table.

"Your ten and another ten."

"Call," Lillian said.

"Last card," Walter said, unfolding his hands and reaching for the deck.

"Freeze, Walter!" Clint said.

Walter froze and said, "Sir?"

"Stand up."

"What's going on?" Cabot asked.

Clint walked around the table to where the dealer was now standing, looking puzzled.

"We're changing dealers," Clint said. "I'm taking over."

"What?" Cabot asked. "Why?"

Clint grabbed Walter's right arm and fished an ace out from his sleeve.

"This is why."

"Mr. Adams—" Walter said.

"Get out, Walter," Clint said. "You're fired."

Walter hesitated, then threw a furious look not at Clint, but at Cabot before he stormed out.

"W-why would he do that?" Cabot asked.

"I wonder," Clint said, taking the dealer's seat. He looked at Lillian, who had watched the proceedings with great interest. "Do you want to continue?"

"What about the rest of the game?"

"It was dealt clean," Clint said. "When he folded his arms this last time he was going to produce the ace."

"I'll play," Lillian said.

"Well, I won't," Cabot said. "Not when the dealer was cheating."

"He was cheating in your favor, Mr. Cabot," Clint said. "Why do you suppose he would do that?"

"I don't know. In fact, how do I know he was going to give me that ace? How do I know she don't have an ace in the hole?"

"The game goes on, Mr. Cabot."

"And if I want to leave?"

"Then you leave with no money."

"You can't do that."

"Sure I can."

Cabot drummed the fingers of one hand on the table. Clint was sure that the man had been paying Walter, maybe even for a long time, waiting for this moment.

There wasn't that much money on the table, not for some-one as apparently wealthy as he was. No, this had to be about beating Lillian Farmer.

"All right, then," Cabot said. "I don't know what's going on here, but deal."

FIFTEEN

Clint peeled Lillian's dress off her shoulders, exposing her skin one lovely inch at a time. She closed her eyes as he pulled it farther down, exposing more and more of the slopes of her breasts until suddenly the dress was bunched around her waist and her breasts were bobbing free. They were large and round, very firm, and her nipples were brown and very large. He leaned over and ran his tongue over them while she shivered and her flesh produced gooseflesh. He held her breasts in his hands, like big, ripe fruits, and continued to devour them, leaving both small red and wet spots, where he alternately kissed and nipped at them.

Finally, he went back to the dress and continued to peel it downward until it was lying on the floor, puddled around her ankles. She lifted first one foot and then the other so that he could finally discard the dress in a corner of the room.

He helped her off with the various undergarments that existed beneath a woman's dress, and finally she was standing before him totally naked. He kissed the pale, smooth skin of her belly and she shivered again. He could smell her musk, wafting up from between her legs, but he wasn't ready for that yet. He kissed her belly some more, poked at her belly button with his tongue, kissed her hip and then, still on his knees, worked his way around to her delightful ass. Her buttocks were full and round and even firmer than her breasts. He licked them, bit them, kissed them, ran his tongue between them, slid his hands up and down the backs of her thighs. The moonlight coming in the window made her flesh glow, as if lit from within. He kissed the other hip, ran his hands down around her ankles, worked his way around until he was on his knees in front of her, again, kissing her belly.

Finally, he moved his mouth farther down. She put her hands on his shoulders and spread her legs for him so that he could delve into her luxuriant pubic hair with his tongue. Now she was not only musky, but moist and the first touch of his tongue did two things. It made her jump, as if she had been struck by lightning, and it covered the tip of his tongue with the wonderful flavor of her. He became so enamored of the taste that he started lapping at her avidly, licking up as much of her juice as he could. At the same time he was sending shock waves of pleasure through her body until her hands squeezed his shoulders so tightly it hurt, and her legs began to quiver.

"My legs . . ." she gasped, her first words since they entered the room. "Oooh, God, I can't stand any more . . ."

He understood and reacted immediately. It was time for

them to move to the bed. He slid his hands up the backs of her thighs again, reached her buttocks and cupped them tightly, then stood, lifting her from the floor. This put her breasts almost even with his face and he licked and sucked at her nipples while he carried her to the bed. Once there he lowered her to it, and she reclined on her back gratefully, as her legs now felt like jelly.

She reached for his belt and he stepped back away from her and began to disrobe for her. Never a vain man, he had been told by enough women that his penis pleased them—both in the way it looked and the way he used it—so he lowered his pants and underwear slowly and then kicked them into a corner where his boots already were. He stood straight and removed his shirt. In doing so, his penis, incredibly erect at this point, pointed up at an angle to the ceiling. The same moonlight that made her skin glow did the same to his shaft, the palest portion of his body. Her eyes widened and she actually licked her lips, but he was still standing out of her reach.

He took off his shirt, tossed it away, and was completely naked,

"I'm on fire," she said, extending her arms out to him. "Come over here."

"This isn't because of that ace, is it?" he asked.

"What?"

"Well," he said, staying just out of her reach, "if you're just doing this out of gratitude because I caught the dealer with that ace—"

"I'm not doing it for the ace," she said, "or for the fourth ten you gave me on the last card to take Mr. Cabot's money. I'm doing it because I want you—and I especially want you *now*! So get that beautiful thing over here!"

"This old thing?" he asked, looking down at his erection.

She got up on an elbow, giving her the few more inches she needed to grab him by the cock and pull him to the bed, saying, "Shut the hell up and get over here!"

SIXTEEN

Clint woke the next morning with the weight of two big breasts on his back.

"I was wondering how long I'd have to lie like this before you woke up," she said into his ear.

"You wore me out last night, woman," he said.

"Oh, I don't think I have the energy to wear you out, Mr. Adams," she replied. She slid her hand down over his butt, caressing first one cheek and then the other. Then she slid down him, nipples scraping his back, until her mouth had replaced her hand. She kissed and licked his buttocks and slid one hand beneath him to stroke his rigid cock. He lifted his hips a bit so she could grasp him. Finally, he got to his knees. She stroked his back with one hand and his cock and balls with the other. Finally, she got on her back and slid beneath him so she could lick him there. He closed his eyes as her tongue went up and down his shaft and then she took him into her mouth, still fondling his testicles.

The angle was bad for him so he rolled onto his side. She went right with him without releasing him from her avid mouth. She reached around with one hand to stroke his ass again, then to clutch it. And then she rolled him onto his back so she could suck him freely, her head bobbing up and down as she wet him thoroughly. When he was slick with her saliva she mounted him, guided him to her moist portal and then sat on him, taking him deep inside.

"Oooh, yeah," she said, "somehow I didn't get to be on top last night."

"Be my guest," he said. "Stay there as long as you like."

She laughed and while riding him up and down said, "We could be here all day, then."

"I don't think so," he grunted.

"And why not?"

"I don't think I could last all day."

She leaned down and kissed him, flattening her breasts to his chest, then moved her mouth to his ear.

"What have you got to do today?" she asked.

"Nothing," he said, "why?"

"Oh," she said, "I just thought we might try testing out my theory."

"Oh, God," he said, "the woman wants to kill me."

She sat up and moved up and down on him several times, taking him in and out in long, deep, slow strokes. It was the most exquisite agony he'd ever encountered.

"Is this a bad way to die?" she asked, teasingly, but before he could answer she said, "I think not!"

•   •   •

After a few hours Clint got hungry and said so.

"Are you giving up, then?" she asked.

"No," he answered, "I'm just saying I'm hungry."

"Well," she said, "I have to admit I am, too."

"Then we'll call a truce and go get something to eat?"

"Sounds good to me."

She swung her legs to the floor and stood up, giving him a perfect view of her perfect butt.

"Wait a minute," he said, and grabbed her.

A little while later they finally got out of the room.

"I'm surprised I can even walk," he said, as they made their way down the hall to the stairs.

"Are we having breakfast or lunch?" she asked.

"I don't know," he said. "I'm not even sure what time it is."

"Well, whatever we're having," she said, "it'll be on me."

"Why's that?"

"Because I won last night," she said. "Remember?"

How could he forget?

Cabot had no choice but to play the hand out, knowing that he wasn't going to get the ace that Walter had up his sleeve. If he did get another ace it was going to have to be on the up and up from Clint.

"Last card," Clint said, and dealt them out.

Lillian got the ten she needed for four tens. Cabot got a three, which did him no good. He stood up angrily and glared at Clint, then seemed to realize who he was glaring at.

"Luke Short will be hearing about this," he finally said.

"Yes, he will," Clint said, sitting back in his chair, "be-cause I'm going to tell him."

"I'm a regular patron here, you know."

"A regular loser, from what I hear," Clint said, "and after seeing you play, I can understand why. If you've got any more of the White Elephant dealers in your pocket—or wallet—Cabot, tell them they better quit before I find them."

Cabot's rage was such that even though he knew who Clint was he still almost attacked him. In the end, though, he simply closed his hands into fists, then turned and stalked out.

"Well. . . ." Lillian said.

"Congratulations on your win," he said to her. "Can I buy you a drink to celebrate?"

"A drink will do," she said, "for a start . . ."

Once they were seated in the restaurant with platters of steak and eggs in front of them, Lillian said, "I have to ask you something."

"What?"

"That ten you gave me last night?"

"What about it?"

"Did you . . . I mean, was that . . ."

"Are you asking me if I cheated?"

"Well . . ."

"Does it really matter?" he asked. "After all, he never improved on his aces. You would have beaten him with three tens, anyway."

"I was just wondering," she said.

"I don't know if I'm even that good a mechanic with cards."

The phrase was not a well-known one, but Lillian was

a gambler and she knew what a "mechanic" was.

"You were good enough to spot the dealer."

"Oh, I can spot somebody dealing in seconds," Clint said, "I just don't think I'm very good at it myself."

She stared at him with a dubious look on her lovely face.

"This steak is so good," he said, "isn't it?"

SEVENTEEN

The next day went by with much tension and much talking by Jim Courtright, who swore to anyone who'd listen that he would run Luke Short out of Fort Worth or kill him. It also brought a bit of a surprise for both Clint and Short.

Clint told Luke Short what had happened with Cabot the night before, and how it had ended.

"Well," Short said, "you may have caused me to lose one of my best dealers and my best loser, but so be it. Cheatin' is cheatin' and if you caught 'em, that's good enough for me."

"You better take a good hard look at your other dealers, Luke," Clint said.

"It don't matter if Cabot's got another one is his pocket, Clint," Short said. "I'm barrin' him from the place. Come on, there's one room I haven't shown you yet."

It turned out to be a billiard room on the second floor and Clint and Short spent much of the afternoon there.

"I heard you and Lillian have gotten real friendly," Short said.

"It's true."

"Lucky man," Short said. "Don't know how you did it, but I figured if anyone could thaw that little gal out it would be you."

"The thawing started as soon as we locked eyes, I guess," Clint said.

"Glad to hear it. Maybe she'll keep you in town a bit longer."

"I'm here until your problem gets resolved, Luke," Clint said. "I'm here to back your play, whatever it is."

"I appreciate that, Clint," Short said, "and so does Hettie. By the way, she wants you to have dinner with us in our apartment tonight."

"Is she going to cook?"

"Not a chance," Short said. "When I had this place built I had a dumbwaiter installed in my apartment, goes down to the kitchen. They can send up anything I want, piping hot."

"Sounds good," Clint said. "I'll be there. What time?"

"Seven?"

"Seven it is."

"Uh, don't bring Lillian."

"Why not?"

"Hettie doesn't like gamblin' women."

"Didn't you say she plays keno?"

"She does," Short said, scratching his head, "but she don't consider that to be gambling."

"I won't mention it to Lillian, then," Clint said. "Besides, we're not quite ready to pick out furniture and be a couple."

Short stood up straight and leaned on his stick.

"You think that day will come, Clint? For you?"

"With Lillian?"

"With anybody."

Clint hesitated a moment, then said, "You know, Luke, I don't. I think that time has passed for me. I'm never going to settle down on a little spread with a wife and have babies. It just isn't in the cards for me, anymore—and maybe it never was."

"Well," Short said, "don't let Hettie hear you say that."

"Why not?"

Short lined up his shot and said, "She'll be tryin' to fix you up with somebody quicker than you can spit."

"Thanks for the warning."

They shot a few more games and then the bartender, Andy, appeared at the door.

"What is it, Andy?" Short asked.

"There's a fella downstairs says he's Bat Masterson, Mr. Short," the young bartender said. He appeared to be equally unimpressed with Masterson as he had been with meeting Clint.

"Dressed like a dandy? Kinda good lookin'?" Short asked.

"Dressed like a dandy, yeah," Andy said, "and the girls are paying attention to him."

"Sounds like Bat," Clint said. "Why not have the boy bring him up?"

"You heard the man, Andy," Short said. "Show the man up."

"Yes, sir."

"What's his story?" Clint asked.

"Who? Andy?"

"Yes," Clint said. "He didn't recognize my name, and now he doesn't seem to know who Bat is."

"Andy's from back east," Short said. "He was in college, where his folks wanted him, but he left after two years and came west. Didn't do much readin' while he was in school, except for schoolwork. He's a little behind in his western legends."

"I just thought of something," Clint said.

"What?"

"What if this fella isn't Bat?" Clint asked. "What if Courtright sent him in to take a try at you?"

"If that's the case," Short said, "he's gonna be real disappointed when he shows up here and finds the two of us. But I got a question for you, if it is Bat."

"What's that?"

"How do you and him seem to show up whenever I'm in trouble?"

"We just seem to know, is all," Clint said. "But hey, we can leave if you like—"

"Never mind!" Short said. "I kinda like havin' the two of you around."

Andy appeared in the doorway at that moment and said, "Bat Masterson, Mr. Short."

Clint stepped to the side, which put him out of Bat's line of sight from the door—or whoever it was claiming to be Bat. As the man walked in, though, he could see that it was, indeed, the one and only Bat Masterson.

"What's wrong with that youngster, Luke?" Masterson was asking as he walked in. "Didn't seem to know who I was."

"There's a fella standing right over there seemed to

have the same problem with my bartender, Bat," Short said, nodding in Clint's direction.

Masterson turned his head and broke into a huge smile when he saw Clint Adams standing there leaning on his billiards stick. While each man was good friends with Luke Short, they were even better friends with—and to— each other.

"Goddamn," Masterson said, "the Three Musketeers all together in the same place at the same time. Must be a helluva storm brewin'!"

EIGHTEEN

Clint and Short took Bat Masterson down to the bar for a beer and to catch him up on what was going on.

"I know Courtright," Bat said when they'd finished. "He's as good with his right hand as he is with his left."

"That's encouraging," Short said.

"Just an observation," Bat said.

"What brings you here, Bat?" Clint asked.

"Just the next stop in my search for the perfect poker game," Bat Masterson said. "It sure looks like I found the perfect gambling palace, huh?"

"You can say that again," Clint said.

"This place is gorgeous, Luke," Bat said. "You've really done it this time."

"Thanks, Bat," Short said. "Now if I can only figure out a way to keep it."

"Well, count me in, whatever you figure on."

"Thanks, Bat," Short said. "I appreciate it. I was asking Clint when you walked in how you fellas always seem to know when I've stuck my foot in it?"

"Huh?" Bat said, looking at Clint. "When does he not stick his foot in it?"

"Thanks!" Short said.

"Is Hettie with you?" Bat asked.

"She's upstairs. We got an apartment up there— Hey! Clint's comin' up for dinner later, why don't you come and surprise her?"

"Oh, hey," Bat said, "it's been my experience that women don't like it when you surprise them at dinner— not when they're cookin'."

"She's not cookin'," Short said. "The food'll be comin' up from the restaurant."

"Oh, well, in that case count me in for dinner, too," Bat said. He looked at Clint. "Any interesting poker games?"

Short remained silent while Clint filled Bat Masterson in on Lillian Farmer.

Courtright sat across the table from his partner, Charley Bull, in the no-name saloon he'd chosen as his headquarters.

"Tomorrow, Charley," he said. "Short goes down tomorrow."

"You sure you wanna do this Jim?" Bull asked. "I mean, Adams is in town and somebody said they thought they saw Bat Masterson come ridin' in."

"Short ain't gonna let nobody else fight his battles, Charley," Courtright said. "I ain't afraid of Luke Short, I ain't afraid of no Bat Masterson, and if Clint Adams wants ta try me I'm ready to increase my reputation by killin' the Gunsmith."

"You sound pretty confident."

"I haven't lived by the gun this long without bein' confident, Charley," Courtright said.

"I still ain't even sure why you're doin' this," Bull admitted.

"That's because you ain't the brains of this partnership, Charley," Courtright said. "If Short gets away with not payin' it sends a message to everyone else, and then we got to look for a new way to make a livin'. You understand that? Luke Short is cuttin' into our livin'."

"Yeah, yeah," Bull said, "I get it, Jim, but I ain't no gun hand and I ain't about to go up against the Gunsmith."

"You don't have to Charley," Courtright said. "That's what I'm here to do. Don't you worry about a thing."

Neither man knew that there was someone within earshot, listening to every word. Truth be told, however, Jim Courtright wouldn't have cared. He wanted Luke Short to know that he was coming for him; that way the little gambler would be nervous.

While Courtright thought that maybe he'd pass the word around the next day, the man at the other table left and went straight to the White Elephant.

Jake Johnson put five one-dollar gold pieces into the outstretched hand of the man who said he had information for him.

"This better be good, Cable," he said.

"It's Courtright, Jake," Cable Kissinger said.

"What about him?"

"He's comin' for Luke."

"Give me back the mon—"

"Tomorrow."

Johnson paused. "How do you know it's tomorrow?"

"I heard him tellin' Bull," Cable said. "I was at the next table."

That satisfied Jake Johnson, and he withdrew his hand.

"Okay, Cable," Johnson said. "Go to the bar and get a drink on the house."

"Thanks, Jake."

As Cable made his way to the bar Jake Johnson caught the bartender's eyes and relayed the message via hand signals that he was to give the man one free drink. The bartender nodded.

Jake knew that Luke Short was having Clint Adams and the newly arrived Bat Masterson up to his apartment for dinner. He also knew that Hettie Short did not like him to come up there. For some reason he could not understand, the woman had taken an instant dislike to him. Still, Short had to be warned, and it might not be a bad idea to do it in the presence of his friends.

Of the two, Johnson knew Clint Adams better than he knew Bat Masterson, but he knew without a doubt that either or both men would back Short's play. That was good, because Courtright had some friends who would back him, although he knew that Charley Bull wasn't one of them. He'd be on the sidelines observing, and so would Johnson, but not for the same reason. Bull simply was not a hand with a gun. He'd be more of a liability with a gun than a help. As for Johnson, as the ex-marshal of Fort Worth he knew how to handle a gun, but he was friends with both men, and did not want to take sides.

Warning Short, however, would not be taking sides. That would just even things up.

He decided to wait awhile, let the folks upstairs finish their meal, and then go up and have a talk with Short.

NINETEEN

The dumbwaiter turned out to be the big attraction of the evening in Luke Short's apartment, followed closely by the food itself.

"By God," Bat said as Short transferred the food to the table, "you'd never have to leave the room if you didn't want to."

"Well, luckily," Short said, "I want to. There's too much to do out there to stay cooped up for too long."

"I agree with that," Clint said. "Still too much to see for me to even stay in the same town too long."

"Me, too."

Both men were suddenly aware that Hettie Short was giving them both dirty looks.

"Of course," Bat added, "finding one town that I can eventually settle down in is certainly something I aspire to."

"You've got it all right here in Fort Worth, Luke," Clint said.

"Don't I know it," the little gambler agreed.

Hettie's expression brightened and both Clint and Bat Masterson knew they were off the hook.

After dinner Short poured some sherry for his two friends while Hettie cleaned the table. She had not been very active in their dinner conversation and once the table was clear she said, "If you gentlemen don't mind I think I'll retire to the bedroom to do some reading. It was very nice seeing you again, Bat."

"And you, Hettie," Bat said. "You're looking even more beautiful than usual."

That earned him a kiss on the cheek, and then she bestowed one on Clint, as well. After a more hearty kiss for her husband she was off to read her book *Huckleberry Finn*, the newest one by her favorite author, Mark Twain. But first she warned, "No cigars, Luke. You've got a whole smoky gambling hall for that vile habit."

"Yes, Hettie."

When she was gone he said, "I sometimes sneak one while she's in the bedroom, but with an open window. I'm afraid that wouldn't help much, though, with the three of us smoking."

"I'll skip it, Luke, if it's all the same," Clint said.

"As will I," Bat said.

"I'll wait until we go back downstairs, anyway."

They were all sitting comfortably when the knock came at the door. Short went to answer it and returned with his partner, Jake Johnson.

"Jake, do you know Bat?"

"We met once or twice," Bat said, and nodded to the man without rising.

"Hello, Masterson," Johnson said. "Heard you were in town."

"Drink, Jake?" Short asked his partner.

"No, thanks, Luke."

"Problems downstairs?"

"No," Johnson said, "I just heard something a little while ago that I thought you should know."

"And what's that?"

"Should we leave—" Clint started, but Johnson put up his hand to stop him.

"No, Adams," he said, "this is something you and Masterson should hear, too."

Clint settled back in his chair. Bat had never moved.

"What is it, Jake?" Short asked, again.

"I heard that Jim Courtright's gonna come for you tomorrow."

"Is that right?" Short looked around the room. "You hear that, gents? Tomorrow's the day. Looks like you got here just in time to see the show, Bat."

Bat sat forward and asked, "How many backing his play, Jake?"

Johnson shrugged. "I don't know. Jim's got a lot of friends, but he won't let any of them near Luke. He wants that, uh, pleasure all for himself."

Bat looked at Clint.

"I guess how many he has backing him will depend on what we do, Clint."

"I agree." Clint looked at Short. "If we stay in the background the play will stay head to head, Luke. How does that sit with you?"

Short made a face.

"I've been tryin' to avoid it," Short said, "but maybe I can't. Maybe I should just get it over with." Then he brightened. "And I might as well make some money out of it, too."

"How do you mean?" Johnson asked.

"When the word gets out, somebody's gonna be makin' odds, right? Takin' bets?"

"He's right," Bat said, before anyone else could respond. "What odds do you think I'd get on Long-haired Jim?"

"Thanks a lot!" Short said. "No, I'm gonna bet . . . ten thousand on myself."

"What?" Johnson asked.

"Yeah, I bet I can get three-to-one."

"My money's on you, Luke," Bat said, seriously.

"Mine, too," Clint said.

"Are you all crazy?" Johnson said. "Courtright's a gun-fighter, Luke. You're not. Nowhere in your rep does it say gunman."

"I can handle a gun, Jake."

"Jim's as good with either hand!"

"I only have to hit him once," Short said, "and it won't matter which hand he's using."

"Man's got a point," Bat said.

Clint brooded. He wanted his friend to win, and he'd bet on him, but the question was, could he take Court-right?

"Adams," Johnson said, "you've got to brace Court-right."

"Will he back down if I do?"

"Hell, no."

"Then why me?"

"You have a better chance at him."

"We'd get better odds on Luke," Bat said.

"Well then you go, Masterson," Johnson said.

"Still better odds on Luke," Clint said, backing the play of both his friends.

"Jesus," Johnson said, "the three of you are crazy. You two are gonna watch Luke get gunned down?"

"I have to do this, Jake," Short said. "I thought I could avoid it, but I guess I can't."

"Jesus," Johnson said, and then again, "Jesus. Either way I lose a friend."

"I'm sorry for that, Jake," Short said.

"Get a bet down, though," Masterson said. "Then you win either way."

Johnson made a disgusted sound and left, slamming the door behind him.

"Well, that was fun," Bat said, "but what are we really gonna do, Luke?"

"Like I said," Short responded, "I might as well make some money."

"If you win," Clint said. "If you win you make money."

"What happens if you lose?" Bat asked.

"If I lose," Short said, "I won't care if I lose the money."

"But we'll care that we lost a friend," Clint said. "Maybe Jake's right. Maybe Bat or I should—"

"No," Short said. "I appreciate the offer, but if you did that I'd have to leave Fort Worth, anyway. I'd have no respect around here."

"Either way," Bat said, "one of us is gonna end up killing him, Luke. We can do it now, or wait and see if he kills you."

"No," Short said. "If I kill him, then neither one of you has to do a thing—except get a bet down!"

TWENTY

The word spread like wildfire that evening. Short was able to get his bet down at three-to-one before he went to bed.

Clint spent the night with Lillian in his room, and that morning they cuddled in bed and she asked him about the betting.

"Did Luke really bet ten thousand on himself?"

"He did."

"Can he beat Jim Courtright?" she asked. "I mean, everything I've ever heard about Luke is that he's a gambler, but never a gunman."

"I guess we'll have to see."

"Are you betting?"

"No."

"Why not?'

"I don't bet on people's lives."

"What about your friend Masterson?" she asked. "Is he going to bet?"

"Probably."

"On who?"

"I expect he'll back Luke."

Well," she said, "if they're each going to risk their money, maybe it's a good bet."

"Maybe it is."

She sat up and asked, "You're not going to help me with this, are you?"

"You're a good poker player, Lillian," he said. "Why don't you stick to that?"

"You don't want me to make money?" she asked.

"Not on my friend's life."

"I'm a gambler, Clint," she said. "That's what I do."

He gave her a disapproving look, and she didn't like it.

"I think I better go," she said.

He didn't respond, and he didn't watch her dress.

"I'm sorry you disapprove, Clint," she said, when she was dressed, "but I'm going to get a big bet down this morning."

"Fine."

She walked to the door, then turned back.

"Don't you want to know who I'm betting on?"

"No."

She hesitated, nodded, and then went out.

It was nice while it lasted, he thought.

"Ten thousand?" Courtright asked.

"That's the bet," Charley Bull said.

"That sonofabitch!" Courtright said. "Maybe I'll shoot his ears off before I kill him."

"Cool off, Jim."

"What?"

"It's just a no-lose bet for him," Bull explained.

"How's that?"

"If he wins he gets rid of you and he wins money."

"And if he loses?"

Bull shrugged.

"What does he care? He'll be dead. He won't care about the ten thousand, or the White Elephant."

Courtright frowned.

"You're only partially right."

"About what?"

"The money," the gunman said, "but not about the saloon. He won't want to leave his wife to face us."

"There are still two other partners, remember," Bull said. "Jake and Adams."

"That's it," Courtright said. "He sold his share to one of them—probably Adams, since he just got to town."

"So if you kill him, you'll still have to deal with Adams, and he won't pay."

"That's okay," Courtright said. "I'll kill Short, and then I'll kill Adams."

"And then what?"

"And then Jake will pay."

"Jake's your friend."

"This is business, Charley," Courtright said. "Jake understands that."

"I guess," Bull said.

"What about our other accounts?"

"Well . . ."

"What's wrong?"

"Nobody wants to pay until they see what happens between you and Luke Short."

"What?"

Bull shrugged. "If he kills you they don't have to pay."

Courtright stared at him.

"If they kill me they still have to pay you."

"Well . . ."

"Wait a minute," Courtright said. "What kind of partner are you? If he kills me you won't keep the business going?"

"Nobody's afraid of me, Jim," Bull said. "They're all afraid of you."

Courtright just stared at him for a few moments and then said, "You know, maybe I should just kill you."

TWENTY-ONE

Lillian was having breakfast alone in the restaurant when Clint walked in and joined Bat Masterson and Luke Short. They did not even exchange a glance.

"Trouble in paradise?" Short asked.

"Paradise sank this morning," Clint said, seating himself.

"What's the problem?" Bat asked.

"She's too much of a gambler for me."

"Sounds like a recommendation, as far as I'm concerned," Masterson said.

"She's all yours," Clint said.

"Not like you to give up a good-looking woman."

"We had problems with our outlooks on life," he said.

"Such as?" Short asked.

"I don't like betting on my friend's life."

"Oh."

Clint looked at Bat Masterson.

"Don't look at me like that," Bat said. "I'm not betting."

"I thought you thought I could win," Short said to both of them.

"We do," Clint said, "we just don't feel like putting out money on a gunfight."

"But we'll be there to back you," Bat said, "in case he brings help."

"You know what you can do to back me?" Short asked.

"What?" Clint replied.

"Get me a lawyer," Short said. "I'm gonna need one after I kill him."

"You think you'll get arrested?" Bat asked.

"On the spot," Short said. "The new police department frowns on gunfights in the street."

"What about in your place?" Clint asked.

"Same difference," Short said, "but I don't want to do it in my place. And I don't want to upset Hettie."

"Can't blame you for that," Clint said.

At that moment a man dressed in black entered and began looking around the room. Clint spotted him immediately and figured him for a newspaperman.

"I was wondering if they'd get wind of this," he said.

Both Bat and Short looked where he was looking and Bat asked, "Reporter?"

"Now that," Clint said, "I'd bet on."

Bat considered the bet then said, "No bet. He couldn't be a lawman, but—"

"Maybe a lawyer," Short said. "I've got ten dollars says he's a lawyer."

"You're on," Clint said.

"I'll take a piece of that," Bat said. "Looks more like a reporter to me, too."

The man spotted them, recognizing at least one, and hurried over to their table.

"Gentlemen," he said, "I hope I'm not disturbing you."

"Well," Short said, "as a matter of fact—"

"Allow me to introduce myself," the man said, plowing right through Short's response. "My name is Alphonse Michael DeKay. I work for Colonel A. H. Belo, of the *Dallas Morning News*."

"Belo is the publisher," Short said. "He's well known in certain circles."

"Doesn't he also have a newspaper in Galveston?" Bat asked.

"Yes, he does," DeKay said. "The colonel has sent me here to get a story."

"What story?" Short asked.

DeKay shrugged and said, "Whatever's breaking. When the three of you get together something happens."

"Wait a minute," Clint said. "Bat just arrived yesterday. How did you know the three of us were here?"

"Uh, I passed through Dallas on my way here," Bat said. "Somebody might have seen me."

"Somebody did," DeKay said, "so I've been sent to see if there's something worth reporting, or writing about."

Clint, Bat Masterson, and Luke Short exchanged a glance.

"Ah," DeKay said, "there is."

"He'll find out anyway," Clint said. "All he has to do is walk down the street."

Short looked at DeKay, who looked all of twenty-five or so.

"Are you a feature writer for the paper?" he asked. "I don't recall seeing your name."

"You read the paper?"

Short smiled.

"I read a lot of papers," he said. "I've never seen your name."

"You will," DeKay said. "I'll soon be making a name for myself."

"On us?" Clint asked.

DeKay shrugged. "Maybe."

Again the three friends exchanged a glance, and then Bat Masterson asked, "Why not?"

"Okay, Mr. DeKay," Short said. "Have a seat."

TWENTY-TWO

DeKay listened intently, taking notes—with permission—while Luke Short brought him up to date.

"So this gunfight is going to take place today?" the young journalist asked.

"Looks like it," Clint said.

"When?"

"That seems to be up to Courtright," Bat Masterson said.

"Why should it be?" Short asked, then. "Why don't I just go and find him and get it over with."

"You said it yourself," Clint replied.

"What?"

"When it's over you'll be arrested," Clint said. "It would be better if you can say you didn't go looking for this."

"You have a point."

"What are you wearing?" Bat asked.

Short knew what he meant. "My shortened .45 on my hip. I cleaned and oiled it this morning. Hettie watched."

"How is she handling it?"

"I'm very grateful that she is not a hysterical woman," Short said, "but she's not happy."

"Where's your watch?" Bat asked, frowning.

Short usually wore a Jurgensens gold watch with an ivory fob and a gold chain in the watch pocket of his embroidered vest. Today the telltale chain was not visible.

"I left it upstairs," he said. "I don't want to take a chance on it being ruined by a stray bullet."

"Wouldn't it stop a bullet?" DeKay asked. "I mean, if you were wearing it and a bullet hit it—"

"It would go right through and kill me anyway," Short said. "What a waste of a beautiful watch."

DeKay looked around the table at the three friends and put his notebook down.

"What's wrong?" Clint asked.

"I get the feeling there's more—a lot more—here than just the story of a gunfight."

"Gunfight's all you've got right now," Bat Masterson said. "Stick to that."

"Right."

Clint wondered at the journalist's youth. He didn't seem at all intimidated by the three men he was sitting with. Even though Bat Masterson and Luke Short were only about half a dozen years older than he was, their reputations made them seem older, worldlier. Clint was older than all of them, his reputation spanning more years. The journalist seemed interested in them only as news—or as a source of a story that would make his name—rather than as legends of the West.

Clint liked him.

• • •

Jake Johnson joined them in the restaurant, acknowledged the introduction to the young newspaperman, but the ensuing conversation between he and Luke Short concerned everything—business, the coldness of the rainy weather—except what they were all thinking about.

As Johnson made to leave DeKay asked, "May I talk to you for a few minutes, Mr. Johnson?"

"Sure," Johnson said, "why not?"

"Gentlemen," DeKay said, rising. "Thank you for speaking with me, and for the coffee."

"Do you think you have your story, Mr. DeKay?" Bat asked.

"Oh, no, sir," DeKay said. "Not yet. Not by a long shot."

He hurried to catch up to Jake Johnson.

After breakfast Short decided to go and get his boots shined.

"No point dying with scuffed boots," he said.

"Want us to come with you?" Clint asked.

"No," Short said, "it's just down the street. I'll be back soon."

Clint and Bat remained where they were as Short left the restaurant, and the building.

"One of us should probably follow him," Bat said.

"He'll see us," Clint said, "either one of us."

"True," Bat said. "So, tell me about you getting a piece of this place. Are you a full partner?"

"No," Clint said, "that was just a ploy to give me a reason to stay."

"But I thought—"

"Oh, that," Clint said. "No, Luke just wanted to draw

up some papers turning his full share over to me in the case of his death."

"Why'd he do that?" Bat asked. "That doesn't sound fair to Hettie—"

"It's so Hettie wouldn't have to deal with Courtright if . . . well . . ." Clint didn't finish.

"Oh," Bat said, "well, I guess that is best, then."

"Yes."

There was an awkward silence and then Bat said, "Do you think Luke can take Courtright?"

"Don't you?"

"Definitely," Bat said. "I was just wondering what you thought."

"Definitely."

More silence.

"I made a bet," Bat finally said.

Clint looked at him.

"Don't fly off the handle."

"I'm not," Clint said. "That's up to you, Bat. You're the gambler, not me. And Luke's a gambler. He'd certainly understand."

"But you don't?"

"I do," Clint said, "I think."

"Clint," Bat said, "you're right about me being a gambler. I mean, I could no sooner pass up a bet on this than I could on a race, or a good prizefight."

"I suppose."

"And the same could probably be said for your friend Lillian."

"I suppose."

Bat decided not to pursue that. He thought that perhaps

Clint was using the argument to simply end the relationship before it actually became one.

They sat in silence for a few more moments and then Clint asked, "So who did you bet on?"

"Who do you think?"

TWENTY-THREE

It was chilly, even for February, and as Luke Short walked through the gambling hall to the door he noticed that there weren't a lot of people gambling. He stepped outside and would have turned up his collar, but that would have ruined the look he cultivated so carefully each morning before he left his apartment.

While he was getting his boots shined an acquaintance walked by and told him that Jim Courtright was in a saloon down the street bragging about what he was going to do to Luke. Short acknowledged the news without comment and paid for the shoeshine.

Next he lit a cigar and walked into the shooting gallery that was situated next to the White Elephant. He had a conversation with Ella Blackwell, who managed the place, and with two men he knew, B. F. Herring and William Allison. He noticed that all three were extremely nervous

to have him in there, so he left and went back to the White
Elephant. Business was still slow, but he knew it would
pick up soon.

Business did not improve until six o'clock. By this time
Short was simply sitting in the billiard room with Clint
and Bat, watching his two friends shoot a game. Jake
Johnson came in, trailed by the newsman DeKay, who,
apparently, had peppered—or pestered—Johnson all day
with questions.

"The rain's let up some, and people are starting to come
in," Johnson said to Short.

Nobody bothered to mention that they were all just sitting around waiting for Courtright to show up. Johnson
left, this time leaving DeKay behind.

"Have you ever played pool, Mr. DeKay?" Bat Masterson asked.

"I've shot a game or two."

"For money?"

"On occasion."

"Are you on an expense account from your paper?"

"As it happens," DeKay said, "I am."

Bat looked at Clint, who turned and offered DeKay his
pool cue.

"If you don't mind," the young man said, "I'd prefer
to pick out my own."

Clint went and sat next to Short to watch.

Bull looked across the table at Jim Courtright, who
seemed to be very calm.

"When are you going over?" he asked.

"About eight."

"Why eight?"

Courtright shrugged. "Why not?"

"Are you really gonna kill him?"

"Deader than dead," Courtright said. "Killing a famous man like Luke Short will send a message to all the other saloon owners in town, Charley. After this we're gonna raise our rates."

Charley Bull nodded. It was fine with him if they raised their rates, but Courtright would have to be alive for that. Whether or not he was . . . well, that remained to be seen. And even if he did kill Short, what about Adams and Masterson? Were they just going to stand by?

"Are you taking some backup?"

"Already taken care of," Courtright said. "They're in place as we speak."

"Inside the saloon?"

Courtright just smiled. He appeared to have everything his own way.

TWENTY-FOUR

It was eight o'clock when Jake Johnson came into the billiard room. Clint and Short had been watching the young Alphonse Michael DeKay give Bat a run for his money on the table. In fact, they could tell that Bat liked the young newspaperman because he had started calling him "Al."

As Johnson entered they all looked at him.

"Luke, Jim Courtright is out front, looking for you," Short's partner said.

"Looks like this is it," Short said, standing up.

"Luke," Johnson said, "I still think we can settle this without gunplay. Let me go downstairs with you."

"You can come down with me, Jake," Short said. "Just stay out of the way."

Short loosened his gun in the custom-made holster he had clipped onto his hip. This allowed him to wear a gun

without the telltale gun belt around his waist. He usually
wore another custom-made holster that was sewn into the
lining of his jacket, as if he were wearing a shoulder rig.
However, that holster would not have served him well in
this situation.

"All right," Short said to the small assemblage, "let's
go."

He went downstairs, followed by Clint, Bat Masterson,
his partner Jake Johnson, and the newspaperman Alphonse Michael DeKay.

Courtright was waiting outside the shooting gallery next
to the saloon. His backup was in place across the street,
just in case they were needed. There were four of them,
wearing handguns and holding Winchesters. Clint spotted
them as soon as he came out of the saloon with Bat, behind Short.

"Across the street," he said.

"I see 'em," Bat said.

"Think Luke does?" Clint asked. "He's concentrating
pretty hard on Courtright."

"He sees them," Bat said, "but maybe we should do
somethin' about it."

"I'm with you."

As Short turned right to head toward the shooting gallery, Clint and Bat turned left. Half a block down they
crossed the street and started back again.

Jake Johnson came out of the saloon and stopped dead.
He'd watch from there. Alphonse DeKay decided to stay
with him. He had a good vantage point from which to
report the proceedings.

Courtright stood with his feet wide apart, the typical
gunfighter's stance as seen on the covers of many dime

novels. Luke Short continued to walk toward him.

"That's close enough, Short!" Courtright called out.

Short kept walking, unnerving Courtright, who expected people to be intimidated by his reputation. When it came right down to it, he thought that the little gambler would be as well, but that was not turning out to be the case.

"I'm warnin' you!" he called.

Short continued to approach him.

"Don't you pull a gun on me, Short!"

This was a familiar shout for this kind of situation. It allowed the winner to claim that he didn't start anything, but Short still did not slow down. He did, however, lift the front of his vest.

"I'm not wearing a gun, Courtright," he called back, when in actuality what he was not wearing was a gun *belt*.

And with that admission Long-haired Jim Courtright drew his gun with deadly intent.

Clint and Bat were successfully able to get the drop on Courtright's backup men. Clint disarmed two of them, and Bat the other two, and they all watched from across the street.

Jake Johnson saw Jim Courtright go for his gun and knew that his partnership with Luke Short was over.

"Damn him," he said.

Later, DeKay would ask Johnson who he was talking about when he said those words.

Luke Short drew his cut-down Colt and fired the first shot. The smoke from the pistol partially obscured Courtright from his sight, so that all he knew was that he had fired the first shot, not whether it had hit its mark or not.

After firing he threw himself to his left and fired again and again until the hammer of his Colt fell on the empty chambers.

When the smoke cleared he saw Courtright lying on his back, half in and half out of the shooting gallery.

He had not fired a shot.

TWENTY-FIVE

A young policeman named Bony Tucker was half a block away talking to his younger brother, Rowan, when the shots were fired, and he was first on the scene. He came up behind Luke Short, who he knew, and hurriedly plucked Short's gun from his hand.

"It's empty," Short told him.

Tucker shoved the empty gun into his belt and hurried to the fallen Courtright. He later gave his account of what he saw, and what he thought had happened.

The first bullet had shattered the thumb on Courtright's right hand, and had also damaged the gun so it couldn't fire. Another bullet had punctured his heart, and a third had struck him in the shoulder.

Jake Johnson had seen Courtright, after the first shot, try to border shift his gun from right hand to left without success. However, even if he had been successful the gun would not have fired. Essentially, Courtright lost all chance of surviving after the first shot.

Across the street Clint Adams and Bat Masterson had returned the guns to Jim Courtright's colleagues, with Clint telling them, "It's all over, boys."

They then crossed the street to stand with Luke Short, who was now unarmed.

Next on the scene were a sheriff named Rea, and a marshal named Shipp. They stood with Bony and Rowan Tucker, discussing how to handle the matter.

They approached Clint, Bat, and Luke Short en masse with Marshal Shipp telling Short, "We got to take you in, Luke."

"Sure, Marshal," Short said.

Johnson came over and told Short, "I'll get a lawyer, Luke. He'll get you out."

Short nodded.

"He didn't give me much choice, Marshal."

"That's for a judge to decide, Luke," Shipp said, "but between you and me, I've heard all the talk during the week. Everybody knows what's been going on."

"Luke," Bat said, "you don't want to go to jail, just say the word."

Suddenly, the sheriff, the marshal, and the policeman all tensed, ready for anything.

"No, that's okay," Short said. "We talked about this before. I'll be fine. I'll see you boys later."

So Clint and Bat stood by and watched as the law took Luke Short to the county jail for killing Jim Courtright. As they passed Courtright's colleagues, though, one of them called out, "You ain't gonna make it through the night to be bailed out, Short."

Clint and Bat exchanged a glance.

It only took them a couple of hours to decide what they wanted to do.

"We'll go over to the jail and spend the night with Luke," Bat said.

"Why do that?" DeKay asked.

"Because Courtright's friends might try something during the night," Clint said. "Luke wouldn't stand a chance."

They were in the billiards room again, and Jake Johnson came in at that point.

"It's amazing," he said, as he entered.

"What is?" Clint asked.

"In the two hours since he died Jim Courtright has made more friends than he made when he was alive, and they're all talkin' about storming the jail to get Luke."

Clint looked at DeKay and said, "See?"

"We'll need some guns for Luke," Bat said.

"Will the sheriff allow you to do that?" DeKay asked.

"He won't have a choice," Clint said, as he and Bat both stood up. "We won't leave Luke in there to be the victim of a necktie party." To Bat he said, "I've got an extra gun."

"That New Line?" Bat asked.

Clint nodded.

"You're the only one who can do anything with that thing," Bat said. "I'll get Luke's Colt back from the sheriff, and Hettie will give me his other gun. I'll meet you downstairs in half an hour."

"Right."

"I'll come, too," Johnson said.

"No," Clint said, "you'll have to keep this place running while Luke's in jail, Jake. Stay here."

"I have an idea," Alphonse DeKay said, running to keep up with Clint. "Can you—"

"Can you tell me on the run?" Clint asked, cutting him off.

"Yes, of course—"

"Then come on."

TWENTY-SIX

Clint Adams and Bat Masterson entered the county jail
heavily armed. Behind them came the newspaperman Alphonse DeKay. It was DeKay's idea to go with them and
interview them throughout the night, while they waited
for daylight to come. Clint and Bat discussed it and agreed
that it would give them all something to do since they
wouldn't be getting much sleep.

When Sheriff Rea saw both men enter so well armed
he pushed his chair back and put his hands up.

"I don't think it's a good idea, gents, to break Luke
out, but I'm not gonna get killed tryin' to stop you."

"We're not breakin' him out, Sheriff," Bat said. "We're
here to keep him alive until morning."

"We'll stay in the cell with him, Sheriff," Clint said,
"and we're arming him. You have our word that we won't
try to break him out."

"The word of the Gunsmith and Bat Masterson?" Rea asked, lowering his hands. "I'll take it." He grabbed the cell keys off a wall peg and tossed them to Clint. "I'll be out here in the office all night. I don't want him to end up dead, either."

"Thanks, Sheriff," Clint said.

"I'll need Luke's gun," Bat said.

"I gotta tell ya," the lawman said, getting it out of his drawer and handing it over, "I'm relieved that you came. I've heard the talk about breakin' him out to hang him and I was worried about keepin' him alive."

"Well," Bat said, loading the weapon, "now we'll worry along with you."

As the three of them started for the cell block the sheriff asked, "Who's this?"

"Alphonse Michael DeKay, at your service," DeKay said. "I'm a writer for the *Dallas Morning News* here to interview Mr. Adams, Mr. Masterson, and Mr. Short about their long friendship."

"We're gonna tell him some stories," Bat said.

"Hell," Rea said, "I'd like to hear some of those. Mind if I come back later?"

"You're welcome to, Sheriff," Clint said. "And bring some coffee with you."

"You got a deal."

When Clint and Bat and DeKay entered the cell block Short rose from his bunk in surprise.

"What are you fellas doin' here?" he asked.

"Keeping you alive," Clint said.

Clint used the key to unlock the door and Bat walked in first and handed Luke his two guns.

"The sheriff is goin' along with this?" he asked.

"He loves it," Clint said. "You may not know it but

there's a rope out on the street with your name on it."

"People are that upset about Jim Courtright bein' dead?" Short asked, surprised.

"He's got friends in death he didn't even know in life," Alphonse DeKay said.

"What are you doin' here?" Short asked.

"He's going to keep us company," Clint said.

"What?"

"We're gonna tell him stories," Bat said.

"About what?"

"About the three of us," Clint said.

"An interview?" Short asked. He looked at Clint, who was making himself comfortable on Short's cot. "You don't do interviews."

"I'll do this one," he said. "We're going to have to do something to stay awake."

Bat left Short's cell and went into the one next to it, to the right, so he'd have his own cot to sit on. Taking a cue from Bat, DeKay went into the cell on the left to do the same.

"The sheriff is going to come in to listen to some of the stories and bring some coffee," Clint said.

Short checked both his weapons to make sure they were loaded, then tucked one into his belt and put the other down on the cot.

"What's Jake doin'?"

"Minding the store," Clint said.

"And does Hettie know about this?"

"She's the one who gave me your extra gun," Bat said.

"Have a seat, Luke," Clint said. "We're going to be here all night."

DeKay excitedly got out his notebook and said, "What's the first story?"

Clint, Bat, and Luke looked around at each other.

"I think," Short said, "you should tell this young man how you first met."

"But that story doesn't include you," Clint said.

"It's a good story, though," Short said, sitting down on the cot with Clint.

Clint looked at Bat. "Where did we first meet? Adobe Walls?"

Bat nodded. "Adobe Walls."

"Well," Clint said, "that *is* a good story. . . ."

PART TWO
ADOBE WALLS

TWENTY-SEVEN

Clint Adams looked across the table at the young man who several people had called "Bat." He had heard the name before and was fairly certain the youngster's full name was Bat Masterson. In a relatively short time this handsome youth who dressed like a dandy had made a name for himself as someone not to be trifled with, whether it be with cards or guns.

At this moment, Clint was trying to match cards with him, and was coming out on the short end.

This particular hand had, once again, come down to the two of them. They were playing draw, so both men were holding their five cards close to the vest. Bat had opened, Clint had raised, and Bat had re-raised. That knocked out the other three players before any cards were drawn.

The dealer, a man named Carson, asked Clint, "How many?"

"Two," Clint said, tossing his discards into the middle of the table.

The dealer gave him his two and turned to Bat.

"Cards?"

"One," Bat said.

Two pair, Clint thought, or had Bat raised him on a four-card straight or flush?

"Your bet, Bat," Carson said.

It was not a high stakes game, since it was being played in the Long Branch, which catered more to the common folk than professional gamblers—storekeepers, cowhands, buffalo hunter . . . lots of buffalo hunters.

So when Bat said, "Twenty dollars," it attracted attention.

Clint stared at Bat, wondering if the man had drawn two pair and made a full house. He looked down at his own hand. He'd drawn two cards to three kings, and amazingly had caught two tens. If Bat was trying to fill a straight or a flush and had done so, he was a loser. If he'd drawn two pair and filled up, then it would depend on who had the higher set of trips.

With three kings, Clint was feeling pretty strong.

"I see the twenty and raise twenty," he said.

"I like the way you play, Mr. Adams," Bat said. "Your twenty, thirty more."

Clint looked around. This appeared to be the last hand of the night, and he was holding strong cards.

"Your thirty, fifty more."

Bat smiled, as if Clint had stepped into a trap.

"Fifty," Bat said, "and a hundred."

Clint was in too deep, even though he felt that he had been expertly taken. Bat had not raised too highly in the beginning, but had allowed Clint to jump the raise to fifty.

No, for a hundred more, Clint had to see those cards.

"I call."

"Four tens," Bat said, spreading them.

"Beats kings full every time," Clint said, tossing his cards facedown on the table.

Bat raked in his money and, as Clint had suspected, the other players called it a night.

"Head to head, my friend?" Bat asked.

"Oh, no," Clint said. "I know when I've been licked. You drew one card to four and made four of a kind? You kept a kicker?"

"I never keep a kicker," Bat said. "You cut down your own chances to improve."

Clint laughed and shook his head.

"You were dealt four of a kind," he said, "and drew a card so I wouldn't know."

Bat put his money away and said to Clint, "Buy you a drink?"

"Why not?" Clint asked. "I might as well get something for my money."

Over a drink they became "Bat" and "Clint" and discovered they were there for the same reason—buffalo.

"The word is this is going to be a hell of a hunt," Bat said. "A lot of money to be made for a man good with a Big Fifty."

"I've heard that Bat Masterson is a very good shot with a fifty caliber—or any size—rifle."

Bat laughed.

"That's what I've heard about Clint Adams. You know, some of us have been shooting for money while we wait for the buff."

"I heard," Clint said. "The word is you can't be beat—not at cards, or with a rifle."

"Well," Bat said, "we've played cards."

Clint shook his head. "I don't shoot for fun, Bat," he said, "or for profit. I guess we'll have to stick to you taking my money in cards."

"Whatever works," Bat said, handing Clint his beer. "Have you heard how many of us are going out?"

Word is fifty."

"That's a lot of men," Bat said. "Lots of competition."

"There are supposed to be enough buffalo to go around."

"Let's have a seat," Bat said, and they carried their beers to a table from which they could both see the entire saloon.

"Word is A. C. Myers is coming out with us to set up shop," Bat said. Myers owned the general store, and some of the hunters had been complaining that they needed someplace closer than Dodge City to outfit, and to sell their hides, if a hunt in the Texas Panhandle was going to be successful. Myers had seen this as a chance to make some extra money. He was going to outfit himself with enough materials to take care of the hunters right at their camp.

"That solves one problem," Clint said.

"And the other?"

"Indians."

"Ah," Bat said. "Comanche and Cheyenne."

"And Kiowa."

"Of course," Bat said, "they might just leave us alone."

"Do you believe that?"

"Hell, no," Bat said. "We'll be taking their buffalo.

Eventually, they'll make a move. We just have to hope we've made enough of a profit by then."

"And that we can get away with our profit."

Bat smiled.

"Sounds like a hell of a time to me."

"I'll drink to that."

Clint was older than Bat, but was able to match the youthful enthusiasm the other man had for the hunt. It would be better than having men Bat's age and even younger trying to prove themselves against him with a gun. Buffalo didn't shoot back.

TWENTY-EIGHT

Over the next few days some more business decided to follow in Myers footsteps. A big Irishman named Jim Hanrahan was going to come along and erect a saloon. Two men named Rath and Wright were going to build a store to buy and sell the buffalo hides.

It took days for everyone to get completely outfitted, and during those days Bat and Clint became good friends. In addition to having common interests, both knew that the other man was completely capable of watching his back. Having a friend like that was rare.

When they were finally ready to leave Dodge and head for the Panhandle, Clint and Bat rode behind the assemblage of mounted buffalo hunters and businessmen's wagons. They both lived by the adage, "Keep everybody in front of you."

"How many of these men do you know?" Bat asked.

"A few," Clint said. "You?"

"Before I got here I knew Billy Dixon, Joe Plummer, some of the others."

"How many do you trust?"

"Two," Bat said. "Dixon, and you."

"Me already?"

Bat smiled.

"I like the way you play cards," Bat said. "Tells me a lot about a man, the way he loses."

"Loses?"

"Anybody can win," Bat said. "Takes a special kind of man to know how to lose."

"I'll take that as a compliment . . . I think."

The hunters crossed the Cimarron into the Texas Panhandle and found a stream known as West Adobe Walls Creek. They followed the stream, which took them to the Canadian River. Eventually they found the ruins of an old Indian trading post called Adobe Walls. They actually set up camp a couple of miles from there and sod buildings were quickly erected for the general store, saloon, and several others. Rath and Wright built their building, meant to store the hides, and rented the back out to William Olds and his wife, who set up a restaurant.

All that was left now was to wait for the buffalo migration, which was late that spring, so they had to find other ways to pass the time.

The most-often used ways of passing the time were still shooting contests, gambling, and drinking. Clint still would not take part in the contests, but he did watch Bat and he was impressed with the man's skills. He didn't know which Bat was better with, cards or a rifle.

The population continued to increase as people heard about the new settlement that had popped up on the Canadian River near Adobe Walls. Among others who joined the party were working women, so that the men now had something to do other than shoot, gamble, and drink.

And then finally, in May, came a sound that sounded like a train passing by, or like thunder. But it was neither.

The buffalo herds had arrived.

The hunters broke up into outfits, and Clint and Bat made sure they were in the same five-man outfit, along with another of Masterson's friends, Billy Dixon.

The outfits moved out onto the plains and took up their positions, and before long the buffalo came within range, and the hunt commenced.

So did the trouble.

The hunting was good, and it gave Bat his first opportunity to watch Clint shoot live targets rather than cans or bottles of bulls-eyes.

"You're every bit as good as I heard," Clint said one afternoon when they stopped shooting long enough to have some coffee.

"Thanks," Bat said. "You live up to your reputation, as well. You're damn good."

"Thanks."

"So good that I wonder how we'd match up."

"You're a better shot than I am," Clint said, and then added, "with a rifle."

Bat laughed and then said, "Okay, I'll accept that. I never claimed to be anything but adequate with a pistol."

"Oh, I think you're probably better than adequate," Clint said, "but I wouldn't want to test it out firsthand."

"No danger of that, I think."

Billy Dixon stepped into the conversation and said, "You know, if we arranged a shooting match between the two of you and took bets we could make a fortune."

"No!" Clint and Bat said, at the same time.

"It was just a thought," Dixon said, with a shrug.

"Rider comin'!" one of the other men shouted. "An' he's comin' fast."

The rider turned out to be Joe Plummer, part of a three-man outfit with Dave Dudley and a man named Wallace, who had set up by Chicken Creek. When he rode in he nearly fell off his horse, but Bat and Clint grabbed him and eased him down. The man was exhausted and couldn't talk right away.

"Let's get some coffee into him," Clint said.

After a few sips of coffee Plummer had recovered his breath enough to talk.

"They're dead."

"Who's dead?" Clint asked.

"Dudley and Wallace," Plummer said. "Both dead."

"How? Who killed them?" Bat asked.

"Indians."

"Which ones?" Clint asked.

"Kiowa, I think."

None of the hunters had experienced trouble with the Indians before this, which had come as a surprise to all.

"I woulda thought Comanches," Dixon said.

"They might be next," Clint said. "Who knows? They've all been pretty quiet up to now. They can't be too happy about us hunting the buffalo."

"We better get back to the settlement and tell the others," Bat said. He was the youngest, but many already looked up to him as a leader, so when he called out, "Let's pack it up for today!" there were no arguments from anyone.

TWENTY-NINE

It was two days later when another hunter came in to report two men from his camp had been killed, and mutilated. The two dead men from Chicken Creek had also been scalped. Soon, hunters were coming in with stories of battles with Indians and it became apparent to all that this was not just the work of a few braves.

Faster than it had filled up the settlement began to empty out. Most of the people there were not comfortable with this trouble happening over a hundred miles from the nearest assistance. They began to leave Adobe Walls and head back to Dodge so that, eventually, only about twenty-eight remained, including Clint Adams and Bat Masterson, who were not willing to give up the hunt at the height of the season.

Others who stayed were some of the businessmen, like Jim Hanrahan and Tom O'Keefe, the blacksmith, because they would not abandon their businesses, as well as Bill Olds and his wife. And A. C. Myers, whose decision to follow the hunters and set up shop to outfit them made him the first of the businessmen to do so—and he wasn't leaving!

Among the other hunters who stayed were Billy Dixon, Mike Welsh, and Bill Johnston, who along with Clint and Bat comprised one outfit.

None of these people—nine businessmen and one woman, and fourteen hunters—would be run off, and some would live to regret it.

THIRTY

A few days after the last of the fleeing hunters had left Adobe Walls the remaining men were getting ready for the day's hunt when suddenly the air was split by a cacophony of wild, savage whoops and suddenly hundreds of warriors were swooping down on them. It soon became clear that the Cheyenne, the Comanches, and the Kiowa were working together to drive the hunters out, or kill them all.

The hunters all reacted the same way. They grabbed their Big Fifty rifles and headed to the closest building. They barricaded themselves in and prepared to ward off the attack as best they could.

As luck would have it the people who built their businesses—mostly from sod—had built them well. The Indians rode into the settlement and began beating on the doors and shutters while the men inside calmly began to pick them off with their Fifties. The buffalo rifles tore huge holes in men and these seasoned hunters were able to deal out death with every shot, their aim sharpened by weeks of hunting. Finally, they beat back the attack of the Indians and both sides had time to evaluate their situations.

They'd lost only a few during the attacks. Two brothers had been asleep in a wagon when the Indians struck, and were killed instantly. The forces were almost evenly divvied up among three buildings.

Clint and Bat had taken refuge in Hanrahan's saloon, and along with the hunters named Billy Dixon, Mike Welsh, Shepherd, Johnston, McKinley, Bermuda Carlisle, Billy Ogg, and a man named McCabe.

The rest of the hunters had split between Myer's store, and the others at Rath's.

The sod buildings had walls that were two-feet deep, and so would not be penetrated by the Indian's bullets or arrows. Also, since the buildings were made of sod, the hunters were not in any danger of being burned out.

"What have we got?" Bat called out.

"We got enough food, drink, and ammunition to hold out a long time," Hanrahan said.

"What about the others?" Clint asked.

"Myers's store probably has more ammunition and less food," Hanrahan opined. "Rath's has to have everything."

"Well," Bat said, "we can hold out, but there's still hundreds of them and how many of us?"

"Twelve hunters or so," Clint said. "Some businessmen—and Bill Olds's wife—who might be able to shoot."

"Only the hunters have got Big Fifties," Dixon said. "The rest, Winchesters."

"We can hold them off," Bat said, "but not forever."

"We can light out for Dodge," Bermuda Carlisle said.

"We'd be cut down before we got a mile," John McCabe said.

"We could leave at night," Dixon said.

Clint turned to Bat and said, "We can't run, not now."

"I know," Bat said. "This is just the beginning. If they drive us out they won't stop until they've driven every white from the area. We've got to hurt them here so they know it won't be easy."

"I agree," Clint said.

"Let's see if we can't get someone else to agree, too."

And so they made their cases to the others, and then two men slipped out to make their way to the other two buildings to relay the message. When they returned they found out that most were in agreement. They should stay long enough to do some damage, but eventually light out for Dodge City.

They had just learned of the others' agreement when the sound of a bugle call cut through the air.

"What the—" somebody said.

"Here they come!" Bill Ogg shouted, on guard at a window.

"They've got a bugler?" Clint asked, but there was no time to ponder this. Once again they were hit and hit hard by hundreds of Cheyenne, Comanche, and Kiowa, and the more they cut down with a deadly hail of .50-caliber bullets, the more seemed to spring up. By late afternoon the Indians withdrew, leaving the ground littered with their dead. In checking their casualties the hunters learned that they had lost only one man, from Myers's building.

When the Indians did not return in an hour the hunters started to leave the buildings to walk around outside. They also had to air out the buildings, which had become thick with smoke.

"Think they're gone?" Dixon asked.

"Not a chance," Bat said.

"They'll be back," Clint agreed.

The hunters looked around at the dead Indians and decided to move them, dumping the bodies in the corral. They had almost finished when somebody shouted, "Riders!"

"Are they comin' back?" Bat asked.

"Hunters," the lookout shouted. "They're ours."

The hunters came riding in and reported that there were others on their way from outlying camps. They brought some horses with them, which were welcome, because the Indians had killed or driven off the animals that had been in the settlement during the attacks.

Among the hunters who drifted in during the early evening was a nineteen-year-old Bill Tilghman, who would later become as famous a lawman as there was in the west. He was introduced to Bat—as they were about the same age—with a challenge.

"This here's Bill Tilghman, Bat," someone said. "My money says he's a better shot than you."

The two young men sized each other up and Bat broke the silence by sayin', "I hope he is. We can use every crack shot we can find."

"How long do we figure this to go on?" Tilghman asked.

"I have a feeling," Clint said, "that's going to be up to them."

"Here they come again!" a lookout shouted, and the men scrambled for their sod fortresses.

• • •

On the fifth day of the siege tempers were beginning to flare.

"Why don't we send one man ahead to Dodge for help?" Hanrahan asked. "He can ride faster alone, and maybe get some help back here to get us out of this."

"We'll need a volunteer," Bat said. "We can't ask somebody to do that."

"Let's pass the word," Clint said.

A man named Henry Lease volunteered to ride out. He would leave as soon as it was dark.

The hunters turned out to wish Lease luck as he mounted one of the horses.

"Be back quick as I can," he said to Bat as they shook hands.

"I hope we're still here," Bat said.

Lease actually shook hands all around from astride his horse and then lit out for what amounted to about a hundred-and-fifty-mile ride to Dodge City.

"Godspeed," Tilghman said.

"He'll make it," Clint said. "He's got to."

The siege was a week old when the men began to get antsy. It was certainly too early for Lease to have reached Dodge, but to some of them it seemed that he had been gone a month.

Some men had already gone stir crazy and started fighting among themselves. The level heads of Clint Adams, Bat Masterson, Bill Tilghman, and some others were able to prevail before much damage could be done.

"If we fight among ourselves we'll be doin' their work for them!" Bat shouted at one point.

"How much longer, Bat?" someone shouted.

"We got to get out of here!" another voice called.

Bat, Clint, and Tilghman tried to calm them, but it wasn't easy.

"I think they're right, Clint," Bat said, "Even though we're got almost a hundred men now, we're still hopelessly outnumbered. I think we might have proven our point and maybe it's time to get out."

Clint looked at Tilghman.

"I agree."

Dixon, Hanrahan, and some of the others agreed, as well. Word went back and forth among the three buildings, and all were in agreement. Indians were stacked in the corral like cordwood and they were still coming.

"Let's get out of here," Dixon said, "and give them a chance to come in and count their dead, see what this cost them."

"Good point," Clint said. "All right, we'll have to plan this. We don't have enough horses for everyone. Some will have to ride double, and there will still be others on foot."

"We should wait a few more days," Tilghman said. "What if Lease rides back here with help and we're gone? They'll be in the same fix we are now."

"That's a good point, too," Clint said. "What do you think, Bat?"

"The attacks seem to be decreasing," Bat said. "We might even be able to spend a day or two without one. Besides, I want one shot at that bugler, whoever he is."

"All right, then," Clint said, "a few more days."

"If we can last that long," Bat added, "without killing each other."

THIRTY-ONE

For the next few days, while waiting for some word from
Dodge, tempers began to flare again in Adobe Walls. The
Indians began to play games with the hunters, choosing
not to attack during the afternoon. Tensions ran high and
one afternoon an incident occurred that lit a spark.

Bill Olds had been standing watch atop the roof of the
Rath store. As he started down to be relieved, however,
he slipped on the ladder and fell, discharging his Sharps
and blowing his own head off.

Men came running out at the sound of the shot and
stood around looking down at the dead man.

"What happened?" Clint asked. "Who fired the shot?"

It was Hannah Olds, the man's wife—now widow—
who stepped forward, hugging herself tightly, in tears.

"It were an accident," she said. "I saw it. Bill slipped
and blowed his own head off."

She started to cry then and the men just stood around, not knowing how to console her. Some of them picked up Olds and carried him off to be buried when they had the time.

Bat walked over to the fallen man's rifle and picked it up. Although he had his own Sharps, Olds's rifle had better range than Bat's and Bat was determined to pick off the bugler who had been signaling the Indians' charges.

"Hannah," he said, approaching the widow, "do you mind if I borrow Bill's rifle?"

"I don't care," Hannah said. "Go ahead."

"I'll give it back when we get out of here," Bat promised.

"We ain't never gettin' out of here," Hannah Olds said. "We's all gonna die here."

Nobody knew what to tell her and she went off to see where they had laid the body of her husband.

Bat looked at Clint helplessly, with Billy Dixon and Bill Tilghman standing nearby.

"I didn't know what to say to her," he said.

"It's hard to know what to say in a situation like that," Clint said, being the oldest of the four. "We just have to give her some time to herself."

"What are you gonna do with Olds's Sharps, Bat?" Dixon asked.

"I'm gonna get that damned bugler," Bat said, "and then I'll give it back to her."

"What if she don't want it back?" Tilghman asked.

"She'll take it back," Clint said. "It'll just be a while before she realizes she wants it."

The men went back inside the saloon while another man went up on the store roof to keep watch.

•　•　•

Over the next couple of days they were finally able to identify the bugler. Somebody actually saw him and excitedly told the others.

"He's a black man," John McCabe said. "I seen him, I tell ya."

"What's a black man doin' with them Indians?" Dixon asked.

"Probably a deserter," Clint said. "Took up with them when he left his company. Indians have funny ideas about black men. They don't hate them the way they do whites."

"Black man shouldn't be too hard to pick out," Bat said, "now that I know what I'm lookin' for. Me and Bill Olds's rifle'll be ready."

And they were.

The next day Bat was eager and excited, and when he heard the sound of the bugle he hurried to the window and leaned out with Bill Olds's Sharps in his hands. The Indians started their charge and everyone else started shooting, but he watched and waited and finally got his chance.

The black bugler did not ride in with the Indians. He sat outside of Adobe Walls, from what he thought was a safe distance away, and blew his bugle.

Bat saw him, sighted down the long barrel of the Sharps, held his breath and fired. The bugle call stopped and the black man flew from his saddle as if yanked from behind.

"You got him, Bat!" Clint shouted.

"Yah!" Bat shouted, reloading. "Somebody blow the bugle now!"

But nobody did, and everyone in camp cheered as the Indians withdrew.

•   •   •

"Okay," Clint said, "it's time for us to leave."

"We can't all leave," Bat said. "We don't have enough horses."

"I'll go on foot," Dixon said.

"A lot of us could go on foot," Tilghman chimed in.

"I've been thinking about this," Clint said. "Whoever goes on foot would probably end up dead. I think we should send out as many men as we have horses for, maybe even some riding double. If we can break through the Indians and head for Dodge some of them might follow."

"Clint's got a point," Jim Hanrahan said. "The best fighters and shots should ride out and head for Dodge. The rest can ride it out here until they get back with help."

"And how do we pick who rides out and who stays?" McCabe asked.

Hanrahan was a businessman, and had formed no great allegiances or friendships with any of the hunters, so it was decided that he would choose the men who would ride out.

Hanrahan made his choices, and included Clint Adams, Bat Masterson, Billy Dixon, and Bill Tilghman among them.

They'd start out in the morning.

THIRTY-TWO

That evening, the hunters who were leaving made preparations in the saloon. However, over at Rath's, Hannah Olds finally decided that she did want her husband's Sharps back, because it meant so much to him. She was worried that Bat Masterson was going to take it with him, though. She approached two of the other men in Rath's, Fred Leonard and Frank Brown, to go and get it back for her.

Leonard said, "Write a note to Bat askin' him to return the gun, and we'll go and get it."

She agreed and wrote the note.

Lookouts saw no sign of the Indians, so Leonard and Brown were able to leave Rath's and go over to the saloon. They found Bat standing at the bar with Clint, Dixon, and Tilghman, having what was left of Hanrahan's beer.

"This is from Mrs. Olds," Leonard said, handing Bat the note.

Bat took the note and read it. It asked that he return her husband's Sharps before he left Adobe Walls. It was something he'd intended to do, but at that moment Frank Brown spoke up and changed the situation.

"She wants that gun," he said, "so give it to us."

The rifle in question was leaning against the bar and Bat picked it up and held it tightly.

"I'm in charge of this gun," he said. "You fellas go and take care of your own business, and I'll return it."

"Uh-uh," Brown said. "She asked us to get it from you. What right have you to refuse?"

Bat, still a young man, felt he was being challenged, and he didn't care for it. He also felt he was being accused, in some way, of trying to keep the gun for himself, when that was never his intention.

"You sonofabitch!" he said to Brown. "It's none of your damn business." He punched Leonard in the jaw, and that prompted the other men in the saloon to take his side. They quickly grabbed Brown before he could even hit the floor, picked him up, and flung him out the window.

Fred Leonard, afraid of more retaliation against him, hurried outside to help Brown to his feet.

"Goddamn it!" Brown said, and drew both his handguns from their holsters.

"Frank, don't!" Leonard shouted.

Brown had only his head in the window when somebody pressed the barrel of a Sharps Big Fifty to his temple and cocked it.

"What do you want here, Brown?" somebody asked.

Brown swallowed hard. He knew full well that the Big

Fifty could blow his head clean off, the way it had done to Olds. Since his hat had fallen off during the ruckus he said, "Uh, I want my hat."

"Here's your damn hat," somebody else said, tossing it out the window, and then shoved him after it.

Several of the other men from Rath's came running over to see what the commotion was. When Leonard and Brown told them, a couple of them drew their guns and threw some shots into the saloon.

With the Indians giving them some time off, the hunters were fighting amongst themselves.

"This is ridiculous," Clint said, sometime later. "The Rath crew are keeping us pinned down in here."

They were shooting at anyone who showed their face in any of the saloon windows.

"What does it matter?" Tilghman asked. "We're leavin' tomorrow, anyway. Bat, are you takin' Olds's Sharps with you?"

"Hell no," Bat said, "I'll give it back to her in the morning. I just didn't want to give it to those two yahoos. I didn't like the tone of their voice when they 'asked' me for it."

"Well," Clint said, "come first light we'll wave a white flag out the window and return the rifle. I don't relish getting my head shot off by a white man when we've stood the Indians off for this long."

Hanrahan came over, gave them each a free glass of whiskey, and said, "You boys all ready to go, come mornin'?"

"We're ready, Jim," Clint said.

He slapped them all on the back and said, "Make me

proud, boys. Get to Dodge alive and bring back some help."

"We'll be back, Jim," Clint said. "That's a promise."

Hanrahan moved away, continuing to pour free whiskey for the others who were going along.

"You promise?" Bat asked. "There's hundreds of Indians out there, Clint. How could you promise a thing like that?"

"I couldn't very well tell him we'd do the best we could," Clint said. "That wouldn't have given him very much hope."

"You really think the rest of them will be able to hold out once we leave?" Dixon asked.

"Why not?" Bat asked. "We held out until Bill, here, and the others came riding in. There was only twenty-eight of us when this started."

"They'll hold out," Clint said, "and we'll send help back."

"I know," Bat said. "You promised."

"Let's find something to use as a white flag so we can give that damn rifle back," Clint said. "I don't want somebody from Rath's shooting us in the back as we ride out."

THIRTY-THREE

In the morning there were twenty-five hunters coming out of Hanrahan's saloon, saddling horses and getting ready to ride out. The first ones out had been Clint and Bat, with a white flag affixed to the long barrel of Bill Olds's Sharps. Bat handed it to Hannah Olds and told her he had never intended to keep it. She apologized for the misunderstanding.

Before leaving, the others came out to wish the twenty-five luck. Bat and Frank Brown shook hands and the men from Rath's apologized for the previous night's shooting.

"We're all getting on each other's nerves," Clint said. "My advice is to try to keep it under control until we get back."

"We'll try," Brown assured him. "We all want to still be alive when you do get here."

There was more shaking of hands and slapping of backs

151

and then Clint, Bat, Tilghman, Dixon, and the others mounted up and started out, assured by the morning lookouts that there was no sign of the Indians.

It was midday when the hunters came upon a deserted camp.

"Whose was it?" Clint asked. "Anybody know?"

Nobody did.

"I got a better question," Bat said, leaning over so only Clint could hear him.

"I know," Clint said. "Where are the Indians."

"I don't know why they let us get this far."

"Maybe they want to let us get far enough away so we won't turn back to help the others when they hit Adobe Walls again."

"Could be."

"We better ride in and see if anybody's alive," Tilghman said, still eyeing the camp.

"Good idea," Clint said.

When they got into the camp they found one dead man. He'd been scalped and mutilated—hopefully, after he was dead.

"Anybody know him?" Clint asked.

"Yeah," Tilghman said, "I recognize him. It's Charlie Sharp, Henry Lease's partner."

"Jesus," Bat said. "I wonder if Henry knows."

"We can tell him when we get to Dodge," Dixon said.

"Let's bury him first," Clint said, and there was no argument.

They decided they'd camp one night and make Dodge the next day.

"A fire?" Dixon asked.

"No," Clint said, "I suggest a cold camp tonight."

"Why not?" Tilghman asked. "All we've got is some beef jerky, anyway."

Tilghman was carrying the jerky and handed it around.

"This turned out to be a disaster, didn't it?" he asked, while they all chewed on the tough, dried meat.

"We knew it had the potential for that," Clint said. "It's more of a disaster for Myers, Rath, and Wright. A lot of the hunters got paid for hides that those men are going to have to leave behind."

"Maybe not," Bat said. "If we can get back with enough men they'll be able to load their hides on wagons and take them out."

"I wonder if Lease made Dodge?" Tilghman said.

"If he had," Clint said, "we probably would have passed him and the men he was bringing back."

"I got a question," Dixon said.

"What?" Clint asked.

"What if nobody wanted to come back with him? What if we get there and nobody wants to come back with us?"

"They've got to," Bat said. "We can't leave the others to die."

"I'm just sayin'—"

"We ain't gonna give them a choice," Tilghman said. "I say we make a pact right now."

"What kind of pact?" Dixon asked, warily.

Clint and Bat waited to hear the answer, as well.

"If nobody will go back with us we'll have to go back ourselves, with horses and guns."

"Agreed," Clint said.

"Agreed," Bat chimed in.

They looked at Dixon, who finally said, "Okay."

"And something else," Tilghman said.

"What?" Dixon asked, as if nothing else could be any worse than that.

"I say we tear that town apart before we leave."

"If all Dodge has in it is a bunch of cowards," Bat answered, "I say why not?"

"Clint?" Tilghman asked.

"I agree."

They all looked at Dixon.

"Well, hell," Dixon said, "at least *that* sounds like fun."

THIRTY-FOUR

They rode into Dodge late the next day and were met enthusiastically. Apparently, the people of Dodge did care about what happened to the hunters.

"We thought you were all dead!" someone shouted as they rode down Front Street.

"We've got to find out if Lease made it," Clint said to Bat.

"Let's just head for the sheriff's office."

They all agreed they'd do that before they looked for a long-overdue bath, meal, drink, and hotel room.

"He sure did ride in here," the sheriff's deputy told them. "Came ridin' in hell-bent for leather and wouldn't let up on the sheriff until he put together a posse."

"And what happened?" Bat asked.

"They rode out a couple of days ago," the deputy said.

"Musta been a hundred of 'em. You musta missed them on the trail."

"Well, we did avoid the main trail," Clint said.

"This is great news," Tilghman said. "They should be able to get the rest of the men out of there."

"The whole town is jumpin'," the deputy said, "waitin' to hear."

"Well," Clint said, "that's what we'll do, I guess. Wait to hear."

"And take a bath," Bat said.

"Get a hot meal," Clint said.

"And a real bed," Tilghman said.

"And a woman," Dixon said.

"Guess we can see where our priorities lie," Clint commented. "Thanks, Deputy."

"Sure are glad you fellas made it back," the young lawman said. "Wish I coulda gone with the posse, but somebody's gotta keep a lid on Dodge."

"It's a big job," Clint said. "I'm sure you're doing fine."

The four men left the sheriff's office and stopped just outside.

"Hotel first," Clint said.

"Dodge House?" Bat asked.

"Sounds good," Tilghman said.

They all walked over to the Dodge House to get a room. After they got their keys they went their respective ways to fulfill their goals, and agreed to meet in the Alhambra Saloon later in the day.

The Alhambra was filled with hunters who had intended to go out and join the party. Now, they were just waiting around to hear the outcome of the Indian trouble.

The four friends each got a beer and found a table in

a corner from where Clint could see the whole room.

"Look at 'em," Bat said. "Chompin' at the bit to get out there and get some of that hide."

"Not going to be any more buffalo hunting until the army can come in and do something about the Indians," Clint predicted.

"I think you're right," Bat said. "Looks like Dodge has about had it, for a while."

"Where are you headed next, then?" Tilghman asked.

"I'm not sure," Bat said, "but I could use some company."

"I just might tag along," Tilghman said.

"What about you, Clint?" Bat asked.

"I might hang around here awhile, just to see the outcome," Clint answered.

"Billy?" Bat asked Dixon. "Why you lookin' so depressed?"

Dixon looked at Bat, then the others, and then said, "I was kinda lookin' forward to tearin' this place down, ya know?"

"Sorry to disappoint you," Clint said, "but it doesn't seem to need tearing down, right now."

"Although there sure seem to be enough hunters in here to tear it down by accident," Tilghman said, looking around.

The four of them drank together for a while, then Dixon went off to be with a whore and Tilghman went off to tend to his own business, whatever it was. He said he'd meet Bat with his horse in the morning, in front of the Alhambra.

That left Clint Adams and Bat Masterson sitting together, nursing beers.

"You know," Bat said, "I wouldn't tell this to anyone else."

"What is it?"

"There was a few moments there when I didn't think we'd get out of there alive," Bat said. "What with the fellas from Rath's tossin' shots in the window—I mean, if the Cheyenne and Cherokee and Kiowa didn't kill us, our own people might have."

"I know what you mean," Clint said. "I had some of the same feelings."

"Well," Bat said, "one good thing came out of it."

"What's that?"

"We forged a friendship that'll last a long time," Bat said, raising his mug.

"I'll drink to that," Clint said.

The present . . .

"We forged a friendship?" Bat repeated, looking at Clint from the other cell.

"That's touching," Luke Short said, looking at Bat.

"I never said that," Bat complained. "That's not somethin' I would say."

"Well . . ." Clint said, ". . . it was something like that."

"I don't think so," Bat said. "In fact, if I remember correctly, I think you said that."

"Me?" Clint asked. "That's not something I would say."

"But," Alphonse Michael DeKay asked, "the rest of it was accurate, wasn't it?" His hand hovered above his notebook as he looked at both of them hopefully.

"Oh, yeah," Bat said, looking at Clint, "the rest was accurate."

"Sure was," Clint said.

"And there were how many Indians?" DeKay asked. "A hundred?"

"Hundred*s*," Bat said, stressing the plural sound.

"Yes," Clint said, "several hundred."

DeKay wrote something and then asked, "And Bill Tilghman *was* there?"

"Bill was definitely there," Bat said.

"And the rest of the hunters came in a few days later with the posse, safe and sound," Clint added. "Myers and Hanrahan and the others; everybody was okay."

"And did the army come in?"

"They did," Clint said, "and there was a big shebang having to do with Quanah Parker . . . but that's something you can look up. Bat and I weren't involved in that."

Actually, he was involved in it, but he didn't want to tell that story now.

"That was an amazing story," DeKay said.

"I thought so, too," Luke Short said. "Simply amazing."

"I thought it was very interesting," the sheriff said. He had walked in halfway through it and distributed coffee to everyone. "You gonna tell any more?"

"Oh, yes, please," DeKay said. "Tell another."

"Well," Clint said, stretching, "we've still got some time to kill." He looked at Bat. "What do you think, Bat?"

"We could tell another," Bat said, "but there are so many. Which one?"

"Hmm," Clint said.

"Tell one with me in it, this time," Short said.

"How about," Bat suggested, "the one about the John L. Sullivan fight."

"John L. Sullivan?" DeKay asked, excitedly.

"This was before anyone knew who he was."

"That was in New Orleans, wasn't it?" Short asked.

"And Mississippi City," Clint said. "Remember? They made us move the fight—"

"And Oscar Wilde was there," Bat said.

"Oscar Wilde?" the newsman said, his voice almost squeaking.

"Well, let's not jump ahead," Clint said. "This was only about four or five years ago . . ."

PART THREE
NEW ORLEANS

THIRTY-FIVE

Clint Adams expected to see Bat Masterson in New Orleans when he arrived. After all, a heavyweight fight was not the type of event Bat was likely to miss, and this one was for the title. Paddy Ryan was considered the heavyweight champion of the world, but a young upstart from Boston had been making all kinds of remarks in the press, hoping to goad Ryan into a title match, and it finally worked John L. Sullivan, after dispatching a whole line of opponents along the way, was going to get his shot on February 7 in New Orleans.

Clint decided to stay in a hotel on Bourbon Street called the Orleans, and when he arrived not only the hotel, but the entire street was jumping with activity. Apparently, this fight was drawing people from far and wide, and from all walks of life.

As Clint entered the Orleans after stabling Duke, his

big black gelding, he was shocked to see two men standing in the lobby, apparently going unrecognized by everyone but him. He decided not to approach Frank and Jessie James, lest he give their identities away.

He registered among the hubbub in the lobby and got himself a room. There were newspapermen all over the place and he wondered if he had chosen the same hotel as one of the fighters. Later, when he came downstairs to have something to eat in the dining room, he discovered that he had, indeed.

As he entered the dining room he recognized Billy Madden, the man who trained John L. Sullivan. Clint knew Madden from other fights he had attended. The man had trained a long line of losers and had somehow managed to come up with John L. Sullivan.

Madden saw Clint and waved him over. Clint had to force his way through a crowd of reporters to reach the table.

"Now, now, gents," Madden shouted to the press, "Johnny's got to get a meal down, so why don't we put off any more questions until later on, huh?"

As Clint approached the table Madden grabbed his hand and said, "Clint, boy, sit down, sit down, have a steak with us."

"How does he rate?" one newsman asked Madden.

The trainer, a bandy-legged little Irishman, drew himself up to his full height of five and a half feet or so and said, "He rates because he's a friend of mine, and because his name is Clint Adams."

"Adams?" the newsman asked.

"The Gunsmith?" another shouted, and suddenly the newspapermen were surging back toward them, sensing another aspect to the story.

"And the Gunsmith," Billy Madden announced proudly—and loudly—"is putting his money on John L. Sullivan!"

That almost incited a riot, and as Madden once again managed to put off the reporters until later, Clint and a man he assumed was John L. Sullivan cast amused looks at each other across the table.

Finally, Madden was able to sit down, and as a waiter came over he said, "Steaks all around."

"Yessir."

"This is gonna be on me, Clint boy," Madden said.

"It better be," Clint said, "since you seem to have committed my money to your boy, here."

"My boy's gonna win, Clint," Madden said. "Have I ever steered you wrong?"

"Fireman Willy Logan?" Clint asked, reminding Madden of one of his former boys, who couldn't take a punch.

"Well . . ."

"The Beast, Ed Fellows?" The Beast could punch, but he was so slow he couldn't *land* a punch.

"Uh . . ."

"Oh, and I liked this one: Irish Seamus O'Brien." Clint looked at Sullivan. "With a name like that Billy decides to put the word 'Irish' in front of it."

"I assume you lost money on all those fighters?" the Bostonian asked.

"Every one."

"Well . . ." Madden said.

"You won't lose money on me, Mr. Adams," Sullivan said. "I guarantee it."

Clint looked across the table at the handsome young man who seemed to be brimming with confidence.

"How do you guarantee it, Mr. Sullivan?"

"I've got my own money riding on me, sir," Sullivan said. "Paddy Ryan and I have a side bet of two thousand five hundred dollars."

"Twenty-five hundred dollars?" Clint asked, surprised. "That's very confident, Mr. Sullivan."

"I am confident, Mr. Adams, "Sullivan said, "and please, call me John L."

"All right, John L.," Clint said, "and since I'm going to have my money riding on you, you might as well call me Clint."

The two men leaned forward and shook hands.

"A meeting of legends!" Madden announced, placing his hands atop their clasped hands. "Why is there never a photographer around when you need one."

"I'm not a legend yet, Billy," John L. said.

"You will be, after this fight," Madden said. He looked at Clint. "Johnny's not only going to beat Ryan, Clint, he's gonna knock him out."

"Well then," Clint said, looking for the waiter, "I guess maybe we better have a drink on that."

"I'll get three beers," Madden said, and started to rise.

"Better make it four," Clint said.

"Why four?"

Clint pointed to the door of the dining room and said, "Because Bat Masterson just walked into the room."

THIRTY-SIX

Bat Masterson joined them and shook hands enthusiastically with John L. Sullivan.

"I'm looking forward to seeing you fight."

"You gonna bet on him, Bat?" Madden asked.

Bat sat down and said, "It's a distinct possibility." He looked at Clint and tapped him on the knee. "How've you been?"

"Good," Clint said. "What's it been? A few months?"

"Seems we always run into each other every few months," Bat said. "I knew you'd be here, though."

"Same with me," Clint said. "What about Luke?"

"He'll be here."

"Luke Short?" Madden asked. "Now there's a gambler. He'll bet on John L."

"I don't know," Bat said. "I think Luke might be a Ryan man."

"Then he'll lose money," Madden said.

The waiter came balancing four steak plates in his arms. As he started to set them down Bat leaned toward Clint to get out of the man's way.

"I saw the James boys in the lobby," he muttered.

"So did I."

"Are they crazy?"

Clint shrugged and said, "Big fight fans, I guess."

The waiter withdrew and the men regarded their dinner plates.

"Best steak in town," Madden said.

Clint knew of a few other restaurants in town that might have served better but kept his mouth shut. Madden was in a good mood, and he was buying.

"Dig in, boys," Madden said. "Eat up, champ. You need to keep your strength up."

"And your stamina," Bat said. "Ryan's a bull who can go all day."

"Oh, didn't you hear?" Clint asked. "John L. is going to knock Ryan out."

Bat looked at John L. in surprise.

"Ryan's never been off his feet."

"I know."

"Who's makin' this prediction?" Bat asked. "You or Billy, here?"

"I am," John L. said.

Bat sat back. Clint knew by the look in his eye that his friend was thinking about money.

"Are you fairly certain on this?"

"I am dead certain," John L. said.

Bat looked at Madden, this time.

"What can I tell you?" Madden asked. "My boy is confident."

Bat looked at Clint.

"He's bet twenty-five hundred of his own money on himself," Clint offered.

"That *is* confident," Bat said. "What are the odds?"

"Ryan's the two to one," Madden said. "You'll get good odds on John L."

"Well," Bat said, cutting into his steak, "I better give this some thought, then." He put a piece of meat in his mouth and then asked Clint, "Who else is in town for this?"

"Just got here a little while ago myself. Maybe after dinner we can go and have a look around, see who we can scare up."

"A walk around New Orleans sounds splendid," John L. said. "Would you gentlemen mind if I joined you?"

"You need your rest, champ," Madden said.

"It's just a walk, Billy," John L. said.

"It's okay with me," Clint said.

"And me, too," Bat said. "I guess we'll feel real safe walking around with the next heavyweight champ."

John L. just smiled and continued to devour his steak.

THIRTY-SEVEN

Clint, Bat, and John L. took turns recognizing people as they strolled around the French Quarter. In turn they were each recognized by someone on almost every block.

John L. saw Joe Jefferson and William H. Crane and Bat saw Nat Goodwin, all well-known, recognizable actors of the time. Clint saw Henry Ward Beecher, a preacher and well-known opponent of anything that had to do with sports or liquor. Apparently, he had come in order to better understand what he was opposed to.

And it was Bat who recognized Red Leary and explained to John L. that the man was one of the most wanted bank robbers of all time.

"Amazing," John L. said, "and he has risked capture to come and watch me fight?"

"Knowing Red," Bat said, "he came to watch and bet on Paddy Ryan."

"Nevertheless," John L. said, "it is I who will put on a show for him."

To repay Bat for pointing out Red Leary to him—and Clint for telling him that Frank and Jesse James were also in town—John L. took the opportunity to point out to them a healthy looking fellow wearing a beaver-collared greatcoat with a sunflower in his lapel.

"That," he said, "is the English writer Oscar Wilde."

"I've heard of Wilde," Bat said. "He's a poet and a playwright, isn't he?"

"He's a little bit of everything," John L. said, "and now I suppose he's a boxing fan."

"What else would he be doing here?" Clint asked.

John L. laughed.

"He's actually on tour in the United States, doing readings. I thought he was going to be in San Francisco, but I guess he decided to detour here."

"To see you fight," Bat said.

"Exactly," John L. said. "Why wouldn't one form of genius come to see another?"

"Oh," Bat said, "you *are* modest, aren't you?"

"Not in the least," John L. said.

Bat looked at Clint.

"You know, I just might make a bet on this fella, after all."

The trouble didn't start until they were on their way back to their hotel. Men and women were overflowing from some of the saloons and restaurants they passed on the way, and out of a particular saloon came half a dozen men who recognized John L.

"Well, well," one of them said, "it's the Boston Strong Boy himself, John L. Sullivan."

John L. stopped in front of the man who spoke and asked, "Do I know you?"

"No, but I know you," the man said. "You're the man who's gonna get a boxing lesson from Paddy Ryan tomorrow."

"Is that a fact?" John L. asked.

Clint and Bat were both conscious of the other men who were backing their leader's play—if there was one.

"I got money says it is," the man said.

"Then I invite you to bet it on Ryan . . ."

"I will."

". . . and say goodbye to it."

"Hear him, boys?" the man asked. "He sounds real confident, don't he?"

"Yeah," one of the other men said, "a little too confident for my money."

"Yeah," the spokesman said. "Hey, fellas!"

He was shouting into the saloon and three more men came out to join him and the others.

"Three-to-one," Bat said. "Not bad odds."

"Let's see what happens," Clint said.

John L. stood his ground as the nine men crowded him.

"Maybe a few bruises will slow him down tomorrow," the spokesman said, "and we'll make some easy money."

"And who among you is going to administer those bruises?" John L. asked. "You?"

The spokesman was a big man, thick through the middle, strong-looking but not in the condition that John L. was in. However, backed by eight other men he might have had a shot.

"You betcha," the man said. He reached back and threw a punch that, had it landed, might have taken John L.'s head off. However, the boxer stepped aside nimbly, avoiding the blow, causing the man to stumble forward several paces before he was able to right himself.

"How's this?" one of the other men asked, and threw a punch, himself. Once again John L. danced aside and the aggressor lost his balance.

"Get him!" the first man shouted.

Two men ran forward to attack John L. but he threw two left jabs that landed with sledgehammer effect, knocking both men off their feet.

John L. danced back. He was breathing heavily, Clint could see, but not because he was tired; rather it was from excitement.

"Who's next?"

The first man said, "Wait," and moved to join his partners. The other men helped the two fallen men to their feet.

"There's nine of us and one of him," the spokesman said. "Let's just all take him at once."

"Gentlemen," John L. said to Clint and Bat, "I just might be in need of your assistance here."

Clint and Bat stepped forward and flanked the pugilist, facing the nine men together.

"Three against nine," the man said to his eight companions. "Still in our favor."

"That's funny," Bat said. "I was thinking how outnumbered you all were, now."

"We'll see," the other man said. "Let's get them!"

THIRTY-EIGHT

Clint, Bat, and John L. moved back to back as the nine men circled them and then rushed in. John L.'s jab lashed out, catching two men on the jaw and jarring them. The third man swung and hit the boxer in the ribs. John L. then dispatched him with a vicious right hand that knocked him out.

Clint, who had witnessed many professional fights and even refereed a few, also jabbed at two men, hitting one with a solid blow, and one a glancing one. The third man landed a punch to Clint's jaw, but it was a glancing blow that stung more than anything else. Briefly, Clint considered pulling his gun, but none of the nine men had weapons in their hands. Shooting an unarmed man, even in the midst of a fight, might be grounds for him to miss tomorrow's fight by spending some time in a New Orleans jail.

Bat, who had been in many scrapes where he was outnumbered, had no compunction about using whatever means was necessary to win. He kicked the first man in the shins and hit the second with a pretty good haymaker. The third man grabbed him rather than trying to punch him, and Bat hit him with a head butt that opened a gash on the man's forehead.

The nine men stepped back, then rushed forward again, more in concert than before. Several blows landed on Clint and Bat, while John L. was able to ward them off, but in defending them was not able to land any of his own.

Three more men came out of the saloon, saw the action, and ran to join. The threesome was now battling four-to-one odds, and taking more blows than they landed. Both Clint and Bat thought it was time to draw their guns, but suddenly the battle was joined by even more men.

Only they were Irish.

A group of Irishman, who had traveled to New Orleans not only to bet on John L. but to support him, came walking down Bourbon Street and saw the battle taking place. They thought it was just a good old street brawl until one of them spotted John L. Sullivan in the midst of the fray.

"Hey, boys," he shouted, "it's John L.!"

There were eight of them, but they were young and strong. They rushed in and peeled the twelve men off John L., Clint, and Bat and began to pummel them.

"We've got company!" Clint shouted.

"Friends of yours?" Bat asked John L.

"I don't know them," John L. said, "but they look like stout Irish lads."

The eight Irishman quickly sent the other twelve men either to the ground unconscious, or running. They then turned to their hero, John L. Sullivan.

"John L.!" one of them shouted. They rushed the boxer and began patting him on the back and pumping his hand enthusiastically. Clint started to think that they were going to do more damage to the boxer than their assailants had.

"We're here to support you," one of them announced.

"And bet on you."

"Well," John L. said, "I appreciate the support, both now and tomorrow. My friends and I all do."

The happy Irishmen shook hands with Bat and Clint also, not because they knew who they were but because they were friends of John L. Sullivan.

The surged toward the saloon that the twelve men had come out of. Clint was surprised the place was so crowded, even with the defection of the twelve men.

"We'll have to buy them a drink for their help," John L. said.

"Fine with me," Bat said, touching his bruised lip. "I could use a cold beer."

Clint had a bruise on his forehead, but a cold beer still sounded good to him.

"Let's go," he said, and they allowed themselves to be carried along to the bar.

Eventually, they secured places for themselves at the bar and armed each of their rescuers with mugs of cold beer. They then managed to separate themselves from the group, telling each other that they would see them tomorrow at the fight. Clint, Bat, and John L. moved to one end of the bar where they could drink their beers without being constantly pounded on the back enthusiastically.

"Wasn't that a great fight?" John L. asked them.

Clint and Bat examined the boxer's face, but it was devoid of any damage.

"Are you all right?" Clint asked.

"I caught one punch in the ribs," John L. said, "but managed to ward off the rest. I'm not known for it, but I happen to be a very good defensive fighter."

"What about you?" Clint asked Bat. "Any damage other than that lip?"

"I'm fine. You?"

"A bump on the head."

"Damn, I enjoyed that!" John L. said, draining his beer.

"The fight?" Clint asked.

"That, too," John L. said, "but I was talking about the beer. Billy won't let me have any while I'm in training— and I'm always in training."

"Want another?" Clint asked.

"Don't give him another," Bat admonished him. "I'm putting my money on him tomorrow!"

"No," John L. said, "I better not have another. Billy doesn't want me to have beer before a fight, or a woman."

"Why not a woman?" Bat asked.

"Billy thinks it weakens the legs."

"I think I can see his point," Clint said.

"Maybe," John L. said, "but I find it hard to resist, especially if we're talking about a fine, red-haired Irish lass—"

Just then the man who had led the burly Irishmen in the rescue came over with three women in tow—all with red hair.

"John L.," he shouted, "these bonnie lasses heard you were here and wanted to meet you."

Clint could see the glint in John L.'s eyes, and he couldn't blame him. All three women were lovely, with pale skin and green eyes.

"These are Shannon, Maureen, and Colleen," the man said. He wriggled his eyebrows and added, "They're sisters."

"What a surprise," John L. said.

"Clint," Bat said, "we have to get him out of here and back to his hotel."

"Don't worry, my friends," John L. responded, "I said I found them hard to resist, but not impossible. After all, I do have my own money on me."

The man with the girls finally introduced himself as Colin as he pushed the three women toward Clint, Bat, and John L.

"A gift," he said, "from Colin."

"A gift very appreciated," John L. said, "but I do have to get my rest before tomorrow. Ladies, meet my friends, Clint Adams and Bat Masterson."

"Clint Adams?" one of them said.

"Bat Masterson?" another said, emerald eyes gleaming.

"You're both famous, too!" the third sister said.

"Goodnight, my friends," John L. said. "Colin, come and see me after the fight tomorrow."

"I will, John L." Colin said, "I will."

"Ladies," John L. said, bowing gallantly, "be very nice to my friends, and come to the fight tomorrow. I will get you in for free."

"We'll be there, John L.," said either Colleen, Maureen, or Shannon.

John L. waved and left. One of the girls cozied up to Bat, another to Clint and the third remained on Colin's arm.

"I'm Shannon," the girl on Clint's arm said. "What do you want to do for the rest of the night?"

Clint tightened his arm around her waist as she pushed small, firm breasts into his arm and breathed sweetly into his face.

"I have a few ideas," he said.

THIRTY-NINE

Clint awoke in the morning with a redhead.

He sat up in bed without disturbing her. She was lying on her stomach, the bedsheet bunched around her waist. Her slender back was peppered with freckles, her hair fanned out and flaming against the pale sheets.

He certainly didn't mind waking up next to a naked, sleeping redhead—the only problem was, he didn't know which one she was.

He vaguely remembered having his arm around a girl who said she was Shannon . . . then later sitting with one of the sisters named Colleen . . . and later still dancing— had they gone dancing somewhere?—with a girl named Maureen.

So which one did he end up bringing back to his hotel with him and taking to bed?

He reached out and traced the graceful line of her back

with his finger until it reached the sheet. Then he moved the sheet and ran his finger down lower, along the crease between her slender cheeks. After that he ran his palm around one cheek and then the other, enjoying the silky feel of her skin. She moaned, coming awake slowly. She pressed her belly into the sheet as his hand moved between her legs, which she spread for him. His slid his middle finger along her already moist slit, then dipped it in just a little. She moaned again, louder, moving her hips and reaching back for him.

He ran his hand back up her back. She propped herself up on her elbows and turned her head to look at him. Seeing her face did not help bring her name to mind. She was a beautiful redhead, but so were all three sisters.

He laid back down next to her, on his back. She slid one hand onto his chest and kissed him, tentatively at first, a light touching of the lips, and then more forcefully until, finally, her tongue slid into his mouth. Then she kissed his back, his chest, ran her tongue and lips down over his belly, leaving a wet trail until she reached his fully distended penis. She hummed to herself and licked him, first the spongy head, then the length of him, wetting him, swelling him even more. She peppered his thighs with little butterfly kisses, caressed his testicles, then ran his lips back up his cock until she reached the head again. This time she opened her mouth and took him inside, began to suck him wetly, avidly. Her head bobbed up and down on him and she moaned, encircling the base of his penis with her hand, holding him in her fist while she sucked him.

At this point it sure as hell didn't matter what her name was.

●　　●　　●

Later she was sitting astride him and it came to him that during the night she had been in the same position, but there had been a beauty mark on her right breast that wasn't there now. Had that been Shannon, with the mark? That would make this Maureen or Colleen. Were the sisters sharing him—or both him and Bat? Were the sisters switching off?

She had her hands pressed down on his chest, lifting her hips and butt up and down, sliding him in and out of her wetly, slickly, biting her bottom lips. Now he had it. Earlier Shannon would keep her tongue out, encircling her lips, as if trying to keep them wet, not biting them the way this sister was.

Suddenly, she clamped down on him, holding him tightly inside of her. As she rode him suddenly it was different. Instead of gliding in and out she was now grasping him with her insides, as if trying to keep him from sliding out. The new sensation caused him to bite his own lip and forget about which sister was which. He had to fight for control so that he wouldn't finish before they were both ready. She leaned down and kissed him, pushing her tongue into his mouth, wetting him with her kisses, pressing her small, hard breasts to his chest, yelping suddenly as she tried to fight her own release, and then finally sitting straight up on him with her eyes wide, her back straight, and then he exploded inside and she was milking him . . .

She kissed him awake later and smiled down at him.

"You're not Shannon."

"No."

"I came back here with Shannon, didn't I?"

"Yes."

"And you're . . ."

"Maureen."

He studied her face, but couldn't see any difference. He took her by the shoulders and moved her away from him just far enough to look at her breasts. Same small, solid globes, same pale nipples, but no birthmark there.

"Shannon has the birthmark," she said. "We don't know how she got it and we didn't."

"Well, just because you're sisters—"

"We're triplets," she said.

"What?"

She smiled.

"Identical in every way, except for that birthmark. Colleen and I don't have it."

"Colleen," Clint said, "was she . . ."

"She was here before," she said.

"And you?"

"I just got here."

"Oh . . ."

Her hand slid down between his legs and started to stroke him.

"I hope they didn't wear you out."

"Well—"

"Oh," she said, as he swelled in her hand, "I see that they didn't."

"Maureen . . ."

"Shhh," she said, putting her finger to his lips.

She slid on top of him, but upside down, so that her face was in his crotch, and his was in hers. Suddenly, her warm mouth engulfed him and his nostrils filled with the scent of her wetness. She braced herself with one hand on each of his thighs and started to suck him avidly. At the same time she pressed her pussy down into his face.

He opened his mouth to meet her, put out his tongue and began to lick her up and down, meeting pressure with pressure.

She groaned around his cock, which seemed to swell in her mouth as she continued to suck him wetly. His tongue pushed inside of her, the taste and scent familiar, and yet subtly different. He stopped thinking about the fact that they were sisters. He reached up to cup her ass and pull her even more tightly to his mouth as he licked and sucked for all he was worth, and suddenly they seemed to be locked in a competition to see who could finish who first . . .

FORTY

When Bat entered the dining room and joined Clint at his table he raised his eyebrows.

"Some night, huh?"

"I'm not sure," Clint said. "I'm still trying to figure out the order."

"You came back with Shannon," Bat said, "I came back with Colleen."

"So what happened to Maureen?"

"According to Shannon she didn't want to go with what's his name, Colin, so she came back here and waited her turn."

"Her turn?"

"In the lobby."

"They let her wait in the lobby?"

"Fought her turn to sleep with a legend. Pretty nice, bein' a legend sometimes, huh?'

"Sometimes . . ." Clint agreed. "I think I left Maureen in my room."

"And Shannon's in mine."

"So where's poor Colleen?" Clint asked. "I didn't see her in the lobby."

"I don't know," Bat said, "but I know one thing."

"What?"

"I sure worked up an appetite."

"Well," Clint said, "I have to admit, so did I."

"How did an older gent like you keep up with those three, anyway?" Bat asked.

"Experience," Clint replied, "something I'm sure you're still working on accumulating."

They were working on steak and eggs when Billy Madden came rushing into the room as fast as his short legs would carry him without actually running. His face was all red as he reached them, and when he sat down Clint thought he was having some sort of attack.

Maybe he'd found out about John L. having a beer last night?

"Billy," Bat said, "are you all right?"

"I can't believe it!" Madden said, bitterly.

"What?" Clint asked. "What can't you believe?"

"They're shuttin' us down!"

"Who's shuttin' you down?" Bat asked. "What are you talkin' about?"

"The locals," Madden said. "They're not lettin' us have the fight here in New Orleans."

"Why not?"

" 'Cause they think it'll cause a riot."

"What makes them think that?" Clint asked.

"Somethin' about a lot of fights on Bourbon Street last

night," Madden said. "What do I care if some jaspers wanna duke it out in the street? We're talkin' about professionals, here. We're talkin' about a lot of money, damn it! Jeez, this is gonna kill John L. He's been waitin' for a chance at Ryan so he could be the champ, and now look. Who knows if we'll ever get him to agree to another fight?"

"Do you think Ryan's people are behind this?" Clint asked.

"Naw!" Madden said. "His people are boxin' people. There's a lot of money in this for them too."

"Billy, what's the panic? Move the fight."

"Today?"

"Why not? You've got all day."

"Move it to where?"

"You said they won't let you have the fight in New Orleans," Clint said.

"Louisiana," Madden said, "they won't let us have it anywhere in Louisiana."

"So?" Bat asked. "Move it to Mississippi."

"But how?"

"Easy," Bat said. "See what the nearest Mississippi town is with a telegraph office and a railroad stop. Send a telegram. Tell them what you want."

"We need an arena—"

"You need a small hotel with a lot of land around it," Bat said. "You erect a tent and put up your ring."

"How do we get there?"

"You charter a train."

"Just like that? I don't know—"

"Billy, there's tons of important people in town, people with connections."

"I don't know 'em, Bat—but you do!"

"Me? Now wait—"

"Would you do it, Bat? Would you help us?"

"Well—"

"With your name and your weight behind it I bet you could swing it for us," Madden said. "Come on, whataya say?"

"I was only comin' to watch, Billy—"

"I'll give ya a piece of the purse," Madden said.

"No, no," Bat said, "I don't need— All right, I'll do it, just so I can get my bet down and see your boy take down Paddy Ryan."

"Okay," Madden said, "let's go!"

"What about Clint?" Bat asked.

"What about me?" Clint asked. "Don't drag me in—"

"Was your referee local?" Bat asked.

"As a matter of fact, he was a local—"

"Never mind," Bat said. "Clint can referee."

"Now wait a minute, Bat," Clint said, lowering his voice, "if I referee I can't bet!"

Bat leaned over.

"I'll put the bet in for you."

"Why are you so anxious— Hey, wait a minute!"

"Billy," Bat said, "why don't you wait in the lobby for us?"

"Okay," Madden said, "but hurry. Time's a-wastin'."

As Madden hurried out as quickly as he hurried in, Clint leaned over to Bat.

"I'm not fixin' this fight, Bat. That's not what I do."

"Would I ask you to do that?" Bat asked. "Even for money?"

"Well . . ."

"The answer is no, not even for money. Come on, with you and me behind this we can make this fight happen."

"What do you want me to do, besides referee?"

"Find a venue," Bat said. "While I find a train and put together this exodus, you find us a place to do."

"That's a big job, Bat," Clint said. "I'll need help—oh, wait. Help just arrived."

Bat looked at the door and saw what Clint saw—Luke Short had just walked in.

"Well, well," Bat said, "Luke don't know it but he just volunteered."

FORTY-ONE

Luke Short was not surprised to be roped into some sort of scheme the moment after meeting up with his friends Clint Adams and Bat Masterson.

"I came here to bet on a fight," he said, as they dragged him into the lobby, "I might as well help make it happen."

Clint and Short went off to find telegraph offices while Bat went to pull some strings with some powerful people he knew. They were to meet back in the lobby in an hour. If they couldn't get something going in that time the odds were slim that it would happen.

As Clint entered the lobby fifty-five minutes later he saw a serene looking John L. Sullivan and an agitated Billy Madden standing there, waiting.

"Jesus, Clint," Madden said, "we're goin' crazy here."

"Take it easy, Billy," Clint said. "I'm meeting Luke and Bat here in a few minutes."

"Luke?"

"Luke Short," Clint said. "He walked in just as we were getting started with this."

"Luke Short is here?" John L. asked. "I've heard of him. Is he here to bet on me?"

"He's here to bet," Clint said. "He didn't say on who."

Madden looked at his watch and shook his head. John L. put his hand on the smaller man's shoulder.

"Take it easy, Billy," John L. said. "This is going to happen."

"How can you be so sure?" Clint asked.

John L. looked at Clint and said, "It's my fate to win this title."

"But today?"

"Well," John L. said, "maybe tomorrow."

"Is Ryan willing to fight tomorrow instead of today?"

"His people say yes," Madden said. "All we need is a place to fight and a way to get there."

"Well," Clint said, "I've got the place."

"Clint, Jesus, man!" Madden said. "Are ya tryin' ta kill me? Why didn't you say so in the first place?"

"The place does no good without a way to get there, Billy," Clint said. "For that we need Bat to come through."

Short came back before Bat and reported that he had not found a place to put the fight on. He was relieved to hear that Clint had. Now they needed Bat, and he came walking into the lobby looking very self-satisfied.

"Well? Well?" Billy Madden asked, anxiously.

"I've got a train," Bat said.

"Yes!"

"And I found a place," Clint said. "Now, if the train can take us to the place we're in business."

"Well," Bat said, "tell me where and I'll find out if we can get there."

"I found a small town on the Gulf called Mississippi City," Clint said. "There's a hotel there called the Barnes. They say they can set up a tent and a ring on their front lawn, and they'd love to have us." Even as Clint spoke he wondered how he had managed to become part of the "us."

"Okay," Bat said, "that sounds good. I'll just double-check and make sure we can get close enough with the train."

"Oh, God!" Madden said, because he thought they already had it.

John L. again put his hand on the smaller man's shoulder and Clint could see the signs of affection between the two of them.

"How long, Bat?" John L. asked.

"Give me ten minutes and I'll have an answer."

"Ten minutes," John L. said, patting Madden on the back. "Come on, Billy. I'll buy you a drink."

"You can't drink," Madden said.

"So I'll watch you." John L. looked at Clint and Luke Short. "Join us?"

"Why not?" Clint asked. "Luke, you haven't formally met John L. Sullivan."

The two men shook hands and the four men went into the bar, where three of them would get drinks and one would watch.

It was fifteen minutes before Bat came in and joined the quartet at the bar. Madden, Clint, and Short were holding beers in their hands while John L. was empty-handed. Actually, Madden was *clutching* a beer in his hands, and almost spilled it as Bat entered and approached.

"Well? Well?"

Bat smiled and said, "We're in business. The train can take us to Mississippi City."

"Ah, Gahhhd!" Madden said, and quickly finished his beer.

"Everyone?" John L. asked. "The train can take everyone?"

"Fighters, trainers," Bat said, "and spectators. We've got twelve coaches."

"How'd you manage that, Bat?" John L. asked.

"The owner of the railroad is here to see the fight," Bat said.

"But how did you get him to go for twelve coaches?" the fighter asked.

"That was easy," Bat said. "I told him to bet on you, and guaranteed him that you'd win."

FORTY-TWO

Amazingly, plans were made very quickly for the participants to board the train. Spectators were left to their own devices to get to the train and get on before it left. On the other end they were assured that the ring would be up by the time they got there.

The fight would happen that night.

John L. refused to have his own car, as did Paddy Ryan. Instead both fighters and their people, plus Clint, Bat, and Luke Short were in the same car, with a crush of other people. Ryan and John L. waved at each other in a friendly enough manner, but they were at opposite ends of the car.

Looking out the window Clint could see waves of people approaching the train and he wondered if twelve cars would be enough to accommodate them all.

Between John L. and Paddy Ryan was a mixture of supporters. There were a lot of Irishmen, including the ones who had rescued Clint, Bat, and John L., and the debate was raging as to who would win. Also, wagers were being tossed back and forth, which reminded Clint that Bat was supposed to place his bet.

He leaned over and inquired about it in a low voice.

"Don't worry," Bat said, "you're covered and you got three-to-one."

"What are the odds on Ryan?"

"They stayed two-to-one."

"What did Luke do?"

"He won't say," Bat said. "Luke likes to play his cards close to the vest."

Having played poker with Luke Short many times, Clint knew that was an understatement.

"Where are our hosts?"

"In the front coach," Bat said, "tryin' not to get crushed."

"I hope John L. can win for them."

"He has to," Bat said. "I guaranteed it."

"Wait," Clint said, "you guaranteed it . . . how?"

"I had to cover their bet."

"You covered a bet made by someone who owns a railroad?" Clint asked.

"That's right."

"I don't even know how much they bet," Clint said, "but I know you won't be able to cover it if John L. loses."

"You got that right."

"Jesus, Bat," Clint said, "what the hell possessed you—"

"It was a challenge, Clint," Bat said, with a shrug. "You

know I can't resist a challenge. Besides, the young man is very confident."

"Have you talked to Paddy Ryan at all?"

"No, why?"

"I'll bet you he's pretty confident, as well."

"I see your point, but it doesn't matter," Bat said. "What's done is done."

"You know," Clint said, "if Luke and I were to help you cover the bet—"

"The three of us probably wouldn't be able to do it," Bat said. "Look, I appreciate the offer, but let's not even talk about it until after the fight, huh?"

"Okay, Bat," Clint said.

They got shoved from behind a few times, and they each patted their pockets to make sure they still had their money. Bat was going to need every cent he had if John L. Sullivan did not win.

"Well, at least you made sure of one thing," Clint said.

"What's that?"

"It'll be a hell of an exciting fight."

FORTY-THREE

The exodus from the train was even more of a mob scene than it had been on the other end. Luckily, the hotel sent two buggies to convey the participants to the site of their meeting.

John L. wanted Clint and Bat to come along, but there was no room.

"Go on," Clint said. "You have to get yourself ready for the fight. We'll see you there."

"Wait," John L. said, at the last minute. "You're the referee. You have to come along."

The buggy was already moving so Clint called out, "I'll get a ride with Ryan!"

Clint had been surprised that the Ryan camp had agreed to let him referee the fight. Riding with them might afford him the opportunity to find out why.

He walked over to Ryan and his manager and asked, "Got room for another passenger?"

Paddy Ryan, a big, strapping Irishman, bigger than Sullivan and bigger than any of the other Irishmen Clint had met on this trip, slapped him on the back hard enough to leave him breathless and said, "Climb aboard, lad, and glad to have ye."

Clint turned and told Bat and Luke Short, "I'll see you there."

He got into the buggy and sat across from Ryan and his manager, a dour-faced man who did not look happy—although that might have been his permanent expression.

"Mr. Ryan—"

"Call me Paddy, lad," Ryan said. "After all, you'll be in the ring with me."

"That's what I wanted to ask you about," Clint said. "If you don't mind . . . why did you accept me as referee?"

"I asked him the same question," the manager said.

"I know yer reputation, Mr. Adams," Ryan said, "and I don't mean with a gun. I mean yer reputation for fairness. And I know ye've refereed fights before."

"Never one of this magnitude," Clint said.

"Ah!" Paddy Ryan said. "A fight's a fight."

"But why go ahead with this one even with all the trouble?" Clint asked.

"I like John L.," Ryan said. "He's a fine lad, but he needs to be taught a lesson. I didn't want to miss my chance to be the teacher. I would have fought this fight on the train if I had to. In fact, I probably would have knocked him out sooner if we did that, since we'd've been fightin' toe to toe."

"And tonight?"

"Oh, he'll move around, run from me, try to jab me,"

Ryan said. "He's a-feared of me power, ya see. But he won't be able to run forever. Twenty, thirty rounds and he'll come down off his toes, and I'll have him for me dinner."

"You sound very confident."

"I'm the champ," Ryan said. "Why wouldn't I be confident?"

"I suppose you're right," Clint said, thinking of Bat's predicament if Ryan won. He wondered if he should excuse himself from the fight because of it. What if a moment came in the fight when he could affect the outcome? Would he make a decision solely because it might take his friend off the hook?

No, truthfully, he didn't think he would, and he didn't think Bat would expect him to, either.

"Can I ask you a question now, Mr. Adams?" Ryan asked.

"Call me Clint."

"Clint, then."

"Go ahead, ask."

"Where's your money in this fight?"

"I'm the referee," Clint said. "It wouldn't be right for me to bet."

"Nonsense!" Ryan said. "I'll be in the ring, and I've bet on me. John L. will be in the ring and he's bet on himself. Why shouldn't you get a bet down?"

"Well . . ."

"It's just us here, Clint," Ryan said. "Come on, where's yer money?"

"I'm afraid it's on John L., Paddy."

"Ah, too bad," Ryan said. "I hate to cost you yer money. What about your other famous friends Bat Masterson and Luke Short?"

"Bat's money is on John L," Clint said. "As for Luke, he doesn't talk about his bets."

"Interesting," Ryan said. "You know, I heard there's a famous writer fella here from England. What's his name?" The question was directed to his trainer, who simply shrugged.

"Oscar Wilde," Clint said.

"That's him!" Ryan said, snapping his fingers. "You know, I heard he bet on me, so I guess not all the famous folk are betting on John L."

"I guess not."

"This'll be a lovely fight, it will," Ryan said. "Lovely— and you'll have the best seat in the house."

"I'll try to stay out of the way."

"Now, lad," Ryan said, "just do your job, that's all, and maybe I'll knock John L. into your arms so's you can catch him and keep him from hurtin' himself when he falls down."

"I wish you luck, Paddy," Clint said.

"A lovely fight," Ryan said, again. "Just lovely."

FORTY-FOUR

When they reached the Barnes Hotel everything was ready and waiting for them, including rooms for John L. and Paddy Ryan. They apologized, but they were unable to supply free rooms for everyone in both fighter's camps. As it turned out, all both fighters had were managers, and they were happy to share their rooms with them.

Clint managed to secure a room that he'd be able to share with both Bat and Luke Short.

When they got there both fighters went to their rooms to get ready for the fight. As referee, Clint went to the tent to check the ring. As he walked in he saw that half the chairs that had been set up for spectators had already been claimed, and the argument over who would win was still raging.

"Hey, Clint!"

It was Colin, the Irishman who had introduced them to

the three red-haired sisters. Clint didn't know what had happened to Maureen and Colleen and Shannon. He and Bat had become so busy with trying to move the fight that by the time they got back to their rooms the girls were gone.

Colin was with his friends and they had all made sure they got seats right down in front.

"Hello, Colin," Clint said. He leaned on the ropes, testing the tension on them, making sure that a man could lean against them without falling out. For a hastily erected ring it was in pretty good shape.

"Is this fight gonna happen?" Colin asked. " 'Cause if it don't, mate, I don't think any of us are gonna get out of here alive."

"It'll happen, Colin."

"Are ye sure, lad?" Colin asked. " 'Cause I got to get me bet down if it is."

"Go and bet," Clint said. "It's happening."

"Saints preserve us," Colin shouted happily, and scampered off to tell his colleagues.

Clint was walking around the ring when he saw Bat and Luke Short coming out of the crowd. Clint went over to talk to them.

"We got seats down front," Bat said.

"How did you manage that in this crowd?"

"We have ways," Short said, and Clint decided not to ask.

"How's our boy?" Bat asked.

"I don't know," Clint said, "I haven't seen him since I got here."

"And how was your ride in with Mr. Ryan?" Short asked.

"Yeah," Bat said, "what kind of shape is he in?"

Clint narrowed his eyes at Bat and leaned over the ropes.

"You sonofabitch," he said. "You told me you made my bet already. Why are you looking for information now?"

"I made your bet," Bat said, "I just didn't make mine, yet."

"Well, what are you waiting for?" Clint asked. "Go and make it."

"On who?"

"That's for you to decide."

"You're a big help," Bat said, and he and Short went off for either Bat to make his bet, or for both of them to. Clint had a hunch, though, that Short had made up his mind a long time ago who he was going to bet on, and had done it. The little gambler rarely changed his mind once he made it up.

He went back to testing the tension of the ropes.

He was still waiting in the ring when a man approached and waved him over. He was in his fifties, sweating profusely, and he had a worried look on his face.

"Are you Mr. Adams?"

"I am."

"I'm Warwick, the hotel manager," he said. "I've been sent to tell you two things."

"What are they?"

"Well, first," Warwick said, "the governor of Mississippi has very hastily signed a proclamation outlawing prizefighting in the state."

"And second?"

"I'm to tell you that we'll be starting momentarily."

"You're not worried about the proclamation?"

Warwick mopped his brow with an already soaked handkerchief and said, "I'm more concerned with what will happen to my hotel if we don't have this fight."

"Okay, then," Clint said, "if anyone asks about a governor's proclamation we'll just say . . ."

". . . what proclamation?" the man finished, hesitantly.

"That's right," Clint said. "Don't worry, Mr. Warwick. Nothing's going to happen to your hotel."

"I sincerely hope not."

A roar went up from the crowd and Clint said to the worried manager, "Sounds like our fighters are here."

"Oh, my God," Warwick said, "I haven't even got my bet down yet. Excuse me."

Warwick took two steps and was quickly swallowed up by the surging crowd.

Here we go, Clint thought.

FORTY-FIVE

John L. was the first to arrive, so that the champion, Paddy Ryan, could make his entrance last. John L. understood what it meant to be champion, and didn't mind going along since he was convinced he would be the next champ.

He came bouncing along the aisle that the crowd had made for him, a towel around his shoulders, his manager, little Billy Madden, leading him. Clint knew that there was a movement to try to get American prizefighters to use the new Marquis of Queensbury rules, and the new boxing gloves, but this fight was obviously going to be bare knuckle, judging by John L.'s gloveless hands.

John L. climbed into the ring with Madden and began bouncing around on his feet, waving to the crowd, which went wild.

Clint pulled Madden aside and said, "We may get

raided any minute. The Mississippi governor has outlawed boxing."

"That's just great!"

"We'll get under way as fast as we can."

Madden nodded and went over to John L., who purposely did not look at Clint. He was treating him like a referee he had never seen before, which Clint thought was probably a good idea.

Next came Paddy Ryan and, if possible, the crowd went even wilder as he made his way to the ring led by his manager. Clint knew that if John L. managed to win, with his personality and charm, he would probably become the most popular champion in history.

All he had to do was beat Paddy Ryan, who looked as if he were chiseled out of stone. John L. had a much sleeker physique than the bulky Ryan, which Clint thought would benefit the younger man if he could last into the later rounds. Carrying all those muscles around might tire Ryan out. All John L. had to do was avoid those ham-sized fists in the early going.

Ryan made his way into the ring and began to wave to the crowd, also, only he stood flat-footed while he did it. In the back Clint could see money still changing hands as betting was still going on. No doubt some men—or women—had made up their minds after seeing both fighters barechested. Men, he felt, would bet Ryan because he looked like a brute. Women would pick John L. because he was more handsome.

He had chosen John L. because he liked the man's demeanor, and his confidence. Ryan had also been confident, but there was something about John L. that just made you believe him when he said he was going to win.

He believed John L., and he had a lot of money backing

that belief. However, he would not let that influence his actions as a referee—not that he could influence the outcome once these two heavyweights began winging punches at each other. He'd probably be lucky to get out of the ring with his own head in tact, so he planned on keeping his distance as much as he could.

Clint was surprised when Oscar Wilde climbed into the ring to introduce the two fighters. Wilde began to expound on his love of the "pugilistic endeavor" and Clint hoped that the writer would not go on too long, giving the governor time to reach them and shut them down. Luckily, the man soon got to the point and introduced both contestants. The champion, Paddy Ryan, got the loudest cheers, but in Clint's estimation, it was not by much.

Clint stepped to the center of the ring and called the combatants to join him.

"We all know why we're here," Clint said. "Let's not have any kicking, eye gouging or any other behavior like that. If I see a foul I'll penalize the fighter. Got it?"

Both fighters nodded, but kept their eyes on each other.

"You two managers understand, too?"

Both managers indicated that they did.

"Okay, then," Clint said, "let's get this show on the road."

FORTY-SIX

After the first four rounds Clint wasn't at all sure who was going to win. John L. was moving around well and blocking a lot of Ryan's punches, but some of the blows were landing. He was amazed, though, that not one punch had yet landed on John L.'s face.

On the other hand, John L. seemed to be able to hit Ryan at will with his left jab, and after four rounds the champ had a lot of lumps and swelling on his face. It didn't seem to bother him, though, as he was smiling when he went back to his corner.

"Punches like a bee sting," Clint heard Ryan tell his manager, as he sat on a wooden stool.

In the other corner John L. refused to sit and just stood staring across the ring at his opponent. His manager kept asking him if he was all right, and John L. would just nod.

Clint saw Bat Masterson and Luke Short in the front row, and both men were red-faced from yelling for four rounds, like all the rest of the spectators.

"You got him where you want him, Paddy!" somebody shouted.

"Finish him, John L.!" another voice yelled.

Clint had to admit that Ryan was throwing the heavier blows, and he thought that if anyone was knocked out it would probably be John L.

Then, as round five started, things seemed to change. Suddenly, John L.'s jab was a lot harder. Clint knew that Ryan could feel it down to his shoes every time it cracked him in the face, because he thought he could feel it in *his* feet.

On top of that, John L. began following the jabs with a right that started to land, as well.

After three rounds of that Ryan was not smiling when he went back to his corner.

John L., on the other hand, continued to stand and looked the fresher of the two. It was then that Clint realized that John L. was chopping Ryan down, piece by piece.

As they came out for round eight Ryan was moving slowly, as if his feet were heavier than they were in the first round—or the seventh. John L. began to jab twice, follow with a right, and then he'd hit Ryan in the body with his left. The man was so thick that it sounded like John L. was hitting a sack of wheat, but the body blows made Clint cringe, so he knew Ryan was feeling them.

He also knew, as the eighth round ended, that John L. was going to win.

Ryan didn't speak to his manager between the eighth and ninth rounds, and neither did John L. The difference, though, was that John L. could have if he wanted to. Ryan was just too tired to form words.

Looking at Bat and Luke Short, Clint could see that they knew, as well. They seemed calmer, and were not shouting as loud. Everybody else in the place, though, was still screaming at the top of their lungs.

Suddenly, everything seemed to be moving in slow motion. John L. jabbed and then he threw a vicious right, packed with more bad intentions than any other punch during the fight. It landed flush on the chin of the champion, whose legs trembled as he tried to withstand it, but finally he toppled and went down.

He went down so hard that everybody in the place was convinced he would not get up.

He went down so hard that it seemed a moot point to even count over him, but Clint did.

He went down so hard that money was already changing hands in the crowd, as Ryan supporters were paying off John L. supporters before Clint had even said, "One."

By the time he got to, "Ten," and waved his hands that the fight was over, the crowd went wild and began chanting John L.'s name.

Clint grabbed John L.'s right arm and raised it in the air.

"You did it, champ," he said.

"I said I would," John L. said. "Hey, let's help him up, huh? He was a good champ."

Clint and John L. went and helped Ryan's manager get the ex-champ to his feet and back to his corner.

"Are you all right?" John L. asked.

"Yeah," Ryan said, groggily, "yeah, I'm all right. You're a helluva fighter, John L. Sullivan."

"So are you, Paddy Ryan," John L. said. "You were a good champion."

"Maybe I was," Ryan said, "but I get the feeling you're gonna be a great one."

Suddenly, there were men in the ring pounding John L. on the back and the situation turned potentially dangerous.

"I gotta get John L. outta here," Madden said to Clint.

"Go ahead."

"I need help."

Clint looked around for Bat and Luke Short and waved them into the ring.

"Get John L. back to the hotel in one piece, will you?"

"Sure," Bat said, "come on, John L."

As Bat and Short began to escort John L. from the ring another man approached Clint, wearing the badge of a U.S. Marshal and holding a piece of paper.

"You the referee?" he asked.

"That's right."

"I got a proclamation here from the governor sayin' this fight is over," the man said.

"The fight's already over," Clint said. "John L. knocked Ryan out."

"I know," the Marshal said. "It was a helluva fight. Here." He pushed the legal paper at Clint, said, "I gotta go collect my winnings," turned and left the ring.

PART FOUR
FORT WORTH

FORTY-SEVEN

BACK TO THE PRESENT . . .

"And what happened after that?" Alphonse Michael DeKay asked.

"Yeah," the sheriff echoed, "what happened?"

"We all got out of there," Clint said, "before the governor could have the place raided."

"First we all collected on our bets, though," Bat said.

"Well," Clint said, "most of us did."

"Okay, fine," Luke Short said, "so I bet on Ryan. After all, he was the champ."

"Have you seen John L. Sullivan since then?" DeKay asked. "I'd love to get an interview with him."

"No," Clint said. "I haven't."

"Me, neither," Short said.

"I've been to a couple of his fights since then," Bat

said, "but didn't spend much time with him."

"What happened to those three sisters?" DeKay asked.

"Is this for your story?" Clint asked.

The young man blushed and said, "Just curious."

"We never saw them again," Clint said, "did we, Bat?"

"Nope," Bat said, "never again."

DeKay looked disappointed.

"I'm gonna check out front," the sheriff said, and left.

Clint took a peek at the small, high window in the cell and saw that dawn was approaching. Still a few hours before court would be in session, though.

"What do the three of you think will happen in court this morning?" DeKay asked.

"Well," Clint said, "since it's not Hangin' Judge Parker's court, I think Luke will probably go free."

"I agree," Bat said. "After all, it was a fair fight."

"You never know what'll happen in court," Short said. Clint and Bat looked at him. "I'm just sayin'," Short added.

"Well," Bat said, "even if he decides to charge you we'll probably be able to bail you out."

"Pillar of the community, and all that," Clint said.

"We'll see," Short said. He didn't hold out much hope. He thought this would just be another case like Dodge City. He'd have to sell his interest for good, take Hettie, and move on.

It was always the same.

The sheriff came back into the cell block and said, anxiously, "We got trouble."

"What kind?" Clint asked.

"There's a crowd out front," the lawman said. "They look mean, and they're armed."

Clint looked at Bat and Short.

"The worst kind," Bat said.

"Somebody's been drinking all night," Clint said. "The drunker they got, the more friends Jim Courtright got."

"So what do we do?" Bat asked. "Wait for them to come in or go out and see them?"

"We've been waiting all night," Clint said. "I'm ready to stretch my legs a bit."

"Give me a gun," DeKay said, "and I'll help."

"Not a chance," Clint said.

"Why not?" the young man demanded.

"Have you ever fired a gun before?"

"Of course."

"Hit what you shot at?" Bat asked.

"Well . . ."

"You stay inside with Luke," Clint said.

"Whoa!" Short said. "I'm not staying inside."

"You're a target, Luke," Clint said. "You step outside and somebody might get brave."

"He's right," Bat said. "Clint and I can go out and handle it."

"And me," the sheriff said. "It's my job."

"Okay," Clint said, "the three of us can handle it. Luke, keep our brave newshound inside and don't let him get his hands on a gun. We don't want him hitting one of us by mistake."

"I'll just watch from the window in front," DeKay said.

"I don't think that's such a—" Clint started.

"I've got to report it," DeKay said.

Clint looked at Bat, who nodded.

"Okay."

They all went out into the sheriff's office. They could hear the sounds of voices from outside. Clint and Bat waited while the man grabbed a shotgun from his gun rack and loaded it.

"Shotgun?" the man offered them.

"No," Clint said.

"We're fine," Bat said.

Each of them still had two guns.

"Okay then," Rea said, "let's step outside."

FORTY-EIGHT

Despite the fact that it was almost dawn some of the men outside were holding torches. There was quite a crowd. Clint estimated maybe forty men were standing out in front of the jail. He doubted that four of them were really friends of Jim Courtright.

"Charley," the sheriff said to a man in front. Clint knew then that this was Charley Bull, Courtright's partner.

"We want Short, Sheriff," Bull said. "He can't get away with killin' Jim like that."

"Like what, Bull?" Clint asked.

"Shootin' him down like a dog!"

"I was there, Bull," Bat said. "It looked like a pretty fair fight to me."

"Short shot him down!" someone yelled.

"Like a dog!" another voice chimed in.

"We want him now!" a third called out.

"Correct me if I'm wrong," Clint shouted, "but wasn't it Courtright who had the reputation with a gun? Luke Short's only rep is with a deck of cards."

"Short is one of you," Bull said, pointing at Clint.

"One of . . . who?" Clint asked.

"You know," Bull said. "He's friends with Clint Adams and Bat Masterson. He knew how to use a gun."

"So did Courtright."

"Jim never got a shot off!" Bull said.

Clint looked at Bull.

"He just wasn't good enough."

"He wasn't as good as he thought he was," Bat said.

"You men should go home and sleep this off," Sheriff Rea called out. "If you stay here somebody's gonna get hurt."

"Yeah," somebody called out, "you."

"We want Short!" Bull said. "Give him to us, or we'll take him."

Rea raised the shotgun, holding it ready but not pointing it at anyone in particular. Clint and Bat produced both their guns at this point and stood with the weapons in their hands.

"The first man who makes a move on this jail dies," Clint said.

"And the second," Bat said.

"Sheriff," someone called out, "are these men deputies?"

"We're friends of Luke Short," Clint said. "That's all you need to know."

"If you're not deputies," someone said, "you can't just shoot us."

"They can shoot anybody they want," Rea said, "in self-defense."

Clint had already decided that although Charley Bull was Courtright's partner, the man was not going to make the first move. He looked elsewhere for a leader, but didn't see anyone. Bull had been leader enough to get them here, but that was as far as his leadership abilities would take them.

"Nobody here wants to die," Clint said. "I can see that."

"If someone does get killed," the sheriff announced, "you'll all be responsible."

"You can't protect Short forever," Bull said.

"Luke will go to court and stand before a judge," Clint said. "What more do you want?"

"Justice," Bull said.

"You don't even know what that means," Clint said. "You and Courtright were shaking down the saloon and gambling hall owners in Fort Worth. What do you know about justice?"

"That's slander!" Bull said. "I'll sue."

"Go ahead," Bat invited him. "We can prove it."

Bull licked his lips nervously. He knew they could prove it, and he wasn't about to push it.

"Bull," Sheriff Rea said, "go home. Unless you're willin' to draw your gun now and lead this mob, turn around and go home."

"Bull," Clint said.

The man looked at him.

"I will personally put the first bullet right in your chest," Clint said. "Think it over."

The mob began to grow restless, waiting for something to happen. Suddenly, a man dropped his torch, turned, and walked away. Several others followed him. They weren't waiting for Bull to make his decision.

"You're starting to lose your backing, Bull," Clint said.

Bull turned and watched as another torch hit the ground and several men turned and walked away. He turned back and looked at Clint.

"This ain't over," he said. "I'll be back with better help than this."

"Bring some professional guns, Bull," Clint said. "Let's see how far they follow you."

Bull pointed at Clint and Bat and said, "This ain't over."

He turned and walked away. The men who were left dropped their torches and scattered. Some of the torches had already extinguished themselves, others would burn for a few minutes.

The sheriff lowered his shotgun and backed into the office, with Clint and Bat covering. Bat went next, and then Clint.

"That was amazing," DeKay said. "The three of you stood off forty men."

"Forty?" Bat asked. "I thought there were eighty, didn't you?"

Clint looked at Bat and said, "Eighty? More like a hundred."

"A hundred," DeKay said, writing in his notebook. "A hundred armed men!"

Short looked at Bat and Clint, and shook his head.

FORTY-NINE

With the testimony of both Bat and Clint as well as Luke Short's own partner Jake Johnson, the judge decided later that day not to file any charges against Short, and released him.

"I can't believe it," Short said, as he walked out of the courthouse with Clint and Bat, his arm around Hettie.

"Why not?" Hettie asked. "What you did was in self-defense."

"Well, I know that," Short said. "it's always self-defense, Hettie, but nobody ever sees it that way but us."

"Well," she said, "maybe times are changing."

"Where are you headed now, Luke?" Clint asked. "Back to the White Elephant?"

Short nodded.

"Got a big poker game in town, startin' tomorrow," Short said.

"I didn't know that," Clint said, looking at his friend Bat Masterson. "Sonofabitch, you knew it, didn't you?"

"Well . . ."

"Why didn't you tell me?"

"Havin' you in the game would just make it that much harder for me to win," Bat pleaded his case.

"Is that a fact?" Clint asked. "Well, it just so happens I'm not in the mood for a big poker game, so you fellas are both safe."

"But you'll stay in town for the game, won't you, Clint?" Hettie Short asked.

Clint was about to say no, but the look on Hettie's face stopped him. It was clear she wanted him to stay. He wasn't sure if she was still worried about Jim Courtright's friends coming after her husband, or if it had something to do with the poker game, but he said, "Well, sure, Hettie. I said I didn't want to play, but that doesn't mean I don't want to watch these two butt heads."

"Excellent!" Hettie said. "Luke, I have to get back to the apartment."

"So do I, sweet," Short said. "I need to wash the jail smell off of me." He turned to face his friends. "Once again I'm in your debt."

Clint waved away his friend's gratitude and Bat said, "We do it so often for each other, Luke, that we're bound to be even."

"I'll see you both at the Elephant later."

"We'll be there," Bat said.

"Luke," Clint said, "you got to buy back your place from me. Don't forget."

"I haven't forgotten, Clint," Short said. "Thanks."

As Luke and his wife went off arm-in-arm Bat said, "Hettie's worried about somethin'."

"I know," Clint said. "Think she's worried about Charley Bull trying something?"

"Bull won't try anything unless he gets a lot more help than he had this mornin'," Bat said.

"The game, then?" Clint asked. "Who's playing?"

"I don't know, yet," Bat said.

Behind them Alphonse Michael DeKay came out, smiling broadly.

"What makes you so happy, lad?" Clint asked.

"I got a telegram from my editor. He wants me to come back and write everything up for the paper."

"Isn't that what you were planning to do, anyway?" Clint asked.

"To tell you the truth," DeKay said, "this will be my first story, my first byline. I been trying to prove myself for months now, but all the stuff I got from you, and covering Luke's arrest has done it. I get to write it all up myself, instead of handing my research to someone else."

"Well, good for you," Clint said.

"We'll be watching for your byline," Bat said.

"You fellas aren't mad at me?"

"For what?" Clint asked.

"Well . . . for making you think I already had a byline? For getting you to talk to me, tell me stories—"

"Hey," Clint said, "telling you stories gave us something to do last night."

"It made the time go faster," Bat said. "And now, to make the rest of the day go smoother, I'm going to go and get some sleep."

"Sleep," Clint asked, "what's that?"

"So you'll be heading home?" Clint asked DeKay.

"Yes, but just to write this story," the young man said. "I'll be back, again."

"For what?" Bat asked.

"I have the feeling," DeKay said, "that the story in Fort Worth is not over."

Clint and Bat walked to their rooms together. Clint had a room at the White Elephant but there wasn't one for Bat, so he was staying at a hotel nearby. Clint had decided that after he got a good night—or day's—sleep he would move out of the White Elephant so Bat could move in. After all, Bat was the one playing in a big poker game, not him.

"Do you think the kid is right?" Bat asked, as they approached his hotel.

"About what?"

"About the story not being over?"

"Bat," Clint said, "when you're us, is the story ever really over?"

Bat chuckled and said, "Good point, Clint, very good point."

FIFTY

When Clint entered his room and sniffed the air he knew he wasn't going to get to sleep anytime soon. The scent was distinctly Lillian Farmer, and when he moved to the bedroom he saw that she was asleep in his bed. She was lying beneath the sheet, which had molded itself to her so well he could see she was naked beneath it. Her luxurious black hair was fanned out on the pillow. Her face was pale, devoid of any makeup, and she seemed younger in repose than when she was awake and wearing her war paint.

He realized then that the reason she was in town had to be for the big poker game, as well. With Short, Bat, and Lillian Farmer in the game it had to be big, but he wondered who else the game was going to bring to town, and what stories this game would yield for young Alphonse DeKay to write about.

Lillian smelled so sweet that, as Clint undressed, he felt bad that he had not taken a bath after leaving the jail. He'd have to do that later. He slid into bed next to her, so as not to wake her. Maybe he could get some sleep before she woke up and realized he was there. Maybe he could even get a bath later before making love to her again.

He drifted off to sleep, vowing to take that bath first thing when he woke up . . .

He didn't know how long he'd been asleep but he was awakened by the feel of soft, silky skin against his and, the feel of large, erect nipples rubbing up against his back.

"You snuck in this morning," she said in his ear.

"We stayed awake in the jail all night to make sure Luke got to court alive."

"How did he fare?"

"He was released."

Clint turned onto his back and Lillian snuggled in against him, putting her head on his chest as he slid his arm around her.

"I smell like a goat," he said.

"You smell fine," she said. "You smell like a man."

"Men smell like goats?"

She giggled and said, "Very often."

She slid her hand over his chest, down over his belly, then felt his thighs before moving her palm to rub his penis up and down. He swelled beneath her touch and soon she had him in her hand, slowly stroking him until he was fully erect.

"Still tired?" she asked.

"Some."

"Too tired?"

"Never."

"I didn't think so."

She slid beneath the sheet so that she was nestled comfortably between his legs. She held him around the base of his penis and began to lick him avidly, wetting him thoroughly before sliding the length of him into her mouth.

No, not too tired at all . . .

"Well, of course I'm here for the big game," she said. "Why else would I come?"

"Maybe just to take Henry Cabot's money?"

She laughed.

"If I'd known Cabot before that probably would have been a good enough reason," she admitted, "but I didn't. I never met him before playing poker with him."

"Do you have any idea who else is playing in this game?" Clint asked.

"None," she said, "and I like it that way. I assume Luke will play, but I'm content to meet the other players at the table, when the game starts. Why? Do you know who's playing?"

"No," he said, "but if I was playing I'd sure try to find out."

"So you're not going to play?"

"No."

"Why not?"

"I didn't know anything about it ahead of time," he said.

"And you need to know that?"

"I'm not a gambler, the way you and Luke are. I'm not always prepared to sit in on a poker game—certainly not a high stakes poker game. So no, I'll pass this time, but I'll be around."

"To watch?"

"Maybe for a while," he said. "I . . . don't have anything better to do at the moment, and Hettie—Luke's wife—seems to be taking some comfort from the fact that I'm here."

"Well," Lillian said, "you did manage to keep her husband alive all night. Does she think he's still in danger?"

"I suppose so."

"Do you?"

"Maybe," Clint said. "We still don't know what Charley Bull, Jim Courtright's partner, is going to do."

"So you'll stick around until you know that?"

"At least."

"Good."

"I'll be moving to the hotel, though."

"Why is that?"

"So that someone who is actually playing in the game can use this room."

"Well," Lillian said, "try to get one nearby, will you? I might want to run over during a break and use you to relieve some stress." She put her hand beneath the sheet to pinch him and let him know she was kidding.

"I'll try to be available to relieve as much stress as I can, ma'am," he said.

"Is Bat going to play in the game?" she asked.

"I thought you didn't want to know."

"Well," she said, snuggling close to him, "I'm just assuming he will, since he's here. I'd love to play in a game with him and with Luke Short."

"Well," he said, "maybe you'll get your wish."

"And if I had one more wish?"

"Yes?"

"I'd wish for you to be in the game, too."

"You want to take my money?"

"I wouldn't mind," she said. "Imagine my being able to say I took money from Luke Short, Bat Masterson, and Clint Adams?"

"Well," he said, "I'll supply stress relief, but I'm sorry I won't be able to donate to your purse—or your reputation."

Lillian remained silent after that, fearing she'd finally pushed him too far and offended him, and they drifted off to sleep for about another hour before they both got up and shared a bath.

FIFTY-ONE

The White Elephant's restaurant stayed open all day, so while it wasn't lunchtime or dinnertime Clint and Lillian were able to get a meal when they came downstairs.

"Well, well," Clint said, as they entered.

"What?"

"In the corner," Clint said, "sitting alone and looking put-upon."

"The handsome man?'

"Handsome?"

"I think so."

"Well, okay, the handsome man," Clint said, "is Ben Thompson."

"Really?" Lillian asked. "He must be here for the game."

"I'd say so."

They were shown to a table, sat down, and put in their orders for steak dinners.

Lillian looked around and said, "This is exciting. Who else do you see in the room?"

Clint looked around and only saw one other man.

"Charlie Coe," he said.

"Coe?"

"Also known as Rusty Coe."

"I know that name," she said. "He's a big gambler, isn't he?"

"Very big," Clint said. "This makes me wonder just how big this game really is?"

"Well . . ."

"Yes?"

"I've got ten thousand with me," she said, finally, "just for this game."

"That is big," he said.

"The biggest," she said. "At least, the biggest game I've ever played in."

"I wonder . . ." he said.

"What?"

"I wonder if you'll be the only woman in the game?"

"I don't know," she said. "Are there any more women who play in high stakes games?"

"One or two."

"And do you see any of them here?"

"Not right now."

"Good. I want the pleasure of taking all the money from the boys myself."

Clint didn't bother telling her that he had seen her play, as well as Short, Bat, and even Rusty Coe and Ben Thompson. She'd last awhile against them, but she wouldn't outlast them.

• • •

After they ate Lillian announced she had to go back to her own hotel to get changed and ready to play.

"The game starts tonight?" he asked.

"I don't know," she said. "I guess it starts when everybody gets here and Luke Short says it does."

She left and he went to the bar to get a beer. There he found Bat and Luke Short having one together.

"You look well rested," Short said.

"Not as well as I'd have liked," Clint said. "Are all your players here?"

"Not all," Short said.

"Ben Thompson is here," Bat said, with distaste. Thompson and Bat were not the best of friends.

"I saw him," Clint said. "Rusty Coe, too."

Bat looked at Short, who shrugged.

"One or two more," he said.

"Then we can start tonight?" Bat asked.

"Why not?" Short said. "We seem to have a quorum."

"Any more women expected?" Clint asked, accepting his beer from the bartender.

"No," Short said, "just Lillian."

"Why didn't you tell me about this game when I got here?" Clint asked.

"Well," Short said, "to tell you the truth, I was a little preoccupied."

"Do you think Charley Bull is going to let this go?" Clint asked.

"I don't know," Short said. "I guess we'll have to wait and see if he tries to collect some money. If he does, he'll have to get it from Jake."

"Why Jake?" Clint asked.

"Because after I get my share back from you I'm gonna sell out to Jake."

"And then what?"

"I'm gonna rent the upstairs and just run some games," Short said.

"What about your apartment?" Bat asked. "With the dumbwaiter, and all?"

"I've got my eye on a house in town," Short said. "Hettie would like her own house."

"Why sell, Luke?" Clint asked. "Why now?"

"Because I can see the writing on the wall, Clint," Short said. "The end is coming for gambling. The owners are gonna be hit hard."

"But you won't own anything," Clint said.

"Exactly."

"And you can continue to run your games," Bat said, "even if you have to do it illegally."

"Right again."

"Our friend is a visionary," Bat said.

"So it would seem," Clint agreed.

"Who knows?" Short said. "Maybe this game will be my last. Do you want to play, Clint?"

"Not me," Clint said. "I'm going to let all you high stakes gamblers have a go at it."

"I'd better get the room ready if we want to start tonight," Short said. "I'll see you boys later."

Short left and Clint and Bat each got a fresh beer.

"Where'd you get ten thousand or so to sit in on this game?" Clint asked his friend.

"Nine," Bat said, "in my case."

"All right," Clint said. "Where'd you get nine thousand?"

"I've got a backer."

"Who?"

"Jim Devine. Know him?"

"Cattleman?"

"That's him."

"He's got a lot of faith in you."

"So it would seem."

They worked on their beers for a few moments and then Clint asked, "Do you agree with Luke?"

"About the gambling? It's possible, I guess . . . here, I mean. There are other places to gamble. In fact, I've been thinking about opening my own place."

"Where?"

"Don't know, yet," Bat said, "but winning this game could give me the stake I needed."

"After you pay Devine back his share."

"Right. I could use a partner, though."

"Not me."

"Why not?"

"I don't want to own anything," Clint said. "Not at this stage of my life. I'll leave that to you big-gambler types."

"You're as good as anyone who'll be sitting at that table tonight," Bat said.

"Except for one thing."

"What's that?"

"I don't have the money," Clint said, "or a backer."

FIFTY-TWO

Charley Bull didn't know what to do.

Jim Courtright had been the brains of their partnership, but Courtright was dead. Without him, the business was dead, too, unless Bull could do something about it. Something that even Jim Courtright couldn't do.

Kill Luke Short.

To do that, though, he would probably have to go through Bat Masterson and Clint Adams, as well. But Charley Bull couldn't do that. He wasn't good enough, and he wasn't brave enough. There was no way he'd ever be able to face any of those men alone, let alone together.

But he knew something that, apparently, even Jim Courtright hadn't known—that there was power in numbers. If Courtright had been backed by more men, he probably would have survived his showdown with Luke Short. So what Charley Bull had to do was get more men—more men than even those three could stand against.

He might not have had the skill or courage of a Jim Courtright, but he had one thing that might make up for it.

He had money.

FIFTY-THREE

Luke Short managed to send messages to all the players who had already arrived in Fort Worth to let them know that the game would start that night. The instructions were to meet on the second floor of the White Elephant Saloon at nine P.M.

After leaving the bar Clint and Bat managed to exchange rooms, so that Clint was now staying in the nearby Sweetwater Hotel. Since Bat now had a room in the White Elephant he was the first to arrive. Clint soon followed, and waited with Bat and Short for the others to arrive.

Lillian Farmer was next.

"Oh darn," she said, as she entered and looked around, "I was hoping to be last and make an entrance."

The three men took in her low-cut red gown, which left breathtakingly little to the imagination.

"You may not be last, dear lady," Bat said, "but you most certainly have made an entrance."

"You're very sweet, Mr. Masterson," she said.

"Miss Farmer," Short said, "welcome to the game."

"Thank you, sir."

She turned to Clint, who shook his head and said, "I don't know how anyone will be able to concentrate on the game."

"My plan, exactly."

Also present in the private room were a waiter, and a dealer. Short sent the waiter to get a glass of brandy for Lillian.

"In fact," he added, "bring a couple of bottles, and a dozen brandy snifters."

"Yes, sir."

Rusty Coe arrived next and did not look surprised to see Bat Masterson.

"I knew you couldn't pass up this game," he said, while the two shook hands.

"Rusty, do you know Clint Adams?" Short asked.

Coe turned to Clint and said, "We've met."

"Once, I think," Clint said, shaking the man's hand.

"Are you playing, too?"

"No," Clint said, "not this time."

"Good," Coe said. "If I remember correctly the last time we met you outlasted me."

"I don't think I won, though," Clint said.

"Who did?" Bat asked. "Do you remember?"

"I do," Coe said. "It was Luke." He turned to face Short. "I'm hoping to fare better, this time."

Short smiled and said, "There's always hope."

· · ·

Ben Thompson arrived next and looked around. He was a slender, dapper-dressed man about Bat's age. The two had a lot in common—the way they dressed, the way they fared with the ladies, their abilities with cards and guns, and the fact that they had brothers. It was sometimes amazing to Clint that they did not get along at all.

"How many are we?" he asked.

"Five," Short said.

Thompson looked around.

"Who's not playin'?"

"I'm not."

Thompson approached Clint and extended his hand.

"Too bad," he said. "You security?"

"If we need it," Clint said, "I can provide it."

"We can start with five, if no one objects," Short said.

"I'm anxious to get started," Lillian said.

"I'm with the lady," Ben Thompson said, looking her up and down.

"You wish," Bat said, under his breath.

FIFTY-FOUR

Charley Bull decided he was smarter than anyone had ever given him credit for—including Jim Courtright, and himself.

"I can do this," he told himself. All he needed was the right men—and he figured the right man to get him the right men was a fella named Austin Healy.

Healy had wanted to work with Bull and Courtright in their business but Courtright didn't like him.

"He's too cocky," he'd said.

"You're cocky," Bull had told Courtright.

"I got a right to be," Courtright had answered, "he don't—not yet. Maybe when he earns the right we'll take him on."

Well, now the question of whether or not to take Healy on was all Bull's.

"You know what ol' Jim used to say about you, Aus-

tin?" Bull asked Healy. They were in the offices that
Courtright and Bull used to conduct their business.

"What did he used to say about me?" Healy asked,
anxious to know. Courtright had been his idol, and he
wanted to know anything the man might have said about
him.

"He used to say you were cocky."

"Yeah?"

"That's right," Bull said, "cocky like him."

"Like him? That's what he said?"

Bull looked across the desk at Healy, who was thirty
but acted like a kid whenever he talked about Long-haired
Jim Courtright.

"Well, almost like him . . ."

"Whataya mean, almost?" Healy asked.

"Well, he said you hadn't earned the right to be cocky,
Austin," Bull told him. "Not yet, anyway."

"Well . . . what do I have to do to earn it?"

"Somethin' big."

"Like what?"

"Well . . . like Luke Short."

"I could take Short," Healy said.

"Have you got some men you can use?"

"I don't need no men," Healy insisted, "I can take him
alone."

"Now, think about this, Austin," Charley Bull said—
although Bull had never been much of a thinker, himself.
"Think it over. Jim thought he could take Luke Short and
look what happened to him."

"Well, you're right about that."

"I know I am," Bull said. "What you gotta do is get
yourself enough help, because Short has help, already."

"He's got Adams and Bat Masterson," Healy said.

"You been payin' attention, Austin," Bull said. He was starting to like the feeling of being the man in charge. "If you could take care of all three—Adams, Short, and Masterson—you'd be more man than Jim Courtright ever was."

"Yeah?"

"No doubt about it."

"I can get help," Healy said. "I know lots of boys who would like to go up against the likes of them—long as they know what they're goin' up against, ya know?"

"Clint Adams, Bat Masterson, and Luke Short," Bull said. "Ain't that enough to know?"

"But they're tough, Charley," Healy said, "real tough."

Bull could see Austin Healy starting to lose his swagger the more he thought about who he'd be facing.

Charley was going to have to nip that in the bud.

"Look, Austin," he said, "A dozen or so men is all you'd probably need to get the job done. A dozen good men, if you know any."

"I know lots of good men," Healy said. "Lots."

"Good," Bull said, " 'cause I got an idea."

"What's that? What idea?"

"You gather your men and I'll tell you the idea," Bull said.

"Okay," Healy said, leaping from his chair. "I'll have 'em all by tomorrow afternoon."

"They're all in Fort Worth?"

"Here, or as good as," Healy said. "I can get 'em."

"Well then, get 'em!" Bull said. "And when you've got 'em all come back here and tell me. I'll be here tomorrow afternoon."

"I'll let you know, Charley," Healy said. "I won't let you down."

"You can let me down," Bull said, "but you wouldn't want to let Jim Courtright down, would you?"

"No, sir."

Bull was glad he'd watched how Jim Courtright could manipulate people. He'd learned a lot from Courtright, but it was time for him to go out on his own, see how it felt to be the man in charge.

"I wouldn't ever want to let Jim down," Healy said. "He was my friend."

Truth was Courtright never thought of Austin Healy as a friend, just a big pain in the butt, but Bull didn't bother telling Healy that.

"Round 'em up and bring yerself back here, Austin," Bull said. "We got a lot of work to do."

Charley Bull was surprised at how his own personality seemed to have changed just since Jim Courtright had been killed. True, he'd backed down outside the jail but then he'd only had a motley gang of townspeople behind him, and he was facing Clint Adams and Bat Masterson, not to mention the sheriff.

Next time, it would be different—and he had a plan. If all went well Luke Short would soon be out of business, permanently.

Austin Healy was excited.

The opportunity to do something that even Jim Courtright couldn't was heady. He needed two things right now: He needed to find Dan Carlton, his partner. He and Carlton had been together a long time. He'd promised his partner that when Jim Courtright took him on he would take him along, too. Between the two of them they could round up enough men to do the job.

Because he was so excited at the prospect of what he might be able to do, the second thing he needed was a woman.

But first things first.

FIFTY-FIVE

The game picked up little steam the first night, with no one taking control by the time they called it to a halt.

As the five players rose to leave, Ben Thompson spoke to no one and simply left.

Lillian Farmer came over to Clint and asked, "My room? It would be easier for me in the morning to get ready."

"Your room it is," he said. "In a couple of hours?"

She looked around at the other men in the room, then said, "All right. It'll give me time to get comfortable."

As Lillian left Rusty Coe shook hands with both Bat and Luke Short, then came over and did the same with Clint.

"Until tomorrow night," he said, and left.

Short and Bat came over to Clint, who said, "Buy you fellas a beer?"

"Let's do it in my office," Short said. "You can sign some papers while we're there."

"Oh, right," Clint said. "I have to give you back your property."

"So you can sell it all over again," Bat said, "only this time I hope you get more for it."

"Count on it," Short said, and led them downstairs to his office.

Minutes later the papers were signed and they all had beers and were sitting around Short's office.

"Have you told Jake yet?" Bat asked.

"That he's gonna buy me out? No, not yet."

"How about Hettie?"

"She knows. She said she'll miss the dumbwaiter, but she's looking forward to living in a house."

"That gonna make you happy, Luke?" Bat asked. "Settling down like that?"

"Why not?" Short asked. "I'll have plenty to do. I'll keep my interests in some smaller places around town." After a few moments of silence he added, "I'll have plenty to do."

Clint looked at Bat. "Is he trying to convince himself, or us?"

"I'm not sure," Bat said. "I think himself."

"You two can argue the point," Short said, getting up from his chair. "I'm going to turn in."

"What other players are you expecting for tomorrow?" Bat asked as his friend headed for the door.

Short reeled off a few gambler's names, all of them familiar to both Clint and Bat.

"And I sent Wyatt an invitation," he finished. "Don't know if he'll show up, though."

"I haven't seen him much since Tombstone," Bat said, then turned to Clint. "You?"

"No."

"Been hearing stories about him goin' a little crazy," Bat said.

"Just stories," Clint said.

"Maybe we'll find out," Short said, "if he shows up. Goodnight, you two. Stay in here as long as you like."

Short left, closing the door behind him.

"I won't be staying here long," Clint said. "I've got a better offer."

"Lillian Farmer," Bat said. "Quite a lady."

"I know."

"Decent poker player."

"I know."

"She's not gonna last in this game, though."

Clint sighed and said, "I know."

"You would, though."

"Let's not start that again."

"Fine," Bat said.

They finished their beers in silence.

"Has Hettie talked to you?" Bat asked.

"About what?"

"About staying."

"Very briefly."

"You don't think Luke's out of danger, do you?"

"Charley Bull . . ." Clint said.

". . . has no guts," Bat finished. "You saw him at the jail."

"I'm not sure what I saw," Clint said. "With stronger men behind him, who knows what would have happened?"

"So you think Bull is gonna take a run at Short? After seeing Luke gun down Courtright?"

"Maybe not himself," Clint said.

"Ah."

"No harm sticking around a bit longer, just to make sure."

"Well," Bat said, "while you're sticking around you might as well play some cards—"

"I'm out of here," Clint said. "Got a willing lady waiting."

"I have a cold bed waiting," Bat said, "so I guess I'll go out into the saloon and see if I can't change that."

Together they left the office, Clint pulling the door closed behind them. They walked through the saloon, but parted company when they reached the bar.

"Good luck," Clint said to Bat before leaving.

"It's the only kind I'll tolerate," Bat said, with a smile.

FIFTY-SIX

Charley Bull looked up as Austin Healy entered his office with Dan Carlton in tow. He knew Carlton, knew that Healy had been trying to get Courtright to take him on, as well. Both men were young, thirty, and impressed by Courtright's reputation. Bull knew Courtright and respected him, but he knew that Courtright's reputation was not something to be impressed with.

"Back so soon?" he asked. It had been hours.

"I told you I could put the right men together," Healy said. "Dan, here, helped. We picked out ten men who can get the job done."

"Ten men," Bull said, "and you two. That makes twelve."

"Thirteen, counting you," Healy said.

"Oh no," Bull said.

"Why not?"

"Because that'd make thirteen," Bull said, thinking fast and actually quite proud of what he had come up with.

"So?"

"Thirteen's my unlucky number," Bull said. "No, you and your boys should be able to do the job nicely."

"What exactly is the job, Mr. Bull?" Carlton asked.

"What did you tell your ten men the job was?" Bull asked.

"We didn't," Healy said, "but they'll do anything for money."

"Anything?" Bull asked.

"That's right," Healy said.

Bull looked at Carlton, who didn't look so sure.

"What about you, Dan?" he asked.

"What about me?"

"Will you do anything for money?"

"Well . . . s-sure."

"Would you kill somebody for money?" Bull asked.

Carlton thought fast. He didn't want to give the wrong answer and then get left out.

"Mr. Bull," he said, "you're hiring twelve men with guns. I think we assume that we're gonna kill somebody."

"You're gonna kill at least three somebodies," Healy said. "Masterson, Short, and Clint Adams."

"Clint Adams?" Carlton asked. He cast an annoyed look at his partner, Healy.

"You got a problem facing the Gunsmith?" Bull asked.

"Well—"

"Not with ten more guns behind us we don't, Charley," Healy said, quickly.

"That's good."

"And for the right price."

"I tell you what," Bull said. "I'll pay you boys, and you

pay the others what you think they're worth."

Bull took an envelope out of a desk drawer and tossed it across the desk. It landed with a good solid thunk, obviously filled with a good stack of greenbacks.

Austin Healy picked it up, hefted it—and to his credit—did not open it and count it there.

"We'll take care of it, Charley," he said to the older man.

"That's good."

"Uh," Carlton said, "can I ask a question?"

"Sure."

"When do you want this done?"

"Tomorrow."

"Where?"

Bull sat forward and folded his hands. He was enjoying playing the part he'd always watched Courtright play.

"I want it done right in the White Elephant Saloon."

"Short's place," Carlton said.

"Right," Bull said, "and if the place should happen to catch fire and burn to the ground . . . well, I wouldn't mind it a bit."

"Burn down the White Elephant?" Carlton asked. He loved that place.

"Not a problem, Charley," Healy said. "But that would cost, uh, extra."

"I think you'll find the amount in the envelope will cover it, Austin," Bull said.

Healy hefted the envelope again and decided that Bull was probably right.

"What about the law, Charley?" Carlton asked. He decided if he was going to kill for the man he should call him by his first name. "The place will be full of people who can identify us."

"That's up to you," Bull said. "If you're not recognized you won't get the rep for killing those three. Any of your men who don't want to be recognized can wear something to hide their faces. Also, there should be so much confusion I doubt anyone would recognize you."

Actually, Bull didn't give a hoot whether they were recognized or not. That wasn't his concern.

"Don't worry, Charley," Healy said. "We'll take care of everything." He turned to leave, but was stopped by Bull's voice.

"Don't be in such a hurry to leave, Austin," Bull said. "There's a few more things you should know."

"Like what?" Both Healy and Carlton looked at Bull, waiting for an answer.

"For one thing," Bull said, "there's a poker tournament going on up on the second floor . . ."

FIFTY-SEVEN

"I think I can win," Lillian said.

They'd spent another pleasant, energetic night with each other and now, in the morning, she woke up wanting to talk about the game.

"Of course you think you can win," he said. "Why would you play if you didn't think you could win?"

"No," she said, "I mean I really do think I can."

They were having breakfast in the White Elephant's dining room and Clint was wondering what she wanted him to say to that.

"Don't you think I can win?" she asked.

Well, there it was. What was he supposed to say to that?

"Anybody can win, Lillian," he said, warily. "All it takes is the right cards at the right time."

"I'm playing in a game with some of the best poker

players in the country," she said, "and I think I can beat
them. I just want to know what you think."

"Lillian—"

"You've seen them play and you've seen me play," she
said, cutting him off. "I just want your opinion. Who do
you think will win?"

"Honestly?"

"Yes, honestly."

"I think Bat and Luke are the best players in the game,"
he said. "I think one of them will win."

"Not me."

"No."

She got quiet after that.

"Now you're mad."

"No," she said, "I'm not."

Just like a woman not to admit she's mad when she is,
he thought.

"Lillian" he said, "you asked me to be honest, and I
was. You can't hold that against me."

"I just thought . . . you'd encourage me."

"I did encourage you," he said. "On any given night
anybody can get the cards and win."

"But you don't think I'm as good a poker player as
your friends are?" she asked.

"No," he said, "I don't—and it's got nothing to do with
them being my friends."

"All right."

Well, he thought, it had been nice while it lasted . . .

Austin Healy met Charley Bull in his office that morning,
without Dan Carlton.

"Are you and your men all set for tonight?" Bull asked.

"We're ready."

"Carlton, too?"

"Don't worry about him."

Bull was worried about Colter because the man reminded him of himself, the way he used to be.

"Just keep an eye on him, Austin," Bull said. "He might be your weak link."

"Don't worry," Healy said, again.

As the man left the office Charley Bull hoped he and his men were ready, because if this didn't work tonight he didn't know what his next move would be.

If it did work, though, he figured he'd be set for life in Fort Worth. Everybody would pay up once they saw what happened to Luke Short and the White Elephant.

Dan Carlton was waiting outside for Austin Healy when he came out.

"So?"

"So what?" Healy asked.

"What did he say?"

Healy started walking and Carlton hurried to keep pace.

"He said, get it done."

"He still wants it burned down?"

"Why not?" Healy asked. "He's tryin' to make a point, Dan."

Carlton grabbed Healy's arm to stop him.

"Austin," he said, "if we set that building on fire it could take the whole block with it."

"Fort Worth has a great fire department, Dan," Healy said. "They'll have it under control in no time."

"Then what's the point?"

"The point is there'll be damage inside and the White Elephant will be out of business."

"And what about Luke Short?"

"Short will be dead," Healy said, "just like his friends. We took Bull's money, Dan. Are you with me on this or not?"

Carlton didn't dare pull out on Healy. They'd been partners too long.

"I'm with you, Austin," he said, but there wasn't much enthusiasm in his voice.

FIFTY-EIGHT

When Lillian entered the room for the game that night, the cold shoulder she gave Clint was very evident to both Bat and Luke Short.

"What happened there?" Bat asked him.

"Trouble in paradise?" Short asked.

"She asked me who I thought was going to win the game," Clint said.

"And you answered her?" Bat asked.

"Honestly?" Short asked.

"Yes to both questions."

"I assume you didn't say that she would win?" Bat asked.

"You assume correctly."

"Who did you say you thought would win?" Short asked.

"None of your business," Clint said. "Did your other players arrive today?"

"Yes, they did. We'll have two tables going tonight."

"Wyatt?" Bat asked.

"Didn't show."

"Too bad," Clint said.

"Clint," Short said, "I didn't hire any extra security because you're here. I figured with the three of us here, and Ben Thompson, we pretty much have it covered."

"That's fine with me."

"But since the rest of us are in the game—"

"I get it," Clint said. "I'll wander around from time to time and keep my eyes open."

"Thanks," Short said. "I appreciate it."

"Me, too," Bat said, patting his friend's back. "My money feels a lot safer without you in the game."

Clint just gave him a look and Bat went to take his place at the table.

Clint knew about half of the gamblers who were playing in the game. The other half he was introduced to. Of those he recognized the names of half. That meant there were only about two or three men at the tables who he didn't know and had never heard of. He would watch them extra carefully while he was in the room, until he was satisfied that they were only there to play poker.

He also noticed that Lillian Farmer seemed intent on throwing her money away that night. He had not expected her to win, but he hadn't expected her to play this poorly. He suspected that she was being foolish because she was trying to prove something, either to him, herself, or both of them. All she was going to accomplish was eliminating herself from the game early.

Clint decided to give her a break and leave the room for a while. Maybe with him gone she'd get her game under control. He headed downstairs to take a look around.

Austin Healy entered the White Elephant first, followed by Dan Carlton, and then the other ten men, one and sometimes two at a time. It took an hour for all of them to get inside, and into position.

The problem with having twelve men in one place, all waiting for a signal from someone is that they all tend to look preoccupied. Ten of the men kept looking over at Austin Healy, waiting for him to signal them.

This is not the kind of thing a man like Clint Adams fails to notice.

When Clint reached the main floor of the White Elephant he took a good look around the place. Most of the men in the place were having a good time, either drinking, gambling, or talking to girls who were working the floor. Just in taking a quick look around, though, Clint noticed three different men—one standing alone, two sitting together—brush away the advances of the girls. He also noticed that they seemed to be keeping their eyes on the bar.

One look at the bar and he was able to locate the man they were watching.

Clint walked to the bar and now he took his time. All in all he saw ten or eleven men who were watching the one man at the bar. He, in turn, kept looking over at them.

Whatever they were planning, it was poorly organized and would probably be poorly executed.

Clint called the bartender over, had a short talk with

him, and then went back upstairs to talk to Bat Masterson, Luke Short, and Ben Thompson.

Luke Short and Ben Thompson were at one table, Bat Masterson at another. That meant that by calling them away Clint was not interfering with either game to the point where they could not continue.

Drawing the three men to one side, Clint filled them in on what he had seen downstairs.

"Are they here to rob the game," Thompson asked, "or is there something else going on that I don't know about?"

Luke Short quickly brought Thompson up to date on the events of the week.

"So what do you think?" Short then asked Clint. "Are they here for the game, or some other reason?"

"I didn't see Charley Bull anywhere," Clint said.

"That doesn't matter," Short said. "Courtright did all the dirty work. Even if Bull wanted to carry on, he'd be hiring other men to take care of it for him."

"Whatever their reason is for being here," Bat said, "they're interfering with the game. Let's get rid of them."

"Brace them?" Clint asked. "The four of us against the twelve of them?"

"We got them outnumbered," Bat said.

"It's pretty crowded down there," Clint said.

"What do you suggest?" Short asked.

"If they want you, Luke," Clint said, "they'll come up here looking for you."

"They'll start a diversion downstairs," Bat said.

"You're right," Clint said, "they will, if they're that well organized."

"Sounds like we're gonna have some action," Ben Thompson said. "Where do you want me?"

"Of the four of us, Ben," Clint said, "you're probably the least recognizable, if only because you just arrived yesterday."

"Right," Thompson said, "so I'll be downstairs."

"I've alerted the bartender," Clint said. "One of them told me they've got shotguns behind the bar. I think I should be downstairs, also, because they'll take their cue from me."

"Okay," Bat said, "so I'll stay up here with Luke."

"I figure if there are twelve of them," Clint said, "eight will make their play downstairs and four will come up here."

"We better be ready for anything, though," Short said. "If this is Charley Bull's play then he's going to want to make a statement."

"You think he wants to do more than kill you?" Clint asked.

"I think he'll want to put this place out of business."

"So what's the easiest way to bust the place up in a hurry?" Bat asked.

The four of them exchanged some looks and then it was Clint who said, "Fire?"

FIFTY-NINE

Ben Thompson went downstairs first, secured a place at the bar. He got a beer from the bartender and made sure the man knew who he was and that he was with Clint Adams and Luke Short.

Clint came down next, ignored Ben Thompson. Luke Short kept a table in the back empty for himself at all times. Clint walked to that table and sat down. From there he could see the entire room.

Both men settled in to wait for something to happen.

Upstairs Bat and Luke Short made similar arrangements. They returned to their games, seated so that they were able to see the door to the room. Anyone wanting to enter had to do so through that door. There was another, but only Luke Short and Jake Johnson knew where that door was. They didn't bother informing any of the other players of what was happening—or what might happen—because they didn't want anyone's nerves getting in the way.

Short would have been just as pleased to have nothing happen on this night, but he had a feeling that wasn't going to be the case. One or two men might come into a situation to take a look first, but not twelve men—unless they're going to do something.

Austin Healy saw Clint and knew who he was. He wasn't worried, though, because the Gunsmith was seated at a table, right where they could see him.

Healy caught Dan Carlton's eye and then looked toward Clint. Carlton nodded, indicating he saw the Gunsmith.

The plan was for Healy to take three men upstairs if one of the men they were looking for—Adams, Masterson, or Short—were downstairs. If not, then eight men would go up.

In this case, four would go, and the four knew who they were. Carlton would remain downstairs as one of the eight.

Healy turned and started for the stairs. As was prearranged, three other men stood up and began to saunter over to the stairs. Four men going up the stairs would certainly not be as noticeable as eight.

Carlton met the eyes of the other seven men in turn. It was the sixth and seventh man who reached down to the object at their feet, picked them up and lit a match.

Clint saw the four men moving toward the stairs. He would have liked to intercept them, but it was going to fall to Bat and Luke Short to handle them.

He checked on the other men in turn and was looking

at the seventh man when he picked something up from the floor, lit a match, and touched it to the object.

Suddenly, two men stood up, holding burning torches.

The man at the bar drew his gun and shouted, "Everybody pay attention! Nobody go for their guns."

The bartenders froze. Ben Thompson looked over at Clint. The patrons in the place all looked up from their drinks, their games, or their women. Mostly, these were men used to guns in one form or another. They were also all pretty mellow at this point, having been drinking whiskey or beer most of the evening. However, no one was drunk enough to panic and go for their guns.

Clint cursed himself for waiting too long. As soon as the men with the torches stood up he should have drawn his gun. Now those men had their torches in one hand and a gun in the other, and the other six men were brandishing their guns.

What were the chances, he wondered, of no innocent people getting hurt, here?

Austin Healy and the three men with him ignored what was going on downstairs. They ascended the stairs with Healy in the lead. In the upstairs hall they formed into a group. Healy had directions from Bull, who had been up here before. He, himself, had never been off the first floor.

He motioned to the men to follow him, staying close. He moved down the hall to the doorway of the room that was used for private poker games.

"We go in fast," Healy said, "locate Masterson and Luke Short, and kill them."

"And the others?"

"Kill anyone who draws a gun," Healy said. "Hopefully, they'll freeze long enough to save their lives."

"Do we kill all of them if we have to?" one of the other men asked.

"You get paid no matter what," Healy said. "If we kill two, or all. Don't wait for a signal from me. Anyone who draws a gun dies. Understand?"

The three men nodded.

"Okay, then," Healy said, "let's earn our money."

SIXTY

Austin Healy was the first man through the door, and the first to get shot. As soon as he entered the room he saw and recognized Luke Short. He also saw Short stand up, draw his gun, and fire. A hot poker of fire hit him in the chest and by the time his three partners came through the door as well, he was dead.

All of the other players performed as Healy had hoped. They froze, but Bat Masterson stood, drew his gun, and fired twice. Only the fourth assailant got a shot off, but it went wild, because he squeezed the trigger only after another shot from Luke Short's gun hit him in the chest.

The four men were on the floor dead and Rusty Coe asked, "What the hell was that about?"

Short ejected the spent shells from his gun and reloaded while Bat was doing the same thing.

"Just some private business," he said.

"Goin' downstairs," Bat announced.

"Right behind you," Short said.

But they could already hear the gunfire.

At the first shot upstairs Clint saw his chance. Virtually all of the eight men lifted their heads and looked up, as if they could see through the ceiling.

Clint drew and put a bullet into the chest of the man at the bar. He thought that if this was the leader of these men perhaps they'd give up when he fell. That was not the case. There must have been a lot of money involved.

When Ben Thompson saw Clint draw his gun he did the same thing. Thompson had not spotted as many of the men as Clint had, and so he chose an obvious target. He shot one of the men who was holding a torch. The man fell and his torch went flying.

Clint turned and fired quickly, once, twice and then again, and three men spun and fell as they were going for their guns. Thompson had killed a sixth man before the bartenders got their shotguns out from under the bar and fired.

One blast from a shotgun struck the second man with the torch. While the first torch had fallen harmlessly to the floor, the second rolled up against a covered gaming table. The cover and table quickly caught fire.

"All right, everybody!" Clint shouted. "Let's get that out before the whole building goes up."

As Luke Short and Bat came down the stairs they saw men tossing buckets of water onto a flaming table. They also saw the floor littered with bodies.

They joined Clint and Ben Thompson, who had come together in the middle of the floor and were reloading.

"Any get away?" Short asked.

"Don't think so," Clint said. "We killed anyone who drew a gun."

"My customers?"

Clint nodded his head to where a bartender was tending to a man's wounded arm.

"One stray shot was all," Clint said. He didn't bother to tell Short that it was one of his bartenders who had wounded the man with a few stray pieces of shot from his shotgun.

Short looked around.

"I'm going to have to explain this to the law."

"You've got plenty of witnesses," Clint said.

"And the torches made it fairly obvious what they were intending to do," Thompson said. "Can I go back upstairs and play poker? This was more excitement than I bargained for."

"Go ahead," Short said. "We can take it from here. Thanks, Ben."

"No problem," Thompson said. He holstered his gun and went back upstairs.

"Sorry, Luke," Clint said.

"About what?"

"We didn't take any of them alive to find out who sent them."

"The torches tell the story," Short said. "Nobody'd want to torch the place but Charley Bull."

"You sure about that?" Bat asked.

Short nodded.

"It would keep the other owners in line if my place burned to the ground," Short said.

"Well," Clint said, "I guess we better pay Charley Bull a visit tomorrow."

"You might not have to," Bat said.

"Why not?" Short asked.

"After what happened tonight just spread the word that we're lookin' for him. See what happens."

"You think he'd leave town?" Clint asked.

"What do you think?" Bat asked. "He sent twelve men here and not one walked out alive. If you had us lookin' for you, what would you do?"

"I'd leave town," Clint said.

"Me, too," Luke Short said.

"There ya go," Bat said.

SIXTY-ONE

The word got around fast the next day that Clint, Bat, and Luke Short were looking for Charley Bull. He was never seen or heard from again in Forth Worth.

The first person eliminated from the poker game was Lillian Farmer. She left Fort Worth the next day, without a word to Clint or anyone else.

The game took two days to wrap up, and it came down to a final hand between Luke Short and Rusty Coe. Coe's four-of-a-kind beat Short's full house.

Clint stayed in Fort Worth until the game was over and the various players had left. He said goodbye to Hettie in the evening over dinner, and had one last breakfast with both Bat and Luke Short.

"Are you leavin' too, Bat?" Short asked.

"Probably tomorrow," Bat said. "Rusty Coe is still in town. I'm going to have a talk with him."

"What about?" Clint asked.

"I thought maybe he'd like to go into business with me."

"What business?" Short asked.

"Well," Bat said, "I've seen how much fun you're having with this place. I thought I might open a place of my own somewhere."

"Fun," Short said, shaking his head.

"Well," Bat said, "if not fun, it sure hasn't been boring."

"I can attest to that," Clint said.

"Coe doesn't strike me as the type," Short said.

"Well, if not," Bat said, "I'll just move on."

"To where?" Clint asked.

"You know where you're goin' next?" Bat asked him.

"I hardly ever know that," Clint said. "I usually just know that I've stayed someplace too long—like here."

"I know it was a little more than you bargained for, Clint," Short said, "but I appreciate the help. You, too, Bat."

"You'd be the first one to come runnin' if one of us got in a bind," Bat said.

"We all know it," Clint said.

Short lifted his coffee cup.

"Here's a toast to stayin' out of trouble for the rest of our lives."

"I'll drink to it," Bat Masterson said, raising his own cup, "but I don't believe it. Clint?"

Clint clinked his cup against theirs and said, "Not a word."

PRAISE FOR DIANE HAEGER'S
COURTESAN

Available from Pocket Books

"Spectacular . . . Diane Haeger explores the fascinating, rich, exciting and tragic life of Henri II's beloved. . . . Lush in characterization and rich in historical detail, *Courtesan* will sweep readers up into its pages and carry them away."

—*Romantic Times*

"Diane Haeger is a master of transporting her audience. . . . You will move swiftly through the pages of *Courtesan*. I've added it to my 'keeper' shelf."

—*Rendezvous*

"Any novel that can keep me awake until four in the morning has to be riveting, and *Courtesan* did that for me. . . . Diane Haeger makes a most auspicious debut with this novel. The love Henri and Diane show for each other will touch your heart as it did mine. I guarantee you'll stay awake nights not being able to put this book down."

—*Affaire de Coeur*

"From the first scene, where the king is arising from the royal bed amidst a crowd of favor-seeking courtiers, to the last, where Diana de Poitiers watches her grandchildren play in the royal gardens, *Courtesan* delivers both a strong romance with believable characters, and a picture of a time and way of life that is long gone from the earth. . . . Powerful . . . a nice, meaty historical romance with a lot of substance."

—*B. Dalton's Heart to Heart*

Books by Diane Haeger

Courtesan
The Return

Published by POCKET BOOKS

THE RETURN

DIANE HAEGER

POCKET STAR BOOKS

New York   London   Toronto   Sydney   Tokyo   Singapore

This book is a work of fiction. Names, characters, places and
incidents are either products of the author's imagination or are
used fictitiously. Any resemblance to actual events or locales or
persons, living or dead, is entirely coincidental.

An *Original* Publication of POCKET BOOKS

A Pocket Star Book published by
POCKET BOOKS, a division of Simon & Schuster Inc.
1230 Avenue of the Americas, New York, NY 10020

ISBN: 0-671-86480-7

First Pocket Books printing December 1993

10   9   8   7   6   5   4   3   2   1

POCKET STAR BOOKS and colophon are registered
trademarks of Simon & Schuster Inc.

Cover art by Lina Levy

Printed in the U.S.A.

For Dick Hanke,
a very special uncle, favorite
traveling companion . . . and great
friend,
with much love

Acknowledgments

I wish to thank Sudershan Chawla, professor of political science at California State University, Long Beach, for sharing his extensive knowledge of the culture and language of India; M. Shafqat Ali, for taking the time to steer my research in the right direction; S. G. Mosdell, mayor of Tetbury, for help with the historical details of his charming town; and James Anderson, M.D., for information regarding facial injuries.

And to the greatest support system/fan club a writer could ever hope to have. My sincerest thanks to Lisa Nordquist, J. P. Jackson, Judi Hayashi, Erin Kelly, Marie Mazzuca, Merrilyn Spicer, and Sandy Lunsford, who laughed and cried with my first novel and made me want to try to do it again.

A special note of thanks also to Al Boroskin for never taking me as seriously as I took myself and for convincing me that there was a niche out there for me. All I had to do was find it.

Prologue

1867

HE WAS STARING AT HER AGAIN.

Even with her back turned, Charlotte could feel the young officer's eyes on the nape of her neck. The sensation was like a splash of icy water. She heaved a sigh and grasped the wet railing as the ship pitched and rolled, heading into the next blue-black wave.

"The gentleman wonders if today you might be inclined to join him for tea."

It was the third afternoon that the ship's steward had been enlisted to ask. Twice before she had politely refused. Charlotte glanced across the deck and saw him nod. Tall, blond, and handsome. Commissioned as well. A splendid catch. Then she looked away. There could never be another man. Not ever. In every man she would always see something: A nod, a turn of the head, and there was Edward. Always Edward.

"I am sorry," she finally replied in a voice so soft that the steward had to strain to hear her. "Please tell the gentleman that I shall be unable to accept."

"You will pardon me, I hope, for saying so, madam, but I suspect he means to continue asking."

1

"Then no doubt before we reach Gibraltar, he shall have grown accustomed to my reply."

Charlotte glanced back at the young officer and saw by the small crown and star on the collar of his uniform that he was a captain in Her Majesty's army. It was all so familiar that her heart strained. The tight-fitting scarlet jacket and sash. The twisted silk cord on his shoulder. Shiny brass buttons. High black jackboots. . . . It was all such a lifetime ago, and yet in her heart it still seemed like yesterday.

She breathed in the briny salt air and gazed across the dark, unending sea through pale green eyes. They were the very color of new grass on a spring morning, Edward had once said. "That I could but look upon those eyes for the rest of my days . . ." She shook her head to chase away the sound of his voice. The memories. For now.

When the ship's steward had gone, she leaned against the railing and let the cold wind and sea spray dash across her face. But it was not the face with which she had been born. Charlotte Langston had been scarred by India. Scarred by circumstances too brutal to recall. The shape of her face was like a heart, the color of ivory. But the features, once perfect, now bore the traces of a moment in time that had changed everything. Her brilliant green eyes, also injured, were still protected by shaded glasses from the noonday sun.

"He's not a bad looking sort a'tall."

The haunting echo of Edward's words faded into the silvery timbre of a woman's voice. Charlotte turned around to see a stout, middle-aged woman, stylishly dressed, wearing a gray silk gown, blue gloves, and a neat straw bonnet tied with a blue velvet ribbon.

"It is just that I am not interested."

"Your heart has been given to another?"

Her reply once again was as soft as a whisper: "My heart and my life."

The woman's round, red-patched face gave way to a mischievous smile. "Well, my heavens. I do hope for your parents' sake he is an officer."

2

"My parents are dead, madam."

The tone of Charlotte's reply chilled Katherine Blackstone to the bone. In a single flash, her mind shot back to the vicious uprising and massacre in Meerut and Delhi ten years before. She had not been in India then, thank Heaven. But by her tone, she knew that this poor young woman had faced that unspeakable tragedy and survived it. Perhaps her husband too, the man who'd claimed her heart, had been among the dozens of innocent Europeans so barbarously murdered by frenzied native soldiers. Gracious heavenly Lord, the acts were too gruesome even to recount.

"I am Mrs. Blackstone. Katherine, to my friends."

"Charlotte Langston."

"A pleasure to meet you. There are so few other ladies aboard ship who have not fallen victim to seasickness."

As both turned to gaze back out at the unending sea, Katherine tried to clutch her hat just as a gust of wind unfurled the loose velvet tie and plucked it from her head. It fell into the water and then disappeared beneath a white-capped wave.

"Blast! That is the third one since yesterday!"

"Then why on earth do you wear them?"

"Oh, my dear girl. You have been away from civilization too long. No true English lady goes out without a proper hat!"

As they faced one another again, Katherine brushed a strand of dusty brown hair from Charlotte's face—a gentle, motherly gesture—preparing to tell her how smart she would look in one of the new Empress hats so popular in London. But before she could speak, Charlotte caught her hand and held it up between them. Her face had gone pale. The woman—this stranger—had moved too quickly, had come too close.

"Forgive me," Katherine gasped, clutching her chest. "I had no idea."

In the awkward silence, Charlotte adjusted her shaded glasses. A nervous movement. Then she lowered her eyes. "It's all right. Really."

"No. It was thoughtless. I had no right when we've only just met."

"It is a long journey, Mrs. Blackstone." Charlotte's voice quivered. "I look forward to seeing you on deck or perhaps in the dining room. But now, if you will please excuse me."

Charlotte picked up her wide skirts. The heavy, rustling silk sounded like the leaves of an Indian tamarind tree. Then she hurried below, down the dark, narrow passageway back to the safety of her tiny cabin. Once inside, she closed her eyes and tried to catch her breath. Only then did Charlotte bring her hand from the pocket in her gown and press the ring to her lips. It was warm from her skin. An opal set in silver. It had belonged to Edward's mother.

Edward had given the ring to her one winter afternoon in their secret place behind Graves House. As she closed her eyes, she could almost smell the scent of curry again. The asafetida. The sweet blossoms from the orange trees in Mrs. Graves's orchard. A moment more and the screeching gulls that circled just beyond the saloon deck became like the drone of the *sitar* in her mind. Suddenly it was not ten years ago but yesterday, and she and Edward were together, rushing home through the Cashmere Gate to their bungalow in the cantonments.

Charlotte lay back on her berth and pressed the ship's monotonous swaying and plunging from her mind. She had made it March again. Although it was warm, the stifling heat of summer was not yet hammering Delhi. It left them free to be a little more wanton in their desire for one another.

She felt Edward's hand on hers; felt her body stir as their ghurrie lurched to a stop before a thatch-roofed bungalow. He gazed over at her, dark hair curling around his face, his eyes such a limpid blue. She saw the glimmer there and knew what it meant. It was what she wanted too.

Her *ayah*, a graceful native woman with kohl-darkened eyes and rich almond-colored skin, moved out from the shady veranda. Rani's blue and gold *sari* shimmered in the afternoon sun as she held an open parasol for Charlotte. Edward whispered something to Rajab, his *khansaman*, a tall well-built man in white turban, long white tunic, cumberbund, and trousers. One glance at the faint flush of roses in the *memsahib's* pale English cheeks spoke volumes. Both of Captain Langston's servants understood. The only sound that followed came from the jangle of the *ayah's* bracelets as she slipped with the butler out of the bungalow.

Even in March, without the gentle sway of the *punkah*, their shadowy bedroom was warm. Charlotte felt reckless and a little embarrassed coming back home unexpectedly so early in the day, but her desire for Edward was as blinding as was his for her. And they were still newlyweds.

A moment later, she was glad to be free of her stiff corset, heavy crinoline, and pantalets. As soon as her underclothes fell to the floor, Edward pushed her back against the door, his need overwhelming them both. She could feel his impatience, full and hard against her thigh as he kissed her lips and then her neck with a warm, open mouth. His tongue was painting her skin with fire, and she felt the sweet, excruciating surge she always did. As a young girl she had never imagined what lay beyond a man's tender caress. But her husband had shown her, taught her; and now Charlotte lived for these intimate times between them.

Edward peeled off his uniform, tossing the red jacket, the blue trousers, and the long black boots in a heap beside Charlotte's lilac silk gown. He was so powerfully built that she still was awestruck when he stood naked before her: broad shoulders tapering down to a small waist and thick, muscled thighs. He was like a statue by Michelangelo or Donatello, his body perfect in every detail. But he was so much more than that. He was a man, and she craved the feel of his very lifeblood pulsing against her whenever he took her into his arms.

Edward's tongue trailed slowly back up the length of her body, along her hips, across her belly, and up to the cleft of her breasts. Charlotte's mind blurred as he tasted one tawny nipple and then the other, his breath hot against her skin. The distant sound of a Hindu servant calling *"Namasté"* across the cantonments drew her away from him. But he would not be put off. He would conquer her now. Here. Edward swept her up in his arms, then pressed her past the delicate mosquito netting and down onto their bed.

"God, you are the other half of me!" he whispered into her hair, and a mutual shudder ran the length of their bodies.

Edward arched over her and looked down at Charlotte with those luminous blue eyes, and they were filled with devotion. It made her twine her legs closer around his buttocks, pulling him deeper inside of her. She could not bring him close enough. He was love. He was life to her. He had made her happier than she had ever thought possible. Like her mother, she had first hated India as a child. Now she adored it because it had brought her Edward.

As he made love to her, Charlotte's mind crossed over the memory of an ancient inscription inside the Golden Mosque. They were the same words he had spoken to her the day he had asked her to become his wife. "If there is a paradise," he had said in a deep, ardent whisper, "my darling Charlotte, this is it. . . . This is it. . . ."

The creaks and groans of the ship as it lurched through a choppy sea roused Charlotte from her memories. She slipped onto her side, tears spilling down her pale ivory face, her slim body awash in perspiration. "How could it be ten years when it is so vivid in my mind?"

"Where are you, my love?" she mouthed the words. "Have you forgotten me, or do the memories of what we shared crowd your mind and your heart so relentlessly as they do mine?"

Now apprehension took the place of the passion that she had felt. Reality brought thoughts of her son—a child Edward had never even known she was carrying—and Charlotte's heart ached. Hugh was the single bit of joy to come from the nightmare she had endured, and she missed him terribly. He was her comfort, her dearest heart. But she had gathered the strength to leave him behind to Jawahar's tender care. It was better not to raise a child's hopes. Ten years was such a long time. Edward believed her dead. Now she would have to find the strength to face whatever that might imply.

This trip had been a risk. The greatest risk of her life. She had chosen not to tell him by letter. To really believe that it was true, both of them must face one another. But now, as the ship sailed steadily nearer England, the uncertainty mounted. She had begun to wonder what they would say to one another once Edward discovered that, despite all of the odds, she too had cheated death. . . .

Charlotte left her cabin a half an hour late for supper. Dressing that night, more than any other night, was almost painful, as her mind reeled with the fresh torrent of memories she had allowed to enter her head and her heart. It had been that way—a devastating onslaught of recollections, flashes of their past together—ever since she had discovered the truth. Edward had not died from the gunshot wound. Her husband was in England. He was still alive.

She would have preferred to remain alone in her tiny, sparsely furnished cabin every night until they docked at Southampton, but she must take her mind off of what lay ahead. She saw Mrs. Blackstone alone at a table near the back of the small dark dining room. Charlotte scanned the room for the young captain who had been so persistent in his attentions. Mercifully, it seemed she was to be spared that continuing nuisance. At least for this evening.

"May I join you?"

Katherine Blackstone looked up, an expression of surprise lighting her bold blue eyes. "Why certainly, my dear. I would be delighted for the company. My usual dining companions fell victim to seasickness as soon as we encountered this new storm."

"They say it can be dreadful all the way through this particularly rough bit of sea," Charlotte agreed, glancing around at the mahogany-paneled room that was only dotted with passengers. A young sailor put a plate of dry roast beef and potatoes before her, and she held it to the table as the ship rose and sank in an unending rhythm.

"I . . . wanted to apologize," Charlotte said softly.

"Whatever for, my dear?"

"I was terribly rude to you this afternoon when you were only trying to be polite."

"I overstepped the boundaries of good propriety. You had every right to be cross."

"But I wasn't cross. It is just that I have a rather . . ." she struggled for the words, ". . . uncertain future ahead of me in England."

Katherine Blackstone glanced across at Charlotte, who wore the same gown that she had that afternoon. While it had been costly once, it was several years out of fashion, and the braid-trimmed sleeves and hem had begun to fray. Her curiosity had been kindled earlier that day. Now it was piqued. Katherine had never met anyone who had actually survived England's greatest tragedy.

"I think it might help if you could talk to someone about it," she said with a sincere note of motherly kindness. "And, as you can see, I've a firm enough shoulder for crying on."

Charlotte forced a bite of roast beef past her lips and chewed it slowly so that she would have a moment to observe the woman she faced. Katherine Blackstone was a big-breasted woman whose stiff corset and side skirts made her aging body voluptuous. Her hair was soft brown, touched with a whisper of gray at the temples and held away from her face in a black net.

Her square jaw set more firmly as Charlotte studied her. She was a woman who carried herself with a regal comportment and dressed not only expensively but tastefully. Her scent, rosewater, was the same soft fragrance which her own mother had once worn. As Charlotte took a long breath, she felt her resistance begin to fade.

"You have a kind face," Charlotte said softly, pushing a boiled potato back and forth on her plate. "And we really do have such a long journey still before us. Yes, it would be nice to talk to someone."

"Good." Katherine smiled as she dotted her lips with the tip of her napkin.

After they had finished supper, the two women went up

on deck. It had begun to rain, a light mist that felt exhilarating to them both after the stale-smelling cabins and corridors.

"My husband believes that I am dead," Charlotte divulged as she clung fast to the wet railing, a strong wind blowing her hair and gown. "Until recently I thought the same of him." Again a breath. "Now I am going to England to try to find him."

"Dear child," Katherine quietly gasped.

She had not needed to ask, and yet her suspicions had been confirmed. The story was all too common. The *sepoy* uprising, which had begun in Meerut ten years before and spread like the most pestilent plague to Delhi, had exploded in a torrent of violence and death. It had destroyed nearly everything in its wake. When it was over, only a fraction of the English men, women, and children had been left alive. "Barbarous savages!" Katherine thought, glad to be out of a brutal land she had never come to understand nor appreciate.

"I am frightened."

Katherine put her fleshy arm around Charlotte's slim shoulder. "Of what, child?"

"Ten years is a long time. People change. India has changed me so that I scarcely recognize myself when I look in the mirror. It is bound to have changed Edward as well."

"Would it not have been wiser for you to write to him first?" she asked carefully. "Seeing you on his doorstep is bound to be a dreadful shock."

Charlotte looked out at the black sea as the rain and the ocean spray wet her face. As always, the memories of Edward and the time they had lost was painful. "That is not something one can say in a letter."

"Perhaps not."

"We were so young . . ." Charlotte whispered, tears shining in her eyes.

"Young and so in love."

"Yes," she whispered.

Katherine Blackstone took a big, heavy breath, wondering

what on earth she could say that would be a comfort when she did not envy this poor dear girl the future that lay before her. Ten years was such a long time. Those who had survived the massacre had done everything possible to put it out of their lives. She could not help but fear that her young man had done precisely that. It would have been the most natural thing in the world to do; to heal a lost love with a new one.

"It is a brutal, awful thing that has happened to you, child," Katherine said. "There is no one in the world fool enough to argue that. So you have made your decision to find your husband, and find him you shall. But not before we work a bit of magic first."

Charlotte dashed at her tears. "I am afraid I don't understand."

"Ah, but you shall soon enough. Perhaps we cannot make you the carefree girl you once were, but we can certainly make you the most stylish young woman who steps off this ship!"

"What is it that you have in mind?"

Katherine's eyes twinkled with delight. "First, will you leave yourself to my care?"

Charlotte knew that she had changed, that she had lost the innocent aspect of her beauty to circumstance. In the hospital that had become her home, she had also lost all sense of fashion and style. Her mind trailed to the fear, the gnawing insecurity. It was the desire to still be to Edward the perfection he would always be to her. For that, she could find the strength to surrender herself willingly to a kind stranger.

"Very well, Mrs. Blackstone. As you wish."

"And as we go, will you tell me about Edward?"

Charlotte took a breath. "It is not an easy story to tell."

"Then I shall listen very closely."

After a moment, she pulled her hand from the wet railing and settled it atop Katherine's. It was such a very long time since she had known the reassuring interest of another woman. Not since Rani. But she felt safe with Katherine

Blackstone. In time, she would tell her the entire story. She would tell her about what they once had shared. Then she would go to England, to Edward; and he would be waiting. Their love would have survived. No matter how her head told her to guard against that fantasy.

It was that, above all, that her heart must believe.

1

Delhi, 1857

"PUT THAT BASKET DOWN OR I SWEAR I'LL SHOOT!"

In Delhi's gold and saffron sunset, Charlotte Lawrence aimed a shiny Colt pistol at the two soldiers crouching in the brigadier's orchard. Each of them held wicker baskets brimming with fat, glistening oranges. Realizing by the glint in her eye and the way she held the weapon that she was a girl who knew how to shoot, Edward Langston and Arthur Moresby dropped the spoils of their dare. Then they stood up before her. Charlotte moved toward them boldly. Her lips parted half in anger, half in surprise, at having found them like this.

"Who, sir, is your superior?"

Moresby, the shorter and more portly of the two, a young man with a neat red beard and mustache, laughed at her question. It was a shrill, noxious sound. "Just a bit of fun, miss. No harm done, really."

"I demand to know who is your superior officer!"

The other man, tall and dark haired, in a captain's uniform, glanced over at his accomplice, but again it was Moresby who replied.

"He is, miss."

Charlotte leveled her jewel-green eyes at him, and her

13

mouth pursed like a tiny pink bud. "What is your name, Captain?"

Edward glanced down at the basket of fruit and across the vast green lawn behind Graves House. She thought he looked as if he meant to try to escape. Until he heard the hammer of the small pistol click back.

"Have you any idea how many *sepoys* will come running if they hear shots fired?"

Her voice was strident, and Edward knew she meant to do it. How anyone so young and beautiful could have become so determined living in Delhi's sheltered English enclave was a mystery.

"The name is Captain Edward Langston," he said in a deep, silky tone, a hint of a smile broadening slim lips. "And since I do not know who you are, it would seem that you now have me at a further disadvantage."

His attempt at levity did little to sway her. She was standing before him with utter self-assurance, her body rigid and the small gun still aimed directly at him. Her thick blond hair was pulled away from her face. In the shadow of the setting sun, Edward thought it a most extraordinarily brilliant shade of gold.

"Shame on you, Captain. You should be an example to your men. Not an accomplice in their misdeeds."

"True enough." He nodded.

As he stared back at her, amused and yet intrigued by her determination, he felt his pulse begin to slow. Then a warm wave of calm washed over him. It was an unexpected sensation, as if he had known her all of his life. She was small with a slim waist, made slimmer still by her corset; but her face, even in anger, was the face of an angel. Heart-shaped with flawless ivory skin. Wide green eyes with long, thick lashes.

There were other young women in Delhi. Officers' daughters. Officers' wives. Widows. Willing native women. But none had ever made such a bold and striking impression upon him. As he gazed at this young girl, Edward found himself wondering, quite against his will, how she would look in a *sari*—the native costume of brightly painted silk that clung to the female form with an almost indecent accuracy.

"What precisely are you leering at?" Charlotte snapped at him.

"I am looking at a young woman who should likely decide whether she is going to shoot us, or if she is going to leave me to make the decision for her."

Despite the curt tone of his reply, Edward was not at all anxious for this curious encounter to end. He had always been in complete control of his life, in control with women; and yet now, suddenly in the presence of this spirited woman-child, he lacked all self-possession. She lowered the pistol. Something had passed between them, something swift and quite unexpected. He knew that she felt it too.

"That fruit belongs to Graves House. The commander-in-chief of Delhi does not take kindly to thieves," she said firmly, and yet Edward could see that her face had softened.

"In the future, I shall consider myself warned," he replied.

When Edward saw a hint of vulnerability in her expression, he seized upon it, bowing to her like a punctuation mark to their encounter. It was a condescending movement, a sorry attempt to regain his self-possession, and he regretted it at once when he saw her frown. Her lovely green eyes narrowed again, and he could see her defenses rise again. He watched the breeze ruffle the little wisps of hair near her face—whispers of gold—and he was enchanted.

"Go before I change my mind," she said after a silence that seemed to go on forever.

Edward looked at her again, and suddenly there was nothing but this girl. No garden. No aroma of rose, hibiscus, or jasmine. No Lieutenant Moresby. Nothing. In that moment, he had an overwhelming urge to ask her name, but that would have been too forward, considering the circumstances.

In the past, with other women, there would have been some clever parting line delivered with a flirtatious nod, but as the girl took two steps out of the orchard, Edward had no idea at all what to say to her. Finally, reluctantly, he too turned away.

"Captain Langston."

This time the girl's voice was so clear and sweet that it startled him. He turned slowly back around.

"You might as well take the fruit with you. Now that you've picked it, it will only spoil if you leave it here."

Edward bent down to pick up the two baskets of oranges as she stood watching him, the pistol at her side. Such contradiction in one so young, he marveled. It had been on a whim that he had come here. Two other soldiers in the officers' canteen had dared them to infiltrate the brigadier's garden in the broad light of day. The monotony of life in India bred the love of foolhardy pranks from idle young men too far from home. He had initiated some of his own over the past five years. But this was more than a lark. Edward Langston had never believed in fate. He was convinced that attraction and meetings of the heart were to be planned like any other element of one's life.

Until today.

"Who in the devil was that?"

"I don't know, Moresby," Edward said breathlessly, once she had gone. "But I certainly do intend to find out."

Graves House, the home of Brigadier Harry Graves, commander of the Delhi garrison, was a grand, three-storied umber-colored building wrapped by a columned veranda. Tonight it was lit with dozens of festive glowing candles just beyond the windows, and flaming torches flickering in the portico. The pounded red-brick drive was lined with gigs and curricles, and the night air was filled with the sweet scent from Mrs. Graves's rose garden. A string of dark-faced *sepoy* guards, uniformed in scarlet, slashed with white crossbelts, stood at attention at the carpeted entrance.

Upstairs in one of the bedrooms that overlooked the drive, Charlotte held fast to the bedpost as Rani struggled to lace the stays of her vast hooped crinoline.

"Hold still!" the *ayah* bid her young charge in her native

16

Hindustani, all the while bewildered that such devices were necessary, much less appealing. To her mind they were not only preposterous but entirely unhealthy.

The moment she was tightly bound, laced, and buttoned, Charlotte moved across the room in a rustle of lemon-yellow silk. She daubed her wrists with the scent of lavender brought back from England and then glanced anxiously into the mirror at her lustrous golden curls threaded with yellow silk. She touched them one at a time, each still warm from the heated curling tongs. Details were important. Tonight, everything must be perfect.

She ran a hand across her brow as the *punkah* slowly stirred the cool, linseed-scented evening air. Outside through the window, Charlotte could hear the click of carriage wheels and the laughter of guests as they made their way up the long circular drive. Brigadier Graves and his wife were having another party, and now that she was sixteen, her father, the brigadier's secretary, had agreed to let her attend.

Colonel Hugh Lawrence's only child was beautiful and innocent, and as a widower in this vast, God-forsaken land, he knew only too well what that combination was likely to mean to the dozens of lonely young officers yearning for English companionship. But Charlotte was a spirited girl, her father's daughter; and denying her this now could lead quite likely to something far worse than a few supervised turns around the dance floor.

The grand ballroom was ablaze with candles. The crystal chandelier glittered in their light and from the movement of the straw *punkahs* that shared the ceiling. Above the doorways were floral wreaths of yellow casia and white thorn-apple trumpets. Charlotte came down the wide, carpeted staircase and stood beside her father, so distinguished in his dress uniform. Her heart was beating like a drum with excitement. He took her hand in his own and squeezed it just as Brigadier Graves and his wife moved toward them.

Harry Graves was a handsome, dignified man; tall and thin, with a neatly clipped white mustache and fashionable tuft of snowy hair beneath his lower lip. His wife was fat and pale but utterly charming. Charlotte curtsied to them in her new yellow silk gown, its flounces embroidered with tiny pink flowers.

"You're looking quite lovely this evening, Charlotte." The brigadier smiled.

"Thank you, sir."

"I understand you have just had a birthday."

"Sixteen yesterday," she replied, and she lifted her chin proudly.

"It is all ahead of you, my dear." Mrs. Graves smiled, her own chin doubling.

"And ahead of you, my good man!" said the brigadier with a wink at her father. Then he glanced up at someone behind them and a broad, welcoming smile dawned on his pale, angular face. "Captain Langston. How good of you to come."

"The honor is mine, sir."

Charlotte heard the voice: deep, silky, and full of self-assurance. She felt her heart quicken and her face blanche. It was the same voice she had heard earlier in garden. It could not be worse. He knew Brigadier Graves personally—he'd probably had permission to pick the oranges; and she had chased him from the grounds like a common criminal! She tapped her satin shoes together nervously beneath her gown.

"Captain Langston, your regiment has been in Delhi long enough for you to know my secretary, Colonel Lawrence, but may I present his daughter, Charlotte. This pretty young thing has just had a birthday."

She turned slowly, crimson flooding into her cheeks and burning them like fire. Edward stood a few feet from her, tall and slim, his dark curly hair now tamed with oil and his smooth lips turned into a pleasant smile beneath a dark mustache. Charlotte thought him breathtakingly handsome tonight in his crimson dress jacket and indigo-blue trousers, with a blue silk sash strung neatly across his chest. The color of the sash enhanced his eyes, making them shimmer. For a moment Edward looked at her without speaking, and she studied his expression. Charlotte could not quite make out

18

if he was mocking her with his elegant smile and if he meant to give her away for her foolish behavior earlier in the day.

"It is a pleasure, as always, sir," he finally said as he bowed respectfully to Colonel Lawrence. "And an honor, Miss Lawrence."

It was clear by the expression on her face, that Charlotte had not expected to see him here tonight but Edward had counted on seeing her. In fact, it was the only reason he could have been dragged to one of these dreary affairs. He had thought of little else as he lay on the cot in his bungalow that afternoon, his mind filled with the scent of her mild lavender perfume.

A few *rupees* to a *chaprassi*, who stood guard at the door after he had come away from the garden, had granted him the knowledge he'd sought. The splendid young girl in the brigadier's garden was Miss Charlotte Lawrence, who lived with her father in Graves House. At the very last moment, Edward had sent his *cossid*, his native runner, to say that his plans had changed and he would be most honored to attend that evening's ball.

"I wonder, Miss Lawrence, would you care to dance?" he asked just as the orchestra struck up another waltz.

Charlotte could feel her father's short, taut body tense beside her, but she saw Mrs. Graves smile approvingly. Captain Langston was a trusted and honored member of the brigadier's inner circle, and she certainly could not refuse him.

"This is my daughter's first ball, Captain," Hugh Lawrence said sternly. "Take care with her."

Edward nodded to the colonel and then led Charlotte toward the dance floor. When they were a safe distance from her father, she said, "I am so terribly embarrassed, Captain Langston. You must forgive me."

Edward took her hand. "Whatever for, Miss Lawrence?"

"I had no idea that you—"

"That I was so intimately acquainted with Brigadier and Mrs. Graves?" The faint glimmer of a smile—the same devilish smile she had seen earlier in the garden—turned up the corners of his lips once again. "It was precisely why the men dared me to raid the garden. As you supposed, I was there today for cross-purposes. You certainly have nothing to be embarrassed about."

He squeezed her hand as they moved in among the other dancers. Waves of muslin and silk, ivory, yellow, blue, and green broke and then formed once again against the tailored crimson and blue dress uniforms. It was now that Charlotte really looked at his face, so different in candlelight than it had been in the afternoon sun.

He was a sharply handsome man, with high cheekbones, clear luminous blue eyes, and a smile that could be as wistful as it was seductive. It was these strikingly classic looks that Edward Langston long before had discovered would see him from the modesty of a small English village and on to a better life than his father had had. Military service had been the path. But he had never bargained on it meaning India.

He had considered himself cursed to have been sent to a land where eight months a year he would be plagued by dusty, choking heat and the constant odor of cow dung. Cursed, that was, until this afternoon. He had known almost from the first moment that this girl, Charlotte, was everything he could ever want in a woman, a wife, and that somehow they were meant to be together.

"If I may say, Miss Lawrence, Charlotte is a lovely name."

"I was named for my grandmother, Lady Charlotte Pearce."

"Ah." He nodded, trying to appear unimpressed.

"Edward is a strong name."

"I was named for my godfather, the man who ran the butcher shop in our village," he said, having battled the urge to come up with a disclosure that would sound more impressive.

It was curious how comfortable he felt with her. Somehow, with this young woman, Edward lacked all ability to keep up his carefully cultivated image. Until the words had passed across his lips, he could not have imagined telling anyone what he had just told Charlotte. It wasn't her innocence particularly, although that certainly intrigued him. Tetbury had been filled with innocent young daughters very willing to trap him into a life like his father's. Perhaps that was it; the utter lack of expectation on her face that had so completely enchanted him.

As the thoughts crisscrossed through his mind, Edward felt himself smiling at her, her brilliant green eyes catching the torchlight, her hair the most brilliant shade of gold he had ever seen. Then, just as quickly, his smile faded. The waltz would be over soon. She would return to her father's protective side, and the opportunity for something more might well be lost to him forever.

"It is rather warm in here," he finally said.

"India is warm, Captain Langston."

"I know it shall seem terribly forward of me, but would you . . ." He could scarcely force the words past his lips; how contrived he knew they would sound to her. "Would you care to join me for a breath of air?"

Charlotte tipped her head, studying him as the music ended, trying to gauge his sincerity. "I don't believe my father would approve."

Edward felt his heart sink. The sensation disarmed him. He had never wanted anything so much in the world as a moment alone with this girl. And yet he understood. After all, they had only just been introduced, and a young lady did not go off together to a dark terrace with a gentleman, no matter what they could both feel was already happening between them.

"Well. I should not want you to go against your father's wishes," he finally said, trying to mean it.

Edward extended his arm properly to lead her back to the colonel, who had been watching their every step. As they moved back through the crowd, thick with rich silk and wide crinolines, Charlotte spoke unexpectedly. She did not look back at him.

"Of course, if you should happen to be on the veranda in half an hour and our paths were to cross, that I suspect would be an entirely different matter."

"Unavoidable." He smiled triumphantly.

* * *

The January night was full of fireflies that glowed like a thousand tiny dancing stars. The air was sweet and heavy with the scent of Mrs. Graves's jasmine and roses. Alone on the wide veranda, the laughter of guests and the clinking of glasses faded into all of the other curious noises of an Indian evening: the faraway howl of jackals, the shriek of parrots, and the chirp of crickets.

Charlotte pulled the white lace shawl over her slim shoulders and gazed off into the night. After only a moment, she could feel Edward standing beside her. He was so close to her that another step would have been indecent. Charlotte's first thought was that he smelled different—more freshly washed than her father. It was a surprisingly sensual aroma; flesh and Castile soap. She felt a sudden surge. The feeling was foreign, one she did not understand. She stood very still, fearing that if she faced him now, he would see this new sensation in her eyes.

"So, Miss Lawrence, tell me, how long have you been here in Delhi?" Edward asked her, both of them pretending that they saw or cared what lay out across the vast, dark lawns before them.

"Ten years," she replied simply, and Edward thought what a lifetime that must seem to her.

"And you haven't minded the summer heat?"

"Everyone in India minds the heat, Captain. It is simply that some of us grow more accustomed to it than others."

"Well, not me. I shall never grow accustomed to it."

"Then you don't like Delhi?"

"Until this afternoon, I was certain I detested it."

Just then Rani slipped silently out of the shadows and spoke to her charge in a whisper of Hindustani. It was a language few English, including Edward, understood, but Charlotte easily answered the beautiful native woman. Then, with a subtle gesture, she dismissed her. Rani moved to say something more but thought better of it. She lowered her head and moved silently back to join a collection of dark-faced native women who had been watching them from a shadowy corner of the veranda. When Charlotte felt

Edward staring at her, she lifted her eyes shyly. Her smooth face was alight in the glow of the moon.

"How did you learn to speak like that?" he asked, and she turned away from the admiration in his eyes. The sensation was warm and familiar and made her feel more lovely, more desirable than she ever had before.

"Rani believed that I should learn," she said simply, feeling a strange yet rapidly deepening power over him. "She wanted me to go inside just now."

He moved a step nearer. "And . . . what did you tell her?"

"I told her that I was old enough now to take care of myself."

"Miss Lawrence, might I say that, after this afternoon in the brigadier's garden, on that score, I quite agree."

Edward had the most overwhelming urge to kiss her. Her youthful confidence, mixed with true naiveté, was positively intoxicating. But it was too soon. He must be very careful not to frighten this spirited young colt. Instead he took a deep breath and contented himself with an admiring smile.

"The pistol belonged to my mother," Charlotte volunteered after an awkward silence, afraid that if she did not keep talking, the moment and this splendid man would disappear forever. "She did not like India very much and she became convinced that a woman should know how to keep her distance and protect herself from so many natives."

"And yet her daughter speaks their language and merits their genuine concern."

"As I said, Captain, one grows accustomed."

Again there was a silence, and Edward glanced down at her hands, both placed on the railing of the veranda. She was clutching it so forcefully that even in the light of the moon, he could see that her fingers had all gone white. He fought the urge to laugh out loud when he realized that she was as anxious as he. In view of her confidence, it had never occurred to him.

"That is quite a stunning bracelet," he said of a band she wore. The gold work was intricate, an Indian design.

"It was a gift."

"From your *ayah?*"

"From my father. It was a birthday gift."

As Charlotte held the bracelet up to the moonlight, Edward took her hand and whispered, "It is exquisite."

She was very aware of his warm hand on her wrist. It was a powerful, masculine grip; and as his fingers pressed into her veins, she felt the same surprising surge that she had when he had first come out onto the veranda. Charlotte had never felt the touch of any man other than her father, and it unnerved her. But even though it was entirely improper, she could not bring herself to pull away. The feel of his warm hand excited her. His pulse beating just beneath the surface of his skin was in the same quickened rhythm as her heart.

When she looked up, she saw that he was staring at her again. His eyes were large and round. His lips were moist and slightly parted. Charlotte had never before known what it was to want to be kissed by a man, but just now she wanted nothing more than to feel those lips pressed against hers. They were no more than a breath apart. He wanted to kiss her too. She could feel it. Then he let go of her arm.

"It is getting late. You had better be getting back inside," he said, and the movement, like the tone in his voice, was sharp and disjointed.

"Yes, of course," she agreed, trying her best to keep the disappointment from her voice as they moved back into the light.

It was then that she saw movement from the corner of her eye and realized that Rani was still watching them. That was why he had pulled away from her so abruptly. Edward too had seen the collection of watchful servant women hidden by the shadows. When he opened the door to the ballroom and knew that their conversation would be drowned by the laughter of the other guests and the chatter and the music, Edward touched her arm. He wanted to hold her back an instant longer, but as he did so they could not risk looking back at one another.

"You know I must see you again," he whispered, as though it were the most natural thing in the world for him to say.

"Yes," she said simply, feeling the same sense of rightness that he did. "Tomorrow."

Her answer was a pale smile. "At teatime in the lanes across the river near the Bridge of Boats."

"I know that what I ask is improper, but I want only a chance to talk with you, free from the reproving gaze of your father or your *ayah.*"

"It is all right. I shall not have long, but I will meet you on horseback. I am accustomed to riding with my father when everyone else takes tea, but tomorrow I shall see that he is otherwise engaged."

The time had been brief, no more than a few moments alone on the veranda, but Edward felt a wild elation as they walked together back into the ballroom. It was the most curiously portentous feeling he had ever had, but he knew then, as he had known from that first moment in the Graves House garden, that Charlotte Lawrence, this spirited, beautiful girl, would be a part of his life.

Forever.

Edward climbed the last stair to his bungalow and paused to stand a moment on his own wide, thatched veranda. On a magical night like tonight, he hated to go inside. He knew what lay beyond that door. Already he could hear the coarse laughter. The ribald jokes. Cigar smoke and whiskey blotted out the last traces of Charlotte's delicate English lavender perfume.

Edward Langston had been in India for nearly five years, having left England on his twenty-eighth birthday, and never had he expected to feel this disconnected from his purpose. And it had come apart so suddenly. Until today, his post in the 38th Regiment had been the most important thing in the world. The only thing. He had pursued it with a singular intensity, determined to change the course of his life from what it would have been as a pub owner's son in the small Cotswold village of Tetbury.

Military service had been the only way, a narrow path open to men ambitious and determined enough to take it.

The price for those of his station was high; if not in India, service was either in Persia or Burma. They were the faraway posts, out of which wealthy young men could afford to see themselves. They paid others like Edward to take their place. But hard work and a little good fortune would see him back on English soil one day, wealthy enough to claim the life he felt he deserved. The life, before today, he had always believed he wanted.

Edward turned the door handle reluctantly and a jumble of light and thick acrid odors sprawled out before him. Four men, all posted beneath him in the 38th, sat around a large, rickety table strewn with a half-full bottle of whiskey, dirty glasses, a Hindustani dictionary, and a half-eaten roast chicken.

"Ho! Langston! You're just in time. These gents are positively murdering me," chuckled Edward's roommate, Arthur Moresby, as he tossed his hand of cards onto the table.

"Not tonight," Edward groaned, wanting to savor the last bit of his encounter with the colonel's beautiful daughter. "It's late. I'm going to bed."

Edward's *khansaman,* a tall, dark native named Rajab, who acted as butler in the small English bungalow, took Edward's jacket and then silently retreated.

"Not tonight," John Evans, a young lieutenant, parroted. "What's that? Now that you've dined with the brigadier in charge of all of Delhi, you're too bloody good for your ol' mates?"

Arthur disregarded Edward's mood and poured his friend a drink. He held it up as a new hand of cards was being dealt in the midst of their cluttered sitting room. Edward hesitated only a moment. Then, more out of habit than desire, he raised the chipped glass to his lips and drank the cheap whiskey. It burned his throat and he closed his eyes just as John Evans lowered his own glass and belched loudly. Edward glanced around the table at the rest of his friends. After a moment, he smiled and surrendered himself to one of the worn cane chairs at the table.

"Perhaps Langston knows something of the situation,"

Henry Dunsford said as he lit a fat Manila cheroot in the golden glow of the single oil lamp between them.

"All I 'know' is that, after I finish my drink, I am going to bed."

"John here was just telling us that he had heard a rumor, quite far-fetched if you ask me," Arthur snipped. "He says the shell casings for the new rifles the *sepoys* will be getting are to be dipped in beef tallow and hog's lard."

"Well, they have to be dipped in something." Henry Dunsford puffed, and a gray cloud of cigar smoke billowed around his face; a square, pale face forever branded by childhood smallpox.

"Can you imagine what the Hindus would do if they got a taste of that!" John Evans smirked. "Them thinking the bloody cow is sacred and all. Not to mention the Mussulmans, who abhor pigs, thinking they are unclean!"

"I hadn't heard," Edward said truthfully, his lips parted in surprise by the implications of such a dangerous rumor.

"I told them it was impossible," Arthur said. "They've got to know what sort of uproar such a thing would bring about."

"The *sepoys* could bloody well revolt over it," Dunsford speculated as he flicked his cigar ashes onto the floor.

"No sense panicking," Arthur interjected. "Even if it were true, how would they ever discover it?"

Edward slammed his glass onto the table, his blue eyes bright with disbelief. *"You* discovered it, didn't you?"

The men hung their heads until Arthur took a long swill of whiskey and then asked, "Do you suppose if you spoke with the brigadier it would do any good, Langston? At the very least, put an end to the rumor?"

"Me?"

"Well, the ol' boy likes you, doesn't he? After all, you were invited personally to a ball at the grand manor," Henry Dunsford reminded, pointing an empty glass at him.

"Along with a hundred other of his most intimate friends."

"I, for one, think Arthur is right," John Evans agreed. "If there is any truth at all to the rumor, we could all be in danger in this God-forsaken place. We're constantly at these poor pitiful natives with our ways and our beliefs, and you know they shall only take that sort of thing for so long."

A scorpion suddenly shivied across the floorboards, making a little tapping sound on the bare wood. Without a word, Arthur lifted his pistol from the table and fired a single booming shot, clipping the offending creature and sending it sailing across the room.

"You really are the only one we can ask," Arthur persisted, without missing a beat. Then, glancing up at the surprised faces around the table, he sneered. "Dreadful little creatures. The sting is really quite nasty."

Edward was tired and he wanted to go to bed. But he agreed entirely with what his half-drunk friends were saying, and the truth of such an abomination would not surprise him. The British had inflicted themselves into a strange culture and then forced innumerable changes upon its people. For the most part, native customs and traditions were treated with a general disregard here. The British found it more convenient to see their role in India as that of deliverers, saving the natives from the oppression of their traditional rulers, rather than as oppressors themselves. The continual annexation of their land under the guise of progress had only deepened the discontent.

"What's worse," Evans fed the silence, "is that I heard it was all intentional. After all, think about it. Those cartridges must be bitten, and if the *sepoys* are forced to do that, they will lose their caste in society."

Henry Dunsford snickered and looked back at his cards. "They'd bloody well be ripe for a conversion to Christianity then!"

Arthur shook his head. "A clever attempt to deliver them completely into what we call civilization."

"This is all so far-fetched," Dunsford huffed.

"Is it?" asked Edward, and the tone of his voice carried a warning.

There was a long, heavy silence in the small bungalow, and the far-off howl of jackals filled the night air. Edward felt as if he suddenly had the weight of the entire British army and their families upon his shoulders, and his own friends had put it there. It was the price of his ambition, he thought, to have established himself in a high enough place to effect change. Like it or not, he had a responsibility. *Good God, if there was so much as a chance that a rumor like that could be true and I did nothing to try and change it . . .*

Edward finished his drink and then rose again. His friends were right about one thing. A great majority of the *sepoys* serving in the army were Hindu. Despite their distaste for British rule, they had never found a cause strong enough to unite them with the Mussulmans. If what Arthur Moresby was saying was true, it was entirely possible that all of that was about to change; and if it did, their very lives could well be in the gravest danger. Suddenly Edward was very tired, and the jubilant effects of the ball had faded back into the bleak reality of day-to-day life in India.

"Very well," he resolved with a sigh. "I shall make an attempt to see Graves about it in the morning. But we do not know if the rumors are true. And even if they are, I certainly cannot promise anything."

"Of course not," said John Evans, sucking in a low, warm breath and fingering his cards. "But, God willing, it shall be enough that you try."

Edward stood there silently a few moments more, angry that the evening should have ended this way; weary just now of having everyone always looking to him for guidance. He swept a hand over his face. He was tired now and he did not want to think of angry *sepoys* or shell casings, or even of danger. Not when there was the fantasy of Charlotte's wanton innocence still clouding his mind.

Rajab came from the shadows in Edward's dark bedroom a few moments later, surprisingly silent for a man of his grand size, and helped Edward off with his boots.

"So tell me, Rajab." Edward sighed, leaning back in a creeky desk chair. "What do you make of the rumor that has my friends so fretful?"

"Sahib?" he asked blankly, looking up as he knelt at the captain's feet.

"Now Rajab." Edward smiled. "We have been together a long time—since Calcutta—and I believe I have come to know you a little better than that. You overheard our conversation."

The *khansaman* took the boots and placed them neatly in the corner beneath the peg that held the captain's crisp red jacket. When he returned, Edward could see the dark frown that had shaded his thick face.

"They are rumors that I too have heard, *sahib,*" he admitted.

Edward came forward in his chair. "Among the men?"

"Among my people, *sahib.*"

"What are they saying?" Edward asked after a moment of silence, struggling to keep the growing concern from his voice. "Please, you must tell me."

"They are saying that death is preferable to the loss of their caste," he replied grimly, and his voice bore a sudden, ominous warning. "I do not believe there is anything the English can do to force this upon us when we have endured so much at their hands already."

"Their hands are my hands, Rajab," Edward reminded him. "I too am English."

The powerfully built *khansaman* whom Edward had hired his first week in Calcutta, just after he had arrived in India, disagreed. "No, Captain-*sahib,* you are not like the others. You have respect for a culture different from your own. You do not seek to change all that you do not understand. It is the only reason I left my home and came away to Delhi to attend you."

He said it more matter-of-factly than complimentary, and Edward felt his stomach twist. He sprang out of his chair so that the two men were facing one another, a fierce tension suddenly between them.

"Then you believe that a rumor like this, whether or not it is true, could unite your people with the Mussulmans in violence against us?"

Rajab lifted his thick dark brows and stared implacably at

Edward. "I think, *sahib*, that it is very dangerous to believe otherwise."

After the lights in the cantonments had all been extinguished, Edward moved away the mosquito netting and sat on his small cot. It was the time of day he liked the best. And the time he feared the most. It was when he finally had no choice but to let down his guard.

It was only in the darkness like this, when there were no more distractions, that the carefully cultivated image of confidence that he forced the rest of the world to see could fade into the pitch black of night. Edward brushed a hand across his face and took a small camphorwood box from a drawer in his bedside table. Inside were a few English coins, a collection of letters tied with a red satin ribbon, and a small opal ring set in silver.

Edward put the ring on his index finger just below the nail and held it up to the single candle flame that lit the room. It was the only memento he had of her. Of Adelaide Langston. Once he had hated this meager ring, because it was all that his father could afford. When he left England, he had thought it the ultimate symbol of the mediocre life he so desperately wanted to escape. But his mother had pressed this simple little jewel into his hand and, with it, bid him not to forget from where he had come no matter where his ambitions might lead him. She died a month later, and Edward had never turned back nor looked at it again, until tonight.

"You would like her," he whispered as he gazed down at his mother's ring, speaking to her memory. "She is clever, like you. She has your spirit. . . . I've really never met anyone quite like her."

There was a girl who had loved him in Tetbury. He had known her since they were children. But he had not loved her. There had been others since then. But none of them had ever made him feel as Charlotte already did. Open and vulnerable. As if all of this ambition of his were really meaningless by comparison. And suddenly, quite to his surprise, this simple piece of jewelry had a significance.

Edward set the ring gently back in the box and blew out the single candle flame, his mind filled with thoughts of Charlotte. He sat in the dark like that, not wanting to sleep, and wondering what happy surprises tomorrow would bring when he saw her again.

The next morning, Edward walked briskly up the stairs and through the entrance of Graves House, residence and headquarters of the brigadier in charge of the Delhi garrison. The night before he had been shaken by the implications of what Arthur and the others had told him. Rajab's words of warning had fueled that fear. But today nothing could ruffle his joy. He was going to see Charlotte again, and he could not recall ever having been so happy about an encounter with a woman. But first he must do as he had promised. He would see Harry Graves and try to put an end to the wretched rumors. He did so detest gossip, especially dangerous gossip like that.

He strode tall and erect past a row of cross-legged *punkah-wallahs* pulling the cords of the wicker fans in rhythmic syncopation. A turbanned *khawasin* salaamed deeply to him as he passed through the hallway and into the office of the brigadier's personal secretary—Charlotte's father.

Hugh Lawrence smiled, coming to his feet behind a large mahogany desk strewn with papers. He was a small, sturdy man with thinning hair, a long salt-and-pepper mustache, and full gray side-whiskers. Lines of worry and too many years in the Indian sun had cut deep patterns into his fleshy face. He motioned to Edward to advance.

"Good morning, Captain Langston."

"Sir." Edward nodded.

"Splendid party last evening."

"Yes. Splendid indeed," Edward replied, quite certain his interest in the colonel's daughter was evident on his young, tanned face. For once in his life, he was relieved to be wrong.

"So glad we could finally coax you into attending one of our little soirées. You know that Brigadier Graves thinks the world of you."

32

"He has always been most kind to me."

"And you gave my daughter her first dance. Quite splendid of you to have humored her that way."

Edward tried his best to sound disinterested. "It was my pleasure, sir."

"But you know how fanciful they can be. I suspect the child will have a terrible crush on you from now on."

"'Child,' sir?"

"Yes, Langston. My daughter has just turned sixteen," he pulled at the tip of his mustache. "One day, in five years or so, I quite expect her to make someone a rather extraordinary wife. But for now, she's still my little girl. You know how it is." The colonel sat back down and crossed his arms over his chest. "So then, tell me. How is it, exactly, that you've come to know our commander so well?"

"Brigadier Graves likes to hunt. I was merely able to help him improve his technique."

"That was certainly not something you learned in London."

Edward linked his hands behind his back and rocked on his heels. "I am not from London, sir."

"Oh?"

"I am from Tetbury."

"Tetbury?" Hugh Lawrence croaked, and his full face wrinkled in a frown. "Where the devil is that?"

"It is a small market town in the Cotswolds, sir."

"You're from the country? Why, I never would have guessed it to look at you. . . . You have all of the bearing and style of an—"

Edward arched an eyebrow. "Of an aristocrat, sir?"

"See here, Langston, I didn't mean to imply—"

"Of course not, Colonel Lawrence. I am not ashamed to have been born the son of laborer. The advantage of poverty is that it gives one a true hunger for achievement, something the leisure class knows very little about."

Hugh Lawrence's sour face turned crimson. He had always considered himself a splendid judge of character, and he had seen men like this before. India was rife with them. Arrogant. Ambitious. Convinced that their appearance and a clever way with words made up for their atrocious lack of breeding and lineage. Thank God Charlotte was still a child and he would not need to contend with a suitor like this. At least not until he had an opportunity to convince his daughter just how utterly disgraceful such a match would be.

"So then," he asked, his speech clipped now, the tone distant, "what might I do for you this morning?"

"I should like to see the brigadier, if he has a few moments to spare."

Hugh Lawrence's reply was a cackle. Fleshly jowls beneath his side-whiskers shivered as he laughed. After a moment, he coughed to stop his laughter and leaned back in his maroon leather chair.

"Sorry, ol' boy. Nothing personal. It is just that I suspect half of Delhi would like the same thing. You shall simply have to get in line."

Edward tensed. "Certainly he has allotted some time to addressing the concerns of his men during his busy day."

"Brigadier Graves sees no one before two, and then even his wife has trouble keeping his attention past a few well-chosen words. Business here keeps him locked up in that bloody office of his from morning until night. Takes it all so seriously."

"I rather think it could be important," Edward pressed. "It is a question of morale among the men. I would hate to have to mention the difficulty I had in seeing him the next time we're hunting . . . especially if this little complexity really comes to something."

Hugh Lawrence rubbed the back of one chubby hand across his glistening brow and studied Edward with cold, gray eyes. For whatever reason, the commander liked this young upstart, and he must take great care not to go too far against that. Finally a canting little half smile turned up the corners of his mouth.

"As I have said, this morning is out of the question," the colonel began tentatively. "But if you can manage to return later today, at teatime, I might well see you slipped in then. No matter how intense he gets about his work, Brigadier

Graves is still an Englishman. Wouldn't dream of missing his tea."

Edward thought of objecting. That was precisely when he was to meet Charlotte, the first woman to draw anything out of him beyond complaisance since he had come to India. And yet he had no choice. Blast! He must do this. If he did not return at the time Colonel Lawrence had appointed him, he might not get another chance to confront the brigadier privately before it was too late.

There was a powder keg of resentment against the English in India, and if the rumors were true, there was no telling how soon things might erupt. There must be a way to get word to her about this change in plans. But how? Trying to contact Charlotte directly would be highly improper, since he was not yet an accepted suitor.

When he should have been filled with excitement about his clandestine meeting with the girl of his dreams, his head instead was filled with thoughts of obligation. Of honor. And the search for a miracle that, after today, would give him another chance to be with her. When he spoke again, no more than a moment later, his voice was tight, his resolve firm. But even then the words came from a commitment to duty. Not from his heart.

"If it must be teatime . . . then, Colonel Lawrence, teatime it shall be."

Edward walked swiftly back through the shadowy corridors and out through the grand portico. She was here, he thought, as he glanced back at the grand, umber-colored manor. So close. And yet a million miles from an explanation of what he must do and why. He must put the concerns of his post and the safety of its people above his own. There would be a way to contact her. There must be.

Edward would think of something.

2

CHARLOTTE CAME AWAY FROM THE WINDOW AT RANI'S INSIS-tence. Her heart was beating like a drum beneath her cambric dressing gown. By chance she had caught a glimpse of Edward beneath her window as he left Graves House. Perhaps he had come to try to see her; to slip her a message telling her that he was as anxious for their meeting as she. How much longer must she wait? Nearly six hours more! *Oh! I shall die before then. . . . I simply know that I shall die!*

She had never done anything so forbidden in her life, and the mere idea of a secret meeting with a handsome military officer sent her spinning. But she trusted Edward. He did not intend to sully her or her reputation. The spark between them was too bright. They had both felt it unmistakably the night before on the veranda. A secret meeting was the only way to see if that spark would become a flame. Her father would have flatly refused him if Edward had tried to call on her openly and honestly. She was too young, he had always said. He was too afraid to lose her, was what he had always meant.

In her sleeplessness last night, Charlotte had lain in her grand canopied bed trying to recall everything Edward had said to her, each look that had passed between them. Her mind still whirled with the memory of it. He had the most beautiful face in the world, she thought; his body lean and graceful, ice-blue eyes, smooth pale lips. How she wished he had kissed her then. She understood why he hadn't. The risk of it, like everything else, had been too great with Rani so near. But this afternoon, perhaps, when they were alone . . .

A smile broke across her face. Charlotte pounced onto her bed in a rustling pile of cambric, immeasurably pleased with herself and quite certain that she would burst with the excitement. She was happy for the first time since that day, in the thick, cloying heat of summer, five years before, when her mother had been claimed by cholera.

When she looked back at her *ayah,* Charlotte's fanciful smile fell by degrees. "Oh, don't look at me that way, Rani," she bade her in English. She only spoke in her own language when she wanted to remind her maidservant of the difference in their positions. It was an act of petulance; something she regretted almost the moment she had spoken. Her next words came again in softly spoken Hindustani. "Can you not see that I am happy? Happy for the first time in a very long time."

"Forgive me, my *bitiya.* But what I see is a young and foolish girl," Rani answered her. "One who is willing to be tempted by evil. It is wrong, and he is wrong to tempt you."

"Captain Langston has only the most honorable intentions."

"He is a man. You are a child. That is temptation in itself."

Charlotte ignored her remonstrations, pulling herself from the bed and dancing around the room in giddy circles. "Oh, is he not the most handsome man you have ever seen, Rani? At least you must agree about that."

"His pleasing face cannot hide that there is trouble for you with him, dear one. I feel it."

Charlotte stopped and faced the beautifully exotic woman with gleaming black hair, black brows, and deeply set eyes. As they opposed one another, Rani's copper-colored skin was in marked contrast to her own pale ivory complexion. Her *ayah's* expression made it clear that she did not approve of any of it. *You cannot ruin this for me,* thought Charlotte angrily. *It is all that I want in the world, and yet one look from you like that to my father and he will know. And that will be it. It will be over even before it has begun!*

"Please do not betray me to Father," Charlotte said instead, and her voice was as smooth as velvet. She caressed Rani's textured cheek with the tip of her finger. "I must do this."

"Then there is nothing further which I can say to influence you not to go?"

"Nothing." Charlotte smiled, her face shimmering with youthful confidence. "And help me choose a pretty dress, hmm? You always know just the right thing for me to wear."

"Very well. Then I shall do as you ask."

After Rani had helped her bathe and covered her pale English body with cream and oil, she began the process of camouflage, dressing for the day, with white muslin pantalets, then the tight corset, the cagelike frame of hoops called a crinoline, and only then the gown. Ruffles of pistachio silk to match her eyes. Her thick blond hair was brushed, then pulled away from her face and knotted. Her head was covered by a small straw hat accented with green ribbons.

Rani stepped back as Charlotte studied herself in the mirror; as Captain Langston would see her. When she thought of him, her heart beat so loudly that she could hear nothing else. She bit her lip as she looked at the reflection. Rani was right: Even in so stylish a gown, she was still a child. He was a man. She was glad to have made her servant pull the corset especially tight so at least she would appear to have a more womanly shape. A man always admired that, her father had told her. She took a series of deep breaths and closed her eyes. She must be calm. Yes, very calm. A man never liked a woman who laughed too freely or was unnecessarily capricious. She had been calm in the garden yesterday. Dead calm. Her anger had seen to that. But things had changed, and swiftly.

Rani was shaking her head as she came away from the mirror. "How is it that you expect to be free long enough to meet him when you always ride with your father in the afternoon?"

"Not today," she replied, her young face radiant with confidence.

"But how? What excuse shall you give for not going riding with him?"

Charlotte turned back around. "You must convince him to take tea with Brigadier Graves. It shouldn't be too difficult, since he is always after Father to join him."

"It is enough that I must keep silent, *bitiya*. I want no part in aiding your deception further." Rani shook her head.

"But you are the only one with charms seductive enough to change my father's mind about anything!"

The tiny lines beside her *ayah*'s dark, mysterious eyes deepened as the words settled between them. It was a relationship about which they had never before spoken. Charlotte reached out and took both Rani's hands, knowing she had crossed a line she ought not have. But she would do whatever she must to see Edward this afternoon.

Her words this time were soft, pleading. "I have kept your relationship with my father a secret. Can you not find it in your heart simply to do the same for me? Please, Rani. There really is no one else I can ask."

You do not heed my warning, my bitiya, *but now you ask me to use my wiles so that you can secretly meet with this man!* Rani's thoughts raced. *Cast away your life! Your innocence! It is wrong. I cannot. I will not. . . .* She stopped when she saw Charlotte's deep green eyes fill with tears.

This sweet child had cried so many tears as her mother lay dying, and long afterward. The house had been filled with the haunting sound. Rani had nursed the feeble *Memsahib* Lawrence, knowing all the while that she would never survive. And she had done her best to take the woman's place in Charlotte's life. The affair with her father had come much later. It had not been so long ago, and she was not so old herself, that she had forgotten what it was like to fall in love. She felt an unexpected ripple of tenderness. Finally the *ayah* gave her a wan smile, and Charlotte fell into her open arms.

"Oh, thank you! You shall see, Rani. I promise. All of your worrying shall be for nothing. Come now. We must get our stories straight for when Father asks you where I've gone!"

An hour later, the same turbanned *chaprassi* whom Edward had paid for Charlotte's name stepped tentatively into Graves House. He bore a slip of ecru paper sealed with red wax hidden safely in his white *dhoti.*

For the same number of *rupees,* the barefoot servant had reluctantly consented to try to get a message to Mistress Lawrence. He had not bothered to disclose to Edward that the interior of Graves House was not his domain and that he had no idea where he might find the young English girl in the middle of the day.

He stepped carefully across the marble entry until he saw the staircase at the end of the corridor. As he neared, he could hear the soft, musical laughter of women. The sound was coming from upstairs. Glancing furtively around the shadowy corridor, the *chaprassi* moved onto the first carpeted step. He closed his eyes for a moment. What he was attempting was dangerous, but he must think of the money he had been paid. If he succeeded, perhaps the captain-*sahib* would have other equally lucrative jobs for him in the future.

He took the rest of the steps quickly, silently, until he stood on the second-floor landing, with a daunting tunnel of sealed doors before him. He had only moments to locate her. He knew that. But where to begin? His heart thumped like a native drum as he turned the first brass handle. Beyond the door, the room was dark and empty. Muttering to himself, he pulled the first door closed again and moved on to the next.

He opened three doors, all with no success, when suddenly he felt a thick, warm hand squeezing his shoulder.

"And what, precisely, do you think you are doing?" a woman's deep voice boomed in his ear.

The *chaprassi* turned around slowly and came face to face with the brigadier's wife, the stout and suddenly very intimidating Mrs. Graves.

"Please to find Miss Lawrence, *memsahib.*" The young man nodded respectfully, his broken English unable to impress the grand lady of the house enough to assist him.

"What is it you wish with Charlotte?" she asked suspiciously.

He shifted nervously, knowing that if he did not hand over the note entrusted to his care, he might well be accused of far worse than trespassing. Reluctantly, he lifted the communiqué from the folds of his *dhoti* and held it out between them.

"I was asked to bear this to Mistress Lawrence."

Mrs. Graves crooked a gray eyebrow. "Who sent it?"

"I know not, *memsahib.* But he paid me handsomely to do it."

Augusta Graves snatched the sealed note from his dark hand. "It was an Englishman, was it not?"

"Han, memsahib," he acknowledged, lowering his eyes.

"I should have known," she huffed, hands on wide hips. "Some sorry infatuated soul, no doubt . . . one who has clearly taken leave of his senses so far from home. Hugh Lawrence is certainly not about to sacrifice his only daughter like that!"

The *chaprassi* glanced around, still hearing the giddy laughter of a young girl beyond one of doors. He had almost succeeded. She was close. Miserably close.

"Well then," Augusta Graves declared firmly. "I shall see to the note. You may leave the proper course of action in the matter to me."

"But *memsahib—*"

Her brown eyes narrowed quickly. "I said that I would see to it. Now, back to your post before I report you myself!" She sniffed condescendingly and turned away, muttering, "Poor motherless chit, completely defenseless against every amorous soldier whose head she turns. Och! My work here is simply never done. It is just never done!"

The sound of shredding paper echoed through the corridors as the *chaprassi* turned reluctantly from the woman who was destroying the note with furiously purposeful snaps. When he could think of no safe way to salvage the task that had been entrusted to him, he ambled back down the stairs and out into the afternoon sun.

It was just as his father had said. Just as he had refused to believe. They were vainglorious power mongers, always insisting that they were superior. Set on the destruction of the traditions and values of the Hindu people. Capable of saying anything, doing anything to cause them to lose their caste as a prelude to it. After today, he had no use for the English, wealthy or otherwise. In that, the simple *chaprassi* was among a dangerously increasing minority.

Four o'clock. Teatime.

Charlotte had gone across the Bridge of Boats and waited alone on the shaded lanes on the other side of the river, her identity concealed by a gauze veil that hung from her hat. Her horse was hidden by the cover of lush kikar trees and thick pampas grass. Her pistachio-green gown made the only sound—a rustle—as she shifted in her saddle.

"Where are you, Edward?" she whispered. "You know that I haven't much time."

Back across the river, up on the ridge, she could see the English cantonments and the thatched-roof bungalows that from a distance looked like dozens of tiny beehives all in long, ordered rows. They were all facing west, in defensive preparation against the searing summer sun, which would soon be upon them. *One of those must be his,* she thought. *Damn him! Edward is not going to come. He has changed his mind. Found something more entertaining to occupy his time. Perhaps someone. It was a game to him. I was just a game.* . . . Fifteen minutes passed as she waited. Twenty. Then twenty-five. It was almost an hour before Charlotte pulled on the reins of her horse and galloped back across the river.

"Rani was right about you. You have made a fool of me once, Edward Langston," she seethed as a tiny vein pulsed in her slim, milk-white neck. "But it shall not happen again. Not to me."

* * *

At the precise moment that Charlotte was pulling her horse behind the cover of trees to wait for him, Edward was mounting the crimson-carpeted steps that led to Graves House, believing she had received his note.

He ignored the *sepoy* guards who lined the halls, their eyes riveted ahead. *Duty first,* he told himself as his footfalls echoed across the marble corridor.

"Well, Langston! My old hunting partner. To what do I owe the pleasure?"

Harry Graves held a blue-and-white china teacup near his lips as Edward was shown into the brigadier's study. Hugh Lawrence sat beside him, with Mrs. Graves's blue Persian cat asleep in his lap. The room was strangely dark for February, shuttered against the light of day. In a shadowy corner of the room, a native boy wrapped in a white *dhoti* quietly pulled a *punkah* cord. The motion teased a sheaf of papers on the brigadier's grand mahogany desk.

Despite the informality with which he had been greeted, Edward stood erect and at attention, hands linked behind his back. "I am afraid it is not a social matter I have come about, sir."

"Well, you have come at teatime. It is the one indulgence I allow myself, so I am afraid, my boy, anything else would be out of the question."

"I suggested he come now," Hugh interjected. "Captain Langston convinced me of a possible problem among the men."

Graves pursed his lips and studied the handsome young officer. "Very well, then. But at least do sit down and have a cup of tea with us. Watching you stand there like that is not a'tall good for my digestion."

Edward let a uniformed *jemadar* fill a third cup and place it on the table between them. But he did not touch it. "To the point, sir: There is a rumor spreading through the compound like wildfire, and quite likely beyond. They are saying that the *sepoys* are getting new rifles."

Graves set down his cup. "Yes. The old Brown Bess they're so fond of is just too heavy in the heat of summer. It slows them down. Our native soldiers shall be receiving Enfield rifles within the month."

"But the Enfield's cartridges must be greased."

Graves's voice was suddenly tight. Edward watched him shift in his chair. "Yes, of course."

"Some of the men were wondering, sir, with what, exactly, the Enfield is to be lubricated. The rumor is that lard is to be used."

Graves and Lawrence exchanged what Edward could plainly see was a worried glance. Colonel Lawrence followed it by shooting him a disdainful glare. There was no mistaking what the look meant. *Great God!* thought Edward. *So then it is true!* He was certain now, in the strained silence, that if he had been more forthcoming with the reason for needing to see the brigadier, this impromptu audience would never have been granted.

After another moment, Hugh Lawrence sprung from his chair. Edward rose to meet him. Hostility was plain in the colonel's voice as he said, "And this is what you found so terribly important that you convinced me to let you interrupt the commander's one brief bit of rest in the day?"

"It is all right, Hugh," Graves said more calmly. "Sit down. Both of you."

He stroked the little tuft of hair below his lip for several tense moments as Hugh and Edward seated themselves again. Hugh's face was still set with a cynical expression, and he sat ready at a moment's notice to spring on this smart young demagogue for his impudence.

"Captain Langston was right to come to me. A great deal of harm can be done from persistent gossip and rumor."

"It is just, sir, that such a thing would be so horrendous," Edward ventured carefully.

Graves took another sip of tea. "I know the rumors, Langston. I am sorry to say that I have been reading about them myself of late."

"Then they are just that? Rumors, sir?"

Hugh Lawrence cleared his throat, plainly uneasy with the line of questioning Langston seemed bent on pursuing.

"Entirely," Graves decreed without hesitation. "If it will set your mind at rest, and those of the men, I shall tell you that in the past week alone I have issued both denials and proclamations to allay any fears that might arise. Before long, there will no doubt be something else we shall be worrying about."

A deserved consequence of such pervasive greed, Edward thought, but he wisely kept it to himself. Instead, he said, "I appreciate your candor, sir. I feel quite certain it shall go a long way toward calming the men. And still, I cannot help but wonder just how such a dangerous rumor could have gotten started, if indeed there was no truth to it a'tall."

Brigadier Graves cleared his throat and looked over at Hugh Lawrence. "Oh really, Langston. Who knows how any of those dreadful things begin," Hugh stammered. "A few of the men are drinking a bit too much one night, and before you know it—"

"Perhaps." Edward cut him off with a turn of his wrist. "But it does cause one to wonder why the men would start a rumor that could quite likely put themselves and their families in the gravest of danger."

"I really don't think that this is the time or the place, Captain," Graves interjected, his voice an octave lower. "Now, I have told you personally that they were just rumors. If you persist in this, I shall have no choice but to assume that you are accusing me of lying. . . . And I am quite certain that was not your intent."

Edward rose slowly, adopting his previous formality. "Certainly not, sir."

The two senior officers stared at him. When Edward saw that the meeting was over, he inclined his head respectfully and moved a few steps toward the door. Then he turned back around with an afterthought. "One more thing, sir: What was it you said the cartridges were to be greased with, if not beef tallow?"

The brigadier stood. His mouth was set in a firm line as he and Edward looked at one another combatively. "I didn't say, Captain."

There was silence—an uncomfortable silence—before Brigadier Graves smiled and moved toward the door. Unexpectedly, he wrapped his long arm around Edward's shoulder, and his stern expression broke. "Edward, dear boy. I do so appreciate your concern. Truly. But why do we not just let me worry about all of that nasty business with the cartridges, and you keep your mind on your men, hmm?"

Graves was smiling, and Edward felt his body stiffen at the pretense. "Of course, sir. And once again, I am truly sorry to have interrupted your tea for the sake of a rumor."

"Not a'tall, Captain. Glad to have been a help."

When Edward had gone, the two men sat back down. Charlotte's father was first to speak. When he did, it was beneath his breath. "It grieves me to say it, sir, but I fear that your young hunting partner there is trouble for us."

"He is an ambitious lad, isn't he?"

"Indeed. He is considered a real leader among the men, and we certainly don't need someone like that stirring up their darkest fears. The bloody *sepoys* are doing a good enough job of that all by themselves."

Graves crossed his legs and straightened his crimson jacket. "Perhaps the good captain's talents would be better suited for an assignment not quite so close to Delhi."

"Have you anything in mind, sir?"

He flicked a hand in the air. "I shall leave the details to you, Colonel Lawrence. But Calcutta is a post that comes to mind."

"Calcutta, sir?"

"I am told they are dreadfully short of good English officers. Perhaps there is a post in a regiment more appropriate for him there."

"That is quite a distance, sir."

"Yes," Graves said calmly. "Precisely."

Charlotte was just finishing supper with her father in his private sitting room when Rani quietly appeared at the table beside them. Her deep red *sari* sparkled in the lamplight, and the exotic fragrance of sandalwood was soothing in the warm evening air.

"I must speak to you privately," she whispered as she stood behind Charlotte.

Hugh Lawrence, drunk from too much whiskey, slammed his glass onto the heavy mahogany table, but he did not look away from his plate. "Kindly speak English in front of me, will you please?" he growled and began to cut another piece of meat.

Rani disregarded her lover's temper and looked back at Charlotte as a bevy of native servants slipped in and out of the room. They were clearing a continuous stream of serving dishes, bringing new ones, and fanning the colonel and his daughter.

"He has sent you a message," Rani said in her deep and exotic Hindustani.

"English!" Hugh bellowed.

Charlotte looked up and knew that she meant Edward. But any reference to or even subtle indication of that fact would instantly bring about her father's wrath. She was not at all certain why she cared. After all, Captain Langston had made a fool of her today. She had risked a great deal for him, stealing from the safety of Graves House by herself in the broad light of day. *How dare he?* she thought. *How dare he come here now and add insult to the injury he has inflicted upon me?*

"No!" she said. Then, realizing she had spoken out loud, she pressed her fingers to her lips.

"What is it, my dear?" said Hugh, his ruddy cheeks full of roast beef.

"Nothing, Father. Only a problem with one of my gowns. Rani tells me she has lost the pattern for the sleeves." She pushed back her chair and stood up.

"Oh really, Charlotte. Must it be now?" He glanced at the *ayah,* whose head was still lowered. "You know quite well how I detest eating alone."

"I shall only be a moment, Father. I promise. Tell Jumai to bring the cake and I shall be back before it is served."

She was gone in an instant, out in the corridor behind Rani, the rustling of silk and jangling bracelets the only sound between the two women.

"He wants to see you, *bitiya*. He says, to explain."

"Captain Langston can have nothing to say which I wish to hear," Charlotte said, her slim arms folded defensively across her chest.

Rani lowered her head and then turned away. "I have done as I was asked."

"Wait!"

The *ayah* stopped but did not turn back around. This child was heading for trouble. She could feel it now, as strongly as she had last night on the veranda when she had seen them together. It had been against her better judgment to come here with his message in the first place. But he had bidden her and paid her fifty *rupees,* and money was always an adequate persuasion to someone who had lived so long without it.

"Is he outside?"

"He waits in the garden."

"Then take a message back to him. Tell him I shall be a fool for no man. Yes. Tell him exactly that."

Charlotte watched her *ayah* until she was out of sight, a whirl of crimson and gold silk and the lingering aroma of sandalwood. She had done the right thing. Let him find another girl eager to play his games; eager to take what he felt inclined to give! How mature she sounded. At an age when her father oversaw everything, it felt good to be in control of something. Charlotte smiled, pleased with herself; and yet, just as quickly as the sensation came over her, it passed, giving way to a chip in her reserve. *He is still the most handsome man I have ever met. Now if only he is half so persistent with his apology as he is with his charms . . .* she thought, heading back to her father's table, her head filled with fantasy.

"So how did it go?"

Arthur had waited up for Edward. He sat alone at the

large table in the center of the bungalow. It was cluttered again with empty bottles and unwashed glasses from the evening's card game. The light from a single oil lamp cast the small room in a saffron glow. Edward removed his jacket and tossed it across the back of a chair, not at all inclined to deal with his roommate or the responsibility that had been so unceremoniously hoisted upon him. He was quite certain that his visit to Brigadier Graves had been useless, and now that Charlotte had refused to hear his explanation, Edward felt a total sense of apathy about the entire affair.

"It was just as I thought," he finally replied, heaving a heavy sigh. "All just a bloody lot of rumors."

Arthur came forward on the edge of his chair. "But what about the rifles? They are getting Enfields, are they not?"

"Yes," Edward said, drawing in a sharp breath as he poured himself a brandy.

"Well, I've seen the Enfield myself, and the cartridges it uses are not going to fit down that barrel without greasing them with something!"

Edward took the full glass of brandy in one swallow. "Graves flatly denied they were planning to use lard or pig fat."

"And you believed him?"

"It is in my best interests to believe my superiors," he hissed, quickly growing angry. "Look, Arthur, I have a few other things on my mind just now besides rifles and malcontented *sepoys*. I did what you all asked of me. Now you shall simply have to accept the reply."

Arthur Moresby let a moment pass before he said anything further. Edward Langston was a complex and moody sort of person, around whom one must tread lightly. "Do you want to talk about it?" he asked carefully.

"No! I most certainly do not want to talk about it!"

Edward took a few heavy steps toward his bedroom and then stopped. The air between the two men was thick and still filled with the echo of Edward's terse reply. Arthur hadn't deserved that. It really wasn't his fault, nor the fault of any of the others, for that matter. He had been given a choice today and he had made it. Edward turned back around slowly, his somber expression giving way to a weak smile.

"Look, I'm sorry, all right? It has just been a dreadfully long day."

"She wouldn't see you, hmm?"

Edward stiffened again. "What are you talking about?"

"The young lady we met rather unceremoniously in the Graves House garden yesterday. I was certain you would have won her over by now."

"Well you were wrong! Dead wrong. I am the last person Charlotte Lawrence wishes to see!"

A flicker of amusement danced in Arthur's narrow, dusty blue eyes as he slumped back in his chair. "Charlotte, is it? . . . Lovely name. I wonder, ol' fellow, what might you have done to earn the wrath of such a pretty young thing since yesterday?"

Edward moved to counter the ribbing, his handsome face filling with hot blood. Then he let the sentence die on his lips and he sank back into one of the chairs. As he spoke, he gazed absently into his empty glass. "We danced together last night at the ball, and we even managed a private moment away from the prying eyes of her father. I felt a real connection between us, and I know she felt it too." He took in a heavy breath. "We were set to meet one another this afternoon across the river."

A flash of understanding darkened Arthur's smile. "And then we asked you to do our bidding with old Graves."

"I understood the urgency. It was my choice to go."

"And she did not understand."

"I tried to send word to her. Apparently she never received it."

The envy Arthur felt—the same envy he always felt when he knew that Edward had met someone or had taken her to his bed—quickly paled at the utterly dejected tone in his voice. It had always seemed so easy for Edward Langston. He was handsome and remarkably confident, a man who knew what he wanted. Or so Arthur had always believed.

But this girl was different. She had dented the self-protective armor with which Edward had insulated himself. Tonight, Arthur Moresby could see a slim streak of vulnerability in Edward that he had not seen before.

"You must not give up without a fight," Arthur said sincerely. "I think she may well be the loveliest girl in all of India. And having seen you in battle, may I say that when it comes to fighting, there isn't an opponent alive—especially one of the female persuasion—who stands a chance against you."

Edward saw her face as it had been in the garden that day, full of a seductive mix of spirit and innocence. Why should she not be angry? She had risked a great deal stealing away to meet him so clandestinely. It must have seemed to her that he had found something—or someone—more entertaining to occupy his time. India was filled with those kinds of salacious Englishmen, about whom her father had doubtlessly cautioned her—and Hugh Lawrence certainly was a powerful force in his daughter's life.

Alone in Edward's favor was the reality of a moment he and Charlotte had shared in the cool, black night. In that moment, he had seen the look in her eyes that said she knew, just as he did, that their paths were meant somehow to come together. Now he had only to convince her of what he had known from the start.

"Charm really is a very potent weapon, Langston," Arthur said when he saw Edward's sharp expression begin to soften.

"Thank you for that, Arthur." Edward squeezed the top of his arm in a gesture of friendship. "For a moment I suppose I just lost sight of that."

The lanes across the river were strewn with the ruins of old temples and shaded by tall kikar trees and clumps of pampas grass. Edward pulled on the reins of his horse and prepared to wait in his saddle, behind one of the tree trunks. "Unless he has business, my father and I generally go riding at teatime," she had told him, and he had remembered every word. He must find a moment to try to explain. Charlotte had not received his note. She was justifiably angry. He had disappointed her yesterday and he could not blame her for refusing to see him either. But Arthur was right. Miss Lawrence was indeed the loveliest girl in all of India, and he would not stop until she understood what had really happened.

Until now he had always lived his life by convention. He knew the rules. He knew what to expect and what people expected of him, and he liked it that way. But now there was nothing he would not do to win Charlotte's favor. Suddenly the meaning of his life was not money or military promotion. It was not service to the Crown. Now all of that was gone, as if it had suddenly disappeared in a puff of smoke. And only the image of Charlotte remained. Charlotte was something of *real* value. It was worth the cost to see where what he already felt for her might lead.

It was another quarter of an hour before he heard the clomping hoofbeats in the dirt; the sound of two horses drawing near. He would need to say something sincere enough so that she would understand, yet vague enough so that he did not alert Hugh Lawrence to his true intent.

He pulled the reins slightly and his horse cantered out toward them. As they drew near, Edward saw Charlotte, attired in a forest-green riding costume and wide-brimmed straw hat, stiffen in her saddle. She lowered her eyes, not quite able to believe that he would have such audacity to follow her here after yesterday. The other thing she could not believe was that she was trembling at the sight of him.

"Captain." Hugh Lawrence nodded as they met beneath the lacy branches of two tall trees.

Edward leaned against the pommel of his saddle, more dashing, more magnificent, than ever. "Sir." He nodded back. "What brings you way out here this afternoon?"

"Father might have asked you the same question," Charlotte snipped coolly. When Edward looked down at her, she glanced off into the brush, trying valiantly to look disinterested.

"My daughter and I try to ride like this most afternoons,

Captain, as my schedule permits. We find that it is one of the lovelier lanes in Delhi."

"Oh, I quite agree," Edward said charmingly. Then, out of necessity, he prepared to lie. "I like to come out here myself. It helps to clear my mind. Although I usually prefer a morning ride."

Charlotte's wide green eyes narrowed suspiciously. "And to what do we owe this unexpected honor this afternoon?"

"To yet another change in my schedule, Miss Lawrence," he answered her, hoping against hope that she would get a hint at least of what he was trying to say. "Unfortunately, the duties of a captain in Her Majesty's army, no matter how firmly set they seem, are always subject to change without notice."

"How well I recall," said Hugh Lawrence, remembering the days before he had become personal secretary to the brigadier.

The tension was still so thick between them that neither Charlotte nor Edward caught sight of the giant black scorpion that had come out of the foliage and shivied up beside her great white mare.

"There is actually quite a grand view of the city from here," Edward said, pointing out across the silvery Jumna.

Hugh Lawrence and his daughter both glanced obligingly in the direction he had pointed. As they did, no one saw the scorpion, tail cocked in defense against the huge opponent, bitterly sting the horse just above the hoof. It whinnied and reared up, startling Charlotte. In a frenzy, the wounded animal broke into a hard gallop, trying by instinct to flee from its offender.

Hugh twisted in his saddle, his lips parted in surprise. "What in the devil!"

"It's all right, sir. I'll go after her!" Edward volunteered, and before the colonel could object, he had turned his horse around and dashed off after her. Hugh Lawrence tried to follow, but he was no match for the younger man's speed.

"Please, Langston! Hurry!"

Thundering hooves churned the dirt as two horses, one

after the other, lashed blindly through the low-hanging branches and patchy scrub. Terror-stricken, and trying her best to remain in her saddle, Charlotte turned around and saw that it was Edward who had followed her.

"Hold fast to the reins!" he shouted as they moved deeper and deeper beneath the canopy of branches that led down near the river. One branch tore the straw hat from her head, and her hair flew out behind her in a golden stream. Her forest-green skirt billowed out like the sail of a ship.

Leaning, spurring his horse on, straining to catch her, Edward could not quite grasp the bridle of Charlotte's horse. Her mount snorted and heaved as it raced blindly through the thick clumps of grass, heading steadily down toward the glistening white sandbanks that sloped like a fringe along the river.

"Charlotte!" Edward called out in a panic, knowing that it was not safe by the river. But she was a hostage to the frightened animal.

From there, it was sudden. A thick of pampas grass concealed the threat of quicksand from her, but not from her horse. As the animal came to a sudden and powerful stop at the marshy place they had reached near the river's edge, Charlotte was catapulted. She fell easily into the fearsome pull of the thick wet sand.

Instinctively she fought, her arms flailing, struggling to grasp anything that could save her. The movement only drew her deeper. In a matter of moments she was waist-deep in the quicksand.

"Edward! Oh, Edward! Help me!" she cried out, fearful tears glistening in her eyes as she thrashed.

"You're all right. You'll be all right," he answered, trying to keep the terror from his own voice. That would do her no good.

He was searching for something with which to pull her out and not be pulled down with her, and all the while she was sinking steadily deeper.

"Don't struggle, Charlotte! It will only pull you faster!"

"Oh, Edward! Please hurry!"

"I've got to find something to pull you out! Just please, don't move!"

As he searched the shore, frantic for anything strong enough to bear her weight, he could tell that she had stopped struggling, but he could still hear her weeping. The sound tore at his heart. She trusted him enough to do as he had bid her, even after what she believed of him.

A branch from a nearby kikar tree would have to do. He tore it from the trunk with a powerful snap and moved carefully back to her. "All right, Charlotte. I'm going to pull you out of there, but you musn't struggle. Just grab hold of this branch!"

She nodded through her tears, the wet sand already up to her shoulders. The sight of such fear in her eyes was enough to bring Edward to his knees, but he had to put all of that aside if he was to save her. Edward steadied himself, digging his heels deep into the firmer sand.

"Oh, sweet Jesus!" Hugh Lawrence cried out, lunging toward the muddy pit, having just that moment caught up with them. He had followed their trail down to the river's edge to see his daughter gasping as she reached for the slim branch Edward held out to her.

"Don't take another step!" Edward warned him. "If she struggles any more she could die!"

"Then for the love of God, save her, Langston! Save my child!"

"All right, Charlotte. Grab hold of it but do not struggle. Let me pull you!"

She was crying now, weeping aloud, and Edward gathered all of his strength and determination to pull against a force that threatened to swallow her.

"Steady, Langston," Hugh urged, his face fully stricken with terror that he might actually lose her, his only child.

Edward pulled steadily, careful that their weight not snap the lifeline between them. Charlotte had been made all the heavier now by the weight of her mud-soaked gown and heavy undergarments.

"Just a little longer. You can do it," he urged her as

Colonel Lawrence watched, silent and helpless. "Come on. That's the way. Hold on."

"Please, darling. Do as the captain tells you!"

Slowly, at Edward's hand, Charlotte finally emerged, mud-brown and soaking. Her elegant riding costume was completely drenched in heavy, wet sand. She collapsed on the riverbank, exhausted and shaking.

"You see? We did it!" Edward smiled, gasping as he fell beside her, his own body awash in perspiration. And Charlotte smiled back at him, her face tear-stained and piqued with gratitude.

But Hugh Lawrence pushed past Edward, and the single intimate moment between them was over, snuffed like a candle. He took his daughter, safe from danger now, in his arms and held her desperately, both of them crying as he blotted her tears with his kisses.

"Oh, if I had lost you . . ." he wept openly.

Edward looked away as he sat back on his heels and caught his breath. He would not interfere between a father and his child. He closed his eyes, and the image of her struggling and vulnerable began to fade, receding into the darkest corner of his mind. Taking its place was the reality that it had been his fault. He had come here, forced them to stop to try to explain, and it had nearly cost her her life. Edward drew a hand across his face and tried to blot out the sound of their weeping.

Together the two men helped Charlotte back to the horses that Hugh Lawrence had tethered to a tree. Then they rode in silence back to Graves House as the last bit of red Indian sun set behind the English cantonments.

While Charlotte was being tended to by a string of servants who rushed to her with various native antidotes, herbs, and compresses, the two men took a drink to steady their nerves. At the end of an hour, in which they had not spoken a single word to one another, Rani came silently through the doors of Brigadier Graves's library and stood before Edward.

"Miss Lawrence wishes to see the captain-*sahib*," the small, dark woman said in English, but in a voice heavily laced with the sing-song echo of Hindustani.

Edward looked over at the colonel for his approval, a man who not twenty-four hours before had made it clear that he despised him. Today, for just a little while, all of that seemed to have been forgotten. But now once again the icy veneer had returned as Hugh Lawrence gazed out the window across the vast green Graves House lawn.

"Be my guest, Langston," he said coldly, not turning around, and Edward's mouth fell open in unmasked surprise.

"That really isn't necessary—"

"You saved my daughter's life, Captain. I expect she has a right to thank you herself. That way any debt she feels she owes you shall have been settled entirely. Rani will see you to her."

Charlotte was in her bed, a dark and heavy-postered thing, surrounded by a ring of native women, when Edward entered her room. The windows were open, and a gentle breeze ruffled her white cotton bedding and the edges of her servants' *saris;* an amalgam of blue, red, and gold. One of the women silently fussed with her pillows, making anxious little movements, while the others stood still, their veiled heads lowered.

When she saw him, Charlotte sat up. Her green eyes sparkled with a curiously serene expression, and her hair, a rich golden yellow, lay softly unbound across her shoulders. She looked like an angel, Edward thought as he approached the bed. Rani nodded, and while the other women withdrew, she remained near the open bedroom door.

"I owe you a great deal, Captain," Charlotte said, and her whispered voice was tempered with softness. "You saved my life today."

Edward shifted on his feet. "I should not have tried to see you again when you had made your feelings so clear."

"But they were not my feelings. Not really . . . I hoped that you would try to see me again," she said sweetly, as a fresh breeze passed across them through an open window. "I hoped that you would try to . . . apologize."

Edward leaned closer. They were gazing at one another,

both of them relieved. There was a gentleness in her expression that told him that, somehow, she finally understood that he had not meant to hurt her.

"I wanted to make you understand that if there had been any way at all, I would have been there to meet you yesterday. For disappointing you, I shall never forgive myself."

Edward's sincere affection for her engulfed her like a heady perfume. It was in his eyes—a pure kind of honesty —and the spark between them was rekindled along with the trust, now that he had saved her life. Edward hesitated; then, disregarding Rani entirely, he bent to gently kiss her forehead. "I am just so awfully glad you're all right."

"I am fine. Thanks to you."

Just before he turned to leave, Edward smiled down at her, his sky-blue eyes crinkling at the corners, and it was at that moment that the single spark between them became a flame.

A WEEK LATER, CHARLOTTE AND RANI STROLLED TOGETHER through the Chandnee Chouk deep in the heart of the old city. The broad, unpaved street was thick with crowds of native women wound in *saris* shaded from dusty rose to brilliant blue and all of them swirled in musk. Dark-haired, barefoot children clung to their mothers amid the aroma of cinnamon, nutmeg, and asafetida.

The two women wound their way slowly through the

broken architecture and buildings of marble and red sandstone, an exotic backdrop for the local bazaar. They passed the stalls of jewelers and spice dealers, but it was a silk merchant's stall that caught Charlotte's eye. Edward Langston sat on a carpet in the front room open to the street, with a leather-skinned tradesman in white turban and *dhoti* who was showing him scarves.

They hung back a moment amid the crowds, and Charlotte watched as the dealer pulled out one scarf at a time and lay it before the crisply uniformed English officer for his consideration. The system was a productive one. A single article at a time was proposed, always saving the best and most expensive for last.

Charlotte watched a moment more as Edward considered an inferior diaphanous red scarf sewn with tiny white flowers. When he asked *"Kitnā hai?"* in his best attempt at Hindustani, she heard the dealer reply with great confidence, "Ten *rupees, sahib."*

"I'm afraid you'd be wasting your money, Captain."

Edward glanced up and was surprised to see that it was Charlotte Lawrence who stood behind him in the company of her *ayah.* "Good morning, ladies," he said, springing to his feet and bowing properly. "I was just trying to decide on a scarf."

"And not very successfully, I am sorry to say."

Edward looked back at the dealer, still sitting cross-legged on the carpet, holding the poorly dyed piece of silk as though it were a precious jewel.

"I'm not very good at this sort of thing, I shall grant you that."

"Perhaps I could be of some assistance. I am rather accustomed to the way they operate in such matters."

"That would be most kind of you." He smiled at her, and when Charlotte thought how incredibly handsome he was, she felt herself blush.

"But of course, you shall have to tell me what it is for, so that I can more properly assist you."

"It is a gift for a young lady."

59

"I see," Charlotte remarked a little too sharply, unable to mask an unexpected burst of jealousy.

"I should like something really lovely."

She paused a moment, studying him, and then said, "Why yes, of course."

"So then, you do not approve of the red?" he asked in a silvery-smooth voice, looking down at the scarf.

"It is inferior fabric, Captain Langston. They shall always save the best for last, hoping to build your interest."

"I had no idea."

"That is precisely what they rely upon," she added, tipping up her chin and stepping past Edward. *"Namasté,"* she said, nodding a traditional greeting to the dealer.

After a flurry of banter between them that Edward did not understand, the slim man with the long white mustache and small dark eyes nodded, rose, and went behind a faded green drapery. Edward watched the *ayah* whisper something to her bold young charge and Charlotte shoot back, *"Chupp karo!"* The phrase for "quiet" was one of the few he understood.

When the dealer returned, he was holding two exquisite silk scarves. One was diaphanous blue edged with delicate gold embroidery. The other was sea-green sewn with gold thread.

"Much better." Charlotte smiled.

"They're lovely," Edward agreed. "So tell me, Miss Lawrence, which would you prefer?"

"It is really not a question of my taste, Captain, but which would most impress your young woman."

Edward's lips turned up in a half smile. "Well, I am not quite certain. She's a very complex sort, beautiful, spirited, and as stubborn as they come."

"And how about her coloring? Is she fair?"

"Oh yes, very," he toyed with her. "Her skin is like alabaster, and her eyes are the green of new spring grass. Yes. They are exactly that color."

"Then I would suggest the green to match her eyes."

Edward held up the scarf to the vendor. *"Kitnā hai?"*

"Fifteen *rupees, sahib.*"

"Ten *rupees*," Charlotte countered firmly before Edward had a chance to reply.

The old man looked up at Charlotte, then at Rani, studying them both. "Ten *rupees*," he finally agreed after several silent moments of consideration. He then took the scarf into the back room to package it without further discussion.

"You are truly a marvel, Miss Lawrence." Edward smiled.

"Never pay more than you must, Captain Langston."

Edward leveled his shimmering eyes to hers. "I have found that there are some things in life worth any price," he said with husky-voiced sincerity.

Charlotte flushed. She knew by the curious gleam in his eye that his reply had nothing at all to do with the purchase of a scarf. The vendor returned a moment later with a neat package, and Edward paid him.

"Well, Captain," Charlotte said with a nod. "Good day to you then."

"Please wait."

Charlotte and Rani both turned back around and saw him holding the package out to her. When she realized that he had all along meant the scarf for her, Charlotte's pale face patched red with embarrassment. Rani's darker face wrinkled with disapproval.

"Oh, I couldn't possibly accept it."

"And why not? You selected it yourself, so I know that it is to your taste. Truly, if I had not met you here today I would have had it sent to Graves House."

"You said it was for . . ."

Edward was smiling as he continued to hold the package out to her. "I said it was for a beautiful young woman as spirited and stubborn as they come."

"But I chose such a costly one. I really had no idea . . ."

"I know that, and I want you to have it. After all, it is the least I can do for inciting your ordeal last week."

"This was very generous of you, Captain."

"Your forgiveness was generous, Miss Lawrence."

She accepted Edward's gift, and the three walked back out onto the busy street.

"Give us a moment alone, Rani?" Charlotte asked.

Her *ayah* was still frowning. "Your father would not approve."

"My father will not know unless you tell him."

The *ayah* moved a few reluctant steps into the crowd, then turned back, her suspicion still bright across her smooth, dark face.

"So then," Edward began, "you seem to have recovered quite nicely from your accident."

"Thanks to you. In fact, I should highly recommend such a scare to all of my friends, so long as there is a handsome captain from Her Majesty's army who rides up to rescue them."

He hid a smile. "I am honored to have changed so favorably in your opinion, Miss Lawrence."

"Tell me, Captain. Do you suppose perhaps we might try once again to find that chance to speak privately?"

They both glanced over at Rani, who was straining to listen and yet pretending to browse at a nearby stall full of pottery. "There is nothing in the world I would like more, but how? You are watched so closely."

"Tomorrow afternoon at five my father shall be meeting with Lieutenant Waite about a transfer of one of the men to Calcutta. It is all very clandestine, and I am quite certain that it shall take him out of Graves House at least until six."

Edward pressed her hand to his lips, not trying any longer to mask his surprise at her boldness. She was always surprising him, this young and beautiful girl with a mind of her own and the courage to use it. "Tomorrow, then. At five o'clock in the orchard behind the gardens where we first met. I shall wait for you there."

Charlotte laughed when she thought how fitting it would be to begin again where it had started off so badly between them the first time. "I'd like that very much," she said, refusing to believe in omens.

He saw her at first from a distance, coming toward him. She sparkled like a handful of precious jewels in the deep red of the late afternoon sun. There was gold and blue, the gauzy silk worn by a native woman, and jangling bracelets. At first he was not certain that it was Charlotte, but as she drew nearer, her fair skin and light green eyes gave her away. Edward was stunned.

She stood before him now, wrapped in an indigo-blue *sari*, her head covered modestly, and she was every dream he had ever had. Every fantasy. He tried not to stare, knowing the danger in wishing she would draw nearer. He had thought her beautiful from the first moment, but this added a dimension of sensuality for which he had not been prepared.

"You take my breath away," he whispered huskily.

"It was the only way I would not be recognized crossing through the gardens at this hour. I bid Rani to loan it to me," she explained. Then, after an awkward moment of silence, she added, "I hope I have not offended you by wearing it."

"You could never offend me, Charlotte."

He said her name as if they had known one another forever, and the sound of it, so familiar, hung in the air between them like her sweet lavender perfume.

"I've . . . brought you something," he struggled to say, and she saw that the adoration on his face was for her as he handed forth a jar wrapped with blue velvet ribbons.

"Another gift?"

"A peace offering."

Looking down at it, Charlotte's face lit with surprise. "Orange marmalade! Where on earth did you get it?"

"I thought something worthwhile should come from my Graves House cache." He smiled.

She seemed pleased, and Edward felt himself breathe a sigh of relief. He had almost not brought it, but his own *khansaman* had gone out of his way to make it for her, having overheard the story of their meeting from Arthur.

"I . . . want you to really understand what happened the other day," he said as she held the jar of sweet marmalade up to the sunlight, still surprised that he would have thought to have had it made.

"That really isn't necessary."

"It is to me." Edward chose his next words carefully, not wanting to frighten her unnecessarily. "My friends had heard a very disturbing rumor. They told me about it late the same night that I met you. They had thought that there might be a problem with the native soldiers."

Charlotte looked up at him. "And is there?"

"I am happy to say that it seems it was all just a dreadful misunderstanding. But I had to hear it from Brigadier Graves personally for the sake of the men. They were counting on me. If it had been anything else but the men . . ."

"Thank you for telling me, Edward," she said simply, without the slightest hint of disbelief or anger. "Shall we walk then?" After they had taken their first few tentative steps, she let him take her hand.

"I never thought of it as beautiful here," Edward said as they strolled together beneath the bristling kikar trees, their pace slow and relaxed. The sun was beginning to set, and the Delhi sky was a magical, shimmering gold.

"To me it has always been beautiful. I remember so little of England."

"You were very young when you left."

"Father says that I hated to leave," she said wistfully. "Now I cannot imagine ever going back."

Edward looked across the river at the cantonments on the dry and dusty ridge. "And I cannot imagine staying here."

"You miss England."

"Not so much England as Tetbury, and nothing could have surprised me more than that."

"Tetbury. What a charming name for a village."

"Once it was all I could think of; to leave that dreadful little place and make a name for myself. To me it was a small town full of small minds and small dreams. I was repelled by it completely."

"And now?"

They stopped at the tumbled, broken ruin of an old temple near a hill that sloped down into a little canyon dense with scrub.

"Now, after five very long years in this place, I finally see the beauty in simplicity. My dream has changed with time and experience. Shall I tell you about it?"

"Please."

"I dream of returning home, with enough money to buy a grand farm with a lovely big house, and working the land ... raising a family with a woman that I adore. I suspect you think that sounds rather foolish for someone once so blindly ambitious as I."

"I don't believe any dreams are foolish, Edward."

He liked the way she said his name, so sweet and full of sincerity. Yesterday they had been "Captain Langston" and "Miss Lawrence" to one another. Now, today, they had become "Charlotte" and "Edward," and already he found that he trusted her with his dreams, and with his heart.

"I may desire a return to the past, but I won't be going back a poor man," he assured her, wanting her to know that he understood the manner in which she had been brought up and that one day, if she should accept him, she would want for very little as his wife. "I have done surprisingly well in India—learned how to succeed here. I have sent back nearly everything that I have earned for my father to invest. He has done well by me, taking risks I never would have taken."

"You did not need to tell me that," she said softly.

"I know. But I wanted to. Oh, Charlotte." He sighed, remembering. "Tetbury is a place where a man can truly feel the earth with all of his senses; the moss on the trees, the cool water skimming over rocks in a stream, and open fields crisscrossed with woodlands as far as the eye can see. You know, as a boy, I used to run through those fields, all carpeted with cowslips, and chase butterflies, with not a care in the world." He inhaled a breath and then sighed again as his mind made the images real. "For everything my ambition has cost me with my family, my dream now is a simple one."

"People change."

"Yes. I suppose they do. At least about some things."

"I believe everything changes sooner or later," she said. They were close now. The setting sun was glistening on her upturned face and her skin was shimmering like diamonds as they stood in the shadow of the temple ruins. "I would like to believe that love is something that can last forever."

"So would I," she whispered back.

Slowly, and with infinite tenderness, Edward reached out and took her face in his hands. When she did not move away, he came nearer and pressed his lips against hers until he was kissing her with every bit of the tenderness and desire he had felt since that first night on the Graves House veranda. When they parted, he was surprised to see that she was smiling.

"Forgive me," he whispered.

"There is nothing to forgive."

"You know that I am in love with you."

"As I am with you."

This time when they kissed, it was languorously. Edward encircled her with his arms and pulled her close. He had never tasted anything so sweet, and his body surged as she willingly opened her lips to him.

"No," he said softly after a moment, pulling himself far enough away from her to lessen the temptation he suddenly felt in her arms.

"Have I done something to displease you?"

Edward took a deep breath to steady himself. "You could never displease me. It is just not proper, that is all. And I want very much to be worthy of you, Charlotte."

"How is it that a kiss could make you less worthy?" she asked, reaching up to brush a strand of wind-blown hair from his eyes.

Her touch, even so casual a one as that, was like fire branding his body, and Edward felt the indescribable surge in his loins. "It is not the kiss, my love, so much as where it shall surely lead if I do not stop us, and I want so much more for us than that."

Trusting that he meant to honor her and what had begun between them, Charlotte held out her hand to him. "Then come with me. I want to show you something that I have never shown anyone else."

They ran together, hands linked, past the temple and halfway down the sloping, densely covered hillside. As they moved deeper beneath the canopy of trees, they were quickly hidden by a mosaic of olive green.

Edward felt her squeeze his hand, and he could not recall ever having felt happier or more carefree in his life. She gave him that. Charlotte. This young dynamic girl, who had wandered so unexpectedly into his life, had changed him, and suddenly nothing else seemed to have much importance but having her.

She paused a moment, then looked back at him, the soft blue *sari* fluttering around her face in the warm evening breeze, beckoning him to follow her. Edward squeezed her hand more tightly and let her lead him until he saw a cave carved out of the rock and hidden by brush and trees.

"This is my special place," she said as they went inside.

The cave was small, and the jagged ceiling was low, so that they had to duck once they had gone past the mossy entrance. When Charlotte lit a candle, Edward was surprised to see a collection of her possessions placed around on two old crates. There were two thick gray blankets, an unopened bottle of wine, and a dusty collection of books. A photograph of a woman in a silver frame was set on one of the crates, draped with white lace.

"It is my mother," she said when she saw that Edward was looking at it. She set the jar of orange marmalade beside it carefully and perked the ribbons. "My father refused to let me keep anything of hers once she had died."

Edward looked back at her. "Her death must have been very painful for him."

Charlotte felt the jealousy rise up inside her as she recalled having actually discovered Rani in her father's bed. "Yes," she said in a whisper. "I am certain that it was."

She spread out one of the blankets, and they sat together on it. "I . . . used to come here nearly every day after my mother died," she finally said, glancing back at the worn picture of a woman with whom she shared the hair color, eyes, and even the smile. "Twice my father thought I had run away, but I convinced him that I had only been hiding between the bungalows. We were living in the cantonments then."

"The brigadier was very gracious to let you move to Graves House when your father became his secretary."

"Yes, I suppose he was. He said it was just more prudent if he needed Father for anything late at night, but I think he believed I should have a proper English model around whom to grow up."

"Mrs. Graves."

"She's not a bad sort, really. But I still prefer our little bungalow. Father just wanted nothing to remind him of my mother after she died. I think that is why he really accepted the offer."

"I lost my mother too."

Charlotte looked over at him sympathetically, brought away from her own grief by his admission. "I'm sorry, Edward."

"I never talk about it, and I certainly try not to think about it."

"Sometimes I wish I did not think about it so much."

Edward squeezed her warm hand. "Be glad you can think of her, my love. That way she will always be alive for you. At least in your memory."

Charlotte felt the pain in his voice, and she brought his hand to her lips. "Oh, Edward. I am really so very sorry."

"It happened just after I had set out for India. She had been dead nearly a year when I finally got my father's letter."

Charlotte nestled against his chest and let him hold her, but now it was not so much passion they sought from one another as consolation. No one had ever understood what it had been to lose her mother. No one had ever even tried to understand. But Edward knew.

"What was she like?" she asked, fingering the buttons on his white cotton shirt.

Edward sighed, letting the image and the memories fill his mind, and as he did, her loss filled his heart for the first time since he had come away to India. "She had the largest blue-gray eyes you can imagine, long dark lashes . . . and her hair always smelled like spring flowers. . . . When she laughed, it sounded just like a song. People said I look just like her . . . like Adelaide."

Charlotte laced their fingers and then kissed his. "I am honored that you chose to share that with me."

"I had not spoken her name since the day I left England," he confessed, and then he kissed her forehead. "Thank you for making me feel that I could again."

"You can tell me anything, Edward."

"I do believe you mean that." He smiled.

"Oh, I do."

"You really are a most extraordinary girl, Charlotte Lawrence."

"I'm glad that you think so."

When the attraction between them had begun to build again, Edward moved to stand. "It is getting late."

"Yes. I suppose we should be getting back."

"I would like to come back here, perhaps talk some more," he said, his voice going lower. "Do you think you might get away again before too long?"

"My father will be accompanying Brigadier Graves to a dinner party for Lord Canning on Saturday night. I am not invited, and so I shall have only Rani with whom to contend."

"And at that, you shall have your hands full," he said with a chuckle.

"Rani and I understand one another. She shall not be a problem for us."

Then they climbed back up the ravine and walked together hand in hand back through the orchard toward Graves House. When they had gone as far as they could together, Edward took her small shoulders in his powerful hands and brought her to him. Her face beneath the fluttering *sari* was bronzed in the last bit of sunlight.

As he touched her he could feel her trembling. *I pray God it shall always be this way between us,* he thought just before he kissed her, his desire twined so inextricably with love. The taste of those lips was enough to intoxicate any man, but already he knew that Charlotte was his, now and forever.

"I truly do love you," he whispered, and he ran a single finger along the line of her jaw.

The adoration he saw in her young face when she looked up at him made him want to weep. It was a long time since he had felt such an overwhelming sensation. He wondered at how such great fortune had finally found him as he held her close in the shadow of Delhi's setting sun.

"I know that I won't sleep a wink, thinking about Saturday."

"Nor, my love, shall I," Edward said.

As he made his way alone across the cantonments, Edward could see Arthur sitting alone on the veranda of their bungalow. He was cleaning his musket by the flickering light of an oil lamp. Arthur Moresby was a good man—a little too loud, a little too garish; but in spite of Edward's reserve, and his desire for something far grander than to what they had both been born, they had actually managed to become friends.

Now that it was dark, the army's compound had come alive with the laughter of children as they played in the dusty lanes around the bungalows. The air was filled with the heady aroma of rice, lentils, and *dhal,* and it buzzed with mosquitoes and fireflies. Protected from the Indian sun by the night, couples strolled together and went calling on one another. This sort of evening revelry was a system borne of the unforgiving heat of summer, when the only time of day worthwhile was long after sunset.

Edward stood amid the activity and watched his friend for a moment before he was noticed. His head was lowered in concentration, the shiny musket glistening in the yellow light of the glass oil lamp. He finally glanced up when he heard Edward kick the loose dirt beneath his boot. Arthur put down his gun and sprang to his feet.

"Well? How did it go? Did you see her?"

Edward fought to stifle the overwhelming joy he felt. He moved up the steps slowly. "I saw her."

"And?"

"And when the time is right, I am going to ask her to be my wife."

Arthur took the other two steps in a single leap and lunged at Edward. "Oh! That is splendid news! Congratulations!"

"I owe you a great deal, Arthur."

"Whatever for?"

They walked together back up the stairs and Arthur poured each of them a drink from the bottle of native *aruck* beside the gun. "I suspect I haven't been the easiest man to share a bungalow with in the past."

"You?" Arthur's thick freckled lips twisted in a sneer at the unexpected confession, just as he handed Edward a full glass.

"I've kept to myself. . . . I certainly haven't gone out of my way."

"True enough," Arthur conceded.

"And yet you were still there for me, urging me not to give up."

They sat down together in two worn cane chairs and both of them gazed down into the city, the crenellated walls, the domes and towers, all bordered by the last bit of flaming orange sunset.

"It actually is lovely here, you know?"

They clinked their glasses in a toast. It was the first positive thing Arthur Moresby had ever heard Edward say about Delhi. "Love will do that to you. It does change everything."

"It certainly has made a changed man out of me," he said reflectively. "I never would have expected it could happen so quickly. I wasn't one who believed in that sort of thing."

Arthur made a gesture as though he had been shot through the heart. When he looked back at Edward he was smiling. "Cupid, no doubt!"

Edward came to his feet and went inside for a moment. When he returned, he was holding the small opal ring set in a tarnished silver band. Arthur took it and held it up to the light.

"Lovely."

"It belonged to my mother. She said it was the only thing of value she ever had in her life. She gave it to me before I left England . . . before she died."

Arthur's face paled with an expression of compassion. He had been allowed to know nothing of his roommate's past, or even his hopes for the future. Until tonight. "I'm sorry, Langston, ol' boy."

"Something good has come out of it, anyway. There is really nothing I would rather give Charlotte than this particular ring. It has come to represent so much."

"Yes indeed." Arthur sighed, leaning back in his chair and looking back out across the horizon. "Life does have a way of setting us back to our course, at that."

"I wanted to ask you, Moresby—" Edward started, then faltered. *"Arthur,* I mean. I wanted to ask you, Arthur, if you would consent to be my best man."

"Me?" He coughed into his glass. "I've never been anyone's best anything!"

"Well, there's a first time for everything, don't you think?"

"I'm flattered, I truly am, but I don't suspect Colonel Lawrence will take kindly to any of this, or even allow it," Arthur warned. "Your intended being his only child, and you being a mere captain."

"I have attained a great deal in Her Majesty's army, including a rank of which I am proud. That I have been determined and clever enough to do it in only five years, and that I turned a handsome profit selling my previous posts, should help me find some bit of favor, don't you think?"

"It will never be enough for Hugh Lawrence."

"Perhaps not. But just now I suspect the good colonel feels slightly more inclined in my direction," Edward said, his blue eyes growing serious as he thought back to his rescue of the man's only daughter. "Let us just say it is a rather good time to call in my marker."

"Oh, speaking of Colonel Lawrence," Arthur said, reaching beneath the bottle of strong native *aruck* and drawing forth an envelope. "This came for you by messenger about an hour ago."

Edward dropped the ring in his breast pocket and broke the seal with his thumb. After he had read the letter, he looked up. "He wants to see me first thing tomorrow."

"What curious timing."

"It would seem so."

"Will you tell him about you and the young Miss Lawrence then?"

Edward finished his drink and looked back at his friend, his straight white teeth shining in the dark night. "Well, of course, he shall want us to have an adequate courtship. For appearances' sake. But tomorrow is as good a time as any to let him know my intentions."

THE MUSCLES IN EDWARD'S FACE TENSED. HIS BLUE EYES darkened.

"Calcutta? Why in Hell Calcutta? And more particularly, sir, why all of a sudden?"

"Sit down, Captain Langston," Hugh Lawrence sternly bid him from his own maroon leather chair.

"With all due respect, sir, I don't understand. Just last month I received a citation for the work I'd done with my regiment at Kabul, and before that at—"

"I said sit down, Captain!" The portly colonel was smoking a *hookah* and leaning back with his feet up as he gazed across the desk. The Indian pipe gurgled as he drew in a puff. Edward fell into the chair facing Charlotte's father with a grunt of disgust.

"I had not planned to call you in here like this, nor offer

you any explanation for your transfer. That, however, was before the incident across the river."

Edward's reply was cool. "As I recall, sir, you made it quite clear that your debt on that matter was paid."

"My daughter's debt, Captain, not mine," he shot back in a bitter tone. "I shall be honest because that's the sort of chap I am. I don't particularly like you. I find you too arrogant, too introspective, and too bloody handsome for your own good. But I am a man who always pays his debts, and, like it or not, I am grateful to you for saving Charlotte's life."

"Then perhaps you will do me the courtesy of telling me why I am being issued so unceremoniously out of Delhi."

The colonel studied him a moment as though trying to decide. "Very well then. I shall tell you. You are a good soldier, Langston, but I am afraid you have committed the unpardonable sin of inflicting yourself into a situation that does not concern you, and then having the gall to press the matter."

"The cartridges," Edward said.

"Quite."

"But you know as well as I that it could have brought about an incredible tragedy if those rumors had persisted."

"There is far more to it than rumor, Langston," Hugh said, and then he puffed his pipe until the room was blue and filled with the acrid aroma of smoke. "The brigadier has his hands full trying to keep that very dangerous fact from spreading."

"Then they *were* planning to grease those cartridges with beef tallow?"

"Look, I am certain you know that the natives here would like nothing better than to be rid of us. The Hindus and Mussulmans have never managed to agree on anything but that. Now that they have got wind of this horrid oversight, the Mussulmans are working to convince the Hindus that we are trying to destroy their caste and turn the whole bloody lot of them into Christians!"

"Which of course you're not."

"Great God, no! The cartridges were changed the moment the error was discovered. But the way rumors spread, it may well be too late already."

"Lying to the men about the risk certainly won't make the trouble go away."

"We cannot afford a panic in the matter, Langston. We have our hands full as it is just trying to put all the gossip to rest. Your well-meaning attitude in all of this could endanger the lives of our men."

Edward sprang to his feet, his body ramrod straight, his fists clenched. "That is absolutely preposterous!"

"The move to Calcutta is a prudent one."

"The move is impossible!"

Hugh Lawrence set down the *hookah* pipe and came to his feet. The two men faced one another like two stags locked in combat, with only the desk between them. "And why precisely is that?"

"Because—respectfully, sir—I am going to marry your daughter."

At first he seemed not to comprehend the declaration. Hugh Lawrence's bushy gray eyebrows merged in a frown as he studied the younger man who had so quickly and completely become his opponent. "Charlotte?" he asked finally in a shallow voice as beads of perspiration shined on his bare forehead.

"Charlotte."

"You shall never have her, Langston!" Hugh Lawrence flared. "Do you hear me? Never!"

"I'm afraid, Colonel Lawrence, it is too late for that."

Charlotte's father lunged at Edward for the implication, and his short, sturdy arms sprung up, his hands closing like a vice around Edward's neck. "You bloody swine! If you have so much as touched her, I shall kill you with my bare hands! I swear it!"

"Then you shall have to kill me as well, Father."

Hugh Lawrence's hands went limp at the sound of Charlotte's voice. He collapsed back into his chair, his face still crimson. "Tell me it isn't true," he moaned as a sudden flurry of tears dimmed his eyes, cut to the quick by their conspiracy. "Tell me, please, I beg of you!"

"I love him, Father, and if he asks for my hand in marriage, I shall give it to him gladly."

"I had hoped that I could ask your permission after we had concluded our business today, sir," said Edward. "I see now that it would be out of the question."

"Great God, Langston, you can have your pick of the women here! There are a dozen widows alone who have been after you. Charlotte is just a child!"

"I am no such thing!" She poised her hands on her hips. "I am sixteen years old, Father. Might I remind you that I am precisely the same age as my mother when you married!"

She had mentioned the forbidden, and Hugh reeled as though he had been struck. "I told you never to speak of her again in my presence!"

"Why, Father? So that you can pretend that she never existed? Well, I exist, and I am just like her! How can you even try to forget her when you must face me every day?"

"I can forbid such an atrocious union!" he hissed, swiftly changing the subject as he sprang back to his feet. "I should rather send you back to England than see you married to a man who would try to blackmail me!"

"I love him, Father, and we want to stay in Delhi. But if you are determined to send Edward away, you may rest assured I shall be with him!"

"Captain Langston shall go to Calcutta at month's end!" he charged, his voice throbbing with indignation. "And by God in His Heaven, he shall go alone!"

Hugh Lawrence punctuated his decree with a fist thumped against his desk, and Edward could see that there was nothing more to be said. Neither side was willing to submit, and the anger between them was too raw just now to come to any sort of compromise.

Reluctantly, Charlotte led him to the door. "Enough has been said for one night," she whispered as they stood in the open doorway together. "He needs time to calm down."

"Yes, I believe you're right," Edward agreed, tenderly touching her face. "He's already had quite a shock."

"So have I."

"I'm dreadfully sorry about that. I wanted to do everything properly: ask your father's permission, and then court you formally for an appropriate length of time."

"But did you mean what you said? Do you really want to marry me, Edward?"

He looked down at her and smiled, having envisioned it so differently than this. "I really wanted everything between us to be perfect when I asked you."

"Oh, Edward." With a sigh, she reached up to touch his hand, which was still against her cheek. "Don't you know, everything already is?"

It was nearly a week before Rani came to Edward's bungalow with a message. She stood on the veranda, her raven-black hair parted in the center and tied in a knot behind her head. Her kohl-darkened eyes glistened with intent. Against all her better judgment, she had come here on Charlotte's behalf.

She knocked softly, two small taps against the door, like a heart beating. Then she glanced furtively over her shoulder and pulled her crimson *sari* more closely around her face. She was not to be seen. Not here. Hugh had decreed it, and she took her life in her hands defying her vehement lover.

"She will meet you tomorrow at noon at the secret place. Her father shall attend church then, and before he departs she shall feign illness, telling him to go without her."

Edward leaned against the door frame, studying the *ayah* before he spoke. "You don't like me very much, do you?"

"As a servant, it is not for me to like or dislike."

"I asked the question, Rani, so it would be right to answer."

"Very well. I believe it is your karma to hurt her, Captain-*sahib.*"

"But I love Charlotte! I want to marry her."

"Perhaps it shall not be through any fault of the man you are today, but there is danger in your eyes, *sahib.* Like pools of evil, they mirror back the God Shiva; one who shall take her down into the depths without a moment's thought."

"Oh, that is preposterous!"

"You asked the question, *sahib*. I am sorry that the answer displeases you."

"I am going to marry her, Rani, no matter what you or Colonel Lawrence or anyone else says!" Edward said defiantly.

"Then you cannot say that you were not warned."

He flicked his hand. "Fine. Yes. Well then. You have delivered your message and are free to leave."

She took a few steps toward the door, her feet bare on his veranda. Then suddenly she turned back, a mysterious and exotic woman whose countenance had gone from contempt to concern in no more than a moment.

"She is the joy of her father's heart, *sahib,* and mine. You will think about what I have said to you? *Suniye?*" she added and squeezed his arm. She had spoken the Hindustani word for "please" with such sincerity that, in spite of his resolve, Edward was shaken.

"Charlotte is my life, Rani," he said, more kindly. "I am going to make her a marvelous husband, and we are going to be blissfully happy together. I'll not hurt her. You shall see."

"Oh, *sahib,*" she said softly, her dark eyes filling with tears. "I should gladly give my life to see that such a fantasy came true."

The powerful punch sent him reeling.

Edward crashed into the dusty, dark cantonment street with a great thud. Later that night, he had just rounded the corner of his bungalow after an evening of billiards at the canteen. Two *sepoys* had been waiting.

Like a shot, he sprang back to his feet, his body rigid in defense, his jaw throbbing from the blow. The tall, powerfully built native soldiers stood boldly before him, their thick legs spread wide, their identities hidden by the cover of night.

"Is that the best you can do?" Edward snarled, leveling his defenses. "Come on, you bloody bastards! If it is a fight you want, then fight me!"

One of them flashed a white-toothed smile and then held

up a tulwar, which glittered in the moonlight. Edward saw it and gave a short, disparaging laugh. "Going to try to kill me with that, are you?"

The soldier lunged at him, his sword poised to strike, but Edward was faster. He gripped the collar of the native uniform with one hand and began swinging at him with his other powerful clenched fist. The *sepoy* lost his footing and fell backward beneath the force of Edward's blow.

The two men grappled in the dirt until Edward forced the weapon from the *jemadar's* hand.

"Not especially good with that thing, are you?" Edward grunted, catching his breath.

But as he held one man down, nearly conquering him, the other loomed over him and, with the force of his boot heel, began to level blow after savage blow to Edward's face and head. Edward grabbed the man's ankle, and with a short, powerful snap, he brought the second rugged *sepoy* crashing onto his back.

"All right, you bloody barbarian! Who sent you?" he shouted, but no reply came. "Never mind. I think I know."

It was a tangle of fists and thighs as each man struggled to his feet and then fell back into the dirt. Grunting. Pounding. Raging. Edward beat the first man until he finally collapsed onto his back, groaning with pain. The tulwar lay shining in the dirt, and Edward grabbed it. He held it up, his chest heaving from the exertion. The other soldier scrambled to his feet and, after salaaming respectfully to the man he had come to murder, staggered off into the night.

"More?" Edward gasped for breath as he stared down at his remaining attacker. He held the sword up as it had been held up to him. "No? Hmm. I thought not." He wiped the back of his hand across his mouth. His jaw had already begun to swell, and the blood was flowing from his lip in a long, red stream.

"Next time you agree to deliver a message like this," Edward warned, his chest heaving, "you would be well advised to see that your intended victim did not have you so clearly outmatched!"

* * *

At noon, as the bells of St. James's Church tolled in the distance, Edward held Charlotte against his chest. She was clothed again in Rani's silky blue *sari*. Each day, the Delhi sun was growing steadily warmer, foreshadowing the raging inferno that would soon engulf everything. Even now, it came like razor-sharp blades through the cover of trees and brush outside the secret cave.

"Oh, how I have missed you," he whispered into her hair. "This week has seemed an eternity."

They kissed, softly first, then passionately, before Charlotte felt him tense against her and pull away. It was then that he lifted his face and let her see the bruises and the cut near his eye.

"Great God, Edward!" she gasped. "What have they done to you? Please, you must tell me!"

"I suppose you could say I wound up on the wrong side of a fist or two last evening," he tried to joke.

"My father's henchmen! I know it! Oh! How dare he do this to you!"

"I suspect it was his way of reminding me just how much he does not want me marrying his daughter."

"But to do this! You could have been killed!"

Edward smiled down at her, his face calm now and full of confidence. "It is fair compensation that both gentlemen feel a far sight worse today than I do."

"So then I suppose there has been no change in the order to send you to Calcutta."

"No, Charlotte. There has been no change. Brigadier Graves has refused to see me, so it is important now that I give you something." He led her into the cave and they sat down together on one of the two blankets kept there. Then at last he drew forth the opal ring. "It was my mother's. It is the last memento I have of her, and I had hoped to make it your betrothal ring."

"Oh, Edward. It is so lovely."

"May I put it on your finger?" he asked as he took her hand. The ring fit her perfectly, and it made Edward think even more than before that she was meant to wear it, no matter what might become of them. But even at this special moment, he must gather the strength to tell her the rest. She had a right to know, because now it affected her too.

"I am being sent to Calcutta tomorrow," he confessed.

"But Father said you would have until month's end!"

"He lied to you so that you would not try to follow me."

"Damn him!"

"He loves you, darling. He obviously considers me a threat. To his mind, both lying and violence are acceptable means of protecting you from that."

"I cannot believe I may never see you again!"

"That is not going to happen," Edward tried to assure her. "We won't let it. He may be able to separate us for a while, but he is not going to part us forever, that I promise you."

He ran a hand softly across her cheek. The feel of it was as soft and sensuous as her *sari,* a feeling like silk, yet warm to the touch. His body surged, the need for her quickly pushing past the desire. No matter what he had said to assure her, this indeed could be the last time they ever saw one another. A man of Hugh Lawrence's influence could certainly see to that.

Charlotte turned her head and pressed the inside of his palm against her lips. Then she looked back at him with wide green eyes, her mouth so full and pink, parted just slightly. As the need within him mounted, thoughts of tomorrow began to fade. Gently, he pressed her back onto the blanket and with infinite tenderness pulled the *sari* from her head. Her hair tumbled onto her shoulders, a golden web, and he took a strand between his fingers. Soft. So soft that he could drown in her hair and her sweet, sweet body. He felt utterly powerless against the wanton innocence of this lovely, sensual child.

Edward kissed her throat, her face, tasting her skin until his lips found hers, and he pressed his tongue into her mouth once again. He felt her shiver, felt her nipples harden beneath the thin silk. He was touching her face, her body, his fingers lost in the tangle of her golden hair.

When he realized where this closeness between them would lead if he let it continue, Edward turned onto his back and watched the shadows from the candle flame dance on the ceiling of the cave. He lay still, struggling to catch his breath, steadying himself. The frenzy must pass before he could look at her again. Even if this was the last time they would ever see one another, he could not bring himself to take her. Not here. Not like this.

After a moment he rolled back over and kissed the tip of her nose. It took every bit of strength he could enlist not to touch her beyond that; her body was so warm and open to him, and she did not fully understand the power she possessed.

"I have an idea," she said with a sudden smile. "A bit extreme, I imagine, but—"

"Well, what is it?"

"Oh, no. You would only try to talk me out of it."

"I don't want you doing anything to compromise yourself, Charlotte," he said sternly.

"This, after what you have endured on my behalf?"

"Your father is so angry now that it may well set him against us both."

"Then that is the chance we shall have to take," she declared, her soft face full of conviction. "Please, Edward, let me try."

They lay in silence a few moments more, surrounded by love, bathed in the safety they had found in one another's arms, in this most unlikely of paradises.

"Tell me about Shiva," Edward said finally when he could see that he would not be able to change her mind about this clandestine plan of hers.

Charlotte twisted up to look at him. "The Hindu God?"

"Is it evil?"

"The Hindus believe there is only one God, but that it has three representations. Brahma is the Creator. Vishnu is the Preserver."

"And Shiva?"

"Shiva is called the Destroyer."

Edward inhaled a deep breath, and Charlotte could see that he was suddenly troubled. "And do you fear this Shiva?"

"If I did, I would certainly not be alone like this with you in the shadow of one of the ancient temples." She chuckled, but his expression remained grave. "Please, tell me it is not I who have put that troubled look upon your face, darling."

"You have brought me only happiness, Charlotte, and so much more than I thought I could ever feel."

"Then what is it?"

He heard Rani's voice echo in his mind: "I believe it is your karma to hurt her, Captain-*sahib*. . . ." The memory of what she had said forced him to choose his words carefully. He did not want her to feel the same dread that he was forced to feel.

"Do you believe, as they do, that each person here on earth has something called a karma, or that a person could be a danger to others through no conscious fault of his own?"

She took a moment before she replied, trying to gauge why he was asking. "That is what the Hindus believe, that a person may pay in this lifetime for the sins of the last."

"But you, Charlotte: Do you believe it?" he asked, desperation clouding his usually confident voice.

Edward turned abruptly and grasped her shoulders. He was squeezing them in desperation. Until she flinched with the pain, he did not even know he had been hurting her. Her reply was a curious half laugh.

"Of course not, darling. I may have grown up here, but after all, I am not a Hindu. Now please, you must tell me what has upset you so. Was it something Rani said to you when she came to deliver my message?"

"No," he lied, not knowing how to tell her that the fear the *ayah* had kindled in him had spread like poison. He would rather die than bring any sort of pain to this sweet, spirited beauty who had so thoroughly captured his soul.

"Then what is it?"

Edward shifted beside her, hoping to avoid her question.

"You know, I am famished. Have you anything to eat with that marmalade?"

Charlotte bolted upright in the makeshift bed and grasped the little glass jar possessively. "You shall do no such thing. This marmalade is not to eat!"

"Oh? And what, precisely, would you suggest we do with it?"

Charlotte plumped the ribbons again and looked back at Edward. "It is the gift that marked our meeting, and I am going to save it forever. I will show it to our children one day and tell them how I caught you stealing these very oranges."

"How you almost shot me?" He grinned.

"I would never have shot you. I've never even fired that thing. But you musn't tell that to anyone. I quite prefer to maintain my mystique."

"Your secret is safe with me." Edward chuckled, then kissed her again.

Their time together was growing short. Her father would return from church soon, and if she was not there, Rani had refused to lie further for her. Charlotte gazed at the lovely opal ring that Edward had given her. He truly did love her, and he had asked her to become his wife. She nestled against his chest one last time, happy to surrender to the blissful contentment she felt in his arms, and anxious to belong to him, entirely. Now and forever, Edward would be a part of her life, and she would be a part of his. She had a brilliant plan, and she meant to see it through. Then the good colonel would not lift another finger to keep them apart. Hugh was not the only Lawrence who knew how to fight for what he wanted.

Charlotte sent her servants away and sat alone at her dressing table. There were always so many servants. Servants for everything. An English woman need literally do nothing for herself in India. Her mother had always said it was one of the few benefits of living in a land so far from civilization.

She ran a single finger down the cleft of her small breasts

and looked back at the reflection in the mirror. Edward had kissed her with such hunger this afternoon; pressed his body so close against hers that she had nearly fainted with desire. She felt as if she had become a different person entirely in his arms. She was no longer little Charlotte Lawrence, the colonel's daughter. Now she was the woman Edward loved. The woman he wanted to marry.

She looked in the mirror for signs of the transformation, but the same beautiful, flawless face gazed back at her. This afternoon she had been so free, a sensual woman wrapped in an exotic *sari*. Now, back at Graves House once again, she was clothed in convention. Corset. Crinoline. Her hair tightly bound. All the trappings of a proper English girl. Her father could kill them both now for the lie she was about to tell. *Forgive me,* she thought, *but, the good Lord willing, soon enough the lie I must tell will not be all that far from the truth.*

Hugh Lawrence knocked twice on the door, pulling Charlotte from her thoughts. He let himself into her bedroom. "You asked to see me, my pet?"

Charlotte came to her feet in a rustle of sheer, amber-colored batiste. "I want to speak to you about Edward, Father."

"Oh, not that dreadful business again. I thought we had been all through that."

"You have been through it, perhaps, but my decision has not been altered. I am going to marry him, and if you force us, we shall both go to Calcutta!"

"You shall not be going anywhere."

"I saw what you had done to him, Father, and it only made me more convinced to fight you. How dare you try to bully him that way?"

"I haven't the vaguest idea what you're talking about," he lied, and his voice rose an octave.

"You had him beaten, hoping that would change his mind about me! Well, it has not changed him, Father, not at all! Edward is not the sort of man who can be bought or beaten into changing what he believes! Not for you! Not for anyone!"

"Charlotte, please. He is not good enough for you."

"I love him, Father!"

"You are so young. What you now believe is love will fade in time. Believe me!"

Charlotte stood firm. "Change Edward's orders, Father, before it is too late."

"Even if I wanted to, I couldn't. The damage is already done. His orders came directly from Brigadier Graves."

"I don't care if they came from the governor-general himself! If you want me to remain in Delhi, you must rescind the order to transfer him!"

Hugh Lawrence moved a step nearer his daughter. "Charlotte, please, I don't understand this. You've never been a petulant child."

"You have never tried to keep me from someone that I love!"

"You must know that I really do have only your best interest at heart in all of this."

"If you force me . . ." She took a breath, steadying herself to say what must be said. For an instant, the pain in his eyes made her falter. But he had left her no choice. She must do this, say this, for Edward. "Then you leave me no choice. I shall go, and so shall the grandchild I carry within me."

It was a moment before the implication of her words passed across the anger, through his consciousness. When it did, Hugh Lawrence struck his daughter hard across the face. The blow sent her reeling to the floor in a mound of amber batiste and crinoline.

"Filthy liar!" he roared. "I did not raise a trollop!"

Charlotte cupped her burning cheek and looked past the heartbreak in her father's eyes. She had not played fair in this, but then neither had he; and besides, she would have said anything to see that she became Edward's wife. Even so bold and scandalous a lie. Rani had divulged just enough about how babies were made. That, coupled with what she had seen when she walked in on her *ayah* and her father, would make the lie believable if he pushed her for proof.

"It is true!"

"I don't believe you!"

"I love him, Father, and we want to stay in Delhi. But if

you are determined to send Edward away, you may rest assured I shall be with him when he goes!"

"I shall kill him!" he raged wildly. "Oh! With my bare hands I shall tear him limb from limb!"

"Kill him and you kill the father of my child!"

It was several minutes more in the charged silence before Hugh could bring himself to speak another word. When he did, he could not look into his daughter's eyes. "Are you certain about the child?" he said with only a slight degree of softness breaking through the rage.

"Very," she answered, desperate enough to perpetuate the lie.

"Good God." He paced back and forth like a caged lion for several moments, his face vermilion with shock and anger. When he finally stopped, he stood before his daughter, stern and imposing. "I want you to answer one question for me, Charlotte."

"Anything."

"Are you absolutely certain that this is the man you want?"

"More than life," she answered without hesitation.

He slumped onto her bed and took a weary, defeated breath. She could see him choosing his next words carefully. "It has not been easy for me since your mother died. I always looked to her to give you the kind of guidance that, as a man, I felt I could not. Rani and Mrs. Graves have tried very hard through the years to assist me in these matters, but I am afraid, in one aspect, I have failed you miserably."

She moved to reassure him, but he held up his hand. "I suppose this travesty is my own fault for having kept you in this God-forsaken place without a mother figure, or at least without the benefit of a proper English maid."

"Rani has been wonderful."

"But she is not your mother. You were my responsibility —this, this travesty, is my responsibility!"

"Don't blame yourself, Father," Charlotte said, feeling a sudden surge of compassion and regret for what she had felt forced to do. "It's no one's fault. Edward and I were fated to be together."

"It is what I once believed of your mother and I, a lifetime ago," Hugh Lawrence said, sighing. His tone was softer now, less combative, and he waited a moment more before he spoke again, as though he was gathering the courage to speak the words. "It would appear that I drove you to this rash behavior you have confessed to me today, and for that I must now pay the penalty."

Charlotte felt an unexpected wellspring of tears sting her eyes as he reached out to kiss her upturned face. It was the first time he had spoken of her mother since her death.

"Then you have changed your mind?" she asked hopefully.

"Don't get me wrong. I think this is all reprehensible. Langston ought to be shot for what he has done."

"But you are going to let us marry with your blessing?"

Hugh Lawrence sighed, then shook his head. "I don't see that I have much choice if we are to avoid a horrendous scandal."

Charlotte flung her arms around her father's neck and kissed his cheeks over and over again, far from proud of what she had done, and trying hard not to feel too guilty about it. "You may have your Edward," Hugh Lawrence whispered with a sigh of resignation into his daughter's sweet-smelling hair. "I shall not stand in the way of your happiness another day."

When Hugh had gone from her bedroom, Rani came from the shadows, her bracelets jangling. Her perfume, the heavy musk, swirled around her. "You are happy then, my *bitiya?*"

"I am delirious! Father has agreed to the marriage!"

"It is only unfortunate—is it not—that you were forced to deceive him to attain your goal."

"You were eavesdropping?"

"One who is quiet hears many things," she said, and her dark face was perfectly calm.

"All right then, yes. You know me too well for me to lie to you. But Father left me no choice. And besides, I hope to bear Edward a dozen children once we are married!"

Rani reached out to her for a moment with a single

caressing hand, then she pulled away. "Perhaps I do not know you so well as I once thought, since I could not have imagined you hurting him in the way you have."

"He left me no choice, Rani. Please try to understand that Father had Edward beaten and then meant to send him all the way to Calcutta just to keep us apart! Tell me, was it not my duty to fight for the man I love?"

Rani's softly spoken reply was kind. "Strength of character is as precious as rubies, *bitiya,* and in that respect, you are a very rich young woman indeed."

"Oh! I am so happy." Charlotte sighed, embracing her *ayah,* and in the powerful connection between them, all was forgiven. "I am in love, and after the wedding we can stay here in Delhi with you and Father. I could ask for nothing more in this world to make my life complete!"

Rani bowed and took two small steps backward, reestablishing the boundary that the British Raj had wrought between them. Secretly, she would have preferred if Charlotte and Edward had been forced to go to Calcutta. She had heard too much about the discontent among her people; the suggestion that perhaps they might well even mutiny against the English. The markets, bazaars, and shops were full of talk. As long as there was even a hint of unrest, Charlotte, this child of her heart, was not safe. Hugh did not agree. Preposterous, he called it, that native soldiers could ever overpower the might of the English. An outright impossibility.

He had forbidden her to speak of it again.

"You told him what?" Edward gasped. He gripped his forehead and sagged against the mouth of the cave.

"We had no other choice. My father would have sent you to Calcutta if I had not done something drastic!"

"But to tell him that we—"

"Well, we *are* going to be married," Charlotte reasoned carefully. "Presumably, one day we are going to have a child."

"That is hardly the point!" Edward fumed, his eyes bright blue with anger. "I would never do anything so entirely dishonorable as take advantage of a young lady in that manner, and that he now believes otherwise—"

"Please, Edward, you mustn't be angry with me," she pleaded, stroking his cheek with her finger, but he jerked his face away.

"You said it was something extreme, but if I had thought for even a moment that you meant to impugn your honor—or my own, for that matter—I would have forbidden you to go through with it!"

Charlotte put her hands on her hips. "And where would that have gotten us? You know my father was against you."

"Well, this kind of deception certainly did not help my standing!"

"Actually, you are wrong about that. He has, just yesterday, given us his blessing."

There was a little pause, and Edward crooked an eyebrow. "Is that true?"

"Of course, silly. It is what we hoped for, isn't it?"

"You know it is," he answered her, and his anger began to slowly fade. "But it still does not excuse what you did to make it happen."

She came back and stood before him, her hands at her sides. "Tell me that you still love me, Edward."

"You are all that I love in this world."

"I know it was dreadful to lie like that, but I did it for us. I would have done anything to become your wife."

There was another long silence before Edward smiled at her with a fascinated twinkle of amusement. "Well. A life with you will certainly be one of surprises!"

"And what more could you ask than that?" Charlotte laughed.

ONE MONTH LATER, ON THE TWELFTH OF MARCH, EDWARD took Charlotte's hand inside St. James's Chapel, the English church in Delhi. The bride was gowned in a whisper of white satin trimmed with chatelaines of orange blossom. The groom stood tall and dashing beside her in his crimson and blue dress uniform, and the sweet fragrance of roses and jasmine was everywhere.

As the curate began the nuptial benediction, Edward glanced over and smiled at the lovely young woman who was about to become his wife. It was the same confident smile that always took her breath away. A rush of love for him shook her, and everyone saw it. Especially Hugh Lawrence.

The colonel sat in the front pew beside Brigadier and Mrs. Graves and several of the other officers and their wives. Rani stood in the back with the rest of the Graves House servants. It was the way it must be, Hugh had told her. Anything else would have been seen as suspect. In that, he had hurt her. They both knew what a special bond she had with Charlotte. But he could not think of that now, not when he had just given up his only child to a mere captain. A commoner, and a ruddy handsome one at that. A man who one day was certain to hurt her. He looked back to the altar and daubed his eyes with a handkerchief.

Charlotte was still gazing up adoringly at Edward as the curate asked her if she would love and honor him in sickness and in health, forsake all others, and keep herself only unto him. Her voice trembled as she answered him that she would. Then she listened to Edward's vow, drinking in every word of his promise to love and to cherish her until death should part them.

Death, Charlotte thought in a fleeting moment before his reply. Their future in India was uncertain. Edward wanted to return to England. She wanted to stay. But wherever their lives would lead them, from now on they would be together. Death was something one need only consider after a long, rich life full of love and lots of children. And they were both young. So young.

They had a whole lifetime ahead of them.

"Oh, Father, I'm so happy!" Charlotte cried after the ceremony. She coiled her arms around his thick neck, and the guests applauded. "Thank you, a thousand times thank you!"

The wedding party had come out into the sun together and stood in the church courtyard. The sweet scent of jasmine and roses from the bridal bouquet sweetened the interminable dust that covered everything in India and signaled the fast-approaching return of the summer heat. As Charlotte turned to kiss Rani, Hugh extended a reluctant hand to Edward.

"You won, Langston. Now I implore you, as a gentleman and as a father, be good to her."

Arthur Moresby came up between them and leaned happily on Edward's shoulder, already holding a glass of champagne. The orchestra struck up their first tune and some of the guests began to dance playfully around the wedding cake.

"Willingly or not, you have entrusted to me the most precious thing in the world to us both," Edward finally answered him, tempering his voice with sincerity. "Rest assured, sir, I shall not disappoint you."

"I hope for your sake I can trust you mean that, Langston," the colonel said gravely. "Because if you don't, this time I truly will see you killed."

Edward's expression sharpened. "So much for denying your involvement in that last miserable attempt, hmm?"

"I would have done anything to try to save Charlotte from you," he said beneath his breath, then simply turned away.

"What was that all about?"

"Just making our own sort of peace, Arthur. Nothing more than that."

"He's a perplexing sort, isn't he? Gruff, and yet there's always a certain hint of desperation in his eyes regarding his daughter."

Edward slapped Arthur's back and then smiled. "He loves her. It is the one thing on which we wholeheartedly agree."

After the bride and groom's first dance together, Edward and Arthur stood together again, watching Charlotte and her father take a turn beneath the bright purple canopy that had been raised for the reception. Hugh was whispering to her, and she was gazing up at him, her white gown flowing like feathers across the floor.

"Your bride looks lovely."

"Yes, she does at that." Edward smiled proudly, watching her.

"I was right, you know," Arthur said after a moment. "She really is the most beautiful girl in Delhi."

Edward tossed his friend a jaunty grin. "You have better taste than I thought."

"I was right about something else. I think she is possibly the best catch around here too."

"Not any longer!" Edward chuckled. "Quite thanks to you."

"You know, Langston, there is something I've wanted to tell you for a very long time; something I never thought I really would have the nerve to say."

"What's that?"

"Since you've been here, I've really envied you."

Arthur hiccuped, and Edward's lips lengthened into a lazy half smile. "And now, my old friend?"

"Oh, I still envy you. You are a bloody fortunate soul, and

far more handsome than anyone has a right to be. But now I will say that I am honestly sorry to lose you at the bungalow. It really won't be the same around there without you to keep us all in line."

Edward cuffed his chin affectionately. "Coming from you, Moresby, that is high praise indeed."

It had been silly to worry about what Rani had said. Edward knew now, as he watched his new wife laughing and dancing so gaily, that he should not have given any more than a moment's thought to the superstitions of a melancholy native woman.

Friends had joined her in dancing beneath the canopy. The music was light and the air was still drenched with the scent of perfume and fresh flowers.

Then the dark thoughts slipped over his happiness and crept back into his mind like a vicious enemy. "I believe it is your karma to hurt her. . . . Perhaps it shall not be through any fault of your own, but . . ."

Edward suddenly felt ill.

"What is it, Langston? You've lost all of your color."

A hand across his back roused Edward from the memory of Rani's dire prediction. No. It simply was not possible. He loved her more than life. She could not have been right. Then he smiled his most charming smile to chase the thoughts away.

"It is nothing, Arthur."

"Are you quite certain?"

"Well, at least it is nothing a few days in Agra alone with my bride won't cure."

Arthur's eyes twinkled knowingly as they both looked over at Charlotte dancing and laughing. "Langston, ol' boy, I shall just bet you're right about that!"

The mystical Taj Mahal.

Edward had always wanted to see it. Agra, once the capital of India, the city that bore the palace dedicated to a legendary love, was forty miles from Delhi. He and Charlotte would honeymoon there and still be close enough to return to his post by the end of the month.

The two silk-draped *palanquins* in which they rode were each carried by four bearers. Eight other native men walked behind them, to replace the first set of bearers when they grew tired. More attendants followed them on horseback, along with a bullock cart for their luggage. The *palanquins* were covered over with rich red fabric and padded with comfortable bedding inside. It would have been quite a luxurious means of travel for a honeymoon trip had the sun not beat down, rendering them stifling inside. So the silk curtains were opened to catch the breeze, at least until the flying dust and the aroma of horse dung forced them to close themselves up inside once again.

"We should be there soon," Edward said, glancing over at her from his *palanquin*. They were being carried closely enough so that he was able to reach out and take her hand.

"I can scarcely wait!" she said excitedly, and she tried to look beyond the string of turbanned, white-clad servants who walked ahead with pointed sabers to see that the road was made clear.

Charlotte and Edward had spent the three nights of their journey at dak bungalows along the royal road between Delhi and Agra. But Edward had not touched her beyond the gentle kiss goodnight he breathed upon her forehead before he retired each evening to a separate room. He could bring himself to do nothing more. Not yet. They must wait until they reached Agra. Until they had a place of their own, without servants and travelers about. Where he would feel free enough to surrender to the passion that denial had only made deeper between them.

Finally, late that afternoon, from across the Jumna River, the grand white dome and minarets of the Taj Mahal came into view, set against a topaz sky. It mellowed the white marble into a sultry orange cream. Edward ordered the servants to stop their train, and he and Charlotte were helped to the ground.

"Is that not the most splendid sight in all the world?" he said as he pulled his new wife close and softly kissed her cheek. "It was right that we should come here. I knew it would be."

"They say that Shah Jehan built it as a monument to his wife," Charlotte remembered. "After her death, he never loved another. He spent the rest of his life in the Agra fort, looking out at the final resting place of his beloved."

Edward turned so that they were facing one another, their faces bronzed by the setting sun. "I am like that. I shall never love another. I mean, if something were to happen to you . . ."

Charlotte smiled radiantly. "But nothing is going to happen to me. I am young and strong, and we have our whole lives ahead of us. Now, thanks be to God, our years shall be together."

"You certainly do have a hold of my soul, Mrs. Langston."

"Mrs. Langston. Hmm," she breathed a musical little laugh. "I rather like the sound of that."

Edward kissed her upturned face, tasting the sweet honey softness of her lips and now suddenly, here away from Delhi, away from Hugh Lawrence and Rani's portentous words of doom, he wanted her. He had never wanted anything so much. Now, soon, she would belong to him completely. Body and soul.

"Shall we go, then?" he asked, taking her hand.

They crossed the Jumna on a bridge of boats, like the one into Delhi, and then passed through a gateway in a battlemented city wall. A train of camels, the halter of one tethered to the tail of another, passed them on the way to market, and the sky shimmered golden with the last bit of daylight.

At dusk, the party drew up in front of the North Western Hotel, an antiquated two-story whitewashed building, and Edward helped Charlotte once again from her *palanquin.* He held her hand as they went together up the steps to the hotel.

The owner, a short, gout-ridden Indian with spectacles and a bushy pepper-gray mustache, met them inside. "You are *Sahib* Langston?" he asked in thickly accented English.

"I am. And this is my wife," Edward said proudly, his arm affectionately around Charlotte's waist.

The old man pushed his gold wire-rimmed spectacles down to the tip of his nose to better assess his guests. "Ah yes. Very pretty. Well, this way." Then he added with a note of annoyance, having dealt more times than he cared to with tight-fisted English soldiers and their pampered brides, "I hope you have brought cash to settle your bill."

"Yes, of course."

Edward winked at Charlotte as they followed the huffing old man up the single flight of stairs. When they reached the end of a long, dark corridor, the proprietor opened a door that made a high squeal like an animal's cry. The white-washed room was spartan and furnished only with a net-draped bed, washstand, night table, and clear-glass oil lamp. Wispy ivory curtains blew with the breeze from an open window beside the bed.

"There are fresh towels and water in the pitcher," the proprietor said abruptly. "Breakfast begins at eight o'clock, if by then you are so inclined."

The inference made Charlotte blush. She went over to the window that looked down onto a crowded bazaar as Edward tipped him generously and held the door open for him to leave.

"Oh, thank you, *sahib,*" the proprietor sputtered, his cool tone completely changed by the officer's unexpected show of good breeding.

"Not a'tall," Edward said crisply, and Charlotte heard the chink of yet another two *rupees* being pressed into the old man's hand. "And that is so that we are not disturbed further this evening with your . . . hospitality."

"Certainly, *sahib.*" He bowed. "I shall see to it person-ally."

When they were finally alone, Charlotte fell back onto the bed in a fit of nervous laughter and flung her arms up over her head. It had been such a long and tiring day, and she was beginning to feel a little nervous, sensing that something very important was going to happen.

Edward came and stood in the first bit of moonlight beside the bed, the netting like a smoky haze between them.

Through the gauzy fabric, he watched her chest heaving from the laughter, and a white-hot passion stirred within him. He parted the netting with uncertain fingers and carefully lay down beside her.

His blue eyes glittered with raw desire as he gently unlaced her gown, peeled back her corset, and then gazed down upon her bare breasts for the first time. They were beautiful: two firm, milk-white peaks with small, rosy nipples. Like the rest of her, they were sheer perfection. But Edward must take great care. He did not want to frighten her with his need. Not this first time between them.

Gently, he reached behind her head and pulled the combs that had properly bound her long golden mane. It felt just like silk, he thought, as he draped it over her shoulders.

He sat back up and removed his boots and trousers as Charlotte lay passively watching him, still half clothed. He liked it that she did not turn away modestly, nor ask to wear a nightgown. It seemed as if, in every way, his new bride was different from every other woman he had known.

Finally free from the constraints of his own clothing, Edward pressed himself back against her, brushing his chest against the tips of her breasts. It was a painfully heightened sort of pleasure, at once like the tickle of a feather and the prick of a pin.

"Do not be afraid," he whispered, pulling away and then bracing himself over her. "I shall do my best not to hurt you."

"I am not afraid," she whispered back. "Not with you."

He fought to hold back the lust, to keep his touch and kisses tender. But he had waited all his life for Charlotte, for this moment between them, and his mind quickly spun beyond his control. He painted a trail of languorous kisses across her breasts, her neck, the lobes of her ears, for a lazy, sensual eternity, until he felt her back begin to arch beneath him—until he knew that she had begun to feel what he felt.

Deftly, he pulled off her lacy white pantalets, and his kisses grew more urgent. It would be easier for her this first time, he thought, if he did not insist she be completely bare.

As he kissed her, Charlotte tried to swallow, but it was impossible. He was still touching her, branding her with his powerful body in ways she had never imagined, making her feel a strange kind of need that forced her to draw him nearer with each wild, pounding heartbeat. His fingers were moving across her body. His lips moved to the vein in her neck. Charlotte moaned softly, her arms solid around his back, feeling a wave of pleasure like a rush of warm water, and suddenly she was drowning in it.

"You are so incredibly lovely," he murmured, his passion rising as his mouth moved over hers once again.

His hand swept to the small of her back, and at the same time, a jolt of pain tore Charlotte from her ecstasy. She felt her body suddenly tense as Edward pressed his hardness between her legs. Once. Twice. She clenched her jaw, forcing herself not to cry out. A third time. And as he moved, still he was pressing his fingers into her skin, bruising her body with kisses. She cried out as he groaned and finally thrust completely inside of her. No matter what she had thought she knew about such matters, Charlotte had no idea. No idea at all.

But holding him tightly against her warm, ripe body, the pain quickly subsided, and Charlotte understood that this most intimate of acts between husband and wife was what he had tried to warn her about. She felt a rush of love deeper than anything she had ever felt for Edward as she looked at his taut face in the shadow of the setting sun, his features shimmering with a combination of enduring love and unabashed lust.

After no more than a moment, her own heightening desire helped Charlotte match Edward's movements. Together they were fluid, both now seeking the same mysterious dark plateau. She wanted to bring him as close as possible, to feel the same sweet agony he was making her feel, when suddenly he stopped thrusting and rolled onto his side, bringing her with him.

He wanted her too much. If he pushed once more that would be the end, and it was not nearly time, Edward told himself. First, there was something he wanted from her. His breathing was ragged as he brushed the golden hair from her eyes and murmured, "Not yet, my love . . ."

Charlotte was too dazed with passion to object as he slid his firm hand gently between them and down the length of her body, lingering at the place where they were joined. It was warm and wet with the two of them, and as desperate as he was for release, Edward had wanted to feel that. Together, they felt just as he had imagined it a thousand times during their courtship, when he had dared to give in to his most private of thoughts.

His fingers toyed there a moment, feeling the soft patch of downy hair surrounding his rigid shaft. Edward watched her eyes flutter to a close, then plunged his tongue into her willing mouth. Tasting her sharp intake of breath, he lost his fight against the raging, aching desire for her.

Edward pressed her back into the bed linens, and as he began again to rock and thrust, he felt Charlotte wrap her arms around his neck to pull him closer. She was meeting his every move completely now. Her sweet breath against his cheek was Edward's final undoing. As Charlotte uttered a deep, primitive cry, he too lost himself to the warm, staggering rush that began to drain his body in furious, pulsing spasms of agonizing pleasure.

Afterward, they lay quietly together, and Edward was gentle with her again, his passion spent. Lovingly, he covered her shoulders with the edge of the sheet and lightly kissed her forehead. "Are you all right, darling?" he whispered.

"I am wonderful." She smiled. "I do so love you, Edward."

Charlotte nestled against his bare chest, and a moment later he could hear a sigh of contentment pass across her smooth, sweet lips. He was glad they had waited. It had been everything he could have hoped for with her now that she was his wife; passion, gentleness, and love. Charlotte's love had washed his mind clean of so many things; the threat that still hung over Delhi, her father's disapproval, and even Rani's ominous warning.

As they lay bound with one another, the furious beating of Edward's heart slowed. His mind grew calmer. Finally he had everything in the world he could ever want, and she was right here with him, safe in his arms.

EDWARD AND CHARLOTTE SAT TOGETHER AT BREAKFAST THE next morning. They held hands beneath the starched white linen tablecloth as a cook served a native breakfast of *chupatties* and curried rice. Kanwar Singh, the old native innkeeper, presided at the table over a collection of guests that included two American Methodist missionaries, an older English couple from Brighton, and a young Italian traveling on his own.

"Will you be visiting the Taj Mahal today, *sahib?*" Singh asked Edward as he sipped thick black coffee from a small clay cup.

"It is the first thing we would like to see," Edward answered him. "It is why we have come to Agra."

"Then please allow me to offer my brother as a guide."

Edward surveyed the crotchety innkeeper, imagining a morning with his brother. "I do not think that would be a very good idea."

Kanwar Singh put down the cup. "Might I ask why not, *sahib?* Forgive me for saying so, but my brother is highly preferable to the English guides who know so little of our history."

"He is right about that," Charlotte agreed, having known of some of the English wives and widows who gave tours of

Delhi in the cool season to pass the time and derived all of their information about the sights from English guidebooks.

"If that is what you wish." Edward squeezed her hand. "Then we shall gladly accept your kind offer."

Singh clapped his hands over his head, and a moment later, a tall, turbanned Indian with a dark mustache and beard came out from behind a drape of Turkey-red cloth.

"This is Dabi, my brother, Captain-*sahib*."

The brothers exchanged words in Hindustani, none of which Edward understood. As he looked to his new wife for a translation, Charlotte flushed angrily and lowered her eyes.

"What is it?" he asked, but she did not answer him.

There was another flurry of charged banter before the younger brother stormed back through the curtains.

"I am sorry, *sahib*. I am most embarrassed, but I am told I have overstepped myself. My brother shall be unable to act as your guide today due to a . . . prior commitment."

"But I don't understand. You made such a point of—"

Charlotte stopped him from springing to his feet by squeezing his hand as he had hers. "It is all right, darling. We shall manage without a guide," she said, then looked across the table to the innkeeper with such reproach that no one present could have been allowed to miss it. "Since I speak the language fluently myself."

The innkeeper's raisin-colored lips parted in an *O* of surprise as he came to his feet. "Forgive me, *memsahib*. I did not know," he said falteringly, and then he backed out of the breakfast room of his hotel, bowing as he went. "A thousand pardons, truly."

"That was odd," Edward said once he had gone.

Charlotte daubed her lips with the corner of a napkin. "Not so odd, for a man who detests all *feringhi*."

The derogatory native term for the English hung in the air like a dark cloud between the curious guests. Everyone at the table knew its meaning well. Especially Edward. The native people were becoming more brazen in their mistrust of the English, just as Rajab had warned. He had seen it steadily worsening throughout Delhi in the weeks before his marriage, but there was little he could do about it. At least not right now. After all, this was his honeymoon, he reasoned, and absolutely nothing was going to interfere with that.

"Well, it is getting late," he said, pushing back his chair and standing. "We had better be going if we are to see the Taj in its most glorious light."

"Yes. Perhaps we should," Charlotte agreed.

They rode together on horseback, followed by three of Edward's servants whom he had brought with them from Delhi. They rode along the bank of the river on a road that cut through scattered ruins and came to an end at an imposing red sandstone gateway—the gateway to the Taj Mahal.

Already the weather had begun to change, foreshadowing the blinding heat of summer that would soon be upon them. One of the servants rode holding an open parasol to protect Charlotte's fair English face.

They passed a train of women bearing roses and jasmine to strew upon the grave of Mumtaz Mahal, the "Lady of the Taj," as a daily tribute. Then suddenly, before them, flanked by two sentinel rows of tamarind trees, like a gem against a cloudless sky, stood the ultimate dedication to a great love. White marble was adorned with semiprecious stones. Where the setting sun yesterday had cast it in a pale orange, today the tall dome and minarets were a blinding white.

"It is breathtaking," Edward said, stopping in the gardens to admire it at a distance that made it seem more like a painting.

"I am glad we came here," Charlotte said to him as she lay her head upon his shoulder.

After he had glanced around to see that they were alone, Edward tipped her chin upward with his fingers and kissed her. "I am only sorry we haven't a guide. I hope that whole dreadful business didn't upset you too terribly this morning."

"No more than it did you," she answered, recalling his face when she had said the word *feringhi*.

"I just want everything to be so perfect while we are here.

Your father may have allowed me to stay with my regiment in Delhi, but he never promised that it he would go easy on me. I suspect there shall be a great deal waiting for me to do when we return."

"You leave Father to me," Charlotte said proudly. "One thing I have learned these past weeks is that I can handle him."

"I do believe you can at that!" Edward kissed her forehead and drew her into his embrace, then smiled his same magnificent half smile, the one that had won her that night at her first ball.

Then they raced one another up the winding stairs of one of the minarets. Edward let her win, knowing that between her weighted gown and her small size she could never have been a true match for a strength that had been honed on the brutal battlefield at Kabul.

It was still early when they reached the balcony, whose sweeping view was of the river, winding like a shimmering snake off into the distance. They stood in awe awhile and then looked back at the majestic structure that had so easily engulfed them as Edward read from his guidebook.

"It says that it took 20,000 workmen nearly twenty-two years to complete. It is covered with semiprecious stones inlaid in white marble."

"Imagine it." Charlotte sighed. "All of this for the love of one woman."

Edward smiled, brushing a strand of golden, windblown hair from her face. "Yes. Imagine it, at that."

As they came out of the Taj grounds in the early afternoon, they encountered a group of vendors selling Agra's most famous commodity, polished stones. There were paperweights of pure jasper, lapis, rose quartz, and bloodstone. There were knives whose handles were fashioned of onyx and beryl. As each tourist came back out into the gardens, the group moved in, seizing upon them with the few broken words of English they knew. But most swiftly upon Charlotte and Edward was a young boy, no more than nine or ten, who held a small tray of nothing but small polished stones.

"Please to buy mine!" He smiled up at Charlotte, his white teeth glistening like pearls against almond-colored skin. His ebony hair hung down into wide, dark eyes, which bore such startling fear that she was drawn instinctively to him.

Charlotte bent down and took one of the small stones, which was the size of the opal in her engagement ring. "Do you have one like this, perhaps in a paperweight?" she asked in Hindustani.

After his initial shock that a *memsahib* so young could speak his language fluently, the boy answered that this was his entire selection. To be polite, Charlotte held a few more of the small odd-shaped pieces up to the sunlight and then told him that she could not decide. Perhaps she should wait, she said, and then began to walk away.

"Please, *memsahib!*" he said in thickly accented English. "My mother will beat me if I do not sell just one!"

Charlotte looked back down upon him kindly. He was thin and more pale than other boys his age, and upon closer inspection she could see bruises on his neck and wrists. "What is your name, child?"

"Jawahar, *memsahib.*"

"'Jewel,'" she said, speaking the meaning of his name in English. "What a lovely and appropriate name for someone from Agra."

"Oh, really, Charlotte. This boy is obviously a professional," Edward huffed. "If you want something, let me buy it for you at the bazaar in town, where children are not paraded out so shamelessly to do their parents' bidding."

In the moment after Charlotte acquiesced to her new husband's will and had turned away again, a stout Hindu woman dressed in a faded apricot-colored *sari* came forward from the crowd of native vendors. Seeing her son's inability to tempt them sufficiently with her wares, she began to beat the boy so furiously that his tray of polished stones fell and scattered across the ground.

"Wait, please!" Charlotte said, pivoting back around in her silk gown and straw bonnet. Responding to her plea, the mother stopped beating the son, and in the interim the other vendors scrambled for the fallen stones. The boy cowered near his mother, his bare back scarred from past beatings.

"I should like to hire your son to work for me in Delhi," Charlotte said. In anger, she spoke the words in English, disinclined to show respect to a woman who beat her children so barbarically.

"Oh, Charlotte!" Edward fumed. "You cannot be serious!"

"Of course I am. How much for your son?"

She asked the question matter-of-factly, knowing better than to think that, as a well-to-do English lady, she would be refused at some price or other. The native people may secretly despise them, but the English were still one reliable source of income for a long-impoverished people.

"Twenty *rupees, memsahib,*" the woman replied, without the kindness to her son of a moment's contemplation.

"Charlotte, please! Think about what you're doing! He's only a boy!"

"Well, I cannot leave him here to face the likes of her! Tell me, would you like to work for me in Delhi, Jawahar?"

"W—What would I do?" The dazed boy grimaced in pain, casting an anxious glance at his mother.

"Not for him to decide, *memsahib,*" Jawahar's mother said coldly. Then she repeated the amount. "Twenty rupees."

"Of course it is for him to decide," Charlotte disagreed, and she extended a hand to help the boy to his feet. "I shall need another *punkah-wallah* with the hot weather nearly upon us, and someone who is able to run with my letters to the other wives when the heat of the day is too dangerous for me."

The boy's dark eyes lit like an onyx flame. "Oh, yes, *memsahib!* Yes, I should like very much to come with you to Delhi!"

Edward studied his new wife, entirely unbending in her

conviction to help this boy. It had been one of the first things he had loved about her: conviction, pure and unswerving. He was not so certain as she was this time, but he knew one thing without a doubt. There would be no changing her mind. She was determined to help him.

"Oh, very well," Edward finally agreed, half angry and half amused that he had been so clearly outmatched today. "I suppose we could use another *punkah-wallah* at that." He reached into his coat for the money as Jawahar hid behind the wide protective skirts of Charlotte's green-and-white-striped gown.

Edward looked back at her, his hungry blue eyes gleaming at the thought of what he was about to propose. "Very well, my love. I have let you have your way in this." He smiled and spoke beneath his breath. "But for my troubles, tonight I shall expect to have something in return."

She looked pleased with herself and with the bargain. Though she was still inexperienced in many of the things that it took to please a man, Charlotte liked the desire she saw in her husband's eyes. She enjoyed this new sense of power it gave her. That much he could see in her expression as they stood surrounded by beggars, vendors, and exotically veiled maidens who had spent the morning praying.

"Have we a deal, then?" he asked.

Her answer was a simple wanton smile.

That night, they knelt together on top of their bed. Charlotte's glistening golden hair was draped sensually across her soft shoulders, the way Edward liked it. The air through the open window was warm and filled with the exotic music of a *sitar* being played in the street below. Tonight it was Charlotte who began the love dance between them.

Slowly, she unfastened his shirt and ran her fingers through the thick, dark chest hair. Instinctively, she seemed to know what to do to please him. Edward found her naive enthusiasm powerfully erotic, and he closed his eyes, trying to steady himself against the agonizing desire that her touch brought.

Teasingly slow, she pressed the white shirt over his shoulders and then ran her fingers down the taut muscles in both of his arms. Such a strong, virile body. Like a god. She kissed his cheek softly, hot breath against his skin. Her lips brushed his open mouth. "Make me yours again," she whispered.

"So then it is time for me to collect my part of the bargain?"

"Oh, yes." She kissed him. "Yes."

He unfastened the hooks with powerful hands and quickly freed her from her gown, the cumbersome crinoline, and her corset. Then he came back to her, his lips and tongue moving down her stomach as her hands tangled in his thick, dark hair. Her body was alive with sensation; her breasts, thighs, her belly—every inch of her responded to him. Then suddenly Charlotte gasped when she felt the moist heat of his tongue move past her navel and between her legs.

She flushed and made a little arching movement to push him away. But Edward was stronger, his hunger more fierce. He locked his hands onto Charlotte's thighs and flicked his tongue against the sweet, moist bud that lay hidden like a precious jewel there. She cried out as the dark sensations shook her to the core of both her body and her mind, pressing her toward a passionate, explosive wave of pleasure.

"Oh, Edward!" she cried out, her head rolling from side to side, her hands gripping his head like a vice, tears streaming down her flushed cheeks. And finally he too was overcome.

It was a hungry urgency that cast away his control and drew him up swiftly. Edward pressed himself against the length of her supple body and pushed his tongue into her mouth. He tasted her gasping breath at the same moment he arched and entered her.

For Charlotte, this time was nothing like the last. There was no pain. No hesitation. Only a mystical pleasure as her body molded to his. His rhythm quickly became her own. Her legs were wrapped around him, pulling him deeper inside of her as he strained with short, rough thrusts.

Edward tried to steady himself, to prolong his own

release, but the pounding inside his head mirrored the throbbing pain that surged downward to the hardness between his thighs. Knowing that his release was imminent, Edward drove himself more forcefully into Charlotte's willing body, his single purpose now the primal, instinctive need to bring himself to pleasure.

His eyes were glazed, his muscles tensed, as he gazed down at his wife, felt her rise to meet him. He cried out her name, losing all control as his body spasmed again and again. When he finally managed to catch his breath, and he could see through the dark haze of passion, Edward rolled onto his back.

They both dozed for a while, drugged by sensual fulfillment. Then, after what seemed like an eternity of silence, he brought her hand to his lips and kissed it.

"It was so different this time," she whispered, her cheeks still flushed with passion, their bodies still bathed in sweat.

"I hope those are words of encouragement." He chuckled, and she lowered her eyes with a shy smile. Edward lifted her chin with the power of a single finger and made her look at him again. "You know it is not wrong for me to give you pleasure as I have, don't you, darling, now that we are husband and wife?"

"It is just all so new and strange."

"And beautiful, I hope."

"Show me," she said shyly, and then to her surprise, he took her hand and pressed it against his spent member.

Charlotte's eyes were drawn down to the strange piece of flesh that began to harden again so quickly beneath her touch and her fascinated gaze. As her fingers wrapped around him, she felt a tug of modesty. But she did not look away. This was her Edward. The man of her heart. He wanted to teach her, and she wanted to learn.

The full moon through the window cast the modest little room in a shimmering silver glow. Charlotte watched him lie back and then begin to writhe again with pleasure as he guided her hand beneath his. She felt powerful now. It was the power of knowing how to excite him as he could excite her, and she was exhilarated by it. When he felt that she understood, he took his own hand away and let her touch him freely.

"Everything is beautiful between us," she whispered finally, uttering the assurance that he craved.

"Yes."

"Oh, I want to make you happy forever."

Edward turned her face to his and gazed into her lovely green eyes. The desire to please him that he saw there touched him at his core. Suddenly, the need for her was again beyond his control, and in a fury of passion and love, he gave himself over to her sweet, inexperienced caress.

"Do you know when I first knew that I loved you?" Edward asked sleepily later that same night, as they lay together, still bound by one another's arms.

"Was it when I held a gun on you?" Charlotte asked with an exhausted sigh, feeling foolish now about how she had treated such an elegant and honest man in their first two encounters. "Or perhaps it was when I would not let you explain about your duty to your men."

Edward smiled as she nestled against his chest, his voice low now and tender. "Your spirit and conviction are very much a part of what I love about you, darling. But neither of those was the first thing."

"No?"

"That first night alone with you on the veranda at Graves House, you were so poised and so incredibly beautiful; and yet when I looked down at your hands, you were clinging to that railing with a death grip. It was then I realized that you were not an angel, but a real, flesh-and-blood woman. You entirely won me over at that precise moment."

"At that precise moment, I thought you were the most handsome man I had ever seen," Charlotte confided as her fingers played at his bare chest. "I felt as if everything I said that night was foolish."

He kissed the top of her head and pulled her closer. "It wasn't."

"Even then I wanted you to fall madly in love with me, you know."

"And I did."

When she lifted her face to look at him, Edward kissed the tip of her nose and felt her small, soft hand run the length of his thigh. "We really should get at least a little sleep, you know"—he smiled lazily—"if we are going to brave the bazaar tomorrow for souvenirs."

"Oh, darling, we have the rest of our lives to sleep," she whispered seductively, her eyes shimmering like two brilliant jewels in the moonlight.

"Do you mean I haven't entirely worn you out yet?"

"Of course." She answered him with a laugh that was sweet and lyrical. "But it really is the most heavenly sensation!"

They stayed another week in Agra, spending the mornings in the crowded Kinari bazaar finding *sari* fabric for Rani and a new silver *hookah* for her father. They explored the Pearl Mosque called the Moti Musjid, and the massive Agra fort. They spent long, lazy afternoons picnicking in the Taj gardens amid the tamarind and the sweet-smelling orange trees that long before Shah Jehan had ordered planted there.

Charlotte and Edward promised one another that one day they would return and bring their children to see the beauty and the mystery of the Taj Mahal. It was important to her that their children learn about India as she had, and not in the way of most other English children, through a thick layer of superiority.

She and Edward spent their nights together, most of them sleepless, in the creaking, iron-framed bed. As their honeymoon drew near its end, they had actually come to think of this room and the hotel as having a certain charm. In the privacy of this little, poorly lit room, smelling of curry from the kitchens below, they spoke for hours about their future. They made plans. And they made love.

In the dark, endless Indian nights, Edward taught his young bride to take the full pleasure from his body and from her own, and in the sweet torment that they could so easily bring to one another. And he was not always the kind and patient lover he had been on their first night. The more Charlotte learned, the more she could excite him with a single skilled touch or a languid kiss. Then his hunger for her would know no bounds, and Edward would take her with the fury of a tempest until she cried out beneath his warm and powerful body, his deft hands, for release.

And when it was over, amid the disheveled bedding, their bodies twined like fine silk cord and bathed in perspiration, he would whisper with still-hot breath into her tangled golden hair, "You are my only love, Charlotte Langston. . . . You are my life. Forever."

Forever. It was what he wanted most in the world.

Forever was what they both believed.

CHARLOTTE HAD ENTIRELY TRANSFORMED THEIR NEW BUNGA-low in the cantonments. She had changed it into a real home, like the one Edward had known as a boy in Tetbury, and the one she had known before the death of her mother.

She hung gold-framed watercolors that she had painted herself and saw that his favorite dishes were made for supper. Imported fresh York ham with cheddar cheese. Roast chicken. Moselle wine. The dining table, once dotted with whiskey bottles and jugs of *aruck,* was now covered with lace, fresh flowers, and her best Derby china. The people they entertained were no longer drunken soldiers content to wile away the long hours with inactivity and liquor.

Thanks to Hugh Lawrence's connections and his daughter's persistence, their guests were the most influentially elite of the British in Delhi. Edward had given her the freedom to love fully and be loved in return. Charlotte repaid him by drawing him into circles that, as a young boy in the lush but modest English countryside, he'd dared not even dream he might one day become a part.

Late one evening in early May, when the cloying heat of the day had retreated for a few brief hours, Charlotte and Edward attended a party at Graves House. There, Charlotte watched her husband chatting easily with the brigadier, the man who, with her father, had plotted to see him out of Delhi. As she watched them now, a smile of satisfaction lit her pale ivory face.

"Never have you looked happier," said Rani, coming up behind her as the guests mingled. Charlotte pivoted around at the sound of her *ayah's* voice.

"Where have you been?" she cried as they embraced. "I've not seen you since we returned from Agra! Oh, I've missed you!"

"And I you, my *bitiya.*"

"You have not been ill, I hope."

"I have been to Meerut. It is my sister who has been ill. Your father did not tell you?"

"Oh, Rani," she said a little sadly, "you know Father never speaks of you to me, not so that I should ever believe that there was anything personal between you."

"Yes, of course," Rani acknowledged softly, like a whisper, lowering her head so that the veil of her *sari* would hide her disappointment. After their silence was broken by a burst of laughter from a group of ladies who stood nearby, Rani lifted her head. "Something has changed. I can see it plainly on your face."

Charlotte tensed defensively. "I'm sorry, I don't know what you're talking about."

"Are you truly with child after all, *bitiya?*" Charlotte glanced around the crowded ballroom, then looked back at Rani. "You need not conceal the truth from me."

Finally she nodded in grave agreement. "All right, yes," Charlotte confessed. "It is possible. But it is still too early to tell for certain. And keep your voice down, or Edward is sure to hear you."

Rani tipped her head. "You have not told your husband what you suspect?"

"No. And I have no plans to do so. At least not until I am absolutely certain."

"Forgive me, *bitiya*, but why would you want to keep such joyous news from the man you love?"

"It is precisely because I do love him that I want to be certain."

"You told me once that your greatest wish was to bear him a dozen children," Rani persisted implacably.

"It is Edward's wish as well, Rani, and I would rather surprise him with the news when it has been confirmed. You know that my flux has rarely come when it should. I simply do not want to disappoint either of us by speaking too soon."

Charlotte glanced across the room again. She saw Edward still engaged in a private conversation with Brigadier Graves. Yes, a child would be the most wonderful gift she could give to the man who had already given her everything. By the time he returned from Ambala she would know for certain.

"I shall tell him. I promise. Only not just now, before he leaves for the demonstration, when he already has such a great deal on his mind. And for your part, you must promise not to break my confidence."

"Oh, my *bitiya*," Rani said, nodding respectfully, "need you even ask it of me?"

Hugh Lawrence joined them a moment later and kissed his daughter on the cheek as the orchestra struck up a new waltz. "Having a good time, darling?"

"Splendid, Father."

"The group seems quite taken with your Edward these days."

"They are only seeing what I have known all along," Charlotte said proudly.

"So then," he began with a concessionary half smile, "would you care to humor one so undiscerning as your old father with a dance?"

He extended his hand to her, but she did not take it. "I am actually a bit weary, Father. But why do you not ask Rani here? She looks lovely tonight, don't you think?"

Hugh's expression changed swiftly, anticipating anger. He looked at each of the two women in his life, trying in an instant to discern complicity. His lips twitched sourly as his eyes narrowed. Another moment passed before he turned and went back among his guests without speaking a word in reply.

"Forgive me. I should not have been so bold."

Rani's voice was soft and kind. "Your father and I are from different worlds. He feels he cannot accept me here among his friends as anything more than his daughter's servant."

"But he accepts you willingly enough into his bed!" Charlotte declared angrily.

There was a little pause before Rani answered her, and as she did a gentle smile lengthened her lips. "Mine are a people who do not speak of such things, Charlotte."

"That does not excuse how he behaves toward you."

"Perhaps not," Rani conceded, drawing in a breath. "But things are as I have accepted them now for a very long time."

"And does he tell you that he loves you?"

"There are many different expressions of love, *bitiya.*"

Charlotte took Rani's hand and squeezed it. "You deserve so much better than that."

The *ayah* looked calmly at Charlotte, and her words came without hesitation or the least hint of self-pity. "We always get what we deserve, my *bitiya,*" she said. "That is simply the way."

Later that evening, Charlotte and Edward took some candles and stole down to the secret cave behind the Graves House orchard. A full moon helped to light their way. After they had made love by the sounds of the throbbing native drums and the far-off howl of the jackals, Charlotte nestled against Edward's chest, comforted by the nearness of the man she so adored. This was a security Rani would never have, and the knowledge of that was unsettling to her now that she was so blissfully happy.

"How is it that love between two people can be so entirely different?" she asked her husband, her fingers twining lazily through his dark chest hair.

Edward was roused from a lazy half slumber by the tone of her question. "Is it that you love me less than you once did, my little enchantress?"

"Oh, no. It's not that. I am thinking of my father and Rani." She sighed.

"Rather sad, isn't it?"

Charlotte turned fully onto Edward's chest, her lustrous blond hair cascading across her shoulders. "You knew about them?"

"For some time now."

"But how?"

"The way the colonel looks at her across a crowded room in the moments when he believes no one is looking; that he has never remarried when there is a wealth of anxious widows here from whom he could easily choose. It really takes very little to deduce what I have."

"But he treats her so poorly."

Edward brushed her lips with a kiss. "My love, he treats her in the only way he feels able. There is, after all, such a world of difference between them."

"That is just what Rani said. But if he truly did love her, would that not give him courage?"

"You know a great deal about these people, so you must know how cruel we often are to them. They tolerate us here because they have no choice. They work for our money and they bow to our rule; clean our houses and feed our children. But they do not accept us, and I, for one, don't blame them. We paint ourselves as superior to them simply because we are stronger—not better. It is that English sense of superiority above everyone else that is the wedge between Colonel Lawrence and your lady."

"You sound so bitter, Edward."

"I told you once that I missed Tetbury. I suppose until now I just never realized how much."

Charlotte sat up. "You really do want to leave Delhi, don't you?"

"All I know is that I don't want to be a party to the oppression of these people any longer," he said, looking down at her earnestly. "Just because we have the might does not make it fair to behave as we do to them."

"What is it that is really bothering you, Edward?" she asked, sensing something greater. "Please tell me."

Things had been getting out of hand lately, and there was no longer any telling where it might lead. They had always been honest with one another, and she deserved to know the truth. But he must take great care not to frighten her. He sat up beside her and braced her shoulders with his hands.

"There have been some rather serious reports of insubordination, darling."

"Among the native troops?"

"It began as a misunderstanding about the composition of the cartridges for the new rifles they're to begin using."

Charlotte's lips parted in a soft *O* of recognition. "So it is true then."

"What?"

"I overheard Colonel Wheeler's wife speaking about it at the party this evening. She was saying that the Mussulmans were setting the Hindus against us and that they were using a rumor about fat-greased cartridges to do it."

Edward ran a hand through his wife's silky, golden mane he so adored and then lay back in the bed of blankets and clothing spread out around them. "Whatever the case, it shall all be over soon enough." He sighed. "Thursday, two companies from every regiment march to their headquarters for a demonstration on how to handle the new weapons. There shall be no doubt then about our intentions with those cartridges."

"And then what?"

"Then finally—God willing—we can lay all of these bloody rumors to rest."

Charlotte pressed her cheek against Edward's chest, feeling a curious desire not to let him go; as if she did, she would never see him again. "For everyone's sake, my love," she said with a sigh, "I hope with all of my heart that you are right about that."

A shadow in the darkness, Jawahar loomed behind a thick of pampas grass. Fearing for their safety, he had followed the *memsahib* and her husband out of the cantonments and down the craggy ravine to the mouth of a hidden cave. After they had gone inside, he drew an agate-handled knife, the only thing he had brought for himself from Agra. Then he stood at attention, barring any intruders.

The captain-*sahib* and his wife had saved his life by bringing him to Delhi, and now he meant to act as sentinel for them. They had not asked it of him. They did not even know he was there. But Jawahar believed that it was his duty. He may be only a boy of ten, but early in life necessity had taught him how to defend himself. It was the only way he had to repay their kindness. They would not be harmed now as they took their pleasure. Nor ever. Jawahar, the stone seller's son, would see to that.

"There is trouble, *sahib.*"

Rajab's voice came through the bedroom window of Edward's bungalow in a whisper later that same night. Roused from his sleep by the words of warning, Edward opened his eyes and glanced over at Charlotte. She was sleeping peacefully beside him. Slowly, he rose from the cot they shared and went alone out onto the veranda, where his *khansaman* waited for him beneath the cover of night.

"What do you mean, trouble?" Edward breathed.

"They have been meeting secretly."

"Who, Rajab?"

"The *sepoys, sahib.* I have just come from them. They seek support from all of us against you. They are convinced they shall be forced to touch the cartridges at the demonstration."

118

"Blast!" Edward thumped the railing with his fist.

"Is it . . . true?" Rajab asked quietly.

Edward was startled by the sincerity of his servant's question. He turned slowly back to Rajab, who had no intention of withdrawing it.

"Good God! The demonstration is to ease tensions, not increase them!"

"Can you be so certain?" he pressed.

"I was assured earlier tonight by Brigadier Graves himself that the native soldiers have nothing to fear."

"I only thought it my duty to warn you of what is brewing, *sahib*. They shall be pushed no further in this."

Edward looked dourly at him. "You don't believe what I have told you?"

"I know not what to believe," Rajab answered truthfully, and the words came with a regretful sigh. "They are my people, and so much has been taken from them by the English already."

"Then why have you come to warn me, the enemy?"

"You are no enemy, *sahib,*" he said with painful sincerity. "You are my friend."

Two days later, Edward's company was ordered to Ambala, headquarters for the 38th Regiment, for the formal demonstration of the new rifle cartridges. Before he left, he had insisted upon posting an English sentry at the door of their bungalow for Charlotte. It was nothing to worry about, he had assured her. Just a precaution. And yet he had held her to his chest so closely in the cool morning hours before dawn that it frightened her.

"Take this with you, my love," she had whispered as she wrapped a scarf around his neck. He glanced down and saw that it was the green silk scarf he had bought for her on the Chandnee Chouk. Now the smooth fabric carried the scent of Charlotte's perfume. Soft, fragrant lavender. It would remind him of her when they were apart, she said.

"God, I don't want to leave you," he said, trying to keep the fear from his eyes. "If there was any other way."

"You shall return to me soon. I know it."

"The very moment I can."

Charlotte helped him tuck the scarf beneath his neat crimson jacket, and then she pressed her hand over his heart. "If there is a paradise . . ." She had whispered back to him the words he loved to say to her. Ancient words that were engraved in a wall of Delhi's exotic Red Fort.

Edward kissed her, then finished the phrase: "If there is a paradise, my love . . . this is it. This is it!"

With Edward away, the days were interminably long for Charlotte, as they were for every other English wife. The ritual began with the early morning sealing of all the doors against the raging hot wind of midday. Then the "tatties" were fastened to the windows and watered down. Her servants stood outside, one tossing water on the scented grass screens, another fanning the water to blow the cool air inside.

During the long daylight hours, Charlotte was a prisoner of the oppressive heat. Only Jawahar, the boy she had brought from Agra, was allowed to remain inside with her, playing game after game of cards to pass the time.

"Tell me, Jawahar, how old were you when you began selling your stones outside the Taj?" Charlotte asked him one day as they sat together at the dining table and she shuffled the deck.

"I do not recall *not* selling them, *memsahib,*" he replied, thinking back. "It was always the way of my family."

Charlotte dealt the cards before she asked, "And for all of that time, did your mother beat you if you did not sell at least something to the tourists?"

Jawahar cast down his cards and moved to stand. There was fear in his eyes, until Charlotte put her hand on his wrist. "It is all right to tell me, Jawahar," she said sincerely. "It is I who am responsible for you now. You know you shall be beaten no more."

"It is my turn to go and pull the *punkah* cord, *memsahib*," he said softly, anxious to escape her probing questions.

"Munsoor is a patient old man. He shall not object if you are a few minutes late to relieve him."

When he could see no clear means of escape, the young boy wiped a flurry of unexpected tears from his dark eyes with the back of his hand, then stiffened into a formal pose. Charlotte saw the self-protective movement. *How long has it been,* she wondered, gazing up at him, *since he was held in someone's comforting arms?* He had come from a family whose struggle for survival had rendered affection nonexistent. Her heart squeezed with compassion for the young man who stood before her, struggling to hide the unmet needs of a child. After a moment, she carefully turned back the conversation, hoping to reach him.

"You know, you are not the only one whose parents were less than perfect. My father and I did not always get on so well either."

"But your father is a great hero, *memsahib*."

"Perhaps. But he has not always been the best father."

"Still, our paths are not the same."

"Loss is loss, Jawahar, no matter what path we walk."

He understood what she was trying to say. "I thank you for that, *memsahib*. But now it is my duty to pull the *punkah* cord," he insisted, standing proudly.

"I believe that being kind to one's self, Jawahar, is the most important duty there is."

"Your kindness has brought me here, *memsahib,* and I know no other means of repaying that than by performing the duty which you bestowed upon me."

Charlotte rose to meet him in her loose muslin dressing gown, her face and neck powdered to soften the affects of the raging heat. The dining table separated them.

"You know, Jawahar, any time that you would like to talk . . . about anything at all . . ."

"Many thanks, *memsahib*."

"Very well then," Charlotte said after an awkward moment of silence. "Perhaps you had better go and relieve old

Munsoor now. But when your turn is over, come back and we shall have another game of whist, all right?"

Jawahar's dark face gave way to a pearly-white smile. Then he salaamed properly, reestablishing the distance between them. But even through the formality, Charlotte could see that she had reached him, and at least, she thought gladly, that was a beginning.

EDWARD SAT ASTRIDE HIS SLEEK GRAY CHARGER, WITH ARTHUR beside him on a grand brown bay. Both gazed out across the sea of discontented *sepoy* faces in the gold and orange shadows of the setting sun.

"I cannot believe the terribly poor judgment in forcing us to test these things so publicly like this in front of the natives," Arthur whispered.

"Our superiors claim that doing it publicly is the only way to dispel those dangerous rumors."

"But they must know bloody well that with all the speculation, certainly no *sepoy* will want so much as to touch these new cartridges, no matter how many of us are paraded out here to convince them to do so."

"No, but if they observe, as they have been brought out here to do," Edward explained, trying to convince himself as much as his friend, "they shall see them being greased with nothing but good old linseed oil, and they shall be forced to give up their fears. At least that is the theory."

Arthur pivoted in his saddle. "Can we really be certain

that the native troops will believe that? Or that we would if we were in their shoes?"

"A public showing is the only way to at least try to convince them."

"They risk a great deal taking an Englishman's word that it is not beef tallow. A Hindu man, soldier or not, who is shorn of his caste could actually be killed if he so much as touches his wife again."

"You don't have to tell me about it, Arthur," Edward said in a strained whisper. "I know quite well what those men have at stake."

"Since it has gotten this far out of hand already, I don't imagine that a single native soldier will be willing to give in on the matter—today, tomorrow, or ever—no matter how we try to coax them."

Edward sighed thoughtfully, then nodded in grave agreement. "Yes, you're quite right, I am sorry to say. If even a specter of doubt remains, I suspect they would all rather mutiny than be forced to lose their caste."

"Mutiny?" Arthur gasped. It was a low sound beneath his breath. "Do you really believe it still might come to that?"

"Moresby, ol' friend," Edward said with a sigh, "I really don't know what to believe any more."

Before them, Brigadier Harry Graves, commander of the Delhi garrison, held up one of the Enfields to demonstrate. Troops sat astride their horses. Others stood in long lines at attention. All except the native troops. The *sepoys*. Instead, before the commander, they scuffed their feet in the dirt and made low hissing sounds, refusing to come to attention. It was their most blatant act of insubordination yet for a circumstance, it was clear, that they did not mean to tolerate.

The words Graves spoke next only agitated them further, and Edward's face went pale with shock. The commander-in-chief in India, the Honorable George Anson, was mindful of the rumors, but he would maintain discipline among his troops no matter what. Observation was not enough. In spite of the fears of the *sepoys*, and the threat that that fear posed, the new cartridges were to be used. Immediately. By every man. Including the native soldiers.

A hush fell over the grounds as a metallic snap drove the commander's cartridge into place.

Edward swallowed hard, his throat as full of dust and discontent as were the *sepoys'*. "God save us, Arthur," he whispered and felt his heart sink. "For only the dear Lord Himself knows where all of this shall lead from here."

A letter from Edward came to Charlotte by courier the next morning in the still, black hours shortly before dawn. Not to worry, he told her on pale yellow paper that still bore the scent of him, but he would not be returning with the rest of his company. He was to be detained at Ambala two days more, doing work for Lord Canning, the governor-general of India. It was an important enough assignment, but one that could have been carried out by any lieutenant. *Doubtless my father's doing to keep Edward away as long as possible,* she thought angrily as she read on.

The situation here is intolerably tense. It appears that General Anson has chosen to ignore the discontent we have all been reporting to him, and he has forced the *sepoys* to use the new cartridges anyway. Fires in the bungalows of the officers and the huts of the native men have broken out every night since the announcement was made, and most of the structures have been burned to the ground. I have been assigned the unenviable task of compiling a full report on the matter for the governor-general in Calcutta. In the dark of night, when I have only my thoughts to keep me company, I find myself wondering where this all shall lead, and fearing the answer.

In the meantime, darling, my heart, take care of yourself, and if there is anything that you need for which you do not feel you can go to your father, go to Arthur. You can trust him with your life. My heart and my life remain yours more now than ever, and my only hope, my single wish, is to return to the love and reassurance I have found in your arms.

Yours always, Edward

Charlotte folded the letter and then pressed it against her belly. There was no longer any doubt. She was indeed with child. Rani was right. She must tell Edward. When he returned from Ambala, they would have a celebration. Cake and candles and a bottle of her father's best champagne. Yes. She would tell him then.

She leaned against a pillar and looked out across the ordered row of thatched-roof bungalows. The sun had only just begun to peak pale pink over the horizon. Inside, the rooms lay in a constant state of twilight, shuttered against the strangling heat that was now only a few brief hours away. But it was the dry stillness of morning, when the dust had settled and the walls had cooled, that drew Charlotte from her bed. A few solitary hours of peace. Time to think.

Jawahar came to her from the range of whitewashed mud huts, the servants' quarters, behind the bungalows and stood barefoot beside her on the veranda.

"Is it wise for a *memsahib* to be out of doors?"

"It is all right," she answered in softly spoken Hindustani. "I am accustomed to the early mornings here."

"You are a *memsahib*, and yet you know the language of my people as if you were born to it," he observed, and in his statement was the question he had longed to ask her since their meeting.

"I was raised in Delhi. India is the only home I have really ever known."

"Then indeed, Delhi is a very fortunate place to have you in it," he said with a slow smile. Then he lowered his head shyly for having broken the bounds between servant and master.

"Thank you, Jawahar." Charlotte smiled back. "Coming from a Hindu, and considering the way things are lately, that is a grand compliment indeed."

She went back inside, and it was several moments before

Charlotte saw that he had not come in with her but remained in the shadows. "Do come in, Jawahar. You needn't stand at the door like that."

"Rajab says it is not proper to make unnecessary conversation with the *memsahib*. If he sees me, he is sure to beat me."

Charlotte's pale blond brows merged in a little frown. "Well, the *khansaman* works for me, Jawahar. Not the other way around. You must not forget that. Nor must he. If he lays a hand on you, I want to know about it immediately. Is that clear?"

"As you wish, *memsahib*." He nodded, his bright eyes lighting his small, dark face at her reply.

In the shadows behind the boy, another figure moved. A tall male in a white turban lingered a moment more and then disappeared. Rajab. Charlotte did not like him, the way he was always lurking about, gazing boldly at her when she spoke to him. But he had been Edward's butler before their marriage, and her husband had grown fond of him. Charlotte was glad Rajab had heard her. It was better that he understand now who it was that was in charge of the bungalow in Edward's absence.

"What time do you pull the *punkah* cord for me today, Jawahar? Perhaps we have time for a game of whist before then."

"Today it is I who shall fan your 'tatties' outside, *memsahib*. I am to begin at midday."

"The 'tatties'? Midday? No, no. I made it very clear that you would be employed as a *punkah-wallah* here in the house with me. It is far too beastly out there for you."

"Your concern is an honor to me, *memsahib*." He nodded respectfully. "But I am of the Sudra caste, worthless to an English lady such as you."

Charlotte tensed, her hands poised at her hips. "Don't ever say that, Jawahar! Do you hear me? It is not a'tall true. You have your own special worth in the eyes of God."

"But it was the gods who saw to my incarnation."

"Well, I follow a very different sort of god, my friend, and in His eyes we are all of us one beneath Him."

Jawahar scanned the room nervously for the furtive return of Rajab. "It is not Brahma or Vishnu or even Shiva of whom you speak, is it, *memsahib?*"

"Certainly not. Mine is a Christian god. But then it would not be my place to try to convert you to my beliefs. I have come to have too much respect for yours. Besides, fear of precisely such conversions appears to be creating enough problems here in Delhi as it is."

Jawahar cupped a hand around his mouth so that he would not be overheard. "They say that the English wish to convert us all."

"I suppose it is true of many of the English here," Charlotte agreed, her voice rising slightly. "But it is not true of me, and it is certainly not true of my husband."

"Thank you for that, *memsahib,*" he said, bowing to her.

"Well then. You are to tell Rajab that I do not wish you to fan the 'tatties,' that you are to pull the *punkah* cord in my drawing room today and every day. If that is not to his liking, he is to see me."

Jawahar pursed his lips and lowered his head to stifle a smile. "It is as *memsahib* wishes," he said, knowing that, from the shadows, Rajab had heard every word.

As the sun went down, the cantonments in Delhi sprung to life. The English came out of their bungalows as a warm breeze stirred the trees and chased away the strangling heat of the day. Jawahar fanned Charlotte with a palm fan as they walked together in the warm night air toward the canteen. It was the only acceptable place where English ladies could play cards and chatter, stringing together an endless series of dark, lazy days and sultry nights during the hot season.

When Charlotte arrived, many of the other officers' wives were already there, taken up with their wicked gossip as they sipped their iced wine, chattering like magpies. She twisted the opal ring on her wedding finger and moved elegantly into the room in her prettiest pale blue silk gown, her hair curled into long, fashionable rings.

Her father stood speaking with Colonel Wheeler and two of the other officers. "Good evening, darling." Her father smiled and kissed her cheek. She had surprised him, coming up from behind him when he had been taken up by a group of fellow officers. "You really must take away this dreadful business for us with that pretty smile of yours."

"And what dreadful business is that, Father?"

"We were just speaking about all of the tension in Ambala."

"Where you left Edward," she replied, without missing a beat.

The officers around Hugh Lawrence averted their eyes and stifled their smiles, secretly amused by his daughter's boldness.

"Your husband was charged with the very important job of writing a report on the situation for Lord Canning." He stiffened.

"To his credit, that is the story Edward maintains," Charlotte smoothly countered.

At first he looked puzzled, not certain if he should be angry. Charlotte was so dazzling tonight—so grown up—in her pale blue gown, her golden hair held back by blue and yellow ribbons. She met her father's gaze squarely, maturely. It was a look that boldly said she was not willing to believe Edward Langston had been chosen to remain in Ambala to serve anything other than her father's grudge. Hugh Lawrence took a difficult breath. His child *had* grown up in these past two months. She was a worthy match for him now.

"Your husband wired Colonel Wheeler just today, informing us that he would be able to return late tomorrow."

"Yes. Edward already wrote to tell me that, and a great deal more that is occurring. So it would seem you have told me nothing I do not already know."

The other officers watched the exchange and were captivated. They had all known her, had seen her as a child. She had become a woman so quickly that not one of them had noticed. Until tonight. Everyone knew full well why Edward Langston had been chosen for the unenviable task of reporting the unrest to the governor-general, and they did not blame his wife for the firm position she had taken. Her new independence was charming.

"Pardon me, Colonel Lawrence," a young uniformed lieutenant interrupted, bringing father and daughter from their confrontation. "I have a letter here just in from Meerut. It has come by special courier for the brigadier, but they say he has retired with a headache. As his secretary, I thought it next best to give it to you."

Hugh Lawrence glanced at the young man and then swallowed the rest of his champagne. Charlotte had soured his mood completely. "I shall wager it's nothing more than an ordinary native petition. Bloody Hindus always hoping to gain the brigadier's attention by making these things *appear* significant."

"I do beg your pardon, sir, but I was under the impression that it truly was of the utmost importance."

The colonel thrust the sealed letter into his pocket with a grunt of annoyance. "There, Lieutenant. That is how important it is to me. Now, you may rest assured it shall keep quite safely there until tomorrow."

The young man lingered, trying to decide whether or not to press the matter. Finally, seeing little point, he bowed to his superiors, walked back into the crowd, and disappeared.

"Perhaps you should open it, Father. It might well be important at that," Charlotte urged, as the two other officers looked on with their own expressions of concern.

Hugh's voice was strident. "I commend your maturity this evening, my dear. It is most entertaining. But kindly do not attempt to tell me how to do my job!"

Charlotte's face flushed beneath her father's cool stare. The edges of his graying mustache twitched with anger, and she could see his body tensing, just as it had that time when she had dared push the issue of Rani too far with him.

For an instant, the vestiges of her newfound confidence urged Charlotte to say something in rebuttal. She still thought it irresponsible to ignore a communiqué by special courier, especially when the situation with the natives had deteriorated so rapidly. It might well be some urgent news.

But Hugh Lawrence was a man of his own mind. In that, Charlotte was every bit her father's daughter.

Fine, she thought as they all stood in the midst of the strained silence that followed. *Let him have his letter and drink his champagne so that he cares about nothing past tonight. If the letter really is important, then it shall be on his conscience, not on mine!*

"Well, if you gentlemen shall excuse me," she said in a small voice before she turned and walked away.

Outside on the veranda, Jawahar was standing alone, swatting at fireflies. For a moment she watched him before he saw her. The evening air was cooler outside than it had been within. She opened her fan again and waved it languidly before her face, bored by her father and his acquiescent friends. Jawahar saw the movement from the corner of his eye and twisted around.

"You desire to leave already, *memsahib?*"

"Yes, Jawahar." She sighed, missing Edward more than ever. "I've tired of nearly everything here."

"But you look so lovely tonight, and you have only just arrived."

Charlotte put her hand on the boy's shoulder as they descended the three steps into the night. "Thank you, Jawahar," she said. "But tonight I have finally seen it all, and, as they say, the bloom is definitely off the rose where the ladies of Delhi are concerned. Tell me, would you like to play another game of whist before we retire?"

He smiled up at her, feeling the pressure of her fingers on his back. The caring nuance was a foreign sensation to him. "Very well, *memsahib,*" he struggled to say. "But only if you do not let me win so easily this time."

"Oh, I am not going to let you win this time at all." She laughed a sweet, gentle laugh. "This time it is all-out war!"

9

ONLY A FEW HOURS MORE.

Charlotte lay alone in her bed, her body awash in perspiration. She was lulled by the steady whirring of the *punkah*, which moved the stifling air in the steely gray hours just before dawn. It was already far too hot to sleep, so she listened to the doors being sealed and the tatties being watered down to ward off the furnace of heat and dust that would soon descend upon them.

Everyone in the cantonments would be riding into town to hear Mass at St. James's Church before long, she thought. But this morning they would have to go without her. Charlotte rolled onto her side and tried not to be sick again.

Once the most splendid time of the day, mornings had now become her enemy as the child within her grew. She reached down and felt her belly, which bore the beginnings of new life. Since Edward had left, she had been sick to her stomach every morning, until she could choke down some weak tea and toast that Edward's increasingly insolent *khansaman* brought. Until then, even so much as the aroma of curry from the kitchens nearby sent her scrambling for a chamber pot.

This morning, to her surprise, it was Rani who brought her tray. She breezed into the dark room at five o'clock, mercifully free of the sandalwood aroma that usually swirled into the room around her.

"What is it?" Charlotte groaned, still unable to sit up.

"First you must try to take some of the tea, *bitiya*. I shall help you."

131

Charlotte forced herself with great determination to swallow the first bite of toast and take a sip of the tea, then another, before she fell back against the cool cotton pillows.

"Better?" Rani asked.

Charlotte smiled weakly, feeling the wave of nausea slowly begin to recede.

"Your father has sent me," her *ayah* said, taking away the tea and pressing a cool cloth to Charlotte's forehead.

"Is he all right?"

"First, he has asked that I apologize to you. I was to tell you that you were right. The letter borne to him at the canteen last evening was of the utmost importance, and he well should have opened it when you bid him. He begs your forgiveness for having been so harsh about it."

"And why did he not come himself?" she asked, feeling sick again and quarrelsome.

"He has sent me to tell you that you are to stay inside until he is able to send someone to tell you differently. He has had to take the guard that your husband left for you and post him elsewhere."

Charlotte cast off the thin cotton sheet and pulled back the netting. "What has happened? Please, you must tell me."

Rani quickly scanned the room, looking for servants who might be listening. "Perhaps nothing," she whispered. "At least not yet."

"You must tell me. Is it Edward? Is he in danger?"

"It is the *sepoys,* my *bitiya.* Quite a number of them have come from Meerut, and they are stirring up trouble down in the city. Your father and two companies have been dispatched to see that they do not advance up here to the cantonments."

"The cartridges!" Charlotte muttered a gasp of comprehension as she pressed her fingers to her lips.

"How is it that you know about such things?"

"Edward hides nothing from me, Rani. He told me all about the horrid oversight of greasing them with lard and

132

pig fat, and what a panic that has incited among the native troops."

Rani lowered her eyes, along with the tone of her voice. "Did he also tell you about the rumor that someone among the English is grinding bones into a powder and mixing it into our flour?"

"Oh! That is horrible! I cannot believe such a thing is true, on top of everything else!"

"But what we believe is unimportant. It is the native troops who believe it, and they see it as yet another attempt by the British Raj to force our men to lose their caste and therefore be vulnerable to a Christian conversion."

Charlotte rose from her bed in the shadowy half darkness of early morning. "This is very serious."

Rani stood to face her. "I believe that it is."

"Might we actually be in danger of some sort of rebellion?"

Lifting her dark eyes to Charlotte's enigmatic green ones, Rani said, "I do not want to believe it could be true. My people are, at heart, a peace-loving people. But if they are roused by the Mussulmans . . ."

"Edward always said the Mussulmans were just looking for a cause to unite with the Hindus against us. It seems as if they may very well have found it in all of this."

"Yes," Rani whispered sadly. "I believe you could be right."

"Then you must stay with me. I have a gun and servants who will stand with us. You shall be safe here."

"It is not I who have something to fear, *bitiya*," she said, and her voice shook with emotion. "You must keep safely out of sight until your father sends word that it is all right again."

"But where will you go?"

"My place is as it has been, with your father. I shall wait for his return at Graves House."

She reached out, and the two women embraced, feeling a shared sense of fear, yet neither of them were able to put it into words. "He does not deserve your kindness, you know."

Rani tried to smile. "Perhaps that is so, child. But he is still the man who has my heart."

She then handed Charlotte a drab apricot *sari*. It was the color and texture a woman wore when she did not wish to draw attention to herself. "What is this for?"

Rani pressed Charlotte's hand into the silk. "I pray you shall not have need of this, *bitiya*, but I thought you should have something to disguise yourself if it comes to that."

"Rani, you're frightening me."

"I want to see you safe. Take it, please. You know how it is to be worn."

Once they had embraced again, Rani hastened to the door, pulling her own *sari* close around her face. As Rajab opened the door for her, she turned back around one last time. "Am I to tell the colonel-*sahib* that you have agreed to stay inside?"

"You may tell my father I shall do as he asks, no matter what."

She held out her hand, and for a moment the two women twined fingers once again. "But if you hear anything from Edward, anything at all," she said, and then the sentence died on her lips. There was no need to say anything more.

As it had always been, Rani understood.

Charlotte sat beside the window, peering out past the shaded veranda from behind the blinds. She still wore her white muslin nightgown, and her lustrous blond hair was pulled away from her face and tied with a pink velvet ribbon. It was more than two hours since Rani had come to warn her. There must be some sort of news soon. From her father. From Edward. From anyone. What she could see for herself was not good, and she struggled to stave off her own increasing sense of panic.

Out in the street, between the bungalows, Mrs. Hutchinson, the judge's wife, was running without a proper hat or gown. Her long, pepper-gray hair was flowing down her back in a half-twined braid, and she was carrying one of her crying children in her arms. Her *ayah* trailed behind her with another. In the opposite direction, servants were scurrying, some in their *dhotis* and turbans, others still in English trousers and red sashes, frantic expressions on their dark, perspiration-washed faces. Behind them were oxen loaded with guns and infantrymen coaxing them with whips to move faster.

Charlotte could hear her servants speaking in hushed tones out on the veranda. The men had stopped fanning the wet tatties, and the rooms of her bungalow had quickly become stifling. She caught only a few disjointed words as she strained to hear them. Inevitable, they said. Important. *Feringhi.* Revolution!

She felt the color drain from her burning face. Her heart thumped against her ribcage. She had never known fear in India, fear of these mysterious people. Until today. But it was happening. A mutiny. The *sepoys* had taken a stand. *Mother Mary, help us all,* Charlotte whispered. As she made the sign of the cross, a knock sounded at the front door. It was an urgent rapping that did not cease until Rajab answered it. Mrs. Holland's native driver had come to bid her join the other ladies in hiding at the Flagstaff Tower.

Charlotte came past the curtains out of her bedroom. The two native men stood speaking in hushed tones in her small, darkened drawing room. "This man says you must hide with the other English ladies," Rajab said to her without bothering to turn around. As he spoke, his voice was hard and sharp.

"I must wait for my father."

A strained silence followed her reply, and then she heard the other man whisper in Hindustani that it was no use anyway whether she came or not. She moved to reprimand his insolence, but after she took the first step, something bid her to remain silent.

"He says the order comes from your commander, *memsahib.* The man you call 'Brigadier.'" Rajab translated coolly, his back still facing her.

By his tone, Edward's *khansaman* had made it clear to her that he did not care whether she chose to go or not. He had, however, discharged his duty by telling her that the order had come from someone she, not he, must obey.

Charlotte thought about going to join the other wives, but Rani had been so insistent. Wait, her father had said. And so wait she must. He would explain her lack of compliance to the brigadier over coffee at the officers' club in the morning, when all of this had passed. After all, any sort of rebellion was bound to be put down quickly. It would all be over by this evening anyway. Yes. In spite of her fear, she must wait. At least a little while longer.

Until the early hours of the afternoon, Charlotte sat alone inside her bungalow, listening to the sounds of panic build to a crescendo outside her door. The steady clop of oxen. Horses. Children crying. Women muttering prayers as they passed. Rajab, with the water carrier and two coolies, sitting out on the veranda, laughing. By three o'clock her nerves were raw and on edge.

Charlotte stopped pacing and glanced up at the ebony clock. Quarter past three. Finally she rang the little crystal bell for the *khansaman*. She would have a glass of Edward's brandy to calm her nerves. Yes, brandy. Her father would be sending a messenger any moment. He had known what he was doing by telling her to stay here, and she trusted him. She rang the bell again. Several minutes later, Rajab strolled into the dark drawing room, wearing only a native *dhoti*. His feet and chest were bare.

"Where are your trousers and tunic, Rajab?" Charlotte gasped at the sight of the nearly naked dark-skinned man.

"They were uncomfortable in the heat, so I have thrown them away," he answered without flinching, daring her with his dark, penetrating eyes to object.

"I would like you to fetch me a brandy," Charlotte said coolly, refusing to let him see her fear.

She could see the resistance in the normally acquiescent house steward, but Charlotte faced him squarely, not so much as blinking an eye as she looked up at him. After an interminably long silence, Rajab picked up the small crystal bell from the table and tossed it to the floor, shattering it to bits. Then, without benefit of explanation or apology, he simply turned and walked out of the bungalow. He had been forced to make a stand. In it, he had chosen to believe his own people.

Charlotte fell limply into one of her mother's chintz-covered chairs and fought to catch her breath. Her mind was reeling, but thoughts were whirling past the fear. Should she run? Hide? Perhaps she should try to find the other wives after all. She must keep her senses about her, she told herself, but it was nearly impossible with the climate of panic filtering through the unbearably still heat, into her room, into her skin—into her mind.

No more than a moment after she had fallen into the chair, she sprang from it and began to pace again. Without the cool watered tatties or the *punkahs* blowing, the sealed bungalow was like an inferno. Perspiration washed across Charlotte's pale alabaster face in the rancid, yellow heat of afternoon. It was like a monstrous weight pressing down on her. She could feel her body dripping beneath the thin, cambric dressing gown into which she had changed. Rajab was lost to her, and she was quite certain now that the devotion of the rest of her native servants had gone with him. She said a silent prayer that Jawahar had remained; that he too had not forsaken her. She called him in a quivering, fear-filled voice. After only a moment he appeared before her, bowing low.

"Are you the only one left?"

"I am, *memsahib.*"

"So be it," she said and then took a deep, steadying breath. "I want you to help me gather my personal belongings. There is a valise there behind the curtain. And do you still have your knife? The one you brought with you from Agra?"

"Yes, *memsahib,*" he said, pulling it forth proudly.

"Good." She smiled an uneasy smile. "We may well have need of it before this day is through."

Jawahar ran to retrieve the valise as Charlotte went into the bedroom she had shared all too briefly with Edward. She stood, trying to decide what few things to take if it came to that. On the nightstand beside the oil lamp was a photo taken on their wedding day. She scooped it up with a trembling hand and tried not to look too long at Edward's smiling face. He had been so happy that day. So proud. *Keep him safe,* she said in silent prayer.

Into the valise went an odd assortment of mementoes. They were the things that came first to her mind in the dark moments of an increasing panic. The photo. The bracelet her father had given her for her birthday. A book of John Keats's poetry that had belonged to her mother. She had always loved best his poem "When I Have Fears." Ironic, Charlotte thought, trying to still her mind.

Next she found the Colt pistol, the one she had held against Edward that first day in the garden. She would probably never need to use it. Of course not. But just the knowledge that she had a weapon helped push the mounting terror a little farther back in her mind.

Just as she pushed the gun into a deep pocket in her dressing gown, she heard the floorboards creak behind her. Charlotte swung around and saw Jawahar standing at the bedroom door. Beside him was Arthur Moresby, out of breath, his summer uniform of khaki frockcoat and white overalls caked with sweat and dust. Relieved to see a friendly face, Charlotte sailed into his arms.

"Oh, thank God! Have you come about Edward?"

Arthur let her hold onto him a moment longer, dazed from the fighting, from the carnage he had seen, and comforted by the soft feel of a woman, so warm and supple, pressed against him. Even if she was another man's wife.

"It is not about Edward. I pray God he shall not return from Ambala in the midst of this!" Arthur finally said as he carefully unwrapped her arms from around his neck. "There is no way to warn him what sort of lions' den he would be riding into."

Charlotte's thumping heart twisted. "What has happened?"

"He asked me to watch out for you, Charlotte, and so I have come to warn you. That much I shall do for a friend before I am called to return to the fighting."

As she stepped back, she saw now how shaken he was. She could also see that the arm of her white cambric dressing gown was covered in blood. His blood.

"Dear God, you've been shot!" she cried, gazing at the area of his arm above the elbow where his shirt sleeve and jacket had been torn away.

"It is just a flesh wound. I shall be all right."

"Then it has happened. The *sepoys* have mutinied."

"They are murdering everyone in their path," he said wearily. "It is the most vicious carnage I have ever seen."

"Here. Come. You must rest," she said, leading him to a chair. "Jawahar, fetch me the brandy and some bandages quickly!"

"They began their evil work yesterday in Meerut, and when they could not kill enough of us off to satisfy their bloodlust there, they came to Delhi."

"The message," Charlotte muttered, remembering the letter her father had gotten, and his apology. Rani had told her that it had been important after all. "It was a warning to my father. . . ."

"I went down to the city this morning when I saw all of the commotion up here in the cantonments. I regret to tell you, Charlotte, that when I entered through the Cashmere Gate . . ."

He took a difficult breath and waited for Jawahar to bring the brandy. Arthur left the glass on the tray and drank straight from the bottle. As he continued his explanation, his voice quivered. "It was the worst thing I have ever seen in my life. All of the officers of the 54th had been murdered and were . . . lying dead. The telegraph wires had been cut. The operators killed. Even that nice family who ran the English bank were not spared."

"God help us," Charlotte whispered, making the sign of the cross again as a flurry of tears stung her eyes.

He could see that telling her this much had been enough. She had been a sheltered young woman, and there was no need to describe the viciousness with which the men had been murdered. Some had been shot in the back, others bayoneted and left to die in the burning sun. The sound of moaning, the death rattle, were things that would haunt him for the rest of his life.

"What should we do?" she asked, dressing his arm with bandages.

"The other women have gone to the Flagstaff Tower, but it is too dangerous for you to try to get there now. All of Delhi is crawling with angry *sepoys.*"

"I don't understand why my father did not send for me."

"At this point, Charlotte, I doubt if he could have gotten to you. I barely managed myself."

"Well, at least I must try to get to the Tower with the others then, musn't I?"

He put his hand on her arm. "Charlotte, this is a fury that knows no bounds. They are butchering women and children too. It would be too great a risk."

Charlotte tried to think, tried to quiet the panic that raced through her mind, making her feel faint. "Well, you will stay with us here then. I have a gun. Jawahar has his knife. Together with your weapons, we shall be able to hold them off if they come."

Arthur's smile was strained by the pain of the gunshot wound that had torn away a part of his arm and by the reality of what he knew he must say to her. "I am glad to hear that you have a weapon," he said, struggling to his feet. "It shall make what I have to do that much easier. I cannot stay. The 38th is mounting an offensive, and I must be with them. These bloody savages cannot be allowed to succeed."

Charlotte fell back on her heels, still at Arthur's feet, and took in a difficult breath. "Of course, you are right. Jawahar and I shall be fine here. Besides, I have no doubt that you shall have them at bay by nightfall."

"Your confidence shall give me strength," he said, trying not to let her see his fear.

She helped him to his feet, and they stood facing one another in silence for several moments, musket fire popping in the distance like firecrackers. Finally, she helped him back on with his dusty coat and shako.

"I really detest leaving you here alone. I suspect all of your servants have gone too."

"This morning." She nodded.

"I shall protect her," Jawahar said proudly, pulling his long, agate-handled knife from his *dhoti* again.

Arthur scowled at the boy, acknowledging him for the first time. He had seen too much carnage today to trust any native, no matter how well meaning his smile.

"I can get rid of him for you, Charlotte," he said coldly. "Or at least do away with that knife. I would not trust him if I were you."

"I am safe with Jawahar," she said, with such confidence that it made the boy's heart swell with devotion. Considering the circumstances, the *memsahib* had just made a huge leap of faith. It was a declaration he would never forget.

"Now you must go," Charlotte said. "And if you see Edward, tell him to take great care, and that I am waiting for him."

"It is promised," he said, trying to smile, then letting her embrace him again. As she did, a sudden desire jerked inside him, the feel of her trembling body so small and helpless against his, and he was ashamed to realize the sensation it stirred within him.

It was the closest Arthur Moresby had been to the feel of a woman's body in a very long time. Before the day was through, the sharp thrust of a bayonet would see that he would never come so close again.

Flash!

The front door of the bungalow blew open to a furnacelike wind and two turbanned, power-drunk *sepoys* burst in. They smelled of sweat and blood, and both were laughing evilly. One held up a musket, the other a sharp tulwar that glistened in a shaft of sunlight behind them.

It was over an hour since Arthur had left Charlotte and her last remaining servant to their destiny. Now, all around the cantonments, bungalows were burning. The thatched roofs were going up like matchsticks in the blazing, dry afternoon sun, accompanied by the sound of shattering glass, the crack of musket fire, and women screaming. The wind carried the smoke in through the windows and through the door behind the two men, surrounding them in a thick, gray cloud, so that they appeared as ghostlike apparitions.

Charlotte and Jawahar clung to one another beneath the gauzy tablecover, as the two men broke every bottle of brandy, whiskey, and wine they could find and spread them across the floor to ignite a blaze. In one hand, Charlotte held the boy in a death grip to keep him quiet. In the other, she held the gun. Jawahar held his knife. If only they were quiet, they might escape through the window after the vicious soldiers had gotten what they had come for and moved on to the next bungalow. But fortune was not on their side.

Laughing and snarling like dogs, one of the *sepoys* began searching for the first thing to ignite a blaze.

"Is ko jalado!" he brayed, his eyes shooting ebony fire.

The Hindustani phrase was clear: Burn it all! The nearest thing was the tablecover. The moment the first orange spark of fire took hold of the cloth, Charlotte clutched Jawahar's hand and scrambled out from beneath it. The furtive movement had cost them the gun as she felt it slip from her grasp near the now blazing table.

The stunned expressions told them that the two soldiers were surprised to find that any of the pampered *memsahibs* had been left behind. The shock quickly faded in the face of one, replaced by a greedy, evil-eyed lust. The other soldier pulled his arm.

"We haven't time for that," he said with a knowing Hindustani reproach.

"I shall make time for one so fair," he answered in a wet-lipped, salivating slur, picking up Charlotte's pistol.

The room had filled quickly with blinding smoke from the burning tablecover, and the flames had begun to ignite one of the chintz-covered chairs. Jawahar stepped bravely before his mistress.

"She has converted! Please have mercy!" he pleaded in their shared language, knowing that his simple, blunt knife was no match for the might of these soldiers.

The two *sepoys* exchanged a glance. The laughter of one incited the other as they stumbled nearer.

"Speak to them!" Jawahar urged her. "It is our only hope!"

"Maafi dijiyè!" Charlotte pleaded for mercy.

But they laughed all the louder and called her a parrot for the way she had repeated the words. As one of the chairs began to burn, Charlotte gasped for breath in the yellow haze of smoke and flames and held her hand across her face.

"Give me your ring!" one of the *sepoys* demanded, seeing the sparkle of opal and silver.

"Never!" Charlotte yelled, their eyes clashing in a combative stare.

"Then I shall cut off your hand to get it!"

"And I shall cut off the other!" His accomplice laughed a cold and blood-curdling chortle.

Charlotte waited a moment before she twisted the opal ring from her swollen finger and tossed it to the ground defiantly. The larger of the two soldiers, the one who had leered at her, bent over to pick it up, and their eyes met again. His were bright with desire.

"Now your gown!"

Charlotte lifted her chin defiantly. "I shall burn first!"

"Remove it!"

The two *sepoys* laughed again and bantered obscenities as they watched Charlotte unfasten her gown with trembling hands. When one of them swaggered toward her, loosening his trousers, the other lunged at Jawahar and held his arms behind his back.

"Run, *memsahib!*" Jawahar cried out, but the soldier pulled her to him and let out a lecherous growl. The sour smell of Palm liquor was heavy on his breath.

Charlotte felt the revulsion through the fear as it rose like a hard fist from the pit of her stomach, and she felt an overwhelming urge to vomit. He was fingering her bare neck and breasts with huge callused hands and pressing her body against his so that she could feel his hardness through his thin, native trousers.

"For the love of God, I am with child!" she cried out. But

her plea only seemed to excite him all the more as he dragged her by the hair into the bedroom amid Jawahar's wailing cries to stop.

In the dark and stifling bedroom, he placed the gun on the bedside table, tossed her onto the veiled bed, and tore away the netting. He was grunting and laughing as he struggled to strip her of the rest of her clothing.

The silver bracelet her father had given her for her sixteenth birthday caught on her sleeve as he pulled it, and it broke. It landed on the floor with her dressing gown.

Charlotte closed her eyes to his evil, sweat-drenched face as he sprawled over her and, with no warning, began the ramming, thrusting invasion of her body. Instinctively, she tensed against him. *Let me die!* she thought. *Surely my death is better than living with the memory of this!*

Feeling her resistance, the *sepoy* arched up and pelted her across the face with such force that she lay stunned, her ears ringing. It had dizzied her just long enough for him to take the advantage he had sought, violating her body with a single, excruciating thrust. Her mind was swimming in pain and revulsion as he writhed over her.

She wanted to die. She wanted it all to be over. But past the horror, the memory of her Colt pistol bled through. She had seen him put in on the bedside table. So near. And he was touching her, kissing her with a wet, open mouth. His foul sweat dripped in her face. No one would blame her. She must try to kill him. *Edward! Oh, Edward, where are you now!*

When she reached, and he felt her body straining against his, he struck her again hard across the face, beating her repeatedly into submission with a hard fist. Suddenly there was blood running down her cheek, and she was gasping for breath. The blood was running like water from her nose. He had broken it. Stirred by the violence against her, the native soldier grew more furious, tearing her fragile body with his need.

Again she reached, fingering, straining for the weapon, and he was gasping as he rocked against her. There was so much of his perspiration falling into her face that it was clouding her eyes, mingling with the blood from her nose into her mouth that she fought the urge to gag. But she would not make a sound. Nothing must alert him. Not now. If she was to survive this, she must reach the pistol before he was done with her.

Now, as she felt his huge, groping body surge, she knew that there were only moments left between her life and death. She had blocked the pain and the degradation with one thought alone. The gun. She must get the gun! She felt the cold steel at the end of her fingertips at the same moment she felt his body arch and begin to spasm inside her. *Must grab onto it . . . Must grab it now . . . Must . . .*

Thud!

A single shot fired into his back sounded as loud as cannon fire in her mind. The lurching *sepoy* fell limp against her, the weight of his hulking body pressing the life out of her. Suddenly they were both covered in blood. His blood. Arthur's blood. Red like a crimson tide. Sweat and blood.

By instinct alone, Charlotte heaved him off of her quickly and crouched down, using the bed as a shield against the other soldier as she aimed the gun at the door. *So help me, God, I shall kill him too!*

But the smoke had engulfed her bedroom. Flames wrapped around the corner and licked the pale pink walls, so that she could no longer see past the bed. Her face throbbed with the pain of her injuries, and her nose was still bleeding. She could tell by the excruciating sensation and the amount of blood that her nose, and possibly more, had been broken. Her hands were trembling so violently that she could not hold the gun steady. At last it fell from her grasp in the choking, acrid air. *It is over for me. I am going to die. . . . And I would rather die, than have to live with the memory of this. . . .*

It was the last thought she had before Charlotte lost consciousness.

DEAR GOD ALMIGHTY! HE WAS PRAYING. DO NOT TAKE HER!

Edward lashed his horse, driving the snorting, thundering animal toward Delhi. *Dear God, I beg You,* he pleaded to a cloudless evening sky as a hot, harrying wind whipped his face, *do not let me be too late!*

He had heard the news of the mutiny five miles back, from a grime-streaked artillery captain who had escaped bloodied and badly wounded. He had stumbled through scrub and prickly pear and was hiding in a thick of pampas grass when Edward stopped to let his horse rest from the sweltering heat. The young man was dying. He had muttered that his own young wife and two daughters had been viciously murdered as they had pleaded for their lives. He had tried to pluck out his own eyes to escape the ghastly memory.

As Edward rode hard, his horse churning the dry and dusty earth beneath him, images of Charlotte passed across his mind. That first day in the garden. Their first dance. Her lemon-yellow party frock. The smell of her hair, always the aroma of lavender. Fresh. New. Not like India at all. And then Rani's words of warning: "You are going to hurt her. . . . That you cannot change."

Edward felt the tears sting his eyes at the mere thought that any harm should come to his wife. She had changed him. Made him see what was truly important for the first time in his life, and he could not lose her now. By the time he reached the outskirts of Delhi, night had begun to fall, and a banner of black smoke streaked the copper-colored

146

sky. He pulled the reins hard, and his steel-gray charger lurched to a stop on a ridge overlooking the city.

Tonight there were no lights sparkling across the horizon, lighting the domes, the soaring minarets, or the crenellated red stone walls of the old city. There was only eerie darkness. And the fires. Pillows of gray smoke coming from the cantonments and the crackle of burning thatch. Edward's face drained of blood as the realization hit him. There was not a single bungalow that had not been torched. No. He would not even consider it. She would not be there. She would have escaped. *Dear God in Heaven, let someone have come for her . . .*

He rode his horse hard without thinking of his own danger, up the rocky terrain and through a dense patchwork of scrub to the next ridge. Mercifully, he saw no *sepoys* as he rode alone into the cantonments, their killing fury likely spent for the night. A few thatched roofs were still ablaze, most of the other bungalows reduced to smoldering embers and a few charred crossbeams. The gardens were full of smashed furniture, broken dishes, burned books, and clothing. The sickening odor of brandy and wine that had spilled from broken bottles. Littering the street were dozens upon dozens of bodies. A few *sepoy* soldiers, but mostly Englishmen. His friends. His countrymen. Their wives. Children. Stabbed. Shot. Decapitated. Slaughtered.

All around him, bodies. And the stench of death. But he must not look or think of that a moment longer. He could do nothing for them now. Now he must find Charlotte. That must be his single thought. He rode toward Graves House, too ill from what he had just seen to feel any fear for himself. He had been forced to leave her alone. He had not been here to protect her. Now he must find her.

When he came up the long, circular drive, the door to Graves House was open and the long glass window panes around it had all been broken. Draperies from the first-floor drawing room flapped ragged in the breeze. At least they had not burned this down. Perhaps she was here, hiding. There had always been a plan that English families could take refuge in the Graves basement if a need arose. *Please, Lord. Let her have remembered that before the panic set in!*

Edward leapt from his horse, thinking only of that. She had survived. Her father had seen her taken to safety.

The beautiful marble portico through which he had so often passed was now washed in a sea of blood and shards of broken glass. It was littered with the bodies of brave English soldiers and the few Indian servants who had refused to betray their masters at the pivotal moment.

All around this once pristine house were hordes of flies, greedily following the stench of death. Edward covered his nose and mouth with his hand and ran down to the basement, but it was empty. His heart was racing, pounding in his ears so loudly that he could not think or feel anything but his own white-hot panic. *Must keep looking . . . Must find Charlotte . . .*

He raced back through the foyer and up the spiral flight of stairs. Her bedroom had been there once. Perhaps there would be a clue. Down the long, shadowy hall of crimson carpet and mahogany doors he ran. Tables were tossed. Crystal smashed. Streaked trails of blood beneath his boots. Edward heard a roaring in his ears, one that he could not silence, as he peered into room after endless room. And then finally he stopped. From the back of his throat came a sound. A little cry.

He moved slowly into the last room. He wanted to run, but something propelled him forward. The need to know. To see for himself what he already knew was there. The blinds had been pulled. A cloud of sandalwood from a broken bottle of perfume masked the rusty smell of blood. Except for the buzzing flies, it was quiet. Deathly quiet. There was a ray of moonlight cast across the bed where two bodies lay. Edward took two more steps forward. The face of one, a woman with large, open ebony eyes, lay on her back, her throat slashed. Her *sari* was torn away. What was left was stained scarlet. The other, a man, lay on his chest, his body draped half over hers as though in a futile attempt to save her.

"Hugh . . ." Edward said, and the name came in a

horrified whisper. It was Charlotte's father and Rani. They had died in one another's arms.

Edward did not recall how he had left the house; whether he had run instantly, or whether he had stood there awhile. Staring. Trying to make himself believe that they were all dead. He seemed to think, in the shock of the moment, that he had tried to revive the colonel, because when he dismounted his horse back at the cantonments, his hands were stained with someone's blood.

Edward leaned against the frame of a charred bungalow and vomited in the street. He wretched until his guts ached, but even then he could not rid his body nor his mind of the images. He had never seen anything like it, nor would he again. So much violence. So much death. When he looked up, he saw his own bungalow through a blur of tears across the dusty, blood-soaked street. Like the others, it too had been burned to the ground.

He charged forward, scrambling through the smoldering ashes for even a clue about Charlotte. But it was gone. Everything they had treasured in their brief marriage. His precious books. Furniture she had brought from her father's house. Dishes. Photographs from their wedding. Mementoes from Agra.

"Charlotte!" he called out in half-crazed fury. "For the love of God, Charlotte! Answer me!"

Edward fell to his knees on the remains of what once had been their sitting room. Hot cinders burned his fingers as he rummaged blindly through the charred remains of a book of verse and a few pieces of silver from a tea service. All things she had brought into his life.

"I am afraid you shall not find her, *sahib.*"

Edward stumbled back to his feet and in the same movement drew forth a loaded pistol, pointing it in the direction of the native voice behind him. It was another moment before he recognized the man as Rajab, his *khansaman,* calling him from the shadowy remains of the cook house beside his bungalow. Edward did not know that this servant had been the very first to have abandoned Charlotte to her fate.

He charged at the butler, his eyes glittering with desperation. "Where is she, Rajab? Take me to her!"

"Please, *sahib*. You must not stand out there like that. It is not safe. There are *sepoys* everywhere."

"Rajab, please! Where is she?"

The servant lowered his coal-dark eyes. He was angry at the British, and he had hoped that an uprising would have meant a call toward change. But he had never expected this. Captain-*sahib* Langston had been good to him. Even in his moment of greatest insubordination, he never would have wanted the *memsahib*'s death.

Bravely, he pulled Edward into the remains of the cook house with him. "I am sorry, Captain-*sahib*. But I cannot do as you ask."

Edward's voice was brittle, his body tensed to strike out at anyone who opposed him. "I am ordering you to take me to my wife! Where have you hidden her?"

Rajab looked down at his master, a man he no longer resented as a *ferenghi*. Now they were just two men like any other men, and one of them had lost the most precious thing in the world.

"I left her here, *sahib,* in the bungalow. She would not leave with the others when she was sent for. Her father had ordered her to stay until he sent for her."

"Surely when it grew desperate she changed her mind!"

"I am sorry, *sahib.*" He took a difficult breath, knowing the pain he was about to inflict. "Two *sepoys* broke into your house. I watched it burn myself. Your wife and her favorite boy, Jawahar, did not escape the flames."

"It was your duty to care for my household and all that was in it, Rajab! You should have seen her to safety! You should have protected her with your own life!"

"You were not here. You do not know. . . ." His voice went down an octave as he watched the utter devastation borne on Edward Langston's face. "There was nowhere she could have hidden from their fury, *sahib.*"

Edward staggered back into the street. *If only I had not been forced to go to Ambala. If only I had listened to Rani . . .* The thoughts played over and over again in his mind like a dirge; a dark, sickening rhythm that he could not silence. She had always had her conviction, Edward thought. It was the first thing he had said he loved about her. Her father had asked her to remain, and so she had. She had gone to her death with her conviction. Damn her!

Edward made a little sound, and it echoed across the silent cantonments as he covered his face with his hands. *Sweet Jesus! Let her not have suffered. . . .* The pounding in his ears grew until it was unbearable, until he felt as if he had exploded. Fragments of his heart, his life, were splattered before him, along with his dreams.

Rajab put a hand to his shoulder, but he cast it off. *You cannot comfort me. . . . For me there shall never be any comfort again!* There was nothing Rajab could say. Nothing anyone could ever say. Charlotte had been his light. His world. She had given him the promise of a future. Now, in the blink of an eye, she had been taken from him.

Tomorrow they would have been married two months.

Blinded by tears, Edward moved to turn away, but as he did, he was pelted with such a force that he crashed onto his chest. The sound of a single gunshot echoed across the cantonments as Edward lay prostrate in a billowing pile of soot and ash.

And suddenly there was no sensation. There was nothing. The numbness rose from his legs and spread across the rest of his body like white heat. He tried to move, to stand, but he had no control. His face was down in the cinders, and he could hear himself choking, but it was as if it were happening to someone else's body.

"Sahib!"

He heard Rajab call out and rush toward him, but as the Hindu butler turned him over, Edward still felt nothing. Saw nothing. Suddenly there was a strange sort of peace washing over him like a cool wave. A calm, and Edward closed his eyes. Charlotte was there before him, smiling and holding out her hand. *Take it,* she said. *Take my hand. . . .*

"Captain-sahib! You've been shot! I must get help!"

Rajab's voice came to him through a long, dark tunnel, beckoning him away from the image of Charlotte. When Edward turned toward the voice, her image began to fade.

"Please, *sahib!* Do not move!"

When Edward opened his eyes, Rajab was hovering over him. His hands and chest were covered with blood—Edward's blood—and yet still Edward felt nothing. No pain. No sensation at all after the bullet had ripped into his back and out through his chest. *Take my* hand, Edward. . . . *Take it.* . . . The voice was soft and sweet, beckoning him.

"Charlotte?"

"No, *sahib,* it is Rajab. You were shot in the back. There must be one of them hiding here. It is too dangerous to go for help, but I must stop the bleeding!"

After that, Edward heard nothing more. There was no other sound. No voice in the cool, white darkness that drew him nearer and nearer.

Not even Charlotte's.

∽11

JAWAHAR SCOOPED THE MUDDY WATER FROM A ROADSIDE POOL into the toe of one of Charlotte's satin-covered shoes. As he had no shoes himself, the boy from Agra had taken the only thing he could find to bear her water.

For four days he had stayed alone with her in the secret cave in the craggy rocks that she had shown to no one but Edward. For three nights he had nursed her fever and the wounds the *sepoy* had wrought, and he had not left her. But now as a fever raged inside her body, burning her like fire, he knew that she must have water to break it. He was glad she was too ill to see what he was forcing her to drink as he tilted the sledgy green liquid down her throat. It was all that he could find without risking both their lives. She gagged and spat most of it back onto her dressing gown—the same dressing gown covered with rusty *sepoy* blood. Then she grew quiet again.

Gently, he pressed her back onto one of the blankets and covered her with the other. Here, hidden by the cover of brush and trees, it was not so hot as it had been in the raging sun, and Jawahar brushed a weary hand across his own glistening brow. She could not die—not now, when he had finally saved her. She had given him a new life. It had been his duty to give hers back in return.

Exhausted, Jawahar leaned against the cool, dank wall of rock and watched her sleep. *It is better that she sleeps,* he thought, *for if she wakes, she shall remember, and there is no memsahib who could endure the memory of what that brutal sepoy had done to her.* It was bad enough that he remembered everything. Being held at the point of his own knife, forced to listen to her struggling in the next room. The creaking bed. The tortured cries. Knowing, yet completely helpless.

When he closed his eyes, Jawahar saw the drawing room painfully vivid before him. It was filled with pillows of thick white smoke. Flames. The hiss of burning thatch and the sounds of a woman's desperation. He could feel his lungs burning. His eyes burning. His vision clouded. And then the gunshot. Not the usual crack, but a thud, heavy and thick. The other *sepoy* had thought it was Charlotte who had been murdered. "Another *feringhi* done with!" He had laughed and then clubbed Jawahar with the butt of the tulwar. He had muttered that it was for trying to save a *memsahib,* just before he'd rushed out into the street to save himself.

Jawahar had wrapped her in Rani's *sari* to conceal her identity. Then, as he had dragged Charlotte Langston's bloody, trembling body through the window of the burning bungalow, he only remembered having had a solitary thought. He must get her somehow to the secret cave. It was near enough to Delhi to make escape possible, and hidden enough to keep them safe until the siege was through.

Charlotte stirred as he watched her. The expression on

her face was so peaceful that Jawahar thought how, even injured, she looked like a little sparrow. So helpless. Her long blond hair hung in a matted tangle near her face, softening the harsh purple bruises, the swollen eyes. Her betrothal ring was replaced on her finger. He had plucked it from the pocket of the dead *sepoy* as he lay sprawled and bleeding on top of the *memsahib*'s bed. She would be glad to have it back when she finally awoke.

Just when he was ready to give in to sleep himself, Jawahar leaned forward on his knees and dotted the tip of her blanket in the murky water. Then he daubed at the dried blood on her cheek, where the *sepoy's* vengeance had broken the skin. Jawahar was a kind, soft-spoken boy who had never wanted to kill anyone. But he was glad that the man who had done this to the captain-*sahib*'s wife was dead. He had no intention of showing allegiance to his people. Not in this.

Jawahar sat back again and felt his eyelids, like two great weights, pressing him toward sleep. The hot wind hushed the trees around the cave, and long shadows cooled the blazing heat from the rocks, but it still carried the odor of burning thatch and human flesh. He had not slept at all the first two nights. That would have been too great a risk. He must instead stand watch in the eerie silence, where the only sound was the occasional far-off pop of gunfire to lull him to sleep.

After the horror he had seen, Jawahar was certain the captain must be dead by now. Nearly all of the English were. He had tripped half a dozen times over a soldier's bloody, lifeless body, as he and Charlotte had hurried from the burning cantonments beneath a cover of smoke and confusion. The ground was littered with them. Bent. Twisted. Bleeding. Broken men who had possessed the arrogance to push a people too far in their own land.

Charlotte stirred again as if she was dreaming, and Jawahar pressed a calming hand to her arm and began softly to stroke it. His own mother had never shown the least bit of kindness like that. But he saw now that her indifference had been a gift after all, for it had given him a will to survive and a desire to live his life differently than she had lived hers.

In the dark of night, when the smoke could not be seen, Jawahar would light a fire of dried cow dung to keep the mosquitoes at bay. He cooked lizards and grasshoppers, chopping them into a paste, and then forced an incoherent Charlotte to choke them down with a taste from the bottle of wine she had left among her things. And at midday, when the heat was at its blistering peak, he would tirelessly cool her with a palm-leaf fan. He would do anything to see her survive. Anything.

After a week, there were signs that she had begun to come around. On those occasions, she would open her matted, swollen eyes and look into Jawahar's kind face, only to have tears begin to rain down her cheeks like a child, and then great waves of grief shake her body. Then Jawahar would patiently hold her and let her weep, as though it were she who was the child. In time, he was glad that Charlotte's periods of lucidity were brief, and he began to cherish the gift of silence in the long, hot hours while she slept.

He waved a white flag and held his breath.

At the end of May, two figures approached the ramparts at the military compound at Kurnaul, twenty miles from Delhi. One, an Englishwoman in a tattered, blood-stained dressing gown, was half walking, half floundering; and the tawny-skinned boy beside her struggled to support her with one arm around her waist. In his other hand he waved a piece of white cloth over his head and prayed that they would see it.

Jawahar would have been content to stay in the cave and wait out the unrest, but the *memsahib* had only grown weaker with each stifling hot dawn. The few scraps he could find for her to eat would surely not be enough now. After the first few days alone with her, he had discovered that she would bear a child. He had wanted to keep her safe himself until he knew for certain that the danger had passed, but it had been beyond the means of a ten-year-old boy. He must return her to her people. They would know better how to care for her.

The noonday sun beat down on them in a savage blaze as Jawahar disregarded his own fate and moved with painstaking slowness toward the ramparts.

"Halt! You there!" a hard, stentorian voice called out across the dusty plain.

Jawahar felt as if his heart had stopped. His own muscles ached from Charlotte's weight against him, and his feet were bloodied from the miles he had walked with no shoes. He had slung her over the back of a dead soldier's horse for most of the journey, until the horse died of exhaustion. Now Jawahar stood completely still, not moving a muscle. And he waited. The silence was broken by whispered words carried through the hot, dry wind.

"By Jove! She's English! Someone else from Delhi, and the bloody native has helped her!"

"Take the woman, but leave the boy to his own kind!"

"Major, please! We would be sending him to his death as a traitor, and this when he has risked his own young life to save her!"

There was another flurry of banter before the senior in command relented. "Very well. Bring them both forward."

"It is all right now, my dear. You shall be safe here," the major tried to assure her once the two were in his presence. But Charlotte did not respond. She only looked past him with a green, glass-eyed stare, her face and eyes still swollen, battered and bruised.

"What in the devil has happened to her? . . . To her poor face?"

For an instant before he spoke, Jawahar considered an honest reply. But he had seen enough of life in Agra to know that the admission of the barbarous crime that had been committed against her by a native soldier could more than likely bring their wrath upon him.

"I cannot say, *sahib*. Only that she has not spoken for many days, but to call out the name of her husband."

"And who, precisely, are you?" The major glared at him contemptuously.

"I am no one, *sahib*. Only a faithful servant."

"What is your name?"

"I am called Jawahar."

The major looked at him over a long straight nose, amber-colored mustache and beard, and a huge round belly. "Well, Jawahar. You are a very brave young man indeed. And your fidelity to one of Her Majesty's citizens is to be commended."

"If you please, I wish only to stay with the *memsahib*. I wish no other commendation than that."

"Do you know the lady's name, Jawahar, so that after this whole dreadful mess is over we might try to locate her family?"

"She is the wife of Captain Edward Langston, *sahib.*"

"Langston, hmm?" The major stroked the point of his amber beard and then frowned. "Can't say as I've ever heard of him. Was he killed over there at that ruckus in Delhi?"

"I know only that I saw no survivors as I left."

"Poor dear young woman." He shook his head. "It must be the shock of it. That she survived that carnage at all is rather a miracle. We've at least a dozen other refugees from Delhi with whom it seems we must now contend. Lieutenant, take her to my quarters and let her rest there until I can determine what to do with her."

As Jawahar moved to follow the soldiers who would take Charlotte to safety and the comfort of a clean bed, another blocked the way with the tip of his bayonet.

"Please, *sahib*. My place is with her."

"We shall tell you where your place is!" the young officer snarled.

"Now, Lieutenant. We needn't be harsh with the boy," the major intervened. "After all, he did save Mrs. Langston's life. Take Jawahar down, feed him, and dress his feet. Those do look like rather nasty wounds. Then escort him to the lockup. I am certain he will be more comfortable there until his mistress is herself once again."

"But she would want me to be with her!"

The major smiled a condescending smile, then looked away. "It really is for your own good, my boy. The sentiment here against your kind is so strong just now, I suspect any one of my men would as soon shoot you as look at you. Let me at least protect you from that until the furor dies down."

Jawahar felt the man's resentment through the polite and well-spoken layer of concern. But the situation had been made clear even to a boy of ten. Separation from the *memsahib* and detention like a common criminal was not a choice.

It was an order.

Charlotte lay in an unending state of oblivion, completely unaware of the war playing out between the rebellious *sepoys* and the regrouped British forces. In a world of her own, she moaned and writhed and occasionally cried out Edward's name. It was a confused haze of dark images and chaotic memories to which she seemed forever bound. Edward's face smiling down at her. Rani's singsong voice calming her with children's songs from long ago. . . . And then the angry touch of a native soldier, snarling over her like a beast.

After the second day, Charlotte was moved from the major's quarters to the infirmary, where she could be watched over by his wife and eldest daughter. Here at Kurnaul, they did not have the facilities to treat this sort of "disorder of the mind," nor her facial injuries, but with all of the unrest just now, neither could they afford the risk of trying to send her down to Calcutta. There were more survivors pouring in from Delhi every day, telling horrid stories of misery and death.

Meanwhile, across the encampment in a dim stone cell, Jawahar sat behind rusted steel bars, his English captors shuffling and muttering outside. "Protecting him." Seven days. He had marked it in the dirt floor. A line for each sunset. But it was easier to pass the time by thinking happy thoughts. Before the mutiny. When the *memsahib* had shown such kindness. It had been worth it. Even this. Now she would survive. In his most lonely hours, he could not keep himself from wondering if she had regained her senses yet. Sadly, the answer that came to him was always no, because he knew in his heart that she would have sent for him if she had.

On the eighth day, Lieutenant Collins, the young officer who had made it clear that he had no use for a poor native boy, stood on the other side of the cell door, his khaki summer uniform crisp and neatly pressed.

"On your feet," he said coldly as he issued him out into the corridor. "The major wants to see you."

Jawahar silently followed the young Englishman through the encampment until they came to a small, dark office shuttered against the fierce midday heat.

The portly, bearded major was sitting behind a huge mahogany desk. His wavy amber hair was brushed away from his face and tamed with oil. The whitewashed walls around him were dotted with huge portraits. One of Queen Victoria framed in a heavy gold frame hung behind his desk chair.

"Your mistress has not improved since you brought her to us," he said in a voice full of control. But Jawahar could see by his eyes that he was deeply troubled. "Her problem, it would seem, is far more serious than anything we are equipped to handle here. Are you absolutely certain you have no idea what might have brought this on?"

Jawahar faltered. For a moment he nearly risked his own safety and confessed the truth. But his sense of duty silenced him. He could not bring himself to shame his beautiful, spirited *memsahib* by admitting the sort of unspeakable atrocity she had suffered at the hands of his own countrymen.

"No, *sahib,*" he lied.

The major dotted his shiny forehead with a handkerchief, and after a few more moments of studying the boy, he came out from behind the desk and perched on the end of it. He was directly in front of Jawahar, their eyes at the same level.

"The doctor here doesn't know what to do for her. She isn't . . . well, she isn't right in the head. Whatever she suffered back there in Delhi has been a great trauma, too great for us to overcome. And she's carrying a child to boot. . . . The point is," he said, taking a heavy, whiskey breath, "perhaps you can be some comfort to her after all. At least until things calm down enough to transport her to a hospital in Calcutta. So I am going to have Collins here take you to her."

"Many thanks, *sahib*." Jawahar lowered his eyes respectfully.

"But I am going to tell you bluntly," he said, his voice going lower, underscored by intimidation, "if you are here in Kurnaul as some sort of spy for your cause, I shall have no compunction whatsoever against disposing of you in the manner which your people understand best."

Jawahar nodded and then turned away quickly, not wanting to show the jolt of fear he felt. But they both knew that he understood. In India, the native punishment for being a traitor was to have molten lead poured down one's throat.

In the shutter-darkened infirmary, Jawahar sat without moving beside Charlotte's lifeless body, his face wet with tears. She looked as if she were dead. Completely motionless. Barely breathing. The harsh brand of a dead *sepoy* was still so vivid on her face. Some of the bruises had begun to fade. Others had turned a sickening yellow, the center still brilliant purple. Her broken nose had changed the perfect line of her face, made her profile more common. Her eyes were still badly injured. But for as long as he gazed at her, willing her to wake and smile at him and laugh as gaily as she once had, she did not stir.

He gazed at her with a heavy heart. India had done this to her. This desolate, unforgiving place. Once, as they had played one of their endless rounds of whist, she had told him about England. Trees the color of emeralds. Meadows thick like carpet, stretching out to a cool azure sky. Shady lanes winding toward villages of gray slate and stone. One day he had even dared hope she might take him there with her. Her husband wanted to return and had described it to her. Jawahar had heard them discussing it once when he had followed them to the secret cave to act as sentinel, and his hopes had soared—before the captain-*sahib* had gone to Ambala. A lifetime ago.

He looked back down at Charlotte, her face so bruised and battered, her pale bloodless lips slightly parted. *Had you only gone with the other* memsahibs *when they bid you*, he thought, gently reaching out to take her hand as it lay linked together with the other across her chest. Sensing his touch, she blinked, then opened her eyes. She looked at Jawahar, but her once lovely face bore the same expression. Distant. Glassy. Recognizing nothing.

"Edward?" she called out in a whisper. "Edward, please, help me . . ."

Jawahar moved to the corner of the bed beside her and brushed a matted tangle of hair from her face. His young heart was breaking. "It is all right," he said back to her in a soothing whisper of Hindustani. "You shall be all right now. They shall not separate us again. That I promise."

He pulled the thin cotton sheet up over her shoulders and bit his lip so that he would not cry. *Only children cry*, he remembered, hearing the echo of his mother's terse words. *And now I must be a man. I have no choice. She has no one else.*

12

"THAT IS THE MOST HORRENDOUS STORY I HAVE EVER HEARD!" Katherine Blackstone whispered, tears streaming down her full face. The cool sea air dried them in long crystal ribbons as she gazed at Charlotte.

"So now you see why I must find him."

"But your Edward, he believes you are dead."

"As I believed of him," she said, looking out at the grand, black expanse of rolling, cloud-darkened sea. "For a long time I had no idea even who I was. I had blocked out the horror that had befallen me by forgetting everything. I felt such shame . . . such unbelievable shame."

"By our dear Lord, it is a wonder you ever managed. That you had the strength!"

"If not for Jawahar, I shudder to think what might have become of me."

The two women stood on the saloon deck as the ship creaked and groaned its way toward the next port. "I am sorry as well about your father and his lady."

Charlotte took a breath and, for a moment, closed her eyes. "At least they died together. It seems it is what they both would have wanted. It is some comfort to know that for all of my protestations, he really did love Rani after all."

"But how, with all of the confusion, did you ever discover what had become of them?"

"Names of the dead were posted when it could all be sorted out. It took nearly a year. I was in Calcutta by then, but the army sent someone to tell me of their fate."

Charlotte took a heavy, pained breath. "The brutal manner in which their lives ended was confirmed for me the same day they informed me that they had discovered Edward's body."

"The Lord giveth and the Lord taketh away." Katherine breathed a soft sigh as she gazed up at a sky full of stars. "And the boy, Jawahar? Whatever happened to him?"

Charlotte smiled unexpectedly, gaining some glimmer of happiness through a sea of troubled memories, at the thought of the boy who had found the courage to save her life. "Jawahar has remained in India to help look after my son."

Katherine's blue eyes widened. "So you had the child? I was not certain after everything if . . ."

"He is my miracle," Charlotte said quietly.

"So I should imagine."

"The doctors tell me I could not even look at him for that first year. Poor darling. But he has become the joy of my life. He looks so much like his father," she said proudly. "He and Jawahar are like brothers now, even with nearly eleven years between them. One day when Edward and I are settled again, I shall send for them both."

Katherine pressed her fingers to her lips. "I can scarcely imagine the shock on the poor man's face when he sees you."

"It can be no worse than what I felt when I discovered that they had made a mistake. That he had not been killed after all."

"But how, after such a frenzy, did you ever discover the truth?"

"That was not for nearly ten years." Charlotte sighed, pushing back the pain of the precious time she and Edward had lost. "My discovering his circumstances was quite by accident."

"Ah, but then there are not really any accidents, are there? That is what the Hindus believe."

"So they do."

"And Edward?"

Charlotte braced herself against the wet railing. "I shall tell you the rest of the story another time. For now, you have promised to go ashore with me."

"I did promise to have one of my gowns tailored to fit you at that," Katherine agreed, managing a weak smile after the incredible story she had just heard. Now she tried to gather her wits about her. "Oh yes, your dress must be beautiful when your Edward sees you for the first time, and you'll surely not want to take the time once we set foot in England to have a gown of your own made. Still, this is your triumphant return to your homeland. You must be wearing the most current style. We shall have your hair done up just as he would have liked it if . . ."

Katherine put out her hand and squeezed Charlotte's chilly fingers. She could feel her trembling. "Anything I can do to make your reunion easier, my dear girl, I shall do it gladly."

Charlotte looked at Katherine Blackstone, as the stout and kind woman's faded blue eyes glinted in the sunlight. "Perhaps now you could tell me why you have been so kind to me."

Very well. She had asked. Perhaps this was an afternoon for confessions from both sides. Katherine's encouraging smile began to fade. "I always wanted a daughter," she said softly. "Once, a long time ago, I did. But to my great sorrow, my dear sweet child died a few days after her birth. Had she lived, she would have been just about your age."

"And you never had others?"

"The doctor told me that I was not able to have more children. Mr. Blackstone found himself another wife who could."

"Oh, Katherine. I am so sorry."

"So was I, for a very long time. But the curious thing about time is that it ends up being a blessing, actually. It helps one to forget."

"I have forgotten nothing." Charlotte sighed. "My memories now are as vivid as if I had married Edward only yesterday."

* * *

The ship had docked at Gibraltar, and passengers were already going ashore. The salty sea air was full of the smell of rope and wood from the crates that were being lowered onto the dock. The two women looked together over the railing at the broad landscape, stark and barren but for a little enclave of whitewashed houses. This was the final stop before the steamer *Indus* docked in Southampton.

The ship's captain had told them about an old woman in the center of town who, he said, could work miracles with a needle and thread. The gown that Charlotte had selected from Katherine's wardrobe must be altered for a slimmer, more youthful figure, and a few other touches must be added to make it her own.

As they looked out to shore, Katherine glanced over at Charlotte. She saw the fear on her face, even through the protective cover of her shaded glasses. Poor dear young woman. What lay ahead of her quite likely would be a greater test even than what she had already faced in India. What could she really expect to find after ten years? Her husband believed her dead. But Charlotte was determined, and Katherine would help any way that she could. No matter what the outcome.

"The more I think about it, the more convinced I am that the thread in that gown is really going to look splendid with your eyes," Katherine said with an encouraging smile. "I have no doubt that your Edward shall simply fall into your arms the moment he sees you!"

She turned toward Katherine, a glimmer of what must have once been a devastating beauty still alive on her small, fragile face. She was no longer perfectly youthful as she once had been. Her hair, which she now wore pulled away from her face, time had made darker but no less brilliant than the adolescent blond she had described. Her nose was no longer perfectly aquiline. Even so, she was still an attractive young woman.

"Oh, Katherine," Charlotte sighed, turning back out toward the sea. "If only wishing could make it so."

They went ashore together and into the marketplace, both of them holding silky, lace-edged parasols against the sun of a balmy May afternoon. They were laughing and chattering like schoolgirls as they wound their way through a narrow, cobblestone courtyard and into the lane of small shops. Number eleven, the dressmaker's shop, had a blue cotton curtain instead of a door and two dirty-faced children playing outside.

"Captain MacDonald has sent us," Katherine said, closing her parasol with a snap.

It was then that an old Hindu woman turned to face them. She was dressed in a faded, ecru-colored *sari,* her dark hair pulled away from her thin face and knotted at the back of her head. Charlotte gasped and pressed her fingers to her lips. In the shadowy indoor light, the woman before them bore an uncanny resemblance to Rani.

"I had no idea, my dear," Katherine whispered at the expression of pure shock on Charlotte's face, certain of what she must be seeing. "We shall find another dressmaker."

"You shall find no other here in Gibraltar," the woman said, her singsong Hindustani accent strong and haunting to them both after the tale Charlotte had just told.

"I do doubt that," Katherine answered in a crisp, combative tone. "Come, Charlotte. We shall ask around town."

The woman moved a step forward, bracelets jangling from her wrists, just as Rani's had always done. There was the haunting swirl of fragrant sandalwood between them. It all tore at her heart. And her memories.

"It is the incidents of ten years past which makes me unsuitable to assist you?"

"We have just come from Calcutta," said Charlotte.

"I left Delhi nearly ten years ago now, just after the mutiny."

"Curious you would refer to it that way," Katherine said crisply. "The rest of your people refer to it now as the great freedom fight."

"A slaughter is a slaughter," she countered without hesitation.

"Yes. Well . . . I simply believe my friend here would be more comfortable elsewhere."

The dressmaker interrupted Katherine with a firm tone of

reproach. "I came away, employed as the *ayah* to a widowed Englishman's children. I helped them survive by covering them in a cart full of hay and daring to pull it past the angry soldiers who were too frenzied by their bloodlust to have noticed me. I am now proud here in Gibraltar to have become his wife."

She emphasized the word *proud*, and Charlotte believed her. Besides, she had nothing to fear from an old woman. She must learn to place the past where it belonged— especially now, when the future had begun again to look so bright.

Charlotte took off her glasses and looked intently at her friend. "Show her the gown, Katherine, please."

"My dear, you really needn't subject yourself—"

"If I am to put the past behind me, yes, I must."

"You shall not be sorry." The woman smiled up at Charlotte, and in her expression, once again she saw a trace of Rani. But this time there was less pain in the recollection. She wanted to remember the woman who had helped raise her. That was a light she was determined to burn brightly forever.

"Oh, yes," she said, fingering the rich fabric. "This is lovely."

"I am afraid it doesn't fit properly."

"When I am finished"—she put a hand on Charlotte's wrist, and the scent of sandalwood comforted her like an old friend—"this gown shall look as if it was made especially for you."

"Then I shall put myself in your hands," Charlotte said, and she turned away purposefully as Katherine winced.

"Charlotte Langston," she said with a little huffing sound. "You do amaze me. I am quite certain I could never be so gracious as you."

Her eyes were wide and green and forgiving. "Oh, I think you would be surprised at the strength adversity gives you."

Katherine was worried.

In the weeks since their meeting, the bond between she and Charlotte had deepened from a tentative acquaintance to a relaxed and trusting friendship. This sweet, vulnerable girl had laid open her heart, and Katherine Blackstone had responded by feeling an overwhelming urge to protect her. She could not seem to shake the feeling that, one day soon, Charlotte was going to need her to pick up the pieces.

"Sit with me," Katherine bid her that evening as they watched the waves splash the railing and a fiery orange sun sink in the distance. "We shall be docking tomorrow, and there is something that has been on my mind for some time."

"What is it?" she asked.

Katherine took Charlotte's hand and breathed deeply. "Now. You do trust that I care for you and that I would never say anything to hurt you more than you already have been."

"I know that." She smiled.

"Well, I simply cannot help wondering if your Edward has not . . . pardon me for saying so, but gotten on with his life. After all, it has been such a very long time, and apparently he had no hope that you had survived."

"It is nothing I have not thought of myself a hundred times," she said calmly, almost serenely.

Katherine's brows arched. "Truly?"

"Of course, I know how possible it is. Edward was a man of great passion. In my favor, however, he was also a man who loved purely and deeply. . . . If I am to go through with this, I must believe that no matter what circumstance these past ten years have forced upon him, the love between us shall have survived."

"Your optimism and spirit are admirable, my dear. And they have certainly been a ray of sunshine for me on this long journey. But are you quite certain you are strong enough to face those possibilities?"

"I have no choice, Katherine," she said, ignoring the little tug at her heart. "I must see him for myself."

Katherine put her arm around her, and Charlotte sank willingly into the easy, motherly embrace as they both watched the last bit of flaming orange sun dip into the horizon. It was safe here, wrapped against her ample, sweet bosom. For this moment in time, so far from any shore, she was protected from harm. Rani had always made her feel that way. Valued. Protected. Loved.

"Now it is I who would like to ask you something," Charlotte said.

"I shall tell you anything that I can."

"Why is it that you never remarried after your husband deserted you?"

She could feel Katherine stiffen against her, and there was a pause before she replied. "I could never find anyone to quite tolerate me," she answered bluntly.

Charlotte sat up and looked into Katherine's eyes. The sea breeze was brushing little wisps of gray hair against her sallow, wrinkled cheek. "I cannot believe that."

"But it is true. I was really very bitter after my daughter died. I blamed the world for what happened to her, and to me." She looked back at Charlotte's tear-brightened eyes. "Oh please, child. You mustn't pity me. It hasn't been a bad life after all. I have a sister in Calcutta who adores me, and more dear friends in London than I can count."

"But . . . what about love?" Charlotte asked tentatively.

Katherine's smile became tender. "Oh, I leave that sort of business to the young. You have the patience and the energy for such endeavors."

"But you are not old!" Charlotte averred, and the sweet tone of her declaration brought a bubble of laughter from Katherine Blackstone.

"Oh, dear child, I feel as old as that ocean out there and, until I met you, nearly as empty."

Charlotte opened her mouth, intending to say something else, but seeing the contented expression in Katherine's eyes, she quickly changed her mind.

At the end of a long and arduous sea voyage, Charlotte Langston stepped tentatively onto English soil for the first time in twenty years. Her heart was racing so that she could scarcely catch her breath. She was close now, no more than a few days' ride from Edward. *At last,* she thought. *Finally, now we shall be able to right the wrongs that fate has so cruelly wrought upon us.*

She stood trembling on the dock at Southampton in a dazzling gown that rippled in the fresh breeze. Topaz silk had been accented with copper braid. Her lustrous dusty brown hair was wound beneath a matching topaz bonnet and tied with copper-colored ribbons. She was the height of fashion. Attractive. Elegant. And yet in appearance, she looked very little like the exquisite child Edward had married.

Behind her, Katherine Blackstone padded down the gangplank in another of her own costly gowns. Violet and white, the bodice sewn with pearls, and all of it thick with crinolines and rustling in the breeze. The two women, whom a sea voyage had made the dearest of friends, stood facing one another as the other weary passengers filed off the ship and huge crates of cargo thumped onto the dock behind them.

"Well," said Charlotte with a sigh, "I suppose this is goodbye, then."

"I know we had planned to part here," Katherine said, "but I have been thinking of seeing you down to Tetbury."

It was really more than the whim she made it out to be. Katherine did not have a good feeling about what lay ahead for this dear girl, one she had so quickly come to care about. In fact, since last night, her concern had turned to dread. She simply did not see how there was a chance that Charlotte could find her Edward alone, as she so wanted him to be.

If what she feared had indeed come true, then Katherine wanted very much to be there for her, for as long as she was needed.

"That is really very kind of you," Charlotte said, "but I believe I have asked quite enough of you already."

Katherine Blackstone tapped her parasol on the moist, spongy wood of the dock and leveled her eyes. "You did not ask, my dear. It was I who offered. Besides, you promised me the rest of that unbelievable story, and I haven't heard yet how on earth you ever managed to discover that your Edward had survived."

Charlotte smiled. "I did promise, didn't I?"

"Indeed you did. And to be quite truthful, I have that huge carriage over there and no real place I must be. I would be glad for your company a little while longer."

Katherine used her parasol to point to a grand-looking brougham with a liveried driver waiting beside it. In India Charlotte had only heard about such costly carriages, and the offer to ride in such luxury was a lure she simply could not refuse. Besides, she could never repay the kindness Katherine Blackstone had shown her. If a bit of company was what she desired in return, then Charlotte would not refuse her.

As she was helped inside by the white-gloved coachman, Charlotte touched the rich, honey-colored leather on the carriage seat. Childhood memories flickered through her mind as she gazed out the glass window at the rolling green hills beyond the port. It felt strange and frightening, and yet splendid to be back.

Out in the countryside, the tips of meadow grass glistened with dew like tiny diamonds in the early morning light. Tree after tree reached out its branches like a feathery canopy, shading the lane down which the carriage slowly rolled. All of it was so verdant, so lush. Daisies. Buttercups. A carpeting of cowslips. And the air was thick with the sweet, heady scent of springtime.

"Though I rather loathe to admit it," Katherine said as the carriage clicked forward, farther and farther away from the port, "that dear old woman was right: The dress does look as though it was made for you."

"All at once now I am frightfully nervous. It is the first time since I discovered that Edward was still alive that I have felt anything but the greatest joy."

"You were going to tell me about that."

"Are you certain you really want to hear so much about me? I've imposed so much on you already."

"I would be honored to hear the rest of your story. After all"—she winked and patted Charlotte's silk-draped knee with motherly affection—"we have nothing but time on our hands, and it is a rather long way yet to Tetbury."

The carriage moved a little farther into the lush country-side as Charlotte smiled and settled against the seat. "You know, Katherine. Besides discovering that my Edward was alive, meeting you was the first stroke of really good fortune I have had in a very long time."

"Let us hope for you, my dear girl, that this is only the beginning!"

"All right then, let's see. It took almost ten years," she began the tale again. "I had been taken to hospital in Calcutta by then, and the worst of my wounds had healed. . . ."

13

Calcutta, 1867

A PERSISTENT FLY NIPPED AT HER NOSE AND CHARLOTTE swatted at it as she dozed in the shaded courtyard of Saint Mary's hospital. All around her near the splashing stone fountain, the flower garden and the covered terrace, there were patients in wheeled chairs, their legs covered over with blue, red, and green tartan blankets. Some of them muttered. Others cried out to no one and nothing, except the memories that still frightened them.

Many of the patients at Saint Mary's were lost to the safe harbor of their own worlds, just as she had been when she had first come here as a patient. Charlotte could reach them like no one else. Because she understood. So when her own wounds had healed, she was asked to stay, to help the other patients still lost to their pain.

Her family was dead. Her husband murdered. There was

172

nothing and no one else to which she must return. There was no reason not to become a part of something here. It was a chance, perhaps, to bring some good from the most horrendous period in her life. So nine years before, Charlotte had chosen to stay on, to help the others, a few of whom had fought and survived the Delhi massacre just as she had.

"Teatime," Jawahar sang sweetly as he set the rattling tray down on the small white wrought-iron table beside her. "Wake up, *memsahib.* Your break is over."

She lay there a moment more, her eyes hidden from the afternoon light by a pair of shaded, wire-rimmed glasses. She often wore them, hoping that if she stayed very still, no one could ever be quite certain if she was awake or not.

She had sustained damage to her eyes in the beating she had endured. When she had first come to Calcutta the glasses had been a necessity against the harsh sunlight. While she had needed them less and less over the years, as the injury to her eyes slowly healed, wearing them like this served two purposes. It also won her a few moments' reprise from the exhausting work and long hours required at the understaffed English hospital.

A warm breeze blew across her face, soft, like a whisper. It was difficult to believe that in less than a month the unforgiving Indian sun would make this time of day unbearable again. But for now it dappled the ground through the trees and warmed her body through the plain cotton hospital shift. Over her head, the leaves rustled like a lady's satin skirts, and birds called out to one another through the endless maze of branches.

Last night the darkness had stretched silently into morning, and she had never gotten up to her room that overlooked the garden from the second floor. She had spent most of those still night hours struggling to convince a young patient not to slash her own wrists with a broken piece of teacup as two doctors had looked on helplessly. Her family was all dead, she had cried, with eyes wide and full of a pain that Charlotte knew too well. There was no reason to keep living, she had said.

Jawahar's soft hand was on her shoulder. *"Memsahib?"*

Oh, sweet Jesus, do be merciful with me for this one day especially! she thought. *If I pretend to be asleep long enough, perhaps he shall go away. Not a likely wish from someone so persistent as Jawahar. . . . But one can always hope.*

"Shall I pour the cream for you, *memsahib?* Or do you wish to do it yourself today?"

She listened to the sound of the china cup rattling against the saucer as he moved to steady it. Then hot tea being dribbled into the cup. Jawahar was whistling merrily and completely ignoring her ploy. *Blasted boy!* she thought angrily. *He has come to know me too well!*

Reluctantly, she opened her eyes and saw him smiling down at her as sweetly as if they had not a care in the world. But Charlotte would never be carefree. Not ever again. Now life was something she must endure. She had found a purpose here at Saint Mary's. But even Edward's son, her precious Hugh Edward, could not give her more than that.

Seeing his sweet cherub's face every day, so full of his father, was bittersweet. For so long, he had been her single reason to go on living. And yet today especially, he was a reminder of the loss. Of her shattered innocence in Delhi. Of loving Edward and losing him. And those memories, no matter how hard she fought them, always wound their way to images of her *ayah.* Her father. Her husband. She still saw their blood in her dreams. The work helped. Here at Saint Mary's, she was needed. She made a difference. And she hid from the loss that, in the dark of night, still managed to consume her.

Charlotte drank her tea and gazed out across the courtyard through the tall black iron fence that separated the hospital from the rest of the world. People were rushing by, arms full of packages and children. Living their lives. *Ghurries* clicking past. Dirty beggars calling for *rupees* from the wealthy English who had come from visiting the hospital and might have felt particularly charitable. But inside the fence, the patients were safe. Protected. And so was she.

Near dawn, the tormented young girl had surrendered the chard of glass and then wept uncontrollably as Charlotte held her. In that moment, she recalled all of the feelings. Her own helplessness. Hopelessness. Her own despair.

"Is he terribly angry with me for not having come up last evening, Jawahar?"

"Your son is confused, *memsahib*. He asked me yesterday and all last evening, and then again this morning, why he would not be seeing you. And I was forced to say the same thing to that sweet face: 'I don't know, child,' I said, again and again."

Charlotte dashed at a sudden flurry of tears as they ran down her pale cheeks. *Why do they not understand that today—especially today—the sight of that child, Edward's child, is worse than the agony of remembering?*

She stared past Jawahar, trying to collect herself, and to chase away the memories. It was not his fault, but still she was angry. Angry that Jawahar was right. Angry that he was forcing her to face her responsibility when all she wanted today was the silence of death; the peace of never having to wake again, to never again see that sweet face. To feel that loss. The loss of dreams. Of innocence. Of the handsome prince whom she had worshiped, but who in the end could not save her. Who had left her to her grief. Her own despair; her wretched emptiness. It was not Jawahar's fault. It was not Hugh Edward's fault.

"Memsahib?"

Jawahar's well-meaning voice jerked in her mind. She looked at him again and thought, *How is it that you do not despise me, child, for how I have treated you? I brought you from Agra with the hope of a future, and I have given you nothing but endless work and broken dreams. Just like my own.*

"Today, Captain Langston and I would have been married ten years," she said in a pained whisper.

"Oh, *memsahib!* A thousand pardons, truly. I did not remember."

"Sometimes, as another year slips away, I wonder myself if it was all just a dream; knowing him . . . loving him."

"But you have your Hugh Edward to remind you that it was true," he softly offered.

"Yes. Edward's son. The very image of his father. And every day of my life he is a blessing, Jawahar. But today, this one day every year, it is too painful even to look upon his face. You do understand that, don't you, my friend?"

"Oh, yes, *memsahib.*"

It was then, through the maze of tears, that she saw him. He was standing at the other side of the wrought-iron fence, talking to an old man as people rushed behind him. She would not have recognized him at first without his turban, and because time had not been kind. Now he was a gaunt and shabby man with a chest-long white beard. The lines on his face were deeper. The circles beneath his dark eyes were heavy. They drew the wide onyx spheres down with the rest of the sagging flesh on his dark face. And yet it was the eyes that called to her. Eyes that had gazed at her once with such undeniable loathing that she had never forgotten them.

"Rajab?" she called out, springing from her chair.

Her teacup and saucer tumbled from her lap, spilling dark liquid onto the blanket as she scrambled toward the fence. But as she neared, he looked vacantly at the curious Englishwoman who called to him, not recognizing her. Then he turned away. "Rajab, please! I only wish to speak to you!"

Her voice was full of such painful pleading that he finally stopped again and turned to face her, his mind searching for a reason that this stranger should know his name.

"It is I, Charlotte Langston! Wife of your Captain-*sahib* Langston!"

She watched him scowl. "The *memsahib* is dead," he said coldly as she neared him. "I knew the *sahib's* wife, and you look nothing like her."

"I know that, Rajab. But just the same, it is I. Do you not remember my *punkah-wallah,* Jawahar? He shall confirm my identity for you!"

Jawahar stood behind Charlotte, staring through the iron

bars at the servant who in the end had abandoned them both for a cause that had ultimately failed. "It is true," he confirmed without emotion.

Charlotte saw the scowl begin to fade as he turned to a boy he had once both envied and despised. Then Rajab looked back at a woman whose face was fuller, her cheekbones less pronounced, and whose nose was no longer straight and pert and small. Nor was this woman's hair at all like the lustrous golden blond the *memsahib*'s once had been. "But it cannot be. You are dead. . . ." he muttered in disbelief, suddenly remembering her eyes, green like sparkling gems. Those had not changed. The eyes alone told him that what she said was true.

"It cannot be! I saw the bungalow burn myself!"

"I suffered, Rajab, yes. Many of the . . . alterations that they tried to correct are permanent. But thanks to Jawahar, I did not die."

The years had aged the captain-*sahib*'s *khansaman* and turned him into a stooped, white-haired, old-looking man. And yet, looking at him now, even in the face of such a shock, Jawahar still felt the raging anger at what his countryman's defection had cost them all. As they had been for Charlotte, those dark days were ones that were forever branded in his memory.

"It is true, I believed you were dead. . . . Or I would never have convinced him so! He searched everywhere for you . . . but we all told him there was no point. . . . Oh! This cannot be. . . . It simply cannot!"

As he rambled nervously, Charlotte's mouth went as dry as Delhi sand. "Who, Rajab?" She fought for a shaky breath, her heart crashing against her ribs. "Who did you convince that I had been killed?"

"Oh, *memsahib* Lawrence!" He began to pale, grasping tightly to the bars, tears of utter disbelief staining his dark, leathery skin, his words springing back and forth between Hindustani and English. "You must forgive me. I beg of you! I had no idea the *sepoys* meant to cause such harm. It was not supposed to be like that! It was not—"

Charlotte clutched both his hands, pressing her own like a vice around his. "Who, Rajab? You must tell me who believes that I died in Delhi?"

He swallowed hard and looked back at her, not certain if he could force the words past his lips. She had changed so much that he still could see only a slight resemblance to the woman he recalled. But he knew the voice. And he knew Jawahar. Along with those eyes, they convinced him that he was indeed looking at a woman whom for ten years, he believed to have died. "It was the captain-*sahib*."

For an instant the shock paralyzed her. Charlotte felt the razor-sharp claws of pain gouge at her heart. "Which captain, Rajab?" she mouthed, fighting for breath.

"Perhaps it would be wise to sit down, *memsahib*." His voice quivered. "I shall come inside and we can speak."

Charlotte's face stained scarlet as her nails dug into his hands. "Rajab! For the love of God!"

Her former servant lowered his eyes. "Captain-*sahib* Langston . . . *memsahib*."

Edward. The sound of his name spun in her mind with the images. His face was smiling through them, more handsome than any man dared to be. *No, it is not possible! No! It is a cruel joke. Rajab, you hate me! You have always hated me!*

Charlotte collapsed into the dry grass at Jawahar's feet, hands pressed to her face, her body racked by sobs. Two English nurses rushed forward. The other patients stared at her. People on the street stopped to gaze through the iron bars as she curled into a ball beneath a low-hanging banyan tree.

"Oh! Make it stop! It is too cruel. . . . Today of all days! Oh, please!"

She was wailing and thrashing at the nurses by the time Rajab and two of the doctors could get to her.

"It is the truth, *memsahib!*" he shouted, trying to make her listen as the nurses fought to restrain him. "I do not deceive you in this! Your captain-*sahib* did not return to you because he could not! He was injured by a *sepoy*. But he did not die, I tell you. . . . He did not die!"

Charlotte looked up slowly, her eyes swollen and full of

tears as she gasped for breath. She felt as if she were beneath a mountain of bricks, and they were crushing the last bit of life out of her.

"It is the truth!" he said again, kneeling beside her with Jawahar. Everyone looked at Rajab. But none of them understood the implications on so many lives of what he was saying.

"How could you not tell me? How could someone not tell me?" Her voice throbbed out the words.

"Until a few moments ago, I had no reason to believe you had not died like all of the others. The captain-*sahib* did not search for you either, because he eventually was made to believe as he all along had been told."

When she could stand, the three walked together back to the terrace, and Jawahar helped her as Charlotte fought to keep her balance. Great God in Heaven, could she ever accept what Rajab was saying? After she learned of the deaths of her father and Rani, she had never dared hope that somehow Edward had survived the carnage. One of the doctors gave her a cool cloth and waited until she assured him that it was all right to leave her alone with this stranger.

"Where is he, Rajab?" she finally asked, and the question brought a new wellspring of tears, which she fought to wipe away.

"I did not see him after he was taken to Jheed."

"Jheed? Dear God, I was in Kurnaul, not twenty miles from there! Why on earth did he go to Jheed?"

"He was hurt, *memsahib,* and it was the only place I could think to take him where he could get help without further risk. I was forced to surrender him to the care of his own people in the dark of night. It would not have been safe for me to seek him out after that."

"But he is alive! You said so yourself!"

"I said he was alive when we reached Jheend, *memsahib.* But his injury was very bad. He had lost a great deal of blood."

Charlotte faltered, and her face went pale. Jawahar put his arm around her shoulder to steady her, and they waited while one of the nurses brought her a glass of water and she drank it.

"Are you certain you are up to hearing this?" Rajab asked with a sincere note of concern.

"I must hear everything you know about Edward, Rajab! Everything!"

They sat together, the three of them, in the shadows beneath the trees, until sunset painted the sky a pale rose-pink. There, Charlotte heard in excruciating detail how her husband had risked his life coming back to the cantonments in search of her. Tears rolled down her cheeks in an endless stream as Rajab told her of Edward's desperation at the thought that, like her father, she too had become an innocent victim of the rebellion. But that was not the worst of it.

Shot in the back.

The words as Rajab finally confessed them were like a knife blade slicing open a vein; her life's blood spurting out with each pulsebeat. She could not bear to think of the pain Edward had endured; nor that, after everything, in the end he might still have died alone at Jheed.

"I am sorry, *memsahib,* that you were left so long to discover the truth. If I had only known. . . ." He put his face in his hands. "Oh, and I was so very cruel to you. . . ."

"It was not your fault, Rajab," she said, her voice full of forgiving. "Those were difficult times for us all. And the bravery you showed in risking your life to save my husband is far more important than any malice between you and I."

He looked up at her again. "For that, *memsahib,* I thank you most truly."

"But how did you come all this way to Calcutta from Delhi?" Jawahar asked him when Charlotte was too overcome to say anything else.

"It was a long time ago now. I came after the . . ." Rajab stumbled on the word. Still, even years later, he could not call it what everyone else did. A massacre. "It was after the uprising. My family lives here, and I had gone to Delhi only to attend the captain-*sahib.*"

Charlotte heard them talking and was glad that neither Jawahar nor Rajab were asking her any questions. Her mind was swimming in a dark pool of thoughts. He had been shot in the back trying to find her. But he had survived. Edward was alive! Somewhere. That was what she now must force herself to believe. And for the first time in ten long years, there was a glimmer of hope. There was a future again.

Oh, Edward. So much time has passed. Circumstance has doubtless made us such different people, you and I. The mutiny has changed me so that I shall never again be that same carefree girl in silk and fragrant lavender water whom you met in the brigadier's orchard all those years ago. I am no longer a child. I am a survivor. So are you. But one thing has not changed: God help me, I still love you so. I shall always love you. Oh, Edward . . . wait for me. . . . Please, wait for me.

Two weeks later, Captain Terrence Willoughby walked into Charlotte's small whitewashed hospital office just as she was finishing a letter to her aunt at her family home in Kent. Finally, Charlotte had reason to inquire about the terms of her father's estate. Until now, it had mattered little to her. She had earned enough here at the hospital on which to live. But once they had been reunited, she and Edward might well need a bit of capital to buy that farm about which he had so often spoken.

Charlotte pushed the cane chair back from her writing table and came to face the captain. Her heart was racing and her mouth had gone dry. He had finally returned with information about Edward.

"Your husband was discharged nine years ago," he said bluntly, reading from a document he had brought out from a small leather valise.

Charlotte sighed as her eyes filled with grateful tears. So then it was true. He really was alive!

"It seems that your source was right," he continued. "Captain Edward Francis Langston was indeed wounded at Delhi and taken to Jheed back in '57. After an evaluation, it was determined that he was not fit to return to his post due to the trauma of his wife's death, and he left for England in October of 1858."

"Does it also say where he went after he left India?" she asked, making fists with both her hands.

The captain looked up from his paper. "I am afraid not, madam. Only that he returned home."

Charlotte nervously twirled her betrothal ring, the opal and silver, around on her finger. "I wrote letter after letter. I spoke to other survivors. . . . Everyone told me that he was dead," she muttered incredulously. "I did not want to believe it. . . . I would not believe it. But then they found a body! They told me it was him!" She looked up at him, her eyes blazing with tears. "How can that be? Tell me how, Captain."

"The army is so terribly sorry about all of this, Mrs. Langston. There was just no way to have kept track of some of the men who did survive during those dark days. Some of our soldiers were still coming wounded out of that region up to a year later. It really was a dreadful mess to try to sort out; reuniting families and all of that."

Outside in the courtyard, an old woman was screaming, and when Charlotte glanced out of her window she saw two of the nurses trying to restrain her until a doctor arrived. The woman had seen her two daughters beheaded by *sepoys*. Her husband had died in her arms, half his abdomen missing. He had simply bled to death. There were only a few others like them here now. Most had returned to England, to what family they had left. This hospital, with its endless sounds of screaming and its pungent scent of camphor, had been her home for nearly nine years. Until two weeks ago she had believed it might just well keep her for the rest of her life.

"If there is nothing else I can do for you, Mrs. Langston . . ." the captain said, shifting uneasily again.

"I really do thank you for coming."

"I only wish I could have been more help."

"You told me what I needed most to know, and for that I am grateful."

He tried to smile, but it looked more like a grimace. She knew he could not wait to leave. *You are fortunate,* she thought as she watched him turn and go through the door. *You still have your innocence. But life here in India shall change that. It always does.* She wondered if so young a man would ever believe, looking at her now—pale skin, the long, unbound hair, this worn uniform for a proper gown—that she had been pretty once. *The prettiest girl in Delhi.*

When he had gone, Charlotte fell back onto her simple cot with its coarse gray covers and wept. She wiped her face, but the tears kept coming. She was glad Jawahar was not there to try to cheer her up.

Just now she really wanted to cry.

 **14**

"MAMA!"

The next afternoon, Hugh Edward leapt into Charlotte's open arms in a single bound, and she cradled his head against her heart. Jawahar stood leaning against the door-frame, trying hard to push away the envy as he watched them. The boy was her son, after all. Still, this was what he had longed for. What he had needed.

"I missed you yesterday, Mama!"

"I missed you too, darling," she said softly, kissing his upturned face.

Charlotte caught her breath when she held him back to really look at him. His eyes, dark and sensual, glittered up at her with the same long lashes. Even at the age of nine, it was Edward smiling up at her. She struggled not to cry again.

"Come. Sit beside me. I have something I want to tell you."

Hugh Edward settled onto the bed beside his mother, then put his hand on her knee. Charlotte looked at his small fingers curled lovingly into the ecru cotton that she wore, and she took a breath. This would not be easy.

"I must go away for a little while, darling."

"No!" he blurted, springing to his feet and pivoting to face her. "You cannot! I won't let you!"

Jawahar came from the doorway into the bedroom and put a hand on Hugh Edward's shoulder. "You must let your mother explain, *béta.*"

"Explain what? That I have no father and now, just when you are finally recovering, I shall have no mother either! You're dreadful for doing this! Really dreadful!"

"Hugh Edward!" Jawahar gasped. "You musn't say such a thing!"

Charlotte came slowly to her feet, her heart pierced by his dagger-sharp words. "No. My son is right. I know that I have hurt him deeply by not being the sort of mother he deserves, and for never having had the strength to explain to him the details of why that is."

"So you plan to make it up to me by going away?"

She braced her hands on the bedpost. This would not be easy, for either of them. But he must be told the truth. After what he had been forced to endure these years as her son, Charlotte owed him that much.

"I am going to England to find your father."

There was a pause in the charged exchange between mother and son, and Charlotte waited, glad for a moment to try and steady her heart. "You're lying! My father is dead! He died in the massacre at Delhi!"

"I believed so as well, darling," she said, trying her best to remain calm. "Until a few days ago. Today I was finally given proof that I was wrong. A man from the army came here to see me."

The child's eyes flicked from his mother to Jawahar, looking for confirmation. One glance told him that she spoke the truth. When he looked back at her, it was with wide, contemptuous eyes full of hurt. "This would not be the first time you've said anything just to keep me away!"

"I know, darling, and I am more sorry for that than you will ever understand. I would like to explain it to you, how it has been for me after Delhi. Perhaps one day when you are older, I shall be able to."

"Your mother endured a nightmare, *béta*. She does not lie to you in this."

Hugh Edward seemed disarmed by Charlotte's honesty, and he sank back onto the bed and she sat down beside him. "Are you really going to find him?" he asked in a softer voice.

She looked into his eyes sincerely. "I do hope so."

"What about Jawahar and I?" he asked, and his voice was even lower now, more full of fear.

"I shall send for both of you once we are settled. Your father still believes that I am dead, so there is bound to be some adjustment at first."

"It is all right," Jawahar said calmly, putting his hands on Hugh Edward's slumped shoulders. "We shall be fine here. We shall come when you are ready."

"Yes, Mama. We shall be fine," he finally echoed, trying to mean it.

Charlotte hugged her son and then Jawahar. "Will you tell him about me?" Hugh Edward asked, suddenly gleeful as his mother folded him into her arms.

"I shall tell him everything." She kissed him affectionately.

"He is bound to be surprised to learn that he has a son, isn't he?"

"No doubt we shall both have our share of surprises, darling." She sighed, stroking his hair.

Later that night, Charlotte sat with a flickering oil lamp to light her desk and tried to decide how to begin a letter to Edward. It was late, past midnight, and the hospital and the grounds beyond her window were quiet. But she must warn him that she was coming to England.

She brushed the dry pen across the paper for the fourth

time, wondering what words one could possibly write to lessen the shock. There was nothing, simply nothing, she could say to prepare him. Her hand was heavy as she dipped the pen into the well of black ink and began.

My darling Edward, I know that this shall come as a tremendous shock. . . .

She crumpled the slip of paper into a ball after a moment and cast it to the floor with the half dozen others. *No,* she thought. *I cannot do it. He is bound to see it, as I did at first, as some sort of cruel hoax.* But there was more than simply that preventing her from finishing any of the letters she had begun. Charlotte wanted to be with him when he discovered the truth. It was something she had been denied: the joy of seeing with her own eyes that it was true; feeling his arms around her to confirm what she so desperately wanted to believe.

She cupped her hand around the flame and blew it out. Suddenly she was in darkness. Charlotte loved the peace that darkness brought. She could hear her heart beating. It was a calming sound. She settled back in the stiff mahogany chair and closed her eyes. *No. I simply cannot prepare him for my coming. How could I? I fear we must face one another for both of us to really believe that it is true. I must put the fear of what I might find aside,* Charlotte thought as she nervously chewed a thumbnail.

"I must go to him unannounced. Yes," she whispered in the darkness. "To Tetbury."

She would not listen to the gnawing fear that he might have met someone new. She could not. She must trust that brief, special time that they had shared, and she must trust the God who had seen fit to make her Edward's wife. Beyond that, there was really nothing else—not if she meant to get back what had been so brutally taken from her. And from him.

It was nearly a week before Charlotte could gather enough of her savings, make the arrangements, and book passage out of India. It had been a week of excitement mixed with apprehension, recalling vividly the sort of arduous voyage that lay ahead of her. Her childhood memories of the ship that had brought her and her parents to India were of the constant rolling and pitching and the retching sounds of seasick passengers. But it was the only means of getting back to England, and she would do anything—anything—to be in Edward's arms once again. But before she left, she must see Jawahar one last time.

He stood in the doorway to her bedroom, a plain white-washed room on the hospital's second floor, which had been her home since she'd agreed to stay on at Saint Mary's. Hugh Edward and Jawahar shared a smaller room down another corridor.

"Doctor Gaylord and his wife have given me this new dressing gown," she said softly as she folded the ivory-colored cotton and packed it into her bag. "And dear old Elizabeth Pemberton knit me that lovely shawl. She said I had been away too long to recall how chilly the evenings in England could be."

Jawahar glanced over at the delicate black shawl tossed over the arm of a cane chair beside the last few items she had left to pack. *"Memsahib* Pemberton would not speak a word when she first came here to Calcutta," he recalled.

"She was filled with so much pain in those days," Charlotte sighed. "As so many of us were."

"Your kind understanding has changed her life, *memsahib."*

Charlotte sat on the edge of her bed, her hands falling to her lap. "Whatever I have given to these people, I have gotten back from them tenfold."

"They shall miss you."

"And I shall miss them," she said softly, then looked up at him. "It has been my own demons I have wrestled with every bit as much as theirs."

For a moment neither of them spoke. Jawahar stood there awkwardly as Charlotte looked at him, and he could see by the expression on her face how difficult it would be for her to leave. "I wanted you to understand why you both could not come to see me off," she finally said, and in her words she breathed a sigh. "I believe it would just be too difficult for my son."

"Perhaps it is so," he answered her in a small voice.

Charlotte moved a few steps nearer the door until they were facing one another. "But I did want to see you privately, Jawahar. You and I have shared something very special these past years."

"You have faced a great deal more than any person should be forced to endure, and you have survived it."

"I can never repay the debt of gratitude I owe you for helping me to do that."

"If there is a debt, *memsahib*, it is I who owe you for taking me into your home and keeping me in your life when you had every reason in the world to hate all people like me."

"There is no one like you, Jawahar," she said, her green eyes shining. "I knew that the first moment I saw you in Agra."

"Agra." He paused, remembering where he had sold stones to pay for his supper—and to avoid being beaten. "If I had stayed there, I can only imagine what might have become of me."

"Ah, yes. What might have become of us both. One without the other," she said, her pale pink lips turning up in a cautious smile.

And then, for the first time in his life, Jawahar saw love for him displayed openly and honestly on Charlotte's pale face. She looked away a moment later, to the photograph of him and Hugh Edward when the three of them had gone on a picnic to Calcutta's Botanical Gardens.

"I don't know what is going to happen once I reach England," she said, gazing down at the image of her son. "But I want you to promise me that you will take care of him. I know that he puts on a good front, but this must all be so terribly confusing to a boy his age."

"I shall do as you ask." He nodded. "You need worry about nothing here, *memsahib.*"

"I know that I can trust you, Jawahar. He is Edward's son,

and despite what my sorrow has often led him to believe, he is the most important thing in the world to me."

His breath quickened, and Jawahar felt the same jerk of envy, a disappointment at the sound of the words spoken in her sweet voice. The brief sensation of love vanished as quickly as it had come over him, and his mind understood what his heart could not accept. He was not her son. He was no longer anyone's son.

"I have come to accept the connection that a blood tie creates," he finally said.

Charlotte looked up at him again. "Blood, yes. And adversity."

Then, in a single fluid movement, she reached out and took Jawahar into her arms. She pressed him tight against her slim body, and he sank against her as if he were a boy as young and full of hope once again as Hugh Edward. This single show of affection was so unexpected, so long desired, that without warning he heard himself begin to weep as she held him.

"I know I have never said it before," she whispered softly into his dark hair, "but I feel as if I have two sons, Jawahar. You were my first; my very special boy that the good Lord in His infinite wisdom brought into my life." She pressed him back gently and tipped up his tawny, tear-stained face with her finger. "And I could not love you any more if you had come from my own body."

There were no more words. There was nothing anyone would ever say to him that would ever mean more. And somehow she knew it. Now at nineteen, Jawahar towered over her, and yet still he lay his head softly on her shoulder as she continued to stroke his soft, ebony hair.

"I should have told you that," she whispered. "I am so sorry I never did before."

When he could tear himself away from her, he opened the door and looked back at her bag, half packed and open on the bed, and his heart sank. He had asked Hugh Edward to be brave, but he did not want her to go either. England was such a long way, a far-off exotic land, and the child within him fought the fear that she might go and never send for them. But unlike his younger charge, Jawahar had seen the captain-*sahib* with his wife. He had seen the flame of love that had danced so brilliantly between them. She had endured so much, and she deserved that kind of happiness again. *The* memsahib *needs me to be strong again,* he thought, glancing up at her one last time.

"Be safe," he called out to her. "Your son and I shall pray for that."

She pressed her fingers to her lips, light like a feather, then softly blew a kiss across the room. "My two sons," she whispered, and as they smiled at one another, no more need be said.

KATHERINE BLACKSTONE'S HUNTER-GREEN CARRIAGE CLICKED across the rolling emerald landscape beneath a flock of fluffy, drifting clouds as the two women jostled rhythmically inside.

"I am sure you miss them both terribly," Katherine said, still overcome by the rest of the story.

"You cannot imagine how much."

Charlotte gazed out of her window across the violet sky. The ancient, sweet-smelling lavender wafted through the window, calling to her from her own childhood. She could see now why Edward loved the Cotswolds so; the remote and mysterious fusing of gray and purple in the late afternoon sky, the violet shadows, the cool wind hushing the trees as sheep grazed along the grassy knolls.

"It looks as if we are nearly there."

"I imagined it so many times when Edward would tell me about it, and in my mind it looked just like this," she said as they crossed the fringes of a quaint country town, its cottages of gray slate and stone and fenced gardens bright with sweet Williams, gilly flowers, and larkspur. "The earth and the sky were exactly this color."

"Would you like me to go with you?" Katherine asked as they passed another handful of cottages, a pub and a church, nearing the town. "Just for the first few awkward moments, perhaps?"

"Thank you, Katherine. But this is something I must do alone."

"Then take this," she said, pressing a calling card into Charlotte's small, moist palm. "Any time you feel you need a friend, I shall come. Or you may come to me. You have but to ask."

The carriage lurched to a stop and Katherine's driver waited outside to open the door. She nodded for him to remain a moment more as she turned back to Charlotte.

"Tell me, will you really be all right?"

Charlotte inhaled a breath. "Now that the time has come, I don't mind telling you that I am actually quite frightened to death."

"Is it seeing him that frightens you, child?"

Charlotte twirled her betrothal ring nervously and looked at Katherine with wide, moist eyes. "I am afraid Edward will not feel as he did once he sees me," she answered softly, vulnerably. "I have changed so much. . . . When I go out, I still must wear these dreadful glasses to protect my eyes from the sun. Plus, you know they broke my nose and fractured both my cheeks. Since I did not get medical attention at first, they never healed quite the same way . . ."

"It is a lovely nose, full of character. Just like the rest of your sweet face."

"But I was . . ." The words caught in her slim white throat. "Quite pretty once."

Katherine sat back against the seat a moment and ran a hand across her lips. It was true. The child she had been in Delhi was hidden now beneath the years—maturity and tragedy. The bright golden mane of hair she had confided that Edward had so loved was gone now. It was darkened by time, into a soft tawny brown, tamed away from her face with combs. Her body too had changed. She was not the rail-slim girl of sixteen who had captivated Edward. Now her body was full and ripe, replete with the willowy curves of a woman. A mother. Her breasts were large, but her waist was still small.

From the moment she had first seen her on board the ship, Katherine had been attracted by her rich, tempered beauty. It was a kind of radiance that, even in the full bloom of her own youth, Katherine Blackstone had never managed to attain. But the expression on Charlotte's face just now was so completely pitiful, so full of real anxiety for what lay before her, that the smile faded softly from Katherine's wrinkled, aging face.

"Would you like me to tell you what I see?" she asked, her words soft as she turned to her. "I see a young woman whose appearance has doubtless been changed by time and circumstance. You are no longer a girl of sixteen, on that I will agree. But your beauty is not gone. Goodness me, look at yourself, dear child! You are a lovely, vibrant young woman with a face full of character and an elegance one does not acquire without surviving a bit of adversity."

Charlotte looked up hopefully. "Do you really believe so?"

"With all of my heart."

"Rajab did not even recognize me at first."

"He believed you were dead."

"So does Edward."

Katherine patted her hand. "Give him a chance, child. Your Edward may well surprise you."

"I can never thank you enough for everything, Katherine," she said, hugging her.

"A new dress and hat really wasn't so much."

192

"No, but listening to the whole dreadful story . . . and being a friend when I needed it most certainly was."

"I have given no more than I have gotten," she assured her in a silky-smooth voice. "I will have my driver take me to that little pub over there," she said, indicating a rustic stone building called the Cock 'n' Feathers. "And I shall wait for an hour. If it does not go as you had hoped with your Edward, I shall be happy to take you back to Oxford with me."

"You needn't wait, Katherine. Really. If I decide not to stay once Edward and I have spoken, I shall hire a coach out tomorrow."

"I want to do this, child," she persisted. "Humor an old woman, hmm?"

Charlotte smiled reluctantly and then took her bag from the driver. "Remember," Katherine called after her. "I shall be waiting if you need me."

She walked alone down the gravel-covered road through the center of town. She was carrying her blue and green carpet bag in one hand and Katherine's eggshell-blue silk parasol and the black shawl in the other. The Langston cottage, she had been told by a young boy who passed her, was the little stone cottage with mullioned windows and a long, slate gray roof at the end of the lane.

Her heart was racing so that she could barely breathe. One part of her mind was filled with fear. It had been so many years. Yet the other part spurred her on. They were man and wife forever. Two halves of the same whole. He would be overcome with joy at what he was about to discover. It would be all right.

It had to be.

She lifted the latch on the rickety white gate and stepped into a neat little English garden. When she heard the sound of children laughing, her heart quickened. Around her there were crocus, tiger lily, lavender, and myrtle. The aroma of the lavender twined with the fragrance of a stew cooking in the kitchen. *This cannot be it,* she thought wildly. *There must be some mistake. This is not a widower's simple cottage, it is a family home!* But the directions had been clear. Last cottage on the right. White shutters. Grand old elm tree in the yard. "I am looking for Edward Langston," she said at the door, taking off the glasses and slipping them into her bag.

A plain, big-boned woman, heavy with child in a drab beige country dress, stood before her, wiping her rough hands on her wrinkled white apron. Her hair was the color of Edward's, dark and full of lustrous waves, pulled away from her pale face and held loosely by two tortoiseshell combs.

"I am afraid he is not here just now," she said as two little girls scrambled around her legs, giggling and squirming. Charlotte glanced past the woman, through the open door and into the modest cottage. It was furnished simply with worn chintz-covered chairs, a table, and it had a large fireplace hearth stained with soot. And then the picture. It was hanging on the wall above the table held by a green cord. It was a wedding picture. The bride was the woman who stood before her now. The groom was Edward Langston. Katherine Blackstone's parasol slipped to the ground, and Charlotte leaned against the doorjamb to brace herself.

"Good gracious me! Are you all right?"

She felt a breeze across her face, but it did not cool her. She looked again with disbelieving eyes. But it was Edward as he had always been. Tall. Confident. So handsome. The way he had once stood beside her. *Oh, Edward . . . no!*

"Who is it, Mama?" she heard one of the little girls ask. The woman hushed her. But it was as if they were speaking from the other end of a tunnel, through which there was light and heat and unbelievable pain. Their words were unclear.

"Dear woman, please do come in and have some water. You look as if you're about to faint."

Charlotte wanted to run back to Katherine. Dash inside her carriage where it was safe and never look back. But it had been such a gruelingly long journey, and now with the shock, she was not strong enough to walk even so far as the pub. Not now. Another word from her lips and she was quite certain she actually would faint.

She let the woman lead her into the kitchen and to a scarred oak table, mercifully far from the framed picture that seemed to dominate the small room. They sat together in two chairs, the woman—Edward's wife—looking at her with concern. Charlotte ran her hand across her brow, and with each breath she trembled. Her worst fear had come true. Edward had recovered from what had happened in Delhi and he had gotten on with his life.

What in Heaven's name am I to do now? she thought as one of the little girls loitered at her knee, smiling and giggling behind chubby hands.

"Is she going to be ill, Mama?"

"I said hush!"

After another moment, the woman got up and poured a glass of water from a pitcher near the stove.

"So how is it that you know my husband?"

Charlotte's heart, pierced by the picture, began to bleed. Now in addition to everything, she must lie. "I . . . don't know him. A man on the edge of town said that you might have a room here to let. He said I should see Mr. Langston."

"Oh? Who was that?"

"I . . . am afraid I didn't ask his name."

There was a pause. The woman turned around with the glass of water and handed it to Charlotte. "That does sound rather curious indeed."

"Well . . . perhaps he was mistaken. He might have meant someone else." She tried to stand, but she felt her legs about to give way beneath her. "I really should be going."

"Nonsense. You are still white as a ghost. Drink this, please."

Charlotte pressed the glass to her lips, not certain how she could swallow anything for the painful lump of shock still there. She could not seem to force her heart to accept what she had found, even though somewhere in the back of her mind she had always known it was a risk just coming here.

"I meant it was rather curious that just this morning,

Edward . . . that is my husband . . . Edward was telling me that I should really look for some help these last few weeks until the baby comes. This one has been so much more difficult than my first."

Charlotte looked away from the well-used collection of cast-iron pots, kettles, and pans and glanced down again at the woman's round belly, and she felt the vomit rise in her parched throat. She took another mouthful of water and choked it down. Then she rose back to her feet. This woman—this stranger—was carrying Edward's child! *God in Heaven above!* she thought. *How much more can You ask of me?*

"I don't believe it is the sort of thing I would be good at," Charlotte mouthed, having no idea from where the words had come. "I was really only looking for somewhere to stay until I am accustomed enough to the area to find a place of my own."

She was still fighting the urge to run from the room with the fury of a madwoman and escape a circumstance that, with her whole heart and soul, she did not want to believe.

"You're not from around here, are you?"

Charlotte looked back at the woman. It was a kind face that met her, one in the full bloom of her pregnancy. Thick pink lips, ruddy cheeks, and a flicker of reserve in her cocoa-brown eyes. But they were tired eyes; the key to a woman who had worked hard all of her life. She was a country woman with heavy bones and thick, rough hands. In every way, Edward's second wife was the complete antithesis of his first.

"My family came from here a long time ago," Charlotte finally said in a low voice, perpetuating the lie, and each word drained her a little more. "When my husband died recently . . . I found that I had nothing else to keep me in London. I have no other family."

"I am sorry."

"Not half so sorry as I," she uttered, speaking her first words of truth between them. "It was after his death that the desire began in me to simplify my life. I found that I wanted to retrace my past, so I came here."

"A fine lady like you comes here with no coachman and no lady's maid?" Her bland face lit with surprise.

"I cannot make a new life as long as I hold fast to those remnants of my past. . . . Perhaps that sounds a bit odd, but I asked them to let me off at the edge of town."

"I see."

Then suddenly, unexpectedly, the deathknell.

"Well then, since we are bound at least to be neighbors, I should introduce myself. I am Anne Langston."

"And . . . are they both your daughters?"

"Oh, no. Just this little minx. This is my daughter, Charlotte."

She glanced over at the shy child who stepped toward her mother, certain she could not possibly bear a single shock more. "Her name is . . . Charlotte?" The question came with the fury of a gun shot, deep and heavy—and fatal.

"Yes. Pretty, isn't it? I wanted to name her Mary, after my mother, but my husband was quite insistent."

Now it was her turn. Charlotte must force a name past her lips, seeing that the truth was certainly impossible to speak. But her mind was reeling, and her face felt as if it were on fire. "I am . . . Katherine—Katherine Blackstone," she heard herself say, and the first name that had come into her mind surprised her.

"Blackstone. Hmm. I seem to recall a family of Blackstones who lived over in Burford when I was a little girl. Or perhaps the name was Gladstone. . . ."

"Burford." Charlotte fought for a tone and a reply that would convince her. "Yes. Well, I've just come from there this morning. But I found nothing suitable. It has been rather a long time since any of my family lived there."

Anne Langston glanced down at her guest's expensive city gown with the copper-colored silk braid. She saw the delicate parasol that lay across the table. "You'll pardon me for saying so, I hope, Mrs. Blackstone, but Tetbury is not a'tall like London. We are simple folks here. Most of us don't trust city types. That may well have been your problem."

Charlotte fought for the strength to stand. "I can see that

coming here was a foolish idea. Perhaps it is true what they say: you can never really go back again."

She turned slowly, her legs like butter. Her only thought was to get away from here, away from this woman who had so unsuspectingly taken her life and was now proposing that she stay to observe it. Charlotte moved toward the door.

"Mrs. Blackstone, please."

Charlotte stopped. She felt as if her heart had too.

"We have a room, and I really could use the help with my daughter. I don't mind telling you, one woman to the next, that I've not been a'tall well. Oh, my friends have been more than kind. But most of them have their own lives to live. Husbands. Children. I can only ask so much. Staying here with us would be a way for you to meet a few people and it would give you time to find a place where you want to settle, either here or back in Burford."

She looked back at Anne Langston, this gentle, unsuspecting woman who truly had no idea who it was that had come into her house. For just an instant, Charlotte wanted to laugh at the incredibly bizarre irony of it all. It was either that or she would surely burst into tears. *I should have written,* she thought. *Why did I not allow myself to believe that my worst fear might actually well have come true?*

"I do appreciate the offer," Charlotte said slowly. "It is very kind of you, but I simply do not think—"

"Yes, of course," Anne interrupted in a good-natured tone, but the expression on her face was full of sudden desperation. "I can understand how a fine young woman from the city like yourself would refuse a simple country wife. After all, we don't have a great deal to offer you."

"It is not that. I simply—"

"We could offer you a room and of course board, but I am certain it is far less than what you're accustomed to."

Charlotte surveyed the kitchen, a room she had managed to avoid for anything more than observation all of her life. "I am accustomed to nothing, Mrs. Langston. I have never worked before."

"No, of course not. But it wouldn't really be any great amount of work here; and it would be just until the baby comes. It would also give you time to decide what it is you really want to do, and a place to do it."

"Mrs. Langston—"

"Please, call me Anne."

Such kindness was a dagger in her heart. "Very well, Anne, then. But how is that you can be so willing to welcome me into your home like this when you don't even know me? I am a stranger here."

"You have a kind face." She smiled. "And Tetbury is not at all like the city. Besides, I really am just exhausted enough to be desperate."

Their discourse was broken off by the long squeal of a door hinge. Little Charlotte, a child of about three, with bright blue eyes and her parents' thick dark hair, scampered out of the kitchen.

"Papa!" she cried. The sound echoed through the house.

"Oh, splendid! Now you can meet Edward himself," Anne said, still smiling. "Perhaps he can convince you to stay."

She could not run now. There was nowhere to go. Hands trembling with fear, Charlotte tipped her bonnet down low over her eyes. She tossed the betrothal ring he had given her into her carpet bag and then fumbled for the shaded glasses. How peculiar to feel so desperate now; desperate to hide her face from Edward, the man she had come halfway around the world to see.

When she looked back, Anne Langston was gazing curiously at her.

"It is the sunlight," she explained in a voice she had made purposely low, a breathy imitation of how Rani had once spoken.

Charlotte was crippled with fear and grasping for anything, not certain how long she could keep up the pretense. But whatever she thought of the man she had married in Delhi, one thing was certain: She could not be cruel enough to confront his expectant wife; to reveal her true identity

199

now. That thought had begun the lie. Now she looked back at the unsuspecting woman and prepared to deceive her further still.

"Light has bothered my eyes since they were injured in childhood, and it is rather bright coming in through the window there. The glasses help."

"Oh, dear me. I am so sorry." Anne rose to her feet, straining with the weight of the child. "You should have said something. Here, let me close the curtains."

Charlotte heard Edward's footsteps behind her as he drew near. She heard the little girl pleading to be gathered up into his arms. Good God, this was some sort of nightmare, and any moment she was going to awake! In Edward's house with his wife and child, hiding her face, her identity, praying that she would find the strength to endure these next few terrifying moments and then escape.

Suddenly Charlotte could feel him behind her; smell his breath on her neck. But it was not sweet as she remembered. Today he smelled of whiskey and cigar smoke.

"What have you got for my supper?" he asked Anne dryly. "I told Paddy I would cover for him tonight since he hasn't been feeling a bit well since yesterday, so I have only an hour."

His voice cut through her heart, already so desperately wounded. It was the single thing that told her no, this was not some grand mistake after all. This man behind her truly was Edward. The man of her heart. Another woman's husband. Charlotte lowered her head further still.

"Must you really go back? I've not been feeling well today myself, and this is the third time this week you've worked from morning until night."

"I know that it is a strain, but it is no longer my father's pub, Anne, it is mine now. You know that," he countered, ignoring the stranger in their midst. "It is my responsibility."

As he spoke, Edward took a glass and bottle of whiskey from the pine cupboard behind her. His voice was harsh and on edge, but beneath it was the most profound undercurrent of sadness she had ever heard. Charlotte was sure that any moment her heart was going to stop. This was too much for any one person to bear. She wanted to spring to her feet and say that she must go, but that would only draw too much attention to herself, and just now she could not risk that, not now when things were so unclear.

Edward slouched in the chair across from her, but he did not look up. For that she was grateful. Finally, in the instant after he had poured the whiskey, she could manage a furtive little glance up at him without being seen. It shook her to the core to see how lost he looked. It was the very last thing she had expected.

The face was the same. The same beautiful, chiseled features, blue eyes lit like a summer morning, with a thick, dark beard now to match his mustache. It was the beard most of all that hid the elegant young military officer he once had been, layering it behind a working-class veneer. Gone was the dashing, red and blue uniform, and the prideful bearing with which he had worn it.

He was still tall and lean and darkly handsome, dressed now in a simple white shirt and gray twill trousers, but he lacked the same spirit; that incredible spark of confidence that had won her over so entirely that first evening at the Graves House ball. He may have remarried, begun again, Charlotte thought; but something had changed, like a stallion broken too swiftly. Too violently. That much she could see from the first.

"This is Katherine Blackstone," Anne said in introduction when it was clear that he was not going to ask. "Her people are originally from Burford, and she's come back to make a new life for herself. I was just trying to convince her to stay with us and help me with Charlotte until the new baby comes, and she can find a place of her own that suits."

Edward glanced up at her unexpectedly.

His expression was disinterested until, for an·instant, his eyes met her glasses-covered gaze across the table. In that one brief moment, she saw a flicker of recognition. Charlotte lowered her eyes, pretending to be demure, and as quickly as it had come, the moment, and the recognition, passed.

Edward swallowed the contents of his glass, then slouched

in the chair, legs sprawled. Though he looked in Charlotte's direction, he did not see her. He did not see anyone. Not his daughter. Not his wife. Not his entire past together with his present, right here in his very midst. It was all so unbelievable.

"So then. Has she agreed to stay?" he finally asked his wife, his harsher tone having softened.

Anne lay a plate of stewed mutton and peas on the table before him. "She hasn't decided."

Of course she could not stay. How could she? Edward beneath the same roof with two wives? Great God in Heaven, the notion of it was completely absurd!

"Well then. Will you be taking the job or not?" he asked into the silence, his head lowered over his plate. "And why is it so dark in here?"

"The light hurts Mrs. Blackstone's eyes," Anne explained calmly, sitting down between them as their daughter played quietly in the corner. "She's had an injury."

Charlotte had anticipated Anne's explanation by coming to her feet so that she would not be forced to face Edward when Anne answered him. "Might I have another glass of water, Mrs. Langston? My throat is rather dry."

"Why certainly, my dear. Help yourself."

She held the pitcher up and tried not to rattle it against the glass. Absurd as it seemed, even in the midst of the fear and the shock, something inside Charlotte was suddenly telling her to accept. That way, when the time was right to confront him, she would know it and she would not be forced to hurt his wife or child in the process. If she left now, she would never understand what had happened to him after the massacre, and this image of the two of them together, Anne and Edward, would live with her forever.

"Well then?" he pressed for a reply, and Charlotte could hear him at the table behind her pouring another glass of whiskey. "What shall it be?"

The tone he had used with her, one of complete disregard, sent a chill coursing through her, and it felt like lightning, cold and sharp and very fast. The Edward she had known in India had never spoken to her with anything but the greatest admiration. Now there was so much futility in his voice that she could not think beyond the grief it brought her. *Oh, Edward, I am your wife!* she thought sadly, drawing in a ragged breath. *It is me, Charlotte, right here in your midst! The woman you searched for, the woman for whom you risked your life!*

"I know he seems a bit mean-spirited, Mrs. Blackstone, but you mustn't let my husband influence your decision to stay. He has been working terribly long hours lately. We recently inherited the pub on Long Street," Anne intervened as Edward finished his supper. "He leaves quite early in the morning these days and I am usually fast asleep when he returns home at night. So I am certain you would have very few encounters with one another if that concerns you."

"Your offer is generous indeed, Mrs. Langston, but this really wasn't the sort of arrangement I was looking for," she hedged, using Rani's reserved tone of voice and keeping her head low to disguise herself.

Edward chuckled at the reply. "There really isn't a great deal of opportunity for a young woman out here in the country, Mrs.—"

"Blackstone. Katherine Blackstone."

"If it is your intention to settle down around here, you couldn't do a great deal better than befriending my wife. Anne knows nearly everyone within fifty miles of Tetbury, and that would certainly make your transition a good deal easier."

"I shall keep that in mind."

"I have got to get back to the pub," he announced, bolting down the last of his supper and then rising again. In all, he had not given Charlotte more than a passing glance. "Whatever you two ladies decide is fine with me."

He bent down to kiss his daughter on top of the head. Charlotte pulled back the curtain to look out into the garden as he kissed his wife. "Well, Mrs. Blackstone, it was a pleasure to meet you," Edward said as she stood with her back to him.

"And you, Mr. Langston," she whispered in reply.

* * *

The real Katherine Blackstone sat alone in a wooden booth inside the Cock 'n' Feathers, more uncomfortable than she had ever been in her life. And more concerned.

She sipped absently at a cup of tea long gone cold and watched the old clock near the bar. The hour she had promised to wait had passed thirty minutes before. She had only managed to stay seated in such a dark and dreary place by bargaining with herself in five-minute increments. *I shall wait five minutes more,* she told herself again and again. *Only five minutes more.*

She tapped her foot nervously beneath the table, painfully aware of the local men who perched at the bar swilling ale and whispering about the mysterious, grand lady in the costly gown. It was the first time in her life that the very proper Katherine Blackstone had ever set foot in a public house—and she was quite certain that it would also be the last.

"I am doing this for Charlotte. Must think of Charlotte," she muttered, choking down another swallow of cold tea.

"Might I bring you anything else, madam?" asked a stocky, balding man who was suddenly looming beside her.

Katherine glanced up at a plump, ruddy-cheeked face set with wide blue eyes and a good-natured smile.

"No, thank you, indeed," she said crisply. "But I should like to sit here alone another few moments, sir, without being constantly fussed over at every turn . . . if you please."

His bushy gray eyebrows merged in a frown. "You shall hear nothing more out of me . . . madam."

"Splendid."

Her concern for Charlotte had made her sound curt. Condescending. She saw the disapproval quickly sour his pleasant expression. He was staring at her. She was staring back, but there was no other dialogue between them. The barman simply shrugged his shoulders after a moment and went back to the bar. He had left Katherine with the most peculiar sensation: that she had no reason at all to feel the slightest bit of superiority. If anything, it was she who was beneath him.

In all, she waited for nearly two excruciatingly long hours in the dim little pub before Katherine finally accepted the inevitable. Charlotte was not going to come. Katherine hadn't expected it to matter so much. And yet it did. She had grown accustomed to the companionship of the extraordinarily courageous young woman. Katherine had hoped for any excuse to have a little more time with her.

By now she had been reunited with her Edward. It must have gone well. Certainly better than she had expected. *Yes indeed, love is better left to the young,* she thought as she placed a few coins on the table. Love—a real love like theirs happened to so few people. She was glad Charlotte and Edward had recaptured it. After everything she had been through, she did so deserve to be happy.

Her decision made, Katherine was anxious to be gone from this provincial little town too full of kind sentiment for a woman who had lived so long without it. She walked out with such purposeful strides that she did not even realize that the man who held the door for her as he was coming in and she going out was Edward Langston, very nearly as Charlotte had described him.

"Who was that, Paddy?" Edward asked, slipping back behind the bar.

"I haven't a clue," he replied, pouring a dark pint of ale for another customer. "Said she was waiting for a friend."

"A friend of someone like that here in Tetbury? Not at all likely." Edward laughed.

As a silver moon glistened in the evening sky, Charlotte stood alone on the front porch of Edward's stone cottage and finally tried to slow her mind of the whirling torrent of thoughts. Anne Langston and her daughter were both safe in their beds, and now finally, for the first time that day, she had a moment to try to collect herself.

She had agreed to stay in Tetbury and help Anne until her child was born. The offer had been too curious a coincidence to have refused it, and Anne Langston truly was in need of assistance. But Charlotte's real motivation had been entirely selfish. She had given her life to this man they now shared. She had come a long way to reclaim him. Charlotte deserved an opportunity to understand.

She took a sip of lukewarm coffee from a chipped china cup and gazed back into the town. Lamps flickered behind a smattering of curtained windows, great puffs of white smoke belched from gray stone chimneys, and all of it lay beneath a heavy shawl of evening mist. It was a charming little village, exactly as Edward had once described it. It certainly was a million miles from their dusty bungalow in Delhi.

The thought of the home they had so briefly shared made her heart ache for Hugh Edward and Jawahar, and she closed her eyes to say a silent prayer that they were not missing her as much as she was missing them.

She must write as soon as she was settled. She had promised. But not tonight. She was not certain she could do much of anything tonight besides fall exhausted into the little bed Anne had provided her in a small room off of the kitchen. Anne had been surprised when she'd insisted upon it, rather than the larger room upstairs across from the one she shared with Edward. But for Charlotte that would have been too much.

She moved quietly back through the house now, looking for even a clue of the Edward she had once known. The dark furniture, the heavy oil paintings—all of it was entirely different from what she would have chosen to enhance a home. But most surprising was that there was not a single souvenir or remembrance visible to tie him to India. Though it appeared he might have wanted to forget what had happened there, he had not sought to do so entirely. He had named his daughter Charlotte—the ultimate remembrance.

From that, she knew he had not even told Anne that he had been widowed. Edward was living his life now as though she had never even existed.

She glanced up at the wedding portrait and forced herself not to turn away from it. The day had made her numb enough and tired enough to look at it now. Edward smiled down from the simple oak frame just as he had earlier in the day, a moment frozen in time. But now, in the lamplight, she could see more clearly that it was not the same expression at all that she remembered from their own wedding portrait.

On this one, his handsome face was drawn. Etched into the beautifully sculpted features was a remarkable expression of despair. *Perhaps that is why he has grown a beard,* she thought. *To cover up what is really inside.* And for the first time since she had come to their door, five long and grueling hours before, Charlotte felt a glimmer of hope. It came with the notion that at least she might leave here knowing that he had not forsaken her.

At least not in his heart.

She wiped at the tears that streamed down her cheeks. "Dear Lord above, give me strength while I am here . . ."

she whispered into the night. "Before I leave Tetbury, please help me to understand."

Charlotte awoke the next morning to the sound of Anne's daughter chattering in the kitchen. Nearly eight-thirty! She had overslept. She tried to sit up, but when she did her body pulled her back beneath the bedcovers as if she were made of lead. She gazed up at the ceiling of the little servant's room. It was an impossibly dreary room with no pictures on the walls and a single, modest window to bring in sunlight. It was smaller than her dressing room at Graves House, How life did change, she thought.

The aroma of cooking bacon wafted beneath the door, along with the smell of fresh coffee. Then suddenly there was Edward's voice edged with that same futility; as painful a sound to her now as it had been the night before. Even so, Charlotte breathed a sigh of relief. If she had not overslept, she would have had to face him in the broad light of day, and she was far from ready for that.

"So exactly how long does she plan to stay?"

"She'll only be with us until the baby comes," Anne replied in a whisper.

"I might remind you that I am not very fond of having strangers in the house."

"Oh, nonsense, Edward. You had a dozen servants of your very own under foot the entire time you were in India. You told me so yourself, and certainly all of them were strangers!"

"That was quite different."

"Why? Because they were employed to wait on you?"

"That is not a'tall what I meant, and you know it. I have been after you to see to some help for weeks. But not a stranger, and certainly not one living right here under foot. And for that matter, where is she if she's been taken on as a help to you?"

"She hasn't risen yet."

"Not yet?" He huffed. "Half the day is gone!"

"She had a long ride down from London yesterday,

Edward. And I heard her roaming around the house until the middle of the night. I thought I would let her sleep in a bit this first morning."

Neither of them said anything else for a moment. The charged silence that Charlotte sensed between them, her ear pressed to the door, was filled by their daughter's laughter. Then she heard a chair being pushed away from the table.

"Well, I have to go. I am late already."

"What time will you be home for supper?" Anne asked, and Charlotte could hear the caution in her voice. "I am fixing lamb."

"You know I can't tell you that," he answered her, and his voice was suddenly full of irritation. "As soon as there is a break in business, I shall try to get home for a quarter of an hour or so."

"Lately that blasted pub is all you think about."

"It is my responsibility. It was all my father had in his life."

Anne's voice was pleading. "Well, you are all that *we* have!"

Charlotte shook her head and closed her eyes again.

She waited until she heard the front door slam shut before she rose and quickly dressed. She pulled her hair back and put on her hat. Once again she hid her eyes with the dark glasses that would buy her the anonymity she needed. At least for a little while longer.

"Well, good morning!" Anne smiled up at her as she stood in the doorway.

"I am sorry I overslept."

"You were exhausted. That is to be expected after a long trip."

Anne looked down at her gown, the same one she had worn into Tetbury with all the hopes in the world. A gown belonging to the real Katherine Blackstone. "Don't you have anything a bit less formal? We are really very simple people here."

"I'm afraid not. I left most of my other things in London until I knew for certain that I could find lodgings here." In truth, the only other dress Charlotte had to wear was the worn and dated one for traveling that had been a hand-me-down from a patient at the hospital in Calcutta.

"And the hat . . ." Anne smiled kindly, looking at the real Katherine Blackstone's fashionable bonnet pulled low again over Charlotte's forehead. "Well, no matter. You can borrow one of my dresses if you like. Until after the baby comes, I certainly won't be needing them."

Charlotte's stomach turned at the thought of wearing her clothes. "I am really quite comfortable just as I am."

"People here can be difficult if they feel someone is trying to put on airs. I know they are not as fine as what you're accustomed to, but after breakfast you'd best choose one of mine. I would hate to see that lovely gown of yours ruined."

Better not to argue, Charlotte finally thought, and acquiesced with a nod as she glanced up at the kitchen window. It felt stifling in here, and she was anxious to have the warm sun on her face and the breeze through her hair.

"I'm sorry. Is the light bothering you again? I shall have to get used to keeping the curtains closed in the morning."

Edward would not be returning for several hours. Charlotte took off her shaded glasses. "It is all right, really. It is only the afternoon sun I find intolerable. But I am so accustomed to these things that sometimes I forget I don't need them."

"I shall try to remember the afternoons."

She lay the glasses on the table and looked up at Anne. In the morning light she was fresh-faced, though already her skin had begun to wrinkle at the corners of her mouth and around her eyes. Charlotte imagined that as a young girl she must have been quite pretty.

"What shall I do first to help you?"

"Couldn't you do with a bit of breakfast?"

"Oh, no thank you," Charlotte replied, getting herself a cup of coffee from the pot on the stove. "I can never bear to eat first thing in the morning."

"Perhaps that is how you manage to keep such a lovely figure." Anne paused to reflect. "I had a nice shape myself once. Edward used to tell me so."

Charlotte took a sip of coffee as she stood at the stove and then swallowed hard. The hot liquid burned her throat. Good, she thought. Better not to feel like talking. The risk of what she might say was far too great if she began now.

"You're a lovely woman, Anne," she finally forced herself to say, and then she gathered her courage to come and sit beside her at the table.

"You're very kind. But I have filled out quite a bit these last years. My clothes tell me so even if my conscience doesn't."

"Is that since you've been married?" Charlotte lightly probed.

"Oh no. Long before that. It was while Edward was away that I lost the girlish figure I once had."

Her heart leapt. It was a painful sensation. "You've known Edward . . . Mr. Langston, for a long time then?"

Anne sipped her coffee. "We were raised together. Almost as brother and sister. My father is the butcher and his father owned the Cock 'n' Feathers pub next door."

"I see."

"They always expected us to marry as soon as we were old enough. But then Edward got it into his head that he should join the army and make something of himself. Since he didn't have the influence of some of the wealthier young men to avoid it, they sent him to Delhi. That's in India."

"Yes, I've heard of it," Charlotte could not help herself from saying.

"He was there for six years."

"Were you not frightened that he might meet someone else, being gone so long like that? A woman, I mean."

Anne settled her cup into the saucer and looked directly across the table. "I suspect he did."

Charlotte paled. "Did he admit—"

"Oh, no. Nothing as obvious as that. But I heard stories about all of the English girls over there; daughters and widows and the like. And Edward is quite a handsome man. Don't you agree?"

"I'm sorry . . . I really didn't see him well enough last

evening to judge," Charlotte answered, trying to sound offhand.

"Well, I knew the risk, and I waited anyway. I had loved him since I was a girl and I always believed he would come back to me. When he did, we had both changed." She took a breath, and Charlotte could hear the words catch in her throat. "He a good deal more than me."

"How do you mean?"

"My husband was in India during the massacre at Delhi, Katherine. He was wounded quite badly; actually shot in the back by one of those wretched native soldiers they call *sepoys.* He has always refused to speak of it, so I don't push him. It was such a terrible tragedy. So many innocent people died. Entire families torn apart." She leaned forward in her chair. "I don't mind telling you, he hasn't been quite the same man since."

"Perhaps it is a part of his life he just wants to forget," Charlotte whispered, and she could not keep the sadness from her voice.

"Yes. I expect you're right. And as to the other women, if indeed there were any of consequence, I can take some solace in knowing that I am the one he married and I am the one who shall bear his children." She patted her belly. "That is consolation enough."

Charlotte stood and began to clear away the breakfast dishes. Heat the water. Collect the basin. Anything not to have to face her eye to eye for a single moment longer.

"I am not entirely certain why I told you all of that," Anne said, breaking the silence that followed her admission.

"It's all right, really."

"I suppose it is just that here in Tetbury, everyone knows about us. Rather hard not to know everyone's business in a small town."

"I suppose so."

"Everyone has always thought of us as the perfect pair."

Charlotte dropped a saucer, and it chipped against the basin. *I can do this,* she told herself silently. *I can* . . . "And you do not?" she asked.

"I did once. Before Edward left for India," Anne replied, and her voice trembled. "In those days, he was carefree and happy. Now it is as if he carries the weight of the world on those broad shoulders of his. I cannot recall the last time I heard the sound of his laughter."

Nor can I, Charlotte thought sadly.

SHE HAD NOT BEEN PREPARED TO LIKE ANNE LANGSTON OR HER daughter when she agreed to stay in Tetbury. But during the days that followed, Charlotte cleaned for them, and under Anne's direction, she even did her best to cook for them. Together they spoke about Anne's childhood, her courtship with Edward, and her dreams for the future, until Charlotte discovered the kind and gentle woman her husband had married.

It only made the pain worse.

For the most part she had managed to avoid Edward. It was not yet time to confront him, and as each day passed, she was not certain it would ever be.

Charlotte had been clever with her excuses so that she was out of his way when he returned home each evening and before he left each morning. But after the first week, she realized that it would not have mattered anyway. Edward lived most of the time in a world of his own, emotionally quite set apart from his family and this stranger in their midst.

He rose early in the morning to open the pub. Then, after

a brief break for supper, he worked into the early hours of the morning, cleaning and preparing for the next day. There was a droning sort of regularity about Anne and Edward's routine to which she very quickly grew accustomed.

One afternoon while Anne rested, Charlotte took her small charge down the lane of stone houses with their gray slate roofs and into the center of town. At first she had hidden in Edward's cottage, fearful that somehow her secret might be uncovered before she was ready to reveal it herself, but as she slowly came to accept the impossibility of such an occurrence, she gained more courage.

They strolled together, Charlotte in her city gown, hat, and shaded glasses, holding the hand of Edward's little country daughter, and nodding to the curious townspeople who passed by them. The scent from gardens was strong with each puff of warm summer wind. The air was hot. Sultry. It called her mind back to India. It was a charming town, exactly as Edward had once described it, and the thought she pressed back just as it passed across her mind was that she and Edward might well have had a life here. Together. Then she glanced down at the gown that the real Katherine Blackstone had given her, and she remembered how far from that fantasy she was truly.

Anne had sent her to buy flour, sugar, and some tea. Charlotte also needed to post a letter to Jawahar and Hugh Edward. It had taken her nearly a week here to find the words. She could not tell them what she had truly found. How could she have explained that she had stayed in spite of it? It would not have been fair with such distance between them, the expectation so high.

Instead she described the beauty of the countryside. How much they would love it. Later, much later, when they were here in England with her, then Charlotte would find the courage to confess the truth.

As they came to the center of town, they passed by the baker, with his grand bow window full of freshly baked tarts, the cobbler, with a worn wooden shoe above the door, and finally the dry goods shop. It was a narrow, shadowy little store, its shelves lined with jars of tooth powder, bars of soap, pins, and bolts of brightly colored fabric.

"Why Charlotte, dear child! We haven't seen you for weeks!" a stout, spinsterish woman exclaimed as she pushed out from behind the counter.

She pressed both her plump hands to her knees as another gray-haired woman with the same long nose and face came out to stand beside her. The smaller and more fragile of the two women, who were clearly sisters, was holding up a fresh ginger cookie. For an instant, Charlotte had thought the woman had been speaking to her.

"I am Katherine Blackstone," she said, removing her shaded glasses and stepping forward to properly introduce herself. "I shall be helping Mrs. Langston until her child is born."

"We know who you are," the more stout of the women declared, and for an instant Charlotte's heart stopped. "Everyone in the village is talking about the stranger who has come to stay with Edward and Anne. Not much gets past any of us in Tetbury."

Charlotte fought a smile, thinking how surprised these two old magpies would be if they knew just how very wrong they were about that.

"What a stroke of good fortune to have found someone such as yourself way out here in the country," the smaller woman chimed in. "That gown you are wearing is really quite grand. I don't believe I've ever seen anything like it."

"It was a gift, actually," Charlotte divulged. "From a very dear friend."

"Some day I should like to see my sweet Emma in a gown so fine."

"Ha!" the stout sister chuckled, and as she did her full cheeks patched red. "It's a city gown, Louisa dear. You're not likely to see anything like that for sale around here!"

"Never you mind. I have big things planned for my Emma," she countered defensively. It was another moment before her lips lifted back into a rosy smile. "Yes, a life in London, a well-to-do husband. A gown like that would surely set her to her course."

"If it were only that simple, my dear Louisa, we would all be wearing elegant frocks and waiting for miracles!" said the heavier of the two as she observed Charlotte with suspicious gray eyes. "Where is it that your family comes from, Mrs. Blackstone? Fairford, wasn't it?"

"Burford," Charlotte corrected her, recognizing the test.

"Oh, why yes of course," she conceded with an insincere half smile.

"Well, welcome to Tetbury," said the smaller of the two women as she picked up Anne's daughter and gave her the ginger cookie.

"Thank you," Charlotte answered cautiously. "It is lovely here."

The more suspicious, the more corpulent of the two sisters advanced a few more steps, still eyeing Tetbury's newest resident. "I am Margaret Evans, and this is my sister, Louisa."

"Your married sister," she corrected, lifting her thin, sallow face proudly in a trace of sibling rivalry.

"Yes, Louisa, quite right. My married sister, Mrs. Perceval Honeycutt," she corrected with an exasperated sigh, then turned back to Charlotte. "Blackstone? Odd. I don't remember ever hearing of any Blackstones from Burford."

"It was a long time ago."

"Yes, it must have been. I know practically every family all the way to Oxford, going back nearly twenty years. It is a bit of a hobby for me."

"She was in need of the hobby, since it was I who caught the husband," Louisa Honeycutt chimed playfully but not cruelly.

Charlotte exhaled, not realizing until then that she had barely been breathing. "That's just about when it was, I believe. Twenty years ago or so. My . . . grandparents lived in Burford until they moved up to London with their married son, my father," she said, finding it essential to further the lie. "But they spoke about this whole area all the while I was growing up, and how terribly friendly the people were. It made me want to see for myself. The city really can become so tiresome."

It was a handsome lie. She nearly believed it herself. The two women finally smiled at one another, both of them convinced that she was harmless, and handed little Charlotte back. She could tell by the pleasant expressions on both their faces that she had passed their impromptu test.

"So what can I get for you today, Mrs. Blackstone?"

"A pound of sugar. Two pounds of flour and some tea. And could you tell me where I might post a letter?"

"Locally?" Louisa asked with interest.

"No." Charlotte took another shallow breath, sensing her voice growing tighter. "It would be going out of the country."

"Oh, well. I could have taken it for you, but outside of England you'll need to do it yourself. The man who can post it for you has a shop outside to your right and down two doors."

She took the tea, sugar, and flour, grateful that the encounter was nearing an end. "You have been most kind."

"We are very fond of Anne," Margaret said, casting a more pleasant smile at the stranger, yet letting the tone convey a warning. "Known her all her life. We're rather glad she is in such capable hands."

"Thank you again."

As she turned to leave, she saw little Charlotte gazing up wide-eyed, her tiny rose-bud mouth open in amazement. Her eyes followed the child's to a shelf holding a delicate china doll dressed in mauve-colored velvet and trimmed with ribbons and lace.

"Might I ask the cost of the doll, Miss Evans?"

"I am afraid she belongs to my sister," Margaret said, going back behind the counter.

"Oh, she's not for sale!" Louisa replied, the words sputtering forth from her pale mouth. "I paid a small fortune for her myself down in Bristol nearly twenty years ago now, before my daughter was born. I leave her up there for all of the little girls to look at. I do take her down from time to time, but for that they must have been very, very good indeed."

She glanced back down at the little child whose gaze was full of only the purest sense of longing. "I wonder, could Charlotte see her more closely for a moment?"

Louisa Honeycutt's hazel eyes narrowed contemplatively. "Oh, she's terribly young." There was a little pause as she considered the request further, and two more customers came in behind them. "But I do suppose there would be no real harm."

Mrs. Honeycutt finally took the delicate china doll from the shelf and bent down to the child's level. She was holding it as if it were a rare piece of porcelain, afraid to let it out of her grasp.

After a moment, Anne's daughter reached out and fingered the lace-edged collar with her small, curled hand. *I had a shelf full of these sort of dolls in Delhi,* Charlotte thought sadly as she watched the child's awe. She had never really understood their value until now as she looked through such innocent eyes.

"Thank you," Charlotte said as she took the doll from the little girl's grasp, a little girl who did not understand and did not want to release her.

Edward's daughter gazed up reluctantly as the doll was finally taken away, and the expression on the small upturned face pierced Charlotte's heart. *So trusting. So unaware of how terribly cruel life can be. You are such an innocent in all of this. Like Jawahar. Like Hugh Edward. . . . And yet one of you is bound to be hurt in all of this. There shall be no way around it.*

They walked out into the afternoon sunlight, the shaded glasses protectively back on her face. One of Charlotte's arms was loaded with packages. The other was clutching the child's little hand. She was looking up and still munching on the ginger cookie that Mrs. Honeycutt had given her—until she caught sight of the drunken man who had come around the corner and was swaggering toward them on the cobblestone sidewalk.

The little girl's face went white as a first snow and she squeezed Charlotte's hand.

"So you're the new hen in ol' Langston's coop!" he slurred once they were facing one another. "I've heard all about you."

He was a tall, shabby-looking man with jet-black hair and gray, unforgiving eyes set in a long, gaunt face. Charlotte knew instinctively that he meant trouble.

Edward's daughter hid behind her skirts as she stood firm, straightening her back against the implied threat. "Please let us pass."

"Such a proper accent for someone living in the country!"

He laughed brazenly, and for an instant, it forced Charlotte to recall another time when another dark and dangerous man, a *sepoy,* had leered at her like that and then laughed when she tried to stand firmly against him.

"I asked you nicely, sir, to let us pass."

He was standing close to her, swaying and smelling of whiskey and unwashed flesh. "I mean no harm, dear lady. We're a friendly group here in Tetbury. To show you just how friendly, I'd be proud to carry your packages."

"I can manage my packages," she replied curtly. Charlotte tried to step aside, but as she did, he stepped with her.

"Oh, come now. You're not all that high and mighty as they're saying, now are you? I'll bet behind those spectacles and all that fancy silk you're a fine-looking woman."

He had his hand on her package of sugar. When she glanced down at his fingers, she could see that they were as dry and cracked as his lips and that his fingernails were jagged and dirty. She felt a flash of revulsion through her fear and glanced around, but there did not appear to be anyone else on the street to intercede.

"Please, sir!"

"Oh, come now . . ."

Another man's voice ended the contest. "You heard the lady, Emery."

Charlotte watched the stranger's back go suddenly ramrod straight and his glazed crimson eyes widen with surprise at the realization of who it was behind him. The man was Edward Langston.

"Aw, go home to your wife, Langston. This one's mine!" he said belligerently, the whiskey obscuring his fear and his better judgment.

Edward spun him around by the force of one hand and seized him ruthlessly by the shoulders. "I said, you heard the lady, Emery. Mrs. Blackstone is not interested in having you carry her packages, nor in frightening my daughter. Now why don't you just go home and sleep it off?"

"And I said mind yer own business, Langston!"

He turned back to Charlotte and tried more insistently to wrestle the packages from her arms. This time as Edward spun him back around, his other fist was waiting. He tried to block the punch, but Edward was stronger. Emery fell to the ground, clutching his jaw. After a moment, he rolled onto his hands and knees, scrambling to stand as he fumed drunken profanities.

"You might want to reconsider that move," Edward warned, looming over his opponent, his arms tensed and his body taut and ready. As the stranger moved more slowly this time to stand, he leered up at Edward.

"And what precisely gives you the right to save all of the women of Tetbury from a bit of male attention?" he growled.

"I took it upon myself," Edward replied, then crooked an eyebrow. "Have you a problem with that?"

The intoxicated man looked at Charlotte and then back at Edward, as though he was trying to decide. Finally the stranger threw off Edward's challenge with a grunt of disgust.

"You know the trouble with you, Langston?" he slurred again, dusting off his loose shirt and trousers.

"I am certain you mean to tell me."

"You think that having been a captain in Her Majesty's army bought you the right to bully anyone you please!"

"What it bought me, Emery, was civility and manners," Edward shot back. "Something you apparently know very little about. Now you had best go home and sleep it off before I decide to send you to your rest personally!"

It was another moment of strained silence before Edward's opponent turned and staggered on down the road.

"Papa!" the child dashed out from behind Charlotte's skirts and leapt into her father's arms once the danger had passed. "He's such a bad man, isn't he?"

Charlotte kept her head low as her heart thumped wildly against her chest. But for the moment she was grateful that Edward had apparently seen her predicament through the pub window. She had no doubt as to where that dangerous encounter would have led had he not come along when he did.

"He's just had a bit too much to drink, darling," Edward spoke sweetly to his daughter. "And it makes Mr. Akins forget how a gentleman should treat a lady. And speaking of ladies, what, precisely, is my best girl doing out here this fine morning?"

"Shopping for Mama with Mrs. Blackstone." She smiled gleefully and looked back at Charlotte.

There was a moment when she was certain her beating heart would come crashing right through her chest. If he looked at her directly now in the bright summer sunlight, Edward was bound to discover her true identity. Her face and hair may have changed dramatically, even her shape. But the essence of the girl he had loved was still standing right here before him.

Suddenly Charlotte let the packages tumble from her arms and bent down to retrieve them. The movement would allow her to keep her head low and buy her the diversion she needed.

"Here, let me help you," Edward said, putting down his daughter and stooping toward the fallen articles.

"No!" Charlotte answered quickly, struggling to drive her real voice deep enough to conceal it. "I can manage."

She picked up the packages one by one, certain that she could avoid his direct gaze if she acted quickly. Until she saw that the letter to India had come loose with the packages of flour and sugar and was lying near Edward's shoe.

Charlotte heard a gasp come from the back of her own throat as he glanced down at the letter. *It is over,* she thought. *Once he sees where the letter is going, he will know it is me, and I am far from ready to have him uncover the truth!*

Just as Edward reached for the letter, his little daughter moved to scoop it up herself. She presented it to Charlotte with an eager smile, wanting to please the woman who had made it possible for a few brief moments for her to hold Mrs. Honeycutt's prized doll as if it were her very own.

"You dropped this, Mrs. Blackstone."

She caught her breath. "Thank you, Charlotte."

She rose back up slowly, her head still lowered beneath the safety of her hat as though demurely.

"It was kind of you to bring the child with you on your errands," Edward said awkwardly, not certain what it was about this woman that had begun to set him so on edge. "With her mother confined as she has been, she gets out in the fresh air so seldom these days."

"It was kind of you to rescue me from harm's way, Mr. Langston," she replied with Rani's breathy voice, recalling another time—a lifetime ago—when he had saved her from certain death in a pit of quicksand.

As she spoke, a curious sensation surged through Edward. It was a flash of recognition. Familiarity. And yet, not quite. He tried to shake it off, but something remained; perhaps something about her voice. He thought that it was oddly familiar. And yet such a thing was impossible. In all his life, Edward had never done anything. Gone anywhere. Except to India. And everyone he had ever known there, everyone who had ever mattered, was dead.

"Will you be all right?" he asked with husky-voiced sincerity, trying valiantly to shake away the feeling.

"I believe so," she answered with a faint smile, one he did not see because she still would not look up at him.

"For future reference, Emery is really quite harmless. The women here are accustomed to his brash behavior, and they put him down post-haste. You, of course, could not have known that."

"I suspect that is what he was counting on." A curious tension had built between them quite suddenly. Both of them felt it. Only one of them understood why it was there. Edward was the first to give in to his discomfort, his body tensing back to a formal pose, the distance between them firmly reestablished.

"Please tell my wife I shall try to be home for supper by eight o'clock."

"I shall, Mr. Langston."

She still did not lift her head as she felt him looking back at her again. She could not take that chance. She took his daughter's hand and hurried back down the road to post a letter to Hugh Edward.

The son they shared.

"You must tell me about London, Katherine."

Anne Langston sat at the kitchen table that evening while Charlotte finished drying the last of the supper dishes. The small house was still thick with the aroma of roast lamb, and a balmy summer breeze blew in through the open kitchen door.

"It is just that I've never been there," Anne said when Charlotte did not move to reply right away. "The farthest I've ever gone was to Bristol. I was taken there for a funeral, but I was only a child then. All I remember was a lot of people crying and the smell of sea air. I know it wasn't like the real city a'tall."

"You never took a honeymoon?" Charlotte asked carefully, thinking of her own trip to Agra.

"Unfortunately not," she said in a soft voice. "Edward was . . . tired of traveling, he said. When he returned from India he told me he did not want so much as to think of far-off places ever again."

"Then you married quite soon after Mr. Langston returned home?" Charlotte probed.

She was not certain that she could bear to hear the answer even as the question passed across her lips. But there was an overwhelming urge inside her to discover the truth. It was why she had come to Tetbury, and why she had stayed.

"What makes you ask, Katherine?"

Charlotte turned back around. "It is just that it sounds like your husband had not entirely gotten over what happened to him in India. I wondered if you married in spite of that."

Anne looked away, her voice a quiet thing as she finally replied. "Sometimes I think he carries it inside him still." She fingered her cup of coffee and then looked back at Charlotte. "We only married a bit over three years ago. It was shortly before Charlotte's birth . . . if you gather my meaning. And yet I thank God for her every day of my life, because it was she who finally brought Edward to believe he should make me his wife."

She could not bear it. Charlotte's mind was a whirling stream of thoughts and she struggled to mask her shock. Edward had married her because she had gotten pregnant! It was not a love match woven from a childhood friendship after all. And he had not married her when he had first returned. He had not betrayed their memory any more than she had.

"But enough dreary talk about me," Anne said after the silence that followed her surprising admission. "Now you must tell me all about London. Precisely how long did you live there?"

Charlotte was grateful for a change in the subject matter, even if it meant she would now have to make something up.

She had heard all that she could bear of the truth for one night.

"Not long," she hedged. Except for the time she had spent there during the Christmas holidays as a child, Charlotte had never ever been to London.

"But I thought you said that you lived there with your husband."

"I did. We had a townhouse there. But we spent most of our time at his estate in Kent."

"Estate?" Anne gasped, and the sound was full of envy.

"It wasn't all that large, really. More of a manor house."

"There is an estate on the edge of town, but I have never gotten any closer than the gate surrounding the grounds." Anne shifted her weight in the chair, the child she carried making it difficult to sit for very long in one position. "What was it like to live so grandly?"

"Really not all that different from the life you live here," Charlotte said, and for the first time that evening, as she recalled her privileged upbringing both in England and in India, she had spoken the truth. "We have families. Husbands. People we treasure. . . . And losses that stay with us forever." She sighed, thinking of Rani. Of her father. Of Edward. "But you don't want to hear about all of that. You want to hear about London."

Anne smiled as Charlotte filled her cup and then her own full of steaming tea. As she did, she prepared a story that was vivid enough to satisfy her hostess, her own mind still quaking with the implications of what Anne Langston had finally confessed.

None of this was Anne's fault. Nor was it Edward's. He had waited for her for nearly seven years, just as she had waited for him, until circumstances had drawn him to someone else. It was natural. Understandable. It was a reality she could one day learn to accept.

As she sat back down, preparing to weave a lovely tale of life in London, the front door clicked and then squealed to open. Charlotte sprang back to her feet. Having believed they would be alone this evening, she was without the protection of either her hat or her shaded glasses.

Anne saw Charlotte's face quickly pale. "It is only Edward. Paddy must have convinced him to take the rest of the evening for himself."

"Yes. He must have." Searching for a way to plausibly see herself quickly from the room, she glanced up at the back stairs. "Isn't that Charlotte crying?"

Anne also looked to the stairs that led from the kitchen to the second floor. "I didn't hear anything."

The floorboards creaked as Edward made his way through the house. They heard him blow out the lamp that Anne kept lit for him near the door.

"I'm quite certain I heard her."

"It's really not good to go to her every time she cries, Katherine. And after all, you were finally just about to tell me all about London."

Charlotte was halfway up the stairs when Edward came through the kitchen door. "I shall just see that she is all right. It won't take a moment."

It was the first thing she could think of to get out of the kitchen. Until that night her system had worked so well. Edward left early each morning and usually returned from the pub only after both Anne and she had gone to bed.

Sometimes late at night, she would lie alone in her little room just beyond the kitchen and listen to him shuffling around after he had come home, searching in the dark for his whiskey or something left over from supper. And with him so near, just beyond the worn wooden door, her heart would ache and plead with her to go to him. Even before she had discovered the whole truth from Anne, she had longed to tell him who she really was, but the complications of each passing day had forced her silence.

Now that she had come to know her, Charlotte must consider Anne. And their daughter. How could she ever ask Edward to give up a woman who had adored him since childhood? What right did she have? She was dead. Edward had buried her in his mind, if not in his heart, and what possible purpose would it serve now to stir all of that up again?

She sat in the dark stairwell just where the stairs turned and went up to the second floor, unable to keep herself from listening. She hoped to hear something that might tell her what to do next.

"How are you feeling?" she heard him ask.

"I am terribly tired. But Katherine has been such a help with Charlotte."

"You do need your rest."

"We were just speaking about London when you came in. Did you know that Katherine and her husband actually had a townhouse there and that she also lived on an estate outside of the city?"

Edward burst out with a disbelieving laugh. "Oh she did, did she? And if that were true, why do you suppose a wealthy young widow would need to be cleaning up after a simple country family like the Langstons?"

"It is just a way for her to settle in here, you know that. She has no other family living, no reason to stay up in London, so she is free to move where the spirit wills her. As to any more of her past than that, she's really quite secretive about it."

"Perhaps Mrs. Blackstone simply prefers to leave the past where it belongs."

"Like you, Edward?"

There was a little silence, and Anne whispered something that Charlotte could not hear. Then there was the sound of a chair being pushed back. "I am going to bed."

"Oh now, don't be cross, Edward. Please. You've only just gotten home. Stay and talk with me awhile. I shall heat you some soup."

"Thank you, but I am not hungry," he said distractedly. "What I really need is to get some sleep."

"Well, I for one shall be glad when this child comes. Then finally, perhaps you shall be able to bear the sight of me for more than five minutes' time!"

"Oh, really, Anne," Edward droned, and Charlotte heard him sigh. "Have we not been through all of this already?"

"I just don't know what to do to please you any more!"

Edward's voice grew suddenly harsh. "Leave it alone, Anne."

"But I am your wife. I have a right to know what you are thinking!"

"Getting me to marry you the way you did was not enough? Now you want to take possession of my mind as well?"

Charlotte could hear Anne weeping in the silence that followed. When he spoke again, his voice had softened. "Look, you got what you said you always wanted. You are my wife. Why can we not just leave it at that without always trying to forage around about things that are better left buried?"

"It's just that I feel you are so much like Katherine," Anne said through her tears. "So much hiding of things that are important, and with both of you it is the not knowing that is so difficult for me to bear."

"You know me," he said more softly, his voice straining to find compassion. "You've known me since we were children. I am the same man you loved then, and the man you say you love now."

"You know that I do."

"Then leave it alone, Anne. I am giving you all that I have to give. Let that be enough for you. Please!"

Charlotte wiped away the tears from her own eyes when she heard them kissing. She was certain that never in her life would there ever be a more difficult sound to bear than that. But she had come here to Tetbury unannounced. She was living in their midst without revealing her true identity. The pain she felt now was a pain she had brought upon herself.

"Come," Edward said, his voice husky now and low. It was a tone Charlotte remembered well. "Let's go up to bed."

She ran on her toes into the dark nursery and sat on the edge of the little bed, her heart beating fiercely. A moment later, she heard footsteps as Edward and Anne moved by, their shadows like one, passing beneath the door. Then a little voice pierced the darkness.

"What is it?" their daughter asked, waking and rubbing the sleep from her eyes.

"It's nothing," Charlotte whispered back, and she felt her heart breaking. "Everything is back to normal now."

Edward tossed and turned. He dreamed of India.

His mind made it all so real again. The heat. The dust. The noxious odor of cow dung. He was back in Delhi. Then suddenly it was not a dream. It had really happened. Memories that he had refused since he had come back to England cascaded forth, and a deep, fitful sleep made him powerless to stop them.

He watched himself walking through the rubble that had once been the cantonments, refusing stubbornly to believe that Charlotte had perished there. He had been kept away for nearly a month recovering from the gunshot wound, forced to wait for the fierce uprising to be brought under control.

Twice he had tried to escape the makeshift hospital and to pay a coolie to take him back to Delhi. He was desperate. He must see for himself. Both times he had been stopped. Finally, for his own good, they said, he had been placed under guard.

Again and again he had combed the list of survivors from his hospital cot in Jheed, praying that her name would be on it. But even the absence of Charlotte's name had not deterred him. She was resourceful. Far too resourceful to have died like that.

A colonel stood beside him now in the ruins. "Well, were there any young girls who did survive? Girls you were unable to identify?" Edward asked desperately.

"I am afraid not, Captain."

The colonel's voice echoed in Edward's mind and he shuddered beneath the blankets. "Perhaps someone you misidentified?" he doggedly pressed.

"Look, Captain Langston, I understand how you must feel. I am a newlywed myself, but all of the civilians were eventually accounted for, alive or dead. I am sorry."

"Well, not my wife!" he fired angrily. "You have no record! You have no body! Perhaps you can tell me how I am supposed to accept that she is dead!"

The colonel's face was distorted now in Edward's memory. His voice came through a long, dark tunnel of time. "There is very little left when a body burns, Captain. I have seen enough Hindu funerals myself to know that."

Edward recoiled. The sensation that the words brought was as vivid and piercing as when they were actually spoken. He watched himself—now an image in his own mind—fall into the ashes and soot, all that remained of his bungalow, just as he had done moments before he was shot.

"Well, that simply is not good enough, Colonel!" he growled, foraging like a madman for even a trace of her. "Not good enough at all!"

"Really, Captain, I do not think—"

Suddenly something cold and sharp pressed into Edward's fingers. He clutched the marred piece of silver and held it up to the sunlight. It was the bracelet Charlotte's father had given her. The one she had worn unfailingly every day that he had known her. *Merciful God, no!*

The rest of the images were fragmented. He had stumbled back to the cave—their secret cave—still holding the sooty bracelet as though it were a piece of his wife. Holding the last shred of hope in his heart that there would be a sign here. Something to tell him that she had survived, in spite of what everyone was trying to make him believe.

Tears ran down his face as he continued to toss and turn beneath the covers, and he felt again the desperation to accept anything but what was being forced upon him. But the cave held no answers. Nothing. It had been ransacked by jackals. Blankets had been carried away. The jar of marmalade had been smashed and was buzzing now with flies.

"What is it?" Anne asked, sitting up beside him in their bed. Never in all the years that she had known him had she ever seen Edward shed a tear, and yet now suddenly he was weeping uncontrollably into his hands.

"Shh," she tried to softly comfort him in the darkness. "It

was only a dream, darling. That's all. . . . It was just a dream."

Understanding.

Painful as it was, that was what Charlotte had sought by coming to Tetbury. Now after nearly two weeks, she had come to understand that there was nothing she could do to bring back the Edward she once had known. That Edward had died in India just as he believed she had. This man had obligations. Commitments that she would not—could not —bring herself to go against, no matter how much she still loved him. And she did still love him with all of her heart.

She would stay until the child arrived. It was a commitment she had made and one she would honor. After that, she would send Jawahar and Hugh Edward to Kent, where her father had always kept a house. Then she would join them there. And she would be sad for a while. She would allow herself that much. But an understanding was what she had sought by staying here; what she had needed. Now her memories of what she and Edward had shared—in India— would be enough. They must be.

Charlotte sat alone, small cold hands bracing her body on the edge of her bed. The moon was full tonight, and it shimmered through her window, casting a silvery shadow across the spartan room. She expelled a long breath and then looked down at the bag full of her last few remaining possessions. It was an embroidered carpet bag given to her as a farewell gift by Doctor Greystone, the man who had convinced her that there was a place for her in Calcutta at Saint Mary's Hospital.

He was a kind old man who understood that she had come out of Delhi with nothing. He said he wanted her to go forth with something to begin her new life in England. The nurses had filled it with a silver-handled hairbrush and comb set, a cotton and lace nightgown, and a new pair of gloves. The shawl that Mrs. Pemberton had knit for her had gone inside at the last moment as the most prized possession of all. It would forever be a reminder that she had made a difference.

She had survived. Then they had all cried that last afternoon, the staff of Saint Mary's, wishing her God's speed and whispering that it was the most romantic tale they had ever heard.

Charlotte closed her eyes, wanting to stop the pictures from flooding into her mind. Even now it was all so vivid. She could see India. Hear it. Smell it. *So many memories . . . One day I pray those images shall be a comfort to me.* She opened the bag slowly and reached inside. Her betrothal ring lay at the bottom beneath her nightgown, the shawl, and the photograph of Hugh Edward and Jawahar. She had not taken the ring out since that first afternoon when she had so hastily dropped it inside to the place where Edward would not see it.

That modest piece of jewelry was a comfort to her now as she slipped it back onto her wedding finger and gazed at it by the light of the moon. She felt the tears sting her eyes as she next brought forth the photograph taken in Calcutta's Botanical Gardens. Her emotions as she gazed at it were a bittersweet tangle of happy memories and longing; for that moment, they were together once again.

Her tears wet the image, and she quickly pressed it down into the folds of her bag. Anne would deliver her second child any day. Charlotte felt a surge of relief at the thought. She had begged the Lord for strength upon coming here, and He had blessed her with what she had asked of Him. But she was tired now, and the longing for her boys had become almost unbearable. The comfort and security they brought her was all that she had left in the world.

Charlotte wiped the tears from her eyes and looked down again at her ring. She remembered the day Edward had given it to her. It had belonged to his mother, he had said. And then he had asked her to spend the rest of their lives together.

It had been the love of a lifetime. For Charlotte there would never be another. She had loved him with her whole heart and all of her soul. She had given him every part of herself, and there was nothing left now for any other man. And he had loved her back in the same all-consuming way.

No matter what had happened since, she would always believe that. It was the memory of that brief time of joy that would have to sustain her. *Oh, Edward . . . be happy with your Anne. . . . Please try to be happy*, she whispered as she lay down on the bed and wept into her hands.

THE NEXT MORNING, AN UNEXPECTED SUMMER RAIN SPILLED forth from a steely sky. It shook the house and rattled the windows for nearly an hour before it slowed.

Upstairs, Charlotte bathed and dressed her little charge while Edward and Anne sat alone together at the table in the kitchen. They spoke in hushed whispers, and this time Charlotte made no attempt to listen to what they were saying. She could not bear it. *Only a few days more,* she told herself. A few days more before the baby came. Then she could leave this place and never look back.

Once Edward had left, she brought Charlotte down the back stairs and into the kitchen for breakfast. Anne had opened the back door, and the fresh scent of wet grass and flowers filled the house like a heady perfume.

"Isn't it glorious?" Anne smiled, her face shining with contentment.

"I take it things have improved between you and Mr. Langston?" Charlotte asked as she scooped a bit of porridge into a bowl, covered it with milk, and gave it to the child along with a spoon.

"This new baby has been difficult on us," Anne confessed unexpectedly. "But it shall all be over soon enough."

Charlotte sat down beside her. "I am happy for you, Anne," she said sincerely. "I may not have known you for a very long time, but I have seen enough to know that you and your children deserve every happiness."

"Thank you, Katherine." She looked out across her garden at the raindrops on the sweet Williams, the roses, and the new gillyflowers. "I love it after a summer rain. Everything is so fresh. So alive. It's always like a new beginning, don't you think?"

"I do indeed."

"You know what I would like? I would adore a stroll before the sun comes out again and spoils this lovely freshness."

"Do you think that would be wise?"

"I think it would be the best medicine in the world for me. I have been cooped up in this house for weeks. . . . Oh, Katherine, please. Say you'll come with Charlotte and I. We won't go far. Just down into town and back."

"Perhaps you are right," she conceded with a hesitant smile. "A little fresh air could do us all some good."

"That's the spirit!"

The two women left together with little Charlotte tottering between them, and they strolled down the path toward Long Street. Songbirds trilled from the lush beech trees that flanked the road and a rainbow crossed the horizon. A few other people had begun to come out of their houses, and Mrs. Bingham's calico cat followed them almost to the center of town.

"You never did manage to tell me much about London last night," Anne said as they strolled, Charlotte now skipping on ahead of them.

"I'm afraid there is not a great deal to tell. It is a big bustling city just like any other."

Anne's brown eyes were wide when she looked across at Charlotte. "You've even been to other cities like London?"

"Oh, no. Not personally," she lied as the images of Delhi, Calcutta, and Cairo flashed across her mind. "My father traveled quite a bit and he always told me that one large city was just like another. The faces and the look of the buildings

234

might vary, but the essence of cities is always the same. They are just huge places in which one invariably becomes quite lost."

"Still and all, I would love to see it one day."

"I am afraid it takes money to see the side of London you imagine. There is as much poverty in that city as wealth."

"Then I suspect I shall never see it. But I have what is most important here in Tetbury," Anne said. "A husband and children, and Edward provides a good life for us."

Charlotte's voice was shallow. "I think you are very fortunate indeed."

Anne looked over at her again, remembering that Katherine Blackstone was a widow, left alone to find a place for herself and a new life here in the country. "Oh, I am sorry. That was most insensitive of me."

"It's quite all right. I am growing accustomed to the way things are," she said, meaning it.

They had nearly reached the Cock 'n' Feathers when suddenly Anne doubled over in the street, clutching her abdomen. Charlotte grasped her arm below the elbow. "What is it?"

"I'm not certain. . . . I think it is the baby."

"I knew we should not have walked so far."

"It's not your fault, Katherine. I insisted. Perhaps if I just sit down a moment . . ."

"Mama!" Charlotte came racing back to her.

"It's all right, darling. Go knock on Miss Evans's door and see if we can come in."

A moment later, Margaret Evans, the stout, ruddy-cheeked woman who owned the dry goods shop, came rushing out of her house and into the street.

"Good gracious, Anne! What is it?"

"I think it's the baby. Might we come in?"

"Of course!"

The two women helped Anne Langston into the sitting room of the slate-roof cottage, and she collapsed onto a faded yellow sofa.

"What can I get for you?" Margaret asked, real concern spiking her normally harsh gray eyes.

"Perhaps just a glass of water."

Little Charlotte was crying, so Margaret took her into the kitchen, promising her another ginger cookie.

"I'm frightened, Katherine," Anne whispered once they were alone, perspiration quickly consuming her powder-white face.

Charlotte took her trembling hand and tried to smile. "There is nothing to be frightened about. You're just going to have a baby. You've already done it once before."

"But I am not as strong as I should be."

"You're strong enough." She squeezed her hand. "I promise you."

Another jolt of pain shot through her, and Anne doubled over again just as Margaret came back from the kitchen with a glass of water. "Oh, my heavens! Perhaps you should go and fetch Mr. Langston!"

"No!" Charlotte blurted. "That is to say, let's wait a few minutes and see. Perhaps it is just a scare. It happens sometimes when the child is close."

But it was not a scare. The contractions remained regular and so intense that Anne could not be moved. She confessed to having had them most of the morning, but not nearly this severe. Now it was certainly too late to move her. Anne would give birth to the child here, at Margaret's house. There would be no other choice.

"I really think we should send for someone," Margaret said, her face blanched with worry. "At least the doctor."

It was the broad light of day, and for once Charlotte had gone out without her hat and glasses, believing the stroll would be brief. Going to the Cock 'n' Feathers for Edward was too great a risk for her.

"Perhaps, Miss Evans, you should go," Charlotte suggested, trying to keep the desperation from her voice.

"Me?" Margaret huffed indignantly. "It is you who work for the Langstons!"

"Margaret, please!" Anne murmured. "Do as Katherine asks. . . . And tell Edward to bring the doctor. It feels as if something is wrong with the baby."

The old Miss Evans turned out her thick lip in a pout of

disapproval. "Oh, very well then. And I shall take the child to Louisa at the shop. This is no place for her at a time like this."

Charlotte knelt beside the couch, her hand a comforting pressure on Anne's knee once they were alone. "What if I lose the baby, Katherine?"

"You are not going to lose it," she answered softly, tenderly running her other hand across Anne's glistening brow.

"Edward wants a son so desperately."

Charlotte gazed off into the house, filled as was Anne's with framed oil paintings, trinkets, and dark, heavy furniture. She was trying to stop the wave of envy that she knew by now would come again with any mention of a son. How sad, she could not help herself from thinking, that Edward would never know that he already had such a fine, strong boy—the son he so desired—in India.

"Breathe deeply, Anne. You mustn't panic," Charlotte willed herself to say.

"Will you stay with me? Please, Katherine."

"I won't leave you. I promise. Not until Mr. Langston comes."

The Cock 'n' Feathers was close enough that Margaret would be back with Edward in only a few minutes. Anne clutched Charlotte's hand tightly as a new contraction rocked her body. It struck her at the same moment that the front door opened and Margaret, Edward, and old Doctor Trumball rushed in, all three out of breath from running.

At the first sight of Edward, Charlotte fought the urge to run from the room, but such a move was bound to inspire far more suspicion than if she remained like everyone else, focused on Anne. She would keep her head low and keep out of the way. Perhaps, in the excitement, that would be enough.

"Are you all right?" Edward asked, crouching down beside the couch and taking Anne's hand away from Charlotte.

"It's the baby. I think it's coming, Edward. But it is too soon for this much pain!"

The doctor, a stately old gentleman with a snowy beard and mustache and a wave of white hair, moved forward. "Let's have a look."

Edward stepped back beside Charlotte and Margaret, nervously brushing a hand through his dark hair. His expression as he looked down at Anne was grave, and it was now, for the first time since she had come to Tetbury, that Charlotte saw it. Perhaps it was not the kind of love they had known in Delhi, but she could see that, in his way, Edward had come to care for his wife.

The pain at such a thought, when it came now, was not so swift and fierce as it had been two weeks before when she had first come here. Living in their midst, watching them with one another, had helped her grow accustomed to the notion that Edward was trying valiantly to get on with his life. He had come through what had happened to them in India the best way that he could.

Charlotte understood when he knelt back down beside Anne and took her hand once again after the doctor had completed his examination. *It is right that he should be with her like this. She is his wife,* Charlotte told herself as she slipped quietly out of the room. *It is my memory he shall always cherish, but it is she who needs him now.*

"Is my mama going to be all right?"

Charlotte held the little child who shared her name after she had collected her from Louisa Honeycutt. Her small, heart-shaped face was puffy and tear-stained from crying, but her blue eyes were wide and seeking. She was determined to know the truth.

"Your mama is going to be just fine," Charlotte assured her.

"Did she have the baby?"

"No. But it will be soon. I am certain of it."

"I want Papa to come home," she whimpered, and her words brought a fresh torrent of tears.

Charlotte felt a rush of tenderness, and she pulled the crying child to her chest. "It will be all right," she whispered, softly stroking the girl's fine, downy hair. "It will all be over soon. . . ."

After another glass of milk and Charlotte had exhausted her repertoire of bedtime stories, Edward's little girl finally fell asleep in Charlotte's safe, comforting arms. They sat together in a worn, overstuffed chair in the sitting room with only the light of one oil lamp for Edward near the door.

Charlotte gazed out of the window toward a sky made brilliant by a full, silvery moon. But everything else was dark. There was no candlelight nor lamps glowing in the houses across the way. She glanced up at the clock. She had not realized that it was so late. It was after midnight. She began to say a prayer for Anne's unborn child just as the front door clicked open. Edward stood limp in the doorway, and even in the shadows she could see that he was exhausted.

"She's had another girl," he whispered to 'Katherine Blackstone,' the woman who held his daughter and who sat cloaked in shadows of her own.

"Is Anne all right?"

He moved inside and closed the door. "There were complications. A lot of bleeding. Doctor Trumball said she cannot be moved. She will need to stay where she is for a few days."

Edward came toward Charlotte and her body went rigid. She lowered her eyes instinctively. Neither of them had spoken again about what had happened on Long Street. But from it a sort of conspiratorial silence had established itself between them. That familiarity danced between them, suddenly vivid and wild, like an evil temptress.

"It was kind of you to stay up with my daughter."

"She's a lovely child, Mr. Langston."

"I shall take her up to bed so that you can retire, Mrs. Blackstone. We won't be needing you any more tonight."

But as he bent down to take her into his arms, Edward caught a glimpse of Charlotte's face in the moonlight, and once again his mind jerked with recognition. It was that same sensation he had felt once before, a more haunting kind of familiarity, as though somehow he should know this woman.

Edward stood up slowly, and as he did so, Charlotte sank back into the shadows. Standing there, his child in his arms, he wanted to ask her, but he could not bring himself to speak the words. Until now he had not allowed himself to see it. There was too much pain in the memory. But the shape of her face, the turn of her long, slender neck, even the haunting green eyes. Yes, the eyes most of all. A wave of numbness passed over him. He had dismissed the thought half a dozen times since she had come here. But not tonight. Tonight he had realized of whom it was that this young woman had all along reminded him. He drew in a shallow, shuddering breath. Dear God in Heaven . . .

She looked just like Charlotte.

20

EDWARD SAT ALONE ON THE FLOOR OF HIS ATTIC, WRAPPED IN memories. Memories of India. Of what he had felt with his first wife so very long ago. A single candle burned beside a nearly empty bottle of whiskey. On his lap he held a small camphorwood chest. Edward looked at it for a long time without opening it. He had not brought it out since the morning before he married Anne. Inside was all he had that remained of his love; all that remained of Charlotte.

For a long time he wavered between tears and a return of the gut-wrenching sorrow he had known. But the helpless rage at what had happened to them was gone now. She had been taken from him. Edward had come to accept that. He had gone on with his life. But there would never be a substitute for her in his heart. Never.

After a long and painful mourning and years of solitude, he had taken a childhood friend to his bed. Anne had wanted him all her life, she said.

She understood that India had changed him, but she would settle for what he felt free to give. She had pleaded convincingly, worn down his resistance, and so in the end he had cauterized his pain with her body. But she was still not Charlotte. He knew that. Every time he touched Anne, it was *her* body that he felt. *Her* long, silky hair that tangled in his fingers and pressed him toward the oblivion for which he longed. But the reprieve was always a temporary one.

He had never told Anne that he had been married in India. He never spoke about it to a living soul once he returned to England. He had tried to put the memories away, along with the few mementoes of Charlotte inside the little camphorwood box. When her image came to his mind, he drank to push it away. And when they were stronger than his will to forget, he gave himself up to Anne's willing embrace, and the dream that it was Charlotte moving so passionately beneath him.

Edward fingered the box and took another long swallow of whiskey. Finally he had the strength to pull back the lid and gaze down at the green silk scarf she had helped him buy on the Chandni Chouk. It was the one she had given him to wear for good luck the morning he had gone off to Ambala. Beside it were a few polished stones that Jawahar had brought away from Agra and given to him as a gift for having saved his life.

That was it, all that remained of a woman he treasured as the other half of himself. He brought the scarf up and pressed it against his lips. So smooth. Delicate. Like her skin. The feel of her was forever emblazoned upon his memory. On the floor beside him, the candle flame trembled as the attic door suddenly opened.

"Mr. Langston, are you all right?"

Edward looked up. It was 'Katherine Blackstone.' She leaned against the doorframe in her sheer cotton nightgown, the shadow of her body willowy beneath it. For the first time since they had met, her dusty brown hair was unbound and draped long now across her shoulders. It obscured her face and neck. But not her eyes.

She had followed him up here, to his secret place, preparing to torture him further with her resemblance to his precious Charlotte. Perhaps tomorrow he would find the strength to be pleasant. But tonight he could not bear it. The weakness had unleashed the memories again.

"Please go away," he slurred, taking another drink, swallowing until the bottle was empty.

The scarf fell to the floor. Charlotte saw it and pressed her fingers to her lips so she would not gasp out loud. Her scarf! He had kept it through everything! He was up here alone, even now, thinking of her, longing for her, when Anne had just given him another child! The mix of emotions she felt strangled every bit of reason she possessed. She moved into the attic, and the shadows helped to conceal her.

"Please, Mrs. Blackstone. I want to be left alone," he slurred, and Charlotte felt the pain in his words as if it were her own.

"I was worried about you," she whispered, coming to sit beside him on the cold plank floor. It was the closest she had allowed herself to be to him since she had come here. The small attic was musty and filled with mementoes from the past. There were two old trunks with worn leather straps, several dusty hat boxes, and a broken rocking horse.

"It is no use," he muttered, gazing blindly down at the camphorwood box. "I try to forget. . . . I have done everything to forget. . . . But still she remains."

"Who remains?" she forced the whispered words past her lips, already knowing the answer.

"Charlotte."

"Your daughter?"

"No, Katherine. Charlotte was my wife."

He held the scarf to his heart and closed his eyes. She

could see the raw pain on his face. It meant everything that he still should grieve for her memory this way. This moment, she thought, would sustain her forever. An impulse followed, old as the love they shared. Older than this life. It was something that forced her to reach out and place her hand over his.

"I am so sorry."

"I've never told anyone about her," he said, gazing off across the attic to a small round window. It had begun to rain again, and beads of water dripped down the glass in a hypnotic rhythm.

"Do you . . . want to tell me about her?"

He picked up one of the stones and the scarf and held them for a long time. His mind was spinning from the whiskey and from fatigue. She knew he had seen a resemblance, but he had not yet made the connection. She would be safe here for a little while longer.

"Charlotte was everything to me. She was my very life's blood. . . ." He dropped the stone into the box. The scarf whispered after it. "And this is all that I have left of her. All."

The candle sitting in a pool of melted wax sputtered. "But you have your memories." She squeezed his hand, and he looked away again, unable to look at her face.

"My memories of Charlotte torture me every day of my life."

The candle sputtered, then burned out, and they sat in darkness. It was raining harder now, and it splashed onto the slate roof above them so forcefully that it pushed out any sound of the world around them. It was as if time had stopped, Charlotte thought, and there was nothing else. Nothing and no one but Edward. When he reached out to her, the movement was swift and disjointed. He took her face in his hands.

"You look like her," he said, drawing nearer as a flash of lightning lit the night sky. "Same smooth skin . . . your shape is slim like she was . . . and your eyes are hers exactly."

They were close now, and Charlotte's heart was thumping against her ribs like a drum. She knew that he was drunk. Vulnerable. Another woman's husband. But she wanted him to touch her. Dear God, she could think of nothing beyond that.

"Oh, Charlotte . . . I miss you so . . ." he muttered in the moment before he pressed his lips against hers.

And as he kissed her, the sound of the words he had spoken shook her, until she realized that the whiskey had distorted his vision. He had spoken to a memory, not to her. Her own thoughts spun with the implication of what was happening so swiftly between them. She could be Charlotte. Here, tonight with him, they could have one special night, safe in the knowledge that he believed she was someone else. The Lord God was giving her this one last night; giving it to them.

It was like a dream. The attic was dark and cold, rain beating against the heavy slate roof, but Edward's arms were around her, cushioning her as he pressed her slowly back onto the floor. He was kissing her with a desperation that rocked her very soul, and she met his lips with the same passion. *This is wrong. I know he belongs to someone else now,* her mind was saying as his kisses grew wild and hungry. But her heart told her that this night between them was a gift, a gift she could not refuse.

His lips traced a pattern of kisses along the smooth flesh of her neck, and her back arched as his arms tightened around her. Overcome with desire, he was still calling out her name. Charlotte's name. As he surrendered to her embrace, to the sweet, familiar taste of his lips, he wept, longing for a woman he still believed had died. And Charlotte wept with him for what she knew, after tonight, they could never have again. But for now she clung to Edward with every part of her body, legs wrapped around his, fingers coiling in his thick, dark hair, her mouth open and warm.

Edward tore the buttons of his shirt trying to free himself from his clothing, and the small glass beads danced around them. He was desperate for her, and in his drunken need he had forgotten to be gentle. But it did not matter to Charlotte. He was hers now. Here, like this. For a little while.

He moved back against her with nothing on but his trousers, and she felt his need through the worn cotton. He let his fingers stray over the fullness of her breasts. Even with her nightgown as a barrier, they felt like Charlotte's breasts. Firm and full. Exactly like. He unfastened his trousers and flung them across the attic floor, thinking only now of the release; the brief bit of peace this stranger's body would give him. He lifted her nightgown and pushed her legs apart, lust driving the reason from his mind. But as Edward arched over her, another flash of lightning lit the night sky, and it was Charlotte's face he saw gazing up at him. The same love. Trust. The same devotion as in Delhi.

Then, as it always did when he thought of Charlotte, the sights and the smells of India came flooding back, pelting his mind like gunfire, and he could not bring himself to push inside her. Edward sagged against 'Katherine's' warm, willing body, and after a moment he turned onto his back. He was panting now and soaked in sweat.

"I'm sorry . . . I . . ."

But before he could utter the words, Charlotte stopped them with her own kiss. It was sweet; a brush of her lips across his. Then she lay down beside him, her head against his bare, heaving chest, and she soothed him as he trembled.

It was still raining.

The morning sky spilled forth a torrent of wind and rain. It beat against the windows with the ferocity of cannon fire. Charlotte made eggs with bread and jam for Anne's daughter, who sat playing at the breakfast table. And she waited in silent anticipation for Edward, knowing that this morning there would be no way to avoid him.

She wore the shaded glasses that had kept her secret for almost three weeks and kept her head low against the pale morning light. She regretted nothing that had passed between them last night, only perhaps that she could not chase away Edward's demons for longer than the few brief, unfulfilled moments they had shared. It was some comfort to know that even in his most desperate hour, her memory had meant more to him than the union he might have shared with Katherine Blackstone.

The floorboards creaked above her and she knew that Edward was coming down. Her heart raced. She had been rehearsing the words all morning, and yet what could she say when it actually happened? What could he possibly say to her, still believing that he had nearly betrayed his wife with a stranger?

It was a tired and drawn man who stepped slowly down the back stairs and into the kitchen. Edward kissed his daughter on the head and then sank wearily into a chair at the table. Charlotte placed a cup of coffee in front of him and turned quickly back to the stove.

"Is Mama coming home today?" the child asked her father.

Charlotte could hear him take a deep, awkward breath before he replied. "Mama is very tired, darling. She will be at Margaret's house a few more days. But you and I shall go and see her just as soon as she is up to a visit."

"What about the baby? Can we bring her home with us?"

Edward was patient with his daughter, his voice gentle now and low. "The baby must stay with Mama so that Mama can feed her. But they shall both be home before you know it."

The eggs were done. They had been done for some time and they were growing dry in the pan. But Charlotte was afraid to turn back around. She could not face Edward in the light of day. Even with her glasses, the risk was too great now that she knew he had seen a likeness between 'Katherine Blackstone' and his own dead wife.

She held her breath when she heard him push his chair back. Charlotte continued moving the dry eggs nervously from side to side in the pan, her head lowered, as he came up behind her.

"We must talk," he whispered.

"I don't think that would be a very good idea," she replied

softly, before she turned away from him and went back to the table. "Would you like some more milk?"

The little girl held up her cup, and Charlotte filled it from a pitcher on the table. Edward turned around and leaned against the cupboard, his head throbbing. He remembered last night in fragments. The birth of his daughter. The exhaustion. The profound sadness at never having had the time to have a child with Charlotte. He remembered being in the attic and holding Katherine Blackstone, kissing her passionately . . . and nearly making love to her. But the morning's light had brought his reason back again. He had taken advantage of this stranger in their midst, and that had been wrong.

"I really think we should talk about what happened between us last night," he said as his daughter drank her milk.

Edward's voice was soft, but he knew that she had heard him. Still, she did not turn around. He could see that she was nervously moving plates and dishes back and forth on the table, trying to avoid him. Edward did not want to push the issue. He did not want to make things worse than they already were. It had only seemed proper that they should have discussed it, and yet, what excuse could he possibly give even if she had been willing to listen? Could he ever tell her that she looked so much like his dead wife that, for an instant, he had been desperate enough to want to resurrect her?

Edward ran a hand across his face and watched her for a moment as 'Katherine Blackstone' tended to his daughter. In the light of day, she was really nothing at all like Charlotte. The hair was different—not the luxuriant, gold mane he remembered—and the nose was completely wrong. The lines of the stranger's face were not nearly so refined, and she was always wearing those dreadful shaded glasses. But in the dark of night—in his desperation, God forgive him—it had nearly been enough.

Suddenly Charlotte heard the back door hinges squeak and then the crash of the door as it slammed shut against the frame. When she turned back around, Edward was gone. For a moment she closed her eyes and braced herself on the back of a kitchen chair. "Only a few hours more," she whispered softly.

Oh, Edward, she thought. *It really is better this way.*

❦ 21

THE SCENT OF WOODSMOKE FILLED MARGARET EVANS'S MODEST country cottage as a blazing fire crackled inside the soot-stained hearth. It was still raining. It had stopped only intermittently since the day Charlotte had set foot back on English soil. What a world away it was from India, she thought as she tried to warm her hands by holding them near the flames. With any luck, today would be her last in Tetbury.

"You can go in now," said Margaret as she came out of the bedroom where, late the night before, Anne had given birth to Edward's second daughter.

"How is she?"

"Weak. The doctor says she isn't gaining her strength back like she should, so you mustn't tire her out. It would be best if you stayed only a few minutes."

Charlotte walked slowly into the small first-floor bedroom, feeling an unexpected rush of guilt. How could she face her? Anne had been nothing but kind and gracious to her since she had first set foot in this quaint Cotswold town. That kindness had changed her feelings, and even her beliefs about what was right and just and fair. She no longer believed she had the right to Edward, which, in the beginning, had brought her halfway around the world. To whom was he really married now? Whom would he choose if he were forced to decide?

All of those thoughts, disjointed, fragmented, shot through her mind in the moments while she stood before the heavy four-poster bed with its thick white pillows and heavy down comforter.

"How is my little darling?" Anne asked weakly. "She must be so frightened after seeing me as I was yesterday."

"She is fine. Mr. Langston explained to her that you would be home soon, and I think she was satisfied with that."

She watched Anne breathe a sigh of relief. She sat down on the edge of the chair beside the bed. In a cradle between them, the new baby slept peacefully, swaddled in white linen.

"We're going to call her Abigail."

"It's a lovely name."

"You know . . . I really could not have made it through these past few weeks without you, Katherine. I want to thank you for that."

Charlotte looked across the room to the window and the rain beating hard against it, uncomfortable now with the kinship she felt with Edward's wife. "I was glad to do it."

"I know you are of a station much higher than my own, and while I am not certain why you're really in Tetbury, I do owe you a great debt of thanks for staying."

Charlotte shifted in her chair. "You owe me nothing."

"Oh, but I do."

She struggled to change the subject. "When does the doctor say you might be able to return home?"

"Not until the end of the week, I'm afraid. I know it's a great deal to ask, but in light of that, I was wondering if I might impose upon you to stay with Mr. Langston and my little girl just a few days more. Until I can get back home and on my feet."

It was what she had dreaded—what she had longed for. A few days more of temptation near Edward before she would leave Tetbury forever. A shade of hesitation passed over Charlotte's face as she considered the plea, and Anne saw it.

"Please, Katherine, I really have no one else to ask. Just until the end of the week."

"Very well then." She inhaled a difficult breath. "Just until the end of the week."

Anne reached out and took her hand. "You've been a good friend to me, Katherine."

"Please don't say that." Charlotte flinched and gazed back down at the baby, sleeping peacefully between them. A child that, if not for the mutiny, would never have been born.

"She looks just like Edward." Anne smiled proudly. "Don't you think?"

The rain stopped.

The air was clear and blue long enough for Edward to walk home from the pub without getting completely soaked again. *Thank Heaven for small favors,* he thought as he trudged along the mud-soaked street. It had been another excruciatingly long day, one made worse by the lack of sleep the night before and a particularly grueling hangover that had only now begun to fade.

Still, he had thought about her the entire day as he'd slung warm, dark ale across the crowded bar and made small talk with men he had known all his life. Her soft, soft skin. The round fullness of her breasts. The feel of her slim body submissive beneath him. But it was not Charlotte's memory that had filled his mind and kindled his ardor. It was Katherine Blackstone.

Edward opened the white picket gate in front of his house, and already he could smell the scent of lamb stew and boiled potatoes filling the air like a lovely perfume. She was a fairly decent cook for an aristocrat, he thought with a half smile. Really a most intriguing woman. No one else had ever intrigued him like this. Not since Charlotte.

When he came into the kitchen, she was standing at the stove, her face masked as it always was—with the exception of last night. *Those bloody glasses!* he thought irritably when she turned around with a plate for him. Her brown hair was pulled once again so taut and severe away from her face. Just as quickly, she turned back to the stove.

"How is Mrs. Langston?" Charlotte asked, imitating the breathy quality of Rani's voice as a means of continuing to disguise her own. Instead of a reply, she heard his fork clank against the plate.

"Are you finished, child?" Edward asked his daughter, who had begun to eat before he arrived.

"Yes, Papa."

"Then be a good girl and go on upstairs now. Mrs. Blackstone will be there shortly to help you get ready for bed."

Charlotte still had not turned around, but she could hear the tiny leather shoes hitting the hard wood floor and then the sound of his daughter scampering up the back stairs.

"My wife is not improving as quickly as she ought," he said in a grave tone once they were alone.

Charlotte turned around halfway, her head still lowered. "I am sorry."

"Yes." He took in a breath. "So am I."

"I went to see her myself this morning. She asked me to stay on a few more days until she had completely recovered."

"And did you agree?"

"I told her I would stay until the end of the week."

Edward came to his feet and moved behind her. Charlotte turned quickly back away from him, nervously plucking a china cup from a basin of soapy water.

He was behind her now. So close that she could smell the ale, the whiskey, and the tangy scent of his unwashed skin. Workingman's skin. It was so entirely different than it had been in Delhi. There he had bathed in scented water and plied himself with the lightest layer of sandalwood. It had been among the first things to attract her all those years ago. She remembered how, as a young girl, he had been the epitome of a dashing young hero to her, almost regal. Now this Edward smelled rough and sensual, and she was surprised how much more it excited the woman she had become.

"I . . . wanted to apologize for last night," he said, his rich voice full of confusion. He was pressed against her dress now, but he did not move to touch her. "I had much too much to drink and I gather I may have said . . . that I behaved badly."

She took a shallow breath. "You loved your first wife very much."

"She was my life," he said in a close, pained whisper.

"I loved someone like that once myself. You needn't explain such grief to me."

"Thank you, Katherine."

Charlotte turned around slowly and he was still there. Close. She kept her head lowered, but the tension between them was powerful and raw. Edward felt it too, and a sudden recollection jerked again inside him. He was surprised and confused by it. Not since Charlotte had he felt anything even close to the attraction he felt right now.

Suddenly, a gust of wind blew open the kitchen door, and the moment between them was extinguished. Charlotte pressed past Edward and hurried to the back stairs. After she had closed the door, she paused a moment and turned back to look at him as he sank against the kitchen counter. *Such a temptation it is to tell him,* she thought. *But the truth can serve no purpose now.*

"Your daughter will be waiting," she said, knowing what he was feeling because it was what she was feeling too. "If you will excuse me, I must see to her care."

Edward sat on the cot in her room and waited.

Whatever it was between them was not over. He was not certain what he meant to say or do when Katherine returned from tending to his daughter, but he could not keep himself away. He sipped absently at a glass of whiskey and glanced around the spartan room. It was curious, he thought, that in the three weeks she had lived here, slept here, she had placed no mementoes or personal effects around the room. He knew from Anne that she was secretive. And yet she must have someone who meant something to her. Perhaps a picture. A remembrance, as he had kept so faithfully of Charlotte.

He sipped his drink and watched the single candle flame flicker on the night table, his thoughts of Charlotte calling to him from another time, another place. The room was dim. Shades of gold transforming the bare white plaster walls into a ballet of dancing shadows.

On a hook near the door hung the costly gown Katherine had worn when she'd first come to Tetbury. He hadn't seen a gown like that since India. It was the sort of fabric with beading and lace that all noble Englishwomen wore. Edward came to his feet and reached out to touch it. The feel of the fabric was rich. Sensual. Nothing had ever reminded him of Charlotte so much as this. He fingered the smooth ripples of topaz silk and his heart and body surged. Why did it never end? No matter what he did, no matter how he tried, he could not make himself forget her.

It was curiosity about this intriguing woman to whom he felt such attraction that led him to kneel before the carpet bag and peer inside, looking for any clue about her. It was the silver-framed photograph he saw first. He pulled it from the bag and held it up to the light. Two young faces smiled back at him. One, a native Indian boy. The other, much younger, was English. Edward felt a cold sharp snap travel up from his spine as he studied their faces. There was something familiar about each of them.

He gazed at the Indian boy first. The somber onyx eyes drew him, and he felt the same flicker of recognition he had so many times since 'Katherine Blackstone' had come into his midst. As he stared at the grainy black-and-white images, frustrated at his inability to make a connection, something caught his eye glittering from the carpet bag beside him. Edward glanced down and saw a ring lying in the folds of a white cotton nightgown. He reached in and pulled out a small opal ring set in silver. His heart stopped. There was no mistaking it. He would never forget.

It was Charlotte's ring.

Edward clenched his fist around the small piece of jewelry that he had long ago given to her when he had asked her to become his wife. Then he opened his hand again. There was a sound like a cannon shot in his mind, and then an echo so that he could think of nothing; feel nothing but the shock.

He stopped and held up the photograph again. He knew the face now. He had grown, but there was no mistaking that it was Jawahar. The face of the younger child beside him had an eerie resemblance to himself as a boy.

Anger rapidly took the place of shock. Where could 'Katherine Blackstone' have gotten such personal articles as these? There were tears running down his face and Edward dashed at them, his mind an incoherent jumble. He looked at the ring again lying in his open palm. There was no mistaking it. This was Charlotte's ring.

"What are you doing in here?"

Edward was still kneeling beside her carpet bag, clutching the photograph in one trembling hand and the ring in the palm of the other. Charlotte stood in the shadowy doorway, looking down at him. The expression of utter shock on his face completely disarmed her.

"Where . . . did you get these?"

Charlotte lunged for the photograph. "You have no right! How dare you go through my things?"

Edward shot to his feet, a breath away from her, the candlelight casting shadows across both their faces. His voice was sharp now, his body rigid. "I asked you a question."

Charlotte's chin trembled as she looked at him. As he looked at her. And suddenly, he knew. She saw it in his eyes. Edward moved a step nearer and slowly reached up to take the shaded glasses from her face. Now the only barrier between them was disbelief that such a thing was possible. At the moment of realization, Edward's hands fell to his sides.

"Dear God in Heaven . . ."

Charlotte's eyes filled with tears as she watched his face blanche and his lips part in utter disbelief. "I don't believe . . ." he muttered. "I cannot believe . . ."

Her words that stopped his were soft, a balm of reassurance: "But it is true, Edward."

"They said there was no hope." Without thinking, without feeling anything but the shock, Edward lunged at her and pulled Charlotte to his chest. "How? My God, my God! How is such a thing possible?"

They were weeping now, both of them, he not knowing why or how they had been brought together again. Not caring. If it was a dream, it was one from which he did not wish to wake. He was saying her name over and over again—"Oh, Charlotte! My God, Charlotte!"—and pulling at her hair so that it came cascading down, dusty brown ribbons framing her small pale face. A face different from the one he recalled. Edward pressed a stream of her hair to his lips as though proof that she was real and not an apparition that his longing had created.

"I thought that you were dead!" he cried.

"I know."

"I swear it! . . . I thought that you were dead! They told me you had burned to death!"

They had suffered so much, endured the greatest cruelty. But now between them it was as if all time had stopped. It was not England but Delhi once again, a gentle Delhi in which they had met, fallen in love, and become man and wife. Edward coiled his arms around her and Charlotte fell willingly against him. His strength and the desire between them overwhelmed them both.

"You are the other half of me. You always have been," Edward muttered as he kissed her upturned face, her neck, and the cleft of her chin.

"As you are the other half of me," she answered, clinging to the strong, taut body that had branded her as his own so very long ago.

He kissed her hard and she gasped as his tongue moved over hers; his desire was to fuse them into one person that could never be parted again. She let him lead her to the small cot, and as she lay back against the cool white linen, Edward stretched out beside her. His hands framed her face.

"I dared hope no longer," he whispered, and Charlotte kissed away his tears. "Rajab told me that he saw you in the house himself and that you did not escape."

Her fingers trembled as she undid the small glass buttons

of his shirt and then ran her hands greedily through his silky dark chest hair. He watched her seeking out the curves of his body, remembering it all. Edward moaned and pressed his fingers into her back as she unfastened his trousers.

Suddenly they were kissing again, lips joined, his fingers tangled in her hair, her soft hands wrapped around his hardness, and he knew that there was nothing they could ever do to make them close enough. There were so many unanswered questions. So many things to say. And yet for now, all of that must wait. Tonight they both craved the same desperate reassurance that God had truly granted them this miracle.

Edward braced himself above her, trying to make his heart believe that what his mind saw was real. As he entered her, Charlotte watched his face shine with all the same devotion she remembered, a devotion that had sustained her through ten long and lonely years. She pulled him close, and he pressed into her again and again, her body molding to his.

"My Charlotte!" he cried in a ragged gasp as she met the full force of his passion with her own. "My precious wife . . ."

They lay together, almost sleeping, in one another's arms until dawn. Neither of them spoke. For hours they had been content just to listen to the rain beat a soothing rhythm against the roof; to braid their fingers and share soft, grazing kisses. As the morning light finally began to stretch its champagne fingers across the small iron-framed bed, it was Charlotte who first moved to speak. Her breath on Edward's cheek was as soft as a new spring breeze.

"I would not have come here if I had known."

Edward brushed the hair from her face and pressed his lips against her forehead. "And you would have deprived me of the greatest joy I have known since the day you became my wife."

"But I have complicated all of our lives."

"Fate has complicated all of our lives."

He kissed her again, softly first, then more urgently, and

Charlotte felt a new rush of passion. But time between them was growing short. His daughter would awaken soon and be needing breakfast.

"I have so many questions," he said against her shoulder.

"I know."

"Are you all right? I mean, truly all right? Your face, your hair . . . you've changed so much."

"What I have endured these past years has not been easy, Edward," she confessed. "But the worst of my wounds began to heal the day I discovered that you were still alive."

"I tried to get to you," he whispered as he ran a finger along her cheek, soft like a feather. "There was so much chaos. Our bungalow was burned to the ground. . . . I found your bracelet among the ashes myself, the one you never removed. Lord God, Charlotte, what did they do to you?"

"It is all right now, darling. All of that is in the past."

They lay together a moment more, tenderly kissing, before Edward spoke again. "I suppose I can understand why you hid your true identity once you were confronted with—" The words caught in his throat, and he took a difficult breath. When he continued, his voice was softer. "But why did you not write at least to let me know you were alive when you discovered what had happened?"

"There were too many things that I thought I should tell you face to face, not least of which was that Rajab was wrong and that I too had survived the massacre."

Edward sat up. "How did you know about Rajab?"

"I saw him not long ago. Quite by accident. It was he who told me that you had not died."

"I might as well have," he said softly, and she understood the sentiment entirely because it was what she had once wished for herself.

They clung to one another again, trying to capture the last precious moments of a night that would remain with them forever, both of them asking questions. Both of them discovering the whole, unbelievable truth, and how desperately each had struggled to find the other.

Then Charlotte rose from the bed and went to the small

carpet bag to retrieve the silver-framed photograph. She sat back down on the edge of the bed and handed it to him. It was time that he knew the whole truth.

"Look at it, Edward."

"It is Jawahar."

"Yes."

He studied the other face so much like his own, and after a moment his eyes widened with the realization of what she was trying to tell him. "I named him Hugh Edward. After his grandfather. And after his father," Charlotte said softly.

"A son?"

"Your son."

Edward lunged at her, kissing her throat and pulling her close to him again. He lay his cheek against her warm breast, more happy and sad than he had ever been in his life. "Oh, God forgive me," he muttered against her. "I didn't know. . . . I swear I really didn't know. . . ."

22

ANNE WAS LYING IN MARGARET EVANS'S HEAVY POSTER BED, soaked with sweat.

"You're looking much better today," Edward lied, looking down at her perspiration-washed face and glazed brown eyes.

"I look dreadful," she murmured.

Edward smiled grimly as he sat down beside her in the early morning hours after he had finally left Charlotte. "How are you feeling?"

"About the way I look. The doctor says I've developed an infection."

He took her limp hand and squeezed it. Her skin was on fire. Anne was right. She did look dreadful. "Is there anything I can get for you?"

"Perhaps just a few more of the years I am not going to have with you and our daughters."

"Now don't talk like that! You're going to be fine. You've only had a bit of a setback. That's all."

"They've taken Abigail. She's with Mrs. Penny. The doctor said it wasn't safe for her to be so near me just now."

He tried to sound encouraging. "It will only be for a few more days."

"Will it, Edward?"

"Of course. You're going to be fine."

"All right then." She squeezed his hand and waited a moment, gazing up at him. "Perhaps you should tell me about Charlotte."

It was a jolt, as if someone had clubbed him, and Edward sat upright in his chair, his heart thumping wildly—until he realized that she had been referring to their daughter.

"She is fine," he mouthed the reply. "Mrs. Blackstone has been wonderful with her."

Anne seemed calmed by his reassurance, and for a few moments she began to doze as he held her hand. "I'm really just so tired."

"Then you must rest. It will be all right. Everything is going to be all right," Edward said with a soft, soothing voice, not certain he believed his own words. Then when she had finally fallen asleep, he quietly left the room.

He did not go back to the pub. The morning had been too much for him. Edward Langston was a man with two wives and, the devil take him, he had no idea what to do about it. One he loved desperately, with every fiber of his being. The other was a woman who had adored him since they were children. Anne had made him her entire life. There was duty in that. But did he not have a duty to Charlotte as well? To the son who had never known his father?

Edward walked blindly through the rain, through a rolling emerald field carpeted with cowslips, and into the thickly wooded forest of beech trees at the edge of town. It was the same field he had crossed as a carefree boy chasing butterflies a lifetime ago.

He passed over an old stone bridge that spanned a tumbling creek, his mind a web of confusion. The lush ash and beech trees were tangled like a protective canvas above him, and the rain was lighter in their midst. He walked and walked, the rain pelting his face, but he did not feel it. He felt only anguish over the choice he would soon be forced to make. Yet how could he ever choose? Honor or love? It tore at his heart that it came down to that.

Edward leaned against a thick tree trunk and he was dazed, his taut body numb with confusion. Last night with Charlotte had been perfection. No sense of duty in her arms, only passion. The good Lord had given him another chance at a lifetime of happiness, but then held Anne up before him as a barrier he must first pass, if he dared.

He sank down on a bed of wet leaves and mossy stones at the base of a lichen-covered beech tree and covered his face with his hands. For an hour he stayed like that, alone in the wind and the rain. He could not believe Charlotte was alive while Anne was near death. *How strange,* he thought. *How bittersweet, to have her back again. So nearly.*

I am going to be a marvelous husband, and we are going to be blissfully happy together. I am not going to hurt her. You shall see!

Edward heard the echo of his own words spoken to Rani so long ago; spoken from the depth of his heart. Now his heart was breaking. *How can you ask me to leave her behind now when I have found her once again? God save me,* he thought. *It wasn't supposed to be this way!*

Edward worked late into the night, avoiding Anne. Avoiding Charlotte. He sent Paddy home and closed up the pub by himself. He had hoped to buy himself the time to sort things out. But the quiet held no answers. It was nearly dawn when he opened the small door to Charlotte's room off the kitchen. She sat up in her bed and held her hand to her eyes against the sudden light as he sagged against the door frame.

"Are you all right?" she whispered, but he did not answer.

He paused another moment, then came and sat beside her. Charlotte held him close. Safe in her arms, Edward touched her cheek, then trailed his fingers down her soft alabaster neck. Her warmth was a comfort, and he let himself give in to it.

Finally, he lay down beside her, fully clothed. Charlotte understood and did not object. She had nearly a month to adjust to their circumstances. He had been given only this one day. She took off his shoes for him and set them neatly beside the bed. After she had covered him with a quilt that had been folded at her feet, she lay back down beside him and let him wrap her in his arms. There was nothing she could say. She knew that. Close to him like this, she craved his body even more than she had last night, the feel of his lips pressed against hers. But she understood.

He had seen Anne today.

It was right that he had gone to her. But it had confused him. The woman had given birth to his child only a day before he had discovered that his wife—his first wife—was still alive.

"I don't know what to say," he whispered to her, his voice sharp with pain.

Charlotte stopped his words with a finger to his lips. "You need say nothing tonight, my love. Only know that I am here for you. Whatever you need."

He turned to face her and trailed his fingers down her neck to the cleft of her breast. "What I have always needed is you."

She clasped his hand and placed it gently over her heart. "Can you feel that?" Edward looked up at her, his blue eyes the color of a stormy sea and as troubled. "Every beat is yours. Now and forever."

The rain had stopped again, and Edward rolled over on his back. Neither of them need say anything more. In the silence, it was almost as if their souls were touching.

* * *

Edward was gone when Charlotte awoke.

She lay alone in the bed they had shared and tried to feel him next to her. But all she felt was the turmoil he had left like an imprint beside her. She had brought that turmoil with her from India. Now the man she adored was drowning in it, and there was not a single thing she could do to save him.

Charlotte swung her legs over the bed and gazed through the window out across the garden. The sun had come out and the sky was full of white puffy clouds. It was going to be a lovely day, and she wondered if the sun was shining in Calcutta. She lifted the photograph of Hugh Edward and Jawahar from the night table and looked at the two of them. As she did, her heart sank. She had hoped to give them a father, but she could not ask Edward to leave. Tetbury was his home. To all the world, Anne was his wife. To believe anything other than that was only indulgent fantasy.

She dressed little Charlotte and sat at the table beside her as the child pushed her spoon back and forth through a bowl of thick porridge.

"When is Mama coming home?" she asked, her lower lip turned out in a pout.

"Soon, I hope, sweetheart."

"Will you stay with us when she returns?"

"No, Charlotte. I have my own home to which I must return."

She looked up, her enormous blue eyes full of questions. "Do you have any children of your own, Mrs. Blackstone?"

"I have a little boy," she answered carefully.

"And . . . you did not die from having him?"

Charlotte stifled an understanding smile, and a ripple of tenderness passed through her. "No, dear child. As you can see, I am quite fine indeed. But bringing a baby into this world can be very, very difficult work. Do you know how you feel sometimes after you've played very hard with your friends, and you need to take a rest?" The little child nodded her head that she did. "Well, sometimes when mamas get very tired, they just need a bit of a rest too. That's all. Your mama is going to be just fine."

Her small cherub's face lit brightly with hope. "Truly?"

"Oh, truly, dear one. Cross my heart," she said, softly painting an imaginary *X* across her chest with a fingertip.

The little girl seemed satisfied with the explanation and sat up to take another spoonful of cereal. "What is your little boy's name?"

Charlotte cleared her throat. "His name is Hugh."

"That is a nice name."

"I think so too." She smiled and took a sip of coffee, more a gesture than a desire.

"Does he look like you?"

"No. Actually he looks like his papa."

"Mama says that I look like my papa too," she revealed, quite pleased with the notion.

Charlotte felt her heart sink, realizing that she was right. How sad it was that these two children, who knew nothing of one another, shared so close and binding a connection as a father—a man only one of them would ever come to know.

"Will you have more children like Mama?"

Charlotte shivered and took another sip from her cup of coffee, anything to keep the sorrow from showing on her face. "You had better hurry and finish your breakfast, sweetheart. We have got a busy day in store for us."

She got up, and when she reached the stairs, the girl stopped and turned around. "You look very pretty without your eyeglasses, Mrs. Blackstone."

"Thank you, Charlotte." She managed a weak smile for such well-meaning words.

A collection of images sprouted tight and vivid in her mind as Edward's daughter scampered up the back stairs. Her reflection in the mirror dressed in Rani's silk *sari*. Her wedding day in Delhi. The violent rape that had wiped away the last bit of her own innocence. The birth of her son had been a golden flicker of hope in a world darkened by pain, and loss, and regret. A sigh whispered across her lips as her mind raged with conflict; what she wanted, what she had a right to expect.

The child was right. How much she did look like Edward.

The shadowy little dry goods shop was crowded with women browsing at bolts of new fabric just in from Brighton when Charlotte walked in holding Edward's daughter by her small hand. She had not bothered to wear the shaded glasses this morning, nor had she tipped her bonnet low over her eyes to hide her face. There was no longer any point. The truth had finally come out.

She waited behind a woman who was trying to decide between red cotton and a yellow-and-blue print. A moment later, she looked down and saw Charlotte gazing wide-eyed once again at the china doll perched on the shelf above the spools of thread and multicolored yarn. She was looking at the doll with unfettered reverence. *How simple are the desires of childhood,* she thought, struck by the purity of this little child's longing. *If only all the rest of life was so simple to handle as that.*

When their turn came, she bought more tea.

"How is our dear Anne today?" Louisa asked as she wrapped the purchase in brown paper, still running the shop alone while her sister tended to Anne.

"Doctor Trumball says she is still weak but she is improving."

"Oh, splendid." She smiled a thick, luscious rose of a smile, and for a moment her bland face lit brightly. "You certainly are a lovely stand-in, but we do so miss her in here every Wednesday."

Charlotte's easy smile fell. "Yes, I am certain that you do."

All the while that the two women did their best to be civil, Edward's daughter could not take her eyes from the delicate and lifelike doll perched so high from her reach. Since Louisa Honeycutt was too busy to be coaxed into showing it once again, the girl settled instead for two ginger cookies and an obligatory pat on the head before they went back into the bustling lane of horse carts, carriages, and people strolling.

They walked back past the cobbler shop and the pub. As they neared the little stone house with the fenced garden, Charlotte saw a man standing at the door. It was Edward. After a moment, Margaret Evans ushered him inside, and the heavy blue door closed behind him.

Charlotte felt as though her very breath had been taken away. Still, she understood now as she had understood yesterday. He had gone once again to see Anne. But her understanding did not come without envy, which today rode a line close to jealousy.

She stood in the street watching the closed blue door a moment longer. Once they had promised to be together forever. Now he knelt at another woman's side, taking her hand. Did he also kiss her? Promise her his devotion? *Oh, Edward . . . To your face I am full of patient understanding. Inside, my heart breaks a little more each day that I am near you and you are with your Anne!*

She longed to confess it to him and beg him to go away with her now before it was too late. But no matter how much she loved him, that was something she would not do. No matter how painful, the decision must be his, and his alone.

Margaret closed the door on the two of them.

"You look better today," Edward said, tempering his uneasy tone with affection as he sat at Anne's bedside.

Duty, more than true concern, had drawn him back to her today. She was his wife, or so the rest of the world believed. He did not love her, but she was a good woman, one who had waited patiently and full of faith that he would return from India and give himself to her. Her faith in the belief that they were meant to be together was so abiding that finally, in the lonely, intervening years, she had convinced him too.

"I feel better." When she smiled lovingly at him, Edward felt a wave of nausa swell inside him, but he struggled to keep his face from showing it. "The doctor says that I am much improved."

"I am so glad. Is there anything I can get for you?"

"I would like to see Charlotte. The doctor said it would be all right now."

"I shall have her brought by this afternoon."

She took his hand and squeezed it, and for the briefest moment she felt him shrink from her, though he did not pull his hand away.

"What is it, Edward?"

"Nothing," he answered her, a little too quickly.

The silence between them that followed was thick and strained. Anne took a breath. When she looked back at her husband, she saw his distraction.

"I had a dream last night," she said softly, feeling him slip away, and she began to squeeze his hand again. "It was a terrible dream. I dreamed that you were suddenly gone. I did not understand, and I was looking everywhere, but I could not find you." Her voice went lower, and she looked up at him. "You know, I could not bear it if I did not have you in my life. You are everything to me, and to our daughters. You know that, don't you, Edward?"

He felt the shock of her plea squeezing the breath out of him. Did she know? How could she possibly? He hadn't known himself until just yesterday. He sat like a stone in the chair, not moving. Barely breathing. Edward felt his heart breaking at the exact moment when he realized that there really was no choice to be made after all. It came with the bitter knowledge that he would never take another truly happy breath again.

He leaned back toward the bed and forced himself to bring Anne's cool hand to his lips. Honor must now be his only thought. "I am here," he resolved. "And I'll not be going anywhere."

She was glad that it was over.

Charlotte let him hold her as she and Edward stood alone in the kitchen late that afternoon. Beyond the relief, the rest of her feelings were fragmented, but she understood that there was nothing else he could have done because she understood Edward. The pride. The duty. He was a man whose very soul was inextricably woven with both.

"I cannot ask you to understand. I can ask nothing of you," he said softly against her neck.

She longed to tell him that it was all right; that she agreed with his decision. She saw that Anne's need was greater. But she could not be that entirely selfless. Losing him once had been painful. Losing him twice was like death.

"I don't want to abandon my son in this."

"I shall tell him all about you," she forced herself to say. "He shall know his father as a good and honorable man."

"I want so much for us to be a family! It is all that I want in the world!"

"You have a family," she could not stop herself from saying.

"Sweet Jesus!" he spun around, angry at himself, angry at Anne, angry at his fate to have been caught up by circumstance. "I just don't know what else to do! I feel as if I have been torn entirely in two!"

"And your heart?" she asked, her voice hollow now, and she felt as fragile as glass. "Has that been torn in two as well?"

"It will be broken for the rest of my life, but not for love of anyone but you." Edward took her face in both his hands and looked down at her. "It is as I deserve for ever marrying again."

"You could not have known. I don't blame you for that. That we both survived is truly a miracle."

"I waited for seven years, hoping. Praying."

"So did I," she said softly. She turned away from him and then looked out through the kitchen window to the garden, where little Charlotte was playing with a new toy.

"Where will you go?" Edward asked.

"My father left me a property in Kent. It is where I lived as a child. My aunt and uncle have been living there since we moved to India. My advisors tell me that, apparently, now I am a very wealthy woman."

"I am happy for you, Charlotte," he said sincerely.

"You've been through a great deal and you deserve every happiness."

"Wealth does not bring happiness, Edward."

"No. And neither does duty."

He moved behind her slowly and placed his hands on her shoulders, wanting to be near her one last time, but he felt her quickly grow rigid beneath his touch. After a moment, it was Edward who pulled away.

"You never bought that farm you spoke of so often when we were in Delhi," she said, her voice on edge now as she turned back around. She was leaning against the counter to support her trembling body. "Why not?"

He sighed before he answered her. "Some time after I returned home my father died, and there was no one to take the pub. It was what he had worked for all his life; what I ridiculed and tried for so long to escape. I suppose, like so many other things, the fantasy of the life I wanted here just gave way to the reality of my duty."

"I'm sorry, Edward."

"You musn't be. Not for me. I brought home enough money from India to feel that my life has been a success. It was why I went there in the first place. Perhaps what I returned to is not the life I would have chosen, but it is not a bad life."

"Anne loves you a great deal."

"Once, perhaps. But now I think it is more that she has come to depend on me."

"As I did."

"Anne is not a strong woman, Charlotte," he snapped defensively, not meaning to. "No matter what it is I want or need for myself, she and the children need me, and it all comes down to the painful fact that I could not live with myself if I simply abandoned them to go off and follow my heart!"

"You needn't explain yourself to me, Edward," she said softly. "I see that she needs you more than I do."

A moment later he had regained his control. "I would like to write to Hugh Edward from time to time, if it would be all right."

Charlotte looked away. "I think it would be better if you didn't. It would only confuse him just now. He's still only a little boy himself, you know."

"Yes, of course, you're right. I'll not fight you on it, then. But perhaps when he is older . . ."

"Yes, perhaps."

In the silence that followed, she walked into her room and came out with the photograph of Hugh Edward and Jawahar that she had taken out of the frame to inscribe. "I want you to have this," she said. "To remember us."

Edward stood before her now, the photograph in his hands, and she thought how ironic it was that perhaps, at this moment, he was more handsome than he had ever been. So tall and majestic, shining now with tanned skin and worker's hands, just as desirable, though in a different way, as he had been in his crisp crimson and blue uniform. And she thought how strange it was that, as some things changed, so did some things remain the same. This proud, complex man who had so often been forced to put honor before love, duty before happiness, would have her heart forever.

As he read the inscription, she watched his blue eyes glitter with tears. Crystal blue tears. "Remember us always as we shall remember you, and keep your thoughts of us close to your heart, for there you shall remain with us forever, Charlotte."

He pressed the photograph to his chest and for a moment closed his eyes. She saw the pain creeping back across his face.

"When do you leave?" he asked in a whisper.

"I shall be leaving in the morning."

"So soon?"

"I think it would be best."

They were interrupted by Edward's daughter, who came tottering in through the back door, her tiny arms filled with the precious china doll from Mrs. Evans's store.

"And where did you get that, my little miss?" Edward asked.

"Mrs. Blackstone gave it to me," she answered him, smiling at her father with such innocent joy that he was able to smile too.

Edward bent down beside her and looked more closely at the exquisite china doll with the gown of velvet and lace, which had been Louisa Honeycutt's pride and joy. Then he looked back up at Charlotte.

"Louisa said she would never part with this. It must have cost you a small fortune."

"Everyone has their price, Edward," she said softly. "Hers was my city gown and shawl for her daughter."

"Papa, may I go upstairs now and make a bed for little Katherine beside my own?" Charlotte asked.

"Is that what you've named her?"

"Yes." She nodded. "Just like Mrs. Blackstone, who gave her to me."

"Go on ahead then. Make her comfortable in your room."

Edward came back to his feet, admiration shining in his eyes as the little girl tottled up the back stairs and out of sight. "That really was not necessary, you know."

"I wanted to do it. Every little girl should have a doll. And after all, she is my namesake."

Edward blanched. "That was so you would always live on for me. I didn't know we'd had a child of our own."

"I am truly touched, Edward, that you would have done that for my memory. Your daughter is lovely."

"I wish with all my heart that she was your child," he whispered. "I wish that none of this had ever happened."

"Oh, Edward." She sighed. "The things I wish now are too numerous to count."

A carriage waited outside on the lane.

Charlotte stood a moment more in the little bedroom off the kitchen, holding her gloves in one hand and her carpet bag in the next. Everything was in order. All of her plans were made. She would go first to Oxford for a week with the real Katherine Blackstone. There she would be free to grieve; to begin the healing. Katherine would give her whatever companionship or solitude she needed. That was the only assurance she had in her life just now—that and the abiding love of her two boys. She had already sent for them and instructed them to meet her at her family home in Kent.

They could have a new life there, the three of them; one that they could never have had in India. Not with all the memories.

Now, as she had only to turn and walk out the door on the man she loved, the man who loved her, Charlotte paused. It was not easy to leave. But she had no regrets about having come here. She had done the right thing. She had faced her past. Her future. She could live with the consequences. After a while, perhaps, she would even make peace with the loss. But not yet. When she finally turned around, Edward was standing in the doorway.

"I cannot let you go," he murmured. "Perhaps there is some way to—"

"There is no way, Edward. We both know that."

"But how can I lose you a second time?"

She moved a step nearer, but there was still a distance between them. "You shall never lose me. Not so long as we both have our memories of paradise. Remember how you used to call it that? 'If there is a paradise,' you would say . . ."

He slumped against the door frame. "Let me hold you, Charlotte. Please, just one last time."

She dropped her bag and wrapped her arms around his neck. Edward's eyes played over her face, memorizing every inch of it for the time, once again, when memories would be all that he had. "I shall never have to do anything more difficult," he said.

"Nor shall I."

Then he kissed her. It was soft at first, their faces so near to one another that it was like a gentle whisper. Then his resistance to her faded into the desire he would always feel, and their kiss became breathless and urgent. The pain of losing her again clenched like a fist inside him as he pulled away and desperately touched her soft, creamy face with the tips of his fingers one last time.

"I thought I could never love you more than I did the day we married," he said, still holding her face in his hands. "And yet today my love for you is a thousand times stronger."

He kissed her again, but this time both of them felt the difference. This time their kiss meant goodbye. Edward closed his eyes as they parted. *Let her go,* he told himself. *You have made your choice; the only choice a man like you could have made. You have a life here. Now you must set her free to find hers.* He took both of her hands and pressed them to his lips.

"If you ever need anything . . . anything at all . . ."

"I won't, Edward," she whispered.

He took a breath. "I know."

She picked up the carpet bag and brushed past him, not pausing to turn around. He closed his eyes again when he heard the latch on the front door click. He heard the driver open the carriage door. The whinny of the horses. Birds chirping from the tree in his front garden.

When he opened his eyes again, he looked back across the little room and saw that she had forgotten her shaded glasses. They were still on the night table. He moved an instinctive step forward, thinking he should go after her with them. It was another moment before he realized that she would not be needing them any longer. Edward moved across the room and took them up in his hand. A piece of her. He wrapped his fingers around the fragile gold wire and two circles of glass as he sank down onto the bed.

His mind was whirling, his thoughts chaotic. "Remember us as we shall remember you and keep your thoughts of us close to your heart, for there you shall remain with us forever." They were the words on a photograph that would have to sustain him for the rest of his life. It was all that he had now. A few mementoes and his memories. Edward heard the driver yell "Whoa!" The crack of the whip followed, and he felt himself begin to die. *No,* he thought. *I cannot die . . . dear Lord above, not when I am already dead!*

CHARLOTTE STROLLED WITH LORD ALFRED LINTON OUT ACROSS the lawn of Briarwood. When they reached the reflecting pond, she turned back around to inspect from a distance the progress on the renovations taking place at her family's ancestral home. This winter had been a harsh one for all of England, and many of the lovely new beech trees she had seen planted in the grove leading back to the house had already died. It was all such a struggle. One step forward. Two back. Just like her life.

Yet even in this perpetual state of flux, Charlotte thought it beautiful here. Beautiful and peaceful. Sometimes the silence so far from the city was as deafening as the noise on Delhi's busy Chandni Chouk. But Briarwood was where she belonged, as she had believed of the Calcutta hospital where she had found work. Here too in England, she had discovered a purpose. There was still a great deal left to be done to Briarwood, but time was one commodity of which Charlotte had an abundance. Now she had time and money and the inclination to make her family's home a tribute to the three people lost to her in Delhi.

Memories of her father and Rani had become easier to bear with the passage of time. There were fewer imagined glimpses of the painful deaths they had suffered, fewer tear-filled, sleepless nights; and more happy recollections to take their place.

A watercolor of each of them hung in the library. Both had been painted by Charlotte from memory, framed in gold and suspended from blue velvet ribbons, one beside the other. Together. In death as they had been in life. An oil painting of her mother as a child hung alone over her bed, a tribute to the first important woman to her. Her first important loss.

Charlotte had retained the staff at Briarwood because they wanted very much to work for Hugh Lawrence's daughter. He was a man they had respected. One who had been fair. The savage way in which he had died only added to the loyalty they felt for his only child.

There were eighteen in all. They were Charlotte's concession to the past. Everything else at her family home in the rolling green countryside was new or in the process of being altered. New upholstry for her mother's Queen Anne chairs. New wallpaper. China. New furniture for the drawing room and for the drafty mahogany and leather library that her father had loved so much. What was old had been neglected until it was unsalvageable. *Thank God for the ancient oaks out in the grove,* she often thought. *They have been unscathed by time. They are my symbol. They remind me that, in spite of everything, I too have survived.*

"Are you not yet getting cold, my dear?" Alfred asked, his slim arm linked through Charlotte's. They stood beside a shadowy ivy grotto, looking back at the rusty-brick house, both of them exhaling cool, white clouds.

"Oh, no. The air is exhilarating!" She rubbed her gloved hands together. "I think it is all those years spent in such dreadful heat."

"How you ever managed to bear it I shall never know."

"One does grow accustomed." She sighed.

And she meant it about so many things. Charlotte pulled the collar of her cape up around her neck, remembering. Her reply was the same one she had given on a moonlit Delhi terrace a lifetime ago. A glimmer of a smile lifted the corners of her mouth. And then as always, the pain followed. But it was a pain dulled by time. Dulled by ceaseless work to occupy her mind. She knew that there would always be the sensation. It came with the love. "How do you bear the heat?" Edward had asked her that first night. She heard the haunting echo of his gentle voice in her mind. Felt the rush as if it were only yesterday. "One grows accustomed, Captain," she had said with a youthful confidence she had believed could never be shaken. How many things had changed since then. How many things were still changing.

"I think things have progressed quite nicely," Alfred said, gazing past the trees, pathways, and lawns up to the house, a modest brick Tudor with Georgian windows that her grandfather had seen added a generation ago.

Charlotte was still smiling, the pain of the memory slowly paling as the cold wind ruffled the hood of her blue velvet cape. "You're very kind, but you are free to admit it. The work is going slow as a snail."

"You must be patient, Charlotte," he said kindly, richly, his voice an elegant baritone. "The house was left untended an awfully long time."

"But I've been back a year already."

"Well, you were away for twenty."

Lord Linton was a distinguished-looking man whose bright gray eyes when he smiled lit his neat mustache and full waves of silver hair like a steely flame. Twenty-four years her senior, the third Earl of Bentham towered over Charlotte, making her seem almost childlike beside him as he stood in his own black cape and tall silk hat.

It was that magnificent stature and elegant bearing that had caught Charlotte's attention when she'd first returned to England, vulnerable and unfamiliar. It was his patient concern and his sense of humor that had elevated their aquaintance to friendship. For Alfred, it had deepened from there to love.

Lord Linton knew the entire story of Edward. He understood what she had endured. He had lost his own wife in childbirth, as well as his only child. Charlotte's father and he had been boyhood friends. There was the bond of history between their two families. In the past year, this widowed nobleman had set out to strengthen that bond by deliberately carving out a place for himself in Charlotte's life.

Alfred Linton was mature, stable, and unbelievably gallant. He owned the grand estate next to her own and also a townhouse in London in the very fashionable Berkeley Square. He was also more rich and more influential than anyone she had ever known, including Delhi's brigadier, Harry Graves. Influence had never meant very much to Charlotte, because in India she had never needed what it could bring to her. But here in England, alone and unfamiliar, with Lord Linton helping her at every turn, she had begun to see the great attraction it could provide.

Since Charlotte's return to England, they had spent countless hours playing whist and croquet and in confessing to one another the most private details of their lives. Confession was easy with Alfred. Natural. That he wished to marry her and she had already twice refused him had done nothing to sully their steadily deepening connection. He understood, he had told her, and then humorously added that, while he still had a few good years left, he would wait.

"After the house is finally back in proper shape, I am going to add a barn over there, and even a henhouse; make it a real working farm," she said, pointing across the sloping lawn to a grassy emerald clearing.

Alfred tried to keep the frustration from his voice with a smile. "I think the cold has gone to your head, my dear. We really should be getting you inside."

"Oh, just a few moments more," Charlotte pleaded, squeezing his arm.

But Alfred was more interested in abandoning the topic of conversation than he was in relinquishing this much sought after moment alone. He knew about Edward's hopes for a farm of his own, and Lord Linton detested the subject. It would be a bloody shrine to the past, Alfred thought irritably. Yet he never let his displeasure show. That was not the way to win a headstrong young woman like Charlotte Lawrence. Patient understanding was the key. The only key. Age and a great deal of experience had taught him that.

"Come now. It's Christmas Eve! How will it look to the boys, their mother out here trying to catch her death?"

When his slightly pleading approach did not appear to be succeeding, he added in a firmer tone, "Besides, what about that friend of yours who has come all the way from Oxford?"

Charlotte's rosy face softened. Katherine. What a God-send she had been. What a dear friend she had become. Having her here at Christmas made the most sentimental day of the year that much easier to bear. "I suppose you're right," she acquiesced with a sheepish little smile before letting him take her arm again.

"Mrs. Blackstone is quite a lovely woman."

Charlotte smiled up at him as they strolled. "The best. She was there for me after I left Tetbury, as devastated as I was. She let me stay with her and weep upon her shoulder until there were no tears left."

"So you told me."

"Oh, did I?" she said with a half smile, truly not remembering.

They walked back toward the house, saying nothing more. It was snowing again. Light fluffy flakes fell like feathers onto their capes, their hats, and even their noses. How different it all was from Delhi, Charlotte thought, looking out across the undulating hills and trees that all belonged to her now. There was peace here. Contentment. But what a world away she was from the only thing that could ever make her truly happy.

She had tried hard to make it a special Christmas, partly for Hugh Edward, but also since this would be Jawahar's first English holiday. The evening before, they had all sung carols by the fire and then decorated the Christmas tree in the library with gilded fruits, paper roses, nuts, and miniature candles. There were garlands of holly and ivy looping the banisters and accenting the fireplace mantels. The best way to survive this, she told herself, was to make it appear as if she were happy. If she could accomplish that, then perhaps one day she might actually make herself believe it.

Everyone else believed that she had begun to heal from the savage wounds wrought upon her in Delhi. Even Alfred believed it, because he wanted so desperately for it to be true.

Lord Linton held open the glass door to the library as they went inside. Katherine Blackstone was sitting beside a roaring fire, explaining to Jawahar about the Twelve Days of Christmas. Hugh Edward was kneeling at the folds of her mint-green gown, entranced by her explanation of the Feast of Saint Stephen.

"Oh, there you are!" she said, glancing up. "We had begun to worry about the two of you."

"You needn't have given it a second thought," Charlotte blithely countered as a housemaid took their capes and gloves. "Lord Linton is always a perfect gentleman."

"How frightfully dull." Katherine smiled a bit like a peevish child, and the sweet expression on her wrinkled face that followed made Alfred let out a little chuckle.

"On that score, Mrs. Blackstone," he said, nodding decorously to her, "you and I do certainly agree."

"Then perhaps Your Lordship would have been better served to have returned through the front door. I saw Mr. Addington only an hour ago hanging mistletoe in the vestibule."

"Katherine, please!" Charlotte showed mock disapproval.

"Well, in any case, do come and warm yourselves," Katherine said, pointing to the fire as they each took a glass of sherry from the butler. "I suspect it is frightfully cold out there."

Lord Linton smiled. "Your friend here says she finds it invigorating. I, however, fear she shall catch her death."

"So again we agree, Your Lordship." Katherine nodded.

"Oh please, Mrs. Blackstone. After all the kindness you have shown our dear Charlotte, I quite insist you call me Alfred."

"It would be an honor," she said. "And you, of course, must call me Kate."

"Agreed," he said with a sweeping bow.

Charlotte smiled, watching them with a prideful gleam in her wide green eyes, like a mother does her children. It was important to her that they be friends. She would have liked it to be even more. Katherine had been alone such a long time. Alfred too. But Lord Linton had made his feelings on the subject of marriage perfectly clear. He meant to wait for Charlotte. Only Charlotte. No matter how she protested that it was never going to happen.

"When may we light the candles on the tree, Mama?" Hugh Edward asked excitedly. Charlotte looked over at him still kneeling beside Katherine, hope lighting his crystal-blue eyes. Edward's eyes.

She could not help but think how much more he looked like his father with each passing day. He would be a tall man when he matured, tall and lean and graceful. Hugh Edward's hair was raven-black, and it fell in soft onyx curls around his smooth child's face. His eyes starring up at her with such sweet crystal purity sometimes made her want to weep. But his resemblance to Edward, once a burden, had now finally become a comfort. After all, now she knew that Edward was not dead. He was simply away. A million miles away.

Charlotte put her hands on her hips, stubbornly pushing the painful comparisons from her mind. She steadied herself by looking out through the wall of paned windows at the fiery orange sunset.

"It really should be dark to light them." She toyed with them by considering the candles another moment. "But it is nearly that now. . . . And I suspect it would do no harm to go ahead."

Her son's blue eyes glittered like the sun on water. "Come with me, Jawahar. I shall show you what we do!" They hurried to the corner of the room, where the heavily laden tree sat waiting.

"Perhaps a bit of supervision would be in order," said Alfred as he nodded to Katherine and Charlotte. He then moved to join Jawahar and Hugh Edward across the room.

Charlotte knew that Alfred had left them intentionally. He was giving the two dear friends a few moments of privacy. He was always doing impeccably considerate things like that, yet never making it seem as if it was something that would require her thanks. It was, after all, not her gratitude that the handsome and exceedingly patient Lord Linton desired.

He had assured her that he would not pressure her into a marriage no matter how desperately he wished it for himself. In the meantime, he intended to prove himself indispensable in her life. Thus far, he had held true to his word in both respects.

But for all his endearing qualities, there was a suspected dark side to the Earl of Bentham. It was a side whispered about in London and even here in Kent. The rumors involved questionable women, incidents of violence, and even the suggestion of murder. But Charlotte believed his explanation. Envy, he had told her. Petty people with petty jealousies leveled against someone who had been blessed with so much.

"So then, my dear, how are you really?" Katherine Blackstone asked in a modest tone as she took a sip of sherry. The question brought Charlotte away from her thoughts.

"I'm all right. I keep busy. I suspect it is how I deal with things."

"The busier you are, the less time you have to think," Katherine said in a voice that came from experience.

"Precisely. Alfred thinks I am positively daft for all the remodeling I am doing around here."

"So then the good Lord Linton prefers a more . . . lived-in style?"

Charlotte held a hand to her lips to stifle a snicker as she considered the state of Linton House with its heavy beams, drab fabrics, and gloomy narrow windows, sorely in need of a woman's touch. "He really has been a wonderful friend to me, Katherine."

"Of that I have no doubt," she said, glancing across the room. "But then he is not your Edward . . . is he?" Katherine saw Charlotte's smile quickly pale. "So tell me, child. Have you thought of trying to contact him? Just to see how he is getting along, of course," Katherine asked as they both pretended to watch the lighting of the tree.

"Nearly every day," Charlotte quietly confessed.

"Well, you could certainly do it under the guise of a former tenant who is inquiring into the health of Mr. Langston's previously ill wife. I should think that would be quite appropriate."

"Choices were made, Katherine," she said, sighing, "on both sides. For the sake of my sanity—and Edward's—I must hold fast to our decision."

It was a love the magnitude of which neither Edward nor Charlotte would ever know again. Katherine Blackstone had known that right from the first. She also understood why it was now a love best relegated to memories. It was all so impossible for them. Edward Langston had gotten on with his life. Now someone must aid poor dear Charlotte in getting on with hers.

Assured by her indelicate questions that Charlotte did not mean to try to return to the past, Katherine set out to advance the only plan with any real merit. As she always said, the best way to heal an old love was with a new one, and there certainly could be no more perfect candidate than the one now in their very midst.

A moment passed before Katherine spoke again. "So tell me, dear. How did you come to meet that very dashing earl of yours?"

"I was out riding and I became lost on his property. I was stranded in the rain at Linton House for over an hour."

"How very fortunate for you."

Charlotte looked over at Katherine and saw the unmistakable spark of admiration for him plain on her full, pleasant face. "Perhaps you and he—"

"Oh, goodness no, my dear. I have never been any good at taking cast-offs!" Katherine chuckled. "Lord Linton shall ever have eyes for only one woman in this room! He is not so obvious as he might be. Doubtless that is due to his fine breeding. But at my age, any man is as transparent as fine silk! And so, to that end, tell me. Has he requested your hand yet?"

"Half a dozen times since last Easter."

"And you have declined."

Charlotte picked a stray piece of lint from her dress. "It simply would not be fair, Katherine. It would always be Edward I would see. Edward I would be thinking about."

"Then Alfred knows about your past?"

"I have told him everything."

"And yet he loves you still."

"So he maintains. But I have every confidence that before long he shall come to his senses. Perhaps thanks to the charms of a splendid woman like you."

"Oh, no! I should like nothing to do with a hornet's nest like that!" Katherine let out a throaty chortle. "Besides, I have been alone for so long now that I have actually grown accustomed to the solitude. I am quite happy as I am. There is a sort of contentment in a life with few surprises."

Charlotte nodded in agreement as they continued to watch the tree lighting across the room. "I too have found that contentment. I have this house to renovate, my boys—"

"Oh, goodness me!" Katherine huffed, interrupting her. "I am practically an old woman, Charlotte. That is quite a different matter. Solitude is certainly not for you!"

Charlotte stiffened slightly, folding her hands in her lap. "And why not?"

"Dearest, you are still a young woman!"

"But you told me yourself that you have been alone since you were just my age," she reminded Katherine.

"Ah yes. But unlike you, child, I did not have so grand a prospect as the handsome and very eligible Lord Linton to sway me from my solitude when my marriage was at an end!"

They had supper together in the dining hall, which, like the other rooms, was festooned with holly and ivy. By candlelight, they ate Christmas goose with fragrant sage dressing, apple sauce, and plum pudding. Then, after being relentlessly coaxed by Hugh Edward to do so, Jawahar captivated everyone with the telling of how he had risked his life to take *Memsahib* Langston into Kurnaul after the mutiny.

"You are a terribly brave young man," Alfred decreed at the end of the tale, a look of amazement lighting his long, rugged face.

Jawahar's reply came in a modest whisper. "Courage is easy to summon when something of such great value is at risk, Your Lordship."

"You are being far too modest, my boy. I know few men who would have acted as you did at the risk of such great peril to themselves."

"But there would be no Jawahar without the kind attentions of the *memsahib,*" he countered, then humbly lowered his shimmering black eyes.

Charlotte, who sat beside him, reached out and gently squeezed Jawahar's hand, which was wrapped around a goblet of water. "You needn't be embarrassed, darling. Lord Linton is quite right, you know. I shall never be able to repay what you did for me over there."

"Well," said Alfred, pointing his fork, "I for one, should like to try."

"Honor is its own reward, sir."

"True enough, Jawahar. But I was thinking of something a bit more substantial than that." Lord Linton dotted his lips with his napkin and pushed himself back in his chair. "I have taken the liberty of speaking to the chancellor at Cambridge University on your behalf. Since I once graced those hallowed halls myself and have contributed sizably to them since then, it seems they would be pleased to have you for the spring term."

Jawahar's head rose slowly from his chin. He looked first at Hugh Edward, who gave an excited yelp. Then his wary eyes shifted to Charlotte, who had straightened and was beaming with pride. "It really is one of the best schools in England," she encouraged.

"But . . . I—I am not English."

"Details, my boy. Details. Your guardian and your benefactor *are* decidedly English. And as I have said, they have already said they would be pleased to have you."

"A real education is what you have always wanted," Hugh Edward reminded him, as if such a comment had been necessary with such an astounding prospect before him. To have come from the poverty of Agra without even being able to spell his own name; to have struggled all those years in Calcutta, trying to make up for a lifetime without formal education. And now such a gift as this!

"You have worked very hard catching up, darling," Charlotte said. "I think you're ready to give it a try."

"Oh, nonsense, Charlotte! The boy shall give it more than a try!" Alfred blustered. "He shall bloody well take the place by storm! With the sort of determination and courage that he has shown, what else could he possibly do?"

Katherine Blackstone and Charlotte both began to clap, and after a moment Lord Linton joined in. Even the black-and-white-clad servants who stood in a semicircle at the end of the dining hall applauded the splendid news.

"Speech! Speech!" called Hugh Edward, clinking the side of his goblet with the tip of his silver knife.

Tears had filled Jawahar's dark, ebony eyes, but they pooled at the corners, refusing to fall. Such good fortune was still too much of a shock. Slowly, he pushed back his chair and stood up, dressed now in a costly gray silk waistcoat, trousers, and a blue silk cravat, the mark of any wealthy young Englishman with a bright future before him.

"I—I know not what to say," he stammered with disbelief. "To—call such a thing my dream would be to bring it too near the realm of what I once considered possible."

"All things are possible," Alfred interjected, his eyes straying to Charlotte.

"Still, I know I shall never be able to repay this greatest of honors, sir. All I shall hope to do is to bring pride to you and to the *memsahib.*"

"That look on your face, my boy, is quite payment enough."

Charlotte had known Lord Linton was preparing to assist Jawahar in some way, but she had no idea he had managed something so splendid. She sat across the table from him, amazed at not only his kindness but his startling generosity. He had done this for her. She knew that. But it did not matter. That he had sought to do it at all, and then actually brought it about, was what mattered most.

Suddenly she was angry at the rumors that had impugned his character. Envy was such a vile emotion, she thought, and he really did deserve so much better than that from the people he considered to be his friends.

"I say we make a toast to Lord Linton," Charlotte said, the fabric of her gown rustling around her as she rose.

"To Lord Linton!" Katherine seconded, lifting her glass.

Later, everyone sat around the tree, watching the candles sputtering their last little bursts of golden light as they exchanged their Christmas gifts. An antique sword for Hugh Edward from Alfred. A new shawl for Charlotte from Katherine Blackstone to replace the one she had left behind in Tetbury. Hugh Edward and Jawahar had gone in together to buy a new French hat for the woman they both adored.

After it was over, the boys sat in a pile of red, white, and gold satin ribbons wound in bright, crumpled paper. A new snow whispered past the drawing-room windows as a constant fire blazed in the hearth to warm them.

"There is one more," said Jawahar, bringing a small, neatly wrapped package out from under the tree.

Hugh Edward took it and handed it to Charlotte. "It is for you, Mama."

"But I have something lovely from each one of you already."

"Well, it would seem you have another."

Charlotte took the foreign package from her son and looked at the blue foil paper. Then she glanced up at Alfred, who sat in a burgundy leather chair on the opposite side of the hearth.

"The ruby earrings were really quite enough, Alfred."

"I am afraid it is not from me, my dear." He shook his head.

A dagger of recognition slashed suddenly in the pit of her stomach. Charlotte's heart leapt. It was a painful slice across a freshly healed wound. "Perhaps I shall open this one later," she said, her hands trembling.

"Oh, open it now, Mama," Hugh Edward coaxed gleefully. "We want to see."

"Who is it from?" Katherine Blackstone chimed, happily sipping her third glass of sherry. But when she looked up at Charlotte's blanched face, those brilliant green eyes of hers shading like an oncoming storm, she coughed into her hand. "Perhaps your mother is right, child. We have certainly all had enough excitement for one night."

Alfred had begun to suspect the same thing that Katherine had, and it showed in the seriousness of his expression. He came to his feet and cleared his throat in the strained silence that had rushed in quickly, like the winter chill through the shadowy, firelit drawing room. "Who is ready for another piece of that heavenly pie? Hugh Edward, would you care to join me?"

"I want to see what Mama has gotten," he said, holding firm to his place at his mother's side.

"Then perhaps you would consent to keep me company, Kate."

Katherine studied Charlotte a moment more, then held out her hand for Lord Linton to help her to her feet. "I should be delighted," she replied, knowing this was something that Charlotte and her son must face alone.

Alfred and Katherine moved silently together across the long Chinese carpet and then turned back around as Charlotte's butler held open the paneled oak door. "Jawahar, my boy, perhaps you would enjoy hearing a bit about Cambridge."

"Indeed I would," he said, understanding. He left the room with the others, closing the door behind him.

"Is it from him?" Hugh Edward asked once mother and son were alone.

Charlotte gazed down at the wrapping and the small white card printed with her name. It was written in Edward's hand. The sloping letters, the heavy way he pressed the pen, were unmistakable. She had told him she would need nothing from him. She had done her best to set him free. And still he had written. Sent a gift! In spite of what they had agreed, Edward was seeking to keep the connection alive.

Perhaps she should toss it into the golden fire that raged beside her, along with all the rest of her hopes and dreams. He had a wife, daughters. He had a life to live that did not include her.

"Do you want me to open it for you, Mama?"

Charlotte looked up at her son, her face drained of its rosy color. Suddenly she was cold. Ice-cold. She handed the package to him and watched as he tore away the wrapping.

Inside a small, velvet-covered box was a letter in a sealed envelope. He handed it to Charlotte and then looked up with an expression of surprise as he withdrew the contents beneath it.

"A silk scarf? That is the best he can do?"

"Green to match your eyes . . ." She heard the echo of Edward's voice and her hands began to tremble. *Dear Lord, I cannot cry. Please do not make me cry. I have no more tears for this.* It was the green silk scarf he had bought for her on the Chandni Chouk. The one he had carried with him for good luck the last time he had left Delhi. She cracked the seal on the envelope with her thumb.

My Dearest Charlotte,

I know you said that you would not need me, but I thought, I hoped, that you might have need of this. I shall always believe this scarf brought me the great fortune you wished upon it in that it spared your life and my own. For that, I shall always be grateful. But you know that I bought it for you with the greatest love, and now I want very much for you to have it back again. It shall give me some little peace to know that you have it.

I know not what your life is since we parted, nor what it shall become, but not a night goes by when I do not see your sweet face in my dreams, and I am still haunted by what once was—what I have tried to accept can never be again. I pray God that you are safe and that one day you shall be happy again. You do so richly deserve that.

Edward

She brushed a hand across her face to wipe away the tears that were clouding her eyes. The first thing she saw was Hugh Edward looking at her, his dark brows merged in a protective frown.

"Mama, are you all right?"

Charlotte was holding the scarf, clutching it as though it were the very line between her life and death. She held the letter in her other hand, open so that Hugh Edward saw the way it began: "My Dearest Charlotte." His bright blue eyes were defensively harsh. "If he bought it for you, why has he been keeping it all this time?"

"I lent it to him," she forced the words past her lips. "For luck."

"Why is he sending it back to you now after all this time?"

She drew in a painful breath and then breathed the words almost in a whisper. "He believes I now need the luck it once brought him."

"Not so lucky when what it cost him was you!" Hugh Edward growled. In a reflex action that shocked her, Charlotte reached out and slapped him hard across the face.

"I'm sorry," she gasped, even before she had brought her hand back down to her lap. "I did not mean to do that."

He lifted a hand to his stinging cheek and stared at her for a long time, as though trying to gauge what she was thinking; what she must be feeling. He wanted to care for this man, the missing part of his life. He wanted some connection, and yet all he felt was protective anger for the pain he was still causing his mother.

Hugh Edward finally heaved a heavy sigh of resignation. "Even after everything, you still love him, don't you?"

"He is still my husband."

"Mama, he is married to someone else!"

"Not in his heart, darling . . . not in his heart."

His blue eyes widened. "Then I don't understand why he

288

cannot be here with us where he belongs. This is not the way it should be, Mama!"

"Sometimes in life, darling, things do not turn out as they should. Your father is a very proud and noble man, and he is going against his heart to do what he believes he must. I love him for the man he is. . . . And you must also."

It was several minutes in the silence that followed before the drawing-room doors clicked opened again and Alfred stood alone in the archway. "There are carolers at the front door. Shall I offer them something?" he asked tentatively, then waited for a reply, to gauge whether or not to speak further.

Charlotte squeezed her eyes to push back the tears as Hugh Edward watched her. Realizing that his mother meant to say nothing more on the subject, he finally came to his feet with a huff and then stalked out of the long, firelit drawing room. Alfred closed the doors behind the boy and came to sit beside her.

"What can I do?" he asked, and it was the kind, patient tone in his voice more than the circumstance that brought a new flurry of tears. "It is all right," Alfred whispered as he took her into his solid, protective arms and kissed away the wetness on her pale cheeks. "You needn't put on a good front for me. Go ahead and cry if you like. You certainly do have every right."

When she had cried until every breath hurt and she could sob no more, Charlotte raised her tear-stained face and looked at Alfred, so distinguished, so full of a comforting kind of experience, in the copper glow of the firelight. It calmed her just to look at him, to have him hold her in his arms.

She wanted to tell him. It always did such good to talk to him about things. The letter had cut her to the quick. The scarf had finished her off. Now her mind was nothing more than a jumble of confusion and pain. God, she wanted to cry out and let Alfred make it all go away. And he could. She knew that. Lord Linton had the power to do anything he chose to do. But he was in love with her, and speaking about her enduring dedication to Edward would be cruel, especially now when the hurt was so open and raw again. When she was likely to say anything.

In the silence, she sagged back against his chest and let him tighten his protective embrace. It startled her to realize suddenly that she was not repelled by this nearness that was fast growing intimate. The hand that was caressing her shoulder was warm and comforting, and it had been such a long time since she'd felt the desire to be close to any man. When she lifted her head again and looked back at him, Alfred's finely chiseled face was flushed with such desire that Charlotte knew he was going to kiss her for the first time.

He took her pale face in both his long, slender hands and gently pulled her nearer. Charlotte closed her eyes as he grazed her lips with his own. When she did not pull away from him, Alfred seized the moment and pressed his lips against hers with forceful abandon. Suddenly it was much more than a kiss. He was sprawling over her, his hands fingering her smooth neck. His body was arched and hard. When he tasted a little gasp in the moist hollow of her throat, he pulled away.

"I have never wanted anything so much as I want you," he whispered as his breath quickened, and she could feel it warm on her face. She was trembling in his arms, but she was not telling him to stop—not with her words, nor with her kiss.

In reply, her hand curled around the nape of his neck and gently pulled him closer again. For the first time with him, she truly wanted to surrender. Perhaps his powerful body and tender words would be the palliative she needed to push away the relentless, dull ache. The emptiness inside of her. In that she was using him, but Charlotte was powerless by any other means to battle a demon that was threatening to consume her. Edward was with *her* tonight. Holding *her*. Perhaps even making love to *her*. Charlotte had every right in the world to want this now with Alfred. Self-preservation, she thought, as his tongue coaxed her lips to open and she surrendered to the primitive desire she had believed completely dead inside of her after Tetbury.

Alfred was pressing her back against the sofa pillows, his body rigid with the need she had kindled. She could feel his heart between them, white-hot pounding. She must stop this, her mind was saying. It really was most improper. But as he continued to kiss her, to touch her, Charlotte fell further and further beneath the murky, beckoning surface of propriety.

As he drew her tongue into his mouth again, Alfred's fingers spread over one of her breasts, instinct calling him to push aside the satin and lace with the palm of his hand. The delicate pearl buttons holding together the bodice of her dress suddenly burst as he pressed his fingers beneath the smooth fabric and onto her flesh. Charlotte stiffened, but the moan of raw pleasure that escaped her lips only spurred him on. His warm lips closed around her taut nipple, teasing it with his tongue. Her body arched beneath his, and Alfred pressed himself against her, wanting her to feel his need.

Suddenly the door to the drawing room clicked and then squealed to open, and a golden light streaked across the sofa like a beacon, lighting them both. Charlotte shot back to the reality of the evening when she caught a glimpse of Jawahar standing in the doorway, an expression of utter shock making rigid his soft, dark face. Alfred had felt her jerk away from him a moment before and now watched her, busily trying to press back the bodice of her dress where the buttons had burst before he realized anyone had seen them.

"They are not in here any longer," Jawahar dutifully called out behind him in answer to an unheard question. Then he looked back at Charlotte with such bewildered innocence that she was ashamed. "His Lordship must have taken the *memsahib* out for a breath of air. Perhaps we should wait for them in the library."

He then pulled the door closed, and they were alone once again. They sat up together, the intimacy having expired between them, and Alfred did not dare try and help her while Charlotte continued fussing with her gown. As she did, he came slowly to his feet and stood over her in the last waning sparkle of firelight.

"Shall I come to you later when the others have retired?" he asked softly, and the awkward tone with which he spoke the question muted the harsh reality of what he was suggesting.

Alfred had every reason to assume that she would have desired such a rendezvous. Some part of herself—a part locked deeply inside her wounded heart—probably did wish the very thing that he did; that he would come to her room in the forgiving darkness of night and make her feel all of the things her heart told her she would never feel again with any man but Edward.

A wave of compassion surged within her and tempered her reply. "Thank you, Alfred," she said softly. "But I think it would be best if you didn't."

"Then perhaps I should say goodnight," he said with a courteous, surprisingly formal bow, then walked quickly across the Chinese carpet toward the door.

"We are still invited for breakfast tomorrow, aren't we?" she called out to him.

Lord Linton looked back at her, sitting on the sofa, holding up the bodice of her gown. A portion of her hair had fallen free from the neat chignon she wore, and she looked as forlorn and desirable as any woman he had ever seen in his life. He was patting at the perspiration on his upper lip with a white handkerchief and trying to press back the desire as he replied, "If you still wish it."

"Of course," she managed to say just as he went out alone through the drawing-room door.

Later that night, she stood alone in the kitchen doorway, watching Jawahar sip a cup of coffee that he had just made for himself. The room was dark except for a single oil lamp that glowed on the table, and the pungent aroma of freshly ground beans lingered between them in the cool night air. No one else made coffee strong and dark, the way he liked it. The way he remembered it in India.

The servants had all gone to bed and he had the kitchen to himself. Charlotte had gone to bed with every intention of surrendering to the fatigue of so emotional a Christmas Eve. But sleep had been beyond her. She had lain alone, tossing and turning, thinking back on all the images of the evening. Edward. Alfred. The scarf. She knew that, after the confusing scene he had witnessed, Jawahar too would be awake. The thought had brought her down where she assumed she would find him.

She moved into the light in a rich burgundy robe. Her hair was long, its dusty brown curls cascading across her shoulders in a manner Jawahar had not seen since the day he'd carried her from the burning bungalow. Charlotte poured a cup of the strong liquid for herself and sat down beside him. To her it was dark and impossibly bitter, but she had always pretended to like it out of deference to him and to the past they shared.

"Do you ever miss anything about India besides this coffee?" she asked him tentatively, searching for the right words to gauge how he was feeling about what he had witnessed earlier.

"I miss nothing about a cruel and unforgiving land that makes barbarians out of peaceful people," he said simply, not looking up at her.

Charlotte leaned back in her chair. "Last summer, there were times late at night when I was nearly asleep, and I actually thought I heard the faraway call of the jackals. When I closed my eyes, I could smell the sweet fragrance of the orange blossoms in the Graveses' orchard. Everything was so unbelievably still. So perfectly peaceful . . ."

"It is not how I remember India, *memsahib.*"

Charlotte inhaled deeply, knowing the darker side of things that had defined his young life. "Tell me then, at least, are you pleased about Cambridge?"

"It is the chance of a lifetime," he replied, his voice suddenly richer and more full of feeling. "No matter what Lord Linton says, I shall never be able to repay him."

"I am quite certain that he expects nothing from you,

darling," she said knowingly. "You have now only to work very, very hard and to realize all of your dreams. You let me worry about repaying the earl."

Before Charlotte spoke again, there was a little strained silence between them at the mention of the man with whom he had seen her so shockingly. "About what you saw earlier, Jawahar—"

"You need give me no explanations, *memsahib*," he countered, again not looking directly at her.

"I imagine you think I am quite dreadful for allowing myself to be compromised in such a way."

"Please, *memsahib*," he implored her, his voice rising an octave.

"It is important to me that you of all people understand, Jawahar. I still love Captain Langston with all of my heart. But sometimes when people are in pain they behave foolishly. As I did this evening. I regret what happened between Lord Linton and myself, and I wanted you to know it shall not happen again."

"It is best not to make those sorts of promises, to yourself especially, *memsahib*."

"I know my own heart."

"Perhaps that is so. But if he brings you some little bit of happiness, *memsahib* . . ."

Charlotte's face was suddenly solemn. "There was only one man who ever made me happy, Jawahar," she said softly.

On Christmas Day, Charlotte stood at the long salon window. She chuckled at the pitiful snowman Hugh Edward and Jawahar were building from the bit of new snow on Alfred's vast east lawn. Katherine Blackstone was standing beside the boys, her hands nestled inside a fur muff, and she was nodding directions about where precisely to put the two lumps of coal that would fashion the eyes.

The scent of fresh cinnamon and nutmeg was especially strong at Linton House this morning, and Charlotte took in a joyous breath. The fragrance that reminded her most of England was courtesy of Alfred's butler, who had risen before dawn to make spice cake and cider. Adding to the festive air in the old dark estate, they had also coiled fresh garlands around the polished oak banisters and looped them across the front of all the fireplace mantels, just as they had been at Briarwood. Sprigs of emerald ivy dotted the base of the dozens of candles that the earl had instructed be set around the dining hall for the Christmas breakfast.

Charlotte was so lost in her thoughts and the pleasing fragrance that she did not realize Alfred was standing behind her until she felt his firm hand on her shoulder.

"Just imagine," he said, gazing with her out across the magnificent, snowy-white lawns, "you could be mistress of all this. Together we would be invincible. We could make quite a statement, you and I."

"Dear Alfred," she said, reaching up to cover with her own the hand still firmly planted on her shoulder. "You deserve so much better than a merger."

"A merger of lives and hearts. What more is there for people of our station?"

When she had turned around, she took his hands in hers and held both between them. "But that is just the point," she said, gently taking great care not to wound him too deeply. "You know you can never really have my heart. No other man ever could."

"I have enough love for us both, Charlotte."

What a magnificent man he was, looking down upon her now with his rugged, masculine face, his expressive gray eyes through which she could see straight to his heart. He would never hurt her. No matter what anyone else said. He would be a wonderful husband and a solid influence in the lives of both her boys. He was everything she could ever have hoped for in a husband. Everything, that was, had she not met Edward first.

"Alfred Linton," she exclaimed, her lips turning up in a sweet smile, "I do believe you are the dearest man I have ever had the good fortune of knowing. However—"

He moved to stop her with his own calm, measured tone. "Charlotte, I am no longer a young man. Yes, perhaps I still retain a measure of my looks; or rather a kind of style that has come with experience and with all of this silver hair of mine. 'Distinguished,' I gather they are calling it these days. In spite of that, however, I am no longer a young man with any grand illusions about what a marriage should be."

"But I do have those illusions, Alfred," she replied, gazing up at him with shimmering, green-eyed conviction. "I know what it can be. I remember it all, and the memory is something I want never to forget."

"Even though it is something you are certain never to feel again if you won't at least try?"

"Even though."

"You know I fully intend to make you my wife," he said with gentle confidence.

"And in spite of my shameful behavior last night, I wish desperately to keep you as my friend. I am certain that if we married you would only end up despising me for what I could never give you."

"I could never despise you, Charlotte."

"It is what you believe now because we have this beautiful friendship of ours built on mutual respect and, I might add, a good measure of fantasy."

His eyes glinted with amusement and then crinkled at the corners. "After last night, I would say that is a bloody respectable place to start!"

"For a dalliance, Alfred. But not for a marriage."

"If you insist on refusing me once again," he sweetly warned, "I shall be forced to wait until I feel that enough time has passed and that you are sufficiently vulnerable."

"I shall always be vulnerable to you."

"A man does dare to dream."

Charlotte held her arm out to him so that he might escort her across the room. "Play a game of cards with me until they tire of that snowman?"

"Only if you let me win for a change."

"Oh, no!" She laughed wistfully. "I'll not make it as easy for you as all that. With me, you shall have to work to win!"

"Dear woman," Alfred said with a laugh, his eyes twinkling, "it is what I am counting on!"

EDWARD SWALLOWED HARD.

The whiskey burned his throat like liquid fire. But it was the only thing that ever helped. He was gazing at but not seeing Anne and little Charlotte as they put the finishing touches on the Christmas tree. He sat on the sofa with his legs crossed as his younger daughter, Abigail, dozed in his arms.

Edward's body was there with them but his mind was a million miles away from the small, firelit sitting room with the exposed oak beams and the fading chintz furniture.

Earlier in the evening, the Langstons had hosted their annual Christmas Eve supper for Paddy Gillam and Margaret Evans. People in Tetbury had been trying to match the town's oldest bachelor with its resident spinster for nearly twenty years, neither of them wanting any part of it. Edward had been the first to come to terms with that fact and to accept their wishes. Christmas Eve at the Langstons' was now a tradition with no motive beside pleasure—and both guests were quite content to keep it that way.

After the goose, the chestnut stuffing, and the mince pie had been devoured, the two men had gone alone to retrieve the Langstons' tree from the back garden. It was considered *de rigueur* not to have one these days, Anne had said, since Queen Victoria and her family prized them so especially. It was one of the few things Anne Langston could insist upon each year to display her knowledge of the social graces to a husband by whom she considered herself so clearly outmatched. She had never been anywhere. Done anything. Her one desire, and the goal of her life, had been to become Edward Langston's wife.

Once outside, neither of the two men spoke about the package Edward had pressed into Paddy's moist, stubby hand the week before and asked him to send to Kent. Instead, Edward had filled the frigid night air with idle chatter about the exceptionally high price of the new pint glasses he needed to purchase for the pub. He had groaned about his discontent with the dreary state of the weather. The burden of taxes. It was as if neither the package nor the request had ever existed.

Paddy Gillam stood now, pot-bellied and balding, leaning against the fireplace mantel. His round, fleshy face was piqued with suspicion as he studied his employer and friend. There was decidedly something more on Edward's mind than the price of glasses and the unabated fall of snow. There could be no doubt about that. He had changed too dramatically this past year. He had been completely transformed into a man who seemed to have lost all hope.

Oh, he went through the motions impressively enough, Paddy thought. Edward opened the Cock 'n' Feathers every day at the same time, and he sat dutifully in the third pew of church with his wife and daughters every Sunday morning. It was all quite plausible. But something vital was still missing. It was the spirit and the drive that had seen him out of Tetbury and off to such an exotic place as India, vowing not to return until he was powerful and wealthy.

Despite the savagery, it was not the mutiny alone that had changed him, nor brought him back. Paddy dismissed that possibility with an audible huff when he considered the Edward who had returned home and had eventually begun this new life with Anne. They had seemed happy enough then, even through the births of Charlotte and little Abigail. Paddy sipped his whiskey reflectively, trying to piece it all together. But some of the pieces were still missing, and he was becoming more and more certain that they were the most important ones.

"How does it look?" Anne asked, then turned back

around toward Edward when he did not answer her. "Darling, I asked you, how does the tree look?"

It was another moment before Edward seemed to comprehend what she was asking him. "T-the supper was wonderful."

"I'm not asking about the supper, silly. I want to know what you think of the tree."

His glazed eyes began to clear, and a slight, mirthless smile curled the corners of his slim, tawny lips. "Lovely. It all looks lovely."

"Would you like to dress it with something? There are a few items left." She pointed, indicating a small collection of nuts and candy.

"No, you go ahead."

"Please, Papa," Charlotte whined. "Come and help us."

"How about if you add a little something for me, hmm?"

"Please, Papa! Please, just one!"

Edward cradled the baby against his chest, searching for a plausible excuse to keep him from having to feign happiness at a circumstance that was slowly choking the life out of him. "Abigail has finally nodded off here. I think we should let her sleep, dear."

"I could take her," Margaret offered, and she moved a step nearer the sofa, lowering her voice. "It would mean a lot to your daughter."

Edward's face went suddenly rigid. "I said no and I meant no! Now that is the end of it!"

Anne put her hands on Charlotte's small shoulders, looking with a blush of embarrassment first at Margaret, then at Paddy. The tension in Edward's face began to fade as he gazed down at his younger daughter, still fast asleep in his arms.

Blast! He had not wanted to strike out like that. Anne was the last person he wanted to hurt. Compassion for her was how he had gotten so mired in this dreadful mess in the first place. But God help him, in the blackest corners of his mind, Edward had started to resent her. The dark thoughts taunted him. It was Anne who was keeping him away from the only woman he had ever truly loved. It was Anne who was denying him his son. And she did not even have the bloody misfortune of knowing it.

It is not her fault, Edward silently chided himself again and again, trying to battle his own dark thoughts, as the two women moved through the sitting room and into the kitchen. He raked a hand through his dark hair to steady himself, but the dark rage inside him continued to build, taking a voice of its own. *I will live here and I will care for her,* he heard his mind saying. *But I cannot give her even a piece of my heart. No! That I can never do to Charlotte. It is the one thing in which I at least have some little bit of choice!* Edward sprang up from the sofa and handed his sleeping daughter to Paddy, who was looking down suspiciously.

"Where are you going?"

Edward plucked his coat and gloves from the peg near the door. "Out."

"When shall I tell Anne you'll be back?"

"I haven't any idea."

"Wh-what kind of an answer is that?" Paddy blustered. "Good Lord, man, 'tis Christmas Eve!"

Edward paused at the open door, and the frigid winter air wafted in between them. "What I mean is that I don't know anything anymore. Under the circumstances, Paddy, it is the only answer I have to give."

He waited alone in the dark kitchen.

A light from the bedrooms upstairs lit the back stairs almost to the landing. Anne was brushing her unbound hair. One hundred strokes every night. The children were asleep. Margaret and Paddy had gone home. Having just returned from an aimless walk, Edward leaned against the pine cupboard that held their chipped blue cups and plates all in neat little rows. By now she was tucking her full, dark hair beneath the white cotton nightcap, he thought. Five minutes more exactly and Anne would be asleep.

He paced across the kitchen, unaware of the draft coming from beneath the back door. He waited a few minutes more after he had heard his wife blow out the lamp beside the bed.

Had Charlotte gotten his letter? The scarf? Had she understood why he'd been compelled to send it, or had she cursed him and surrendered them both to the fire, as he might have done in her place? It hurt him to consider that possibility, but in spite of the risk, still he'd needed to send it. That scarf was a symbol. A sign of the love that would always be between them.

The five minutes had passed. Anne would be asleep now. Slowly, Edward moved up the back stairs, not intending to go to bed just yet. The floorboards creaked beneath his leather shoes. Beyond the nursery was a second, more narrow flight of stairs. They were the stairs to the attic. With a single sputtering candle to light his way, Edward held the banister and took the steps two at a time.

Once inside the musty-smelling attic, he closed the door and moved past the dusty beams to the green-painted chest with the worn leather straps. The little camphorwood box was hidden safely inside of it. His life and his heart were inside that box.

Christmas was a time for remembering. For sentiment. Tonight the temptation had been the strongest it had ever been to confess the truth to Anne and to tell her that he was leaving. For a moment, when he had snapped, the desire had even been unbearable. Sending the scarf had been a compromise to the battle that had raged inside him since the day Charlotte had left Tetbury. To have come so close to happiness again—and then to have been forced to let her go from a sense of duty!

He knelt on the cold plank floor and opened the small chest he had carried with him to Delhi and back again. Edward took out one polished Agra stone at a time and held them up to the candlelight. There was comfort in them now. And to think he had almost forbidden Charlotte to bring Jawahar back with them to the cantonments. That boy at whom he had scoffed had saved her life. There had been a special bond there from the first, one Edward had never been able to understand. *Thank God I did not listen to my own objections,* he thought gratefully, knowing that she had a friend for life in the stone seller's son.

Edward glanced back down and saw her shaded glasses, but those he did not lift out of the chest. The pain of simply looking at something that had been so close to her skin was intense enough. After a moment, he moved them aside and slipped out the photograph of Jawahar and Hugh Edward. His precious son.

He stared at the image for a long time, seeing snatches of Charlotte and of himself in the small, slim boy who had smiled for the camera. He was a beautiful child. *What he must think of me, of my absence.* Edward sighed painfully. Hugh Edward was the age now that he had been when his mother had first fallen ill. The protective way a boy felt about his mother paled everything else. There was so little she could say on his behalf to change that. This unknown child of his heart, this child of so great a love, quite likely despised him. Now the fates were asking him to learn to live with that.

He would rather have died in Delhi.

"Come to bed," he heard Anne say later as he stood at their bedroom window, gazing out across the horizon. The sun was just beginning to come up, pale pink behind the neat row of slate-roof houses.

Edward had fallen asleep in the attic that Christmas Eve, holding the photograph bearing the image of his son. He had believed himself to have been up there no more than an hour, but he had awakened to find that it was nearly dawn. He shivered now and looked back at his wife, buried beneath a mound of fluffy goosedown pillows and blankets, only her face and a white linen nightcap peeking through.

"Go back to sleep," he said softly.

He heard the rustle of sheets as she sat up. "It really isn't worth it, you know."

"What?" he asked, and his voice broke a little, wondering what she must think.

"Whatever it is that has had you in such a state this past year."

Edward looked at her again, the plain, pale oval of her face etched with well-meaning concern. Her eyes were as dark and expressive as they had been in childhood. He really should go to her and take her in his arms. It had been so long since he'd taken her as a man takes his wife; even before he had discovered Charlotte was alive. Anne had never once complained, but he knew that his withdrawal had hurt her.

He moved to the bed and forced himself to sit down beside her, trying desperately to call up the desire that had led to the conception of two daughters. They remained together like that for several moments, looking at one another, neither of them speaking.

"Perhaps one day, if we are married long enough, you will tell me why it is that you always look so sad," Anne finally said, covering his hand with her own.

Edward felt a slash of guilt, cold and hard as slate. It had gone right to his heart. He expelled a long breath, wondering how he could ever tell her what she wanted to hear. There were so many lies already. For the second time that evening, he wavered between the truth and the deception.

His voice when he spoke again was hollow and on edge. Once again he had taken the only side his conscience had left him. "There is nothing to tell you, Anne. . . . Nothing at all."

"You know I don't believe that."

"Believe what you will."

"I try to make myself believe that you still love me."

Edward stood back up and turned away. He could not bear to look at her any longer. There was too much heartbreak in her eyes. All the passion he had tried to enlist again for her as he had left the attic and come to their bedroom now was wiped away with that one pleading glance between them. He should never have come back. Whatever he'd been hoping to find by coming into their bedroom in the early hours of morning was not there. Nor would it ever be.

"I'm so sorry," he said in a whisper.

Anne closed her eyes and then opened them again. "Not half so sorry as I."

"So, Edward my boy, tell me, how can I help?"

Late the next evening after closing, Edward and Paddy

were alone, separated by an empty bar and by the lingering fragrance of ale and stale smoke. Edward could sense that he knew something. They had been friends a long time. But how could he ever bring himself to tell him this?

"There's nothing you can do," Edward said, struggling not to sound harsh.

"I've a good enough pair of shoulders, you know," he gently prodded, pouring Edward a drink. "I've known you all your life, Edward my boy, and there is something eating you alive, as sure as I'm standing here."

"You cannot help me, Paddy. No one can."

He leaned against the bar on rough elbows. "Are you so certain of that? I may not have been to the far corners of the world, but I've packed a good deal of living into this old body of mine just the same."

Paddy's tone made Edward smile. He was only trying to help. And telling him probably would help. For a few brief moments, at least. But no matter what temporary release he might gain, the burden of his secret was too great a one to ask of such a dear old friend. After all, this was not a simple tale, and Edward was not altogether certain that Paddy would be able to keep it from Anne, even if he could find the words to confess it. The pity for her would be there in his voice, the heartbreak for her would shine brightly in his eyes; and she would know because she knew the kindly gentleman as well as he did.

Paddy Gillam had sung at their wedding. In his gravel-voiced, off-key tenor, he had chortled out a love song to which the bride and groom had danced. *More children. Marriage,* Edward thought, torturing himself now. *Why did I not wait? Why?* He surrendered his face to his hands, heaving a painful, heavy sigh.

"Have you done something you ought not have?" Paddy pushed a little further.

Edward looked up again after a moment. Paddy was relentless, and Edward was suddenly too weary to fight him. "Old friend." He sighed. "You don't know the half of it."

Paddy pressed two fleshy fingers to his lips. "'Tis a woman, then."

"There was a woman once, back in India. But it is over now," he said, trying with everything he possessed to mean it.

"I thought as much."

Edward straightened, and Paddy chuckled at his surprise. "You don't give your old chum much in the way of credit, now do you, Edward Langston?"

"I'm sorry." He smiled a weak half smile.

"Unrequited love is always the hardest to leave go," he ventured, leaning back, eager for an opportunity to wax philosophic.

Edward took a long swallow of scotch and balanced his own elbows on the bar. "Tell me, Paddy. How does a lifelong bachelor know so much about affairs of the heart?"

"I never married"—he winked—"but I never said I hadn't been in love."

"I had no idea," Edward replied, unable to mask his surprise. "Who was she?"

"Oh, 'twas a long time ago, my boy . . . before you were even born. But she was a vision then. Long silky hair dark like onyx and as brilliant. . . . And she had the most exquisite eyes, bright China blue."

Edward paled. "You're describing my mother, Paddy."

"That I am, lad." He nodded. "That I am."

Paddy ran a limp cloth along the surface of the bar in the silence, then filled both their glasses again before he continued. "I loved her for as long as I can remember. I used to carry her books home from school, and on the way we always shared our deepest secrets."

"What happened?"

"A chap named Charlie Langston happened," he said matter-of-factly, glancing up at Edward, the hurt long gone from his voice and from his eyes.

"I had no idea."

"Of course not. Looking back, I'm not certain even Adelaide knew how much I loved her. Your father was as far as she could ever see once they discovered one another."

"And you never even tried to fight for her?"

"He made her happy, Edward," Paddy said softly, his

own blue eyes becoming moist. "I could not take that away from her, even if it meant I would never have the only woman I ever loved."

"Wh-why didn't you ever tell me?"

Paddy lowered his eyes, leveling them at an amazed Edward. "Dear boy, 'twas your mother I loved!"

"Well, just the same, I wish I'd known."

Paddy crooked a bushy gray eyebrow. "Now, what purpose might that have served if you had?"

"I don't know exactly," Edward conceded, raking a weary hand through his hair. "You might have let me be a comfort to you somehow."

"Like you are letting me be to you now?"

Edward exhaled and gazed across the bar contemplatively. It had been such a long time since he'd anyone in whom to confide. And Paddy was here now. A dear friend offering him a caring ear. "I loved her with my whole soul, Paddy. When I lost her, it really was the end of me."

"And Anne will never take her place," Paddy added knowingly.

"Never. Does that shock you?"

"That you loved a woman before Anne?"

"That I love her still."

"Life doesn't always come in those neat little packages we wish it would." He shook his head. "Once you accept that, there is really very little left to shock you."

"Perhaps you're right."

They sat in commiserating silence for a while, both of them gazing down absently at their glasses. Edward finished the rest of his drink and set the empty glass reluctantly back down onto the bar as Paddy glanced up at the clock.

"You'd best get home to her, lad," he said kindly when Edward made no move to leave. "No matter what it was you had with that other woman, and no matter what you still may feel for the memories, you have a wife now who adores you. One who, I'll wager, is waiting for you as we speak."

Edward forced himself onto his feet and Paddy reached

across the bar, taking hold of his wrist. As he did, an expression of compassion swept across his face.

"We can talk about the past all we want," he said in a tone of concern. "We can keep it alive in our hearts and our minds for as long as we like, but that'll never change one fact. There it shall remain, lad, in the past."

If you only knew, Edward thought.

"PIGS?" HE GASPED.

"Yes, pigs, Bickers." Charlotte looked up from her writing desk at the butler who stood in open-mouthed amazement at her directive. "And chickens and geese. And a cow or two, if you can find them."

"But madam, if you will pardon me for the observation"— he gulped a deep breath—"those are farm animals."

"Precisely, Bickers." Charlotte smiled. "Now, can you see to it, or shall I ask someone else among the staff? The henhouse will be finished by week's end and, as you know, the barn is already completed and just waiting for the lovely little creatures to come and grace Briarwood."

"H-have the eggs or meat I've seen to in the past not been to madam's liking?" he asked, trying to keep the indignation from his formal, resonating voice.

He watched her as Charlotte put down her quill and rose in her blue and yellow gown. Her smile was as sweet and endearing as any he'd ever seen, and he would have been quite taken by it had she not been trying to reorganize a household that for longer than her years he had been running quite efficiently, thank you.

"It is not that a'tall, Bickers. I've just been longing for my own fresh milk and eggs like I had in India." She lied smoothly as to her motivation. "And I thought it would be quite lovely to have them again."

"I see."

"Have you a problem with my wishes, Bickers?" she asked, knowing full well that a servant would not dare resist her wishes.

"No, madam." He shook his head and clasped his hands so tightly behind his back that he cut off his circulation. "If it is pigs madam desires here at Briarwood, then it is pigs we shall have."

He nodded. Then, without waiting to be dismissed, and knowing he dare not spend a single moment more in her presence, he turned away and quietly left the room.

"Splendid," Charlotte said, pleased with herself as she sat back down and then unlocked her desk drawer with a small silver key she wore on a black silk ribbon around her neck. Inside the drawer, beneath Edward's letter and the green silk scarf, were sketches she had commissioned of the additions to her family's estate. Among them was the farm about which Edward had always dreamed. It was the life he had so desperately wanted for the two of them, before the mutiny —before Anne.

That somewhere in the world there should be a place where his dreams were being realized, if not in his own life, was of the utmost importance to her now. It was the goal that occupied her mind, her resources, and her heart.

"I've come to say goodbye, my dear."

Charlotte was so deep in her thoughts of the great working farm she would create that she had not heard Katherine Blackstone come in behind her. She turned with a start and then shot suddenly back to her feet.

"You're not leaving already!"

"Alas, I must. I promised Mr. and Mrs. Covington that I would sit with them in their box at the opera the first thing after the New Year."

Charlotte reached out to take Katherine's hands. They were warm and soft, and through them she could feel the enduring friendship and love that precious confidences had begun to build.

"You truly do not have to go, do you?"

"The Covingtons await, my dear." She smiled blithely, neat and elegant in her slate-blue traveling gown and bonnet.

"You're really going because of Alfred," Charlotte declared, her eyes narrowing. "Because you believe you will impede the course of his intended courtship if you stay."

Katherine looked thunderstruck as she straightened her back. "My, how perceptive you've become in my absence."

"I cannot love him, Katherine, and I do not intend to let him court me, no matter whether you stay or not."

They walked to a sofa and tea table near the fire and sat down together, their hands still linked. "I do recall how firm you can be when you've made up your mind about something."

"You do, do you?"

"Have you forgotten the persistent young officer on the ship as we sailed back to England?"

Charlotte fought a smile at the recollection of her rebuff of a young captain who had waited every day for her out on the saloon deck, hoping that she might accept a simple invitation to tea. "I was rather impolite to the poor man," she conceded. "But I simply see no purpose in leading someone to hope when there is no hope a'tall."

"Dear girl." Katherine sighed heavily and reached out to touch Charlotte's pert chin. "Fate certainly has been less than kind to you in matters of the heart, I shall grant you. I only wish that there was something more I could do about that. I was only trying to help."

"There is nothing anyone can do, Katherine," she said, her voice lowering an octave. "Edward is with Anne, and that is where he must remain, but his heart will always be here with me," she said, pressing her hand lightly against her breast. "And as long as I know that, there can never be anyone else."

Katherine arched an eyebrow. "Your Edward is a far more fortunate man than he realizes."

"Edward knows what he had," Charlotte assured her. "He also knows what he sacrificed. We both do."

They hugged one last time.

"Must you really leave? It seems as if you've only just gotten here." Charlotte sighed as the driver helped Katherine into her packed and waiting carriage once everyone else had bid their goodbyes.

"Dear heart, our visits are never long enough."

"I shall miss you."

"Will you write?" Katherine asked hopefully.

"You know that I shall."

"Then it shall not seem so long until we see one another once again."

"It shall seem like an eternity to me," Charlotte countered. "I detest having my dearest friend at such a distance."

"You know I shall be coming back in the spring."

"Do you promise?"

"It is promised," Katherine assured her, then patted Charlotte's hand through the window of her elegant green brougham. "I know what you said, but in my absence, tell me you'll at least think about accepting Lord Linton, won't you? He may not be your Edward, child, but now that there is no hope he is a far sight better than your ending up alone like me."

With her question and her final declaration hanging as thick and heavy as a rain cloud between them, Katherine tapped her parasol on the roof of the carriage. It lurched and then pulled off down the drive before Charlotte could say anything further. Her well-meaning friend had done it quite intentionally.

She had wanted to give Charlotte something to think about.

In the weeks that followed Christmas, Edward kept busy assuring Anne that his father's pub needed the bulk of his attention now. But neither money nor the success of the already profitable Cock 'n' Feathers was really at issue. He and his family had been left more than comfortable after the death of his father, who had spent a lifetime being smart with his money.

The truth of the matter was that being with Anne now—facing her, carrying the painful secret that he did—was torture for Edward. Circumstance forced him to be a hypocrite. A liar. Most days he left the little slate-roof cottage early and then worked late, unconsciously forcing the wedge between them to deepen into something that could never be closed again. Distance was better, he thought. Better than the truth.

He had told himself that he expected nothing in return when he sent Charlotte the scarf and the letter, but in his heart now, as the days drudged onward with no reply, Edward realized that had been a lie. Alone now, he tortured himself by playing the scene over and over again his mind. The discovery. The unbelievable truth. The excruciating farewell.

Could he have acted other than he had? Could he have forced himself to follow his heart, abandoning Anne and his duty to two small children after all? He knew the answer even as he asked the question. Regardless of how he felt, Edward had willingly taken on that responsibility when he married again. For that he must pay the price. He could not leave. He could never leave, and there were only two things that made staying even bearable: Charlotte and Abigail.

Each night when he gazed down into his daughters' sweet faces to kiss them goodnight, he saw the reason he had remained, mirrored back at him. There had been no other choice than the one he had made.

There would never be.

"Tell me a story, Papa," little Charlotte pleaded one night as Edward sat on the edge of her bed, trying to coax her to close her eyes.

"Only a short one," he bargained sternly. "Then will you go to sleep?" When she nodded her head in agreement, he began. "Very well then. Let me see. . . . A long time ago, in a faraway land, there was a dashing, dark-haired prince, who fell in love with a beautiful princess. . . . She was a beautiful girl with long golden hair and eyes the color of new spring grass. That was what the prince used to tell her. When they got married, they lived together in a wondrous palace that the people could see for miles and miles, all in white marble and glittering jewels."

Her dark eyes lit brightly. "What was it called, Papa?"

"It was called the Taj Mahal," Edward said fondly.

"Where was that?"

He hesitated a moment, then smiled. "In a land far, far away, darling."

"What happened to them?" Charlotte asked sweetly.

"Well, one day, quite suddenly, the beautiful princess was lost to her prince. Someone very evil had stolen her away."

The child's face darkened. "Who stole her away, Papa?"

"A dreadful enemy called Fate took her away, darling," Edward answered, his voice full of remorse.

Charlotte turned her lower lip out slightly. "Was the prince very sad?"

"Yes, he was."

"And did he search for her?"

Edward averted his eyes, not quite certain what it was that was possessing him to tell her all of this. And yet he wanted as much as she to hear the rest of the tale, intent on giving it the ending he would always believe their love story had deserved.

"The prince searched high and low, but he could not find his beautiful princess for a very, very long time. And then one day, when he had lost all hope of every seeing her again, a kind old woman found her wandering lost and alone, and she brought her back to him. And the prince was so filled with joy and love that he laughed and laughed, until they both cried."

"And did they live happily ever after, Papa?"

"Of course they did." Edward smiled, wanting to believe as much as she did in fairy tales.

After his daughter was asleep, Edward once again lost the battle within himself. He had fought hard not to return to the attic and those few treasured possessions from the past. It had been days since he had gone up there. With the start of the new year, he had promised himself to try and put the past to rest. To leave his memories alone. For Anne's sake. For the children's sake. For his own. But tonight his need had taken over his senses. It had also made him careless.

Anne had not gone to bed, as was her custom, and he had not heard the creaking floorboards as she came alone up the attic steps behind him. She had received an anonymous letter that morning after Edward had gone to work. It had been written on curiously expensive paper, in a heavy masculine hand, one she did not recognize. "Do not be deceived," it had bidden her. "Do not ignore the truth that lies in your very own house. Not all of the past is really in the past. . . ."

She stood in the doorway now, her shadow large and looming before Edward on the wall. The letter was tucked safely away. The memory of the strange warning was not.

"What are you doing up here so late?" Anne asked, and his heart skipped a beat. He furtively closed the lid of the camphorwood chest and turned around.

"I was just looking for something I thought might be up here, that's all," he lied, coming to his feet in front of the chest and trying not to look like a child who had been caught.

"Did you find what you were looking for?" she asked, straining to see, past the light and shadows, what it was he was so obviously hiding.

"No . . . it wasn't here after all," he said, coming across the attic to where she still stood in the doorway.

"Shall we go to bed then?" Anne asked hopefully, the tone in her voice suggesting more than sleep.

Edward closed the attic door behind them once they were out in the corridor, trying not to let the distaste show on his face. They walked down the narrow flight of stairs, which came to an end in front of their bedroom door. Edward kissed her cheek.

"You go ahead and brush your hair," he said kindly. "I want to get a glass of milk. I won't be a moment."

He started down the back stairs, not giving Anne an opportunity to object. Then he waited silently at the bottom until he finally heard their bedroom door squeal to open and then close again. Edward stood there a moment more, breathing in a sigh of relief. That had been close. Too close. He had been careless with his mementoes, and it must not happen again. He knew what it would do to Anne to discover the truth. What it would do to them all.

Edward lit a lamp on the kitchen table and slowly opened the door to the little room she had used in his house as 'Katherine Blackstone.' He stood there silently for five minutes; perhaps it was ten. He saw her in the bed, waiting for him as she had done that final night when they had only held one another, both of them knowing what the dawn would bring.

The air in the long-sealed room was cool now and musty. All trace of Charlotte was gone. He had not allowed the door to remain open since the morning she had left him. He could not bear it. Edward fought the urge to come in here, but somehow there was always the belief, the tiny spark of hope, that like that single miraculous night, he might one day open the door and see her there looking up at him.

When the reality of how unfair those thoughts were to Anne and to himself streaked harshly across his mind, Edward turned away reluctantly and extinguished the candle. Then he went back upstairs. His legs felt like two huge weights, holding him back. His heart felt twisted. It was still so badly broken.

He knew that he should make love to his wife. She had been hoping for some time that they might, but Edward could never quite make himself believe he felt the things he needed to feel to make it happen. Now that he knew Charlotte—his true wife—was alive, there was a kind of betrayal in the notion of that kind of intimacy with someone else. It was a lie that he was living; one they were all living. But it was better than the truth, he told himself as he set one weighted foot in front of the other. Anne needed him. His daughters needed him.

"I'm sorry," he whispered in the darkness as he sank into

bed beside her and softly kissed her cheek. "I don't honestly know what has possessed me lately. I only know that you don't deserve this."

He pulled back a moment and looked at her. She smelled of dish soap and country cotton. Edward ran a hand along her broad forehead and brushed back the hair that had come free from her nightcap. How could two women be so different? he wondered as he studied the angles and ridges of Anne's full face.

"You're a good mother and a good wife," he whispered, safe in the knowledge that she was already asleep. "You have not deserved any of what fate has done to all of us."

He watched her for another moment, the gentle rise and fall of her chest beneath the blankets, her face free of the concern he so often saw there these days, and in that moment he felt a little less of the guilt.

I do love you, Anne. Not in the way I know that you desire, he thought as his mind bent and swooped toward slumber. *But it is enough to keep me by your side. And I know in my heart this is how it must be.*

Anne waited motionless until she knew by the rhythm of his breathing that Edward was asleep. Then she opened her eyes and looked at him in the silvery moonlight through the window. The most handsome man she had ever seen. It was still worth the price she had paid to have him—even knowing that he did not love her as she wished to be loved.

She touched a hand to his smooth cheek and then fell asleep, wondering what secrets she would find tucked away in that attic when she went looking there tomorrow.

IT WAS IMPOSSIBLE TO COME TO BRIARWOOD WITHOUT SEEING Charlotte. Three months after Christmas, it was one of the few certainties Alfred Linton could depend upon until the day she would finally agree to become his wife.

To that end, he cleverly and persistently organized hunting parties. Initiated card games with Hugh Edward. Croquet. Whatever the pretext, he constantly found ways to keep himself firmly routed in her life.

"Easy with her. She's about ready to have that calf as it is." Charlotte directed with a pointed finger as four shabby-looking country farmers led a brown and white Jersey milking cow onto the sloping emerald lawn. Two pink, snorting pigs and a gaggle of honking geese followed. Alfred stepped down from the sleek black stallion he had named Sophocles and then handed the reins to a Briarwood servant.

She was really going through with it, turning a charming country manor like Briarwood into a working-class farm. There was no stopping her when she believed enough in something. He fought a smile. Charlotte Lawrence was exasperating; but she was also a truly amazing woman. Alfred did not always agree with her. In matters of business he rarely did. But in his life he had never known a woman so guided by purpose as Charlotte. It was one of her many equally infuriating and entirely seductive qualities that had so thoroughly captivated him. He laughed out loud as the notion drifted like a spring breeze across his mind.

Charlotte turned suddenly, hearing him behind her. "Oh, Alfred, is she not wonderful?"

He removed his riding gloves a finger at a time, fighting a wry smile. "*Wonderful* isn't the word," he replied coolly.

Charlotte pressed her hands against her hips with a huffing sound. "Oh, now you're mocking me."

Alfred covered his lips with a single reed-long finger and rocked back onto his heels. "I would never mock you, my dearest," he said genuinely. "I adore you."

"You think my animals are common," she accused.

"I think your animals are very fortunate indeed. That is, until you have them killed for supper."

A goose sidled up beside Charlotte, honking loudly, and she bent down to stroke its smooth white neck. "Oh, I am not going to kill them, Alfred."

"No?"

"Of course not." She laughed her sweet, musical laugh. "I am going to keep the hens for their eggs and the cows for their milk."

"And the pigs?" He grinned.

Charlotte held out her arms expansively. "They are for the ambiance!"

"Ambiance?" Alfred chuckled.

"Certainly. Every farm needs pigs!"

And suddenly, through his amusement, Alfred Linton remembered the reason she was so bent on this transformation of Briarwood. Edward. Still and always Edward. He fought an overwhelming urge to turn away from her, his eyes blazing with a sudden jealous fury. All of the progress he had made would have been dashed in this instant—had it not been for his brilliant plan. Had it not been for that, he knew there would be no hope for him with Charlotte.

It was no more than three short months ago that she had lain against him, her arms pulling him as close as the clothing they had been wearing would allow, kissing him with the most rapturous sincerity that he was certain he had nearly won her.

She was the most nearly perfect creature he had ever had

the fortune of knowing, and her only real fault was this persistent preoccupation with a man she could never have again. And so he had been moved to take steps so that Charlotte would never have him in her life again. A simple letter. That was all it had taken. A warning to someone else whose possessiveness and insecurity was more powerful in this delicate situation than his own. Anne Langston was the only other person who could help him keep the lovers apart.

Alfred had been a good student. He had listened to Charlotte's stories for months. He knew every detail of the situation. The people involved. Every nuance. He even knew about the camphorwood chest Edward Langston kept full of mementoes in his attic. Charlotte's grief and his own expert sympathy had made her free with specifics.

So now he had needed only to hint at the truth in a letter and then wait for the rest of the pieces to fall into place. The plan was brilliant in its simplicity. He would finally gain that which he desired most in the world. After what would undoubtedly be a bitter confrontation, Langston's wife would recapture her husband, and Lord Linton's noble hands would, as always, remain sparkling clean. Clever man, he thought proudly, lifting his aristocratic nose. So very clever indeed.

"Gray Ashton is having a party tomorrow night, and I would like you to come with me, Charlotte," he said firmly, coolly. It was the reason he had come to Briarwood today. But the joy of such a perfect opportunity for them to be seen together paled a little with Edward Langston's farm animals in their midst. It made him even more impatient than ever for the little country wife to take a solitary trip to her attic.

Charlotte looked up as though she had not heard him correctly. Her pastel lips were parted slightly and shining from where she had just licked them. "Oh, Alfred, I don't think so. But thank you."

He was not quite certain that her tone was not a condescending one, and his silvery brows sharpened into an unexpected frown. "Good God, woman. It is only a party!" he blustered. "I require a dinner companion. You require an evening out of this prison of yours."

"And I thank you for thinking of me, truly I do," she calmly countered. "But I really cannot accept."

The patient expression on her face made him feel like a petulant child, and he detested that almost as much as her rejection. "You're not even going to give yourself a chance to love me, are you?" he said belligerently as one of the pigs sniffed his trousers.

"Really, Alfred," she said, her voice lowering, "have we not been through this already?"

"Then perhaps you could tell me why, precisely, you allowed me to kiss you so scandalously as you did on Christmas Eve!"

Everything stopped. The animal noises. The rush of the wind. The men who had brought the animals. Everything quieted with the sound of Alfred's very inappropriate question.

In the silence, he watched a red fire stain Charlotte's rosy cheeks, and he knew he should not have said it. He had betrayed her in so grand an admission before servants and hirelings. That much was written all over her face. But it was too late for apologies, even if his pride would have allowed it.

Two of the fieldhands who had brought the animals had begun to whisper and Charlotte caught a fragment of the question one asked the other. "Did he say, a scandalous kiss?"

Thank the dear Lord, she said in silent prayer, that Alfred had chosen not to vent his ire in the presence of anyone of great import, or both their reputations would have been ruined. She waited a moment. It was more than she would have given to anyone else, hoping that he meant to apologize for his impudence. But he simply stood there, anger darkening his rugged face, as if she was the one to have breached a trust.

"No matter how rude, I shall take the silence as your disinterest in replying," he said stiffly. "I am sorry to have troubled you with my concern for your welfare yet again."

With that, Lord Linton stomped off back across the lawn to reclaim his horse. Charlotte, her servants, and the fieldhands all stood silent, in utter amazement at what had just occurred.

It was a side of him she had never seen before.

A side that frightened her.

"I know what Katherine would tell me to do," Charlotte muttered to herself later that evening as her maid stood behind her, brushing out her luxuriant brown hair with a silver-handled brush. "She would tell me to get out. To mingle. 'It will put the roses back in your cheeks!' she would say." Charlotte could almost hear her voice.

It would be lovely to get out. To dance. To laugh again. There was no denying that. But was it not giving Alfred false hope of something more between them? If there had been any doubt in her mind, he had certainly made the depth of his feelings clear to her earlier in the day. He had also revealed the great force of his temper to her for the first time.

But in fairness, Charlotte thought, he had a right to be angry. Although she may have continued to deny his proposals, she had accepted both his companionship and his assistance. She had even allowed him to kiss her that once.

Charlotte hated that she felt so indecisive where Alfred was concerned. From an early age she had known her own mind and she had never hesitated to act upon it. She had learned to speak fluent Hindustani when it was most unpopular for a European child to do so. She had gone against her father and Brigadier Graves to keep Edward from being transferred to Calcutta. She had also married him in the face of great opposition. Now things seemed so fragmented in her mind. Edward. Alfred. Desire. Betrayal. Heartbreak. None of the decisions or the feelings were as clearly cut as they once had been.

Her maid folded back the crisp bed linens and waited dutifully for Charlotte to climb into bed. "Thank you, Theresa," she said, taking the lamp from her dressing table and biding her goodnight.

Charlotte waited for the door to be closed before she surrendered to the downy soft bed that was all posters and polished mahogany. She was tired tonight, but not so her mind. The images sifted through her consciousness long after she had closed her eyes.

She wondered about Anne; if Edward ever took her dancing. She chased such thoughts away when the imaginary picture grew too vivid. And then quite suddenly the pain turned sharply, distinctly, toward anger. Her heart squeezed, thinking of them together.

It was the first time she had felt anger erupt from beneath the stoic exterior she fought so hard to maintain; the veneer that said Edward was where he belonged. Tonight it bothered her, even reviled her that they were together and she was here—alone, warmed by downy soft blankets and not by the man who loved her. The emptiness. The longing. All of it merged suddenly and fiercely into that same great ache.

Her overwhelming thought was of stopping it.

Charlotte pulled the covers up to her chin and closed her eyes again. The sheets around her face were icy, and when she rolled onto her side her skin quickly turned to gooseflesh. It would be so wonderful to feel a man lying beside her again. Bare flesh against her own. Warming her. Helping her to forget. Not anyone, particularly. Just someone who could make her feel the things she had felt so long ago. Her helplessness at what had become of her life made her more susceptible now to Alfred's protestations than her loneliness did.

His face in the firelight that last dreadful Christmas Eve, bright with desire, had imprinted itself like a stamp on her mind. She could still feel his lips pressed against hers, his tongue hot and seeking in her mouth.

Charlotte squeezed her eyes, remembering how at that very moment her heart had felt as if it had been shattered. Even as he was kissing her, it was Edward's lips she had imagined. Edward's body she had longed to feel pressed against her own. The memories and the anger prickled through her mind, threatening to take control. *You're never going to have him again!* she scolded herself, buried deep beneath her covers. *So you may as well stop trying to resurrect him!*

321

After a while the anger faded. Like a gently flowing stream, her thoughts wandered away from Edward back to Alfred. He really was a handsome and charming suitor. Trying to let him into a tiny corner of her heart might actually help take away the relentless longing for Edward. The pain. The indecision about the rest of her life.

Everyone in London already assumed they were lovers. There seemed little sense in arguing the issue when the man she loved had those sorts of marital obligations to someone else anyway. Why should she waste away fallow when there was no chance of him ever returning? There were balls to attend. Theatre. The opera. It was her heart's defense. She knew that much. But it still did not change the facts. Edward was gone. Gone! And he was never coming back.

"The Earl of Bentham really would be a splendid catch if not for some of those questionable rumors. . . .

Lady Bennington's words streaked harshly through the pleasing images that Charlotte had conjured. It was preposterous, she thought angrily. Alfred was a perfect gentleman. He had done so much for all of them this past difficult year. He had helped her with her finances. He had been a companion and confidant. He had even seen her precious Jawahar into one of England's finest schools. Given him a future. Alfred's angry outburst earlier that afternoon had been an aberration. She quickly pushed the unseemly memory from her mind along with the rumors, refusing to examine it further. A moment later, Charlotte bolted upright in the pitch-dark bedchamber.

"Theresa!" she called out to the maid whose small servant's room was beside her own. "Theresa!"

Her small bare feet slapped the wood floor as she came back down the corridor and returned to Charlotte's bedchamber. Her own long dark hair was half brushed and she was already wearing a nightgown.

"Yes, ma'am." She nodded, surprised and out of breath.

"Bring me a pen and paper!"

"Now, ma'am?"

"Yes, now, Theresa!"

Her maid went to the desk, her white cotton nightgown

whispering across the floor. She brought back a silver tray with pen and ink and several sheets of fresh paper. Hastily, Charlotte scribbled a note and then folded it over.

"Have Bickers take this to Lord Linton at once," she instructed, her pale face bright with color.

"But ma'am, 'tis very late."

"It is all right, Theresa. Lord Linton shall not be asleep," she assured her maid, knowing that Alfred's own anger and frustration over the scene on the lawn that afternoon would have kept him awake drinking brandy well into the night. Theresa, who had witnessed Lord Linton's tirade and her mistress's embarrassment over it, glanced up at her quizzically one last time, fearing what this communiqué might mean. Then, dutifully, she left the room with it.

Charlotte blew out the lamp again and pressed her head back against the soft, downy pillows. Her heart was racing. But she refused to believe it had been a mistake. No, she convinced herself.

It was self-preservation.

Across the undulating and expansive lawns at Linton House, Alfred sat beside a blazing fire, a brandy in one hand, as he read the words Charlotte had written:

I was wrong to so flatly refuse such a kind gesture of friendship this afternoon. If you have not already chosen another partner, I should be honored to join you tomorrow at Lord Ashton's dinner party.

Charlotte

Alfred pressed the page to his lips and closed his eyes. Finally. Yes, finally she was beginning to come around. He still regretted having embarrassed her as he had that afternoon, but if anger was what it took to make her see that they belonged together, then he was not entirely sorry he had done it.

He dropped the letter into his lap and then raked a hand through his waves of silvery hair. He was trying to imagine Charlotte's body, bare and unencumbered by crinolines, corsets, and the layers of fashionable silk. Her breasts were perfection. That much he knew and could recall, even beneath the fabric of her stylish gowns.

He especially liked the blue moiré with the whisper of white lace that breathed a bit of innocence onto the sensual rise of her bosom. He could feel his body stir and the slow burn begin again as he imagined peeling the smooth fabric carefully away from her warm, moist body, she lying sprawled on his ancestral bed, ready and willing to conceive his heir.

The lack of a child to carry on his name and to care for Linton House had not bothered Alfred particularly until the day that Charlotte Lawrence had returned to Kent. He had heard in those first early days after her return that she had been mysteriously widowed in India. The fact that she had reclaimed her maiden name, however, had given him the first bit of hope that she was not completely lost to the past.

The twinge of regret about children began when he had allowed himself to recall Charlotte as a little girl, before the Lawrences had left for India. She had been an exquisite child, a sweet, happy angel, and he knew that together they would produce magnificent offspring.

Alfred's blood simmered now, red rivers of unfettered desire, and his body grew rigid with need at the image of them coupled together like that. He had never been with anyone so sweet and yet wanton at the same time, and his lust for her was open and raw when he thought about it.

The prostitutes he sought out when he was in London, the ones who most closely resembled her, let him call them Charlotte. He plunged into their willing bodies with a thundering ferocity that anticipation of her always kindled and then unleashed like a wildfire inside of him. He always paid extra to call them by another name. But it was not the same thing. Rarely was it even close.

Alfred touched the writing on her letter. The ink was barely dry. Perhaps soon there would be no more need for such a poor imitation. Alfred Linton was blissfully close to the real thing.

He was wet with sweat when he came to his feet and found

the bell pull in the shadowy darkness of his drafty mahogany library. A few moments later, his butler Cravens, an old stoop-shouldered man with snow-colored hair, shuffled slowly into the room.

"You rang, sir?"

"Yes, Cravens," he replied, his voice ravaged and low. "Inform Miss Mills that I wish to see her privately."

"Miss Mills has retired, sir, along with the rest of the staff."

"Well then wake her! I wish to discuss her wages, and I haven't had a moment before now to do it."

"But sir—"

"Wake her, Cravens!"

"Very well, sir." He nodded, shrugging his bony shoulders as he shuffled back out into the corridor.

Alfred poured himself another brandy and drank it in one swallow, hoping to push back his misgivings. He had not summoned the upstairs maid to discuss her wages. He had no intention of discussing anything tonight.

Jenny Mills was a willing and foolish young girl from the wrong side of London who, thanks to his finely honed powers of persuasion, considered it an honor and a duty to service the master of Linton House when and how he desired it. He might play the kind, older gentleman for Charlotte, but with Jenny he need not bother with such pretenses.

Still, Alfred was not entirely without conscience on the matter. Each time he had called for her this past year in the forgiving dark of night, he had paid for his weakness with a generous bonus, which she had been able to send home to her family. He tried to push away the image of himself as a lecherous old roué as she smiled now and knelt before him in her heavy white nightgown, beginning to unfasten his trousers.

"So already you know what I desire, hmm?"

She looked up at him, wide-eyed and eager. The copper-colored spirals of loose, frizzy hair softened a full face and long, flat nose. "I recall sir," she whispered, and the words came in a thick, working-class accent.

"Splendid." Alfred muttered an upper-class growl—thinking of Charlotte.

Charlotte primped nearly the entire afternoon for the Ashtons' dinner party. She gave herself over completely to the pampered luxury of it, something she had not allowed herself to do since her return to Briarwood. Nails. Hair. She had even submitted to a massage for her feet.

In the torturously long months between then and now, Charlotte had concentrated all of her energy on outward things, declining all social engagements. There was the renovation of the music room, new furniture for three of the guest rooms, and of course, the creation of the farm to which she must personally attend. In those endeavors she had consciously neglected herself. It was easier that way. Less need to confront what was missing inside her heart. What always would be.

Theresa came out of the wardrobe closet, holding a new beaded ivory gown with delicately embroidered sleeves. Charlotte had ordered it shortly after her return to England, but then she could never quite gather an interest in wearing it. "Ooh, isn't it lovely," she cooed now, as if she were looking at it for the first time.

"Will you wear it with your pearl necklace, ma'am?"

"No, Theresa. I believe I shall wear the ruby earrings that the Earl of Bentham gave me for Christmas."

"They shall look lovely with this dress," her maid concurred, and Charlotte actually felt a twinge of excitement. She had not danced since that fateful evening at the Delhi Club where she had seen her father and Rani for the very last time. It would be eleven years tomorrow.

A bit of her exuberance faded into her dark memories of that afternoon, the ones filled with people she would never see again. But that night at the Ashtons', Charlotte Lawrence was a vision. Everyone said so. After supper, Lord Linton stood proudly among the men, his chest bowed out like a crowing rooster, as he watched her from across the room.

"Lovely girl, your Miss Lawrence," observed Lord

Abercrombie, a somber-faced walrus of a man standing beside him.

"Isn't she, though," Alfred agreed, nodding to an earl who was twenty years his senior, with a big pot belly and long white mustache.

"Well then, tell us, Linton ol' boy. Do you mean to marry her or not?" asked Gray Ashton, the evening's host. "You've been hinting about it for months."

Alfred fought a wayward smile. "Some things, gentlemen, simply cannot be rushed. Miss Lawrence is not only beautiful, but she is quite thoroughly independent. I cannot simply go ordering her about, hoping she will bow to my will."

"Doubtless a bow to something of yours is precisely what you are hoping for," drawled Abercrombie. The improper gibe sent the others into a mirthful explosion of laughter.

"Now see here, Abercrombie," Alfred boomed indignantly, his spine stiffening. "I shall not have you making light of this whole affair simply because it has not come off precisely as you and the others deem reasonable. I discovered long ago that Charlotte Lawrence is a prize well worth waiting for!"

"Waiting is a state to which you shall doubtless grow accustomed, by the look of such a beauty," Gray Ashton chuckled petulantly. "She has tossed little more than a solitary glance your way all evening."

"You do know what they say about making a beautiful woman your wife!" Abercrombie pressed gaily.

"You shall have trouble the rest of your life!" chimed Ashton.

Charlotte had not heard their good-natured taunting at first. She had been too taken up with Anne Ashton's recipe for the perfect punch, the one with which the guests had been plied all evening. Some, like Lord Abercrombie, had surely had more than their share. But she had heard quite clearly their last accusations, and she had seen its subsequent effect on Alfred.

"Of course, it is spiked, you know!" Anne Ashton confided, a firm hand cupped around her mouth. The woman with wide-set dark eyes and a little prune mouth was entirely oblivious to the storm cloud that was brewing in her very own salon. Charlotte, however, was not. "A bit of gin to make things interesting, I always say!"

"If you will excuse me." Charlotte smiled, nodding politely. "I believe I see Alfred waving me over."

As she came up behind him, all the guffaws quickly ceased. "If you insist upon making light of the relationship between Miss Lawrence and myself," Alfred said politely, but with cold, almost ruthless conviction, "I shall have no choice but to challenge you to a duel."

Audible gasps were heard thundering through the silence. "Certainly you know dueling is quite illegal, Linton ol' boy," Gray Ashton warned nervously.

And yet he meant to do it. Charlotte was absolutely certain. They had pushed him too far with their drunken jests. She knew the steel-eyed look of determination. It was the same one he had shot at her the afternoon before, when his pride had been as assaulted as he believed her honor was now.

It was a side of Alfred she had not seen before yesterday, and it caused her, for a brief moment, to wonder if what people so often whispered about him might actually be true. But the thought was quickly replaced by the realization that she must stop this before it got any further out of hand. After all, Alfred had not technically challenged him. At least not yet.

"Excuse me, gentlemen," she said, batting her long, luxurious lashes as expertly as any coquette and cleverly ignoring the air of combat between the two men. "But I have a rather serious bone to pick with my escort, and I feel pressed to do it presently."

Everyone looked at Alfred, whose face was stained crimson at the notion that Charlotte was about to make an even bigger jest of their friendship than Lord Abercrombie had attempted to do.

"Not now, my dear," he gritted. "There is a score here to be settled."

Charlotte wisely ignored his rebuff, smiling and looking as flirtatious as her conscience would allow. "Alfred, you are really quite wicked. You're absolutely neglecting me way over here in favor of your gentlemen friends," she said sweetly, linking her arm through his. "And I simply won't have it another moment. Dance with me," she coaxed, tugging playfully at his hand.

Abercrombie's mouth fell open like a loose hinge at the sight of the mysterious and beautiful young woman whose intentions he had quite clearly misjudged.

"Not until Lord Abercrombie sees fit to apologize," Alfred said stubbornly.

"I do indeed!" the other man quickly countered, sobered by the dangerous rumors he too had heard about the Earl of Bentham. He was also quite unwilling to discover personally whether or not they were true.

A proper apology obtained, Alfred turned sharply with a little huff and stalked off to the dance floor, with Charlotte's arm wound tightly in his. "You didn't have to do that, you know," he said once they were safely sheltered by the other dancers.

"What do you mean?" she asked vacuously.

His gray eyes narrowed. "Do not make it worse than it already is by keeping up the coquettish pretense!"

"Oh that," she said, lowering her luminous green eyes, though not managing to hide her smile from him. It seemed to irritate him all the more.

"I warn you, Charlotte, do not make light of this."

"I wasn't, truly," she bubbled, thinking he looked a little silly trying to be so cross.

"They were inferring dreadful things about us. Only your quick and rather clever improvisation saved Abercrombie from certain death."

"Oh now, Alfred. Let's not spoil a perfectly good evening with that sort of nonsense, shall we?" she coaxed blithely, then smiled up at him until she could see his defenses begin to melt away. His expression softened, as it always did when she looked at him. A moment later his own smile returned.

"I suppose you deserve my thanks," he said penitently.

"I do indeed," Charlotte agreed as they whirled through the waltz.

"Still, I shall wager your precious Edward never defended your honor so boldly as I did this evening."

She was not certain if he was trying to wound her or to bolster his own confidence with such a statement, and there was a sudden urge to confess the truth of Edward's bravery. But Charlotte kept silent. At the moment, Alfred was still too volatile for that sort of important correction.

She found his reaction flattering and a bit confusing, but certainly very intriguing. It was actually quite seductive to be fought for, to be desired so openly once again. "What matters is that you were very noble indeed," she skirted cleverly. "And for that it is I who must thank you."

He calmed with the sound of her praise. His eyes widened and his rigid jaw slackened. A moment later he was smiling again. "So tell me, my dearest. Between the two of us, just what is it, precisely, the ol' boy has that I haven't got?"

Charlotte breathed a faint sigh. "Only history, my dear Alfred," she replied, finding the strength to lie again.

Later that night, as his carriage sat before a candlelit Briarwood, cloaked in a thick blanket of fog, Alfred kissed her lingeringly. He had not tried again to press his advantage since Christmas Eve, and he was surprised now when she did not pull away nor urge him to stop. He trailed a single fingertip across her smooth, milk-white throat and felt her lean closer to him. As his warm lips covered hers, Alfred shivered with desire. She was completely convincing. Charlotte had given him no idea at all how hard she was trying to make herself want him.

"My God, you taste like honey," he muttered into Charlotte's lustrous pale brown hair, trying to keep the triumph of finally winning her from his voice.

She moved away from him only slightly as the carriage lurched with the restless pull of the horses. "You have been very kind to me since I came back here, and certainly very patient."

"It has not always been easy."

She looked up at him in the moonlight with smoldering green eyes, her sensual lips parted slightly. "I know that. For a long time I did not want your kindness. I was too badly hurt," she softly confessed. "But there has always been this attraction between us."

"Yes," he averred.

"At first when I returned here to Briarwood, I believed it was because you reminded me of my father." Alfred felt a thud of disappointment at her admission, and it showed on his slim, chiseled face. "But I have not believed that for a very long time now."

"No?"

She touched his face softly, seductively, with her fingertip. "No." It was what he wanted to hear. It was also what she must say if she was ever going to rescue herself from the past.

"So then you will let me escort you publicly again?"

"If it is what you still desire."

"Dear heart." He took her hand. "I think you know quite well that it is only a part of what I desire."

Charlotte tried to smile, but she knew it looked more like a grimace. "Let us just take it a step at a time, shall we?"

"People are bound to talk," he gently warned, secretly not caring a stitch what people said or thought.

"No more than they already do."

"Yes. The society in London believes we are already lovers."

"Then the fact that we spend a good deal of our time together should not surprise them." She smiled, her face full of radiant confidence as she gazed up into his hungry gray eyes. "I must face the fact that Edward has gotten on with his life and, as Katherine says, I must get on with mine. Yes, dear Alfred . . . it is time I begin getting out, and I can think of no one with whom I would rather be seen."

He took both of her hands and brought them to his lips. They were the words he had waited to hear for over a year. Granted, it was a small victory. But he was winning. Now Charlotte really would be his. It was only a matter of time.

"But you are still refusing my proposal of marriage?" he asked cautiously.

"I shall give you what I can of myself and I shall hope that shall be enough."

Alfred pressed his lips against hers once again, but this time it was a violently sensual kiss. He locked his hands around her waist and pulled her close against his rigid erection with such force that she could not have pulled away. "How I do desire you, Charlotte Lawrence," he murmured hungrily; then, loosening his hold on her, he tried to catch his breath. "I'm sorry I was so harsh with Abercrombie this evening, but if it has done anything at all to influence you, then I would do it all again."

He made his confession with a slick smile, knowing he would have done far more than that to win her. But he was too arrogant to see that her decision had nothing whatsoever to do with him.

The sun began to rise, luminous pink over the lush grove of oak trees along the drive, long after Alfred had bid her goodnight. In the gray early light inside the house, Charlotte finally drew herself from her bed and threw open her window. She rubbed her bare arms and listened to the birds singing sweetly from the rooftops as a lacy morning mist veiled the ground below her.

Theresa had not yet risen to light a fire, and her room was chilly. It was several moments more before she noticed the glistening rope of pearls. They were lying on a swatch of red velvet on a table beside her bed.

Charlotte moved toward them and took them up into her trembling hand. They too were cold. Cold and smooth and very elegant. Alfred must have had them with him, and had Bickers leave them while she was preparing for bed. She looked down at them again and remembered him kissing her. They were a string of perfect pearls. They had cost a small fortune. She should have been grateful. She knew he had meant to please her. Just the same, they made her feel exactly like a whore. She grimaced at the thought, the memory of his touch, and quickly hid them in a drawer.

After putting on a heavy velvet robe, Charlotte went in bare feet down the hall, not yet touched by morning light, and into her son's room on the other side of the house. Hugh Edward was still asleep. She thought how his small, pale face looked exactly like an angel's. *Such sweet purity*. She sighed, wanting to capture some little bit of her own, and yet still feeling so completely dead inside.

Lingering beside the bed, she gazed down at her son. His soft lips slightly parted. His eyelids were gently fluttering. So peaceful. So precious. She shook her head to keep herself from crying. There was no benefit in tears now. What was done was done. She had opened the door to Alfred. It was self-preservation, she reminded herself, trying to push away the sick feeling inside her.

Suddenly Hugh Edward awoke. His crystal blue eyes gazed up at her, full of concern. "What is it, Mama?" he asked quietly.

Charlotte pulled the covers up over his shoulders and smiled down at this precious child of her heart. "Nothing, darling," she whispered. "I just wanted to look in on you. Is that all right?"

Hugh Edward brushed the sleep from his eyes with a curled hand and then yawned as she lay down beside him. "Are you going to marry Lord Linton?" he asked, and the sincerity of his question surprised her. Especially after last night.

"Why would you ask such a thing?"

He nestled against his mother, comforted by her nearness and by the way she stroked his hair—gently, rhythmically. "I know that he loves you."

"How would you feel if he began to play a bigger part in our lives, darling?" she asked, reminded of her commitment to finally try to put the past behind her.

Hugh Edward frowned, considering the question in a long, tentative silence. "He's a nice enough fellow. He was terribly good to Jawahar. . . . But then what would you do one day when my father came back for us?"

Charlotte felt something catch in her throat. No matter the lengths to which she went in order to force Edward into the past, somehow he always came to the forefront again. God! Her heart was being strangled so that she could scarcely breathe. Charlotte stroked her son's temple, wondering how she might answer a question for which, after last night's concession, she was not prepared.

Her reply, when it finally came, was calm and measured. "Your father is not ever going to come for us, darling. He cannot."

"Yes he is," the boy insisted. He bolted upright in his bed and turned back to look at her, lying there on the pillow beside him.

"No, Hugh Edward," she said softly, as sincerely as she could manage. "I'm sorry, but that is simply not going to happen."

"Then why has he sent me these?" he charged, pulling out a collection of polished stones he had kept beneath his pillow.

Charlotte gasped, taking them up in her cold and trembling hand. "W-where did you get these?"

"I told you, from Papa."

She had not remembered that Edward had them. Like so many other things, she had blocked the memory because it was simply too painful. But she remembered now, as vividly as if they were still in Agra together. The stones had come from Jawahar. A token of thanks for rescuing him. But Edward had prized them more as a reminder of their very special honeymoon.

"I knew that you would be angry if you discovered that he had written to me, so I didn't tell you."

"I—I am not angry, Hugh Edward," she said, fighting to keep the wounded tone from her voice and knowing that her son was right. "I only wish that you had felt free enough to confide in me about it. That's all."

He tipped his head to the side and a dark curl fell onto his smooth, pale forehead. "Are you certain?"

"Of course, darling. After all, he is your father."

"But I have not forgotten how upset you were when he wrote to you at Christmas. . . . When he sent you that scarf."

The memory stabbed at her like the blade of a dull knife. She wanted to run. To hide. From the memories. From the future. Oh, those stones! The Taj Mahal. Huge. White. Majestic. Symbol of such grand and enduring love. Their love. Where so many hopes had begun. She could see it all in her mind even when she closed her eyes.

"What did he say in his letter?" Charlotte asked tentatively, not certain she could bear to hear the reply.

"He said these stones were the last thing of value that he had in the world," Hugh Edward divulged, studying his mother carefully. "He wanted me to know how precious they were to him. That you both had once dreamed of taking me back to see the place where they had come from. That he dreams of it still."

Charlotte sat up beside her son, feeling suddenly sick. Sicker than she had ever felt in her life. It was all too much. Alfred. Edward. The stones. The relentless memories.

"I don't understand, darling. Whatever gave you the idea that your father was going to come back to us?"

"I just know," he said simply, emphatically.

"But how can you be so certain?"

"How can you be so certain that he won't?"

"As I have always told you, Hugh Edward," she said, measuring her response, "your father is a very noble, a very wonderful, man, and I am glad that you feel better about him than you once did. But you must accept, as I finally have, that he has another life now. He is married to another."

"But not in his heart. . . . Isn't that what you told me?"

The pain was so sharp that Charlotte flinched. How could she expect him to understand this? He was a child. An innocent. His heart had not been broken. His dreams had never been washed away by an overwhelming tide of circumstance.

"I simply don't want you to be disappointed, darling," she said, chucking his chin with her finger.

"Papa is coming for us one day. You'll see," he insisted, and his youthful sincerity almost made her believe that it might actually one day come true.

Charlotte smiled and brought her son to her chest. "Perhaps there really is no harm in wishing."

"Then you're not going to marry Lord Linton?"

"No, darling, I'm not going to marry anyone."

"I'm so glad," he said with a relieved smile as she held him. "Because that really would be a dreadful mess!"

❧27

WHILE CHARLOTTE WAS SEEKING COMFORT FROM HER SON, Anne Langston stood at the dark base of the attic stairs. An amalgam of curiosity and fear shot through her at the prospect of what she might find if she gathered the courage to trespass farther.

From the time she had moved into the cottage once owned by Edward's parents, the attic had been her husband's domain. He had been insistent about that. His things from India were kept there, things he had told her he did not care to remember or to see again. And she had always believed him. Because she wanted to. Because she loved him so desperately.

Anne understood about the atrocities that had occurred in Delhi. Everyone had read about them in excruciating detail. She had surmised by his inability to speak about India that he had witnessed the deaths of many of his friends. But there was something more in that attic, something dark, ominous, and very powerful driving a wedge between them. "Do not be deceived," the letter had said. "Do not ignore the truth that lies in your very own house. Not all of the past is really in the past. . . ." If the truth was in this attic, thought Anne, she must somehow gather the courage to discover what it was.

At the top of the staircase, she twisted the doorknob slowly, and it let out a single, long squeal. Anne looked back around instinctively, knowing that her children were safe in their beds and Edward would be at the pub for several more hours.

The oil lamp shook as she held it out before her, searching for anything that appeared to hold some of the answers she sought. Answers the mysterious letter said she would find. The attic was musty and dark. Apprehension and fear paraded through her mind when she saw the sealed green trunk across the attic. It must be inside there, she thought. The answer—her opponent.

Anne Langston believed with all her heart that if she at least knew what sort of opposition was slowly tearing her marriage apart, then she might well have a fighting chance of saving it. She consoled herself with that thought as she lifted the heavy lid. She was surprised to find remarkably little inside. There was an old white summer military uniform starting to yellow, a few tarnished medals, an old pistol, and a small camphorwood chest. The chest was plain, with tarnished brass hinges and a small brass nob.

She drew in a steadying breath and, completely determined, brought it out into the lamplight. Anne felt her heart pounding like a drum as a dark fear began to quake through her. *It is like Pandora's box,* she thought as she held it in her lap. *If you choose to open this . . . you must forever face what is inside. You will never be able to close it again.* But Anne had come too far to turn back now, no matter what the risk.

She lifted the lid and looked down at a single grainy photograph. It was quite perplexing. Until she saw the shaded eyeglasses neatly placed beside it. Anne Langston had seen that sort of spectacles only once in her life. They had belonged to Katherine Blackstone.

She fought against the thick mire of confusion quickly clouding her mind as she brought the photograph closer and looked at the two faces on it. One was a Hindu. The other was the very image of Edward as a child. The architecture behind them was a garden but clearly Indian. On the back of it was an inscription. Anne glanced down, her eyes playing over the signature: "Forever, Charlotte."

And then the violent jolt of comprehension. "Not all of the past is really in the past."

The photograph whispered to the floor as the pieces began to come together with frightening clarity. Anne dashed at the tears running down her face. "Damn you, Edward!" she heard a voice say, realizing that the photograph was not of Edward at all. Over the roaring in her ears, she did not realize that the voice had been her own.

Her heart splintered into a thousand tiny pieces, like broken glass. The truth lying here in her very own house—the truth a stranger had warned her about—was that this boy . . . this boy who had clearly lived in Delhi, had to be Edward's son! Katherine Blackstone—the woman who had signed her name as Charlotte, whose eyeglasses he kept neatly beside the photograph—had to be the child's mother!

It all fit. She must have become his wife in India. God in His Heaven, of course he would have married the mother of his son! She knew from personal experience that Edward would not have brought a child into the world any other way.

She closed her eyes, but she could not chase the images away. All of the lies. The betrayal. Katherine had been her friend—and her husband's lover! His wife! She had told the most personal things to a woman after whom Edward had secretly named their daughter!

Merciful God, she thought, had they made love right here in this very house as she sat so lovingly, trustingly ignorant, filled with yet another of Edward's children? The pain was gripping her heart, squeezing it to death. "Do not be deceived. Do not ignore the truth. . . ."

And through the paralyzing agony came a single thought —small at first, like a whisper: *I suppose I always knew deep inside that there was someone else who possessed his heart. It was why he could never completely give himself to me. Dear Lord above! Take me back to the ignorance, I beg You! I don't want to know! Oh, the ignorance is better than knowing this!*

She gazed back down at the photograph through a raging torrent of tears. Who was the Hindu boy? Had Edward known all along that he had a son? And why were they not together? There was a story to it, one she would never know because they were a part of the woman called Charlotte—part of what the two of them had shared in India and then collectively agreed to keep from her.

Her entire life with Edward had been a lie. Their family was a lie. He was still in love with this woman. That much was clear. He had stayed here—oh, it was too humiliating to acknowledge! He had turned away from love and stayed with her—out of duty.

Anne did not even have the satisfaction of despising the woman because she had made the ultimate sacrifice. Katherine—Charlotte—had given up her own husband, a man whom she had rightfully first possessed, and she had done it without so much as a fight.

She sat back on her heels, her body beginning to go numb as she wiped her eyes. But the tears kept falling. Like rain. Like a torrent of wretched, pitiful rain. "I have no pride left," she sobbed. "The love has taken it all away. I want to hate him. I want to hate her. But I cannot. I am too afraid of the life that would bring me if I told him to go to Hell and take her with him!"

Anne felt as helpless as a child and as devastated as if she had heard that Edward had died. And in a way, he had. For her. His heart was not here with her. With their children. And she knew now that it had not been with them for a very long time. This was the problem. This was what had been eating at him, torturing him since the day Katherine Blackstone had left Tetbury.

It took all of her strength to stand again and place the camphorwood chest back inside the musty trunk. Beside the pistol. Already, through the grief and shock, a plan was forming in her troubled mind. Like Pandora, she might never be able to return to the bliss that had kept her safely ignorant for such a long time. But she could keep her secret now that the truth was out. She could press what she knew deep inside her broken heart and close it off. She could pretend this evening had never happened. That Charlotte had never happened. She could keep her family together because at least now she understood. After all, that was what the stranger had tried to help her do by warning her with a letter. It was also what Edward was trying to do by staying. By being so damn noble!

God forgive me. . . . Charlotte forgive me. . . . Perhaps you want him back now. But that cannot happen. I have two children of whom to think. I cannot change. Or perhaps I do not want to change. But whatever the truth, the reality is still the same. Edward is mine now. I will not give him up.

The stale aroma of ale and smoke came into the bedroom before he did. Pretending to be asleep, Anne listened to all of the little noises she knew so well. The sound of him washing at the basin at foot end of the bed; the thick, husky sound of his breathing; floorboards creaking beneath his shoes. How comforting those noises had always been, she thought as he began to undress. *What I would not give to know that peace again. . . .* She squeezed her eyes to press back the tears, *hoping* vainly that tomorrow it all would not hurt so much. *Knowing* that the bitter pretense between them had only just begun.

"OH, WELCOME HOME! WELCOME HOME!"

Charlotte flung her arms around Jawahar's neck and kissed his cheeks, one after the other. "Let me look at you!" she cried, stepping back but still holding his hands out between them.

He stood proudly in the drive of Briarwood, dressed in a handsome English frockcoat with striped silk cravat and black trousers. The fresh morning dew glistened on the flowers and shrubs and the sun shone down on his dark, smiling face. The month of June had chased the rain away, and in its place the garden was filled with sweet and fragrant flowers. Primroses. Jasmine. Newly blooming hollyhocks.

"So, my boy, tell me," Alfred asked, stepping up beside Charlotte and extending his slim hand. "How are those hallowed halls of Cambridge treating you?"

Jawahar beamed. "Even after a grueling first term, sir, it is still the most wondrous place I have ever been."

Suddenly a door slammed shut and everyone looked back up at the house. Hugh Edward was taking the stone stairs two at a time to get to Jawahar. "Why did no one tell me that you had arrived?" Hugh Edward cried, charging at the boy he had long considered his older brother.

The two young men embraced, and Charlotte felt the happy sting of tears in her eyes. It had been a dreadfully long six months for her, with Jawahar away at school and Hugh Edward constantly taken up with card parties or some other social event. Through it, Charlotte had come to feel disconnected. At times it was as if she had lost her purpose in the two people who had helped her the most in maintaining her sanity throughout this whole dreadful ordeal.

Even after Edward had sent her the scarf bidding her a final farewell, and the concession to Alfred she had then made to forget her husband, Charlotte still dreamed of him in her sleep. She still wondered if the longing for what they once had shared would ever end. But through the worst of it, Alfred Linton had been there to cosset and protect her and remind her almost daily that there was at least one well-bred man in England not fool enough to let her go. Honor or not.

"Do come in." She smiled at Jawahar and brushed away the happy tears. "Bickers has seen your favorite breakfast

341

prepared this morning, and there is an urn full of coffee, strong and dark, just as you like it."

Jawahar kissed her cheek. "It is good to be home, *memsahib.*"

They all sat together on the terrace behind the library at a black wrought-iron table. A greedy bee, half drunk with nectar, buzzed above the table as they ate fresh bread, eggs, and bacon and everyone heard all about Cambridge.

"I understand your marks are very strong this term," Alfred said, pressing a forkful of eggs past his smooth, tawny lips. "I knew from the first that it was the right place for you. You're a very bright young man indeed."

"I am learning so much," he replied, his dark, exotic face filled with the joy of the limitless future now before him. "Thanks to Lord Linton's kindness."

"Have you had much trouble with your classmates this term?" Hugh Edward asked tentatively, taking a sip of orange juice.

Jawahar put down his fork and dotted his lips with a napkin before he looked back at the boy. "None of which to speak. I believe the curiosity as to the color of my skin has rather run its course."

"Good," Charlotte chimed. "Then surely now they shall all be able to see what a splendid young man you really are."

"I think perhaps you are just the slightest bit partial," Jawahar supposed, his lips quirking into a smile.

"Of course I am!" she replied, her own radiant smile widening to match his. "That, I believe, is a mother's prerogative!"

After breakfast, Charlotte gave Jawahar a personal tour of the house to show him all of the work that had been done in his absence. There was new yellow and green wallpaper in the dining room. Splendid new china from France to grace the table. A new Chinese carpet in the drawing room. And he loved it all because she had chosen it. Arms linked, they strolled alone out into the newly blooming garden, the warm summer air causing them both to feel a little more carefree.

"So, how are you, truly?" Jawahar finally asked. When he spoke, his voice was filled with such entire understanding of who she was, who she had been, that Charlotte felt not the slightest inclination to bother with the pretense.

"I am still taking it one day at a time."

"Does that maxim still hold true in the matter of Lord Linton as well?"

Charlotte stopped beside a lush bed of pink roses, remembering what he once had seen—his knowledge of the lengths to which that Christmas Eve had eventually led in her valiant effort to put the past to rest. She closed her eyes and turned her face up to the sun, feeling the radiant warmth, trying not to remember Alfred's greedy kiss, or to feel the regret.

Since the night of the Ashtons' dinner party, the night she had agreed to be publicly escorted by him, Alfred had made no secret of his belief that her resolve was weakening. She had ignored her heart and made a concession, hoping to get on with her life. But it was never going to lead where he desired. Not to marriage. No, it would never lead to that.

Not with Alfred, nor with anyone else.

When she looked back at Jawahar, Charlotte said wearily, "I still have not accepted his proposal, if that is what you mean."

"And will you?"

"I do not see how I could, no matter how everyone else presses me and I press myself to get on with my life. There is no way to entirely get round the fact that I am still married."

"Then that is the excuse you give him."

"It is not an excuse, Jawahar," she said, tensing. "It is quite simply a fact. I cannot, in all good conscience, become a bigamist."

"Nor a self-deceiver," he said calmly. Charlotte looked at Jawahar, his dark face filled with knowing as his startlingly accurate observation hit her like a pointed dart. "You know you would only be deceiving yourself, *memsahib*, if you accept more from him than you already have," he said more softly. "Have you been firm with him? Told him that there is no hope for a future between the two of you?"

"Almost constantly since you left." She sighed. "But I believe the Earl of Bentham is a man possessed by the romance of it all, and he is completely convinced that persistence shall one day win my heart."

"He has been a good friend," Jawahar observed.

"That he has. He is a wonderful man. And if I were anyone else . . . But, whatever choices Captain Langston was forced to make, I cannot forget the past, no matter how many people wish it were otherwise. It is simply not in me to do that."

"You have a big heart, *memsahib,*" he still insisted upon calling her. "I am certain it is part of what makes him love you."

"Ah, Jawahar," she said, squeezing his arm, "it is this heart of mine, I fear, that one day shall be my final undoing."

It was not until the next afternoon that Jawahar and Hugh Edward went down across the back lawn to the freshly painted white barn to see the advances Charlotte had made on her farm. Jawahar stroked the back of a large brown-and-white cow with a brass bell around her neck as she grazed on sweet summer grass.

"What was he like?" Hugh Edward asked in a silence that had followed a barrage of small talk between them.

Jawahar understood what he was asking and hesitated only a moment to consider his reply. "Perhaps that is a question better asked of your mother, *béta.*"

"I cannot ask her. Even the mention of my father's name brings pain to her face. I heard her tell Alfred once that I look just like him. 'More every day,' she said. His blood courses through my veins, Jawahar, and yet I know so little about him, other than the story of why he chose to stay in Tetbury."

They went into the barn and sank down together in a soft, golden bale of hay. "Ask what you like," Jawahar finally agreed, pressing a blade of straw between his lips. "I shall tell you what I can."

"Was he handsome?"

"Very. He was about as tall as I am, and your eyes and hair are his exactly." He leaned back on his elbows and thought a moment. "The captain-*sahib* carried himself with more pride than any Englishman I had ever seen. I was quite certain the first time I saw him in Agra that he was among your country's nobility. Of course, I was only a child then."

Hugh Edward was silent, trying to piece together the fragments of description in his own imagination. "Was he good to my mother?"

"He adored her," Jawahar firmly assured him. "He did not want to leave her, even to go to Ambala with his regiment. They had been married such a short time then. But I have always believed it was something more than that. It was almost as if he knew, or had a premonition that something would go awry. I know in my heart that if it was not for that wretched mutiny . . . they would be together still."

Hugh Edward gazed across the barn at three white geese parading out into the shaft of warm summer sunlight. He was trying to imagine his parents together in a faraway land that had begun already to fade from his child's memory. "She always told me that none of this—the way things are—none of it was his fault."

"I believe she is right," Jawahar softly agreed. "He really had very little choice but to stay where he was. Your mother told me once that the other woman would be quite helpless without him."

"I want to respect him for his decision, I truly do," Hugh Edward confided, the tone of his voice growing troubled. "I know that is what she wants of me. But it is just so difficult when I see what the loss of him . . . twice, has cost her."

"Perhaps if you allow yourself to think about what the captain-*sahib* lives without every waking moment of his life," Jawahar gently offered, "that being the woman he loves and the child born of that love, you will feel less of that anger I see so bright upon your face just now."

His voice broke. "I wish I had at least met him."

"I am quite certain, *béta*, that there is not a day which goes by that your father does not wish the very same thing."

* * *

Alfred Linton walked briskly away from the brothel on South Bleecker Street, pulling the rim of his dark top hat down over his eyes. Even his coachman would not wait for him in this shabby London neighborhood. But Alfred smiled as he tapped his cane on the cobblestones and tried not to breathe too deeply.

Even this early in the morning, the summer air had already turned foul. The breeze when he had come here late last evening had been more forgiving. But now in the harsh light of day, women emptied chamber pots from second-story windows and their contents mixed with the garbage and mud and splashed against the houses into the streets. He was glad that the narrow old buildings kept the street dark. Kept him anonymous.

In spite of the risks of being in this part of the city, it was not his first visit here and it certainly would not be his last. At least not so long as Charlotte Lawrence continued refusing to become his wife. She had also refused his entreaties into her bed, continuing to string him along in this excruciatingly endless game of cat and mouse.

Most of the time the contest between them was precisely what encouraged him. The excitement. The challenge of it. In his long life there had not been many who had refused the charms of the Earl of Bentham, and Alfred had grown accustomed to having his way with them. He had also grown bored. Charlotte Lawrence certainly did keep him guessing. It really was her great allure. And with her hand to strive for these days, Alfred Linton was anything but bored.

Everyone expected them to marry. All of the papers said so. They had accepted that she had been widowed and taken back her maiden name as a testament to what she felt for the earl. During the London Season they were inseparable. In spite of her outward devotion to him, however, the gossip was that the rather mysterious Miss Lawrence was causing the Earl of Bentham to wait for her hand. It was clearly not the other way around. She had discovered his more dangerous side, they supposed, and it had become an issue between them.

He had been with Charlotte one morning as she read

those veiled suppositions over her tea and toast, and he had breathed a sigh of relief when she found them all quite comical. Dangerous indeed, she had chuckled. "Perhaps you have a bit of a temper," she had said. "But speaking from experience, I can honestly say that the Earl of Bentham lives his life like a perfect gentleman!"

He stepped carefully now through a slushy street of foul-smelling debris, a gloved hand pressed against his mouth, mindful not to soil his costly new leather shoes. *If only she could see me now,* he thought.

He had dozens of things to do today, and now that his lust had been sated by the expert charms of a big-breasted prostitute for whom he had a particular affinity, he longed to return home as quickly as possible. He crossed the street and kept walking briskly until he saw his coach waiting before a tavern whose door was open to the street. Alfred did not look inside. After last night, he had partaken of enough wine, women, and song to last a lifetime. Or at least until the next time Charlotte refused him.

Charlotte. Her face lit before him like a candle flame as he settled into his carriage and it lurched out into the street. He thought about how it would be to make love to her. Her skin so soft and sweet, her body replete with gentle curves. It may not have happened yet but, yes indeed, he was wearing down her resistance. In addition to escorting her publicly when at first she had refused him, he now spent every afternoon with her at Briarwood playing whist. Suppers twice a week. Soon enough, she would not be asking him to take his leave at nightfall.

It was true what they said. Patience truly was a virtue! He smiled a slim, Cheshire cat grin. One day not only her body but her heart as well would belong to him. He lay his head back against the velvet seat cushion and closed his eyes, suddenly feeling exhausted.

He had not slept last night, and today his body felt heavy and spent. Reality loomed more clearly now than when he was with her, caught up in the moment. *What on earth is a man of your tastes doing chasing after a young innocent like Charlotte Lawrence?* he asked himself. *Once the novelty has worn off, you shall grow as weary of her as you were with all the others.* The thought skipped across his mind and then disappeared as quickly as it had come. The answer now, as it always had been, was simply for the challenge of it all. He had killed a man for less. Taken mistress after mistress, caring little for their reputation or what would become of them once he left. But Charlotte was different. She would bear his children. Satisfy his desire—and his curiosity. *Then,* perhaps, he would be rid of her.

Once they were safely out of London, Alfred's carriage swayed to a halt. A moment later, a young liveried driver leaned his head in through the window. "Where to, sir?" he asked, waiting for Alfred to open his eyes.

"Home, Branford, my good man." Alfred smiled wearily, still smelling of cheap perfume and spilled wine. "I have need of a bath and a change of clothes before we set out for Briarwood. We certainly cannot have the lady of the manor seeing me like this if we ever are to win this bloody contest between us!"

THE SECRET HAD BEEN LIKE ACID.

It had eaten away at Anne Langston's heart and mind during the long months since she had discovered it. There had been so many times, an avalanche of times, when she had longed to confront Edward with what she knew. But always the same thing stopped her: Anne feared that if the truth was out between them, that he would see no impediment to leaving.

After all, why would he stay? He did not love her. It was obligation that had chained him to Tetbury when his body and soul longed to be elsewhere. If she came at him like a shrew, hurling accusations and blame, it was likely to give him the courage to run right back into Charlotte's waiting arms. Even that name pierced her heart when she thought of it. Their daughter! Their own little girl!

Anne sat alone in the darkness at the kitchen table, cauterizing the pain with sherry. Lots of sherry. Far too much sherry. It had taken this—this unspeakable secret— for her to understand why Edward drank so much since his return from India. It really was the only thing that helped one to forget.

Her children had gone to bed hours before and her husband would be home soon. The quiet time between those two events every night was the most excruciating. For Anne, it was the time of day when she could not help but think. And so she drank to stop the thoughts.

"My husband." The words moved to her lips and then passed across them, tasting like venom. She drank the rest of her sherry and then poured herself another.

Eager to have a friend, she had told Charlotte things she had never told another living soul. Dear Lord above! She had even confided in her about her eldest daughter's un- timely conception. But the shame of it all had passed now into a grinding ache. Like the memory of a vicious beating, the scar remained.

She sipped absently at the sherry and gazed down at her wedding band. She had not taken it off her finger since the day Edward had placed it there on the day of their marriage. Oh, deception! They were not really even married. How could they be when the woman he had first taken as his wife was still alive?

Anne heard the front door click open just before mid- night, but the sherry had made her heavy in her chair. It had also left her vision blurred. Most evenings she drank enough to fall asleep by the time Edward returned from the pub so that they would not be forced to face one another without the cover of their children. Without them there to shield her, Anne Langston had grown afraid of herself. Of what her conscience might force her to confess. But tonight she had not had the energy nor the inclination to be out of his way. She sagged back against the chair and waited helplessly.

"Good. You're still up," he exclaimed in a surprised, slightly weary voice, as he pulled off his heavy brown jacket and slung it over the back of the chair beside her.

"I wasn't tired."

"I'm exhausted."

Anne tried to focus on Edward as he sat down beside her, but his image was distorted. It was like looking at his reflection in water. He moved, and she felt ill.

Edward glanced at the nearly empty bottle and tried not to let his irritation show. "Are you all right?"

"W-why wouldn't I be?"

In the silence after her question, Edward poured two glasses of milk from a glazed ceramic pitcher and handed one to Anne. He hoped that it would help. "I have something for you," he said cautiously, waiting for her to lift her eyes and look at him. When she did, her once smiling brown eyes were glassy and distant, as though she was not really there. It had been that way since Christmas, Edward thought, completely unaware of what she knew.

In the palm of his hand he held a locket on a delicate gold chain. Anne looked down at it and then back up at him. "What is this for?"

"For your birthday, of course," he said with a faint smile. "Have you forgotten it was today?"

"Yes. I suppose I had." She took the locket in her trembling hand and held it up to the lamp he had brought into the kitchen, trying hard to focus on it. The venom she tasted was choking her. *I cannot live with this!* she thought desperately. *With the lies. With knowing. A year ago, I thought that I could. God, how much I wanted to. But every day it becomes a little more unbearable.*

"It is very lovely," she said flatly, suppressing her thoughts.

"I'm sorry I wasn't here for supper. Especially tonight," Edward said in a strained but sincere tone. "I meant to be. I truly did. It just got so bloody busy. It took both Paddy and I to see everyone served."

"The Cock 'n' Feathers is important to you," she said, drawing in a strangled breath as a single tear faltered on her cheek. "I understand that."

Edward put his hand on hers—the one that held the locket—and squeezed it. "So is my family."

Anne tore her hand away and sprung to her feet. The room began to spin. She could not bear to hear a single word more of his hypocrisy. She was drowning in the lies. Edward's and her own. "All of a sudden, I am very tired," she said.

He tipped his head, puzzled by the change in her. He had come home intent on their spending time together. Intent on making another attempt at some sort of reconciliation. Especially on her birthday. He had told himself that he owed them both that much. "I thought that you said—"

"I know what I said, but I am tired now!"

He could see that once again she had drunk too much. He had been hiding the sherry for weeks, but she always managed to find it while he was away.

"Then at least let me help you up to bed."

"I don't need your help!" she lashed out, her eyes like melted chocolate, narrowing angrily on him.

Edward bit his lip to stop himself from saying that help was precisely what she did need. "Very well. I shall be up in a few minutes then."

Anne clung to the railing, taking the back stairs slowly. She was halfway up the stairs when she stopped. Edward saw only her legs in the shadows. "Thank you for remembering my birthday," she said, her voice quivering.

"You're my wife, Anne," he called back to her. "It is my duty to remember things like that."

"Yes, your duty," she said with a strange little mocking laugh, then continued on up the stairs.

Charlotte plucked a rose from one of the bushes in the garden and handed it to Hugh Edward, who held a wicker basket for his mother. She looked back at the basket heaped with plump pink and red flowers snipped from what had once been all brambles and weeds. She felt a real sense of pride in all she had accomplished here at Briarwood in only two years.

As she once had transformed a simple Delhi bungalow, so now too had Charlotte enriched the house and grounds. Once again it was the small yet elegant manor that her ancestors had envisioned. Refurbished with great care, it was a much sought-after place to attend suppers and card parties once again. A surprise to everyone, especially Alfred, was that her little farm was also flourishing. It had actually become quite fashionable for the estates nearby to purchase their eggs and milk from her supply. They found it quite chic to buy from someone in Society. Edward would have liked the irony in that.

England was beautiful in September, Charlotte thought as she looked out across the grounds. Such gloriously verdant land on which the cows and horses leisurely grazed; puffy white clouds against a brilliant azure sky. But before she knew it, the air would be turning again. The cool crispness of autumn would steal away her roses and the beautiful blue horizon. Once again the drafty old brick manor would hold her captive through the long, cold months of winter. She dreaded that, like a little death.

Charlotte felt so much more strength in the sun. It made her feel bright. Alive. It had been that way since she was a child in Delhi, having grown accustomed there to the sun's nurturing warmth. Charlotte pressed another long-stemmed pink flower to her nose and inhaled the sweet, heady fragrance. *I am so far from that child I was in Delhi*, she remembered sadly. *That precious little girl with hopes and dreams died such a long time ago.* She thought of Edward's dreams, dead now too in a camphorwood box. So many sacrifices. So much pain.

But time had healed the most excruciating part of that pain; the part that had bidden her to let Alfred kiss her those few times and to pretend she had actually enjoyed it.

During that second year, even when Charlotte told herself and everyone else that it was over, she had not really believed it. There had always been that tiny glimmer of hope that, if she wished for it hard enough, or waited long enough, one day Edward would return to her. It was that relentless hope against which she had struggled that had driven her so briefly into Alfred's arms.

But that period of her life was all over now. She had let go of the futility of hoping for a miracle. She had fought instead to cherish the precious memories they shared and to tuck them away inside her heart, in the same place she kept the memories of Rani and her father.

Charlotte had grown and she had survived. She liked the woman she had become. Mother. Businesswoman. Trusted friend. Being alone for the rest of her life would not be so awfully bad in the full light of that.

"What are we going to do with all of these flowers, Mama?" Hugh Edward asked. The straw-colored basket he held for her was already brimming with them.

Charlotte turned around, looking with what he thought was a curiously serene smile, the ends of her hair tipped golden by the sun. "We are going to fill the house with them, darling," she replied resolutely, "so that we can make everything smell like summer for as long as possible."

She then handed him three more roses and turned back to snip another.

Edward felt a thump of panic.

"What do you mean, she's gone?"

"I don't know, Papa," Charlotte confessed as he stood exhausted just inside the front door, facing his eldest daughter. It was late and it had been such a miserably long day. His face was drawn. His mind was preoccupied, and he hadn't the strength for this. "Mama took a bottle of sherry, something else that looked like a pistol, and then walked out of the house."

"But it is pouring rain outside! It has been all evening long. Did you not try to stop her?" he charged.

The child averted her china-blue, panic-stricken eyes. "I did not know what to do, Papa. She was . . . not herself. You know."

Edward knew what that meant and he was ashamed of himself for even asking such a thing of a child. Anne had been drinking again. Good Lord in His Heaven! She had changed so that now he scarcely remembered the woman he had married. If it was possible, Anne had lately seemed almost more tormented than he.

"Blast!" He slammed the front door behind him. "What could she have been thinking to have gone out on a night like this?"

Suddenly his daughter began to weep, half out of fear, half out of concern that this was somehow her fault. Edward saw the heartbreak in her eyes and brought her to his chest. "Oh, now you musn't cry, sweetheart. Everything is going to be just fine. You took good care of your sister while Mama has been away, and I'm very proud of you for that. But now I must go and search for her. She might have gotten lost in the dark wind and rain, and I am going to get some men to help me." Charlotte nodded through her tears that she understood and then she looked back at her father. "Do you think you could be a good girl a little longer and help me?"

"Yes, Papa."

"Good." He smiled and kissed the top of her head. "I need you to be a very brave girl and put on your coat and hat and run across the back garden. Tell nice Mr. Morris what you have just told me and ask him to meet the lot of us over at the pub in ten minutes."

"Are you going to find her?" she asked, starting to cry again.

"Of course I am, sweetheart. Now run as fast as you can!"

30

ANNE LANGSTON SWAYED AS SHE STOOD ON THE EDGE OF THE
spring, swollen by days of rain, the dark thoughts fusing in
her troubled mind. The rain, fierce now and steady, had
soaked entirely through her clothes several hours before. But
she did not feel it. She felt nothing. Her body was numb with
cold. Her mind was numb with regret.

As she stood watching the dark water swirling below her,
Anne's thoughts turned to Edward. To the woman who had
called herself Katherine Blackstone. Then she imagined
them together in the same cruel, self-punishing way she had
done every day since she had discovered the truth. The pain
to her heart of that truth was like a physical blow. Hard and
sharp. Relentless. But the guilt at having kept them apart
had brought the strongest part of the pain.

Now there was nothing she wanted so much as peace from
all of it. It had been her single, unending thought for days.
Her only regret in so doing was that she would have to leave
her children. Abigail would not remember her at all. Charlotte's memories would soon be clouded with time. But
Edward was quite a different matter. She had never really
been a part of his heart. She was certain that leaving him
would bring him little more than relief.

Pain and guilt had made her weary of this life she had
manufactured for herself, cleverly orchestrating her first
pregnancy to trap him into marriage. Anne had managed to
convince him that she was helpless. That she needed him.
Adored him. *Yet it never could have been enough, could it?*

355

she thought sadly now, but honestly, because no matter how desperately she had loved him, he could never really have come to love her. She hoped that this Charlotte, this woman from his past, would be a good mother to her children.

Of course Edward would return to her once it was over. That much she knew was fated, and Anne felt some relief now from the guilt at that prospect, knowing that she had been responsible for keeping them apart.

None of it had happened the way she had planned it. The white pain of discovering such an awful truth had blinded her judgment. It had made her believe that she could actually live a life filled with that kind of deception.

In those first dark, dreadful days, Anne had tried again to make him fall in love with her. As usual, she had tried too hard, and her obsession had only pushed him further into his secret past. Now it was time to give him back to the woman he loved. Death was the only way she knew to let him go.

By now they were searching for her, but even Anne did not know exactly where she was. She had been stumbling blinding in the rain for hours. She sank slowly down into the mud and curled her arms around her legs, hoping, praying that the earth and the water would simply swallow her up. That death would come to claim her. It took an hour more before she felt calm enough to aid the process. When a sudden jerk of courage came, she pulled Edward's loaded pistol from a pocket in her cape and pressed the barrel against her heart.

$$\mathcal{C} \hspace{-0.2em} \sim \hspace{-0.2em} \mathcal{P} \hspace{0.3em} 31$$

IT WAS A SIMPLE FUNERAL.

Edward laid some hollyhocks on the plain pine casket and watched the grave digger lower it into the waiting earth. He and Paddy were the last to leave the little cemetery beside St. Mary's Church as the rain came down in long white sheets around them. After a last goodbye, Paddy linked his arm through Edward's and the two men walked alone back across Tetbury toward the Langston cottage.

"I just don't understand why," Edward muttered, still shocked that his wife's mysterious and pervasive grief could actually have caused her to take her own life.

"'Tis a mystery." Paddy shook his head. "She used to be so happy."

"I really tried to give her what she wanted," he said, and his deeply wounded voice sought approval from an old friend.

"I am sure there was really nothing you could have done. Everyone in this world has their own demons to face. You must know that."

"I only wish," said Edward with a sigh, "that I had known what Anne's demons were. Perhaps I could have stopped her."

Everyone else was already there by the time Paddy and Edward arrived back at the cottage. Somber murmuring filled the dim rooms like a dirge as people who had known Anne Langston all of her life ate and drank and spoke of the great tragedy.

From Margaret Evans's arms, both his daughters ran to his side, seeking comfort. For a moment, their nearness helped to clear his mind. Edward bent down in the middle of his sitting room crowded with friends. He held them both against his heart, trying vainly to give them what they so desperately needed; an explanation. But Edward had no idea what he could possibly say to them. Even now that their mother was buried, the words would not come. Every explanation he had offered since her death the day before seemed wholly inadequate, because Edward did not understand it himself.

After receiving condolences from the mourners who crowded into his drawing room, people who had attended Anne and Edward's wedding and the christening of their children, Edward excused himself. His wife had just died. Everyone understood that. What they did not understand was that he had begun to feel a curious sense of responsibility. He should have been able to save her. He should have known what was wrong. He went upstairs alone to the bedroom they had shared, his head bursting with unanswered questions.

Sagging against the door frame, Edward gazed at the bed where they had made love those first years, where little Charlotte had been born. Where his wife had been washed for burial yesterday morning.

He glanced around the room still so full of Anne. As he studied the articles she had left behind, the noises from downstairs slowly faded away. A moment later, he heard only the silence. It was curious, Edward thought, that he did not feel the great relief he might have at her death. There was no sudden burden of weight lifted from his shoulders. No real sense of freedom that he need no longer keep up the pretense and deception.

What he did feel was regret that she had felt desperate enough about something to have done this. They had known one another since they were children. Shared so many secrets. He had seen for months how unhappy she was, but he had honestly not seen this coming. This mysterious, unexplained ending. And Anne Langston had taken any real explanation of why with her to the grave.

That night, alone in the cottage, Edward went down to the little room he had so briefly shared with Charlotte. But he did not go there because he wanted to think about her on the night he had just buried Anne. It was that he could not bear to lie again in the bed they had shared. He was relieved that the children would be spending the night with Margaret Evans. Edward was certain that once everyone else had gone home he would not have been able to bear their little faces gazing up at him full of hurt and questions. He had no answers. Damn! He had nothing.

Methodically, carefully, that night, he had packed away all of Anne's dresses. Her perfume. Her hairbrushes. Anything to keep his mind busy. But as he worked in small, hopeless movements over her things, the scenes played over and over again in his mind.

Had he done anything, said anything, that could have caused this? The answer his conscience always gave him was the same: He had stayed when his heart's desire had been to leave. He had been noble rather than passionate in his resolve. How could he have been to blame for thoughts he had kept safely buried inside his heart? No. It had been something else. It must have been something else.

He thought of her body lying so still and white, so cold, on their bed as he had gone to see her one last time this morning. Margaret Evans and her sister, Louisa, had washed away the mud and grass and he thought how, in her entire life, Anne had never looked more at peace. She had looked as if she were only sleeping. As if she would awake any moment and look up at him.

Edward had kissed her palm and then lay it gently back on top of her other hand as a way of saying farewell. "Sweet dreams," he had whispered, breathing a gentle kiss onto her forehead. "Whatever it was that troubled your heart so is gone. Now you shall have nothing but peace. . . . A safe and gentle peace."

Until now, his calm had been like armor, protecting him

from more loss in his life. More pain. He had lost something very special in Anne, and Edward felt that loss profoundly. Perhaps he had not loved her. But she had been the mother of his daughters. A precious childhood friend. They had shared a history. It was only now, alone with the memories and the regrets for a woman who had loved him—a woman he had never been able to love in return—that Edward felt free to grieve for her loss. And for all of his other losses.

Paddy brought fresh rolls and a full bottle of whiskey for their coffee early the next morning. He found Edward alone at the kitchen table, gazing blankly out into the back garden through the open door.

"You look like a man who could use a bit of this," he said, holding up the bottle. "Didn't sleep much, hmm?"

"None," Edward confessed wearily. "I just keep playing it all over and over again in my mind. Searching for answers."

"Edward, my boy." He sighed, plunking down heavily into the chair beside him. "I believe there are some questions in life just not meant to be answered."

"Well, that is just not good enough!" Edward thumped his fist onto the table. "How am I supposed to make peace with what she did if I haven't a clue why?"

In the silence, Paddy poured a generous amount of whiskey into each of their cups of coffee and then took a long swallow of his own. "All right then. Had you done something to cause your wife to feel desperate?" he asked pointedly, setting the cup back down on the table.

Edward grimaced. "Not that she would ever know. I made a promise to myself in that."

"I see," Paddy breathed accusingly as he slumped back into the chair.

Edward's eyes dilated as they shot back up from his cup. "No, you don't see, Paddy! You don't see a'tall. No one does!"

"'Tis the woman in India you told me about who came between you."

"Leave it alone, Paddy," Edward brayed like a wounded bear. "I'm sorry I ever said a thing about it."

"Oh Edward, my boy, how bad can it have been? You know what they say. A little confession is good for the soul. . . . Come now! You can tell me."

The urge to confess was strong within him. But he must not. Not today with Anne so newly buried. There would be a kind of betrayal in that. "Paddy, you wouldn't understand."

"You've been unfaithful. Is that it?" he pestered. "And the guilt is tormenting you. Well, is that it? Is it?"

"Yes! All right, yes!" Edward surged furiously out of his chair, causing it to crash back behind him. "For the love of God, yes. I have been unfaithful! But not to the wife you believe!"

Paddy gasped against chubby fingers. "I . . . don't understand."

"Yes, you understand exactly, Paddy. I have another wife!"

"You . . . married the woman you knew in India?" he gasped incredulously.

"Long before I married Anne!"

"Oh, saints preserve us!" Paddy moaned. Then he too surged out of his chair and walked briskly to the back door for some air. He needed a moment to try and quiet his mind; to accept what Edward was saying. It was so impossible to believe. "I really don't think I should be hearing this, Edward." He shook his head.

"Oh no you don't!" Edward charged, grabbing Paddy by the shoulders and spinning him back around forcefully. "You wanted to know the truth, so I shall tell you! All of it! Charlotte, my wife, died in the massacre in Delhi two months after our wedding. She burned to death when they destroyed our bungalow—or so Her Majesty's army led me to believe for almost ten excruciating years. I never loved anyone like I loved her, Paddy. Our hearts were joined in a way I never thought possible with another human being. When I thought she had died I was destroyed."

Paddy's tone reflected a gentle knowing. "That is why you

wouldn't marry Anne for such a long time once you returned?"

"I couldn't," he said with an aching honesty. "I still grieved for Charlotte and the brutal way in which I believed she had died. I grieved for what I had lost, until the day she showed up here in Tetbury as Katherine Blackstone."

"The Devil you say!"

"It's true, Paddy. Every word of it, so help me God. She too believed I had been killed. My wife came back to England to find me and to tell me we had a son, only to discover that I had married someone else, and that I had two other children."

The expression on Paddy's round face was one of real horror, as though he could not quite convince his mind of what Edward was saying. His thick lips were softly parted and his eyes were wide as saucers. "The woman who stayed in your house, who cared for your daughter . . . was another wife?"

They both sat back down and Paddy drank the rest of his whiskey-spiked coffee, hoping that it would steady him while Edward considered how to make him understand. "It is all rather more complicated than that," he finally said. "Anne urged her mercilessly and Charlotte, who thought perhaps she would find a more private moment to confront me with the truth, agreed to stay only until Abigail was born."

Paddy was shaking his head again. "This is all just so impossible to believe. That it was going on right here beneath my very nose, and I hadn't a clue!"

"Nor did I, at first. It was quite by accident that I ever did discover who she really was. After being here for a while, and seeing Anne and I together, Charlotte had decided that she could not be the one to come between us. She really had no intention of confessing the truth to me."

"I remember that she wore those shaded glasses a great deal, but I cannot imagine that you did not even recognize your own wife in all that time!"

"She was injured quite badly in the mutiny, Paddy," Edward explained, and his lifelong friend heard the overwhelming sorrow in his voice that he had not been there to protect the woman he loved. "What ten years' time had not altered, the vicious *sepoys* had."

"And knowing all of this," he murmured, "you stayed with Anne. Dear Lord, it must have been an excruciating choice."

"Not the choice so much," said Edward with a sigh, remembering. "I knew how much Anne depended on me, and upon the life we had made here together. It was letting Charlotte go after only just finding her again that was truly unbearable."

"Oh, my dear dear boy, I am really so terribly sorry."

Edward reached across the table and grasped Paddy's shirt-covered arm. "I have never told another living soul that story."

"Do you suppose . . . Great Heavenly days, it is too dreadful to imagine, but do you suppose Anne somehow discovered the truth?"

"Of course not," Edward huffed, dismissing the notion.

A stray memory, soft as a feather, whispered across his mind even as he spoke the denial. He saw Anne behind him in the shadowy attic as he knelt at the foot of the open trunk. But just as quickly as the image came, Edward dismissed it.

The alternative would have been unthinkable.

"I believe it is a sign," Paddy confessed.

Edward turned around on Long Street the next evening after he had locked up the Cock 'n' Feathers. Paddy was standing in the glow of the moon, his full face all luminous silver and shadows.

"What is a sign?"

"Well, I've been thinking about what we spoke about yesterday, and I believe the advent of Anne's passing might well have been a sign from above. Perhaps the good Lord is giving you permission, at last, to follow your heart."

Edward's tone was suddenly clipped, self-protective. "That is impossible."

"But why? She's still your wife. And you still love her—that much I can see in your eyes."

"Love has nothing to do with it, Paddy," Edward said, his

voice going suddenly lower. "It has been nearly two years since she was here. I sent her and my son each a gift. It was my way of saying goodbye. I cannot open that door again now. Not when I have put her through so much already."

The clouds had broken again, beginning to spill a soft, new rain as they moved together out into the dark night. Paddy saw the raw pain ripening on Edward's face at what he had suggested. That pain made him think of his own lost love. Of Adelaide. Of what he had surrendered by not trying harder.

"Go to her, boy," he urged. "See for yourself. Don't lose any more time without knowing for certain that she does not still want you."

"I know you're only trying to help and I appreciate that, Paddy," Edward said, trying to keep the frustration of so many things from his voice. "But it is over between us. It's done. My damnable sense of honor saw to that."

32

CHARLOTTE KNELT DOWN INSIDE THE BARN ON A THIN BED OF golden straw and stroked the tawny neck of the newest Briarwood calf. The animal gazed at her with wide eyes.

"Isn't she precious?" Charlotte asked, smiling proudly up at her butler, who had accompanied her most unhappily in the rain to see this latest addition.

"Divine, madam," he said dryly.

"Oh, Bickers, don't be such a dotard, hmm? What has gotten you in such a foul temper on so fine a morning?"

"I have been trying to tell you all the way down from the house, madam. It is Lord Linton. He has sent yet another message. Rather insistent, he still is, to speak with you."

Charlotte looked up. Her hand froze on the calf's neck. "And what have you told him?"

"The same as I told him the half dozen times he has sent word, that Madam is unwell and not receiving."

Alfred was doubtless livid by now. She had declined to see him for the past two days, relying on the same pale excuse. Since they had become so familiar that one Christmas Eve, when her desperation had taken over her good sense, Alfred had behaved more every day as if their marriage was only a matter of time. She knew that he had even boasted about it.

She had wanted to care for him. In the beginning she had tried her best to convince herself that they might actually be able to develop some sort of comfortable understanding. Lately, however, his constant pleading was like a noose around her slim white neck, tightening a little more each day. Charlotte knew how confused she had made him with their few stolen kisses and the large amount of time they had spent together.

She winced now when she thought of it. *Oh, Alfred. I am so sorry. I did so try to give you what you wanted,* she thought sadly.

But the sharp pain in her heart was less each day. Time had continued to see to that. And with the pain, so too had gone Charlotte's need to use extremes in attempting to heal the wound. Being with Alfred—seeing the hope in his eyes—had become unbearable in light of that. The needy possessiveness that had forced him to behave more and more rash toward her with each passing day was suffocating her. It had become like some sort of contest between them, their betrothal the prize. Alfred would not rest until Charlotte agreed to become his wife.

Of that much she was certain.

He really would be such a splendid catch if not for those dreadful rumors. She closed her mind a moment and willed the thought away.

"You may continue to inform Lord Linton's driver that I am still unwell and that I shall not be receiving again today. Leave the consequences of that prevarication to me."

"As you wish, madam." He nodded mechanically and then moved back toward the open barn door to wait for her.

"She's lovely, isn't she, Will?" Charlotte then asked the man to whom she had entrusted the well-being of her precious animals. He stood behind her, a stocky, red-bearded man, a worker's green felt cap held between two chapped hands.

"That she is, ma'am," he agreed, far more sincerely than her butler had now that they were alone. "She will fetch a fine price in town once she's grown."

"Oh, goodness no, Will. I'm not going to sell her either. This sweet animal has a home here at Briarwood for as long as she lives."

Charlotte could see that her words had surprised him. Even to him, animals were on this earth to provide a function. They either produced something or they were eaten. Their only value was in what they could bear.

Will Clarke cocked an eyebrow. The mistress had a fondness for these silly animals like nothing he had ever seen before. She was different, all right. Attractive. Wealthy. And yet passionately connected to the earth and its creatures like someone of far simpler means. Perhaps it was all those years in India, he reasoned, an impoverished, far-off land of simple people and even simpler values. Whatever the cause, Will liked working for Mistress Lawrence. Yes, he liked it very much indeed. No employer had ever been so kind to him or treated him more fairly. Whatever the reason for her preoccupation with this portion of her estate, Will Clarke meant to accommodate her in any way that he could.

"Good work, Will," Charlotte said, rising back to her feet. "Thank you for feeling certain I would want to see our new little addition."

"I remembered what you said about this place," he humbly told her. "I'm pleased I acted properly."

"You may come to me any time," she said, squeezing his shoulder. "It is a pleasure to have a kindred spirit in this," she said, glancing back at her butler, who was clearly growing impatient with their presence in this foul-smelling enclosure.

It was not until they were nearly all the way back up the hill to the house that Charlotte saw him standing there. Waiting for her.

"ILL INDEED!" ALFRED HUFFED.

She could see the irritation on his face, a hard, scarlet mask. His long, slim body was rigid as he stood tapping the gravel with the ivory tip of his long mahogany cane. "Charlotte, why do you insist upon playing these games with me?"

"Perhaps because you insist upon making me feel like some sort of prize to be won!"

She looked at his face in the single golden ray of sunlight that had come through the clouds, and she was sorry already that she had been so harsh. He was still so elegant-looking, with his neatly groomed silver waves of hair and his bright gray eyes. He did not deserve this indecision on her part, and yet he was so impossibly, so grimly possessive lately he had elicited little else from her than her desire to avoid him.

She went inside, followed by Bickers, then Alfred. In the beginning she had made excuses for this dreary temper of his. Now she no longer cared why it possessed him. All she knew was that she was quite tired of dealing with it—and with him.

She walked into the breakfast room, where her tea and

toast was waiting for her. It was set out on rose-dotted china and a crisp white lace-edged cloth. Alfred sat down heavily in the chair that faced her. From the corner of her eye, she could see the expression on his face slowly turn to one of desperation. *How I detest that expression even more than the anger,* she thought as she took a piece of toast and buttered it, pretending to be unaffected by his presence.

"Look," he said in a voice gone suddenly soft, nauseatingly vulnerable, "I love you. You know that. And I thought that you loved me. Or at least that you had come to feel some little bit of affection for me. So tell me, why must we torture one another as we do lately?" A sudden jerk of guilt blanketed her, and Charlotte sipped her tea to keep it from her face. "You said you needed me in your life, and I accepted that. I accepted whatever you wanted to give. But never did I agree to be your own personal whipping boy! Never!"

"I care for you, Alfred. I do—"

He interrupted her. "But you love Edward!"

"Oh, Alfred, please!" She rolled her eyes, slamming her cup into the saucer. "Must you always do that?"

He lurched across the table, seizing her hand. She could see the purple vein pulsing in his neck. "I cannot help it. You positively bring me to my knees. No other woman has ever managed to do that to me before, and I detest you for it!"

Charlotte looked up with surprise, her lips slightly parted. *What am I supposed to say?* she thought. *The sort of reassurance he wants I can never give him.* He may have made himself *available,* but still she had used him, and they both knew it. In aiding her own shattered heart, it appeared that she'd been breaking his. She believed that she alone had incited this desperation, still knowing nothing of the game of challenge as which it had begun.

"Look," Charlotte said, preparing to offer a concession, "why do you not come back this evening and we shall have supper? I'm certain the boys would be glad to see you."

"And you, Charlotte, will you be glad to see me too?" he asked flatly, still gripping her small hand, despising the name of Edward Langston. "Will you welcome me to

Briarwood as you once did, a wounded little bird in need of mending? Or will you merely tolerate me at your table now because, having shared such intimacies, your good breeding cannot permit you to do otherwise?"

Their eyes locked. "You're hurting me."

"Then perhaps you have some idea of how I feel."

"Alfred, let go of my hand!"

"Not until you tell me it is not over between us!"

It has been over between us for a very long time, she thought, but chose to say nothing that would anger him further. "Come to dinner," she said instead, wrenching her hand from his desperate grasp. She felt that she owed him at least that much for what he had done for the boys and for her. "I shall have the cook prepare something special just for you."

Wanting to believe her but refusing to let go of his hatred for Edward, Alfred took her hand again and this time pressed it softly against his lips. "Dreadfully sorry about that. You know I would never intentionally do anything to hurt you."

"Of course not," she said, standing up and hoping he would take it as his cue to leave. "Say, eight?"

"Perhaps it would not matter so much if I did not love you," he said, smiling sheepishly for his behavior.

Charlotte winced. *I warned you in the beginning not to fall in love with me,* she thought, recovering her pleasant smile. *I told you all along that my heart was lost forever. You have already had more of me than you were ever meant to. Why can you not just be happy with that?* "Shall we just put this regrettable little incident behind us then?" she asked him instead.

"I should like nothing more," he replied, being artfully led toward the door. A further step in his plan—now one of revenge against his enemy—began to gel in his mind. "Eight o'clock?"

"Eight o'clock it is."

Charlotte waited until she heard the front door click to a close before she sank back down into her chair at the table, her face pressed into her hands. *Oh Edward,* she thought sadly. *How could I ever have thought that he—or anyone else—could take your place?*

"So, can you see to it or not?"

By the next afternoon, Lord Linton's plan for Edward Langston, a plan he had been formulating for weeks, had become more than a cruel fantasy. His London banker, however, sat across from him in the cavernous, paneled Coutts Bank, shaking his head as business was carried on around them. He was trying to discern from the earl's expression what could possibly be motivating the desire for such a curiously poor business venture. But there was no explanation to be had in those cool gray eyes. Eyes that told only so much as the calculating Earl of Bentham meant to tell.

"Frankly, Alfred, I simply don't understand," he finally hedged in reply. "You know as well as I that a property like that, out in some small country village, cannot possibly be worth the investment."

Seeing that the banker meant to continue, Alfred leaned back in the stiff, creaking chair, a long polished mahogany desk between them, and placed his neat gray gloves across his lap.

"Look, ol' chap, I have been your banker for twenty years—your friend for thirty—and I simply cannot in all good conscience advise you to make such an unsound purchase."

Alfred leveled his eyes, suddenly unwilling to hear more. "Do you mean to see to the transaction for me or not, William?"

The banker, a man with a thin face, pointed silver beard, and thin gold spectacles, raked a hand through his thinning hair. Then he exhaled a breath. "But Tetbury? It is such a modest country town. I have checked it out myself, and the butcher shop and pub in the building will not possibly be able to pay you enough rent to make the investment profitable. Then, with one or both of them gone, where will you be?"

Alfred stifled a wayward smile. *But that was just the point, wasn't it?* he thought evilly. And those who could not afford to pay, sadly, would have to be evicted. Unless, of course, they could come to some sort of agreement about certain things. . . .

Either way, he would be rid of Edward Langston at last. Yes indeed. That is where he would be. This new and more drastic measure would not have been necessary, he consoled his conscience, if that mouse of a wife of his had done her part after receiving his anonymous letter. Now Alfred had begun to lose his patience. He had had quite enough of Langston's great power over Charlotte, which was always ruining everything. Now it was time that someone had that same command over him.

"Look, William," he began in a cool, measured tone, "I absolutely mean to have that building. It is a personal matter. Now, do you plan to represent me, or shall I be forced to find someone else who will?"

Reluctantly, the banker pulled forth a black leather portfolio and drew out a series of papers. "Since it would appear there shall be no changing your mind," he said, shuffling the documents that would be begin the procedure.

"None at all."

William dipped a pen in the inkwell between them. "How much should I offer for it, then?"

"Whatever it takes."

The banker thought of objecting again. It really could be quite costly if there was the least bit of sentiment attached to such a building. But then he thought it prudent to hold his tongue. He had objected all he dared. And money could never really be considered a factor for the wealthy Lord Linton, even if he did lose a significant amount on such a curious venture.

Besides, there was something far more driving this than what had been presented to him. That much was clear, and it was scarcely worth losing such a valuable client, even if it did prove to be the reckless investment he believed. Personal, Alfred had said. Revenge was more likely. It would not be the first time the venerable London banker had been a witness to the earl's ruthless determination to have his way. And God help the poor people of Tetbury.

Or whoever it was who had stirred the Linton ire this time.

34

HE WAS GOING TO HAVE TO SEE CHARLOTTE.

Edward knew that now. Whatever it would mean. But it was almost three months after Anne's death before he accepted the inevitability. It was like a scene that must be played out. The final chapter of a book one must read to see how it was going to end.

Paddy was right. It could be a *sign*. That conversation between the two old friends had played itself over and over in his mind relentlessly until finally he had no choice but to listen. He must see Charlotte. He must meet his son. Whatever else happened, at the very least, he had a right to that single bit of joy.

Edward cantered his elegant gray and white mare up the long gravel-covered drive, knowing for the first time how Charlotte must have felt coming to Tetbury those two long years ago. As he slowed his horse with a gentle tug at the reins, Edward could feel his heart thumping hard against his ribcage. He tried to catch his breath.

This was foolish, he thought. Two years. By now a woman like Charlotte had certainly gotten on with her life. And he had no one else to blame for that but himself. He had offered her no other alternative when he had chosen to stay with Anne.

There would have been dozens of eligible men waiting to snap her up. And looking at the impressive size of her family's estate, remembering her beauty and wit, he could see what a splendid catch Charlotte would be.

"God, grant me the strength to do this," he muttered as he jerked the reins harder, bringing his horse to a stop in front of the small Tudor manor.

When no servant came to attend him, Edward pushed out of his stirrups, bounding onto the ground. He looked out across the vast green lawns. They were carefully manicured. The flowers were in full bloom and perfectly arranged. It was early afternoon, and the summer sun was warm on the back of his neck. A slight breeze stirred, making it bearable, bringing a sweet fragrance up from the rose garden. *Of course she would have roses. How like her,* he thought.

Edward surveyed the grounds as he stood beside his horse. He was trying to imagine the sweet, simple girl in her *ayah's sari* who long ago had claimed his heart, now running such a grand enterprise as this, when suddenly he caught sight of two people. They were strolling in his direction up from a collection of bristling willow trees surrounding a shimmering pond. One of them, a woman with dusty brown hair pulled away from her face and dotted with a straw hat, was holding a feathery parasol above her head. The other, an elegantly dressed older man who towered over her, was holding her hand. Instinct forced Edward behind the thick trunk of one of the old oak trees that lined the drive. As they drew near, Edward saw finally that the woman was Charlotte.

Obscured from their view, he strained to hear what they were saying when they stopped a yard away from the tree. The man, distinguished and considerably older, was giving her something. A moment later, they embraced. To his frustration, Edward still could hear none of the discourse between them.

"Oh, Alfred, it is lovely." Charlotte smiled, gazing down at a huge, flawless diamond. "But you know I cannot accept it."

"Of course you can."

Charlotte looked up, her smile fading slightly. "It is not a betrothal ring, is it?"

"Not unless you are ready for it to be." She frowned just slightly, and Lord Linton let out a throaty chuckle. "At least for now, why not think of it more as an atonement for my dreadful behavior these past weeks. . . . Please say you will not refuse it, or I shall never be certain you have entirely forgiven me."

He saw her hesitation, but before she could say anything further, he took her left hand and held it up. "Here. Let me help you put it on."

It was then that he caught a glimpse of the simple opal ring set in silver still on her finger. She had worn it unfailingly every day that he had known her. Though he never asked, and she never confessed it, Alfred was certain that such a plain little trinket must have been given to her by the illustrious Edward Langston.

"Shall we replace that one with this?" he asked innocently, indicating the two rings, one far more extravagant and costly than the other. He was suddenly irritated that, even in this, he was still competing with the past.

Charlotte retracted her hand sharply. "Don't touch that! Don't ever touch that!"

Alfred's eyebrows arched and he stepped back. "If I have offended you in some way, my dear, I am sorry," he said, suddenly indignant.

Charlotte knew better than to confess the truth about the ring's origin. They had gone around far too many times on the subject of Edward already, and she had grown weary of the battle. But still she must take great care not to offend Alfred too much. No matter how her personal feelings for him had changed these past months, the influential Earl of Bentham was a favorable ally, and there was still a reason to keep him present in her life. He had helped her a dozen times this year alone with financial matters regarding Briarwood that were too complex for her to have dealt with alone. She trusted him. That she could not replace.

Alfred had taught her how to manage her father's sizable estate. Finally, last year, he had even relented and showed her how to make a success of her little farm. No matter how she felt about him personally, the role he had cleverly carved out for himself in her life was one she could not deny.

"Why do we not put it on this finger?" she asked, slipping the ring onto her right hand and holding it up to the sunlight.

"It matches those lovely green eyes of yours," he said, trying not to think of the slight she had just accorded him. He had spent a small fortune on that ring. He had meant for it to duly impress her. It would have worked like a charm on any other girl in England. But not Charlotte. No, she was more taken with cheap silver studded with a minuscule piece of insignificant rock.

"Thank you, Alfred. I really am very touched."

Alfred gripped her shoulders and pulled her closer. "Ever the optimist, I was hoping for a little more ardent display of gratitude than that," he said, his voice suddenly low and husky.

For everything in this world there is a price to be paid, she thought. So now, too, even for friendship. Charlotte cringed, feeling his mouth wet and open against hers.

"Now, that is much better," he growled, then gave another throaty laugh, ". . . as a beginning!"

Edward had not heard a word between them, but he had seen enough. He led his horse from behind the oak tree as Charlotte and her companion moved farther out across the pristine landscape, away from the house. He prepared to mount the waiting mare again and gallop hard out of Kent and out of Charlotte's life.

A devastating sense of finality marking his face, Edward pulled the bridle, turning his horse around, only to look down suddenly upon a young man with a hunting rifle in one hand and two sleek, black dogs at his heel. For Edward, it was as though he was looking into a mirror from his own childhood. The boy before him, on the brink of adolescence, was lean and fit and tanned, with thick dark hair and brilliant crystal-blue eyes.

"Are you the new banker, here to see my mother?" he asked. "If so, I believe you are a trifle early."

Edward could not speak as he gazed down at his son for the very first time. "No . . . I am not a banker," he finally managed to utter through his amazement. "I am an old acquaintance of your mother's."

"She has only gone for a stroll. She should be back within the hour," Hugh Edward said. "Why don't you come inside and we can wait for her together?"

"No . . . I cannot wait. But I thank you."

Hugh Edward's crystal-blue eyes, so much like his father's, began to darken with vague recognition. "Then may I at least tell her who it was that came to call?"

What could I possibly say? Edward thought in the split second that followed the question. All he had ever done for this boy was send him a few stones and tell him how much he regretted things. He did not have the right to introduce himself now as the boy's father—no matter how desperately he wanted to do it.

"Just an old friend of hers from India. . . . You may tell her that."

They were gazing at one another now in the still, warm sun of a summer afternoon, both of them knowing, yet neither confessing, the identity of the other for the shock of their first encounter.

"You have grown into a splendid young man, Hugh Edward," Edward said, speaking again after a long and strained silence. "Your mother should be very proud of you."

"And my father?" the boy asked tentatively, hoping for so much more than this unexpected jewel of a moment between them. "Would he be proud as well?"

"I am certain he would be," Edward finally said. Then, when he could not bear a single moment longer faced with the life he could have, Edward spurred his horse hard and galloped as fast as he could away from Briarwood and out of Kent.

* * *

"I didn't know who else to tell," Hugh Edward whispered to Alfred that evening after supper as they stood alone in the drawing room. "It is just that Jawahar won't be home for another two days, and I really thought that this could not wait before I came to a decision about what to do."

Alfred Linton calmly sipped a sherry from a crystal glass and leaned on the fireplace mantel. "You have acted wisely, my boy," he said in a cool, measured tone. "News of his visit here would only upset your mother, and she has been through far too much already. . . . His coming here in a moment of personal weakness could only have meant heartbreak for her."

"That is just what I thought. But I really don't like to keep things from her."

"Why do you not think of it more as keeping her from harm's way? That is a son's responsibility, after all."

"I would like to see them together again," he confided, certain that, as his mother had once assured him, there was no hope of a serious liaison with the earl. "But I don't suppose that is why my father came here as clandestinely as he did."

"I am afraid I would be forced to agree." He waited a calculated moment, certain he could make the question he was about to speak sound cast-offish. "So tell me, Hugh Edward. Who else have you told that your father was here?"

"No one."

"Are you certain of that?"

"I have spoken to no one, Alfred," Hugh Edward assured him.

"Did any of the servants see him?"

"I don't believe so. He was alone when I saw him."

"Splendid," he said, forgetting himself. When he realized how his expression of relief must have sounded, Alfred smiled and wrapped his arm around Hugh Edward's back. "That is to say, you have behaved splendidly in this, my boy. Shown real maturity. I'm quite certain that it wasn't easy for you."

"I wanted to tell him that I knew who he was."

"He made his choice two years ago," Alfred said spiteful-ly. "It would have come to nothing if you had."

They were interrupted when Charlotte returned to the drawing room in a whisp of rose-colored satin and white lace. "I am sorry," she said sweetly. "Just a misunderstand-ing with the cook about tomorrow's menu. So now, what have the two of you been speaking about while I was away, with your heads pressed together so closely?"

Alfred said nothing, deferring to her son. After all, he had his own plans for Mr. Langston; plans that would put an end to this folly of any sort of further liaison between them once and for all.

After a moment's consideration, Hugh Edward, who had secretly wanted nothing so much as to see his family reunited, came to a difficult decision. Looking at the Earl of Bentham, trusting him, he resolved instead to keep silent about the most fateful encounter of his young life. Alfred was right.

He must do it, he thought, for his mother.

 **35**

"YOU DID NOT EVEN SPEAK WITH HER?" PADDY BLUSTERED incredulously.

Edward swallowed a gulp of warm ale and leaned on his elbows across the bar. "I saw all that I needed to see."

"Balderdash!"

Edward's head perked up. Paddy scanned the regulars, making certain no one would overhear them. Then he coughed nervously and leaned a little nearer. "You have waited all these years for the woman of your dreams, and now you are willing to give her up to some aging competitor without so much as a good row?"

"She may well have already married him, Paddy. I don't believe I could bear to face the sort of thing she did when she first came here!"

"So not knowing is better?"

Edward heaved a contemplative sigh. "I think that it might well be, yes. . . . You didn't see them together as I did. And my own son took no steps to encourage me to remain once he realized who I was."

Paddy took a moment, grabbed a damp cloth, and began to mop the bar. "Edward Langston, you disappoint me." He shook his bald head. Finally he looked up again, his steely eyes blazed with conviction as the other men around them laughed at some unheard jest. "Good Lord, man! The boy believes you are still married! How else would you expect him to behave?"

"I saw her myself, I tell you! She was with another man!" Edward brayed. "I have got to make an end of it, Paddy. I have put them both through too much already. She and my son have a right to their happiness!"

"And you have a right to yours," he persisted doggedly, even as he watched Edward's drawn face tense. "Look, my boy. Go home. Get some rest. You cannot make so grand a decision as this without some real consideration. Margaret can see to the girls a few days more."

Edward raked a hand through his thick dark hair, feeling more weary and more hopeless than he ever had in his life. "Thank you, Paddy."

"Eh, you would do it for me," he said blithely, cupping his own chubby hand over Edward's slim one. Then he answered a call from the other end of the bar for another pint of ale as Edward walked alone out onto Long Street.

He walked home quickly. He had gone to see Paddy directly from Briarwood, and suddenly now he felt an overwhelming desire for a hot bath. It was a need to wash away not only the dust but the disappointment of what he had seen there.

He tried hard not to think of her or to recall it. He could rationalize the circumstances all he wanted to, but the image of Charlotte—his Charlotte—being kissed so passionately by a man old enough to be her father had stunned him. None of this was fair, he thought, opening the white gate to his front garden. This garden, once Anne's single prized possession, was being taken over now by the slow yet strangling growth of weeds. Anne had suffered. Charlotte had suffered. Oh, the Good Lord help him, Edward too had suffered.

He had fought to do the noble thing. He had stayed when he had wanted nothing so much in the world as to go. And now for that his world had crumbled down around him until there was nothing left but memories. It was so unfair, every last bit of it, he ammed the gate.

Alfred knew at once that it was him.

Charlotte had described his features perfectly. She had not, however, detailed what a surprisingly elegant and dignified man Edward Langston was. Alfred Linton removed his gloves and black silk top hat and moved farther inside the low-ceilinged, rustic Cock 'n' Feathers, amid the curious stares and whispers of the local patrons. This revenge would be sweet. So sweet.

Edward had seen him too as he entered the pub. He recognized the stranger to Tetbury as the man who had been with Charlotte at Briarwood. He wore a dark blue waistcoat, trousers, and matching cape, which he pulled off with a flourish and flung over his arm as he drew near an open space at the bar. It was clear by the expression on his face that the man did not desire libation.

"I have come to tell you to stay away from Charlotte," he said crisply, arrogantly, not caring who heard. "She has finally gotten over you, Langston, and she does not need you coming to her home, hoping to stir things up again."

All the chatter and whispers around them ceased. No one had missed a word of what the stranger had said. "Why do you gentlemen not take this outside, where there is more privacy?" Paddy suggested, anxious to help keep Edward's secret from small-minded townspeople who would not understand.

"You made your decision, ol' boy," Alfred said crisply, lifting his bearded chin. "Regrets or not, you cannot have it both ways now, and I mean personally to keep you to that."

Edward surged across the bar, grabbing the lapels of the fine waistcoat in both his clenched fists. "No one has that sort of power over me!"

"Oh, really?" Alfred laughed and tossed forth the freshly signed deed to the building that housed the pub. It was the moment he had waited for. Planned for. And now he took great pleasure in the ultimatum he was about to deliver. "I own you now, Langston. Read it for yourself. Try to see Charlotte again and your father's beloved public house, the one for which he worked all his life, will be reduced to scrap before you can so much as beg my forgiveness. And I would do it like that"—he snapped his long fingers—"to keep you from her. Believe me."

Edward's handsome face blazed with contempt as he surged once again toward Lord Linton, and Paddy did his best to hold him back. "Please, son!" Paddy pleaded, trying to temper Edward's frustration and rage. "This can come to no good!"

"Perhaps not," he gritted, "but it will make me feel a far sight better!"

"Your friend is right, you know. Hitting me will change nothing, Langston. You had your chance. Two of them, as I see it. I've simply seen that there shall not be a third—"

Edward cut off his cruel jibe with a powerful blow to the jaw. Alfred reeled back, collapsing onto the floor amid the stunned gazes of the pub's regular patrons.

"Oh, you shall be sorry you did that!" he moaned, gripping his flame-red jaw and staggering back to his feet.

"I don't think so."

"I had come here as a gentleman, Langston, intending only to warn you about what would befall you if you continued on. But under the circumstances, I've changed my mind. I no longer have the slightest desire to spare you from the truth. At long last, dear sweet Charlotte has consented to become my wife. . . . Ah! So I see by your expression that now I have wounded you. Good!"

"You're a bloody liar!" Edward surged forth again, but Paddy held him back.

"Am I?"

"Now that I've met you, I know that Charlotte would never consent to give herself over to someone so vile as you!"

"But your own eyes have told you otherwise, haven't they?" he asked ruthlessly, dusting off his waistcoat. "You saw us together that day. Your son told me as much. You saw with your own eyes that there is more between your—" he stumbled purposely on the words. "Between Charlotte and I than innocent friendship."

Edward broke free of Paddy's strained grasp and leapt over the bar, tumbling half-full pint glasses and bar stools in his wake. "I'll kill you! I swear I'll kill you!"

Three of the patrons, men who had known him all his life, held Edward back as he struggled. "Go ahead and hit me again if you like," Alfred said smugly, swirling the dark blue cape back across his shoulders. "It will change nothing. As this building is, so now too Charlotte Lawrence is mine . . . in every way. Our marriage will only formalize that which has already been ordained by the good Lord Almighty!"

He tapped his dark hat back on his head like a punctuation mark and then smiled as Edward's face continued to fill with hot blood. "Leave her alone, Langston, before you lose what little you have left. After all, it really is over between you!"

Two days later, Edward still felt as if the breath had been knocked out of him. The Earl of Bentham's revelations had imprinted themselves on his troubled mind, seizing him ruthlessly.

Sleep was beyond him. It had been since he'd returned to Tetbury the week before. So was any real sense of peace he had ever found here among his memories of childhood. Now he counted plates, cups, saucers, neatly set in their racks, as he sat alone in the kitchen of his cottage. He did anything to pull his mind from the images of Charlotte with that sort of man.

He wanted to go to her, as Paddy had encouraged him to do. At the very least to stop her. Rescue her. No matter how influential or wealthy the earl might be, no matter what it was likely to cost him if he pushed too far, Charlotte marrying someone so malicious as that was a mistake—the greatest mistake of her life. Edward felt it in the core of his soul. It welled up from there like a spring. *What if she needs you?* Paddy had asked. *The poor young woman at the mercy of a scoundrel like that?*

But he must let his conscience guide him now. He could rely on his heart no longer, no matter how the two battled within him. The conflict was always the same. Relentless, dogged, never ending. *Don't let love slip away! It is the only thing that really matters,* his heart hounded him. *You gave her up. You made your choice,* his conscience replied. *Now you must let her make hers.*

I must! he doggedly declared, doing his best to refuse his heart's desire.

That evening, Edward sat at the kitchen table by the light of a single flickering lamp with his two young daughters. He was doing his best to look as if the food before him was pleasing. Eating had become such a chore in light of all that had happened. Sleeping, too, was beyond him. Since Anne's death, it took all his determination just to choke down enough of his meal not to cause little Charlotte concern, and then to lie alone in their bed until morning came.

"Very tasty," he said, leaning back in his chair and struggling to smile at the two precious little faces that gazed back at him expectantly.

"You've barely touched it, Papa," Charlotte replied, looking across at his nearly full plate of stew cooked by Margaret Evans.

"It has just been a very long day, that's all. The meal is wonderful. Truly."

"You need your nourishment," she countered protectively, her face suddenly grave. "Abigail and I cannot lose you too."

His daughter's sweet concern caused a genuine smile to blossom on Edward's drawn face for the first time in days. He leaned forward again and took a large spoonful of the stew. At that, even Abigail smiled. It broke her heart that they should have to worry about him now too. They had already been asked to deal with so much after the unexplained death of their mother. They could have no idea all that he still faced. They should not need to. They looked to him for security. For love. And he must be there now, both mother and father, to give it to them.

"I don't want either of you to worry about me," he said, smiling gently, trying hard to reassure them. He leaned closer across the table and took one hand from each of them. "I know how difficult this has been for the two of you and I wish I could help you understand why Mama had to go away. But I can't. Still, you must believe me when I tell you that your papa is never going to leave you. I will always be there for you. Always."

He saw one small face soften and then the other, and he felt himself breathe a tiny sigh of relief. Nothing in his life was certain just now but these two beautiful children, and he would guard their happiness and their security to the death.

"Now drink your milk. Both of you." He smiled, trying to sound firm.

My dear Mrs. Blackstone,

Although we have not had the pleasure of a meeting, it is my firm belief that you and I have a great deal in common . . .

Paddy lay the pen down beside a stack of fresh paper on his writing desk in the dim candlelight. Then he read aloud the words he had just written, hoping to see how they might sound to her.

The situation had clearly gotten out of hand, and Paddy

Gillam was not about to let it continue a single moment longer than necessary. Since Edward's miserable encounter with the grand and rather unctious Lord Linton two days before, Paddy had racked his brains, searching for a way to help two young people desperately in love. He wanted to help them find their way back to one another since this new and open path had so clearly obscured itself from their view. Since the evil Earl of Bentham now threatened to take away what little Edward had left. That dear boy could use a bit of good fortune. And after the unbelievable story of love and sacrifice he had heard, so, he thought, could Charlotte.

That was when the idea had first come to him. Brilliantly simplistic. Flawless. A woman who cared about her, bound together purposefully with a man who cared about him. In the days following Edward's startling confession, Paddy had heard the tale of the real Katherine Blackstone, a kind and generous woman who had befriended Charlotte on the ship back to England. During their brief reunion, Charlotte had told Edward, that the wealthy widow from Oxford had since become a trusted friend.

Paddy glanced back down at the letter. This first tentative introduction was too soon to propose his plan. First he must convince her of his sincerity. To do so, he must confess the entire story. She must be told about Anne's death and about Edward's subsequent trip to Briarwood.

> My interest is in the happiness of Edward Langston, a good and noble man, recently widowed, whom I have known all of his life. I believe you bear the same interest in Miss Charlotte Lawrence, a young woman I came to know during the time she bore your name here in Tetbury. . . .

He touched his fleshy cheek and smiled. Brilliant. Simply brilliant. Someone must help those two lost souls find one another again. *Someone needs to give fate a little push in the right direction,* he thought, smiling. *It might just as well be me.*

Paddy added a few more well-thought-out lines about desiring her participation in this most romantic of adventures and then signed it, "Eagerly, Padraic J. Gillam."

He stroked the fat tabby cat who lay sprawled and purring on the desk beside him and leaned back in his chair. "We have to help our boy, McGee," he spoke to the animal. "With a bit of conniving and a little good fortune to boot, one day soon our Edward shall actually see those dreams of his come true!"

36

"WHAT IN HEAVEN'S NAME HAPPENED TO YOUR JAW?" Charlotte cried, coming toward Alfred.

"It is nothing," he lied, kissing her cheek. "Just an unfortunate tangle with a wily branch on my afternoon ride yesterday. Wasn't a'tall watching where I was going. Really all of my own fault."

"A branch gave you a nasty bruise like that?"

"Curious how those things happen sometimes. . . . So tell me," he said, changing the subject, "how was London?"

"Crowded, as always." She sighed. "The best dressmakers in the city are still exorbitant. But how are you?"

"Not so wounded as my pride, I'm afraid," he replied, buoyed by her genuine concern as they sat down together. "I've been riding since I was a child. I really should have been more careful."

"Does it hurt much?" she asked, reaching up to touch his cheek.

"Only when I laugh."

"Can I get you something? A cold compress, perhaps?"

"One of your smiles would do better. And a kiss, perhaps."

Charlotte leaned forward obligingly and pressed her lips softly against the bruise. "Better?"

"Much," he replied, and then, without warning, he sought out her lips for a more passionate, open-mouthed kiss.

Charlotte's eyes flashed a warning as she sprung back to her feet and went quickly across the room to pour them each a sherry. In the silence, she collected herself.

"So now *you* tell me. What did you do with yourself for the two days I was away?"

Alfred crossed his long legs and leaned back against the settee. "Just a bit of business," he said evasively. "Nothing at all about which you need concern yourself, my dear. I would much rather hear what lovely creations you are having done up for next season."

Charlotte handed him a sherry and then sat back down, though this time there was more of a distance between them. "Oh, I don't want to bore you with those sorts of trivial female things," she said more modestly, secretly not wanting to discuss something so familiar with him. "Are you certain that it does not hurt? It really does look dreadful."

Alfred thought of Edward's face so full of rage, facing him across the crowded bar, wishing that he had gotten in just one good punch. What would Charlotte think if she knew how he had really gotten that nasty purple bruise? Would she be so free with her sympathy then?

"Look, my dear, I was waiting here at Briarwood for you to return for a reason. There is something about which I must speak with you."

"That sounds rather serious."

"It is to me," he said, taking both her hands. He was pleased to find that she was still wearing the diamond. It meant that there was still hope. He had so little time now to act upon the lie he had told, since he could not be certain that he had convinced Edward to stay away. He must extract an acceptance from her before it was too late.

"Charlotte, I want you to marry me," he said forcefully. "Now. Today."

Her green eyes quickly narrowed. "Alfred, you know I—"

"I have waited patiently for two very long years for you and I know well your objections. You do not love me. You shall never love me like you did *him*. But we are good together, you and I. You know that. And honestly, Charlotte, it is time someone spoke bluntly to you about this Edward of yours."

"Alfred, please—"

"Allow me to finish." He held up a firm hand.

"Edward made his choice two years ago. If he was ever going to return to you, would he not have done so by now?"

She turned her head to hide the heartbreak in her eyes. "I don't want to hear this!"

"You must hear it! You are wasting your life on memories when there is a flesh-and-blood man here who wants you desperately! I can assure you I would never make the same miserable mistake of leaving you that he did!"

Charlotte's eyes blazed with contempt. "That was beneath you, Alfred!"

"He chose another woman over you! I'm sorry if that hurts you, but it is quite simply the truth—a truth you one day must accept!"

"Damn you, Alfred Linton!" she cried, unable to halt the sudden flurry of tears that rained down her smooth, pale face. She tried to turn away from him but he grabbed her arms, pressing his fingers around them like vises. The breath was thick and rapid in his chest. His eyes were suddenly glazed.

"You know how good we are together. It hasn't been so long ago that you could have forgotten that," he murmured, licking her throat, tasting the sinful sweetness of flesh he remembered. "Say you will marry me, Charlotte. . . . Say it!"

He was still kissing her and touching her, trying to keep her from thinking. Her mind was a barrage of images as his hands groped her rigid body. The echo of her promise to love Edward and to honor him until death should part them rang in her ears like a resonating bell. He was pushing her, trying to make her reply without thinking. Alfred's tongue was darting behind her ear in expert licking kisses, trying to rekindle that faint spark that had once so briefly been between them. And even though she knew what he was doing, all she felt for him now was revulsion.

Like the distant memory of being raped.

Katherine Blackstone read the letter again.

What in the world was going on there? she wondered. Edward's wife dead! Charlotte's happiness in jeopardy! And who in blazes was this total stranger writing to her on their behalf?

She thought of dismissing the entire affair as dangerous meddling. That dear child had already sustained more wounds and disappointment in her young life than any one person should be asked to bear. She screwed her wrinkled face into a frown at the thought. Still, it did sound well-meaning enough. And if there was so much as half a chance that Charlotte and Edward might actually find their way back to one another after everything they had endured, it was her duty to aid this stranger.

She tapped a finger on her knee. Padraic J. Gillam. Hmm, she pondered. It was a kind, simple-sounding name. Honest. Proud. It had doubtless taken the man a great deal of courage to intercede with a total stranger on Edward's behalf.

And for her part, Katherine was partly to blame for the way things seemed to be turning out on their own. She had, after all, encouraged that relationship with the dreadful Lord Linton. But that had been before she'd heard the rumors. Persistent. Dark. Ugly rumors. London was rife with them. It was not just the women. Those questionable women. There was more. Whispers of embezzlement. Violence. Even murder. They said the Earl of Bentham stopped at nothing to attain what he desired. And, God save her, what he apparently desired at the moment was Charlotte.

He was boasting all over London that they would marry any day now. Sanctimonious reprobate! She could not allow her dear sweet girl to be taken over by someone like that! Absolutely not.

Katherine had always considered herself a splendid judge of character. This was such a humiliating and dangerous miscalculation. What harm could come from answering a simple letter? A friendly call for help? She weighed the alternatives, remembering Charlotte's face on board the ship that first time she had spoken of their great love. The first time she had confessed her hopes for the future with Edward as they had sailed toward England. Now his other wife was suddenly dead. That simply had to be more than coincidence. Yes indeed, there was a greater force at work here in their favor than two well-meaning friends.

Katherine took a sip of tea and drank silently to their happiness. Great heavenly days! It looked now like it might actually be possible for them. She lifted a fresh sheet of paper from a drawer in her writing desk. It really was a most romantic adventure, she agreed, entirely in accord with a man she believed herself never to have met.

A man she once had thoughtlessly snubbed.

"She wants to see me, Paddy," Edward said in wide-eyed amazement.

A letter written by Katherine Blackstone but forged in Charlotte's hand lay open on the kitchen table. Paddy sank down into the chair beside Edward. It had worked perfectly, he thought. By the hopeful look on his handsome face, Edward did not suspect a thing. It had taken four letters each way between the two romantic conspirators to fully explain the situation on both sides and to devise an acceptable plan.

"What else did she say?"

"Only that it concerns our son," Edward said, drawing in a small, shuddering breath.

"Well then, you have no choice but to go to her, do you?"

"None at all," Edward agreed, glancing down at the words

he believed Charlotte had written, caring not what it might cost him to cross the man who now had the power to ruin him entirely. Not when it came to the welfare of his son. Then he looked back up, his eyes two shimmering crystal flames. "Do you suppose she wants my blessing to marry that charlatan?"

"Perhaps," Paddy said carefully, hoping to incite enough anger to set Edward on his way to Kent before nightfall.

"It shall never happen!" he raged, springing to his feet with the full force of a geyser. "He is not nearly good enough for her!"

"He is an earl, Edward," Paddy expertly prodded.

"Charlotte doesn't care about such things as money and titles! She is a sweet and vulnerable woman who has obviously been taken in by him!"

Paddy lifted a single bushy brow. "All the more reason to stop their union while you are still able."

"You're right, you know. I cannot let it happen like this," Edward agreed with a sigh, after pausing. "I know I told her I would stay away. I know what it is likely to cost me when he catches wind of my involvement. But I love her, Paddy. God help me, I cannot let her make the biggest mistake of her life!"

"Certainly not!"

"I should go to her now."

Paddy came to his feet, meeting Edward in the center of the kitchen. "Absolutely."

"There is no time to spare."

"Not a moment!"

Edward pulled Paddy to his chest, a stout little man who came up only so far as his collar, and embraced him fiercely. "Thank you, old friend."

"I did nothing."

"You have been more than understanding. You knew Anne, and you cared for her for a very long time."

"So did you. But you have always loved another. I suppose you could just call me an old romantic at heart. I have a real soft spot for those happy endings."

"Say a prayer for me, Paddy," Edward asked, excitedly grabbing his coat and hat, which had been tossed over the back of one of the kitchen chairs. "And watch over my daughters while I am away. Tell them every day for me that I love them dearly, will you?"

Paddy Gillam smiled and nodded. "Make haste, my boy!"

Edward felt his heart break a little more.

Abigail and Charlotte stood side by side near the front door, looking up at him like two brave soldiers. They were doing their best to hide their fear at the prospect of his going away. He stood there, jacket slung over his arm, hat in his hand, resisting the overpowering urge to lift them up and take them with him. Even though he had assured them he would only be gone for a few days, Edward could tell by their expressions that they still did not believe him. He had promised always to be there for his daughters.

Now, it seemed, he was breaking that promise.

Edward stooped down and held them both close to his chest. "I promise you I will be back soon," he whispered. "This is not a'tall like Mama going away. You both know that, don't you?"

Dutifully, each of his girls nodded their heads that they did. Charlotte struggled to keep her face from showing anything, but the unshed tears darkening Abigail's blue eyes told the truth.

"Paddy will be here for you, and you both do so like Mrs. Evans. You will scarcely know that I am gone, and I will come back to you both the very first moment that I can. When I do, I am going to bring you each a very special present. . . . You would like that, wouldn't you?"

He was trying to appease them. His action was a bit too blatant, but Edward did not know what else to do. He was a man torn between two families. Two obligations. Children on both sides who needed him. He would hate himself for leaving. But he would hate himself even more if he denied Charlotte and their son yet again. They were in danger, and they had called out for him.

"Go ahead, Papa," little Charlotte said, her jaw jutting

out bravely. "Abigail and I will be fine here . . . if you truly are coming back."

"I swear it," he vowed, his voice breaking as he hugged them both close again. "I shall be back before you know it."

AT LEAST THE EVENING WAS OVER.

It was one of the best things Charlotte could find now to say about the one they had just spent at Lord and Lady Upton's. It had been one of the longest and most dreary in recent memory.

Having the company of Hugh Edward along with her and Alfred tonight had been the one saving grace. This handsome young man of twelve had taken his mother's arm and escorted her into the grand blue drawing room ahead of the Earl of Bentham. In so doing, he had thoroughly charmed the rest of the guests.

Already Hugh Edward had the regal bearing and witty charm his father possessed, Charlotte had thought proudly. He had even managed to charm the cantankerous old Countess of Lambourne.

They came into the Briarwood library, all gleaming mahogany and gold firelight, just before midnight. They were all laughing at a story Hugh Edward had been telling about Lady Upton's pet lap dog and a certain unsuspecting trouser leg belonging to the very blue-blooded Sir John Barrow. Their heels tapped together on the polished oak floor.

"You have a guest, madam," Bickers said from inside the

library at the very moment Charlotte saw a man stand up beside the crackling fireplace. The gold flames shadowed his face, but she could see enough to know that it was Edward. As they stood still, looking at one another, the conversation and laughter softly faded away.

"I warned you not to come," Alfred snarled beneath his breath, his face flushing red.

"So you did," Edward replied calmly. "But I never have taken too kindly to threats."

"By God, you shall pay for this!" Alfred brayed.

"It is him, isn't it, Mama?" Hugh Edward asked, breaking the unexpected tension between the two men who should have been strangers.

But Charlotte did not reply to her son's question. The room was blurring, and she could not think of what to say. Charlotte was so completely disarmed to see Edward here at Briarwood now that she could not move. Nor could she comprehend the whispered exchange between him and the very disgruntled Lord Linton, both of them fiercely protective of the woman who stood now between them.

"Let's give them some time," Hugh Edward suggested, his voice cutting into the strained silence.

"Not on your life!" Alfred spat out a whispered refusal. "I'll not leave her alone with the likes of him!"

But finally, reluctantly, when Charlotte looked at him in a silent plea, Alfred did follow the boy out of the room, leaving her and Edward alone, separated by a Portuguese carpet and two very long years.

"He is a very handsome boy," Edward said tentatively. "You should be very proud."

"Why have you come? I thought we had made a decision."

Edward tilted his head slightly. Still so dashing, she thought. So incredibly handsome, even in a simple pair of brown wool trousers and a tan cotton shirt, the sleeves rolled up casually. "You sent for me."

"I did no such thing." She frowned slightly.

"I received a letter."

"I did not write it."

Edward studied her expression full of so many things—

the same things he was feeling—and he knew that she was telling the truth. But suddenly, now it no longer mattered how they had been brought together. Only that they had. Now she was here. Charlotte. Standing before him and looking more radiantly beautiful, more serene, than she ever had before, and he knew that he must say something.

He took a difficult breath. "Anne died three months ago."

He had not said it in a tone to elicit her sympathy. He had merely spoken it as a fact and let the words hang in the heavy air between them. Charlotte moved a step nearer, beginning to bridge the great chasm time and pain had wrought between them. "Oh, Edward. I am so sorry. She was a very special woman."

"As are you, Charlotte Langston. . . . And I shall despise myself until my dying day for ever having a reason to let you go."

She flinched at the sound of her name woven with his. She had not used it for such a long time. It had been a symbol of union, a joining of souls that for Anne's sake she had denied these past two years. "A great deal has happened," she said softly, painfully, knowing what he was feeling.

"But there was never any question where I wanted to be. . . . Or where in my heart I always belonged. You know that. In spite of that, I have not come on my own behalf, even when I thought that you might have sent for me. Regardless of how my circumstances have changed, I no longer have a right to expect anything of you. I know that. . . . Only tell me," he said, drawing a step nearer and then stopping again. "I must know. Have you . . . married him yet, Charlotte?"

The hand she had lifted to her lips was shaking. A moment later, she answered him. "Lord Linton has been a terribly big help to me with Briarwood, Edward. And he has been a friend. But I shall have only one husband in my life."

"Thank you." He glanced up and muttered a silent prayer as Charlotte moved closer to him.

"So then, is that the only reason you've come? To tell me I mustn't marry Alfred."

"I know when we parted last you said that you thought it

best that I not come, but I was also hoping for an opportunity at least to finally meet my son."

Charlotte's breath caught in her chest and she swallowed her disappointment. "At least?"

She could see him straighten nervously and lean for support against the back of the chair in which he had been sitting. "Charlotte, I have no right to ask anything more from you. I did not leave Anne. . . . She took her own life."

"I don't understand," she whispered, her eyes widening.

"She shot herself with my pistol. The one I brought back from India."

"Oh, Heaven above!" Charlotte gasped, pressing her fingers to her lips. "But why?"

"I don't know. . . . I don't suppose I ever will."

It seemed so unbelievable. The woman had gotten everything she had ever wanted. She had gotten Edward. Two of his children. What could possibly have made her unhappy enough to have ended her own life? Charlotte waited in the awkward silence for him to say something more.

"She is at peace now. Like me, I am sorry to say, she hadn't been happy for some time."

"I am glad you did not leave her, Edward," she said, moving nearer still, watching him grip the back of the chair.

"How can you mean that after all I have asked you to bear?"

"Well, I do. We both knew it was what was right . . . then."

"And now?" he asked tentatively.

Charlotte paused a moment and then took his hand in hers. "Come with me, Edward. I want to show you something."

They walked together silently out into the night—a starry, moonlit night—still holding hands. Both of them were trembling as they walked across the dark, spongy grass and down the knoll to the freshly painted barn and clearing where geese, sheep, and cows roamed freely beneath the stars.

"I wasn't certain what sort of farm you dreamed about," she said softly as he stood in complete astonishment. "We never spoke about that. So I have all sorts of animals. The geese I saved from slaughter. The cows shall be only for milking, and—"

Edward turned to her. "You did this for me? Even after I chose—"

Charlotte turned now too and stopped his words with a single finger pressed lightly against his lips. Her gaze lingered on his. "I did it for us. For the dreams we once shared. And so that at least somewhere in the world, your part of that dream could come true."

"My God." He gripped his forehead. "I cannot believe you would have gone to such lengths for me."

"I would go to the ends of the earth for you, Edward," she said softly, her eyes wide and vulnerable. "Still."

Edward exhaled a breath and looked back out across the grass to what was a real working farm. His dream. His heart swelled. Everything he had ever wanted for himself was here at Briarwood and now, like a dream, so was he.

"You say that you expect nothing from me," Charlotte said in reply to the question he had asked her back inside the house. "Well, I don't believe that because, Edward Langston, I most certainly do expect something from you."

"You may have anything I have to give," he said in a voice raw with emotion.

"I expect you to give me the lifetime we should have had; the one we were denied. That is, if you still want me."

"Want you? God, I have never stopped."

"Nor have I."

"And you could actually find it in your heart to forgive me after what I was forced to do?"

"You could take the time to try."

Edward's lips quirked into a strained half smile, trying to push back the magnitude of what he felt at the sound of her voice so free of accusation and blame. "Would the next thirty or forty years do?" he asked.

"For a start," she replied, her own tentative smile matching his.

He lurched at her awkwardly, and she molded into his embrace as if no time had passed at all since Delhi—since the day she had become his wife. His mouth covered hers hungrily.

"I did not want her to die," he muttered, still kissing her, breathing his love onto her lips, her skin, and her neck. "But somehow it has led me back to you, and for that, God help me, I can never be sorry."

There was such unbelievable happiness in her body, in her soul, that Charlotte trembled and wept against his heart. "Oh, please don't, my darling," Edward whispered, tasting her tears. "I cannot bear to hear you cry when I have brought you so much pain already."

"These are tears of joy, Edward. Everything is going to be all right now. Finally," she said, pressed against his chest, listening to the beat of his very noble heart.

They sat alone on the dewy grass, watching the stars twinkle in the black night sky, his rough country jacket now a blanket beneath them. They talked about their children. About what challenges the morning would bring. But through all of the uncertainties, both of them were content just to be together, to slowly find their way back to what a few short hours before had seemed impossible.

Edward was still awed by what she had done for him here at her family's ancestral home. But in all the years that he had known her, Charlotte was a woman who had never ceased to amaze him. She was the most resourceful, the most splendidly determined woman he had ever met. He sat beside her, gazing across the grass, still not quite able to believe the depth of love that she still felt—in spite of everything.

"I had given up believing that this would ever happen for us," Charlotte softly whispered as she sat with her head on his shoulder, the lights from the house casting shadows on the ground around them.

Her words were so sweet and honest that they made his heart ache. "As had I," he replied, his voice a ravaged whisper. "I came here tonight honestly believing that it was too late for us. That you really belonged to someone else."

"Finally, I belong to myself, Edward," Charlotte said, her

magnificent green eyes shimmering in the moonlight with hard-won pride. "But my heart has always belonged only to you."

"It tore me apart the day you left Tetbury. *My* heart shall never recover from that."

"No. Neither of ours ever shall."

Edward turned and took her face softly in his two hands, his own expression suddenly somber. "No matter what we may still feel for one another, I want you to know that I don't expect to just waltz back into your life now and for things to be the way they used to be."

"Things can never be the way they were in India."

Edward let out a heavy sigh. "No. I suppose not. And there will be a great deal to explain to Hugh Edward. I suspect this shall not be easy for him to understand."

"Nor shall it be for your daughters. They will all need time and patience—and a great deal of understanding."

"But there is more that has changed between us since India than the coming of children, isn't there?" Edward asked her, and Charlotte heard the strain in his question.

"I suspect there is very little that was left as it was."

"I was speaking of you and Lord Linton," he quietly confessed, and Charlotte's lips parted softly in surprise. "I know about the two of you."

"You do?"

He plucked a blade of grass and held it up to the moonlight. "I had no right to expect that you would wait for me. I put you through a great deal, I know."

"You did what needed to be done. We both agreed."

Edward shook his head. "Tell me how you can always be so understanding about my circumstances when the very thought of you with that lecherous old reprobate actually incites murder within me."

Charlotte leaned back on her elbows, scrutinizing Edward's face for the longest time before she spoke again. "Perhaps you should tell me why you detest Alfred so when you scarcely know him."

"I know enough."

"The two of you have met somewhere before tonight,

haven't you? I could tell by the look on both your faces the moment you saw one another."

Edward heaved a sigh, not certain what it would do to her to tell the truth about the man she considered a friend, yet knowing that he did not want there to be any secrets between them ever again. Reluctantly, he chose to confess.

"He came to see me in Tetbury."

"Alfred?"

"He . . . came to tell me to stay away from you. He warned me that if I chose not to heed him, he would close down my father's pub and evict me from the building, which, it would seem, he has just recently purchased. It was a maneuver, I gather, he thought fair since you had accepted his proposal of marriage."

"But you know that I hadn't."

"I know that now, but not when I first came here."

Edward watched Charlotte's eyes darken first with disbelief and then with anger as she sat back up. "Alfred has done some drastic things to win me, that is certain, but in this he has gone too far. Good Lord, I fear those rumors about him may actually be true after all."

"Shall I handle him for you?" Edward offered, wrapping a supportive arm around her shoulder. "You know I will."

"No. This is something I must do on my own. It is enough that you are here for me."

"I shall always be here for you, Charlotte."

"Always?" she asked playfully, and Edward took her palm and softly kissed it.

"You just try to get rid of me."

"I was hoping that you would say that."

They lay down together in the soft damp grass, lulled by the chirping of the crickets, she wrapped in his strong, solid arms. For a time, neither of them spoke.

"I had better get you back to the house. It'll be light soon." Edward sighed reluctantly, never wanting to let her go again.

Charlotte turned onto her chest, smiling serenely. She could see him trying to gather the strength to push her away, and in that movement she knew exactly what he was feeling.

She wanted to be with him as much as he wanted to be with her. There would always be that same fierce passion between them, no matter what forces took them apart. But they both knew their time had not yet come. There was Alfred to be dealt with first. And before that, Edward had a son to meet.

"Let's not go back," she said softly, laying her head against his chest, content to hear his heart beating with hers. "Let's just stay here exactly like this, holding one another until the morning comes. For the first time in a very long time, Edward, I feel so completely happy."

Birds were singing in the oak tree outside the drawing-room windows and Bickers had just placed a fresh pot of tea and three china cups on a table before the sofa. Edward and Charlotte sat together, both happily exhausted, as they waited for Hugh Edward to join them.

"I don't believe I have ever been so apprehensive about anything in my life," Edward confessed nervously as he perched on the edge of the sofa.

"You will be fine," Charlotte assured him, taking his hand. "He really has grown into a fair and honest young man. Just like his father."

"I am just not certain I will know what to say to him."

His wife brought his hand to her lips and kissed it tenderly. "I am certain your son is feeling precisely the same way that you are."

"He has suffered without a father, Charlotte."

"But I know you shall make it up to him."

"Do you really believe that I still can?" he asked, his voice bitter with self-accusation and regret.

"You plan to make it up to me, don't you?" She smiled.

Edward pressed his lips softly against her cheek. "For the rest of my life."

Suddenly he was standing in the doorway, looking at them together. It was a sight their son had dreamed about all his life. Edward came to his feet and Charlotte followed.

"Darling," she said calmly, yet feeling more trepidation than she had ever felt before. "I would like you to meet your father."

For a moment, an eternity, no one moved. The tall painted ebony clock near the fire ticked rhythmically in the silence. The birds continued to sing beyond the windows. "It is a pleasure to meet you," Edward finally said, the first to break the silence, as he extended his hand across the great chasm between them.

No one could have known the utter joy Hugh Edward felt in seeing his parents together for the first time like this. He still felt a conflict at never having been able to have this man in his life. There was much to be worked out between them. But his mother had a radiance he had never before seen, and there was nothing that he wanted so much in the world as her happiness. No one had ever made her happy like Edward Langston. No one else ever would. The rest of it, between father and son, would take some time.

The night before, Katherine Blackstone had come to him secretly when everyone was asleep. She had come to town clandestinely, knowing from Paddy that Edward would be here too and thinking perhaps she might be needed.

She and Hugh Edward had sat together here in the drawing room by the last of the firelight, and she had told him the entire story. About the death of Edward's other wife. About Alfred's visit to Tetbury. The threats. And about her own clever attempt at matchmaking with Paddy Gillam. Hugh Edward was sorry that a woman had died. That he would wish upon no one. But he could scarcely be somber, knowing that what he had hoped for all his life was on the verge of finally coming true.

"It is a day for which I have waited a very long time," Hugh Edward finally said with a reserve-tinged voice. "Mama too . . . I told her it would come if she just believed."

Edward's eyes clouded as they both moved across the room, taking the first steps toward bridging the gap between them at last. Charlotte hung back, intent on giving father and son their moment.

"I know that I have a great deal to make up to you," Edward said tentatively, studying the boy's expression. At last he was looking at the same beautiful face as in the photograph Charlotte had left with him back in Tetbury. The one he had looked at nearly every day since then.

"I only wish we hadn't lost so many years together."

Edward heaved a heavy sigh, understanding entirely. Knowing that this would not be easy. "No one wishes that more than I, Son, believe me."

"Mama was always honest with me, though. I always knew exactly why you stayed there, and I tried my best to understand it."

"And did you? . . . Understand, I mean."

"Not all of the time," he said truthfully, a little of the boyhood hurt bleeding through. "I wanted you to be here with us. And Mama—there were so many times she really needed you here."

"You have every reason in the world to despise me," Edward said carefully, knowing he could not chase away all of the bad feelings with just a word or a gesture. It was going to take time between them. A great deal of time. "I have no illusions about this being easy for the two of us. All I ask for is a chance to find our way with one another—much as I have asked of your mother."

"We could give it a try," replied Hugh Edward, his reserve falling away a little.

"Then we will just take it a day at a time. If that is all right with you. . . . Perhaps after breakfast we could take a nice long walk. Just the two of us."

"I'm really very sorry about your other wife," the boy said, directing the conversation away from himself.

Edward's expression quickly sobered. "How would you know about that?"

Again a silence. Charlotte moved beside her son and touched his arm lightly. "It is all right, darling. You can tell us."

Hugh Edward looked at one parent and then the other, recalling the romantic tale of surreptitious letters between his mother's dearest friend and his father's; realizing that perhaps he had just now inadvertently broken a confidence. "Mrs. Blackstone told me," he reluctantly confessed, hating to lie to his mother.

"Katherine is here?"

"She is staying at the Boar's Head Inn, Mama. I saw her last night after the two of you had retired."

Edward arched a brow suspiciously. "And I wonder who it was who told your friend Katherine about Anne."

"You mustn't blame Mr. Gillam," an authoritarian female voice boomed through the arched entrance to the drawing room. "He had only both your best interests at heart."

Everyone looked up at the sturdy, middle-aged woman who stood nobly in a fine silk yellow morning dress and matching ribboned hat.

"Katherine!"

"Darling girl, something needed to be done. I am not ashamed to say that I supported Mr. Gillam's plan entirely."

The two friends swept across the room toward one another and embraced. "When did you arrive?"

"Just yesterday when I knew your Edward would be here. Mr. Gillam and I agreed that we needed to let this dear son of yours in on the changing situation, before he was entirely put off by Edward's coming here."

"The real Katherine Blackstone," Edward said with a genuine smile, stepping forward slowly.

"In the flesh."

"I suppose we both really should thank you."

"Yes," she agreed, her gray eyes twinkling mischievously. "Indeed you should."

"What a blessed day." Charlotte sighed happily. "At last I have everything I have ever wanted, and the three most important people in the world are here to share it with me."

"I'm relieved to see that you're not angry," Katherine said.

"We really should be furious," Charlotte said, then paused, as Edward wrapped an arm around her waist. They looked at one another in mock indecision. Then they both smiled. "How could I ever be angry with you? You're my dearest friend in the world!" Charlotte laughed sweetly.

Edward was still smiling, but his voice sounded suddenly

stern. "I, however, shall deal with my own dearest friend, Padraic, later. He tricked me into thinking you had written that letter, Charlotte."

"Technically speaking, Mr. Langston," said Katherine, beaming proudly, "we both tricked you."

Applause broke the sound of their shared laughter, and everyone looked to the open drawing-room door. Alfred Linton was leaning against the door frame in a hazy shaft of morning sunlight. His face was rigid and sober, and he alone was clapping.

"What a truly touching family scene," he exclaimed icily. Edward felt his wife stiffen. "Leave Lord Linton and I alone, please," she said, not taking her suddenly mirthless gaze from Alfred. Her voice was cool and in control.

"Are you certain, darling?" Edward whispered.

"No. But this is something I must find the strength to do alone anyway," she whispered.

"How could you, Charlotte?" Alfred asked accusingly once the others had filed out of the drawing room. "After all that we have meant to one another!"

"How could *I?*" she gasped in disbelief.

As he moved nearer, he suddenly seemed to change from anger to a kind of crazed despair, and Charlotte was forced to take a step back. A man advancing on her too quickly would always remind her—it would always bring the memory back.

"It is not too late, you know," he said. "Even now. I shall forgive you your little indiscretion of last night with that bigamist. We shall chalk it up to a dreadful case of nostalgia. If you ask my forgiveness in this, rest assured you shall have it. You have only to say the word."

"Oh, I have a word to say to you, Alfred," Charlotte brayed angrily. "In fact, I have several. Through these past years I have made excuses for you, for your temper and for your possessiveness, because I felt alone and frightened after all that had happened. I needed someone, and in that I was wrong to have used you. But your sin is far greater than any I may have committed against you. No matter how you may pretend, you are not a kind or a decent man."

"I have no idea what you are talking about."

"Oh, please, Alfred. Do not insult me more than you already have! I know everything. I know about Tetbury. That you went there behind my back, that you not only blackmailed Edward, but then you lied to him about you and I, hoping to keep the two of us apart!"

But she did not really know everything. No one knew what he had done to Anne; how he had been responsible for the beginning of that woman's undoing by simply sending her a letter. But that he had managed to hide the fact did not matter now anyway. Now he was losing everything he had sought to gain by his cruel and systematic manipulations. And for a man like Alfred Linton, losing something he had wanted so much was nearly punishment enough.

"Really!" he huffed indignantly. "After all that I have done for you and your family, you are going to take that dreadful man's word over mine?"

"Any day of the week, Alfred."

"Well, I certainly don't need to stand here and listen to this!"

"Fine, since I have said nearly all I have to say."

His face was white and pinched with rage, and his lips quavered as he moved his mouth to speak again. "I hope you know that you have insulted me to the very core!"

"In that, we appear to be even. Now, I should like you to leave. I have a reunion to attend to."

"Great Scot, woman! You're certainly not going to take that man back, are you?" he sputtered out the question.

"Lord Linton, I believe that my mother has asked you to leave."

Hugh Edward had returned with his father, both of them having heard the heated nature of the discourse between the two angry friends. Father and son were standing united now in the same arched doorway through which they had so recently left.

Alfred spun around, his eyes blazing. "Not you too?" he asked the boy whom he had long ago won over with cleverly calculated gifts and endearments.

"You not only lied to my mother but you lied to me. You told me my father was here to hurt her."

"I believed that was true!"

"You thought that you could win her for yourself if you had me on your side," Hugh Edward countered. "You used me against my own father, and I shall never, ever, forgive you for that!"

"After everything I have done for you and that . . . that Indian street urchin, now you as well have the temerity to betray me?"

Charlotte's green eyes blazed as she slapped him so hard across the face that her hand stung. The sound echoed in the silence between them. Charlotte stepped back only slightly, her body still a rigid line at the unconscionable slight to an absent Jawahar. "Get out of my house, Alfred, before I have you thrown out!"

"Charlotte, please! After all that we have meant to one another!"

"I believe you heard the lady," Edward said firmly as he took a commanding step forward, his crystal-blue eyes blazing with the same contempt as Charlotte's.

"Oh, do keep out of this, Langston," Alfred snarled. "Or have you forgotten already the sort of revenge of which I am capable?"

Edward was standing so close, looming over him, that he could feel the earl's hot breath on his neck. But he did not deter. He was steady and very, very certain; a rock for the family who needed him now.

"I haven't a care what you do to me or what you try to do to my business, Linton. But when you harm my family, you bring yourself dangerously close to death. By the look of that bruise still left on your face, I cannot believe *you* have forgotten the sort of violence of which *I* am capable! Now, I strongly suggest that you do as she asks and get out of here, before I take it upon myself to remind you!"

"Fine. I shall do precisely that and leave you to your bourgeois fate," he finally snipped at Charlotte. Alfred turned away from her halfway and then, as if an afterthought, pivoted back, giving her one final attempt to come to her senses. "You could have had the world with me; anything your heart desired. But perhaps this fate of mediocrity is what you deserve after all."

"This fate, as you call it, *is* my heart's desire," Charlotte rebutted as Lord Linton turned with a grunt of disgust and finally left Briarwood.

That night after everyone else had retired, Charlotte took Edward's hand in the darkness and led him upstairs. They had banished Alfred and they had begun the healing with Hugh Edward. They had taken care of everyone else. Now, finally, their time together had come at last.

They both felt a little nervous with one another; as if once again it was the first time between them. Agra. The North Western Hotel. But what was between them—what had always been between them—was far too powerful to deny a moment longer.

Edward pressed her back against the sealed bedchamber door and kissed her bare white throat until he evoked a little whispered cry. A sharp pain of desire jerked inside of him, but he must force away his own wild need. A need that had gone unmet between them now for nearly two years. To Edward's mind, tonight was Charlotte's night. A way to begin the atonement for how much pain and loneliness he knew he had caused her.

Edward was kissing her, pushing his tongue between her smooth lips in tiny erotic thrusts as he moved his fingers deftly beneath the bodice of her dress and onto the sheer white flesh of her breasts. He touched one nipple tentatively and then the other, and they hardened beneath his fingers.

He leaned closer against her, and Charlotte could feel his need hard against her thigh. She wanted nothing so much as to feel that part of him inside of her once again. Her head was pounding—a hot, white pounding—so that she could not think. All she could do was feel. His lips. His fingers. The pressure of his powerful erection. Charlotte was certain that she had never wanted anything so much in her life as she now wanted Edward. But even as they kissed passionately, she could feel him holding back.

"Edward!" she cried out, shaken, her body quaking with desire.

"Not yet, my love," he answered, taking her into his powerful arms and carrying her to the open four-poster bed across the room.

"But I want you and I know that you want me."

"Shh." He hushed her with another languorous kiss. Edward was in complete control with his rugged body arched over hers, her wrists pressed into the bed by his straining fingers, as he painted a trail of feather-light kisses across her bare breasts.

Finally, he reached down to unfasten the buttons of the rest of her gown, and when she saw his hands trembling, he let her help him. She arched her back as he slid the cool fabric over her shoulders and down past her slim waist. Charlotte lay beneath him then in only her stockings and chemise—white silk against smooth ivory flesh—and he gazed down at her as the need flared inside him again.

Edward doggedly ignored the powerful urge, kissing her softly, her cheeks, chin, and the tip of her nose, moving downward, and for Charlotte the sensation was excruciating. She moaned and caught her fingers in his silky black hair, trying to pull him closer. But Edward was stronger. He still arched over her, tearing away his shirt and trousers with one hand. Then he flung them atop her dress beside the bed.

That splendid body, Charlotte thought from the drugged ecstasy he had wrought upon her. It never seemed to change. Firm, muscled shoulders. Soft curls of hair across his chest. Long, tight legs wrapped around her own. So in control. But finally something did change. He had begun trying to steady his breath. She could hear it. Ragged and short. Little gasps. When she opened her eyes, she could see that his were tightly closed. His face was pinched from the effort. He thought it was too soon, and he was trying to hold himself back from what they both so desperately desired. He was trying to give her everything and take nothing for himself.

It had been a long time since the unhurried days and nights of lovemaking in their bungalow in Delhi, but not so long that Charlotte had forgotten how to please him. He had taught her those secrets patiently, and she had learned them well.

Charlotte pressed her rigid fingers into his back, sliding them down across his buttocks, pressing her nails into his skin until she felt his hips begin their rhythmic, uncontrollable thrusting.

"No," he murmured against her smooth cheek. "I want tonight to be for you."

But she was undeterred. Expertly, it was she who kissed him now, opening his lips with her tongue, tasting the gasps of desire, tasting the waves of tension as they shot through him. He tried to draw in a breath but he could not. At last, he too was entirely possessed by the passion.

Charlotte slipped her fingers across his hips and cupped his rigid erection in her hand. "Oh, God, don't!" he pleaded, but with her touch he was lost, and Edward finally abandoned his fervent attempt to hold himself back. Finally plunging into the sweet splendor of her willing body, he cried out in a long, aching groan, and this time it was Charlotte who quieted him with a devouring and sensual kiss.

They were wound tightly with one another, molding like one flesh—arms, legs, grasping fingers—and suddenly they were as attuned to one another as if they had never been apart.

As he thrust fiercely into her again and again, Edward abandoned all restraint. So did Charlotte. Her nails bit into his muscled back. She sucked the violently pulsing vein in his neck, willing him deeper and deeper inside of her. Both of them were gasping for air.

"Charlotte!" he cried out her name at the moment he poured himself into her, his body jerking spasmodically over her, her own wet with sweat and torn with the violent tremors of fulfillment.

It was a long time before either of them could speak, or wanted to. They were wound in one another, their bodies still joined beneath a silver shaft of moonlight through the open window. A cool night breeze began to cool them as Edward stroked her damp hair. Both of them were more contented than they had been in a very long time. It was a kind of peace that both Charlotte and Edward had learned to live without, yet neither of them need speak about what they now felt. They were so close, so attuned to one another, that words were unimportant.

A sense of joy that this was not a dream swept over them both at the same time, and Charlotte closed her eyes, drinking in all the sensations of this old familiar Eden as Edward pulled her closer.

"You really were something with Linton this morning," he said softly, then turned over to look at her, cast in moonlight and shadows. "You know, Charlotte, you were a splendid young girl when I first met you all those years ago, but you have grown into a truly magnificent woman."

She lifted her chin proudly. "I doubt you shall have any problems with your pub in Tetbury now."

"How can you be so certain when he despises me for taking you away?"

"Because Alfred's reputation is far more important to him than whatever it is he feels for you. If he pursues this insane grudge any further, he knows full well that I shall say publicly why we ended this supposed engagement of ours. That it was due to a scandalous incident with that very wicked and infamous temper which he tries so hard to hide from the world."

"An incident which, of course, is untrue."

A clever smile dawned across her face, lighting her eyes. "Lord Linton is certainly not the only one who knows how to manipulate the truth, you know. . . . Remember how I got my father to let me marry you?"

Her voice was so confident, her expression so provocative, that Edward felt his reservation begin to dissolve into a new wave of hot ardor for this woman he had loved and lost—and who, by a miracle of fate, he had somehow found once again. She really was such a magnificent woman.

He turned her onto her back with the force of his own

powerful body, and his warm lips descended onto hers yet again. "God, how I adore you," he murmured, hands gripping her hips as Charlotte welcomed once again his very skillful seduction.

38

THE NEXT FEW DAYS WERE BLISSFUL.

For Edward and Charlotte, it was as if no time at all had passed. They both understood that all along this had been meant to happen; that fate had intended to grant them this miracle. During the days they took long walks across the grounds, so that he could see and begin to appreciate all that she had done to create the farm of his dreams. It was her tribute to a man whose soul would belong to her forever. They also had quiet suppers, so that Edward had an opportunity to better get to know his son. There was so much lost time to be made up between them.

The nights—their private times—were never long enough. Charlotte gloried in the sweet ecstasy Edward could still so masterfully weave upon her body. She loved to feel him taut and full of need poised above her, patiently teasing her into unparalleled rapture. But those times when it was he who lost control brought the wildest, most primitive passion from her.

Then he would gasp against her cheek and drive into her with deep, powerful thrusts, until both their bodies were awash in perspiration and Charlotte was crying out in agonizing pleasure. Then Edward would hold her tightly against his wildly beating heart and whisper that there would never again be someone else to come between them. At last, they were where they both belonged.

It was nearly a week before Charlotte and Edward began to examine the future that lay before them and to look at the past that had brought them so miraculously back together for this second chance.

Charlotte held a gauzy blue parasol over her head as they stood together beside the pond and watched the ducks gliding across the glassy surface of the water. Edward's face was tense and he was looking straight ahead.

"I have put this off for as long as I can," he said in a low, hard voice. "But there is something about which you and I must speak."

It was curious, Charlotte thought, but she knew even before he spoke the words what Edward was going to say. And as it had always been, she understood because she understood Edward.

"I must return to Tetbury."

"I know," she whispered back, pretending to watch the bristling willows shading the pond.

The resolve in her reply so surprised Edward that he softened as he looked back at her. "I owe a formal period of mourning to my daughters."

"And to Anne's memory."

Edward reached up, taking her face in his hands, and he softly kissed her cheek. "Have I told you lately how magnificent you are?"

"I think it has been at least since yesterday," she replied, her lips curving into a faint smile.

"I must stay for the rest of the year."

"It is what is right. One day it shall mean a great deal to Charlotte and to Abigail that you did it. Besides, they need time to adjust to what you must tell them."

"Then you're not angry?" he asked, his tone suddenly tentative.

"Of course, I shall miss you desperately. But your great sense of honor is part of why I love you so. Besides, we can still write to one another."

"I shall write to you every day."

"You had better!" she playfully warned, and Edward brought her to his chest.

"God, it shall be the longest eight months of my life."

"And of mine."

"But then we can truly begin our new life together—all of us as a family."

"It is what I shall dream about."

"And when I return, sweet love of my life, I want to marry you."

"Again?" she asked, her soft smile lighting his heart.

Edward took her hands between them. "So much has happened since Delhi. I think it is important that we renew our vows. If, of course, you will have me and two new daughters."

"It would be an honor to become your wife again, Edward," Charlotte replied, as a sudden flurry of happy tears glistened like tiny jewels in her brilliant green eyes.

"Then while we are apart, it is important to me that you have this," he declared, holding out a ruby set in gold between two diamonds. "It is my promise of what is to come."

"Edward, it is so beautiful!" she gasped, the tears spilling now onto her pale cheeks. "But you cannot afford something this extravagant, can you?"

"I told you back in India that I would be able to provide well for you, and I have not been foolish with my money these past years since. It was one of the many important lessons I learned from my father. He was a man of far greater wisdom than I ever knew. My inheritance when he died bore that out. You and the children shall always be comfortable."

Finally, she held out her hand for him to put the ring on her finger—the finger that had worn Alfred's ring, which she had long ago surrendered to her jewelry case upstairs. To her surprise, after a moment, Edward released her and took her other hand instead.

"Shall I replace the opal with this, as a symbol of our new life together?" he asked. "That one is bound only to remind us both of the past."

"Not all of which was bad."

"True enough," Edward conceded.

"I want to keep it," she said softly. "This ring shall always be special."

Charlotte's calm face in the sunlight, so different now but so much richer, sparkled with the promise of the future, and Edward tenderly kissed her with all the love and devotion that adversity had wrought between them. Then he slipped the new ring onto her other finger.

"Oh, my soul," he whispered into her smooth brown hair. "Only April shall bring me to life again."

"It shall be here before we know it," Charlotte promised. "And then nothing shall ever tear us apart again."

Epilogue

STANDING IN THE GARDEN AT BRIARWOOD BESIDE PADDY, Edward watched Charlotte and his two daughters greeting guests after their wedding. Abigail, three years old now and eager for the reassuring presence of a mother, clutched fast to his wife's hand. In her pink and white lace dress, she looked up with Anne's wide dark eyes at the string of tall strangers offering their congratulations.

Charlotte, who had just turned six, stood beside her younger sister and gazed up adoringly at the woman who had given her her first and only doll, a gift that had begun their friendship. One day she would know the whole truth, Edward had promised himself. Both his daughters would. There would be no more secrets in the Langston family. But for now he had decided to let his two precious little girls revel in childhood. That part of life was over all too soon anyway.

"You're a very lucky man, Edward my boy." Paddy proudly smiled, patting him on the back.

"I am indeed," he replied, remembering suddenly that they were the very words he and Arthur Moresby had exchanged after his first marriage in Delhi thirteen years ago. It was a poignant memory, vivid as the day it had happened. Life was odd that way. Edward smiled to himself. The things that go around do so often come back around.

"When do you leave?" Paddy asked, taking a sip from a pint of warm dark ale while everyone else drank champagne from delicate crystal.

"Our ship does not sail until week's end."

"'Tis bound to be an excruciating journey," he kindly warned.

"But one Charlotte and I have both taken before. And the children are all young and strong. They shall fare just fine. It shall be an adventure. Besides, India is a place we promised ourselves long ago that our children would one day see."

"Will you be going back to Delhi as well?" Paddy asked, and Edward heard the caution in his reedy voice.

The two old friends exchanged a tentative glance before Edward replied. "We shall be staying there, Paddy. We have agreed, Charlotte and I, that it is the best way to finally put what happened to us in the past."

"You're a brave man, Edward Langston."

"No," he said with a chuckle, dragging his gaze from Paddy across the garden to Charlotte, laughing gaily as she danced with Jawahar. "I am just a man in love. My wife suffered far more than I did in that city, and it is her wish to return there. If it is within my power, from now on, there is nothing I won't give to her."

It was several moments amid the lively music, the laughter, and the warm afternoon sunlight before Edward spotted Katherine Blackstone newly arrived. She was up near the house, being greeted by Hugh Edward.

"Well, well. If it isn't your fair partner in crime," Edward remarked, breaking into a jaunty grin. "I did not expect to see the illustrious Mrs. Blackstone today."

"She's here?" Paddy exclaimed with surprise. "Charlotte told me that her friend was likely to miss the wedding."

"Well, it would seem that she at least has made it to the festivities."

"Jolly good! Let us have a look at the old girl. All of this time in all of those letters, a man conjures up an image."

Edward shot him a glance of surprise. "You mean, for all your meddling, the two of you have never met?"

"'Tis a fair distance between Oxford and Tetbury, Edward my boy." Paddy grinned, reminding him. "Bring her over, would you?"

Edward moved through the maze of guests and well-wishers as Paddy stood rocking on his heels in anticipation. The letters between he and Katherine had gone on long after the reconciliation they sought had occurred. He had kept them all; long, beautiful missives in which they had slowly shared more and more of their painful pasts, the secret of their years of loneliness, and their desire not to remain alone forever.

"You!" Paddy gasped.

"You!" Katherine primly countered as they faced one another. "I had no idea," she exclaimed, remembering their brief and unfortunate encounter in the Cock 'n' Feathers that single afternoon when she had so reluctantly left Charlotte to her fate.

"Nor did I, I assure you, madam," Paddy blustered, stiffening into a more formal pose.

"Then the two of you have met after all?" asked Edward.

"Our encounter was mercifully brief," Paddy answered him coolly. His disappointment at the woman before him was lost on neither of them.

In response, Katherine stiffened equally, and they stood facing one another like two opponents on a battlefield, rather than as willing accomplices in such a delicious and worthy deed of love. But even so, Edward saw a spark of something.

Uncertain of precisely what it was and unwilling to engage himself as a referee today of all days, he bowed and left them to discover between themselves just what precisely that spark might be. It certainly seemed an unlikely pairing, he thought as he tromped across the grass in his blue-black wedding suit to retrieve his bride. But then again, love did have a way of striking the most unlikely of targets.

"You know, I never get tired of looking at you," Edward said to Charlotte as they danced, the wind blowing little wisps of brown hair free from her lace and rose headdress and casting them like feathers against her face.

"I hope you feel that way a year from now back in India."

"Oh, no." Edward smiled handsomely, glad to have her safe in his arms again.

"No?"

"A year from now I shall love you much more."

It was a magical afternoon full of happiness and joy. Obligations behind them, at long last their new life had begun, and they were surrounded by the good wishes of friends and family. It was curious to Charlotte that as the afternoon wore on, Katherine and Edward's friend, Paddy Gillam, had become an odd-looking yet inseparable duo. She was taller and more slim. She was gowned in amber silk with a velvet collar. He looked entirely out of place in a poorly fitting button-down jacket, trousers, and a brown felt bowler hat.

Still, by the time the sun was nothing more than a rosy stain in the evening sky and Jawahar had called for a toast to the bride and groom, they were huddled together as if they had known one another all of their lives.

Katherine took two goblets from a servant's silver tray and offered one to Paddy as everyone else was taking theirs. "No, thank you indeed, my good woman," Paddy deferred. "I make it a practice never to drink anything that tastes precisely like a lady's perfume!" His declaration spoken with fervor, Padraic Gillam then lifted his ever-full pint of warm dark ale—mercifully supplied by Edward—in a toast like the others.

"Tell me, Mr. Gillam," Katherine huffed. "Are you always so gruff?"

"Absolutely always. And you must tell me, Mrs. Blackstone, are you always so persnickety?"

Katherine's pursed expression melted slowly into a smile as they gazed at one another, having seen far more of one another than these glaringly opposite exteriors in their long months of correspondence. "You know, I doubt whether either of us is going to change much," Paddy said wryly.

"Highly unlikely."

"Well, at the very least, tell me you don't detest bacon and eggs by firelight and moonlit strolls beside a sparkling spring."

"I adore them." Katherine smiled, and then she began unexpectedly to giggle. The sound was soft and unassuming, like the laugh of a schoolgirl.

Edward and Charlotte, who had been standing in front of their two dearest friends for the toast, had not been able to help but hear the curiously amorous exchange. It made them both smile together to imagine the very dignified Katherine Blackstone as a simple country wife.

"Still, I actually think they shall be good for one another," Edward said in a whisper. "If they don't manage to kill each other first!"

"I do believe it is a romance made in Heaven." Charlotte chuckled quietly, careful not to turn around or to let them hear.

"A romance like ours?" Edward asked.

"Oh no, my love," she replied, linking their hands as the last burst of summer sun dipped reluctantly below the horizon. "There shall never be another romance like ours!"

Dear Reader,

My heartfelt thanks for your willingness to follow me on this exciting and unpredictable journey, so far, from Renaissance France with *Courtesan*, and now here to Victorian England and India for Charlotte and Edward's story.

Your gracious comments and enthusiasm continue to inspire me, and it is a privilege to hear from each of you.

Diane Hagger

P.O. Box 9136
Newport Beach, California 92658